1984

It Takes All Kinds

IT TAKES
ALL KINDS

By

Louis Bromfield

Harper & Brothers Publishers

NEW YORK and LONDON

1939

The story BETTER THAN LIFE was originally published serially under the title of AND IT ALL CAME TRUE and is
published in England under the title of IT HAD TO HAPPEN.
The story McLEOD'S FOLLY was originally published
serially under the title of YOU GET WHAT YOU GIVE.

CONTENTS

*

It Takes All Kinds

I

McLeod's Folly

A S SHE grew older Mrs. McLeod found that she needed less and less sleep and so took to the practice of rising early, a little after dawn, to work at her book. This allowed her two hours for work and an hour for bathing, dressing and arranging the business of the day with Aida, the cook who had lived in the house for nearly thirty years, ever since the sad morning when J. E. McLeod had the first of the heart attacks which finally carried him away and left the *Daily Shield and Banner*, then Plattesville's leading newspaper, without an editor.

Mrs. McLeod was childless and one might have thought that the business of the day was a simple enough affair, but this was not the case. In the first place the house was enormous, and in a well-advanced state of dilapidation. Then there was Jane Baldwin, her niece by marriage, the daughter of J. E. McLeod's sister, who lived with Mrs. McLeod and had a way of getting herself into a great many romantic and sentimental complications. And then there were the stray men who passed the night and sometimes part of the day in the cellar of the house. And there were Aida's relatives, dark in color and vast in number, who had come to look upon Mrs. McLeod as a kind of family deity who could straighten out all their troubles. She could help to feed those who were broke and see the magistrate who sat in judgment upon those members who woke up in jail on Monday morning, and help through school those members of the family who felt intellectually inclined.

All this and a great many other complications pertained to the realm of housekeeping, but all this represented only the beginning of Mrs. McLeod's day. As a rule, the world of the big house known as "McLeod's Folly" ended at eight-thirty in the morning to begin again in the evening at the hour when she returned, exhausted but happy, from the office of the *Daily Shield and Banner*—an hour which was frequently nearer to nine than to six P.M. In between Mrs. McLeod belonged to the *Daily Shield and Banner* and to the town of Plattesville.

When Aida came up from Darkietown, she was in her thirtieth year, a buxom, high-yaller girl with plenty of life in her and plenty of admirers. She had a no-good husband who died in a saloon brawl the same year that J. E. McLeod passed away from heart disease, and the two widows found themselves occupying the vastness of the great house on San Antonio Street. Since that year their lives had grown together in a relationship which was now, years afterward, less that of servant and mistress than of old friends who forgave each other anything.

On the whole there was not much to be forgiven on either side. The worst Mrs. McLeod had to forgive was Aida's bullying, and the worst Aida had to forgive was the muddle-headedness of her mistress and friend. There was no longer—there had not been for many years—any question of wages; they lived in a communist state. When there was money they both spent it as if they were millionaires. When there wasn't they both stalled creditors and pinched and scraped, not merely to make ends meet but to feed the stray men in the cellar and to keep what was one of the best tables in the whole of the Southwest. Mrs. McLeod always said, "You can economize on everything in the world but food." Aida in her younger days privately added to this philosophy "And love," but Aida was old now, like Mrs. McLeod, and didn't have any longer to keep philandering bucks from Darkietown in pocket money. As the years passed and the circulation of the *Daily Shield and Banner* slipped down and down and the advertisers grew fewer and fewer, there was less and less money for Aida and Mrs. McLeod. Luckily the *Daily Shield and Banner* existed, for if money was sometimes scarce, the newspaper did represent a kind of credit. Most of the grocer's and butcher's bills were paid by free advertisements in its columns, and there were times when even the plumber had to be satisfied with a quarter column in the pages of the *Daily Shield and Banner* as payment for repairs to burst water pipes and stopped drains.

The great house had been built long ago in the early eighties by J. E. McLeod's father—the famous "Possum Jack" McLeod, out of his profits in cotton and cattle and real estate, and long ago as the house, beam by beam, nail by nail, raised its rococo splendors above a frontier town of shacks and saloons and humble dwellings, it had promptly been given by the simpler inhabitants of Plattesville the name of McLeod's Folly. Now, nearly sixty years after, when there were a hundred finer and bigger houses along Alamo Avenue and in the suburbs, the name still stuck.

Although it was a huge house there was really very little room in it, for the architect and Possum Jack McLeod both showed a taste for the grandiose and the fantastic. The rooms were few but enormous and there was a colossal amount of space wasted in a profusion of turrets, oriel windows, stairways and baroque cozy corners. It stood upon a large and valuable (although much mortgaged) plot of ground surrounded by an old-fashioned

[2]

wooden fence in a bad state of repair, amid a shaggy overgrown jungle of lilacs, syringas and magnolias, the whole overshadowed by huge and ancient cottonwood trees which littered an unkempt lawn in the late summer with a drift of white down.

Once, long ago, McLeod's Folly had been the heart of Plattesville's residential district, but gradually, during seventy years of growth and prosperity in Plattesville, the residential district had retired, leaving the fantastic turrets and oriel windows to overlook a vista of garages, filling stations, cheap restaurants and coal yards. To have painted McLeod's Folly with all its angles, brackets and fretwork would have cost a small fortune, and no amount of free advertising had ever tempted a painter to attack the nightmare job, and so for twenty years no virgin paint had touched its walls and in this shabby nakedness, bits of fretwork and cornice had rotted and fallen away.

I

Like a garrison perpetually besieged and holding out heroically, Mrs. McLeod and Aida shared the old house with their single lodger, Mrs. McLeod's niece.

More sophisticated people than the citizens of Plattesville would have said that Mrs. McLeod was a rank sentimentalist and that all her troubles had arisen from her romanticism and lack of common sense. The truth was that in her youth she had been that rarest of all things—a woman who loved passionately and was loved in return, a woman who had found perfect happiness with one man. The daughter of a Calamos County cattle breeder, she had fallen in love at nineteen with the twinkling blue eyes, the big mustaches and the six feet two of J. E. McLeod and married him. For fifteen years, until the day he died, she had been happy with him, and afterward for thirty years she was happy in the memory of him. When he died she determined to carry on without him the newspaper which he had loved nearly as much as he loved her, and she determined never to give up that fantastic house known as McLeod's Folly but to go on living in it, afflicted though it became with increasing shabbiness, until she died.

She was perhaps a sentimental woman, but she had integrity of purpose, and money as money didn't mean much to her. She wore clothes, fashionable or not, until they were worn out. She was hospitable and she liked good food, and this Aida provided for her on a miraculously small expenditure of money. Her whole life, which had never known a holiday, was spent between McLeod's Folly and the office and printing press of the *Daily Shield and Banner*. She was untidy because, since the day of J. E. McLeod's death, she had never found time nor reason to make herself attractive. After he

[3]

died she became merely a kind of machine intent on carrying on the ideas of J. E. and concerned with the welfare of Plattesville, which was the only town she had ever known and which she loved very nearly as much as she had loved J. E. McLeod. And in thirty years McLeod's Folly, the *Daily Shield and Banner* and her own open-handedness had devoured the whole fortune which came to her as his widow.

She was tall and thin and very straight. In her youth she had been a beauty, famous in Calamos County and the Southwest, and now in old age, in spite of all her worries, her untidiness and her distraction, she remained a handsome woman, although now the beauty lay more in the voice, the eyes and the expression than in the body. Although the face was wrinkled, the cheeks sagged and the hair hung in wisps from beneath a worn and dowdy hat, there was something about her that arrested a stranger and made him think, "That must have been a fine, handsome woman."

Until J. E. McLeod began to have the heart attacks which finally killed him, it had never occurred to her that she could write more than the simplest letter, but when he fell ill and had to lie for days propped up in bed, there was nothing for her to do in order to quiet him but go to the office herself to take charge of things. There, because J. E. was the kind of man who did nearly everything himself, she had been forced to learn a great deal overnight. She had even to write editorials which some people thought better than those of J. E. himself. And then, after he died, the idea came to her to write a novel about him and his family, about the people of Calamos County and Plattesville and the pioneer life on the great plains, dusty in the summer, windswept in winter, where she had spent the whole of her life.

Once she began it, she found that there wasn't much time for writing; she had to do it in odd moments, in the early morning or late at night, and as she finished each chapter she put it away in a blue paper envelope and stowed it in an old cowhide trunk in the vast turreted attic of McLeod's Folly.

She belonged to the country; it was in her blood as it was in the sap of the rugged old cottonwoods that rattled their leaves just outside the window. She had no idea what she meant to do with the novel when she had finished it. It simply *had* to be done. And no one knew anything of its existence but Aida. Not even her niece, Jane Baldwin, suspected that for two hours before the dreadful sound of the alarm clock roused her, Mrs. McLeod had been working away like a beaver, in the little room on the second floor which had once been J. E. McLeod's den, where J. E.'s fountain pen and pipe and tobacco jar were left untouched exactly as he had left them on the evening he dropped dead. It was a little room which Mrs. McLeod did not even trust Aida to clean and put in order; she kept it locked, a sacred place, like the rooms of the Prince Consort in Osborne.

[4]

At eight o'clock on the morning which marked the beginning of the revolution in her life, Mrs. McLeod left J. E.'s den after writing for two hours, locked the door behind her and went down to a breakfast which was one of Aida's best efforts. There were waffles and ham fried in butter (paid for by two paragraphs of advertising in the columns of the *Daily Shield and Banner*)—ham which was crisp round the edges and pink in the center. There was strawberry jam (made in the sun on the roof of the back porch of McLeod's Folly) and spoon bread and honey and black currant jelly and eggs fried in butter and coffee that was sublime, coffee with an aroma more wonderful than all the perfumes of Araby.

Aida, with advancing years, had grown as round and fat as Mrs. McLeod had grown lean, and as she came through the door from the pantry bearing a plate of crisp waffles, her bulk filled the whole doorway. To her, Mrs. McLeod, faded now, old and weather-beaten, was still the pretty young woman she had come to serve when J. E. was still alive, a big vigorous man with the curling mustachios of the wide open spaces and a bartender's curl on his forehead. To look at Aida one would never have suspected that she was a "worrier." It wasn't natural to her; the habit of worrying had come over her during the long years of days spent alone in the morbid solitude of the vast rooms of McLeod's Folly. Aida would have liked a cozy little house with bright curtains at the windows and a heating system which wasn't cracked, expensive and dirty. Instead of that she dwelt in a vast mausoleum that was like a museum of the eighties with its huge windows and plush curtains, its horsehair furniture and its Axminster carpets. In a way she liked the size and importance of McLeod's Folly despite its shabbiness, but it was a house which made a lot of work and Aida suffered from a vague and perpetual dread that some day it would tumble down on top of herself, Mrs. McLeod and Miss Jane. Meanwhile she worried over the dwindling importance of the *Daily Shield and Banner*, over Miss Jane's friendship with the scalawag son of Old Dougherty, the Democratic boss, and she worried over the men in the cellar and the prospect of one day sharing a cell in the Plattesville jail with Mrs. McLeod. On the whole she kept her worries to herself because she knew Mrs. McLeod had plenty to worry about at the office of the family newspaper.

So when Aida came through the door her café-au-lait face was cheerful and she said with a grin, as she had said every morning for thirty years, "Well, Mis' McLeod, I hope you all slept well."

"Fine, Aida, fine."

It wasn't true. She had lain awake for hours worrying about money to pay for newsprint and whether she would be able to collect the bill for advertising out of the wreckage left by the bankruptcy of Fillman's Bazaar. But for thirty years she had always replied, "Fine, Aida, fine," and it was too late to change now, even when she felt tired.

Aida distributed the food on the table, making small side remarks which had always been her way of conversing with Mrs. McLeod. She said, "I s'pect The Book is gettin' on pretty big by now?"

"Yes, it's getting on. Not much more to do now."

"Jes' what part is you at now, Mis' McLeod?"

"About the part where Mr. McLeod's grandpappy got caught out in a blizzard when he was eighty-six."

"That must be right near the end?"

"Yes, it's pretty near the end."

Aida gave another side glance at her mistress, "Ain't you all eatin' your spoon bread this mawnin'?"

"Yes, Aida, you know I always finish with that."

Aida pretended to be looking for something in the vast intricacies of the immense Gothic sideboard. When she emerged, she said, "I guess maybe that book you're writin' will make us rich again, Mis' McLeod."

"Don't have too big hopes, Aida," she laughed. "Maybe it'll be just another McLeod's Folly—big and empty."

"What you all gonna call it?"

"I haven't thought about that."

"I kinda think 'McLeod's Folly' would be a good name for it."

Mrs. McLeod stopped eating. She hadn't any appetite but she had been stuffing herself to please Aida. She hadn't even been listening to Aida's chatter, but through the cloud of worries which oppressed her, she did hear the last sentence. Aida, bending over, exposed only a vast backside covered with calico, and her voice seemed to come from the inside of the Gothic sideboard, like the voice of an oracle and prophetess accompanied by an echo.

For years Mrs. McLeod had thought and thought about what to call the book and now Aida had hit the nail on the head. "McLeod's Folly!" That was it! A rich and sonorous name with an echo of grandeur in it, summing up, enveloping, a whole epoch, encompassing all the rich, wild, fantastic life of the plains country in the days before the county had been shut in and fenced with wire, the days when Plattesville was a wide-open town filled with strong, colorful, strapping men and women with frontier manners and appetites, the days before there were women's clubs and lecture courses and Greek restaurant keepers and Irish politicians like Old Dougherty. The picture raised a sudden, sickening wave of nostalgia in Mrs. McLeod. Suddenly she saw Plattesville as it had been nearly fifty years earlier, when she was a wild young girl riding into town with her grandfather on a pinto pony called Satan, down the main street, past the saloons and general stores, to tie Satan to the hitching rail in front of the El Dorado saloon and dance hall run by Gashouse Mary's father, hoping all the while that she'd meet young J. E. McLeod on the steps of the *Daily Shield and Banner* office.

It was a fine town then, not so big or so rich; but clean and wild, where every citizen was free and most of them honest. It wasn't this garish over-grown town dominated by Old Dougherty sitting like a spider in the center of the web collecting graft off every saloon and brothel, stealing money meant for street repairs and new sewers. No, that old life had a dreamlike quality now. Whatever had been harsh and wrong or corrupt had vanished from the image which remained in the brain of Mrs. McLeod at sixty-seven. She wanted desperately to change it, to make a crusade to clean it up and drive Old Dougherty out of power. She wanted to organize a committee of vigilantes once more as her grandfather had done long ago during the land rush when Plattesville was filled with all sorts of unruly people, gamblers and strumpets and professional "badmen" and crooks of every kind. It was almost as bad now as it was in those days, worse, perhaps, because all the vice and crookedness wasn't open and wild and carefree as it had been then but hidden and corrupt and sordid. She sighed so heavily that Aida said, "What's the matter, Mis' McLeod? You all ain't got a misery?"

"No, it's nothing."

She didn't tell Aida that she was sighing because she didn't have a son, a big two-fisted son like the McLeods and all her own people, a son who could have carried on the *Daily Shield and Banner* and waged a crusade and whipped a man like Old Dougherty. All she had was Jane Baldwin for a society editor and Willie Ferguson, an elderly, untidy, broken-down reporter whose only desire and ambition was to get drunk on Saturday night as soon as the *Daily Shield and Banner* had gone to press.

Again Aida, watching her stealthily, interrupted her thoughts, "I guess Mis' Jane must have gone to sleep again. She oughta been down ten minutes ago. I never seen such a girl for dozin' off."

"She's young, Aida. Young people need a lot more sleep than old ones like us. Maybe you'd better go and see if she's gone off to sleep again."

Aida started for the door and then turned, "What's this, Mis' McLeod, about her courtin' with that Dougherty boy?"

"Nothing, I guess. Where did you hear that?"

"Gawd-a-mighty, Mis' McLeod, everybody in town knows about it. That's why she's so sleepy, staying up every night to go traipsin' about with that poor white trash."

"You mustn't say that, Aida."

"Well, Mis' McLeod, they ain't nothin' but shanty Irish and I hate seein' a nice girl like Mis' Jane marryin' into a family like that. What would her

[7]

poor old grandpappy say if he was alive? Like as not he'd have given her a good whalin'."

Mrs. McLeod sighed again and said, "Well, Aida, it's not the same now as it once was. I guess it isn't any of our business what Miss Jane does. And the Doughertys are rich and Jimmy Dougherty isn't as bad as the old man. And he's mighty good-looking."

"It ain't his looks I'm worryin' about. He's a good-lookin' enough feller," Aida retorted with something like wrath. "They're bad people, the Doughertys." She snorted, "Money! Anyway we get on without money, don't we? *We* ain't had a cent for years."

She wanted to explain to Aida's muddled brain that they had had money of a kind, out of the advertising columns of the *Daily Shield and Banner* and that even that might not go on forever. The *Daily Shield and Banner* might die at any moment and then poor Aida would find out what it was like to be without money.

Aida opened the door and as she did so, Jane Baldwin, society editor of the *Daily Shield and Banner*, came in. She wasn't very big, and the immense size of the doorway made her seem even smaller. She was pretty, with golden hair and blue eyes, a stubborn mouth and a turned-up nose, which wrinkled up when she laughed. She was twenty-three but she looked eighteen, a fact which made Aida treat her always as if she were a small child of undeveloped mentality. She was hurrying now, a little stricken in her conscience because she had wakened, turned off the alarm clock and deliberately gone to sleep again, and a little frightened for fear Aida was going to give her a lambasting because she wasn't there when the spoon bread was fresh out of the oven.

"I don't know what's got into me," she said, as she sat down. "I guess it's spring fever. I promise I won't be late again."

Aida pridefully refused to give any response in words, but with a snort far more eloquent, rolled across the room and through the door into the kitchen to bake up waffles for the culprit. Miss Jane could eat a powerful lot for a little thing her size.

When Aida had gone through the door Jane said, "I don't see what right Aida's got to take on as if she was my mother."

Mrs. McLeod laughed, "She hates anybody being late for meals. She's like any good cook. She's an artist—Aida is."

She wanted to ask Jane if she had been out again last night with Jimmy Dougherty. She had heard her come in late, after midnight, while she was lying awake, worrying. Sometimes Jane told her when she went out with Jimmy, but she told only once out of five times, and that showed, Mrs. McLeod knew, that she had a bad conscience. It meant that Jane was ashamed before her of going around with Old Dougherty's son. It worried

Mrs. McLeod because Jane was headstrong, not a bit the way girls had been when Mrs. McLeod was young. In spite of her smallness and youth, there wasn't anything gentle or dovelike about Jane.

Jane said, "I suppose I'll have to go to that Starburger wedding this afternoon. It'll be one of the showiest affairs Plattesville has ever seen."

"And don't forget it's county correspondence day."

"No, I wish I could."

Then a silence fell between them. Neither the old lady nor Jane could think of anything to say although both knew what the other was thinking. They were both thinking about Jimmy Dougherty. The old lady didn't favor him because he was the son of corrupt Old Dougherty, but she had other objections as well, principally a dislike of the idea that one of the McLeod family who had come to Plattesville long ago and grown up with the country should marry the son of an upstart politician who was a new-comer. There wasn't any need to tell all this to Jane, because the girl already knew it. She had grown up on a McLeod ranch and she knew what her own family was like; she knew their pride and their honor and their sense of decency. She knew, too, that no matter how poor they were, none of them would ever do a dishonorable thing for the sake of money. For more than fifty years the whole county had looked up to the tribe of McLeod and depended on them for order, and duty, and good government. But that was changed now; with Plattesville booming there didn't seem to be any need of the McLeods and their old-fashioned standards. They were all out-of-date, as out-of-date as McLeod's Folly itself, sitting in desolation among its ancient cottonwood trees.

Presently Mrs. McLeod coughed and pushed back her chair and stood up. "Well," she said, "I'll be off. I've got a lot of people to see this morning." Then she turned and called toward the kitchen door, "Aida!"

A voice answered, "Yes, Mis' McLeod!" And the solid figure rolled through the door.

"I'll be in for supper." Hesitating, she turned toward her niece and said, "What about you, Jane?"

Jane gulped and said, "I'll be out."

Mrs. McLeod didn't say anything, but Aida could not contain herself. "You're gonna have a bad stomach, Mis' Janey—eatin' around like you do— all sorts of trash. You're lookin' powerful peaked lately. If you was mine I'd give you a good dose of sulphur and molasses."

"Leave her alone, Aida," said Mrs. McLeod. And Aida went back to her kitchen not saying anything audible on her way out, but muttering and grumbling all the while like a volcano.

She went on grumbling and talking to herself while she baked up another heap of waffles and fried more eggs. She wasn't cooking her own breakfast;

she would have that when everyone in the house, visible and invisible, was fed. When the cooking was finished she loaded up a huge tray with waffles, jam, eggs, spoon bread and coffee and pushing open the screen door of the kitchen with one foot, she descended the steps of the back porch and after ten steps turned and went down the outside stairs into the cellar. On such occasions she always had to go outside the house to gain the cellar; the inside stairway was too narrow to permit the passage of so large and so heavily laden a tray.

Once inside the cellar, she put the tray down on a cheap wooden table and called out, "Hey! You all! Your breakfast is awaitin'," and after a moment two figures appeared out of the warm furnace room beyond. One was that of a stooped and graying man of about sixty, dressed in shabby clothes of decaying, humble, middle-class respectability. The other was a boy of about nineteen wearing a blue denim overall stained with grease and dirt. At the sight of the tray of hot food his blue eyes grew bright with excitement.

Aida said, "There it is. Better get at it while it's hot. And if you want more, all you got to do is pound on the ceiling. Ma stove is right over your heads."

Then she went away and in a little while the sound of pounding set her to work at the waffle iron once more.

3

In the huge hallway Mrs. McLeod took down from a coatrack, carved out of wood in the form of a tree with bear cubs climbing up it, a worn blue serge coat which had turned purple along the seams, and a red fox fur which had come long ago to look more coyote than fox. On top of her screwed-up hair she placed a hat with a little worn plume sticking upright on one side. Then she opened the large worn leather bag which was a kind of trade-mark, to make sure that she had plenty of pencils and copy paper, and with a quick glance in the mirror, turned and went out the door. Coming down the weed-grown path between the ancient shaggy laburnums and spirea, the figure of Mrs. McLeod had about it a curious, almost ghostly quality, as if McLeod's Folly were an enchanted place in which time stood still. It was the figure of a woman who was dressed in shabby worn clothes of a style that had passed like that of McLeod's Folly itself, years ago. Meeting her as she passed through the gateway, you might have thought Mrs. McLeod a ghost, save for the light in the eyes. It was the glance of someone who at sixty-seven was still very much alive, the glance of some-one who, despite the fact that she had never been farther from Plattesville than Galveston and Memphis, missed very little that happened about her and knew very nearly everything there was to know of the human race.

She was setting out upon the morning round of news collecting. Years ago she had arranged it so that in the morning she visited certain shops and places of business; Jane in the afternoon visited another series of establishments and Willie Ferguson had the district where lay the railroads and factories, all save Franklin Street with its sinister houses, grim and shuttered by day, glittering and raucous by night. It was no good letting Willie visit Franklin Street. Long ago she had permitted it, but the visits only ended two times out of three with Willie getting drunk and disappearing for a day or two, and then Willie's wife, Myrtle, the cashier in the *Daily Shield and Banner* office, would become hysterical and the whole office would be upset for days. So for a long time Franklin Street, except from six o'clock Saturday night to nine o'clock Monday morning, was out of bounds for Willie. What he did during those hours was his own affair so long as it did not interfere with the business of the *Daily Shield and Banner*.

From long experience she knew where to find the news. At the undertaking establishments she checked up on deaths and accidents. Hostetter was a modern undertaker who had a funeral chapel, wore elegant clothes and called himself a mortician. Beyond grim facts his establishment never yielded much news. The office, a sort of waiting room for Charon's ferry, was done in violet and black with a dark green carpet and a rich mahogany desk behind which sat Mr. Hostetter himself, dressed even on non-ceremonial occasions in suitable heavy black broadcloth. The place and the too smooth personality of Mr. Hostetter himself always dampened the spirits of Mrs. McLeod. There was something unctuous and heavy about the establishment which not only brought death very near but made it seem a pompous and boring affair like the reception of a visiting notable. And Mr. Hostetter himself never had any gossip or any tips. In the aloofness of his role as Charon's assistant he seemed to have no contact of a human sort with his fellow citizens.

So the visit there was always brief.

"Good morning, Mr. Hostetter."

"Good morning, Mrs. McLeod."

Mr. Hostetter rose and came forward, washing his hands, to greet her. The greeting always alarmed her a little, for it seemed to her that the cold green eyes of the undertaker were always regarding her as a prospective client. More than once she had thought grimly, "When I die he can't take out his bill in advertising because the *Daily Shield and Banner* will die with me."

"Any news, Mr. Hostetter?"

"No, Mrs. McLeod. Nothing since the Jones funeral yesterday. Were you able to attend?"

"No, I can never get away at that hour."

"A pity. It was one of the best conducted funerals Plattesville has ever seen."

"I don't like funerals much," observed Mrs. McLeod, moving slowly toward the door.

Anticipating her, because even the publicity of a dying paper like the *Daily Shield and Banner* had its value, Mr. Hostetter reached the door first and held it open for her. "You mustn't think of funerals like that. It's just a passing through the gates."

"Yes, Mr. Hostetter, I expect you're right, but . . . (she couldn't say that she disliked his unctuous way of preparing the gates) . . . but, well, I've got so much work to do. I don't like to think that far ahead."

"Good morning, Mrs. McLeod."

"Good morning, Mr. Hostetter."

Once in the street, she took a deep breath of that good, fresh, dry air for which Plattesville was famous. She put away her pencil, snapped her bag, and set out for the next stop, which was Jim Newman's Undertaking Parlors.

Jim belonged to her generation and tradition, so she felt at home there and approached the place with none of the dread which chilled her bones as she opened the door of Mr. Hostetter's mortuary. Jim she had known since he was a boy. He came from Calamos County, which was the site of her father's own ranch. Mr. Hostetter came from Brooklyn. Jim's undertaking establishment occupied a comfortable old building of red brick that stood back from the street with a stable at one side which sheltered the black hearse and the ebony horses. Mrs. McLeod liked that; it made her feel that there remained in the world at least one pair of horses which could conduct her to the grave with dignity. The thought of being whisked off to eternity in Mr. Hostetter's Buick hearse did not please her.

When she opened the door she found Jim and a half-dozen cronies seated about the iron stove. The air was hot and filled with tobacco smoke and the faint scent of embalming fluid, but somehow you noticed the faint acrid smell no more than you would notice the stale scent of beer in Hennessey's saloon. It belonged to the place and there was nothing sinister about it. The cronies were all men about Jim's age, all of them over sixty, belonging to the county, with childhood memories which matched those of Mrs. McLeod. She knew them all. They came from the ranches and farms out on the plains. Because it was Saturday they had all come into town in old Fords and Chevrolets. One of them, Sam Henderson, a die-hard, wouldn't even own a motor. He drove the twenty miles from his place in a buckboard drawn by a couple of piebalds in which he took great pride. They all greeted her as she came in, Sam shooting a great jet of tobacco juice into the box of sawdust by the stove and calling out, "Hello, Vinnie. You get younger every time I see you."

Jim told Sam Henderson to get up and give her his chair because here Mrs. McLeod never remained standing as she did in Hostetter's ante-chamber to Heaven; here she sat down and chatted. Here she garnered bits of gossip and news and hints of births and deaths and marriages to come in all parts of the huge county. Here she took out her pencil and sheets of copy paper and wrote in her scratchy illegible handwriting item after item in the saga of the great rich country she loved so much.

Jim Newman himself was a fat man, monstrously fat. When he sat down his stomach fell forward and rested on his knees. He did not rise when Mrs. McLeod came in: he rose and lifted the stomach off his knees as seldom as possible. He only grinned at her and said, "Well, Vinnie, what news?"

"Nothing," said Mrs. McLeod.

Sam Henderson handed her a Mexican cigarette, lighted it for her and said, "Henry Goddard's girl is gonna marry Jim Wilson's boy."

"Which one?"

"The one that was to St. Louis to the hairdressin' school."

"I guess that means she'll give up hairdressin'," said Jim, "in favor of diapers."

Out of the worn bag came the copy paper and pencil.

"How's the old rag getting on?" asked Sam.

"So-so," said Mrs. McLeod writing away on her copy paper.

"What you need is an up and comin' young fella to help you," said Jim. "We ain't as young as we once were . . . not even you, Vinnie."

"Where am I gonna find him?"

"Try prayer," said Hal Pierce; "the Methodists are having a big revival over to Little Canyon. You might go over and ask the parson to put in a word for you."

One by one they brought out more items from the life of the county and Mrs. McLeod wrote them down. The *Daily Shield and Banner* was a good county paper; it never lacked county news, and subscriptions had never flagged among the villages and ranches beyond the borders of the town. All that was *her* country and *her* people. She knew them. It was in the town that the newspaper seemed old-fashioned and a little empty. Mrs. McLeod never understood the Greeks, the Italians, the Irish. She couldn't fathom or like very much the sort of people who huddled together in cities. While she jotted down her notes, the five old boys from the plains went on making jokes and kidding her, smoking and spitting into the sawdust box. All of them had known her since she was a little girl, and now, when she was old like themselves, they still treated her as if all of them were still young bucks and she was the belle of some county gathering which had happened long ago when nobody thought anything of driving forty miles across the plains in open wagons. They knew that the worn coat, the shabby fur, the funny hat with a plume in it were a little ridiculous, but they knew too the sturdiness, the integrity, the honesty, the heart beneath the odd exterior. And all of them had been friends of J. E. McLeod and all of them knew the strange willful streak of pride and indefatigability that was in every member of the McLeod family, even in Jane Baldwin, who had been East to school.

"It's catching," Jim Newman used to say about the McLeod pride and stubbornness. "Everybody who marries into the family comes down with it —not that Vinnie McLeod didn't come by a big share from her own family."

4

When Mrs. McLeod found she had gleaned everything there was to be got out of the gossip about the stove, she said, "Well, boys, I got to go along now. If anything good turns up, write to me," and she went out to a chorus of "Good-by, Vinnie. Good luck."

As she left them, she walked across the little plot in front of the house feeling cheered and strengthened, but as she turned into the street once more a subtle depression settled over her like a cloud. It was always fun calling at Jim Newman's, especially on Saturdays when the boys came into Plattesville from all over the county; but what lay ahead of her did not raise her spirits. She had to visit the courthouse, which was dull, and the police station and the magistrate's court, and then she had to make a call on Old Dougherty, and if there was time she would call on Gashouse Mary. The last was the only visit in which there was any prospect of friendliness or cheer.

As she walked along the street, about one out of every three citizens she passed said, "Good morning, Mrs. McLeod." Once she had known every citizen in the town, and now she knew nearly all the old ones. Some of the old ones thought her funny and nearly all the new ones did. Half of those who said "Good morning" were negroes, some of them as old as herself and older. She walked down Louisiana Street and into Main Street, which she had known since the time it was a dusty unpaved thoroughfare with saloons and hitching rails and gambling houses on each side. Now it was like the main street of any one of a thousand American towns, lined with shops and chain stores and movie houses and office buildings and parked automobiles. It was the sight of Main Street more than anything in the town which made Mrs. McLeod feel old. No matter how many times she

[14]

saw it, there was always a faint contraction of the heart, and a faint sickish feeling of nostalgia.

She didn't much want to call on Old Dougherty, but his office was on the way to Gashouse Mary's and she had decided suddenly that calling on Gashouse Mary would cheer her up. After that she would go to the magistrate's court, which would probably be finished and closed until Monday, and then go to the police station where, with a little luck, she would find nothing but the routine record to copy.

The drama and the misery of all that concerned the police she would have avoided every day in the year if it had been possible; the spectacle, especially as it was conducted under the régime of Old Dougherty and his henchmen, filled her with pity and despair. But it wasn't possible to avoid the spectacle and be a good newspaper reporter. The subscribers of the *Daily Shield and Banner*, she knew, liked news of burglaries, murders and rape, and sometimes in the police court she came across a good human story, and good human stories, she knew, were the life blood of a newspaper's circulation.

There wasn't any humanity or even any intelligence to be found in the administration of the police court and the jail. Bill Flynn, the magistrate, always seemed to her to be less a judge than an exploiter of human ills. And he was hardest of all on the poor devils who drifted through Plattesville looking for work, not the tramps who knew the place and had it marked and avoided it, but honest fellows trying to find a job and make a new start. Bill Flynn never took any notice of the difference between a professional bum and an honest man looking for a job. None of them ever had a chance, because each one meant money in the pockets of the Dougherty gang. The charge of "vagrancy" covered almost anything. It meant that any stranger out of work might be clapped into jail for two or three months to work for Old Dougherty. For two or three months the poor wretch would have to work digging ditches, laying bricks, collecting garbage and refuse, for the city of Plattesville, but his work brought no saving to the taxpayers because Old Dougherty charged the city with a whole payroll and took the money himself. It was, Mrs. McLeod knew, a vicious system all round because it kept citizens of Plattesville out of work which otherwise might have been theirs. She knew all about that too, but she couldn't think how to go about cleaning up such a situation. You couldn't bring accusations unless you had proof and the money to back it up.

She was still worrying and dreading what lay before her when she turned off Main Street through Cherokee Alley to make the short cut that would bring her to the Dougherty Block. The alley was narrow and dark and in it were the Busy Bee Lunch and the Eureka Beer Saloon which attracted unfortunate strays by the cheapness of their prices. Once they left the river

[15]

front they came here like bees to clover, and Dougherty's gang, knowing this, always had a policeman somewhere about to pick up new workers on charges of vagrancy. Mrs. McLeod always took this short cut, not only because it was a short cut but because often enough she might encounter an unfortunate or two and warn them out of town before it was too late. Now, as she turned into the alley, she forgot her depression and looked about her sharply for any shabbily dressed man who might be looking for a job.

Before she had gone a dozen yards she saw coming toward her the tattered figure of a middle-aged man who was clearly down on his luck. He needed a shave. His felt hat, once a dark green, was faded by wind, rain and sun to a bilious shade of yellow green. His clothes were worn and bagged at the knees and elbows. In the discouraged face there was a look of weariness, despair and actual fear, like the fear of an animal which has been beaten and kicked for too long. She knew all the signs. She had met them a thousand times in the last three or four years.

She watched him come toward her, and as he was about to pass, she said as brightly as she could, "Good morning."

He stopped, looked at her for a second in a startled way, then he answered, "Good morning."

"Out of work?" she asked.

"Yes, ma'am. You don't happen to know of a job?" A note of despair came into his voice. "Any kind of job."

"No, I don't," she said, "but you oughtn't to be walking around this town looking for one."

"Why not? All I want is a chance to work."

"Well, this is the wrong town. If the police see you, they'll pick you up for a vagrant and then you'll get a couple of months working for the city."

The man only stared at her as if what she said was the last straw. So she went on. "See here. I'll tell you what to do. You go straight ahead of you up that first street on the right and when you get to the top of the hill turn right and walk two blocks up the street and you'll come to a big house with a big yard all around it. It's the only big house in the street, so you can't miss it. When you get there, you go to the back door. You'll find a colored woman. Just tell her Mrs. McLeod sent you. She'll give you a good meal and you can have a bath and press your clothes and hide away, and tonight you can get out of town again."

The man looked at her silently with a puzzled expression. "If anybody—a policeman, I mean—stops you, just say you're going to work for Mrs. McLeod. Now," she added briskly, "have you got all that straight?"

"Well," said the man, "pretty straight."

She repeated the instructions again, slowly, and then added, "If you get lost, just ask anybody where McLeod's Folly is. That's what everybody calls the house. Anybody can tell you."

"All right, ma'am," said the man. He still looked a little dazed, but he lifted his hat and said, "Thank you, ma'am," and then went on his way, crossing the street and going up the hill. For a moment she stood there, watching him to make certain he was following her directions. Once he turned and looked back, still with an astonished expression. When he saw her still standing there, he raised his hat again.

The encounter cheered her a little. If the man got beyond Main Street he'd be very likely safe until Aida hid him in the cellar, and at nightfall with a little luck, he could get out of town either by a passenger local or by one of the night freight trains. She knew the train schedules. Tom Higgins, the station agent, even kept her up-to-date on freight trains. She knew all the spots where trains stopped for water or slowed up for long pulls. It was all part of the system worked out between herself and Aida. Aida liked all the mystery—she liked having tramps hidden in the cellar. (She kept them in the cellar and locked the door of the inside stairway.) But most of all she liked feeding up people who hadn't had enough to eat for weeks. It cost both money and trouble, and if Dougherty's gang ever got wind of the "Underground Railway Station" in McLeod's Folly, the thing might become serious.

Odd kinds turned up in the shelter—men who borrowed through Aida books from J. E.'s dusty classical library, one man who said he had been president of a bank, another who had been a professor, and one who said that he was an Italian count. Most of the refugees Mrs. McLeod discovered in the part of the town which lay along the river; the others nearly always were rescued from the teeth of the police in Cherokee Alley. If a day passed without her sending along some unfortunate to McLeod's Folly, Aida was disappointed and grew ill-tempered.

As she emerged into the Courthouse Square, she ran full into Sam Hildreth, the policeman on duty to round up the strays of Cherokee Alley. He saluted and called out, "Good morning, Mrs. McLeod," and at the sound of his voice she started and blushed furiously.

"Good morning," she said.

"Looks like you were in a hurry. Going to a fire?"

Her heart beat furiously and she had to use all her will-power to control her voice. "No, but Saturday's an awful busy day."

She hurried on until she reached the Soldiers' and Sailors' Memorial Fountain in the center of the Square, and there, as she hurried round it, she came upon another man who lifted his hat and asked politely, "Excuse me, ma'am. Could you spare me something for a cup of coffee?"

He was a young man, dressed in a gray flannel suit that was stained with

[17]

dirt, and the hat he held in his hand was faded and the band missing. It astonished her that he stopped her because such men usually passed her by, judging no doubt from the dowdiness of her clothes that she was not worth a touch. Nearly always she had to speak to them first.

Hastily she opened the leather bag and took out a quarter, and as she passed it to him, he said, "Thank you," and it occurred to her suddenly that there was something about him that was very like J. E. McLeod when he was a young man. He had no mustaches and no curl on the forehead, but there was something about the set of the big shoulders and the jaw and the look in the blue-gray eyes which called up a swift vision of J. E. standing long ago on the steps of the *Daily Shield and Banner* office.

Looking quickly behind her, she said, "You better take my advice and get away from here before you're picked up for vagrancy."

"Thanks, ma'am, I'll follow your advice."

Then she drew aside so that the fountain was between them and the figure of Sam Hildreth, now standing in front of Hennessey's saloon. "Listen," she said, and gave him the same directions she had given the man in Cherokee Alley.

The young man did not seem to pay very close attention to what she was saying. He kept looking at Sam Hildreth and then back at her. So little attention did he give to what she was saying that she felt suddenly as if she were talking to herself and said, "Are you paying attention?"

"Yes, ma'am," said the young man.

"Well, you'd better get out of here quick before that policeman sees you or you're as good as in jail for two months."

"Thank you, ma'am," said the young man.

Then she hurried away, looking back timidly once or twice over her shoulder. When she turned the corner to go in the direction of the Dougherty Block he was still standing there by the fountain watching Sam Hildreth.

"What's the matter with him?" she thought. "You'd think he *wanted* to be arrested and clapped into jail."

All the way to Old Dougherty's office she kept thinking about him. There was something about him that was puzzling. It wasn't only that he looked like J. E. He had, too, an air of determination, almost of authority. He didn't have about him that look of despair and defeat which most vagrants had, and his clothes, despite their stained and rumpled condition, obviously weren't tramps' clothing. Being a reporter, for thirty years, even a bad, rather sloppy reporter, had sharpened her powers of observation. His accent told her that he was an Easterner, and when he said, "Thank you, ma'am," like an ordinary tramp, the speech didn't quite ring true. It was more as if he were an actor, and a ham actor at that, repeating lines.

"Well," she thought, philosophically, "if he wants to be taken up, it's his business. I guess he doesn't know how tough we are on tramps here in the West." She was a little troubled, too, by a suspicion that she had made a fool of herself and that even now the young man was chuckling at her expense.

5

Old Dougherty's office was on the top floor of the building which bore his name, the one skyscraper in all Plattesville which you could see ten miles out on the plains, if the day was clear. On the glass door were printed the words, "W. M. Dougherty and Son, Contractors." The "and Son" meant Jimmy Dougherty, who was running about with Jane. In a growing town they did a rousing enough business as contractors, but that, Mrs. McLeod knew, was not the source of most of their fat income. It came from graft, from protection paid by people like the poor women in the grim houses along Franklin Street; from every sort of petty political corruption. Old Dougherty had the Democratic party in the palm of his hand, and in Plattesville the Democratic party was practically everything.

As she climbed the stairs, a little wearily, she thought again how fine it would be to start a crusade and clean up Plattesville, to smash the machine of Old Dougherty and throw him out of control. She was always reading about editors in other parts of America who started crusades and cleaned up towns. Vaguely she thought of medals and prizes given to editors for services to their own towns. It was all something she dreamed of, something she thought of in the nights when she lay awake unable to sleep. But her hard, common sense always answered her: "You can't get away with that with nothing but an old-fashioned, out-of-date machine like the *Daily Shield and Banner*. You have to have a lot of money and a lot of energy and a lot of influence and I haven't got any of those things. You're old and tired and mortgaged up to the hilt."

Sometimes when she felt especially well and strong there were moments when she dreamed of the novel solving everything. She saw what Aida always called "The Book" finished and sold to a publisher. She saw it sweeping the country like wildfire. She remembered vague tales of the fortunes authors made by selling stories to movie producers. In an occasional excess of health she sometimes even went so far as to cover pages of copy paper with figures based on the hypothetical fortune "The Book" would bring her. With money which did not exist she bought new linotype machines, repaired the old-fashioned press that was always breaking down, gave McLeod's Folly a good double coat of paint and brought in two or three "investigators" to help her in the crusade against Old Dougherty.

But when the excess of health and spirits had passed, she knew that all the dream was nonsense and all the figures rubbish. No matter what Aida said about the parts that had been read to her, the novel was old-fashioned and too long, and anyway in these times nobody would be interested in the history of a pioneer family. Worse than that, she knew, in the shyness which had tormented her since she was a girl about anything which she herself had done, that she would never have the courage to send away to any publisher that mountain of manuscript that filled the old cowhide trunk in the attic of McLeod's Folly. No publisher would even trouble to read it through to the end.

6

In his office Old Dougherty was dictating two or three letters to wind up the week's work before he went fishing. He was a big red-faced man with a bull neck, the shoulders of a wrestler and tiny Irish blue eyes. His hair was pepper and salt, and coarse black hair covered the backs of his big hands. He was an ugly man, a kind of Iberian aboriginal out of the bogs of Ireland, but there was a kind of magnificence in the animal strength of his healthy body, and now and then there came into the small blue eyes a twinkle which disarmed even his worst enemy. And he was an actor by temperament, one of those flamboyant actors who, in the closing years of the nineteenth century, toured opera houses and auditoriums throughout the West, playing wild and sentimental Irish melodrama.

When the office boy came in to announce the presence of Mrs. McLeod he hesitated for a moment, thinking, and then said to his secretary, "I suppose I might as well see her and get it over with. Tell her to come in and then you can go home."

He knew her well enough. She had come to see him before, now and then, when she wanted a bit of information about street improvements or the plans of the Dougherty wing of the local Democratic party. He had hesitated not because he was afraid of her—what reason was there for a man with all his power to be afraid of a funny old thing with a dying newspaper like the *Daily Shield and Banner*? He was not afraid of her, but she had a way of making him feel vaguely uncomfortable which, for all his shrewdness, he could not quite understand. She belonged, he knew, to a vanishing world. She was respectable and a little fantastic. She had integrity and tenacity. But these were not reasons why the lined face and clear blue eyes beneath the funny plumed bonnet should always make him squirm a little inside himself. He was cynical in all his dishonesty, telling himself that if he didn't get the graft, someone else would, so it was not his conscience that was stirred by the sight of Mrs. McLeod. Partly perhaps it was because she was a woman—a woman who was plain and old now but who had once been pretty, perhaps even beautiful. If the editor of the *Daily Shield and Banner* had been a man, Old Dougherty would have given him a cigar, slapped him on the back and sent him away loaded with bilge instead of information. But a woman like Mrs. McLeod?

The door opened and she came in, shyly, stopping for a moment in the doorway and peering at Old Dougherty's heavy, coarse figure sprawled in the swivel chair.

"Good morning, Mrs. McLeod. Come in and sit down. What can I do for you?"

She came over and sat down and suddenly she could not think why she had come here or what it was she had meant to ask of him. On the way from Jim Newman's, she had gathered up her courage and decided to ask him directly why the new waterworks were taking so long and why it cost so much. And she thought of asking outright why the new lights along Hillyard Street had never been installed. And she had meant to protest about the brutality of the police and the magistrate toward vagrants whose numbers, in spite of everything, went on increasing.

But now all the questions quite flew out of her head. She saw that the proper source of information on these subjects was the Mayor and the City Council and that that was the only answer she would get from Old Dougherty. It didn't matter that he knew the answers better than the Mayor or the City Council or anyone in Plattesville and that she knew that he knew them. She understood now that if she asked such questions he would treat her like the fool she was. And something in the sight of his big body and corrupt, heavy, masculine face made her feel helpless and feminine. She knew that feeling all too well: more than once it had betrayed her. If it hadn't been for that feeling, she would have been a better newspaperwoman and a better editor.

Now she sat quietly on the edge of the chair and said feebly, "There wasn't anything special. I just dropped in on a chance that you might have a bit of news." And suddenly she found herself flattering this corrupt bullying man whom her whole nature held in contempt. She heard herself, with shame, saying, "I think editors should keep more in touch with important men in the town."

Old Dougherty grinned. "Thanks, Mrs. McLeod, for the compliment." He took the cigar out of his mouth and turning in his swivel chair, shouted, "Jimmy, come in here a minute." Then to her he said, "Jimmy knows more about what's going on than I do. I've kind of retired from things."

A voice from the next room called back, "I'm on the telephone. In a minute."

[21]

And Old Dougherty turned to Mrs. McLeod with a kind of leer and said, "That's a mighty pretty cousin you've got working for you on the *Shield.*" "It's a niece," said Mrs. McLeod, "my niece, Hally Baldwin's daughter. Hally was a McLeod. J. E.'s sister." And then she was aware that all this family history couldn't mean much to a newcomer to the county like Old Dougherty, and she felt a fool all over again.

"Sweet girl, too," he said. "Jimmy has taken kind of a shine to her. Brought her to the Elks' dance Saturday. We had a couple of beers together."

Mrs. McLeod experienced a kind of sick feeling in her stomach. Jane hadn't told her about the Elks' dance. The thing must have gone farther than she knew.

Weakly she said, "Yes, she was educated in the East at Wellesley."

"Too bad you haven't got a good man in your office to liven up the *Shield* a bit. Never thought about selling it, have you?"

She felt her cheeks growing hot. He was patronizing her now, treating her as if she were a comic town character. She said, "No, I don't expect I'll ever want to sell it. When J. E. died, I promised I'd keep it going."

He crushed out the end of his cigar and lighted a fresh one. "Well, if ever you think about selling it, let me know. I'd kind of like to own a newspaper. I've got a big interest in the *News*, but I'd like to own a newspaper outright. I've been thinking about it lately. Anyway, there's too many newspapers in Plattesville for a town this size."

She felt suddenly weak because for the first time it occurred to her definitely, as a fact, that some day if things kept on going the way they were going, she might *have* to sell the *Daily Shield and Banner* at a forced sale and then this old monster could buy it at his own price. The *Daily Shield and Banner*, J. E.'s paper which he had loved so much, the paper that had always belonged to the McLeods, going to Old Dougherty!

Then the door opened and young Jim Dougherty came in. She had known him, vaguely, ever since he was a little boy. She had seen him about town, growing up, seen him when he came home from the State University, seen him now and then at political meetings, but she understood suddenly as he came in the door that she had never really seen him at all until this moment, because always before he had simply been one of Plattesville's forty thousand citizens, and now she was seeing him as Jane's "young man."

What she saw was a young man who was an improvement on Old Dougherty, an improvement even on what Old Dougherty must have been before he grew heavy and gross and hairy. He was tall and wiry, with wavy black hair and Irish blue eyes and he wore his clothes well. And there was an engaging frankness about his grin as he came toward her. At sight of him she thought, "Well, I can't well blame Jane." His mouth was perhaps a little too sensual and the angle of his jaw was so sharp as to give an impression of willfulness that might approach cruelty. And perhaps he was a little too sure of himself and had an indefinable commonness. But there was no denying that he was handsome and personable.

He said, "Good morning, Mrs. McLeod," and crossed the room to shake hands with her. "We don't see you very often."

"I called you in to see if you might know some news for Mrs. McLeod," said Old Dougherty.

Jimmy Dougherty grinned, "Don't know of much happening that you or Jane don't pick up. I pass along to Jane whatever I hear."

"Yes, so she tells me," said Mrs. McLeod, lying. Jane had never told her anything of the kind, but she had to say it in self-defense, especially as both men seemed to regard Jane already as one of the family. She couldn't let them think that Jane hadn't told her everything.

"Still," said Jimmy, "there's the annual barbecue of the Democratic Club. We're making great plans. You could get out a good half a column about that." He turned and said, "Wait a minute, I'll get you a copy of the program." In a second he was back with a carbon copy. "This year it's going to be at Millersville. There's going to be prizes for the most fish and the biggest fish caught and a gold cup for the prettiest baby and a bathing beauty contest, free bus service—and a lot of other things. The biggest ever!"

She took the paper, folded it and put it into her bag. Then she rose, still with an odd feeling that they were treating her as a kindly old fool. "I guess I'd better not keep you any longer," she said, timidly.

"Drop in any time," said Old Dougherty, as he rose and went to the door with her. "Always glad to see you."

When the door was closed the father and son looked at each other, grinning.

"Might as well be kind to the old fool," said Dougherty, "it ain't much trouble and it's better to have her on our side. Even that old rag of hers might stir up trouble."

"Anyway," said Jimmy, "she's gonna be in the family before long."

"Has that girl said yes?"

"Not yet, but she will."

"Well, don't go getting her into trouble like that Ritchie girl."

"Hot chance, even if I wanted to," Jimmy grinned. "You don't know that girl."

7

Mrs. McLeod left the Dougherty Block with a feeling of depression. Although the sun was shining—that great sun of the Southwest, sometimes so kindly and benevolent, sometimes so fierce and relentless—she was not aware of it. If you had asked her if the day was bright she would have told you that the sky was overcast and there was no sun, for in her spirit, her own sun had gone out. She was ashamed of her own femininity and weakness, ashamed that somehow the Doughertys, father and son, had made her seem a fool. She had never been any good at dealing with people who were crooked and ruthless; they made her feel foolish, and her own mind immediately became incapable of coping with them. Again and again she had told herself, "You must fight fire with fire. It takes a thief to catch a thief!" But whenever she attempted Machiavellian methods they failed, leaving her stranded and a little ridiculous. Long ago it hadn't mattered so much, but now the failure made her seem old and tired and discouraged. And she was ashamed of having been so weak and feminine as to like such a scamp as Jimmy Dougherty when she saw him with Jane's eyes.

She had left McLeod's Folly intending to go to see Gashouse Mary down on Franklin Street, but now as she walked along Main Street, scarcely seeing the people who smiled and bowed to her as she passed, it seemed a useless thing to do. What good was it to try to discover evidence of the Doughertys' wrongdoing when the Doughertys had only to talk with her for ten minutes to muddle and defeat her.

She would have abandoned the project but for Gashouse Mary herself. In spite of everything she had always liked Mary. There was a kind of strength in her, a sense of reality, uncontaminated by cynicism, from which she herself drew strength. Gashouse Mary, she thought, wasn't a silly vaporous romantic like herself, writing novels and hiding them away timidly in trunks in the attic. Gashouse Mary was always down to brass tacks.

And Gashouse Mary might have news, the kind of underground news which you couldn't find elsewhere in Plattesville.

So when she reached the corner she found herself, almost without knowing it, turning down the hill toward the river and Franklin Street. With each step in the direction of the river the street grew a little more shabby, a little less well-kept, a little more sordid. Even the trees seemed more tired and discouraged than the sycamores, the oaks and the cottonwoods higher up in the town.

Franklin Street lay along the river, a short street only three blocks long, in a district which in one spring out of three was flooded when the river, fed by the last rains of winter, rose above the levees. The flood had just passed, leaving behind it a thick layer of mud which, drying, still filled the air with the heavy scent of fertility. Boards had been laid down to protect the high-heeled feet of the shady ladies of Franklin Street from the mud, and along these Mrs. McLeod made her way past the dozen or more houses, dingy and unpainted, with large windows on their façades. They

[24]

were all shuttered and closed now; they would, Mrs. McLeod knew, come to life after sundown. Then the dreariness of Franklin Street, concealed by the darkness, would change to noise and lights and frantic gayety, with the sound of mechanical pianos filtering out from behind closed windows.

The last house in the street was different from the others for two reasons; it had had a fresh coat of white and yellow paint and at one side there was joined to it a large flat structure, one story high, bearing across the front both in enormous painted letters and in electric lights, the name: EL DORADO BAR AND DANCE PALACE. The house itself was of the same fancy architectural epoch as the other houses, the same in fact as the vast bulk of McLeod's Folly itself, but it made no effort at concealing itself or hiding behind shutters. This was because Gashouse Mary, its proprietor, was the only tenant in the block who operated within the law. For Mrs. McLeod the sight of the low flat building with the legend EL DORADO BAR AND DANCE HALL always roused to life a long chain of memories; it carried her back to the days of her childhood when Plattesville was a wide-open frontier town and there had been a dance hall called the El Dorado on the Main Street where the Dougherty Block now stood—a dance hall with a hitching rail in front of it, lined with ponies of the cattlemen. Gashouse Mary was the daughter of the proprietor of the original El Dorado. She had carried on the tradition in another day in another part of the town.

Mrs. McLeod crossed the mud-soaked front yard on a walk made of boards and rang the bell, not without a stirring of excitement in her heart. There was something about the whole district and about Gashouse Mary's place, something free and wild and unrestrained, that never failed to touch the romantic in her. As a little girl waiting in a buckboard for her father outside the Ranchers' Bank, she had listened to the singing and shouting and wild music that came out of the original El Dorado on Main Street: and afterward, throughout her life, she had known moments when she experienced a fierce longing to see, just for one night, what life was like behind the swinging doors of such a place. But she had never been able to see it at first hand. As a young girl it would have been unthinkable for her to visit such a place, and after she was married it became even more impossible as the wife of J. E. McLeod, first citizen and owner and publisher of the *Daily Shield and Banner*. In spite of being a newspaperwoman and the owner of a newspaper, she could never quite escape the mold of the old-fashioned Southern lady.

So, when the door opened and she found Gashouse Mary's colored parlormaid, Minnie, not yet dressed for the evening but wearing a faded gray wrapper and carpet slippers, her heart leaped with excitement at the glimpse of what life was like inside a place like the El Dorado.

She said, "Good morning, Minnie; is Mrs. McGovern up yet?"

"She's just gettin' up," said Minnie. "Come right in."

"I don't want to disturb her."

"You ain't disturbin' her," said Minnie. "She's always glad to see you all. And how's Aida?"

"Aida is fine," said Mrs. McLeod, now inside the hall.

"Give her my respecks," said Minnie. "She doan speak to me no more since I'm workin' in Franklin Street."

"Aida is kind of peculiar," said Mrs. McLeod kindly.

Minnie opened a door and showed Mrs. McLeod into Gashouse Mary's parlor, saying, "You all just wait here." In the doorway she turned. "Maybe you all would like some beer or some coffee?"

"Some coffee, Minnie."

"Mrs. McGovern'll be right down."

"Thank you, Minnie."

She had seen the room in which she was sitting many times before. Ever since she had found it impossible to send poor broken-down, drunken old Willie Ferguson into the district and had taken to coming herself, she had always come to Gashouse Mary's for news and had been received as a re-fined and superior visitor in the parlor. It was a big room with an ornate mantelpiece full of pigeonholes, each containing a bit of hand-painted china. Plumes of dusty pampas grass stood before the mirror, and opposite there was a portrait of Knobby McGovern, the third-rate prize fighter, who for twenty years had been Gashouse Mary's husband and chucker-out wherever she had a bar and dance hall. The portrait was an enlarged photograph, hand-tinted, of a man with huge mustaches, cauliflower ears and a flat nose, with a wistful expression in the blue eyes. Mrs. McLeod had never seen him, but she liked his looks. He looked like a lot of the men she had seen in her childhood along Main Street.

The rest of the room was crowded with furniture, furniture which was very like that in the parlor of McLeod's Folly—gilt chairs and a loveseat, a vast black walnut sofa and a carved teakwood table with a plush cover, an album and a dusty palm. The whole room was now veiled in the feeble light which came through the cracks of the closed shutters.

Minnie returned in a little while, bringing in coffee and hot buttered toast, and while Mrs. McLeod ate and drank, her spirits began to rise again and her romantic imagination to work furiously.

What, she asked herself, had happened in this funny shuttered room? Whom, besides herself, had Gashouse Mary received here? What had Mr. McGovern really been like, with his battered face and his mild childlike too-blue eyes? But most of all, she kept asking herself just how bad Gashouse Mary was. Her house wasn't like the others in the street. Ostensibly it was a dance hall operated with a license: and yet . . .

[26]

The neighborhood was unsavory and she couldn't make herself believe that Gashouse Mary, for all her friendly manners, hadn't a finger in other pies besides the dance hall. There was, she was certain, some understanding between Gashouse Mary and Old Dougherty. Slowly her indignation began to rise again, and with it the old desire to overthrow Old Dougherty and expose him. It might be just possible that Gashouse Mary could give her aid and information. There was only one thing to do and that was to take her courage in both hands and put it directly to Mary.

She had just finished her coffee when the heavy walnut door opened and Gashouse Mary came in. She was a big woman, so big and powerful that in the underworld of Memphis and Natchez and New Orleans there was a legend that in her prime she had acted as her own chucker-out. There were stories that the battered appearance of the late McGovern had come about as much from Mary's prowess as from his ill-starred fistic career. There was something grand about her even now as a woman in her sixties, entering the darkened respectable middle-class parlor. She was magnificent and impressive. Something came into the room with her—something big and wild and full of vitality. She was dressed in a peignoir of purple cut-plush and was wearing red mules trimmed with ostrich feathers. Her figure, corseted very high in an old-fashioned way, was full to overflowing. Her hair was mahogany red and her coiffure was, even at this early hour of the morning, an intricate and elaborate affair of coils, rolls and knots, fastened at the top with a tortoise-shell comb studded with brilliants. About the whole picture there was an air of something splendid and indefatigable, a remnant of those earlier days when Plattesville had been a wide-open town.

Now she smiled, showing her fine double row of false teeth and said, "Good morning, Mrs. McLeod." Mrs. McLeod put down her cup, rose a little, timidly, and said, "Good morning, Mary."

Long ago on Saturdays, when Mrs. McLeod was a little girl, waiting for her father to finish his business before driving back to the ranch, she and Mary had played together in the little square of open land in front of the El Dorado Dance Hall. The little square was a park row, with a soldiers' and sailors' monument in the midst of cottonwood trees, and she and Mary were well past sixty. She always called Mary by her Christian name as she had done long ago, but ever since Mary had returned from her wanderings in the great world, she had always addressed her childhood playmate as "Mrs. McLeod." This troubled Mrs. McLeod, but she never complained of it for fear of embarrassing Mary.

Mary said, "Why didn't that dumb Minnie open the shutters? You can't see to get the cup up to your mouth." And with that she pushed up the windows and flung back the shutters with a vigor that raised a clatter to be heard the whole length of Franklin Street.

Then she seated herself and offered Mrs. McLeod a cigarette. Mrs. McLeod did not as a rule smoke because it gave her no pleasure and cost money that was needed to keep the *Daily Shield and Banner* alive and pay the devouring interest of the mortgages that encumbered McLeod's Folly, but she always smoked when she came to see Gashouse Mary, because it seemed to bring the two of them nearer together.

"And how have you been?" asked Mary.

"Very well."

"And the *Daily Shield and Banner?*"

"Pretty well."

Gashouse Mary detected in the voice of her friend a shadow of weariness and despair and said, "What you need for that paper, Mrs. McLeod, is some new blood. Neither of us is as young as we once were."

"Where am I going to get it?"

"Well, that's kind of hard to answer. Too bad you never had any children to carry it on." And then, fearful that she might have hurt Mrs. McLeod's sensibilities, she quickly added, "I never had any either—anyway none that lived. But I guess if you haven't got 'em you just have to carry on by yourself."

"My niece Jane has come to work on the *Shield.*"

"Yes, I've seen her in the street. Looks to me like an uppity young woman."

"She was educated in the East, but she doesn't mean to be uppity."

"What you need is a good tough, two-fisted young fella that knows his business."

"Yes, I guess so."

There was an awkward silence and then Gashouse Mary said, "I ain't got any news for you this week. Nothing much has happened down here on the line."

Mrs. McLeod coughed and then plunged. "It wasn't news I was worrying about," she said. "It was something else." Then she came to a dead halt.

"Well, what is it?" asked Mary. "I guess you don't need to mince words with me."

"Well," said Mrs. McLeod, "I've been thinking and it seems to me that this town is due for a good clean-up."

"You said it," said Mary. "But how?"

Mrs. McLeod's hands were trembling now. "Well, I thought I might start a crusade in the *Daily Shield and Banner*—you know, exposure and facts, etc. . . . . about graft and how the taxpayers' money is wasted."

"You mean attack Old Dougherty and his gang?"

"Yes, I guess it would have to be that."

Gashouse Mary grinned. It was a hard grin full of false teeth and experience and knowledge of a corrupt world which had never been quite able to defeat her because she was a realist and took no chances; she had never been a romantic like Mrs. McLeod.

"Who's gonna do it? You and your uppity cousin and old drunken Willie Ferguson?"

"Well, I thought I might get others to help—honest citizens like you and me who are scandalized by the open goings-on."

"Yeah?" asked Mary. "I've found out it's no good depending on honest citizens unless you've got something to offer 'em. Get a good leader and a good organization and they'll follow—mebbe. I've been through plenty of clean-up campaigns up and down the Mississippi River, but damned few of 'em ever came to much. Just when you need 'em most, the good citizens back down. I've always kept inside the law because I've found it paid better, cost less in money and trouble. So nobody's ever been able to chase me out of anywhere. I'd like a clean-up myself. I've got plenty to settle with Old Dougherty, and there ain't anything he can do to me by law . . . not a damned thing."

Mrs. McLeod drew a deep breath. "You mean that you'd be willing to help?"

"Sure I'd be willing if we had the right outfit. You can't ask the *Daily News* to help. It's in Old Dougherty's pocket. And it ain't much use going to Hoppins up in the *Chronicle* when he owns half the property here on the line. It's always the same story. I've been through a lot of clean-ups. Most of the time the crooks are too well organized, and most of the town don't want to be cleaned up for fear it might lose a little dough in the process."

Mrs. McLeod didn't say anything and Gashouse Mary warmed further to her subject. "I don't say there ain't a lot of unsavory people down here by the river, but they ain't as bad as the crooks that live off 'em. Right now I'm paying money to that outfit."

"How?" asked Mrs. McLeod. "Your business is legal."

"A hell of a lot of difference that makes to Old Dougherty." She caught herself and said, "Excuse my language, Mrs. McLeod, but it burns me up."

"Sure," said Mrs. McLeod. "But tell me how?"

Gashouse Mary drew her chair nearer to Mrs. McLeod. "If I tell you," she said, "you'll have to give me your word not to use it in the paper. A woman in my position can't afford to get in wrong with Old Dougherty—anyway, not unless we had an outfit strong enough to lick him."

"Of course what you say is confidential."

"Because," said Gashouse Mary, "if you did print it, I'd just deny I ever told you anything." She lighted another cigarette and said, "You see, I always liked Plattesville ever since I was a kid, and when poor McGovern died I decided to clear out of New Orleans and come up here and open a bar and dance hall like Pappy had. I thought it would be a good idea to spend my old age here." Again she glanced at Mrs. McLeod and said, "I've always kept orderly places within the law and that's what the El Dorado is. It ain't in a very nice part of town, but nobody can say it ain't run right."

She blew rings of smoke for a moment as if hesitating whether to go on. After a time she said, "Old Dougherty's been collecting protection money right along from Mamie Furnoy and Estelle Laverne and the other girls down here, and as soon as I opened the El Dorado one of his guys came to me and proposed that I make a weekly contribution to the City Orphans' Fund—that's what this particular graft is called. So I said, 'Why? I don't need protection. The El Dorado is a straight bar and dance hall. What do I need protection for?' Well, he went away and a couple of nights later a lot of bums turned up in the El Dorado, started a fight and smashed about two hundred dollars' worth of furniture and glass. I sent Minnie for the cop on the beat and called up headquarters, but the cop on the beat wasn't there and by the time the cops from headquarters came, the bums had disappeared. That kind of thing never happened in a place of mine before, but it happened again the next week and the next and then I got word from the Mayor, who is just Old Dougherty's stooge, that if it happened again, he'd have to close the El Dorado as a public nuisance."

Again she was silent, her face now bright red with anger and indignation. Mrs. McLeod asked, "What did you do?"

"What did I do?" asked Gashouse Mary. "The next time Old Dougherty's man called on me, I made a fat contribution to the Orphans' Fund." She crushed out her cigarette. "It burns me up," she said. "In the old days when you and I were kids, Mrs. McLeod, they used to call Plattesville a wide-open town full of bad men, but it was a kindergarten compared to this town now. Every place you turn, some guy from Dougherty's crowd has got a hand held out. It's a damned shame, that's what it is—to see a fine town like Plattesville spoiled by a gang of crooked politicians. Something ought to be done about it, but who's gonna do it?"

"I don't know," said Mrs. McLeod weakly. "I wish J. E. was still alive."

Then for a time Gashouse Mary and the editor of the *Daily Shield and Banner* sat silent and brooding. They were both thinking about the old days during the land rush when there wasn't any Dougherty Block on Main Street and when there was a row of saloons and dance halls opposite the Park and a vigilant committee which gave everybody a square deal. In their memories McLeod, the late J. E. McLeod, came alive again, tough, honest, a valiant citizen struck down in his prime by death. J. E. would have fixed Old Dougherty and his gang in no time. But what could his widow do, with no money and only herself and old drunken Willie and Jane?

At last she said, "Well, you think, Mary, and I'll think, and maybe we can find some way of fighting them."

"Think?" said Mary. "I've been thinking of nothing else except clearing out of Plattesville for a decent town. Only I never been licked yet and I don't want to be now."

Suddenly Mrs. McLeod felt a wave of affection for Gashouse Mary and her valiance. They belonged to a day when life had been simple, direct and full of savor. Then suddenly she saw with a sense of despair that Gashouse Mary was, like herself, a relic, a left-over. For a second she even saw that Mary and herself must seem awfully funny to most people in Plattesville, curiosities to the younger ones of the place.

She sighed and rose. "Well, Mary, if that's all the news you've got, I'll be going."

"That's all," said Mary, "and mind you don't even print a hint of what I told you."

"I promised you."

They moved together toward the huge walnut doors.

"Drop in any time. I usually sleep until about ten-thirty, but after that I'm on my feet. It's an awful job running a place like this all alone. I never knew what a help McGovern was until he died."

They passed into the hall and Gashouse Mary went with her to the door. As she stood in the full light from the outside she seemed, despite her handsome, tight-corseted physique, despite the dyed hair with its complicated coils and studded comb, despite the rouge and powder, to turn old and tired and raddled.

"Give my best to Willie Ferguson," she said. "I miss him down here, but for Gawd's sake don't tell him that, or he'll be wantin' to come down here again."

"Okay," said Mrs. McLeod.

8

The courthouse was a depressing building constructed in the eighties in that same gaudy once-fashionable style as the houses in Franklin Street and McLeod's Folly itself. Two years earlier it had had a bright, shiny, new copper roof out of which Old Dougherty had made ten thousand dollars. Through it passed the official life of the whole county, and as Mrs. McLeod entered its ill-lighted corridors smelling of stale tobacco smoke and spittoons, she was greeted by cattlemen and ranchers come into town to pay taxes or register deeds or check up on boundary lines. Most of them stopped to chat, addressing her as "Mrs. McLeod" and sometimes as "Vinnie." They exchanged gossip and hearty handshakes and three or four invited her "out to the place" to spend a week or two. But she had to decline their invitations, saying that she would like nothing better but that she was busy all the week with the *Daily Shield and Banner* and on Sundays she was too tired and had to wash her hair and do a little house cleaning.

They delayed her progress so that by the time she reached the magistrate's court old Judge Flynn had already gone. With the clerk she went over the morning's record, thankful in her heart that she hadn't been there to witness the hearings which were recorded simply and sordidly in the book of the clerk. There wasn't news in any of the cases—just a dreary record of drunkenness, wife-beating, adultery, petty thievery, and at the end, three cases of "vagrancy," which meant three more jailed workers whose pay Old Dougherty would draw. When she had written down the simple facts she put her copy paper and pencil back into the bag, snapped it shut, thanked the clerk and left.

Then she passed through the ornate doorway, out of the musty corridor and crossed the street to the police station. Here, as in the courthouse, she was allowed all the privileges of a newspaperwoman. She knew all the "boys" and liked most of them. The Chief, Harvey Bingham, was, she knew, crooked or he wouldn't have kept his job, but outside of that he was a good fellow and kindly enough and he had eight children to support. She liked Harvey Bingham; she had known him always, and before him his father and mother. He belonged to the county; he wasn't a newcomer like Old Dougherty and most of his gang, bringing corruption with him. Harvey, she told herself, wasn't naturally crooked, he was just easy-going. If Old Dougherty and his gang hadn't spread their net over the whole town, Harvey would have been just a simple straight citizen.

She found him in the room where prisoners were brought in to have their records taken down, sitting with his feet up on the desk. When she came in he said, "Hello, Vinnie," put down his feet and added, "How's things?"

"The same."

Two other policemen greeted her, grinning a little as they always did at the sight of her thin figure, her wispy hair and her old-fashioned clothes.

"I was just going to eat," said the Chief. "Anything I can do for you?"

"I was just looking for news."

"Ain't none around here but the same old stuff."

She went over to the record and began looking through it. The Chief stood up, put on his hat and said, "Well, Vinnie, if there ain't anything I can do, I'll run along and get me something to eat."

"Okay," said Mrs. McLeod, without looking up.

She went on copying the record. She heard the door close and then, after a time, open again and was aware, without looking up, that a policeman had come in with a prisoner. Automatically one of the other policemen seated himself at the table beside her, opened a book and took up a pen. There was nothing new in all this. Because she had stayed so long talking with Gashouse Mary she was late already and the Saturday evening edition with all the county correspondence was always a bother. She went on writing, scarcely hearing the answers to the questions asked for the record.

Vaguely she heard the name "Thomas Richardson" and the address "New York," age "twenty-nine," born "Boston, Massachusetts," business or profession, "newspaperman," charge, "vagrancy."

At the words "newspaperman" she looked up and there before her, looking down at the policeman who was writing in the book, she saw the young man she had left standing by the Soldiers' and Sailors' Memorial Fountain. She thought, "The damned fool! I told him if he hung around there he'd be picked up," but at the same time she couldn't really make herself feel irritated at him. Now, in profile, he seemed to resemble J. E. scarcely at all, but he was none the less the kind of young man for whom she had always had a fancy, ever since she was a young girl. There was something about the set of the shoulders and the square angle of the jaw which made her feel very feminine, and for thirty years now, Vinnie McLeod, the most feminine of Southern ladies, had had to run a newspaper and compete with men and pretend she was a man. There were plenty of men, even Old Dougherty for example, who had square jaws and broad shoulders, but this young man had something else—something which J. E. had had—a quietness about him which gave the shoulders and the jaw an augmented attraction. It was that quietness which had made it possible in the old days for J. E., unarmed, to dominate a whole barroom full of brawling gamblers and frontiersmen. That was what made this young man seem like J. E.— it wasn't really that he looked so much like the husband who had been dead for thirty years. It was the quietness.

While she was watching him, he turned, and recognizing her, grinned and said, "Hello." It was a friendly, almost affectionate grin, the kind of grin she might have expected from her own son if she had had one.

"Hello," she said and with her eyes tried to say, "I told you so."

The man at the desk looked up and said, "Do you know the prisoner, Mrs. McLeod?"

Quickly she said, "No. Only he touched me for a quarter this morning."

"You oughta have turned him in."

"I guess I didn't have time," said Mrs. McLeod. "I was in a hurry." She blushed suddenly and bent her head again over her copy paper.

With a kind of malice the policeman at the desk said to the prisoner, "Well, it looks like you'll have to spend Sunday in the calaboose. It's Saturday and there ain't any more court till Monday."

The young man did not answer him and Mrs. McLeod knew that both policemen felt malice toward him because he was young and good-looking, and because of the way he held himself, and because you could see at a glance that he was no fool. There was something pugnacious and challenging about him, in the very way he held himself, a kind of defiance and contempt which Mrs. McLeod knew would do him no good in Plattesville. And the quietness made his manner seem worse. It put an extra edge on the defiance and contempt. The two policemen were grinning as if they thought, "We'll soon take that cockiness out of you, young fella. This town is famous for taking the freshness out of guys like you."

"Take him away, Jim, and lock him up," said the policeman at the book.

Mrs. McLeod looked up and almost spoke. She wanted to say, "Let me speak to the prisoner for a moment," but quickly she stopped herself, thinking, "If I talked to him they might get a suspicion about the men in the cellar, and then all that would be spoiled." She wanted to ask if she could send him books or something special to eat from Aida's kitchen, but she dared not risk it.

When the policeman had led him away to a cell she asked, "Where did they pick him up?"

The policeman at the desk grinned. "In the park by the Memorial Fountain. He practically asked to be picked up. He walked straight into Sam Hildreth's arms. He must be a hell of a sap, hanging around the center of a town like Plattesville. Acts to me as if he was a little goofy."

Mrs. McLeod put away her copy paper and pencil and snapped shut the voluminous bag. No, he wasn't goofy certainly, but she couldn't make him out.

"We'll take care of him," said the policeman. "Looks to me like he's pretty husky. We need guys like him to wrestle garbage cans and dig that new Bellmore Avenue sewer."

All the way back to the office Mrs. McLeod couldn't get the young man out of her mind. It would be a pity to see such a nice-looking young man digging sewers for two months.

9

It was after one o'clock when Mrs. McLeod reached the office of the Plattesville *Daily Shield and Banner* and went through the door past the grill where Willie Ferguson's wife Myrtle sat to register subscriptions and accept the rare money which was paid in for advertisements. The cashier was a chill and angular woman filled with the unassailable egotistical integrity of the woman of her day. She wore an old-fashioned white shirtwaist with a high collar, a skirt with pockets in it, and over her arms from the wrist to the elbows, sleeve guards of black alpaca. On the ridge of her narrow Roman nose dangled uncertainly a pair of pince-nez which were attached by a gold chain to a button fastened to the shirtwaist. These were of use to her only when regarding figures and accounts; talking to a subscriber or an advertiser she was forced to tilt her head forward and look over the glasses.

At the sight of Mrs. McLeod entering the office flushed and distracted, Myrtle Ferguson simply said, "Good afternoon," in a clipped, pettish fashion, but by the tone of her voice she managed to say a great deal more. She said without saying it, "William's and my pay is two weeks behind. The gas company wants to be paid. I haven't been able to get a cent out of old Weissman on his account. And I suppose you've been gallivanting around Plattesville with some crazy new idea in your head."

But Mrs. McLeod, thankful that she said all this only by intimation, hurried past lest Myrtle should change her mind and become more articulate. She was thankful too when she reached the back stairway leading to the composing room, and the door banged behind her, leaving Myrtle to her sour reflections.

The *Daily Shield and Banner* occupied the same building constructed for it at the time of its founding, seventy years earlier, by J. E.'s father. Bigger, more modern and more prosperous buildings had grown up round it facing on the square—buildings which squeezed the little two-story red-brick structure in the relentless embrace of an inexorable progress. About its façade with the big sign in dingy gold letters—"THE PLATTESVILLE DAILY SHIELD AND BANNER"—there was something quaint and sad. Clearly the structure belonged to another era; it stood among its more modern sisters a little like a belle of the sixties at a rowdy country club dance.

On the ground floor at the back of the business office the clumsy old-fashioned presses thumped and groaned in the late afternoon and on the floor above, the precious old linotype rattled away, melting, molding its miracle of print beside the racks of type where Zimmerman, the ancient compositor, picked and set and corrected from nine in the morning to six at night.

In the front of the building on the second floor overlooking the square there was a big room with a cubbyhole built of matchboarding in the corner. This was the sanctum sanctorum of Mrs. McLeod, from which she directed the destinies of the *Daily Shield and Banner* in her vague distracted way. Here she received complaints and attempted to keep accounts which in thirty years had never once balanced properly. In the large room outside there were rows of cupboards filled with ancient dusty files of paper, and a long table on which were kept daily copies of the *New York Times* and the *New York Tribune*, the *Kansas City Star* and the *St. Louis Post Despatch*, all papers which J. E. had admired and which provided the *Daily Shield and Banner*, a day or two late, with most of its national and foreign news. On one side, against the wall, stood the desks of the remaining members of the staff—Mrs. McLeod's niece, Jane, and Willie Ferguson, the one as neat, as orderly, as clean as Jane herself, the other a confusion of clippings and copy paper, half-smoked cigars, pencils, paste pots, paper clips and packages of chewing gum—for all the world like Willie.

The whole room had a smell of paste and dust and ancient tobacco smoke, tempered sometimes by a faint smell of lavatories or with a faint whiff of Bourbon from the bottle which Willie kept in the bottom drawer of his desk. It was a friendly, dirty place, reeking with the atmosphere of fifty years of old-fashioned intimate journalism.

Although the desks of Niece Jane and Willie Ferguson stood side by side, there was little communication between their two occupants. It was rare indeed that any word was spoken which had to do with anything save the pressing business of the paper itself. Jane thought the disorder of Willie's desk a disgrace and Willie himself a drunken old reprobate; and Willie, in his turn, thought Jane uppity with a whole set of cold-blooded efficient Yankee mannerisms picked up at school in the East. In his opinion—which he never hesitated to utter when the spirit and reinforcement from the Bourbon bottle moved him—the place for women, even Vinnie McLeod herself, was in the home and not in a rough place like a newspaper office where they were in daily contact with all sorts of sordid and unladylike facts which women were not supposed to know. He was old, Willie, and cantankerous and he had grown up in the grand tradition of Southern chivalry. It was his earnest belief that even the mother of ten children should never admit, even to her husband, that she suspected how it had all come about.

He did not like to hear words like "illegitimate" and "rape" and "criminal assault" in the mouth of a nice young woman like Niece Jane, and twice he had been caught by Mrs. McLeod suppressing stories in which such words occurred simply so that they should not reach the eye or ear of Jane—an action symbolic of the unwelcome chivalry which Jane was determined should not be forced upon her. In his heart he had never forgiven J. E.'s widow for taking him off the Franklin Street round and herself going to see Gashouse Mary, and in his heart the resentment was born less of his own deprivation than of his horror at the picture of Lavinia McLeod and Gashouse Mary sitting down together for a chat in a house on Franklin Street.

He was a small man, very thin and wiry, with a mocking blue eye and large shaggy mustaches, who always had the air of being lost in his own clothes. In general, he was sour, with the agreeable sourness of a dill pickle, but there were moments when temper would rouse the small elderly figure into a rage which was more like the tantrum of a small child than the fury of a grown man.

When Mrs. McLeod pushed open the door from the composing room, she found the atmosphere of the editorial room charged with that unmistakable sense of strain that invariably followed a quarrel between Niece Jane and Willie Ferguson. There were two other more definite signs: Willie was reinforcing his temper with a generous swig from the bottle of Bourbon, and Jane had turned her chair so that she sat with her back directly to her enemy. Before her on the neat table stood a carton of coffee and a bag of sandwiches.

"You aren't going out for lunch?" asked Mrs. McLeod.

"No, I've got to finish editing the county correspondence."

Willie rose, pulled up his loose trousers, buttoned his shabby coat and said, "Well, I'm going to have some *hot* lunch. There's nothing ruins the stomick quicker than slops and cold food."

For a moment he stood looking at the back of Niece Jane with a faint expression of hope on the thin, discouraged face—hope that somehow he would goad her into answering back. But Jane gave no sign whatever of having heard his remark, and hope died out of Willie's face to be replaced by that look of sour and humorous discouragement that was habitual. He could think of nothing better to do than to slam the door violently as he went out.

When he had gone Jane put down her pencil and said, "I don't see why you keep that old drunk here."

Mrs. McLeod said, "He's not so bad."

"He couldn't be worse. He's never sober. He can't remember anything. He muddles every story and he gets on my nerves."

"He worked for J. E. I can't turn him out."

Then for the first time Jane was rude to her Aunt Vinnie. She said, "The paper will never be any better so long as the office is filled with rubbish. It'll just get worse and worse."

Mrs. McLeod regarded her for a moment reproachfully. "What would happen to Willie if we turned him out? He can't do anything else."

"He could go to the county poor farm."

"No, he couldn't. It would kill Willie." Jane was silent and Mrs. McLeod added, "And Myrtle. Think of Myrtle's self-respect."

Jane took up her pencil again and went back to her work but Mrs. McLeod remained there for a time standing behind her. At last she said, "You see, you don't understand about Willie's pride. You aren't old enough yet, my dear, to know what Plattesville and the county used to be like."

But Jane had nothing to say. She shrugged her shoulders and went on with her work. Her aunt went into the little sanctum and shut the door, the only sign of disapproval anyone in the office had ever known her to make. When Mrs. McLeod shut the door of her tiny office it meant that things were not going too well.

<h2 style="text-align:center">10</h2>

She hadn't shut the door because of what Jane had said about poor Willie; that she understood. She understood that Jane was young and ambitious and impatient, and had the hardness and intolerance of youth, and she understood that poor old drunken Willie was cantankerous and meddlesome and bitter at his own weakness and failure in life. You couldn't really blame him for the Bourbon bottle in the bottom drawer of his desk.

It was Jane herself who worried her—Jane and Jimmy Dougherty. She knew that Jane was having her lunch in the office because she wanted to get away early, and she divined that Jane was made irritable not by the childishness of Willie Ferguson but by that persistent bad conscience.

Mrs. McLeod was innocent of anything which might be called an intellectual process, but she had plenty of instinct. Muddled intellectually and overemotional, she *knew* things about people without thinking them out. What troubled her most was the difficulty which she and Jane had in understanding each other. It wasn't, Mrs. McLeod saw, only the great difference in their ages but a difference in upbringing and generation and point of view. Jane and all her generation always made her feel shy and a little frightened. She could not quite understand what they meant when they spoke of falling in love, and in her heart she could not quite see how any man could fall in love with anyone so hard and sure of herself as Jane seemed to be. She could see with her own eyes that Jane was pretty enough and even that there was something brilliant about her. A man would certainly be attracted by her fine complexion and her figure, but there were other things which mattered, perhaps even more than complexions and figures, in the long run. Love, for Mrs. McLeod, had always been something soft and tender with humility in it and adoration. And she could not see how any man could feel tenderness or adoration for anyone as pert and confident as Jane. And as for Jane's feeling tenderness or humility or adoration for any man, this to Mrs. McLeod was inconceivable. Jane, she knew, thought her old-fashioned and sentimental. Jane in her heart thought her a fool to have kept the *Daily Shield and Banner* going on year after year, ruining herself slowly, because she had loved a man who had been in his grave for thirty years. And Jane had hard, new, bright ideas, picked up, most of them, in the East, about woman's freedom and independence and what she called "a woman's right to her own life." Mrs. McLeod wasn't afraid of Jane's being seduced, even by a good-looking boy like Jimmy Dougherty with the reputation of being Plattesville's

Don Juan. Jane would never get into trouble out of weakness. But she might get herself into trouble out of recklessness and defiance.

She felt that something must be done about Jane, that some warning must be given her out of her own long years of experience and watching the world about her, but how this was to be accomplished she had no idea, because whatever she said, Jane would simply think her an old fogey. What troubled her most was the fact that when Jimmy Dougherty had come into the old man's office and she had seen him for the first time with the eyes of Jane, he had seemed to her, even in spite of her prejudice against the Doughertys and everything they stood for, a handsome, attractive and disarming young man. With the ghost of a blush she thought, "At her age I might have been seduced by a man like Jimmy Dougherty."

She might have sat there by her old-fashioned roll-top desk for hours staring out into the square seeing nothing, but for the tinkle of the telephone. Starting, she took up the receiver and heard a voice saying, "Is this Mrs. McLeod?"

"Yes."

"Well, this is Tom Higgins."

"Yes, Tom."

"Well, there's been a wreck on the P. and W. two miles beyond Spoonerville siding and I thought you'd want to know about it in time for the paper. It happened after Willie was here this morning."

"Anybody killed?"

"No, just a freight train. Engineer has a broken arm and fireman a broken leg."

"What's their names?"

"Don't know yet. I'll telephone you as soon as I find out."

"Thanks, Tom."

"Good-by."

"Good-by."

The call cheered her a little without her knowing why. People all over town had a way of helping her out, people like Tom Higgins, the ticket agent of the P. and W. station, who called her up and told her news. They were really reporters for the *Daily Shield and Banner* who never got any pay. They were always helping her out. That was something that Jane didn't understand—at least not yet. It was the kind of knowledge which came of age and experience. Jane didn't yet know that you get back from the world just as much as you give to it of friendliness, of generosity, of understanding.

Then her eye fell on the alarm clock which stood on the top of the roll-top desk and she saw that it was nearly two o'clock and that she had less than an hour to get in whatever news was to come out in the Saturday evening edition.

Opening her bag, she took out the sheets of copy paper covered with erratic, hastily written notes and turning J. E.'s ancient swivel-chair about she went to work picking out with one finger on the noisy old typewriter the news she had collected.

There wasn't much, nothing at all in fact save the records of the police station and the magistrate's court and what she had picked up at Jim Newman's funeral parlor. The longest bit she had to write was the story of the plans for the coming barbecue given by the Doughertys each year for the entertainment of their henchmen and their families. That occupied half a column which she needed to fill up the paper. Gashouse Mary's story, which would have shaken the town and started trouble, she had promised not to use. Depressed, she felt now that she would never be able to use it. She was too old and too tired and too silly. She had set out this very morning with vague ideas for starting a big clean-up campaign and she had returned to pound out on the typewriter nothing but the story of the barbecue which only helped the Doughertys instead of hurting them.

While she was finishing the barbecue story the telephone tinkled again and when she answered it, she heard the voice of Willie Ferguson. He had begun his week-end drinking early, for by the sound of his voice and the way he spoke his words she knew that he was already a little drunk.

"I've got a good story," he said. "I won't be in till late."

"What is it?" asked Mrs. McLeod.

"A woman down here is having children. She's had three and Doc Hazlett says there are more coming. I guess she can't make the dead line."

"What's her name?"

"Mary Kowlski . . . k for kitten, o for Osbert, w for Willie, l for lulu, s for sugar, k for kitten and i for idiot."

"Okay."

"Her husband works in the Chain's factory, address 62 Franklin Street. His name is Jan . . . like jam only n for Nettie at the end."

"Yes. Call me back as soon as they know how many."

"Okay."

"Where can I call you back?"

There was a moment's hesitation and then a weak voice said, "Gashouse Mary's."

"Okay."

Suddenly she felt discouraged again. Willie had broken his word and gone to Gashouse Mary's before the Saturday paper went to press.

Again she went to work picking on the typewriter. "Mrs. Jan Kowlski of 62 Franklin Street gave birth this afternoon to quadruplets. Her husband is a worker employed at the Plattesville Chain Mill. Mrs. Kowlski, it seems, will be the winner of the generous prize offered by W. M. Dougherty for the largest number of children born to one family during the year."

As she typed the last word, Alf Lyman, the linotype operator, thrust his head in the door, his hatchet face beneath his eyeshade giving him the appearance of a voracious crow.

"Any more copy, Mrs. McLeod?" he asked.

"Just this," she said, handing him the barbecue story and the story of the freight wreck, "and here's a woman who had quadruplets . . . anyway she's had three and there's more on the way, so I've said quadruplets."

"Foreigner?" asked Alf.

"Yes, Pole."

"Better set that last. She might have a litter."

"Okay. Put it in a box."

The sudden excitement put her in a better humor and when ten minutes had passed, she rang Gashouse Mary's bar and asked for Willie.

"Paper's going to press," she said. "Any more?"

"Five," said Willie, "and Doc says that's all. They're celebratin'."

Quickly she ran through the room. "Five there are," she called through the door to Alf above the rattling of the machinery. "Quintuplets!"

"Was I right?" Alf shouted back.

Then as she closed the door again she remembered the line about W. M. Dougherty's prize. She had meant to attack him, and tonight the *Daily Shield and Banner* would seem no more than a Dougherty organ bent on giving Old Dougherty publicity.

II

While Mrs. McLeod worked behind the closed door of her cubbyhole Jane went on with the writing of her society column and the editing of the county correspondence. The wedding didn't happen until four o'clock but she had been to see Mrs. Vanderpool, the bride's mother, and got all the information necessary—the decorations, the list of guests, the description of the wedding presents, the menu. The rest she wrote out of her own imagination, using the flowery phrases which Aunt Vinnie said the people liked. She hated every word of the story and was ashamed of herself for writing it. Mrs. Vanderpool had been silly and tiresome, saying over and over again, "Please be accurate. You newspaper people make so many mistakes." Anyway, thank Heaven, she didn't have to go to the wedding itself and see Hazel Vanderpool simpering in her wedding gown, beside pimply Herman Starburger under an arbor of smilax and lilies. At four o'clock she would be free to join Jimmy and drive down to Millersville for supper at the roadhouse.

The wedding out of the way, she tackled the county correspondence.

When she first came to work on the *Daily Shield and Banner* she had ripped it apart unmercifully, changing the wording and the phrases to make it sound up-to-date, condensing and killing the floweriness which was a passion with the old maids and widows who sent it in each week from the villages which dotted the county. Mrs. McLeod, preoccupied with many troubles, had let it go through without looking at it, and became aware of the sacrilege committed by her niece only when the *Daily Shield and Banner* received a flood of protest from the correspondents and their friends. After that she said to Jane, "It doesn't matter how it sounds. They're the ones who read the county correspondence. They've always written it like that and they like it that way."

"Why, it isn't even grammatical," Jane had protested.

"What does grammar matter? You can't hurt their feelings. They love to see in print what they've written just as much as you do."

"It does matter. It's one of the most important things in the world."

But Aunt Vinnie had only smiled and said, "Be a good girl and let it go through. Just watch the spelling, that's all."

When Aunt Vinnie was like that Jane hated her, mostly because when Aunt Vinnie was gentle and smiling and firm, it always made her feel terribly young and stupid. It was worse, almost, than if Aunt Vinnie scolded her the way Aida did. So after that she let the county correspondence go through exactly as it was sent except for correcting the spelling.

It wasn't funny any more to her when she read:

"Mrs. Curtis was over to the Henry Billings place Sunday. Brought back two hams and some fresh eggs, gifts of the generous Henry."

Or:

"Mrs. Bert Pease has a bonny new boy. Congratulations Bert!"

Or:

"Miss Elvira Sefton is expected at any moment to announce her fiancailles to Homer Banks from over Geneva way."

At first when she came home from college in the East, the county correspondence always caused a warm feeling of superiority, but lately that too had gone, leaving only boredom in its place. These were her own people. She had grown up with them. She knew them all, the second and third generation of the pioneers who had built a great rich state out of the wilderness. If her mother at home on the ranch near Pottstown had written the county correspondence, it would have sounded exactly like the copy she spent half a day each week reading and correcting. So at rare moments she felt ashamed of herself for being what Gashouse Mary and Aida called "uppity."

She might not have been "uppity" if she had not also been unhappy. She was unhappy for a great many reasons, because the ranch at Pottstown had been yielding less and less ever since the war, because she didn't really belong in Plattesville and could not find any way to make herself fit into that somewhat special picture, and most of all because she felt that she wasn't getting anywhere. Sometimes she lay awake in her big room in McLeod's Folly and thought, "I'm twenty-three years old and I haven't got anywhere. Just working on a broken-down, old-fashioned newspaper where I don't even get a regular salary. No nice clothes, nothing. Not even married yet. I'll be an old maid grumbling away in the office like Myrtle Ferguson downstairs."

She didn't want to be married and settle down with a husband in a little house in Plattesville. She wanted a big house and a couple of cars, and enough money to help out her parents and the Pottstown ranch which she loved better than any place in the world. She wanted to have a lot of money and to be somebody. She had, she decided, been poor long enough. Now, looking back, she hated those years in the East when she had worked in the college tearoom to help pay her tuition and board.

It was ambition which made her unhappy. It was herself who had chosen to go East to college instead of going like other girls in the county to the State University. She had wanted to get out into the world, but somehow she hadn't really escaped at all. She had only gone away for a little while, and here she was back again, worse off than if she had never seen the East at all.

But she was unhappiest of all over Jimmy Dougherty. He made her unhappy because she was falling in love with him and she really didn't want to. It was, she knew, a betrayal of Aunt Vinnie and her own parents and all they stood for, and a betrayal of herself as well. There were even times when she was out with him in a restaurant when she felt ashamed to be seen with him before people she met there. She deceived Aunt Vinnie and Aida because she was ashamed. Yet she couldn't help going out with him. Lately she had even taken to sitting in the office staring at the wall for a long period of time, trying in spite of herself to see the black hair and blue eyes and good-looking face and the engaging, unmoral, mocking grin. And always there was a terrible small voice saying, "If you married Jimmy Dougherty you could have a wonderful house and two automobiles and trips to New Orleans and St. Louis and even New York. You'd be somebody then. After a while you'd be able to fix it so that people wouldn't even mind his being Old Dougherty's son."

But he hadn't even asked her to marry him yet, and she was afraid that when he did ask her, she would say "Yes" just because of the black hair and blue eyes and grin and because with all the money he had she could do all the things she liked. Both reasons made her ashamed and unhappy. Scottish Presbyterian blood stirred in her veins and made her feel that neither reason was good enough. All the same she lay awake at night thinking, "I'm twenty-three already and I haven't got anywhere."

At four o'clock she put her desk in order, closed the drawers, and went to the dim little mirror advertising Reiselman's Cigars, where she rearranged her hair and put on her hat. She did it with a nervous self-consciousness, fearful that before she got away the door would open and Willie Ferguson would come in. She wanted desperately to get out of the office without seeing Aunt Vinnie and without some acid remark from Willie, so she hurried as much as possible, but as she turned from the mirror she discovered Willie standing unsteadily in the doorway. He was regarding her with a tipsy air of mockery, and as she turned he said in his richest Bourbon voice, "Goin' sparkin'?"

She tossed her head and didn't answer him and the Bourbon voice said, "Better look out for that Dougherty squirt, he ain't up to no good."

She felt her face go red with unbearable rage. She heard herself saying, "I can take care of myself. You mind your own business, you drunken old sot."

But all the response she got was a cracked laugh and the sound of the Bourbon voice saying, "When I was your age I was kind of uppity too, but I had to come down off my high-horse. Wait'll you get married and have a dozen kids. Wait'll you get to be my age. You'll change your tune."

She started to answer him but the door of the cubbyhole opened and Aunt Vinnie came out, her hair in wilder disorder than ever, her face and hands smudged from the struggle of trying to put a new-fangled ribbon into an old-fashioned typewriter. The sight of her, just as she meant to escape, was not quite the last straw; the last came when Aunt Vinnie said, "Will you be home for supper?"

In spite of herself she answered wildly, "You know I won't. You heard me tell Aida."

Aunt Vinnie didn't lose her temper. She just said quietly, "I guess I must have forgot."

Then as she opened the door, she heard the Bourbon voice behind her saying, "Young woman, you got no right to speak to your Aunt Vinnie like that." And all she could do was to slam the door, which only made her feel worse than ever. By the time she reached the bottom of the worn stairway tears were streaming down her freshly made-up face—tears of rage and shame and heartbreak.

In the office behind her Mrs. McLeod was saying to Willie Ferguson, "You leave her alone, Willie. She's a good girl."

"Mighty pert!"

"Well, I can remember, Willie, when you were mighty pert yourself. I can remember when you were the struttinest lady-killer in the whole Southwest."

But that only pleased Willie. The lined old face broke into a grin. He gave a hoarse chuckle meant to be rakish and wicked and took the Bourbon bottle out of the bottom drawer.

"How about a little drink, Mis' McLeod? It's Saturday night."

Surprisingly she answered, "Don't mind if I do."

The old-fashioned press was rolling away belowstairs. The day's work was done and she felt oddly tired and defeated and old.

Willie fetched two paper cups from the water cooler, poured a drink into each and raised his cup. A queer distant look came into the small, shrewd blue eyes. "To J. E.," he said. When he had swallowed his drink he added, "Somehow Bourbon don't taste right out of paper cups."

12

Because of the tears Jane had to stop in at the Boston Store and go into the ladies' room to make up her face all over again. And that made her late and failed to improve her humor. But Jimmy Dougherty was waiting for her already in his new olive-green roadster in front of the Dougherty Block. Both the sight of the roadster, all shiny and new, and the sight of Jimmy himself, jumping out and grinning at her when she came up, made her feel happier. Which had the stronger effect she was unable to judge.

"Sorry I'm late," she said, "but everything has gone wrong today."

"You're worth waiting for, any time."

"I hate pretty speeches."

They both climbed in and he started the motor. "You're the most defeating girl I ever knew."

"Why?"

"Always saying things like that. Always snapping me up."

"I'm sorry, only that kind of stuff always sounds like something out of the movies."

She didn't really hate the speech itself. She loved it; only she had the feeling that he had talked like that to a hundred other girls. Her instinct told her that Jimmy was that kind of man; worse than that, he was attractive because he *was* that kind of man. It made her feel cheap that she liked the speech, and liked him for saying it. Worst of all there was something inside her, some sort of unhappiness which made her say things like that even to people she liked most.

After a moment she said, "Anyway, I'm cross today."

"Why?"

"Everything has gone wrong since I got up this morning."

"What, for instance?"

"Nothing. Never mind."

She could not and would not tell him the story beginning in the morning with Aida's scolding. She would not tell him even one incident of the day because to tell him any of it would be a betrayal of her Aunt Vinnie. That was one of the things which upset her friendship with Jimmy—that she

[45]

couldn't be frank or confide in him without betraying Aunt Vinnie and all the McLeods as well to the Doughertys. And she told herself, "I would rather cut off my right arm than do that."

"Anything I can do to help?"

"No."

He grinned, using that weapon which always disarmed her. "You'll be all right when we get to Millersville and have a cocktail."

"Maybe."

"Anyway, it's a swell day."

What he said was true. The day could not be finer and he had a kind of animal appreciation of its fineness. The early summer had brought a thick cloud of green over the plains and along the brooks and ditches. It was an evening when everyone should have felt the simple glory of being alive as Jimmy felt it and here she was riding beside him, fretful and unhappy. They drove on for a time in silence across the flat plain dotted with ranch houses, ending at last in a barrier of low hills which were already turning opalescent in the sunset; and as they drove her mood changed. The tenseness of her nerves slackened a little and a kind of peace stole over her.

Presently he said, "Your aunt paid us a call this morning."

She divined a mockery in his voice and knew that he was grinning, but she would not look at him for fear of losing her temper. She said with a certain tartness, "What aunt? Mrs. McLeod?"

"Yeah, I don't know any of the others."

"I've got aunts all over the county. The family have been here for a long time." She had managed to hit back at him in return for the mockery, but almost at once she felt ashamed of herself.

"We're always glad to see her."

"Yes, I suppose you have a good laugh as soon as she's gone."

This time he didn't answer her, but presently, after they had driven for a long time in silence, he said, "You're one of the most disagreeable young women I've ever met. I don't know why I should bother about you except you're so pretty."

"Thanks."

"And because you aren't really like that."

"I know what I'm really like," and she wanted to say, "I'm selfish and nasty and quarrelsome," only she wouldn't give him such an advantage.

"The right man could do a lot with you."

This she found too insulting to bear. The tears came into her eyes, blinding her, and filling her with a new fury. She said, "If you don't stop talking about me, I'll jump out and walk home."

He did not answer her and to her astonishment he drove the car to the side of the road and stopped the motor. Then he said, "Now look here.

[46]

We've got to settle this. There's no use in going on to Millersville if we're going to quarrel all evening."

"I'm not quarreling."

"Well, I don't know what it is, but anyway neither of us is enjoying himself very much."

"I'm sorry. I'll behave myself, but it's your fault too."

"Maybe."

He took her hand. It was a big handsome comforting hand. He said, "I'll behave myself if you will."

Reluctantly she said, "All right. If you don't speak again until we get to Millersville."

"Okay."

He started the motor and they drove off in silence, and as they drove she thought again as she had thought so many times, lying awake in the middle of the night, that she was a fool to go on seeing him when she knew that everything was against any good coming out of it. She told herself that this was the last time she would see him. After tonight she would be finished with him and then maybe she would have peace and her disposition would be better. And everybody would be pleased—Aunt Vinnie and Aida and even that horror, Willie Ferguson.

They were silent for nearly half an hour until they came into the foothills and then without thinking or willing it, she said, "I love this country, I'll never leave it."

"Not even to go back East?"

"No. There's no room in the East. Out here you can breathe."

"It *is* pretty big."

Big! Was that all he saw in it? She wanted to laugh with scorn but controlled herself. What could he, a newcomer, know of this country where every stick and stone was somehow associated with the great tribe of McLeod?

As they climbed out of the flat plains into the hills toward Millersville, she forgot the quarrel and the ill temper passed away. There was something about the hills that always lifted the spirits of the people who lived day after day, year in and year out, on the vast plain. The old cattlemen and their families had always looked on the hills as a place of spiritual refuge, going there on every holiday to picnic and fish in the little lakes that lay hidden away in the more remote valleys. The hills worked a kind of magic on them, and the same magic was working now in the soul and spirit of Jane. Here there were trees and wild shrubs and wild flowers and all sorts of wild small animals. The first touch of summer had brushed the hills and they were glorious in the sunset.

They climbed again for a long time in silence and then suddenly the car came over the crest of a hill and below them lay Millersville with its groves and trees, its little hotel and tourist camp built just on the edge of the little lake that was a deep sapphire color in the blue sunset shadows which filled the little valley. It was a spot which Jane knew well, which she had known since she was a small child. Millersville and the little lake belonged too in the tradition of the McLeod clan, for the Miller who had discovered the lake and built the hotel was a brother of Jane's grandmother. Millers still lived there and Ira Miller, the grandson of the founder, still ran the hotel and the tourist camp which had brought new prosperity to the place. She knew the deep blue lake and every tree of the groves which grew down to the edge of the water, and now the sight of the place as they descended the winding road leading down to it swept away her restlessness in a flood of happy memories. Suddenly she no longer hated Jim or Aunt Vinnie or herself or even poor drunken old Willie Ferguson. In the sunset she felt a sudden blossoming of the spirit, a kindliness that approached love for everyone she knew. All at once, because she was very young, she was happy.

13

Before the slow valley twilight slipped into darkness, they went for a row on the little lake in one of Cousin Ira's boats, talking scarcely at all, drifting now and then along the edge among the water lilies, watching the startled birds which flew up with wild cries as the boat slipped among the reeds. And presently she found herself watching Jimmy Dougherty as she had never watched him before, stealthily, speculating about him—what he was really like when he was not wise-cracking and trying to impress women, what it was exactly that he wanted of her, what there was in him exactly which made her want to see him in spite of everything, why the thought had ever occurred to her that in a weak moment she *might* really marry him. She knew his shortcomings—that he was too gay, that he made love as easily as any tomcat, that he was not too well educated. It always troubled her that he would not talk about plays or books or economics or even of politics outside the small world of Plattesville, where he knew politics only too well. He could talk of nothing except that which touched him at the moment—what had happened during the day. He lived, it seemed to her, from moment to moment, unaware of fine and subtle things, of all the things she had learned in the East to admire. Always she told herself that she could never marry and live with a man who had neither background nor cultivation, for it was a part of her dream of being important that she would have in Plattesville a kind of *salon*. She would wake up the people of Plattesville. She would bring lecturers and symphony orchestras and singers and exhibitions of pictures. She would . . .

And then she forgot all this in a sudden flash of insight about him. It was born of a sudden glimpse of him as he sat opposite her, turning his head a little to correct the direction of the boat. He had taken off his coat and rolled the sleeves of his shirt above the elbows and he was rowing with the easy strength of a man who knows his own body, a man in whom body and spirit are perfectly coördinated with no complications, no fears, no nonsense. In that flash of insight she thought, "He belongs here on this lake, among the trees, as any wild animal belongs here. He belongs much more than I do." That was why he fascinated her. That was why he was irresistible—because he was such a healthy animal. It was very clear to her suddenly and she was ashamed at the quick intimation of what love really was, ashamed because she had believed herself above such emotions. And she was frightened too. Something about him as he sat there opposite her, driving the heavy boat through the water, made her want to cry.

Then the sudden instant of revelation passed and in the next second she could not remember what it was that had been revealed to her. She heard him saying, "We'd better go back and have a cocktail." And quickly because the shadow of her sudden fear still clung to her she said, "Yes, it's getting dark."

Changing the course of the boat, he rowed in silence for a long time, grinning at her once or twice as if to tell her that it was a beautiful evening and that he was happy with her sitting there opposite him. Then as they drew near the little pier, he said, "There's something I've got to ask you later."

In spite of herself, her heart leaped. She did not want him to ask her to marry him because she would have to refuse him. Yet the idea was agreeable and titillating. She wanted to go on seeing him, but if he asked her to marry him she would have either to say "yes" or "no." She could not say "yes." There were too many things against it. And if she said "no" she would have to give up seeing him and that she did not want to do. She felt herself blushing, and feeling thankful for the twilight, she answered, "All right."

By the time they reached the little pier, the open space in front of the hotel was filled with cars of every sort. Half the younger world of Plattesville was there for the Saturday night dance.

It was a world which she did not know very well because before she went to college in the East she had lived mostly at the ranch, seeing only those people who belonged to the old cattlemen's world, and when she came home again and went into Plattesville to work for Aunt Vinnie, she had made little progress because she felt strange and unadaptable and almost alien. The world of these motors was the world, not of the county, but of the town, a world made up of the children of bankers and lawyers and merchants, and in it she never felt at home. It was the world too of the country club and for that world neither she nor her own family nor Aunt Vinnie had ever had enough money.

So when she entered the big dining room she felt shy and embarrassed, shy because of Plattesville's younger set, and embarrassed of being seen out with Old Dougherty's son. And at the same time she felt defiant, and ashamed because she was ashamed.

She knew some of the people, not well, but enough to show her recognition with an abrupt nod of the head which conveyed defiance, resentment and even contempt. Jimmy knew a good many of them and those he knew he spoke to, always showing that wide grin which had so evil an effect upon Jane's feelings—that grin which made him seem so attractive, but with which he was too generous, giving it to everyone—the grin of a young man who had come to terms with life and so could afford to be pleasant to the whole world.

They had cocktails and then danced, and presently Cousin Ira Miller came to show them their table. He was a big man, nearly sixty, with big hands and feet, a rough-hewn, rather grizzled head and sharp blue eyes. He had inherited Millersville and a little hotel, rotting and in need of paint, and he had kept both, barely making ends meet for nearly twenty years, hunting, fishing, farming a little, begetting eight children and living a kind of idyllic life very near to the trees and the birds and the animals. And then when he was middle-aged the automobile brought prosperity to Millersville and the old-fashioned lakeside hotel. It brought people during the long summer evenings from Plattesville and towns much farther off; it brought people to fish and people to spend the week end; and it brought people to stay in the tourist camp which had grown and grown until it filled all the little grove behind the hotel. Ira's father had been the first white man to see the little lake and now, sixty-five years later, Ira was profiting by the foresight which had led his father to lay claim to the whole country round it.

Ira kissed Jane and asked after the family and Aunt Vinnie and said, "You mustn't go without going into the kitchen to say hello to Ella. She's awful busy on Saturday nights seein' that everything goes right."

When he had gone, Jimmy said, "I always like to see Ira. There's something about him that's like a good western film."

They had a good dinner with trout out of the ice-cold water of the hatchery which Ira had built at the back of the grove, and the best cut of sirloin which the plains below could offer. They drank St. Louis beer and danced some more and then Jim said, "Let's go and have a row by moonlight," and she thought, with pessimism rising in her heart, "Now he's going to propose and I can't stop him. Oh, why can't we just go on as we are?"

On the lake they rowed for a long time without speaking at all, silenced by the beauty of the night, but Jane kept thinking, "What will I say if he asks me now? What will I say?" She didn't want to marry him. She could not. But . . .

Then she heard him saying, "I told you there was something I wanted to ask you." And faintly she answered, "Yes?"

"How would you like a good job on the *News*?"

The question startled her and she thought, "What a funny way to begin." But she said, "What do you mean?"

"I mean I can get you a good job with good money. I've been thinking about it for a long time. You're never going to get anywhere on the *Daily Shield and Banner*. I hate to see you wasting your time on a broken-down, old-fashioned paper like that."

Her pride flared up. She was suddenly wild with anger. She wanted to cry and she wanted to strike him all at the same time.

"It's a good enough paper," she said, with a wild effort to control herself. "I wouldn't think of leaving Aunt Vinnie," and at the same time she realized that this was really all he had to say, that he had never thought of asking her to marry him, and in the merciful moonlit darkness she felt her face growing hot with shame and rage. It was as if he had insulted her.

"I didn't know," he said humbly. "I thought you might like it."

"Anyway, I wouldn't touch a dirty, filthy sheet like the *News* with tongs."

He didn't answer her but she knew that he understood what she meant— that she would have nothing to do with a newspaper that belonged to the Dougherty gang. That was too much—that the Dougherty gang, even Jimmy himself, dared to offer her, a McLeod, favors. It was the first time there had ever been between them an open hint of the truth that she was a McLeod and he was Old Dougherty's son, that she came of the people who had made the county and he was no more than the son of a shrewd and crooked politician who was a newcomer.

Now he didn't answer at all but merely turned the boat in the direction of the little pier. When they landed he said in an odd voice, "I think maybe we'd better go home."

"Whatever you like."

But she knew by the queer sound of his voice that she had hurt him.

Together they found their way to the motor. Together, side by side, they drove back to Plattesville. But they never spoke during the long drive and when at last they drove up before McLeod's Folly, he got out, opened the door and helped her out of the car. Without a word he opened the rickety gate and she said, "You mustn't come all the way up." But he answered, "I'm not going to have you go alone up that path through the bushes." And she wanted suddenly to cry and say, "I've been a damned fool. Don't let's quarrel! We mustn't! We mustn't!" But she said nothing and passed through the gate with a stiff dignity which she knew in her heart was ridiculous. But she could do nothing about it.

When they reached the door and had put the key into the lock he said, "Your aunt oughtn't to keep those bums in the cellar. Some day one of them will try to murder her."

She could think of nothing to say but a melodramatic, "What do you mean?"

He only took off his hat and said "Good night," so there was nothing left for her to do but to open the door and go into the house.

Alone in the gaslit hallway of McLeod's Folly she realized that he hadn't said, as he always did, "What are you doing Thursday?" or "When am I going to see you again?" He had simply said, "Good night," and gone away. Then she thought, "How did he know about the tramps? He's known all the time. Now he'll make trouble for Aunt Vinnie." But in her heart she knew that he wouldn't.

Upstairs in her own room, after she had undressed and climbed into the huge walnut bed, she could not sleep for pondering what it was she wanted in life. It had been an awful day and everything had gone wrong from the beginning. What Jimmy had said about the tramps in the cellar began to trouble her so that she could not rest until she had got out of bed and locked her door, a thing she had never done since she had come to live at McLeod's Folly. Then suddenly she had visions of strange men springing at her out of the tangled lilacs and syringas, of unshaven desperadoes haunting the huge shadowy halls of the old house.

14

At home Mrs. McLeod had eaten listlessly one of Aida's best dinners, suffering because of her indifference and lack of appetite the unceasing reproaches of her cook, so that it was a relief to her when at last the meal was finished and Aida could no longer scold her. Before she said "Good night," she told Aida about the young man she had seen at the police station.

"Too bad you all didn't see him before the police," said Aida. "I hate to see a nice young man get caught up by that Old Dougherty gang."

When Aida had gone to bed Mrs. McLeod put out all the lights except the one in the hall and went upstairs to have a bath and wash her thin, gray hair. It seemed to her that she had never been so tired before, and for an hour she lay in the hot water, fretting about what was to come if now, when everything was going so badly with the *Daily Shield and Banner,* she was to lose her strength when she needed it most.

After she had gone to bed she lay awake until she heard the sound of a motor at the gate and then the sound of the front door closing. Then quietly she rose and went into the hall, meaning to say "Good night" to Jane. There was friendliness in her intention, for she knew that Jane was unhappy, but there was no curiosity, for she knew well enough with whom Jane had spent the evening. As she made her way along the big, dark hallway, she was again filled with a desire to help the girl, but how she was to do it she did not know. Then as she neared the door of Jane's room, she heard the sound of sobbing and stopped, a little frightened and uncertain. Now, because she had never had any children of her own, she did not know how to behave. For a moment she even felt that Jane was wiser and had more experience than herself. Jane, after all, had been to school in the East and she belonged to another generation which knew what it wanted and how to get it in a fashion she had never known. For a long time she stood there and at last, overcome by the sense of her own foolishness and inadequacy, she went back again to her own room.

But there was no sleep. In the darkness she lay awake, oppressed by her own weariness and all the worries which tormented her. She thought about the Dougherty gang, and Jane, and the bills for newsprint paper which were long overdue, and the mortgages on McLeod's Folly and the *Daily Shield and Banner*, and about the nice young man brought in by the police who was spending Sunday in jail, and about what Gashouse Mary had told her; and thinking about Gashouse Mary made her remember the town as it had been long ago when they were both little girls. And she thought, "I must be growing old," because she found more pleasure in contemplating the remote past than in thinking of the present or planning the future.

Presently the past became so dominant that she rose and put on a worn and woolly old dressing gown of gray flannel and, taking a key out of the lacquer box which Cousin Helen, who was a missionary in China, had given her long ago, she went into the hall once more and down the stairs, striking matches as she went to light her way. At the bottom of the stairs she reached J. E.'s den, and unlocking the door went in and lighted the old-fashioned gas chandelier. When she had seated herself in the familiar leather chair, she remained for a time gazing at the heavy mahogany desk, at J. E.'s pen and his meerschaum pipe and the little tray of pencils which remained exactly as he had left them, thirty years before. And memories of her old happiness swept her away and made her young again and humble and thankful. For she knew that she had had what few women had ever known, a kind of perfect happiness and a love that was complete and satisfactory and eternal—the sort of love she wanted Jane so desperately to have, the sort of love which Jane, so young and headstrong, could not value or understand, the sort of love that Jane would call sentimental and impossible.

The surge of old memories drove away her weariness, and presently she took out a sheaf of copy paper and pencils from a drawer in the desk (not J. E.'s sacred pencils but her own) and set to work on The Book.

She wrote now, rapidly and furiously, with a power and a facility she had never known before, the closing pages of this book into which shyly she had poured out all the wealth of memory and tradition and experience which was hers, all the fire and passion which in thirty years of widowhood had had no outlet, never thinking in her humbleness that the small life which she had known in Plattesville and the county was in its essence no different from the life of the great world outside. She wrote because she had to write, because there was something inside her which had to be told. There was a richness there which was long since ripe.

She had begun The Book long ago, ashamed of her own pretensions —that she, Lavinia McLeod, should have the presumption to think herself a writer. She had meant simply to write down what she knew and what she remembered of the old life, and somehow it had become a novel and J. E. had become the hero, and it had gone on and on until it was immensely long, hundreds of pages stored away in the old cowhide trunk in the vast dusty attic of McLeod's Folly. Nobody would ever see it, not even Jane, until after she was dead. The Book was, in a way, her child, the child of her childlessness upon which she lavished all the love that since the death of J. E. had had no object save Aida and Jane, and the defeated tramps whom she sheltered in her cellar, and the poor of Plattesville, and strange people out of the old life like Gashouse Mary and poor drunken Willie Ferguson.

She wrote on and on until at last the darkness outside the window turned to gray. Then suddenly she was tired with a weariness she had never known before; it was as if her very soul was empty. Wearily she put away the pages of manuscript in the drawer along with the worn pencils and rose and turned off the gas. She was cold now, and as she climbed the stairs she thought how miserable and bleak was the sensation of coldness, and of how cold all the poor tramps must be who had no place to sleep. And that made her think again of that poor boy who had been brought in by the police, and suddenly an idea occurred to her, an idea so logical and so obvious that she was astonished it had not occurred to her before. There was a way of rescuing him, a way to save him from sleeping every night in jail, from working at cleaning the streets and building roads and hauling rubbish. He was a newspaperman. She would offer him a job and then he would no longer be a vagrant. It wasn't too late because by good luck there wouldn't be any court until Monday.

He hadn't yet come up before the magistrate. Harvey Bingham, the police chief, was an old friend; he would help her to manage it. She couldn't offer the boy much in the way of salary but he might not mind that. He might be willing to share what there was over out of the dubious weekly earnings of the *Daily Shield and Banner*. He was young. He looked strong and energetic. He might be just the person she was seeking, sent by God. Anyway, working on the *Daily Shield and Banner* would be better than hauling garbage for the city of Plattesville and spending every night in a cold and cheerless cell.

Still shivering in her imagination she lay in the great bed she had shared long ago with J. E. until it was daylight, when at last she fell asleep on the Sunday she had meant for rest. But on Sunday Aida never dreamed of waking her, so she slept all the day until four in the afternoon.

15

On Sunday evening Jane had supper with Mrs. McLeod and afterward she went straight to bed. The conversation was not sprightly and they did not mention the Doughertys. Nor did Mrs. McLeod give any hint of her plan about the young man who was languishing in the Plattesville jail. She kept silent because she knew that Jane would say that the plan was foolish and idiotic, that she did not know anything about the young man, and that he might be a thief or a murderer. Indeed, Mrs. McLeod was not so much afraid of Jane's arguments as of herself; if she talked the plan over with Jane she knew she would never carry it through, because, as her own common sense told her, it *was* both reckless and stupid. But she had been reckless and stupid all her life and she had always enjoyed living enormously, even after J. E. had died and she thought there was nothing to live for. Even if the young man did turn out to be a bad egg, it would not make much difference to anyone, and it would be exciting to see what happened. You got about what you gave in this life, and out of all her foolish generosity in the past she had, she knew, already reaped a great harvest, certainly not in money, but in good will and kindness and respect.

So on Monday morning, she had breakfast half an hour early so that she might reach the jail before the magistrate's court had opened and have a talk with the young man. If she were late, he might already have appeared and been sentenced to two months as a vagrant.

The change in the breakfast hour made Aida suspicious, and each time she came into the dining room with eggs or hot bread and coffee, she sent out feelers—stray remarks and hints that were calculated to make Mrs. McLeod give herself away.

With Aida curiosity was a devastating vice. She had to know everything or she sulked or had the "miseries." Before breakfast was finished Mrs. McLeod detected the familiar signs of a fresh attack of the "miseries" in the baffled Aida. She shuffled her feet and slammed the door as she went out. She regarded her mistress with sullen, almost sinister, sidelong glances. At the very end of breakfast she moaned slightly as if stricken with some secret and fatal pain.

At this point Mrs. McLeod knew it was her cue to ask the reason for the moans and when she asked, Aida, with the air of an early Christian martyr, said, "It ain't nothin', Mis' McLeod, but the same old misery. It's gonna carry me off one of these days."

Brightly Mrs. McLeod said, "Nonsense, Aida. Nothing's going to carry you off. Where is the pain—in your stomach, your jaw, or where?"

"It ain't in no special place, Mis' McLeod. It's all over me."

"I'll tell Dr. Craig to come and see you."

And with a huge sigh Aida answered, "It ain't doctors that'll do me any good, Mis' McLeod. It's a misery of the speerit."

For once Mrs. McLeod remained adamant before the spectacle of a stricken Aida.

She left her dragging one foot after the other with the mien of a doomed woman, knowing that if she returned with the young man the "misery" would be cured instantly.

With foreboding in her spirit, she set off down the path between the syringa bushes. Monday was always a bad day at the office. There was never any news, and Willie Ferguson if he turned up at all would be suffering from a headache and dyspepsia, and belowstairs in the business office his wife Myrtle, with her prim high white collar, would be sour and disagreeable because Willie had been drunk at Gashouse Mary's and hadn't come home at all on Saturday night. And now, Jane had the sulks because of her bad conscience and because something had gone wrong between her and Jimmy Dougherty. No, Monday was always an awful day when it seemed to her that she had to carry the whole of the office and half creation on her own thin shoulders.

16

She had no trouble with the chief of police. She had to wait for him to arrive, and when he came in she went right to the heart of the subject.

No, he said, if she wanted to give the young fella a job, he wouldn't make any objection and he guessed the magistrate wouldn't make any. The young fella, he said, seemed a harmless nincompoop who spent all his time reading the books that were stuffed in his pockets. Anyway, the chief said, he didn't seem to be the regular sort of bum that came through

Plattesville. He probably wouldn't be any good at repairing streets and emptying ash cans. If he had a job, of course, he wasn't a vagrant so the law couldn't do anything about it, technically.

"Anyway," he said generously, "I'm always ready to do you a favor, Vinnie. You've always been square with me."

When he said that she felt suddenly traitorous and ashamed, but she held her peace and said doubtfully, "Maybe I'd better talk to him first before we do anything."

"Sure, that would be a good idea. One of the boys will take you over to the jail."

She shook hands and thanked him, not minding any more the fact that this was Monday, because something exciting was going to happen.

17

The prisoner was shaving when she arrived and asked for a moment to wipe the soap from his face before she came in. He looked much neater and much nicer than he had when she ran across him near the Memorial Fountain, and at sight of him behind the bars she had an impression that by nature he was a precise and rather neat young man, and the rumpled and spotted suit and old hat were like a costume one might put on to play charades. The warden unlocked the door of his cell and ordered him into the corridor where he left him with Mrs. McLeod.

She said, "Good morning," and he answered, "Good morning," and then nothing happened until she said, as if she were a hostess, "Won't you sit down?"

"Thank you."

He looked at her coldly out of gray-blue eyes which until now she had not noticed especially. They were honest, matter of fact, and like his voice, a little cold.

She said, "I'm Mrs. McLeod . . . Mrs. J. E. McLeod."

"Yes," he said without interest. "What can I do for you, Mrs. McLeod?" And then she realized that being Mrs. J. E. McLeod might mean something in Plattesville but that it could mean nothing in the world outside.

"I'm the proprietor of the *Daily Shield and Banner*, the oldest newspaper in Plattesville. I'm a newspaperwoman myself."

"Yes." The tone was still reserved, with a little shadow of mockery in it.

"I've come to get you out of jail."

"Thank you."

Then again, sharply, it struck her that there was something strange about him. It seemed to her that he did not mind, in spite of his well-cut clothes and superior appearance, having been arrested and locked up in a common cell. He was behaving with a curious dignity, almost as if there were some honor in his situation. It made her feel suddenly silly and ridiculous, so that she said abruptly, "But don't you want to get out of jail?"

She felt her face growing red, and she thought, "Maybe he's a forger or something and wants to hide away in the Plattesville jail."

Then nervously she told of seeing him brought in and how she divined at once that he was a superior sort of person, and that it was a pity he should be locked up and put to work digging ditches and emptying ash cans. He did not seem perturbed by the horrors she described, so, still more and more nervous and ill at ease, she enlarged upon them—telling about the excessively long hours, the poor food (and with a glance over her shoulder in the direction of the warden), of the cruel treatment prisoners suffered. She became so earnest that she exaggerated and ended by drawing a picture which resembled more a medieval prison with a rack and wheel than the county jail of Plattesville.

When she stopped for breath, he said, "I don't mind all that."

She said, "I'd give you a job on my newspaper and then you wouldn't any longer be a vagrant. It's all fixed. You'd like a job, wouldn't you?"

"Not especially . . . right now."

"Do you want to stay in jail?"

"Yes."

Wildly she thought, "Am I crazy or is he?" Aloud she asked, "Why?"

"I can't tell you the reason."

So, she thought, he must be a forger or a murderer or something. Only he couldn't be with a face like that.

She felt that she was being made a fool of, and knew that she should have risen with dignity and left the stubborn young man to his fate, but it was Monday morning and she had set her heart on the plan, and besides there was in her something young, even childlike, which would not let her give up without a struggle. And she was a little angry because she was aware, from the manner of the prisoner, that he thought her a meddlesome, sentimental woman.

So, with another glance over her shoulder in the direction of the warden who still remained at a distance outside the grating of the corridor, she said, "You see, I make this sort of thing my business." And she told him about the "Underground Railroad Station" for unfortunate men out of jobs which she and Aida had arranged in the cellar of McLeod's Folly. She touched upon the corruption Old Dougherty had brought to the town, about the graft and the inhumanity of the whole system. And as she talked a strange and youthful light came into her tired and wrinkled face.

She saw that the face of the prisoner softened a little and that a light of interest came into his eyes. Presently his whole expression changed and was no longer either hostile or mocking but quite friendly.

She finished by saying that for a long time she had hoped to start a reform movement, a clean-up campaign that would make Plattesville the fine place it had once been.

When she had no more breath, she paused, and the young man smiled at her. He said, "I owe you an apology. If I was indifferent to your help it was because I thought you were just one of those meddlesome, sentimental women who get a kick out of visiting prisoners. There's a lot of women like that."

"No, it wasn't that. I thought you might like a job and I need an up-and-coming young man."

He looked at her and grinned, "Thanks for the compliment, but I want to stay in jail."

Again she asked, "Why?"

"Because I want to know exactly what it's like. And I came here to Plattesville and got picked up on purpose because I heard this was one of the toughest spots in the whole Southwest." This time it was he who glanced toward the warden. "If they knew why I was here they'd drop me like a hot cake. You see, I'm writing a series of articles on how badly the wandering honest fellow out of work is treated. They're to be published afterward in a book, so that the whole country will know about it."

She nearly said "Oh!" and then felt a sudden shock of disappointment. She had set her mind upon rescuing an unfortunate young man and now he did not want to be rescued. He actually wanted to stay in jail, caught in the net of Old Dougherty's system. And he had a good reason, the kind of reason she understood, the kind of reason J. E. would have respected. It was the kind of thing J. E. himself might have done. She made a desperate effort to gather her scattered wits and put forth a proper argument, for she was not yet willing to give up. And the more she talked with the young man, the more she liked him. And her woman's intuition told her that she was herself having a success with him, that in spite of her age and her dowdiness he liked her and was even a little impressed.

So she said, "You and I could do a lot together."

"How do you mean?"

"I mean, I've got a newspaper with about ten thousand subscribers and if you're out for reform it's yours. I've been looking for a young fellow like you for a long time. You can do with it as you like."

"I'm afraid I couldn't. Not just now."

"There's an awful big job of clean-up to do right here." She waited for him to speak but he said nothing, so she continued, "You could get

[59]

plenty of information for your book here and in other places at the same time. You could live right here and know everything at first hand."

He looked at her for a moment, speculatively, with a look of interest in the clear gray-blue eyes. Then he said, "Perhaps."

At this sign of encouragement the enthusiasm of Mrs. McLeod burgeoned, and drawing a little nearer to him, she told him more and more of Old Dougherty's iniquities, and of her own helplessness with so little money and only Jane and Willie Ferguson for a staff.

"You could kill two birds with one stone," she said. "And that is always better than one."

"Yes," he said, "if you can hit both of them squarely." He coughed and looked away from her in silence for a time. Then he said, "I'd have to think it over."

"But you haven't got time. You'll be hauled up before the magistrate in an hour, and it's a sure thing that you'll get two months."

For a second he was silent, and it seemed to her that the gray-blue eyes were looking through and beyond her. Then he said, "It's extraordinary."

"What's extraordinary?"

"That a man could get two months just because he's looking for honest work."

"Well, that's the way it is, and worse." Then eagerly she added, "You've no idea how bad it is . . . how shocking."

"I could think it over for an hour," he said doubtfully.

"Yes, but I've got to know beforehand so that I can step up and say you've come to Plattesville to work for me."

Again he thought for a time. Clearly he was not a young man who jumped headlong into things. At last he said, "Well, we can do it this way. When I come into court I'll make a signal to you. If I raise my hand and scratch my head it will mean that I've accepted your offer."

"It's a great chance to do good."

"Perhaps you're right. Anyway we'll see." He rose and took her hand. "Don't you want to know anything about me?"

"You said you were a newspaperman?"

"Yes, but I might be a crook too."

"I don't think you are. Anyway, if you *were* a crook, there isn't much you could steal from me."

"Well, I'm not. Good-by and thank you for your interest. I'll see you in court."

"Okay."

He called out, "Warden!" And when the warden turned he said, "Come and lock me up."

Mrs. McLeod waited, watching, until the warden had locked the door of his cell and came to release her.

"A very strange young man," she thought. "I suppose he is cold and stiff like that because he was born in the North."

18

The courthouse clock showed 9:05 on its brazen face and that left her only about half an hour to hurry to the office and see that all was going well.

Willie and Jane were both there, Willie rather less damaged than usual on a Monday morning. As she came in she had the half-born intention of telling Jane what she had been up to, but a glance at Jane told her that this was not the moment. The girl was sitting with her back turned squarely to Willie, a sign that there had been another quarrel between them. And Mrs. McLeod saw at once that Jane had been crying. As for Willie, there was no question of breaking the news to him, especially on a Monday morning when the stuffy air of the office was impregnated with the perfume of Bourbon. It would be bad enough if and when the newcomer put in an appearance at the office.

So after a perfunctory "Good morning" she went to her cubbyhole, collected the telegraph news, opened her correspondence and brought whatever work there was to do and gave it to Jane.

She said, "I've got a special job to do at the courthouse. I'll have to leave everything to you till I come back. I don't exactly know when I'll be in."

By the time she returned to the courthouse the magistrate's court had opened, but there was no sign of the young man. So she had to wait, listening to the sordid cases which always depressed her so profoundly—two waitresses from the river district charged with soliciting (guilty); a Mexican charged with beating his wife (guilty); two tramps charged with vagrancy (guilty). And then the door opened and, accompanied by a policeman, her young man, the brand she meant to snatch from the burning, came in.

In the hour since she had left him, her romantic imagination had run away with her. While she walked along the streets, even while she was in the office talking with Willie and Jane, she had been thinking of him. It was almost like making up a novel. She invented a whole long and complicated story in which he helped her to clean up Plattesville, to rejuvenate the decrepit *Daily Shield and Banner*. He changed the whole of her existence. He even fell in love with Jane and wooed her away from Jimmy Dougherty. He had become in an hour a legendary figure. Unconsciously she had put him in the place of the son whom she had never borne.

And now as he came in, accompanied by the grim reality of a policeman, her heart sank because he seemed suddenly distant again and cold and unfriendly in his Northern way. The sight of him made her see herself in turn as a nit-witted, romantic fool who was always trying to make the world a better place than it could possibly be. Why, he wasn't yet even out of the clutches of the law; he might not even want to be freed.

With beating heart she watched him cross the room and take his place in front of old Flynn, the magistrate. She heard him answering the questions asked him about his name, his age, his occupation, the reason he had come to Plattesville. He hadn't even looked about the courtroom to see if she were there.

Crossing her fingers, she prayed to herself, "Oh, God, make him come to work on the *Daily Shield and Banner.*"

Then as the magistrate asked him roughly what work he had expected to find in Plattesville, she saw him raise his hand and scratch his head. In the same second, she was on her feet, hurrying down the aisle of the court to a seat just in front of the magistrate.

The rest was easy so far as procedure was concerned, but not so easy with regard to Mrs. McLeod's emotions. She was not good at plotting and she had not been so upset since J. E. proposed to her more than forty years earlier. She blushed and she could not make her voice do what she wished. But after twenty minutes, during which all of them save the prisoner discussed the case from all sides, the magistrate finally said, "Well, I'll tell you what I'll do. The prisoner is certainly guilty on two charges (her heart sank): First, of vagrancy and second of defrauding the P. and W. railroad. Owing to the intervention of Mrs. McLeod, a citizen of prominence and character, I will be lenient and release the prisoner on parole of good behavior in her charge for two months."

Suddenly she felt that she was going to faint and sat down. The magistrate said, "The prisoner is free to go at any time."

Then she pulled herself together and said, "Judge, I'll keep an eye on the young man," and in her enthusiasm she added, "I'll even have him board with me."

It wasn't what she had expected. She had wanted him free with no strings attached, and the parole attached a string to him by which they might pull him back at any time. If he helped her in a crusade to clean up Plattesville, they could clap him back into jail on some pretext and put him to digging ditches. Old Flynn, she saw suddenly, was shrewder than she thought. And now she was faced by the reality of having a strange young man thrust into her care. Now, when she looked at him, he wasn't any longer just an agreeable, rather good-looking young fellow who might be her son, a kind of character in a novel. He was a perfect stranger, about whom she knew nothing whatever, for whom she had accepted every responsibility. She was aware that he was standing there opposite her, free, and that they were looking at each other in an awkward silence. She had to do something so, almost sternly, as if he were a little boy, she said, "Better come with me."

19

It was a brilliant day in June, and the escape from the stuffy magistrate's court with all its sordid stories into the clear, cool air raised her spirits. She said, "I suppose we'd better get you some clothes first."

"Yes, that's not a bad idea. If you can get them, I'll pay you later. You see, I didn't bring any money with me. I set out without a penny just like any man out of work. I wanted my information to be authentic."

Quickly she said, "Maybe you'd like some cigarettes?"

"Yes, I would . . . more than anything."

She waited until they reached the next doorway and then she stepped into it where she couldn't be seen by passers-by and took a five-dollar bill out of the confusion of the worn bag stuffed with copy paper, lozenges, pencils and memoranda.

"Here," she said. "Take this. It'll be an advance."

"Thanks. I can pay you back in a few days."

And she said suddenly, "We haven't discussed salary or anything. What a fool I am!"

But he said with nonchalance, "Don't worry about that."

He left her at once and went across the street to the tobacco shop, and while he was gone she pretended to be interested by the display of breakfast foods in the window of Hanselman's grocery store, but she didn't really see anything in the window or even the reflection in the glass of her own distracted, eccentric figure. She was thinking what a fool she was to have given him a five-dollar bill instead of a twenty-five cent piece. Five dollars! She and Jane and Aida could live on that for a week! And she had tossed it away just like that, as if it were no more than a scrap of paper, to a man she knew nothing about.

And then suddenly there he was beside her, not with a package of cigarettes but with a whole carton. A young man of lavish tastes indeed!

Perturbed by the sight of the carton of cigarettes she changed her course, and instead of leading him to Blackmore, the tailor, she took him to Frendlich's Perpetual Bargains in Gentlemen's Clothes. There patiently he tried one ill-fitting suit after another until he at last had chosen a very quiet one which bagged in fewer places than any of the others he had attempted. When he emerged from the dressing booth, she felt a wave of shame at her suspicion and economy, for he had really looked much better in the stained, worn suit which had been cast aside.

[63]

To Mr. Frendlich she said, "Just put that down to your advertising account." And then, as she and the young man left the shop, she said, "And now about lunch. You'd better come home with me."

But alarmingly he said, "No, if you don't mind, I'll go to a lunchroom and then I'll have a look about town to get acquainted with it."

There was nothing to do. So she said with all the firmness she could muster, "I'll expect you for dinner. Anyone can tell you where my house is. Just ask for McLeod's Folly."

"What time?"

"About half-past seven."

He held out his hand and she took it. "Thanks," he said, "I think we're going to get on fine."

Then with his hands in his pockets and a cigarette between his lips he turned and went off down the street.

20

For a long time she stood looking after him. Certainly he was a strange young man. He wasn't, she saw now, in the least like J. E. and she couldn't think why the likeness had occurred to her except that in her foolish way she was always looking for young men who reminded her of J. E. in his prime. There was something cold about him and secretive—that was the word, "secretive." He hadn't told her anything, and now he had gone off with her five dollars and a new suit of clothes for which she had paid.

Alarm took possession of her, and for the first time she had intimations of the full depths of her folly. Very likely she would never see him again. Very likely he would disappear, and she would become the laughingstock of half the town when the story got out. She had meant to tell Jane about him when she went back to the office, but now she could not do it. She would wait to see whether he ran away or turned up again. If he disappeared she need never tell Jane, and Jane might never hear of the story at all.

She went back to the office to find, with a certain relief, that Jane had gone out somewhere leaving a message that she would return after she had had her lunch. That, too, she found odd, for as a rule Jane either had lunch in the office or went home with her to profit by Aida's cooking. After a moment in the presence of Willie she wished that he had gone out too instead of making his lunch in the office on Bourbon and a hamburger sandwich as he always did on Mondays.

"Monday," she thought, "was the wrong day altogether." But on the other hand, if she hadn't acted on Monday she would have lost her young man altogether. By now he would be emptying garbage cans into a large truck along with three or four other vagrants.

[64]

But the steady hang-over gaze of Willie interrupted her thoughts. She felt it there on her back as she bent over Jane's desk. For a time she resisted it, stirring about among the exchange newspapers, but in the end she had to give in as she always did when Willie was in this condition. Sober, Willie was timid in the knowledge that he was a failure; half-tipsy he became a combination of a lion and an old Southern colonel who regarded all women as poor foolish things.

Worst of all he spoke, calling her by her Christian name, "Now, Vinnie," he said, "what have you been up to?"

She tried to look annoyed and even indignant, but she only succeeded in blushing like a schoolgirl.

She asked, "What do you mean?"

He chuckled. "You can't fool me. Don't tell me you've been out all morning just walking around the Square." He cocked his head and asked, "Been down to Gashouse Mary's again?"

"No, I haven't."

"Well, you've been up to something, Vinnie, and don't think I won't find out."

Then she not only blushed, she became angry. "You won't find out," she said. "Anyway, it's none of your business, Willie."

She turned and, going into her cubbyhole of an office, she slammed the door, now more angry at herself than at Willie, because she had done just what he wanted her to do—delivered herself into his hands. Although the door was shut between her and Willie, she knew perfectly well that he was sitting there, still grinning half-tipsily at the door which separated them, grinning with a grin which said, "All women are poor, helpless creatures, and now Vinnie has got herself into another mess."

Sitting in front of J. E.'s littered old roll-top desk, she felt as flustered as the young girls courted and tormented and seduced by Willie long ago had done. She couldn't think why she had gotten herself into this mess except perhaps that the young man had for a fleeting instant looked a little like J. E.

21

The rest of the day was no better. When Jane returned she was in a bad temper, and as the afternoon wore on, no amount of Bourbon from the bottom drawer was able to put off the penalties of Willie's week-end carouse. He grew more and more querulous and disagreeable until about four o'clock she said, "Willie, you'd better go home and sleep it off," and Willie, in silence, with an aching head, took down his worn overcoat and battered hat and, for once, went without an argument.

When he had gone Jane, red in the face, turned round in her chair and said, "What are you going to do about him, Aunt Vinnie? He's getting worse and worse. This afternoon he tried to pinch me."

"Well, it didn't hurt you very much, did it?"

Jane lost her temper. "Don't worry, it didn't hurt me. He never touched me, but he got a slap that he'll remember for a long time."

"Well, that's the way to treat him. A woman always has a right to defend herself."

"So that's all you're going to say?"

"What do you want me to say, Jane? You're old enough and strong enough to take care of yourself. You could knock him down with your little finger—the little pip-squeak. Anyway, he wouldn't do anything."

"That's a nice way for one Southern lady to talk to another."

Mrs. McLeod wanted to laugh suddenly at the idea of Jane calling herself a Southern lady, but she managed to keep silent. Coming a little nearer to Jane she said, "Listen, Jane, Willie is a poor disappointed old man."

"I don't care what he is."

"If I fired him it would kill him."

"Well, it's him or me, I've had enough."

"The only importance he's got left is being a reporter on the *Daily Shield and Banner*. If you took that away from him there wouldn't be anything."

Jane rose and picked up her hat and coat. "Well, I'm going back to the ranch."

"You can't do that, Jane. I'd have to give up."

Jane burst into tears and ran out of the office. At the door she cried, "I'm sick of it. I'm sick of Willie and the *Daily Shield and Banner*. I'm sick of everything."

When she had gone, Mrs. McLeod stood for a moment in the center of the room, and then, dead weary, dropped into Willie's chair and covered her eyes with her hands. Suddenly she wanted only one thing in the world—to go back to McLeod's Folly and go to bed and stay there forever, never to see again people who were difficult, never again to worry over where the money was coming from to keep the *Daily Shield and Banner* going, never again to have to see Old Dougherty or to think of his evil doings. She knew suddenly that she was a fool for always believing people better than they were. That had always been her folly and J. E.'s folly before her. If only she and J. E. had been ruthless and dishonorable and self-centered, believing always the worst of people instead of the best, the *Daily Shield and Banner* wouldn't be where it was today. And now Jane had deserted too, not, she knew, in a sudden burst of clairvoyance, because Willie tormented and tried to pinch her, but because, in spite of everything, she had been in love with Jimmy Dougherty and something had gone wrong between them. Why, she thought from the depths of her long experience, was human nature so cussedly complicated and difficult? Why, because Willie had once been the Don Juan of the county and now was old and a failure, should he become drunken and cantankerous? Why couldn't Jane be simple and direct instead of being complicated and sullen, making her and Willie and even Aida pay for the folly of herself and Jimmy Dougherty?

And in a sudden burst of despair she was sure that the young man had made a fool of her. He had got a carton of cigarettes, five dollars, and a new suit of clothes out of her. He had even gotten his freedom and run away, making her a fool and once again the laughingstock of the town.

She wanted only to go home to bed and never again set foot on the floor as women did in the old days when life had defeated them; but that, she knew, she could not do because in the scheme of things it was not permitted to women like herself. Wearily, she rose and, going to the untidy washroom, she put cold water on her face so that Willie's prim wife Myrtle downstairs would not guess she had been crying. She struggled with her untidy hair, which had given her an exciting unruly look when she was young and pretty, and now was no more than a nuisance. When she had done this, she returned and put Willie's desk in order and then Jane's and finally her own, shuffling the pile of bills that always encumbered the top drawer, to see what bills *had* to be paid at the end of the week. She thought wildly, "I've got to carry on somehow. I can't let the *Daily Shield and Banner* die."

It would be like dying herself—even a little worse—for if she died everything would be over and she could rest forever. If the *Daily Shield and Banner* died she would go on and on, sick for its troubles and worries, for the smell of dust and paper and paste, sick even for the smell of the Bourbon that hung over Willie's desk, oddly enough, the only clean smell in the whole office.

At six o'clock she went downstairs to ask Willie's wife, Myrtle, for a little money to take the place of the five dollars she had given to the young man who made a fool of her. From Willie's wife she got no sympathy; the cashier sat behind her rusty cage, grim, high-collared, an old-fashioned school marm, distrustful of everybody and everything. Any day in the week Myrtle was bad enough, but on Mondays, after Willie's week-end carouse, she was insufferable.

Coldly she said, "I guess I can let you have a dollar and a half, Mrs. McLeod. The gas bill has to be paid or the linotype'll have to stop running."

With the dollar and fifty cents in her big, untidy bag, she walked home through the dark, along the familiar streets and across the Square where long ago she and Gashouse Mary had played when Plattesville was a wide-open town. Two blocks from the Square she came upon McLeod's Folly, huge and fantastic against the clear blue of the late spring night. The sight

[67]

of it surprised her, for she had, like an old woman, been dreaming of the town as it was when she was a girl, before McLeod's Folly had been built.

Opening the rickety gate, she walked up the path between the ragged lilacs and syringas toward the dark house, depressed now by the fact that she had no appetite for supper and that Aida, with pleadings, cajolery and finally threats and abuse, would force her to eat against her will. The house was dark because Aida was a great saver of gas. Without troubling even to strike a match, she groped her way along the huge familiar hall, through the great dining room and as far as the pantry. Then she heard voices from the kitchen and knew that Aida was not alone. One voice was unmistakably Aida's, the other voice that of a man. For a second, because she was still a little confused as to past and present, she thought that Aida had returned to her old tricks and was entertaining an admirer, but almost at once she realized that Aida was nearly as old as herself and for a long time had had no admirers in the romantic sense.

With an effort she summoned the determination to push open the door, and when she had done this she saw Aida, busy over the oven, and beside her on a chair a figure which was unmistakably that of the young man who had run away. He had a notebook and was writing in it and Aida was saying, "And a lot more than that happens here. You all oughta stay in Plattesville for a spell! What you'd see would raise the hair off'n your haid."

In a second the depression left Mrs. McLeod and her appetite returned. Aida's "misery" was gone. She was chippy as a lark and God had sent her what she wanted most. The young man was a born reformer; he was already at work, making notes.

22

Once her tears had subsided after running out of the office, Jane experienced a sudden vacant feeling about the heart. She found herself in the street without any idea of where she was bound. She had meant, later on, if she had left the office at the usual time, to go to the Presbyterian Church and help serve at the annual supper to raise funds for the Missionary Society; but now she was an hour too early, and if she went there directly she would, she knew, have to help with the peeling of potatoes, the setting of tables and a great many other tasks in which she found no pleasure at all. Worse than that, she would have to talk to the other women and listen to their gossip of babies and housekeeping and small town doings. Once these things would have amused her, but since she had been to school in the East she looked upon such small human interests as beneath her. Nevertheless, there was in her heart a feeling of warmth and anticipation about helping to serve at the Missionary Supper. Part of this feeling arose out of tradition, because her mother and her grand-

[68]

mother had both occupied themselves with the affairs of the Missionary Society and because she herself had always "helped," except for the years in the East, from the time she was fourteen. And in her heart, she really liked the simple, friendly wives and mothers whom she would find there. They were, after all, *her* people—the old people of the county, not the country club set which she did not like, nor outsiders like the Doughertys.

So, when she came out of the office, she acted, in the perversity of her mood, against her own natural inclinations, and instead of going straight to the church, she set out to walk around the Square. Inside, she was feeling sick and angry, so she got no pleasure out of the familiar shop windows which now, in the violence of her mood, looked not only strange to her but without interest. When she had finished one complete tour, she still did not know what to do with herself, so she made a second tour. This time, perhaps on account of the physical action, her mood changed a little and she began to feel sorry, less for herself than for the way she had behaved to Aunt Vinnie and even to Willie Ferguson. And as she softened her confused emotions gradually cleared and sorted themselves out, and she found herself thinking of Jimmy Dougherty and wanting to see him. If only she could meet him by accident, and he would come up to her and say "Hello!" as if nothing had happened . . . that would be wonderful. For that she'd even chuck the Missionary Supper in spite of all her promises and go to the movies with him. And aimlessly, in spite of herself, she found she was walking toward the Dougherty Block, her head filled with romantic imaginings of what would happen if suddenly she saw him coming along Main Street toward her.

She had almost reached the doorway of the Dougherty Block when her mood changed again and she thought, "What am I doing? I'm running after a man like any cheap servant girl. I ought to be ashamed of myself." And then almost at once, logic prompting her, she thought, "What am I after anyway? I won't marry him. I can't marry him. I must be crazy."

Quickly she changed her direction, but she did not go toward McLeod's Folly or toward the Presbyterian Church. She crossed the street and went into the Boston Store thinking, "From the doorway, I can see him come out." Once inside the door she knew that she must buy something because Miss Hamilton and Miss Reeves behind the nearest counters would wonder what she was up to and begin to talk if she just came inside and stood around. So she gave them each a bright "Hello" and took a long time looking through spools of thread to match a mythical dress which she found herself describing in nervous detail. And all the time she kept glancing toward the big, lighted entrance of the Dougherty Block. With a little jump of the heart she observed something which in her excitement she hadn't seen before —that the olive-green roadster was standing two cars away from the entrance.

After a time even the description of the imaginary dress gave out and she knew that she couldn't go on and on pretending, and she hadn't enough money to make other purchases, so she paid for the spool of thread and said "Good night" to Miss Hamilton and Miss Reeves and went out of the door, aware that they were watching her, and that as soon as she was well out, one would cross the aisle to the other and begin talking about her.

Outside she found herself almost without knowing it walking to the opposite side of the street. Then as she stepped on to the curbstone, Jimmy came out of the big entrance and crossed the sidewalk to his car. At sight of him she wanted suddenly to do two things at once—one to sink out of sight, melting away into the very asphalt of the street—the other to run up to him and say, "I'm sorry about the other night. Let's be friends again?"

In fact she did neither thing. She simply stopped and stood there on the curb, feeling foolish and idiotic and ashamed. But the worst was that she could not be sure whether he saw her or not, or even sure whether he wanted to see her or not. In any case, he walked past her, climbed into the car and drove away, leaving her, when he had gone, with a feeling of sickness and disgust, thinking, "I must be crazy. I must be out of my mind. I'll never speak to him or think of him again."

23

All the time she helped with the serving at the Missionary Supper she had a bad headache. She tried not to talk to anyone and she was as polite as she was able to make herself. She served badly and spilled things and she kept thinking, "I ought to do what I threatened to do. I ought to go back to the ranch and maybe marry one of the county boys." And almost at once she began making plans for going to the state agricultural school. She decided to forget the useless things she had learned in the East which seemed only to bring her trouble, and to find out all about dairies and cheese and butter and diets for cows. By the end of the evening her headache was gone, and she was already planning how she would revolutionize her father's ranch and build up a big dairy business in Plattesville. For a time she even forgot Jimmy.

But at last the serving was over and she had eaten her own supper—a great deal more than she had meant to eat when she arrived—and there was nothing to do but go home. And as she walked along the streets from the Presbyterian Church to McLeod's Folly she thought about many things, wishing that she was not so healthy that even in the midst of sorrow and melancholy she always had an excellent appetite. For the first time it occurred to her how really lonely she was, and how odd it was that you could be lonely in the midst of a big town like Plattesville. Even at home in McLeod's Folly she was lonely because she really didn't know Aunt Vinnie or Aida. And she saw quite clearly that it wasn't their fault; they wanted to be friendly; they wanted to share everything with her. Indeed they were always pushing and prying and hinting, trying to be intimate with her and share her happiness and her unhappiness. It certainly wasn't their fault so, she thought, it must be her own.

"There must be something about me," she thought, "that puts people off. It isn't even any better on the ranch. It must be that which has put Jimmy off me . . . whatever it is."

By now she had reached the gate of McLeod's Folly, and thinking of Jimmy made her think of the perils which he had suggested might haunt the ragged bushes bordering the path, the tramps who might spring out of the shadows and attack her. She had never even thought of such things before, but now as she opened the old gate, the mere squeaking of its hinges made her hair rise on her head. For a moment she stood in the shadows listening, unable to screw up her courage to run the gauntlet of the friendly ancient syringas and lilacs. It was after ten o'clock, and as far as she could see in both directions there was not a person in sight in the shadows beneath the cotton-woods and live oaks which lined San Antonio Street, not a soul to come to her aid when she screamed.

At last she told herself, "I can't stand here all night. I've got to go up that path." So she counted ten and then started, trying not to run, although her legs kept carrying her along at a speed far too rapid for dignity and self-respect.

And then suddenly she was up the steps and putting her key into the lock. And nobody had attacked her.

As she opened the door she saw that the hallway was not as black as the economical Aida usually kept it. At the far end there was a faint glare of light that came from the half-open door of J. E.'s library and she thought, "It must be Aunt Vinnie working late. I'll go in and say good night and apologize for having been so nasty." But it was odd that Aunt Vinnie had chosen to work in the rarely used library instead of J. E.'s den.

Taking off her hat and coat she hung them on the mahogany coatrack and started toward the library door, but she didn't arrive there, for as she reached the foot of the stair the door opened all the way and against the light appeared the figure of a man.

In a second all the terrors of the dark path swept over her again and she screamed, wildly, violently, not so much in terror of the actual figure as of the images Jimmy's warning had raised in her mind. At the sound of her screaming, the man did not stop but continued to come toward her, and between screams she heard him saying, "It's all right. It's only me," and her body collapsed at the knees and even the dim light in the library went out.

24

When she opened her eyes she found herself in one of J. E.'s big worn leather chairs with Aunt Vinnie and Aida in their wrappers standing over her, and just beyond them a young man with dark blond hair and steel-rimmed spectacles. Aunt Vinnie was saying, "It's all right, dear. He won't hurt you. He's living in the house." All of which made no sense at all, even when she considered that it was Aunt Vinnie who was saying it. Then Aida gave her some whisky—a big oversized drink—and Aunt Vinnie explained that this was a young man called Mr. Richardson who was coming to work on the *Daily Shield and Banner*, and how she had snatched him from jail, and he was an investigating reporter and was going to live in the house as a boarder. And while Aunt Vinnie was explaining all this, Jane, feeling much better and much clearer in the head than she had ever dreamed was possible, examined the young man.

Even while she listened to the latest and most fantastic of Aunt Vinnie's exploits, she saw that the young man, while not exactly handsome, was nice looking. The steel-rimmed spectacles gave him an intellectual faintly owlish look, but he wasn't feeble and skinny and anemic like most intellectual young men; he had big shoulders and a fine frame beneath the suit from "Every Day a Bargain Day" Frendlich's. Even in her weakness and excitement she couldn't help thinking that his presence would make life less dreary in McLeod's Folly.

He said, "I'm very sorry to have upset you. I was looking over the library and found Grant's *Memoirs*. I always wanted to read them, but never seemed to have a copy about when I thought of it. So I just sat down and began to read."

She assured him that it was all right, and then there was a moment's awkward silence to which Aida tactfully supplied an end by saying, "Ah'll make you all some cocoa and sandwiches. That'll calm down your nerves."

So they all followed Aida into the big kitchen, and while Aida made the cocoa, Mrs. McLeod and Jane made up some sandwiches, and as the whisky began to stir in Jane's blood she suddenly felt very gay and thought that after all housework and even cooking which she had always scorned might be very pleasant. The young man didn't act at all like a stranger. He helped with the sandwiches and chatted and made jokes, rather bad jokes, Jane thought, which set Aida off into gales of laughter.

When everything was ready, Mrs. McLeod and Jane and the young man sat at one table and Aida served them and took her place at another. It was all very agreeable, and after a time the young man began to tell them about his adventures he had had bumming his way from New York into the Southwest. After a time, listening, Jane forgot about herself and was quite happy again. She was especially happy when he said that he had been to Harvard.

"Now," she thought, still a little tipsy from the whisky which had revived her, "I'll have an intellectual equal in Plattesville." For a moment she even forgot about the agricultural school and doing farming and considered him as a new matrimonial candidate. At any rate it would be nice to have a man about the house.

It was after midnight when at last they all went to bed, leaving Aida to clean up the kitchen and turn out the lights.

25

On Tuesday morning Mr. Richardson went to work, and from the moment he arrived at the office of the *Daily Shield and Banner* a change came over the place. In the make-up room the linotype operators punched and rattled their machines into new activity, old Zimmerman, who had been picking up and dropping type for forty-eight years, found a new interest in the worn old bits of lead. Belowstairs, even Willie Ferguson's wife, Myrtle, unbent a little inside her cage and for the fraction of a second was seen by Mrs. McLeod to smile in a wintry fashion.

Abovestairs, in the editorial office, the newcomer was given an old desk placed near a window overlooking the Square, where he sat with his square, powerful back turned on Jane and Willie. In honor of the occasion Mrs. McLeod put on a new foulard dress. For Jane, it was again like the first day she had come to work on the *Daily Shield and Banner*, fresh out of college, filled with ideas of how to make the paper over into a modern go-getter kind of journal. (That was before she grew discontented and was finally defeated by the debts and bills, the inertia of the whole staff and the muddle-headedness of Aunt Vinnie.)

Now, as she contemplated the broad capable figure by the window, she felt a new confidence, a new excitement. Again and again during the morning she stopped in the midst of her work to study the back covered by the cheap suit from Frendlich's. There was something about it which was solid and emanated confidence. Everyone else in the *Daily Shield and Banner* was so old and so tired and bored. They all belonged to another day which Jane, in her modernity, felt was finished. Here was a young man who was modern; he was a radical; he was writing a series of special articles on the treatment of the wandering unemployed.

So far he existed for her more as an abstraction and as a symbol than as a man. Even though she had made a fool of herself by fainting at their first encounter, even though they had sat together with Aida and Aunt Vinnie in the kitchen, talking until after midnight, she felt that she did not know him.

She thought him pleasant-looking—perhaps without the steel-rimmed spectacles you might have considered him handsome—but there was a kind of secrecy about him, a kind of coldness and efficiency, a way of looking at things in an abstract fashion which put her off. It was as if he held you at arm's length, as if even in the intimacy of the kitchen, he had been regarding them all simply as specimens. Perhaps, she thought, that was because he was a Yankee, and a little perhaps because he was an intellectual.

And in spite of herself she thought again of Jimmy Dougherty, and how different he was. Even while she looked at the broad capable back she kept seeing Jimmy with his blue eyes and black hair and wide, warm, friendly grin. You knew Jimmy right away. It was as if he said without saying it, the moment you saw him, "The world is a fine place. Let's be friends." She felt that no matter how long Mr. Richardson was about you would never really *know* Mr. Richardson.

But in her minx's mind she already began to make plans. Perhaps, she thought, the newcomer wouldn't be so bad after you got to know him. Yankees were stand-offish and not easy-come, easy-go, hospitable fellows like Southerners. Perhaps he might fall in love with her and marry her and take her back to the East where she could be somebody. But even if none of these things happened, he could still be of use to her as a beau. He could take her to the movies and out to dinner at the Beauregard Hotel and to lots of places where Jimmy would see them. Never again would she have to sink to the level of buying a spool of thread in the Boston Store simply to get a glimpse of Jimmy leaving the Dougherty Block. Now she could show him that he wasn't the only pebble on the beach.

It was true, she had to admit, that on the first morning, Mr. Richardson took very little notice of her. He spent half the morning repairing efficiently the cast-off, broken-down typewriter Aunt Vinnie had given him, and the other half studying copies of the *Daily Shield and Banner*, going over them carefully, line by line, peering intently through the steel-rimmed spectacles. She tried to ignore him and to take no notice of his indifference, but she wasn't quite able to manage it.

Out of the *Daily Shield and Banner* staff only Willie Ferguson seemed unstirred by the sudden appearance in the office of the newcomer. In him the tempo of daily existence was not quickened. Partly this was because, although he no longer suffered from a hang-over, he was in the third or Tuesday phase of his weekly reformation, when he felt sour and virtuous and disapproving of everyone. Partly too he looked upon the introduction of the newcomer as one of Lavinia McLeod's follies, and a major one at that. Being a conservative he did not like change, and having a good deal of instinct he divined before any of the others, indeed almost at once, that the young man was going to do a good deal of upsetting. And most of all he disliked the young man, because, even in the Frendlich "bargain day" suit, it was clear that he was efficient, clear-minded and energetic—all qualities which in the philosophy of Willie took the savor out of life and made of it a poor thing. And he was a Yankee and Willie did not like Yankees. But for the Yankees and General Sherman he would now be living in luxury, surrounded by slaves and mint juleps on an inherited plantation in Georgia, instead of eking out a miserable existence in a cow town in the Southwest. The Yankees, he believed, had ruined his destiny before he was born. He had been meant by fate to be a gentleman and the Yankees had cheated him out of it.

So Willie sulked, resorting more frequently to the lower drawer than was usual on a Tuesday, and now and then giving vent to an eloquent snort or a derisive belch of which the newcomer seemed to be maddeningly unaware.

Side by side with the elation which accompanied the appearance of the newcomer, there was in the office also a sense of emotional strain. Even old Zimmerman setting up type was aware of this. It was a friendly old-fashioned office in which all save Willie Ferguson were willing and ready to take the newcomer into their arms and make him feel at home. Somehow, as the day wore on and the excitement lowered a little, the staff, one by one, became aware that this was not possible. It was not that the stranger resisted in any way, not even that he was unfriendly. He was just nothing at all, a little like a new piece of furniture, an adding-machine perhaps, wondrous and working with astonishing efficiency, but without warmth of personality.

Most of them were puzzled and made uncomfortable. Willie, as the day wore on and the uneasiness increased, grew a little triumphant as if he were saying, "See! I told you so! You can't mix Yankees down here. They're too cold-blooded!" Only Jane actually resented it. She felt, rather than reasoned, that she had a right at least to the notice of the newcomer. When she stared at the square back she expected him to turn round and speak, or at least to give her a friendly smile. Heaven knew, other men paid attention to the blue of her eyes, the amber color of her hair, the pink of her cheeks, the trimness of her figure—plenty of other men, stupid men, men who didn't even know her. But now she stared at his back and he never so much as turned, except occasionally to ask her a question about the preferred style of the *Daily Shield and Banner* or Mrs. McLeod's taste in headlines, or the name of some prominent citizen.

26

For the whole of the first week it went on like that. He did not even come home for supper but spent his evenings in the town, where, neither Jane nor Mrs. McLeod was able to discover. Usually he came in after all of them were in bed and went for a time to the library to work. He had taken the second volume of *The Memoirs of Ulysses S. Grant* off the shelves to read himself to sleep with and kept it on the table beside his bed. Five mornings out of the seven they came down to breakfast to find that he had already eaten and gone to the office. Aida said that after the third morning a letter sent by air mail and postmarked "Boston" arrived every morning for him. At the end of the week Mrs. McLeod was able to report triumphantly to Magistrate Flynn that the young man in her parole had behaved, as far as she knew, in an exemplary way and was in the process of being a worthy citizen of Plattesville.

Certainly he had done nothing criminal. He had been sober, orderly, polite. But Mrs. McLeod, nervous again, was beginning to have her doubts. He was not what her romantic mind had planned; he was not playing the role she had created for him. He was not as she had hoped and believed—a ball of fire. It seemed to her that he had done nothing at all but sit at his desk, ask questions and read newspaper exchanges. Troubled, she began to think for a second time that she had been made a fool. She began to suspect that she had simply taken on a lodger with whom, in her softness, she would be burdened for the rest of her life. Out of the labor squad she had, she began to believe, simply picked up a gentleman of leisure.

What made it worse was that Willie Ferguson, aided by Bourbon, became steadily more triumphant and exasperating.

And then on the following Friday the change occurred.

In the first place, Mr. Richardson appeared in the morning dressed in a different suit, one which was not new but obviously expensive in cut and material. The shirt, tie and shoes were different, and they all had the same look of having cost a great deal of money. Mrs. McLeod was not the only one to notice this; Jane saw it at once. He now dressed and looked like an Easterner, like those negligently dressed, self-assured young men whom she had seen in hotels and at a distance on the street in Boston. At the sight her heart gave a little leap, and the snob in her thought, "Perhaps he isn't as bad as I thought."

About eleven o'clock, carrying a bundle of copy paper covered with voluminous notes, he knocked at the door of Mrs. McLeod's cubbyhole and asked if he might speak to her for half an hour, a request which she granted with mingled apprehension and delight.

Closing the door behind him, he sat down and placed the bundle of notes on the end of her untidy desk. Then he adjusted his spectacles and looked at her and said, "I'm sure, Mrs. McLeod, that you feel that I haven't been earning my board and lodging for the past week, but I assure you I've been working hard all the time. I was a stranger here and I had to find my ground and get used to the place." He took off the spectacles, and when she looked at the honest gray-blue eyes, she knew again that the impulse at the police station had been right.

[76]

He said, "I hope you won't think me impertinent. I have a lot of suggestions to offer."

"Not at all . . . not at all . . ." said Mrs. McLeod. "I hoped you'd have some suggestions."

"Shall I begin first about the paper itself?"

"Yes. . . . Yes." Her tired worried face brightened, and her excitement concentrated itself in her fingers which began to drum the top of the desk.

He grinned apologetically, and for a fleeting moment he again looked like J. E. If he had had J. E.'s flowing mustaches he would have looked very like him.

Again he said, "I hope you won't think me impertinent."

"No, certainly not." That was what she wanted . . . suggestions, change, organization, efficiency, energy.

"Well, Mrs. McLeod, I think what the *Daily Shield and Banner* wants is waking up. I like the name. It has a fine old-fashioned, crusading sound. It ought to be a crusading newspaper."

"That's what I want it to be . . . only . . ." For a moment she fumbled and then finished lamely, "only I don't know how to crusade."

Again he grinned, "Well, perhaps I can help. How did the paper get its name?"

"It was J. E.'s father who founded it and called it the *Daily Shield and Banner* . . . just after the Civil War during the Reconstruction." Then she remembered that although everybody else in Plattesville knew who J. E. was, Mr. Richardson wouldn't know, so she added, "J. E. was my husband. I took over after he got ill and died."

Surprisingly he said, "Yes, I know. I've found out all about him. He must have been a remarkable man." Then he picked up the papers and said, "I'll begin with the newspaper first." And putting on his spectacles he added, "I haven't forgotten about the crusade. I've got some notes on that too."

"Good."

One by one he went over the suggestions, changes of make-up of style, added human features, a column of gossip about people in the town, perhaps even a special Saturday edition given over to the farmers and ranchers. "Their interests," he said, "are so different from those of the townspeople . . . articles on cows and chickens and new vegetables . . . all that sort of thing."

While she listened Mrs. McLeod grew more and more excited. The ideas, she thought, were wonderful. Why had she never had them? And then she remembered that she had had most of them, at one time or another, one at a time, but somehow nothing had ever come of them. Always they seemed to have got lost.

"You see," he said, "what we must do is to make over the paper and attract attention and get more subscribers and then the advertisers will come to us. You see, before we can be a force as a crusade, we have to have an audience. Then when we begin the crusade, subscribers and advertisers will come in by leaps and bounds."

The excitement inside her was almost more than her heart could bear. The *Daily Shield and Banner* important again! The *Daily Shield and Banner* a power in the community as it had been in J. E.'s day! The *Daily Shield and Banner* a great crusading paper! But a small voice kept speaking to her, presently with such force that she said aloud, "But all this will take a great deal of money. I've told you the *Daily Shield and Banner* was hard up, but I never told you how badly off we really are."

"No," he said, "it won't take much money, hardly any at all to begin with. I've figured it all out. But it'll take a lot of work." He took off his glasses again and lighted a cigarette.

"Miss Baldwin," he said. "She looks young and strong. She's willing to work, isn't she?"

"Yes, Jane . . . . why Jane's as strong as an ox. Sometimes she's difficult though."

"Yes," he said, with a faint grin, "I've noticed that. I think work would do her good. It might make her less difficult."

For a moment Mrs. McLeod resented the remark, thinking it presumptuous and even "fresh." He saw the look in her eyes and said, "Forgive my saying that, but if we're going to do this thing, we must all feel friendly and frank and confident."

"Oh, that's all right. We can manage Jane, I guess."

"I don't suppose Ferguson will be much help."

"No, but I can't get rid of him."

"Well, I guess we can manage."

And then he took up the second sheaf of notes. "And now as to the crusade. I've been digging about a bit into that." He took up the notes and said, "I've been getting acquainted in town. You see, it's no good working a job like this till you know your ground."

Then he told her what he had discovered, here and there, in poolrooms and restaurants and saloons. He couldn't be as unfriendly as he appeared to be, because he seemed to have made friends with all sorts of people and got all sorts of information out of them, bits and oddments which had never reached the ears of Mrs. McLeod herself, fresh scandals and hints of villainies perpetrated or contemplated by Old Dougherty and his gang. And as she listened Mrs. McLeod grew more and more excited, the weariness went out of her, and she felt young again as she had in the days when J. E. was still alive and attacking corruption wherever it raised its head. It was all wonderful, all far beyond her expectations.

When he had finished she said, "Well, I must say you haven't been wasting your time."

"There's still the question of State politics. I don't know exactly how this man Dougherty stands with the State party organization."

"What's that got to do with it?"

"Well, a crusade is no good unless you've got plenty of backing and power. If we're going in for politics, if we're really going to clear out the Dougherty gang, we've got to know where we stand."

Mrs. McLeod was silent for a moment, thinking, and then said, "Well, I have heard stories about a feud between Dougherty and Swain. Bill Swain is the State boss. But I don't know how true it is. They say Old Dougherty's got an ambition to take Bill Swain's job away from him."

A new light came into the gray-blue eyes. "Well, if that's true it's fine. It's just what we're looking for. I heard rumors of the same thing."

"When can we begin our crusade? Next week?"

Mr. Richardson laughed, "Not so fast. I'm still on parole as a vagrant."

"What's that got to do with it?"

"Well, until that parole is up they can clap me back into jail any time and put me to work digging ditches."

"How, if you don't do anything?"

Again he laughed, this time at her naïveté, so that she was ashamed and blushed. "Oh, they'd find a way. They'd *make* me do something. That's easy enough." His face grew serious again. "No, for the next couple of months we'll make over the *Daily Shield and Banner* into a first-class modern newspaper. And by that time we'll have all the cards ready."

"You mean you're going to stay in Plattesville for a long time?"

"Sure, I'm going to stay here until the job is done."

She held out her hand and he took it, "Then it's a bargain."

"Yes."

"The paper is yours to do with as you like."

"That's what I wanted you to say."

At that moment, quite suddenly, she thought of Gashouse Mary. She'd have to go right off to see Mary and tell her what had happened. She couldn't tell her before now; she couldn't tell her about the young man until she was sure of him. Now she *knew*.

Aloud she said, "Have you been to see Gashouse Mary?"

"You mean the woman who runs that dance hall by the river?"

"Yes."

"No, I don't know her."

"Well, I'll take you there. When shall we go?"

"Tonight?"

"Tonight."

Then he left her, and when he had gone she sat for a long time staring out of the dirty window into the park, seeing nothing, bubbling inside with elation. It was wonderful to feel young again, to feel that thirty years had slipped away suddenly. Wildly she thought, "I must pull myself together and be efficient now." And feeling that she must begin at once, she thought, "I must straighten up my desk first," so she went to work on it sorting out papers, trying to produce some order out of the chaos, doing her best to make it look like Mr. Richardson's desk—neat, precise, orderly. And in her heart she knew all the time that by the next day chaos would have returned.

When she had finished she went outside to find Jane, for she had planned to have lunch with Jane in the Pasadena Cafeteria and tell her everything that had happened; but Jane was not there. Willie said she had gone out half an hour earlier saying she wouldn't return until two o'clock. She knew what that meant. Jane was sulking again.

27

It was true. Jane *was* sulking. Unable any longer to bear the sight of Mr. Richardson's indifferent, tweed-covered back, she had flounced out to have lunch alone, and no sooner had she found herself in the street, than she found herself walking toward the Dougherty Block.

Impatient, she had, after a week, given up hope of rousing interest in Mr. Richardson; all she wanted now was to forget him. She wanted Jimmy and his grin back again more than she had ever wanted them. She wanted something that was human and impudent and even wicked. She wanted to show that conceited Yankee Mr. Richardson a thing or two.

Three times she walked up and down the street in front of the Block, but there was no sign either of Jimmy or the olive-green car. And then, as if a fever had suddenly gone out of her, she came to her senses and thought, "I must be crazy. What will people think if they see me walking up and down here like an idiot? What is it that gets into me and makes me like that?" And angry now at herself, she turned and went down toward the river to Kirschbaum's restaurant where she was sure she wouldn't see Aunt Vinnie. At that moment, she felt, Aunt Vinnie's simplicity and calm would have been insupportable.

The lunch was good, but she was unaware of what she ate. With the first volume of Grant's *Memoirs* propped in front of her she sat there for an hour, trying to make out what on earth Mr. Richardson found interesting in such a book. And now and then she would find herself staring for a long time at the pages without seeing anything but Jimmy's grin and blue eyes.

When she returned to the office, Mrs. McLeod called her into the cubbyhole and closing the door, told her everything. As she listened, she seemed untouched by enthusiasm, and when her aunt had finished she only sat there silent and a little sullen.

"Well," said Mrs. McLeod, "why don't you say something? Isn't it wonderful?"

"Yes, if it's true—if it works out."

The remark was like a dipperful of cold well water on Mrs. McLeod's enthusiasm. She said, "What do you mean by that?"

"I mean that your Mr. Richardson hasn't got enough pep to carry anything through. He's nothing but a cold fish."

Mrs. McLeod saw through that and felt better. Calmly she said, "Well, we'll see. Anyway, it'll be more interesting. Only you mustn't tell anyone. If anyone finds out, it would ruin everything. They might clap Mr. Richardson right back into jail."

Jane rose with an air of great weariness. "Who could I tell in this cow town?"

Then Mrs. McLeod took the bull by the horns. "Jimmy Dougherty," she said, and waited for the explosion.

There wasn't any. Jane only opened the door, and on her way out said, "I never see Jimmy Dougherty. What do you think I am, going around with shanty Irish like that?"

After the door closed, Mrs. McLeod felt dashed for a moment and then understanding came to her, and she knew that Jane wouldn't have talked with such violence about "shanty Irish" if her feelings had not been strong. She knew it was true that Jane hadn't seen Jimmy Doughtery for a week, but she knew now that Jane wished she had seen him.

She thought, "That's going to make the crusade all very difficult—with her doubting Mr. Richardson and feeling as she does about Jimmy Dougherty."

A month ago everything had been clear and simple as crystal, and now suddenly it was all complicated again. She turned to her desk and discovered that already in some mysterious way it was in utter disorder, a disorder rather like that of her own mind.

"It's no use," she thought wearily. "I can't keep anything straight."

Then she took up the telephone and asked for Gashouse Mary's number. When the familiar voice answered, she said, "He's turned up."

"Who?" asked Mary's voice.

"The young man I was looking for . . . the one who's going to help me with the crusade." Then hastily she told Mary of how God had sent him to her.

But Mary's voice was cautious. "Are you sure of him?" she asked.

"I've never been surer."

"It's better to be careful, Mrs. McLeod. You know how you are."

"Yes, I know. I'll bring him down tonight after supper and you can see for yourself."

"Okay, I'll be in the dance hall. But I wouldn't talk too much over the telephone."

After that she forgot the untidiness of her desk and felt better again.

28

Gashouse Mary's evening began early, vaguely about eight o'clock, depending upon the number of barges and river boats that were in town at the moment. The El Dorado dance hall was nearly as garish as the original had been in the days of the land rush. Moved by a sentimental feeling for the past, Mary had modeled the new El Dorado as nearly as possible upon the old. It was a vast barrack-like room with a long beer bar at one end and a lunch counter at the other, where sandwiches and hamburgers and hot dogs were to be had. Along one side there was a kind of cattle pen where the "hostesses" were kept between dances. Overhead the beams were left bare and ornamented with garlands of colored paper and the flags of all nations. The center was given over to dancing, save for the railed-in square at one side where the negro jazz band played from eight o'clock until there were no longer enough customers to make it profitable. Notably it differed from the old El Dorado in two things: there were no tables of roulette and faro and poker, and the hostesses were, as Gashouse Mary put it, "refined," which meant that, herded together in their pen, they looked rather like a convention of gay but respectable school teachers. Actually they were girls who worked during the day, some as clerks, some as hired girls, some in millinery shops and department stores. At the El Dorado they could dance in the evening and earn money as well, five cents on every dance and two and a half cents on each glass of beer. Gashouse Mary would not have at the El Dorado what she referred to as "professional doxies," adding, "of course I can't say what the hostesses do after they leave here, but while they're here they've got to be refined."

And so, despite the clientele of river men and roughs from the town, a kind of hard-boiled decorum prevailed in the El Dorado. Watching the spectacle, studying the lined, hard-worn faces of the men, a stranger would have wondered what it was that kept their passions in control. There were, in fact, several reasons: there was no hard liquor, and Gashouse Mary allowed none to be brought into the place; there was something about Mary herself, elegantly dressed, and seated at her table near the long bar, which imposed a restraining influence—something in the dignity of that tightly corseted figure crowned by the complicated coiffure of dyed hair that filled the heart of the toughest longshoreman with awe and apprehension; and in case the dignity

[82]

failed, Mary had the best chucker-out on the whole river. His name was Jake, and he was built like a gorilla. He was not quite bright, and peaceable enough under normal conditions but a demon when roused. A blow on the head from a bottle actually gave him pleasure.

The El Dorado was, in fact, an efficient and money-making institution, the result of sixty years of experience in frontier and river towns, beginning long ago when Mary had first played in the Square during the days of the land rush.

It was nearly nine o'clock when Mrs. McLeod and Mr. Richardson arrived, and the dancing was already going full blast; every seat at the bar and the lunch counter was taken, and all the girls from the cattle pen were busy with customers. Gashouse Mary was waiting for them at her table, dressed in a tight-fitting dress of purple merino, in the style which she described as "semi-evening" and wearing all her collection of garnets. It was clear that she had made a special effort for the occasion. She sat facing the door and the dance floor as she always did, so that she might keep an eye on the proceedings. From this position she was also able to watch the bar and the amount of business done there. Mrs. McLeod and Mr. Richardson took seats opposite her.

When she had ordered beer for them she said to Mr. Richardson, "Well, I certainly am glad to meet you. Mrs. McLeod told me about how she picked you up in the police court."

While she was ordering beer and inviting them to sit down, she had been engaged in a process she called "taking in." This meant that shrewdly, out of years of experience, she was drawing her conclusions about the young man. She had no preconceived notions and no theories; she simply relaxed and allowed her instinct full play. She liked the shape of his head, and the stubborn chin and the rather thin mouth, the straight nose and the square forehead. But most of all she liked the honest, almost innocent look of the eyes behind the steel-rimmed spectacles. Almost at once she told herself, "This fella is on the level. If you crossed him he might be a tough customer. He ain't a natural fighter, but if he got ideas about something he'd fight to a finish. He ain't the kind of man I'd choose for myself, but he might be all right for other things."

They talked for a time about this and that—the girls, the weather, the music.

"Good music," said Mr. Richardson, raising his voice to make himself heard above the cacophonies of the negro band.

"Not good but loud," said Gashouse Mary. "That's what they want. Excuse me a moment." She rose and crossed the dance floor to a couple who, lingering near the rail, were jiggling up and down. As she crossed the room her

[83]

companions saw for the first time that the purple "semi-evening" had a slight train.

She spoke to the couple and they moved off. When she returned she said, as she sat down, "I don't allow no rough stuff here." Then suddenly, as if she felt that they had talked banalities for a long enough time, she said to Mr. Richardson, "Now, tell us about yourself."

While permitting her instinct free play she had noticed two or three things—one that his clothes were much too good for a newspaperman; they were too expensive and they showed too much taste and care in selection. They were what she called "tony," not what the late Mr. McGovern with his taste for checks and red neckties would have called "tony," but the real thing. She knew "tone" when she saw it, although she had not seen it more than a half-dozen times in her checkered life. It was something special, expensive and careless. And his speech, like his clothes, was "tony." She knew what that was too. To herself she thought, "He ain't any common ordinary newspaperman if he's a newspaperman at all. And he's not as slow as he looks. Maybe Vinnie McLeod has found the right guy." And for a second, hope rose in her vast bosom and excitement at the thought that here might be the means of getting back at her enemy, Old Dougherty.

But Mr. Richardson held his ground and revealed nothing more than he had already told Mrs. McLeod. Then suddenly he grinned, a grin that was both unexpected and illuminating. It lighted up the impersonal bleakness of the face and revealed unsuspected depths of warmth and humor and experience. At the sight of the grin, Gashouse Mary's instinct told her, "He's been around too. He's no parson."

He said, "I guess you think I'm pulling your leg, but I'm not. I've done everything there is to do on a newspaper. I know it all sounds sort of fishy, but you've got to take my word for it."

Then, before she could answer, the door opened and her trained vision told her that someone unusual was coming in the door. She was silent and Mrs. McLeod followed her glance, turned and saw Jimmy Dougherty stepping across the threshold. He was a little drunk so that he moved unsteadily, and with him was a girl in a green suit and a red fox fur with a tiny hat placed on the back of a head covered with platinum curls. She was young, but she had a hard face and a big mouth. Mrs. McLeod remembered having seen her somewhere before now. She was very different from the dance hall girls, with their cheap dresses and home-set waves.

Gashouse Mary leaned forward a little and started to rise, then thought better of it and sat down again.

"I don't like him coming here and I don't like her either."

"Who is she?" asked Mrs. McLeod.

"She is the daughter of poor old Hedges, the plumber. Gone gay. It's bad for the morals of the girls when they see her fox fur. I don't like doxies coming here. I've told her to keep out. She wouldn't dare come in except with Jimmy Dougherty. He's got a nerve too—after what I told him and his old man the last time I saw them. I'd throw him out too, only I've just got things patched up again and it would cost me money."

Then Jimmy Dougherty turned and saw them, and leaving the platinum-haired girl at the bar, he came unsteadily over. When he reached the table he said, "Good evening, Mary. Good evening, Mrs. McLeod." Then he turned directly and insolently at Mr. Richardson without speaking. To Mrs. McLeod he said, "I just wanted to tell you to give my love to Jane."

"I'll tell her," said Mrs. McLeod.

"Thank you."

Then abruptly, unsteadily, he made his way back to the bar. Intoxicated men, all except Willie Ferguson, always made Mrs. McLeod nervous, and now she felt a little sick at the sight of Jimmy Dougherty because she couldn't help liking him.

Gashouse Mary was saying, "He'd be all right if he'd get away from that hellion of a father. Jimmy ain't a bad sort himself."

But Mrs. McLeod scarcely heard her because she was thinking of Jane and wondering whether she should deliver Jimmy Dougherty's message. If she told Jane the whole story, about where he was, and what condition he was in and whom he was with, it ought to finish off the whole thing and leave her hands free for the crusade. But somehow she didn't want to deliver the message or tell Jane anything of what she had seen.

Gashouse Mary said, "I guess I can get away for a minute. Come on into the parlor." She raised her voice and yelled "Jake!" and the chucker-out, who was standing near the door, lumbered over to the table, his huge hands hanging somewhere about his knees.

"Listen, Jake," she said, "if there's any trouble send for me before you do anything."

"Okay!" said Jake.

Gashouse Mary rose and with dignity led the way through the door near the bar into the parlor. There, beneath the enlarged portrait of the late Mr. McGovern, the three of them held a conference which lasted for more than an hour. It was Gashouse Mary who outlined the campaign. She knew about politics. She had a political following of her own and she volunteered to warm them up discreetly, without giving away anything, to the idea of running the Doughertys out of power. Mrs. McLeod was to get hold of Sam Henderson and Jim Newman and start them to work quietly organizing the old-timers in the county. Mr. Richardson was to go ahead with modernizing the *Daily Shield and Banner* until the time came for them to act. There was plenty of time—nearly eight weeks before Mr. Richardson's parole would be up. The light of battle came into Mary's eyes. She trusted Mr. Richardson. She had given her instinct time and her instinct had told her that Mr. Richardson was okay.

"Maybe it'll be Old Dougherty instead of Gashouse Mary who's chased out of town." She slapped her big thigh with a loud whack. "That'd be good. That would." Then her eyes narrowed a little and she said to Mr. Richardson, "And you'd better not try any double-crossing, young man." She said that just in case her instinct had been a *tiny* bit wrong.

"You can count on me," said Mr. Richardson.

"The only thing I can't make out is why in hell you're taking the trouble to help clean up a cow town full of strangers like us."

"I guess it's just because I like cleaning up places. It's kind of a disease with me. . . . I like fighting and I like fighting for the underdog."

And out of her long experience with reformers, Gashouse Mary said quickly, "I suppose it *is* kind of a disease." It was the first time she had ever found herself on the side of the crusaders. She didn't like them. She didn't feel at home with them, and even now she wasn't quite sure that she was safe.

When they went back again into the dance hall, Jimmy Dougherty and his girl were gone. They had another beer, and as soon as Jake, the bouncer, saw them, he came over to the table, scratching his head.

"Sorry, Mrs. McGovern, but I had to throw out young Dougherty."

"My Gawd! Why?"

"He knocked a guy down who said something fresh to that moll with him. There wasn't time to come and tell you. I threw 'em all out, the moll too."

"Okay," said Gashouse Mary. "Only I'd like to have been here."

When Jake went away she said, "Well, I suppose that means more trouble." But her spirits weren't crushed. In the bright old eye there was a new light. She liked politics and she liked a good fight and she hadn't had one since Mr. McGovern died.

29

Outside in the remnants of the mud from the flood Jimmy Dougherty picked himself up. The man he had knocked down was already vanishing in the mist that rose in the moonlight from the river. He felt dizzy and his head ached, and Fern Hedges, the plumber's daughter with the platinum hair, was standing over him.

"Why didn't you hit him?"

"I knocked him down, didn't I?"

"I don't mean him. I mean Jake."

Jimmy looked at her. "Are you crazy?" he asked. "You might as well try to throw a rhinoceros."

"Anyway, how dare an old bat like Gashouse Mary throw us out?"

"She didn't know anything about it."

"Oh, yeah? She's been after me for months. She don't like my competition."

"Maybe." Jimmy, in the dim light from the single bulb over the door, was trying to remove the mud from his clothes. He did this laboriously, painstakingly, without much result.

For a time Fern stood watching him, then she said, "Well, are we gonna stand here all night?"

"I don't want to go back to town looking like this."

Her voice softened a little as she said, "We don't need to go back to town. You can go home with me and I'll clean you up."

"I'm not going home with you."

"Why not?"

"Because I don't want to." He set his hat straight and said, "Come on, I'll walk back with you."

Through the mist they walked past the shuttered houses and the bawdy music of Franklin Street and up the hill toward the town. Neither of them said anything for a long time. It was Fern who spoke first. She said, "What's the matter? I was countin' on your comin' home with me."

"Nothing's the matter."

"Drunk . . . that's what you are."

"I am not."

"I suppose it's that girl reporter on the *Daily Shield and Banner*. I know you've been running around with her. Thought you were pretty smart, but I knew it. Everybody knows it."

"Leave her out of it."

"I won't leave her out of it. Why should I? She's no better than I am. I know about her."

"If you don't shut your trap, I'll sock you too."

She stopped and began to shout, "That's what you would do. I know you—a Dougherty. Dirty Old Dougherty's son. The old pimp. You can't talk to me like that."

Finally he took her by the arm. "Stop that yelling," he said, shaking her. "Stop it, right now!"

"I won't! I won't! Let me go!" And now instead of shouting she began to scream, "Help! Help!"

He let her go and started on up the hill, but she did not follow him. She simply stayed there screaming. Without turning he walked on, and in a moment he heard the sound of her footsteps running to catch up with him. As she came up behind him she said, "That's right. That's just what you would do . . . leave me alone in a part of town like this, full of bums. Anything might happen to me. . . ." Then she placed herself in front of him so that he couldn't advance and cried, "Anyway, I couldn't meet anybody who'd treat me worse than you have . . . laying hands on a woman. You're no gentleman—if you were a Southern gentleman, you'd know better. You're nothing but a damned Irish Yankee. I'm going home alone and if you dare follow me I'll scream for help. I'll scream till you can hear me in Memphis."

She turned and hurried away up the hill, and he remained where he was standing, looking after her. At the corner under the street lamps she turned her head quickly to see if he was following, then she went on again, a little more slowly. When she had passed the light he turned up a side street. He didn't follow her so she had no need to scream again.

Walking along the dark street he was, in his tipsiness, lost for a time. It was a narrow street lined by dreary cheap houses that pressed in like the walls of a shabby narrow canyon. He did not much care whether he was lost or not. He felt sick and corroded by disgust at himself and over the behavior of Fern. He had known her always, since the days when the Doughertys were new in Plattesville and few people knew them or spoke to them. He had gone swimming with Fern on spring days when they were both ten. He had known her in grade school and in high school where as the "fast girl" she went brazenly her own way and sometimes his. He had come to think of her as an old friend and now she behaved like any street-walker.

"Which, I suppose," he thought tipsily, "is what she is." He couldn't imagine why he had never thought of her like that before, except that he'd always known her. Then he felt sudden remorse at his condition, and instead of going to Hennessey's saloon as he had planned to do, he turned his steps as he reached the end of the narrow street, toward home.

Once, when the Doughertys had first come to Plattesville, it would have been a short walk but now it was a long one, for since nine years Old Dougherty had lived in the best part of town in a big florid house that represented his Gaelic idea of splendor. Built in the Tudor style, which had very little to do with the Southwest, it stood back from Fleming Avenue surrounded by clumps of the most expensive shrubbery laid out by a landscape gardener from St. Louis. It was, in its way, the McLeod's Folly of a later generation.

In half an hour Jimmy, still a little unsteady, turned in between the globular lights which marked the steps leading up to the big veranda. There was, he saw, a light in what the architect had called the library, so he knew that his father was still awake. He wasn't pleased at the prospect of seeing the Old Man, not because his father would object to his condition, but because Jimmy was aware, more and more of late, that he was twenty-six years old and it was time that he was settling down.

When he had let himself in with his latchkey he went directly to the library, steadying himself with a great effort of will in the hope that his father would not notice his condition. He had, he thought, succeeded admirably until the moment he entered the room where the small shrewd blue eyes of the old man looked up from the pile of papers that rested on his chest and he said, "Well, been at it again, have you?"

He was lying on the sofa, his shoes off, his feet resting on the end. He was smoking a cigar and had, it was evident, been making figures on the sheets of foolscap that adorned his chest. Behind, in the shadows, were the dim rows of shelves almost innocent of books. For the first time in his life Jimmy was aware for some reason of their bareness.

He grinned, a little foolishly, the effort making his face feel as if it belonged to someone else. "Sure," he said, "why not? I was out with Fern."

"Hitting it up, ain't you?"

"Well, now and then a fellow's got to enjoy himself."

"You don't look as if you'd been having much fun. Who threw you in the mud?"

He had forgotten the mud. Looking down at his blue suit, he saw that he looked as if he had been rolling in the river bottom. If he had remembered he would have sneaked upstairs somehow, in spite of everything.

Again he grinned, "I got thrown out."

"Where from?"

"The El Dorado."

"Didn't you fight back?"

"I might have once. Did you ever see that bouncer Jake? It wasn't worth getting a black eye and maybe a chewed ear."

"Glad to see you're getting some sense." He sat up and put his feet on the floor. "But Gashouse Mary's got a nerve—throwing a Dougherty out of any place."

"She didn't know anything about it. She was in the parlor talking to Mrs. McLeod and that new guy she's got working for her."

"What new guy?"

"That guy she saved from a vagrancy charge. He's a reporter."

"Oh, him!" The old man took up the whisky bottle and poured his son a drink. "Here, sit down and take some of this. I want to ask you a couple of things."

Jimmy sat down in his big loose way and took the drink. "Shoot," he said.

"What's been the matter with you these last ten days?"

"Nothing. I haven't noticed anything. . . ."

"Seems to me you've been off your feed."

[89]

"Mebbe."

"Workin' too hard?"

"Mebbe."

"How'd you like to take a couple of weeks off fishin' at Galveston?"

"I'll think about it."

"And there's something else."

"Yeah?"

"You get around a lot more than I do. What's old Mrs. McLeod up to?"

"I don't know. Nothing, I guess. I haven't noticed anything."

"What about tonight?"

"I hadn't thought about tonight."

"Well, I've been thinking ever since you told me. What was she doin' at Gashouse Mary's?"

"Mebbe she's gonna write a story about the place."

"She ain't modern enough for that. And what did she have that bum along with her for? What were they talking about in Mary's parlor?"

"I don't know. I wasn't in there."

The small blue eyes of Old Dougherty narrowed. He crushed out his cigar and said, "Well, it smells bad to me. Gashouse Mary would like nothing better than to fix us—the bitch! And old Mrs. McLeod has been bitten by reform ideas for a long time—ever since J. E. died." He lighted another cigar and said, "What's the reporter guy she picked up like?"

"I don't know. He looks all right—looks pretty smart. He's an Easterner. It's written all over him."

"What's he meddlin' around here for?"

"Don't know."

"Well, it looks to me like he might be one of them damned radicals." For a time he studied the end of his cigar. Then the jaw hardened and the mouth grew thin and straight and he said, "You get around more than I do. It's up to you to find out what's going on. If the old lady has got any reform ideas we'll just have to strangle the paper. That's easy enough to do." He looked directly at his son and said, "You been going around with that niece of hers, haven't you?"

"Yes."

"Well, you might get some information out of her."

"That's no good. That's busted up."

"What's the matter? Wouldn't she give in?"

"It wasn't like that. She's not that kind of girl."

"There must be something wrong with your technique."

"Let's lay off her."

"Okay."

Jimmy finished the drink in silence and put down the glass. After a minute his father said, "You look kind of peaked to me. Better go to bed and sleep it off, and tomorrow we'll talk about that fishing trip." Jimmy rose and started toward the door. "Only remember what I said. If they start anything, we've got to stop it quick before they even get started. It wouldn't have made so much difference a couple of years ago. But with Bill Swain in strong at the capital it's different."

"Sure," said Jimmy and went out of the library and up the huge stairway to his own room. But when he got into bed, he couldn't sleep. For two hours he lay awake in the darkness trying to collect and put in order his thoughts and emotions. He was dissatisfied with himself and he could not discover why. He had never felt like that before in all the twenty-six years of his life.

30

Belowstairs in the library Old Dougherty finished his figuring and put away the papers in the safe built into the wall just beneath the portrait of his wife. Then he lay down again on the sofa and for a long time looked up at the picture. It was not a good painting, but it had a certain photographic quality which he had always liked and which now brought her back to him very clearly. It was the portrait of a gentle, serene face, with graying hair and the same blue eyes that looked out of Jimmy's handsome face. It had been painted for this room in the "new house" which had marked an upward stage in the fortunes of the Doughertys—the "new house" built for her in which she had never set foot because she was dead before it was finished.

He missed her tonight. He had never ceased missing her. In the beginning she had come of a much better family than his own, and she had been willing to marry him in the face of every opposition, and she had, he knew, put up with him and a great deal of which she disapproved, because that was the way she was. Jimmy was like her in his looks and in his easy-going nature; and when she died Jimmy was only seventeen, and she left her son in his care, hinting gently that the boy should take up some other career than politics. If Old Dougherty ever knew a troubled conscience, it was over his failure to follow her hint. He hadn't paid much attention to Jimmy one way or another. He'd always been so busy working and fighting that Jimmy had grown to young manhood without much guiding. But he was, Old Dougherty reflected, a good boy—wild, yes, but he wouldn't have wanted a son who hadn't a bit of the devil in him. And after all, it was inevitable that Jimmy should go into politics. Otherwise that good-looking face and the personality and manner which charmed people would have been wasted.

The old man felt tired tonight, with a weariness which had come over him more and more often of late. Lying on the sofa in his stockinged feet he was sick of politics and the worries that went with them. He would have liked nothing better than to have gone to Galveston himself, only it wasn't possible for them both to be away at the same time, and Jimmy looked and acted as if he were the one who needed the change.

Presently, for lack of attention, his cigar went out, and in disgust he threw it away and fell to dreaming about how good it would be to go back to Daytona, maybe go there for a whole winter with nothing to do but drink and play horseshoes and fish and muck around a bit on the beach. He wouldn't regret leaving the house because he had never been attached to it; it was too big and so pretentious that when he took off his shoes and made himself comfortable, he felt ashamed. And with no woman to run it, it wasn't a home anyway—just a big ornate barracks which had been a mistake from the beginning. His wife would have liked it; she had had enough class to dominate it and she could have made it human. He couldn't blame Jimmy for going out every night in the week and only using it as a place to sleep. It was pretty dreary for a young fellow; a boardinghouse would have been livelier.

The striking of the big, showy, expensive clock in the hall roused him to the knowledge that it was two o'clock and time he got some sleep. Thrusting his big feet into his felt slippers he switched off the light, leaving the library with its empty shelves in darkness and climbed the stairs. He would send Jimmy to Galveston tomorrow morning for a couple of weeks. He was always afraid of Jimmy's drinking, and it was a good idea to nip it right at the start. And he wanted Jimmy to be in the best of spirits and behaving himself when the annual Democratic barbecue and home-coming came off. In his Irish bones he had a feeling of presentiment. Somehow this year, the barbecue and home-coming was going to be of greater importance than it had ever been.

31

When Mr. Richardson and Mrs. McLeod returned to McLeod's Folly the house was in darkness, and they discovered that Jane had already gone to bed. In the hallway, while Mrs. McLeod was taking off her hat and coat, Mr. Richardson said to her, "Do you mind if I work late in the library? You see, I'm writing some articles, and I'll have to do it late at night, outside office hours."

"Of course not." Because she was sure of him and feeling full of warmth and friendliness, she wanted to cry out, "I'm writing a book too." But in the same moment the old shyness swept over her so that she found herself blushing at her presumption and quickly added, "Use anything you like in the house. I want you to feel at home here. Act just as if it was your own place."

Suddenly she felt like settling down to a good talk. Excitement and confidence had driven all weariness out of her, and she wanted to break through that odd wall of reserve which surrounded her "discovery" and find out what he was like. She hadn't any reserve herself, and she always felt friendly and intimate toward everyone.

The desire came to nothing because before she could even propose a cup of hot cocoa in the kitchen, he was saying politely, "I won't keep you up any longer. I've a lot of work to do," and left her no choice but to go upstairs to bed. For a moment she thought of going to J. E.'s den to do some more revising on The Book, but she quickly gave that up. She was far too excited to do any work of that kind. Tomorrow would be Saturday, and she would go to Jim Newman's and tell the old boys who gathered there about her clean-up campaign. She must set to work quietly organizing the county.

Upstairs she passed Jane's door and stopped for a moment to listen to the quiet breathing which told her that Jane was asleep. She was glad of that. Now she wouldn't have to give Jane Jimmy Dougherty's message and have to say where she had seen him and with whom and that he was a little drunk. Tomorrow she could pretend to herself that she'd forgotten.

32

On Monday morning the revolution began. It began the moment that Mr. Richardson arrived at the office and seated himself at the old desk overlooking the Square. Everyone in the office, even Willie Ferguson through a haze of Bourbon fumes, knew it at once by something in the atmosphere. The change became definitely apparent when at ten o'clock Mrs. McLeod, with a stagy air of authority and confidence, emerged from the cubbyhole and announced that there was to be a conference—the first conference in the long history of the *Daily Shield and Banner*. For a conference it was necessary to have a table, so while Mrs. McLeod went into the composing room to summon old Zimmerman, the make-up man, Mr. Richardson cleared off the files of newspapers which occupied the long table in the center of the room.

Days, weeks, perhaps months and years had passed since the sacred files had been moved and the table properly put in order, and Mr. Richardson's activity raised clouds of ancient dust which filled the room and set both Jane and Willie coughing. Jane coughed loudly out of injured vanity, and Willie with immense ostentation in order to demonstrate the evil and unsanitary effect of innovations. And at last Jane opened the windows admitting, in an unconsciously symbolic gesture, the fresh balmy air of the early summer.

When all this had been done, chairs were placed round the table and the staff seated themselves, Mrs. McLeod at one end, Mr. Richardson at the other and Jane, Willie Ferguson and old Zimmerman at the side. Mr. Richardson was about to open the conference, when Willie uttered an objection.

"If this is going to be a real conference," he said, "I think Myrtle ought to be here—seeing as how she runs the business end."

Mrs. McLeod said, "You're right, Willie. Go and fetch her. And tell Alf he can lay off the linotype and keep the business office until we're finished."

Gloomily, with foreboding pantomimed in every line of his skinny body, Willie descended to fetch Myrtle while the others sat in strained silence. When the husband and wife returned, Myrtle, in her high immaculate collar and with her most disapproving air, took her place at the table beside Willie and everything was ready. At the table only Mrs. McLeod seemed enthusiastic and stirred by the joys of anticipation. The others, all save old Zimmerman, were hostile. He betrayed no emotion whatever; he simply went on chewing tobacco.

Mr. Richardson rearranged the papers on which he had made notes, and clearing his throat, began:

"Mrs. McLeod," he said, "has kindly asked me to submit suggestions for the reorganization of the *Daily Shield and Banner*. I have outlined some changes and improvements, none of which is very difficult and none of which requires the expenditure of much money."

At this Myrtle gave a sniff rich with meaning, and at the sound Mr. Richardson smiled at her respectfully and said, "Mrs. McLeod has explained to me the financial difficulties of the *Daily Shield and Banner* and I have taken all that into consideration. It is my hope that in a few weeks or a few months the changes and improvements will show such results that we shall be able to undertake larger and more comprehensive ones."

He paused for a moment, and going through the papers said, "In the beginning the burden of work involved will very likely fall on my shoulders, a situation which I am quite prepared to accept."

Around the table, one by one, the confreres began to be impressed, first by the seriousness and dignity which young Mr. Richardson managed to impose upon an occasion which none but Mrs. McLeod had meant to take seriously and without cynicism; secondly, they liked the sound of the big, slightly pompous words he used—the young man had authority and it was evident that he was used to speaking in public. Mrs. McLeod beamed with pride and pleasure like a mother whose son has won everything on school prize day. Myrtle fussed with her jabot and sniffed as if struggling to resist. Jane was really impressed, because what he was doing was exactly what she had meant to do a year ago when she first came to work with her Aunt

[94]

Vinnie. She was impressed, too, by the firmness, clear-headedness and decision of Mr. Richardson. She felt suddenly that he was the kind of man who took hold of life firmly and calmly and bent it to his own ends. In Willie's heart admiration and resentment struggled for domination. Old Zimmerman simply sat, his face growing more and more solemn, giving no sign of life save the rhythmic cowlike movements of the jaws as he chewed.

Quietly, firmly, Mr. Richardson went on, outlining one by one the changes he proposed to make, taking them up one by one with the persons concerned, so that each one of them was in turn flattered by his deference and attention. Jane, brightening, put in her own objections and some new ideas about a whole page devoted to the county and another given over to the interests of women. These she volunteered to take on herself. At first, Myrtle objected to everything on the grounds of expense, but slowly, with a knowledge which surprised her and made her humble, Mr. Richardson brought her round to his side. With tact and flattery he suggested that Willie Ferguson should undertake a gossip column full of small items of news, personal and flattering, concerning the citizens of Plattesville. And Willie, because he was a born gossip and had a sense of humor, and sometime during every day put his nose in the door of every poolroom and saloon in Plattesville, liked the idea and in spite of its being Monday morning, warmed up to it. When it came to old Zimmerman's turn, he accepted every suggestion, not by words but by gulping noises. His face, old and leathery, seemed to grow paler and paler beneath the strain of Mr. Richardson's impressive conference manner.

The conference lasted for more than an hour, and at the end Mr. Richardson said, "We'll begin the changes with the Monday edition. In the meanwhile we'll say nothing about it to anyone, and on Saturday I'll write an editorial calling attention to the new *Daily Shield and Banner*." He paused, took off his glasses and added, "We can only accomplish this by coöperation and working together as good fellows for the pride of the job and the tradition of what was once and will be again one of the great newspapers of the Southwest."

This was actually received with applause by Jane and Mrs. McLeod into which Myrtle joined with a slightly acid tapping of the hands. Willie, reinforced by a stealthy visit to the bottom drawer, actually cried, "Hear! Hear!"

"If you all agree," continued Mr. Richardson, putting on his spectacles once more, "we will make these conferences a weekly affair—say every Monday."

"Yes, yes," said Jane with enthusiasm.

"Thursday," said Willie, thinking of Saturday night and Sunday, "would be a better day."

"All right, then," said Mr. Richardson, "let us make it Thursday."

Old Zimmerman, quite white now, gulped his approval.

Then Mrs. McLeod, beaming, rose to her feet and said, "Now I think we should all give some sign that we are in agreement with Mr. Richardson and his ideas. I think," she said (remembering her Women's Club days), "that a vote of thanks would be in order. All in favor will say 'Aye.'"

There was a chorus of "Ayes" about the table from all but old Zimmerman. Suddenly, inexplicably, in great haste, his face green now with anxiety, he leaped from his chair and ran from the room. For a second there was a startled silence, and Mrs. McLeod said, "What on earth is the matter with Mr. Zimmerman?"

It was Willie who answered with a wicked chuckle, "There ain't nothin' the matter with him except he's never been to a conference before. He's been swallowin' tobaccy juice all through the goings-on."

33

During the rest of the week Mr. Richardson devoted moments now and then to the individual encouragement of each member of the staff. With Mrs. McLeod this wasn't necessary; on the contrary he was compelled to exercise restraint now and then to prevent her getting ahead of herself; she bubbled and boiled with enthusiasm and herself kept having ideas which, as Mr. Richardson was forced to point out, were far beyond the narrow limits of the cash they had to work with. But the spirits of the others rose and fell, according to their moods. Jane, in a personal way, was certainly happier than she had been and scuttled about, now to the library, now to the bookstores to purchase women's magazines and agricultural papers from which she shamelessly stole ideas, suggestions, and whole articles, rewriting them in her own glib style for the new woman's page and the page devoted to gardening, poultry and the dairy.

"What we want," Mr. Richardson kept saying, "is individual stuff, with a personal local touch. All this bought-up mat stuff will never get us out of the hole."

Her doubts as to his ever having been a newspaperman were quite vanished now; he knew his stuff; he knew every technical term; he knew even how to run the linotype and set headlines. In short, he seemed to her to know everything, to be, indeed, God-like in his journalistic all-knowingness. There was only one thing he did not know and that was how to be intimate and warm. He was, Jane thought, much too much of an efficient machine.

Nevertheless, the new régime pleased her; for one thing she was no longer treated to the spectacle of a tweed-covered, incommunicative back.

It was not only in the realm of ideas and plans that Mr. Richardson busied himself; there was the simple matter of house cleaning. For the first time within memory the editorial office was set by the ears. Cupboards and files were opened; mice nests and ancient documents were discovered, even a whole packet of J. E.'s editorials written in his own hand, for which Mrs. McLeod had been searching vaguely for years. Dust rose in clouds. The ancient floor was scrubbed and Willie Ferguson's spittoon placed on a square of metal. The ragged old files were bound together. And last of all the whole was given three coats of fresh new water-green paint. When Mrs. McLeod grew troubled about the expenditure, Mr. Richardson only said, "Leave that to me. Don't trouble your head about it—you'll see!" and again for the moment she had a new doubt—that she had rescued from prison a man who was bent upon ruining her.

At last came Saturday night and Mr. Richardson's editorial about the new *Daily Shield and Banner*.

It was calm, dignified, impressive and a little pompous, like his speech at the conference, and it occupied a whole page near the center of the paper. It began by reviewing the glory of the origin and the past of the *Daily Shield and Banner* with dignified compliments to the memory of J. E. McLeod and of his father. Then it proceeded to the history of Plattesville itself, from its beginning as a settlement on the frontier, through the days when half-wild cattle and horses roamed the whole range of the big country, through the wild wide-open days of the land rush, to the importance of Plattesville's modern and latest stage.

"The *Daily Shield and Banner*," wrote Mr. Richardson, as if he were Plattesville's oldest inhabitant, "has always been representative of the best life of the county and the new *Daily Shield and Banner* will continue to be so, burgeoning, we hope, into a new and modern version of the excellent newspaper founded long ago by old Angus McLeod who helped to rescue the great Southwest from the villainies of Mexican tyrannies, and carried on so ably by his son, the late J. E. McLeod, and latterly by his widow, Mrs. Lavinia McLeod."

Originally he had written—"his widow, one of the best known and respected citizens of our community." But Mrs. McLeod, assuming all the authority she was able to assume, objected to the phrase and had it cut out because, she said, it made her feel foolish.

In closing the editorial Mr. Richardson quoted gracefully from the earlier writing of the late J. E. himself, out of one of his own editorials found among the mice nests at the bottom of the cupboard.

"Plattesville has always been a city in which we may all take pride; our county with its plains and hills and salubrious climate might well be the envy of all citizens of this great and glorious nation. It has always been an honorable and forward-looking community and the *Daily Shield and Banner* means to fight eternally to keep it so."

It was, even Willie and Myrtle Ferguson agreed, a mighty fine editorial, which restored the self-respect and roused the spirits of everyone connected with the *Daily Shield and Banner* down to the boys who delivered it to the scanty list of Plattesville subscribers. And outside the office it was a bombshell which, an hour or two after the last copy was off the press, had set half the town to talking. Those who did not yet know about Mr. Richardson thought with a certain cynicism, "Just another of Vinnie McLeod's brainstorms," and others said, "Where on earth is Vinnie getting the money?"

By Sunday morning most of the town was awaiting the Monday evening edition with impatience and anticipation.

34

Probably the most interested of all Plattesville's citizens was Old Dougherty. That Saturday night he sat with his stockinged feet up on the end of the sofa, reading the editorial through again and again. He did not like the sound of it, and he wished that Jimmy were here to discuss it with him instead of fishing in Galveston and trying to forget that niece of Mrs. McLeod's.

As he grew older he felt more and more the need of Jimmy at his side to back him up. When the boy was away there were times when he felt tired and old and lost.

More ominous than anything in the whole editorial was that last paragraph in which J. E. McLeod, who died before Old Dougherty ever came to Plattesville, spoke from the grave. He did not like the smell of that line which read, "Plattesville has always been an honorable and forward-looking community and the *Daily Shield and Banner* means to fight eternally to keep it so."

Old Dougherty had no illusions; he did not deceive himself. This declaration was in direct and blatant opposition to his own ideal for the future of the city. He meant to keep Plattesville in his pocket.

That night Old Dougherty did not fall into a heavy sleep the moment he climbed into the vast bed in his pseudo-Tudor palace. He lay awake for a long time thinking and planning and making notes on the memorandum pad which lay on the night table beside him—notes of information he must ask from Hirsh, the new business manager of the *News*, about the *Daily Shield and Banner's* debts and its dealings with paper companies. Hirsh would undoubtedly know the answers.

Like a great spider he lay in the Grand Rapids Louis Quinze bed, spinning the web with which Mrs. McLeod and the *Daily Shield and Banner* might, if necessary, be caught and destroyed.

In his heart he didn't want to ruin Mrs. McLeod because he liked her the way you like an old worn-out pair of shoes, but if she started anything he might be forced to ruin her in order to save himself from ruin, perhaps even from prison. He wasn't afraid of her, but he was afraid of the ball which she might start rolling. And that little squirt whom old Flynn, the magistrate, had permitted her to nip out of jail under the very noses of all of them! If they'd only guessed what he really was, he'd be emptying garbage cans at this moment into municipal street-cleaning trucks. Old Dougherty knew well enough where the editorial had come from. It wasn't from the pen of poor muddle-headed Lavinia McLeod. It was written by somebody who was damned smart—too damned smart for his own or anybody else's good.

35

On Monday the new *Daily Shield and Banner* appeared. Although the type was unchanged, it had been so reorganized and so rearranged that the whole paper gave the effect of having been reborn. It was, a great many people said, like a brand new newspaper. Where it had been old-fashioned and rather stuffy in appearance, it now seemed thoroughly modern. The news stories which once had been lifted bodily a day late out of metropolitan papers were rewritten, each with a twist which gave local interest. And the choice was different. Mr. Richardson left out the dull stories and took those which had human appeal.

The Monday edition included as novelties, Willie Ferguson's gossip column and an article by Jane Baldwin on the subject of making Plattesville a floral city with flowers and gardens where only empty lots and rubbish heaps had existed before. And there was a special article by the editor, Lavinia McLeod, upon old-fashioned recipes for jams and preserves, recipes which had been forgotten, save by a few old women living in villages and on ranches in the county who still exhibited their jams and preserves each year at the county fair. Although her name appeared nowhere it was Gashouse Mary who had contributed three of the recipes. Also there was another editorial by Mr. Richardson, in which he declared that although the paper intended to guard and cherish the tradition of the old *Daily Shield and Banner*, it had a new policy which was to make the DAILY SHIELD AND BANNER *the* newspaper of the town and the county, a newspaper so personal, so typical of the county itself that people all over the United States would know and even perhaps read it.

It was the first time that an article signed by a name had ever appeared in the columns of the *Daily Shield and Banner,* and this lent to the newspaper a personal touch and warmed the hearts of those who signed the articles. Even the veteran, Mrs. McLeod herself, felt at the sight of her name in print, a new youth and something approaching celebrity.

Willie's column was excellent, a compound of small bits of personal intelligence, stories and bits of observation gained from a long life of Bourbon and lady-killing, and for the first time in twenty years he appeared in the office utterly sober on a Monday morning. He was, in his anticipation of the great day, so sober that he felt self-conscious and a little ashamed before the astounded glances of the whole office.

On Tuesday, a little before noon, the first new subscription was received by Myrtle Ferguson in her cage belowstairs. By three in the afternoon there were seven more, and the day closed with a total of nine. There were, too, telephone calls of congratulations which kept Mrs. McLeod flurried and inefficient throughout the afternoon. And late in the evening just before the office closed, Mrs. Mabel Urquahart Jenkins, president of the Women's Civic Club of Plattesville, telephoned to Jane to say that at the meeting of the club during the afternoon her article about beautifying Plattesville had aroused so much interest that a committee had been formed to undertake the planting of flowers and shrubs. Would she, Mrs. Jenkins asked, accept an honorary membership in the club and act as one of the committee?

Flushing with pleasure and embarrassment, Jane accepted, and when she left the office she went at once to the library to take out books on gardening, and as soon as she arrived home she wrote for a dozen seed catalogues. She knew nothing whatever about gardening, but now that she was garden editor she would have to learn, not only about flowers but about vegetables, and enough so that the committee would never discover her ignorance. And it wasn't only gardening that occupied her mind. She had her page for the women on Thursdays and the county page on Saturdays. Life, it seemed to her, for a whole day, had never been so full and so exciting before.

That night, about eleven o'clock, they held a celebration in the kitchen —Mrs. McLeod, Jane and Mr. Richardson—with cocoa and spoon bread and Aida seated apart at a small table, listening. Although there was nothing stronger than cocoa they were all a little drunk. Even Mr. Richardson seemed pleased in his detached way. It was, in fact, simply another conference from which Willie and Myrtle Ferguson and old Zimmerman were absent.

Mr. Richardson's head, it seemed, was simply a repository of inexhaustible ideas for brightening up the *Daily Shield and Banner*. One after another he brought them out and they took them up and discussed them. Aida too joined in the discussion, and presently she too had an idea.

"What about the colored folks?" she asked. "We ain't got any newspaper. We ain't got any way to read about ourselves. There's a powerful lot of colored folks in Plattesville and they all buy vittles and clothes and they all got votes too, and a lot of 'em have got money too."

And so, from Aida's suggestion, was born the Friday night page given over to the recording of fish fries and births and deaths and the doings of the African Baptist Church.

Mr. Richardson asked, "But who's going to do it? It ought to be a colored person."

Aida supplied the man. "My cousin Athena's got just the boy. He's been to Tuskegee. He's a poet but he doan make much money at it, and he'd like to pick up a coupla dollars a week extra money."

"Aida, you go round tomorrow morning and tell him to come in and see Mrs. McLeod. Tell him she's got a job for him."

And then he had another idea. He said, "There ought to be somebody in the county who could write some articles about Plattesville in the old days. That would go big with all the old citizens, and there are thousands of new ones who'd like to know about all that—some good colorful articles like that ought to attract a lot of interest, not to mention paving the way for the crusade." He turned to Mrs. McLeod and said, "Do you know anybody who could do them?"

The question threw her into confusion. She blushed and stammered, and at last she was able to say, "No, I don't, but maybe I could find somebody."

It was Aida, in her enthusiasm, who revealed the secret. She said, "Why don't you tell him about The Book, Mis' McLeod?"

"No . . . no," said Mrs. McLeod, blushing more wildly than ever.

"What book?" asked Mr. Richardson.

"What book?" repeated Jane.

"It's nothing," said Mrs. McLeod.

Aida was determined now. Putting down her cup of cocoa she said, "Why, Mis' McLeod has been writin' away on a book for years. It ain't about nothin' else but the old days in Calamos County."

Jane regarded her with astonishment, and Mrs. McLeod, still miserable, said, "It's nothing at all—just some things I set down so I wouldn't forget."

"Let me see it," said Mr. Richardson, "it might be just the thing."

"If you want to . . . I guess it would only bore you. Anyway, I guess you couldn't read my writing. Nobody can but old Zimmerman."

"We could get it copied out by a typist."

"It's awful long, and it would cost a lot of money."

"I guess we could manage that somehow. It would be worth it to the paper. It would soon pay for itself."

Mrs. McLeod didn't answer him because she couldn't. She simply felt speechless and shamed. But Mr. Richardson, as she already knew, was not one to give up. He said, "You give me the manuscript and I'll get in a stenographer."

"She couldn't read it either," said Mrs. McLeod.

"Well, she can come to the office and work near you, and when she gets into trouble you can help her out. Agreed?"

"I'd rather not."

Mr. Richardson laughed, "Come now, you're a veteran journalist—you're no schoolgirl."

"All right . . . maybe." But she blushed like a young girl, and it was clear that Mr. Richardson had won another victory.

And then the old kitchen clock banged twice and Mrs. McLeod said, "For heaven's sake, it's two o'clock and we've all got to work tomorrow."

So they all rose, and when Mrs. McLeod stayed behind to give Aida belated orders for the next day, Aida said, "What I tell you, Mis' McLeod. That young man's a ball of fire, he is. . . . And now the colored folks is gonna get into the newspapers. I knows a man when I sees him. He's a mighty white fella even if he is a Yankee." She gave a wicked, triumphant chuckle. "And now I'se gonna read that book. I've been itchin' to read it for several years now."

36

Wednesday, Thursday, Friday brought new subscriptions and for the office a growing sense of excitement. The very character of Willie Ferguson, gossip writer and columnist of the *Daily Shield and Banner*, began to change, and with the change and the stream of subscriptions, Myrtle Ferguson in her freshly painted cage belowstairs began also to alter. She grew softer, less forbidding; the high old-fashioned starched collar itself disappeared altogether to be replaced by feminine open collars, crocheted at home in the evenings. In the composing room old Zimmerman changed his shirt in the middle of the week, an event unknown before in the history of the paper. On the second Monday he wore a collar and necktie the entire day, and Willie hurt his feelings by asking him if he was all dressed up to go to something special.

Mr. Richardson went right ahead rising early, working all day at the office, circulating in the town during the evening and returning late to McLeod's Folly to sit up till the early morning writing in J. E.'s library at his book. But in spite of all this activity it was evident that he was becoming slowly aware of Jane. Seated at the same desk, they went over the paper together each night as the first copy rolled from the old-fashioned press, criticizing, looking for ideas and improvements. At first he sat at one side of the table, but after three days, he looked at her suddenly and said in his stiff odd way, "May I come and sit beside you? I think we could work more easily that way."

And Jane, with a rush of pleasure, moved her chair a little further to one side and said, "Of course. Please do."

Sometimes they went together to the library to seek information, and sat in the reading room going over magazines which had to do with architecture, gardening and city planning. And there were more cocoa parties in the kitchen late at night when he seemed for a time to relax and grow almost human and intimate.

But his behavior and his very personality continued to puzzle her. She had never before met a young man who seemed so completely indifferent to her charms. He had a way, despite all her efforts to the contrary, of keeping everything between them on a perfectly professional level, and this attitude only made her the more interested. She didn't hate him any more, perhaps because he no longer treated her as if she were a provincial half-wit, but took her into his confidence and asked her advice; or it may have been simply that she was growing used to him. And slowly she began to discover that he was not dull-looking at all but handsome. There were things about his appearance to which she became definitely attached—things like the angle of his jaw, and the back of his neck and the little ghost of humor that came and went in the gray-blue eyes behind the steel-rimmed glasses, and of course the big shoulders under the worn tweed. One morning she even wakened thinking, "Maybe after all, I was just a fool about Jimmy Dougherty. Maybe it didn't mean anything at all." But all the same the minute she thought of Jimmy his presence returned, and suddenly she couldn't any longer see the square jaw, and the humorous gray eyes and the big shoulders, but only Jimmy's carefree grin and dark head. And she felt suddenly hungry for his warmth and the way he had of reaching over and touching her hand or arm when he felt a sudden wave of affection.

For ten days she did not know what had become of him. When she passed the Dougherty Block by accident now, since the paper and Mr. Richardson absorbed her interest, and never driven as she had been before, there was no sign either of Jimmy or the olive-green car. It was Willie Ferguson's gossip column which enlightened her. On the second Monday she read it: "Jimmy

Dougherty, we have just learned, caught a record barracuda last Tuesday at Galveston where he is spending a couple of weeks on vacation. Two days earlier he landed one of the biggest sailfish ever caught in the gulf. He expects to return on Monday next."

The information gave her a sudden shock. She thought, "So that's where he's been . . . off enjoying himself, going away without saying a word to me." She knew now. She was sure that he never wanted any more from her than he could get from a girl like Fern Hedges. And she blushed at the memory of that evening on the little lake at Millersville when she had been foolish enough to imagine that he meant to propose and he had only asked her if she wanted a job on the *News*.

So, quite firmly, she resolved to put him out of her mind, and concentrate on Mr. Richardson—not that she meant to capture the newcomer or to marry him, but only because if she concentrated on him she would forget Jimmy more quickly.

The annual barbecue of the Democratic party was still weeks away, and long ago Jimmy had asked her to go to it with him; but that, of course, had been before the quarrel at Millersville and she supposed that the invitation no longer held good. But she couldn't help wondering, at moments when her mind was not under control, whether, when he returned, he might not use it as an excuse to patch up the quarrel. And she knew in her heart that if he asked her she would go.

Then suddenly one evening Mr. Richardson said to her, "I think we've all been working pretty hard. What about coming out to dinner and going to the movies with me? Everything is going fine on the paper. A little relaxation would do us good."

They dined at the Beauregard Hotel and had cocktails, and Mr. Richardson relaxed more than she had ever seen him do before. The dinner was excellent—thick Texas steak and French fried potatoes and fresh little green peas. They began talking about the paper, and suddenly Jane said, "I thought we were going to relax and not talk shop?"

He laughed and said, "You're right. I forgot. The trouble is, I can't think of anything else. I've never enjoyed myself so much before."

What she wanted, what she hoped for, was that he would break down and talk about himself, about his book, about the letters always in the same handwriting with a Boston postmark, which were waiting for him every evening on the table in the vast hall of McLeod's Folly. In spite of his efficiency, in spite of the fact that he was twenty-nine and she was only twenty-three, she sometimes felt the older of the two. She experienced a growing desire to help him to enjoy himself, to give him some of that reckless animal abandon which Jimmy had in too generous a quantity. She wanted, in fact, to loosen him up and at the same time she wanted, as a woman, to satisfy her curiosity.

"Have you always worked on newspapers?" she began awkwardly.

"Ever since I was a kid, except when I went to college."

"Oh, I see. A self-made man."

At that he laughed. "Yes, I suppose so."

"Well, I must say, you don't show any signs of it."

"What do you mean by that?"

"Well, your clothes for instance."

"Yes, what about them?"

She leaned over boldly and felt the tweed of his sleeve. "Well, don't forget I've been in the East too. I know what clothes cost, and I've seen how self-made men dress—I mean that boys who work their way through college don't wear that kind of tweed."

He laughed, "You should have been a detective instead of a newspaperwoman." Then after a drink of wine, he said, "Well, I'll tell you. There's nothing mysterious about me. I'm a professional newspaperman and, if I do say it myself, a good one. And some day I'm going to have a lot of newspapers of my own. I'm a radical in politics. I believe in change. I believe it so much that I had a row with my father before I came here. And when I told your aunt I wanted to stay in jail, I meant it. Nothing could have got me out except your aunt and her proposition. The times are changing. Something died about 1920 and it's only beginning to admit it and lie down. The future is going to belong to the fellows who understand what's happened and are ready for it." He laughed again, "And maybe some day if I have some time off I might run for President of the United States. For the present that's all I'm going to tell you."

"Which isn't any more than I knew before," said Jane, "except maybe the running for President."

He had made her feel young again and that made her angry. And she didn't like the way he came right out and hit the nail on the head.

"By the way," he said, "I've got to go up to the capital for a few days next week and I want to leave you in charge."

"Why?"

"Because you've got the best brains and the clearest head in the office."

"Aunt Vinnie's been running the paper for thirty years. I guess a couple of days won't upset her."

"It's not the same thing."

"Why?"

"Well, because she's tired and you're up-and-coming and have the makings of a first-class newspaperwoman. When I have to leave for good you'll have to carry on."

"Maybe I won't want to stay on forever working on a newspaper."

He grinned and said, "Well, I don't say that it isn't pretty certain that you'll get married. Even so you could carry on. Married women nowadays have jobs—lots of them."

"Thanks. I've got other plans."

He didn't say anything to that but asked for the check.

During the silence while he paid, she watched him narrowly, a little surprised that she felt about him the same way she had felt about Jimmy in the very beginning. It was an emotion oddly compounded of admiration, liking, resentment and fascination. In the beginning she had resented Jimmy's attitude about women; he treated them as pretty, silly creatures whom he adored and who were made for his delight and entertainment. Now in Mr. Richardson she felt something of the same attitude, only with him it was more mental, perhaps, she thought, because he was a radical and an intellectual. There were times when they both treated her as if she were a joke, a very pretty and charming joke, but a joke all the same. "That," she thought angrily, "is because of the way I look. If I wore flat heels and horn-rimmed spectacles and didn't use any make-up, they might respect me as a person." But in the same moment, she knew that she couldn't do without their admiration. It was to win their admiration that she dressed as prettily as her slender income allowed; it was for that she looked at herself twenty times a day in the mirror. "Why," she thought, "couldn't Mr. Richardson leave sex out of it?" But at the same moment she knew that without the titillations produced by sex, their relationship would be excessively dull. Why, only a week or so ago she had been furious because he paid her so little notice. "I'm a fool," she thought, "just a plain muddled fool. I've got to get things straight, if I'm going to get anywhere."

He had lighted a cigarette while the waiter poured more coffee and said, "I've been reading your aunt's book. The first chapter is typed out. It's pretty good and just what we're looking for."

"What do you mean by pretty good?"

"I mean, it's original stuff, and the first chapter is swell. If she keeps it up all the way through there's money in it for her."

"I hope so. She deserves it."

"I wouldn't have believed it. I mean I didn't think she had that much sense of organization in her."

"Maybe it wasn't organization. Maybe it was something else. That old life she loved better than anything in the world."

"Yes, that's true."

He finished his coffee and waited for her to finish hers. Then he said, "Shall we go?"

But she didn't answer him. She didn't even hear the question. She was looking over his shoulder at the doorway. Instinctively, he turned to look.

In the doorway was standing Jimmy Dougherty. He looked thin and hard and sunburned. He glanced round the room and then saw them. For a second he simply stared; then he bowed and turned and went out.

Mr. Richardson said, "Who's that? I've seen him some place."

"It's a man called Jimmy Dougherty." Her voice sounded weak and far away.

"Oh, yes, now I remember. I was at the El Dorado when he got thrown out."

"Thrown out?"

"Yes, he and some platinum blonde. He sent you his love. I guess he must know you pretty well. Didn't your aunt give you the message?"

She stood up suddenly and, turning away from him, said in an odd, quiet voice, "If we're going to the movies, we'd better be on our way."

The film wasn't very good but it was heavily sentimental, and halfway through the picture Mr. Richardson leaned over in the darkness and took her hand. "Do you mind?" he asked. "It really doesn't mean anything."

Quickly she withdrew her hand and said, "I do mind. If it's just a question of holding something I can get you a department store dummy." And suddenly she was aware that the tears were running down her face and that she dared not let him see she was crying, because he might think it was the idiotic film or even himself who had caused the tears. The funny thing was that she'd been hoping all along that Mr. Richardson would take her out and even hold her hand, and that Jimmy would see them together. She had meant to show him that he didn't mean everything to her, and that there were other men who thought her attractive. But now she hadn't any sense of triumph at all. It wasn't at all the way she had expected it to be. She only felt sick inside and desperate.

37

Mr. Richardson's visit to the capital was made to call up the State Democratic leader, Bill Swain. Only Mrs. McLeod, Gashouse Mary and himself knew this and none of them betrayed the secret, for as each week passed they became more and more secretive. It was, of course, simple enough for Mr. Richardson, whose very nature was tight and secretive, and with Gashouse Mary she had learned long ago out of experience with tough politics in river towns to keep her own counsel. With Mrs. McLeod, it wasn't so easy. She went about the office and the town looking like the cat that had just swallowed the canary, wanting to cry out to everyone, "If you knew what I know. If you knew the tornado that is going to break over Plattesville on the third of next month!" There were moments when she had to bite her tongue to keep silent, moments especially after she had paid a visit to Gashouse Mary and Jim Newman's undertaking establishment and heard how the organizing was going along the river front and in the county. There were moments when, in her excitement, she felt she must jump up and down and shout in order to contain herself any longer. For the first time in her life she began to have an exciting feeling of importance, and she made fresh efforts to smarten up her clothes and keep her hair neat, although the efforts came to no more than they had ever done.

There wasn't only the excitement of the coming campaign against Old Dougherty; there was also The Book. Day by day, a wretched stenographer, called Miss Willet, seated beside her inside the cubbyhole, struggled to decipher the secrets of the mysterious scratchy handwriting, interrupting Mrs. McLeod a hundred times a day when she found herself absolutely stumped by a word or a phrase. To Mrs. McLeod the emergence of The Book into the realm of human communication was a breathless experience. Each night as fresh pages emerged clear and neat from the typewriter of the stenographer, she read them, fingering each page lovingly. The emergence was to her a kind of miracle, as if a new book had been born with which she herself had had nothing to do. The feeling helped to stifle her morbid modesty and self-consciousness, and she found herself thinking, "But it's really pretty good. I can't have written it. I must have been possessed." And she began to ponder about spirit writing, and whether she was a medium and The Book had been dictated by some spirit—perhaps the spirit of J. E. himself while she sat there locked in his sacred "den" working. And shyly she watched Mr. Richardson and his reaction to each new dozen pages.

All he ever said to her was, "It's good. It's just what we need. We'll begin using it the day we start the campaign." And he said it casually, with indifference, leaving her disappointed. What she wanted was someone to tell her that it was marvelous, that it was the greatest book ever written. There were times when she wished that Mr. Richardson would be enthusiastic just once, about something, anything at all. She told herself that he behaved thus because he was a Yankee; that fact, to her as to Willie Ferguson, always explained anything queer about Mr. Richardson.

On the other hand, his cold-bloodedness was, she found, a great asset to the *Daily Shield and Banner*; there was never any danger of Mr. Richardson going off half-cocked, or undertaking anything which had not been carefully prepared in advance. Look what he had accomplished already, all those new features, and twelve hundred and seventy-nine new subscriptions!

So when he went to the capital to see Bill Swain, her heart sank and she asked herself what she would do while he was away. It didn't seem possible to her that she could run the paper even for two days without him. But she felt better when he came in just before leaving for the train and said, "I've left all instructions with Miss Baldwin. I didn't want to burden you with a lot of details. You're busy enough as it is—what with The Book and everything."

She wished him good luck, and after he had gone, as she watched from the window his square shoulders moving across the Square, she knew that she needn't worry. He would probably get what he wanted. He had a letter in his pocket to Bill Swain from Gashouse Mary, introducing him and explaining that he had come to seek support of the Boss against Old Dougherty. Bill Swain and Gashouse Mary were old friends, and it wouldn't be the first time they had found themselves fighting shoulder to shoulder. Usually the battle had been against reformers, but this time they were themselves the reformers, which struck Mrs. McLeod, as indeed it struck Mary herself, as being pretty funny.

But when the shoulders had disappeared in the direction of the railway station she felt depressed again, because she knew that Mr. Richardson had left the office in charge of Jane instead of herself, not for the reasons he gave but because she was nothing but an old flibberty-gibbet whom he couldn't trust. But she was glad for Jane's sake. It would give her a feeling of superiority and make her get on better with Mr. Richardson. "If only," she thought, "Jane would fall in love with Mr. Richardson and marry him instead of crying over an attractive scamp like Jimmy Dougherty." Then maybe Mr. Richardson would stay on forever and the *Daily Shield and Banner* would be safe and secure and prosperous until she herself died, and even long afterward.

38

In his office in the Dougherty Block the wily old spider knew that Mr. Richardson had gone to the capital, and he knew exactly why he had gone and even the day and the hour when he had a conference with Bill Swain.

The feud between Old Dougherty and the State leader was not a new one. It had been going for twenty years, since the moment the two men met for the first time at the State Democratic Convention. At that time both men were bursting with ambition, and the goal of their ambition was the same—to become State boss, and after that an influence in national politics and finally a senatorship in Washington. At that time Bill Swain had a great advantage over Old Dougherty: Bill belonged to the county. He stood six feet two in his stockinged feet and was thin as a rail and had a long narrow leathery face. And he was still near enough to the land rush days to go shamelessly collarless in hot weather, wear a ten-gallon hat, and be able to hit a spittoon at twenty feet. Old Dougherty, who had not yet become "Old" Dougherty, was squat and powerful with the bullneck of a wrestler, and he spoke not with the broad drawl of the Southwest but with the echo of a Galway brogue. Bill's methods in politics were those of the frontier barroom and dance hall; Dougherty's were those of a Boston ward heeler. But what Dougherty lacked in background he made up in evilness. At double-crossing he far outdid Bill Swain.

At the very moment they met for the first time they bristled with mutual dislike like a pair of strange fox terriers circling about each other with every hair standing upright. Bill Swain regarded Dougherty as an intruder, a "furriner," an immigrant invading territory to which he had no right, and he let Dougherty know it. And because Dougherty had a feeling of inferiority upon the subject of being a newcomer and an outsider, the knowledge did nothing toward making him love Bill Swain the more.

So for twenty years, in the politics of the Southwest, they had battled or bargained with each other, moved by hatred and ambition; and at the end of twenty years Bill Swain had the advantage. He ruled the party in the State and had an influence all through the Southwest. But Old Dougherty was strong; he had Plattesville in the palm of his hand and all one corner of the State under his thumb, and he had built up an organization on the model of Irish politics in Boston and New York, a far more solid and efficient and menacing model than the loose-built machine of Bill Swain.

And Bill, sitting in his hot office in the State capital, knew that in the whole of the region he controlled, there existed only one menace to his power and authority and that was Old Dougherty. He would have liked to have crushed him, the way one steps on an insect and crushes it, but he was a little afraid that Old Dougherty might turn out to be a scorpion rather than a mosquito, and as yet he could not quite do without him.

So when Mr. Richardson arrived in town with a note from Gashouse Mary broadly hinting at what was up, Bill Swain took his long legs off his desk, spat ten feet, hitting the spittoon accurately, and said to his secretary, "Telephone the hotel and tell Mr. Richardson to come right over heah."

They liked each other on sight. Bill Swain said, "Take a seat and tell me, how is Gashouse Mary? She's been a friend of mine for mighty near forty-five years." He grinned and spat and said, "Matter of fact, it was Gashouse Mary who taught me about life. I was just a kid about eighteen, ridin' the range and knowin' more about horses and steers than wimmin. She was a pretty good teacher too—better'n any I've found since."

At this intimate revelation of Bill Swain's past, Mr. Richardson grinned too, and said, "She's all right. Seems to be doing pretty well except that she doesn't get on very well with Old Dougherty."

"No, I guess she wouldn't get on with that maverick. He never did understand people like me and Gashouse Mary." Slowly, like the opening of a carpenter's rule, the long legs unbent, straightened, and found a resting place on the desk. He picked up Mary's letter written on mauve paper with gold initials and said, "She writes me that you all are renovatin' the *Daily Shield and Banner*."

"Well," said Mr. Richardson, "that's what we're hoping to do. It's succeeding very well up to date."

Bill Swain put down the letter and turned his tiny shrewd gray eyes on Mr. Richardson. "You all had much experience with politics?"

"A tolerable amount."

"Where?"

"In the East mostly. In Illinois too."

"Gashouse Mary tell you anything about the sitchasin' here?"

"Yes. Gashouse Mary and Mrs. McLeod and I've picked up a good deal on the side."

"Vinnie's a mighty fine woman, but she ain't got much sense."

"No," admitted Mr. Richardson, "I guess she hasn't."

"It's a long time between drinks, as the governor said," remembered Bill Swain, pounding on the table with his iron fist.

The door opened and a pretty young woman came in. "Miss Bradford," he said, "tell that black Ananias to bring in the Bourbon."

The young lady vanished and in a moment an elderly negro came in bearing bottles and glasses. Bill Swain poured two stiff drinks and said, "Here's to crime," and emptying the glass, said to the servant, "Leave the bottles here and skedaddle." Then addressing Mr. Richardson he said, "And now we'll get down to instances."

For two hours they talked and on the next day Mr. Richardson came back again and they drank more Bourbon and talked some more, and on the third day when he came back to bid Bill Swain good-by, Bill slapped him on the back and said, "Good luck to you, son. I'm for you. Let me know how things are gettin' on. Only remember one thing, Bill Swain's never gone off half-cocked yet. You gotta show me a good clean bill of sale. If I believe in it, I'll come in with all four feet." He spat and then said, "And give my love to Mary and tell her I never forgot what she done for me when I was young and in need of instruction."

On the third day Mr. Richardson returned to Plattesville and came directly to the cubbyhole. When he had asked the stenographer to go out and get some air in the Square, he took off his coat, sat down with deliberation, put on the steel-rimmed spectacles and took a sheaf of papers from his pocket. While she waited, Mrs. McLeod thought she would burst with anxiety. At last, when he was settled, he said quite calmly, "Well, it's all right. He'll back us up to the very end. He's wise to the fact that Old Dougherty is double-crossing him and trying to take over his job. He'll be ready with the works when we open the campaign, only it's got to be a good campaign."

He showed no enthusiasm. The only sign he gave of an inward excitement was that he used slang words.

39

From the moment of his return, one thing after another happened in quick succession. On the following morning there was a telephone call for Mr. Richardson, and when he answered a gruff voice said, "This is Mr. W. M. Dougherty speaking."

"Good morning," said Mr. Richardson.

"I guess you know who I am."

"Yes," said Mr. Richardson.

"I'd like to have a talk with you."

"Yes."

"Could you come into my office this morning about eleven-thirty?"

"I'm very busy about that time. Could you make it the office of the *Daily Shield and Banner*?"

There was a little silence and a cough and then the gruff voice said, "It's a private matter I wanted to discuss. I think we'd better discuss it in my office."

For a second, Mr. Richardson in his turn was silent. Then he said, "All right. I'll arrange it . . . at eleven-thirty."

When he had hung up the receiver he went into the cubbyhole and again sent the stenographer out for air. When she had gone, he said to Mrs. McLeod, "They've found out."

"Who?"

"Dougherty and his mob. He just telephoned asking me to come over and see him."

"Are you going?"

"Yes."

"He'll try to bully you."

"Yes, I know that. But I might get some information we could use."

Then Mrs. McLeod looked at him anxiously. "They may try to beat you up."

He laughed, and there was a hint of actual excitement in his voice. "Don't worry about that. If they try anything I'll run like hell."

She looked disappointed, and he said with a grin, "My parole isn't up for ten days yet. I'm not going to give them any excuse to clap me back in jail on some trumped-up charge of assault."

"I see. I guess you're right. You seem to know a lot about those things."

"I do," said Mr. Richardson.

And then Mrs. McLeod noticed an odd thing—that the veins in Mr.

[112]

Richardson's temples and in his throat were swollen and throbbing. She noticed too that while he was talking with her he had broken a heavy copy pencil clearly in two with one muscular hand. It surprised her. She hadn't thought of him as a passionate man.

40

They hadn't, it seemed, meant to bully him. When he arrived at the office of W. M. Dougherty and Son, Contractors, a secretary took him straight into Old Dougherty's office. There were three men there—a short, fat, smooth little man with pink cheeks and shiny eyeglasses, a lean, hollow-cheeked, rather gray man with a stoop, and a heavy, partly bald man with the look of a retired all-in wrestler. The last, Mr. Richardson divined at once, was Old Dougherty. The second was the editor of the *News* whom he already knew by sight, and the first, Old Dougherty said, after he had introduced himself and the lean, gray man, was Mr. Hirsh, the business manager of the *Daily News*.

Mr. Richardson bowed and then a door opened and Jimmy Dougherty came in. The old man introduced his son and Jimmy and Mr. Richardson shook hands. In the gesture there was something of hostility, something of suspicion and something of wariness.

They all sat down and Old Dougherty said, "Have a cigar?"

"Thanks," said Mr. Richardson. He took the cigar and lighted it, and while he was thus engaged, nobody spoke at all. They simply sat watching him as if the mere lighting of a cigar were some fascinating trick of sleight of hand. Mr. Richardson seemed completely unmoved by the scrutiny.

At last Old Dougherty himself broke the silence. He said, "We've been talking about the job you've been doing with the poor old *Daily Shield and Banner*. You've done wonders with the old rag."

"Thank you," said Mr. Richardson.

"Yes, a mighty fine job," said the tall lean man. He spoke nervously as if he wanted to jump off the edge of the chair.

"There's some good new features in it," said the business manager. "I suppose you've had a reaction in the subscriptions?"

"Yes," said Mr. Richardson.

"I should think a pretty big reaction," said the editor.

"Yes," said Mr. Richardson. "Plenty."

There was a moment's awkward silence and then Old Dougherty said, "Well, it's fine to see a grand old paper like the *Daily Shield and Banner* have a come-back."

"That is—if it lasts," said the pink-cheeked Mr. Hirsh. "I always say, it's easy enough to get new circulation. The hard thing is to keep it."

[113]

"Yes," said Mr. Richardson.

Jimmy Dougherty didn't say anything. He simply sat on the opposite side of the mahogany table and stared at Mr. Richardson. There was nothing smooth and friendly in his manner, as there was in the manner of the older men. Now there was just plain hostility and contempt in the blue-eyed stare. He sat on the very edge of the chair as if at any moment he were ready to spring off it and sock Mr. Richardson on the jaw.

Another silence intervened. Each silence became more awkward than the one before. Each silence became a little more demanding. Each silence placed more and more responsibility upon the broad shoulders of Mr. Richardson. The shoulders, however, appeared strong enough to bear the burden. All they could get out of him was a quiet "Yes." He went on, unperturbed, smoking Old Dougherty's expensive cigar.

It was the *Daily News* man, the editor, who broke down first.

He said, "We're always interested in promising young men. We've been watching your work and think you have a lot of talent."

"Thank you," said Mr. Richardson, with a shade of irony in his voice.

Then the business manager spoke up, "We're always on the lookout for new talent." He took off the shiny pince-nez and began polishing them. "It occurred to us, Mr. Richardson, that you might want a new job. . . . I mean a good, well-paid job."

"What sort of job?"

This time Old Dougherty spoke up, "Well, I think we might as well be frank with you, young fellow. Mr. Winterbottom, here, the editor, would like to retire year after next. We've been thinking that we might take you on the *News* as associate editor and then, by the time Mr. Winterbottom retired, you'd be broken in and could take his place." He looked expectantly at Mr. Richardson, as if he had counted upon his accepting an offer so magnificent with enthusiasm, but the face of the visitor was quite blank of all expression. Apparently he was thinking.

"It's a very fine opportunity," said the business manager, "especially for a young fellow who's unknown—who's just out . . ." Then he halted, awkwardly, and Mr. Richardson finished for him.

"Just out of jail," he said.

"Well, I hadn't meant to say exactly that."

"You might add that I was thrown into jail simply because I arrived in Plattesville without a job." It was the first time any emotion of any kind had entered Mr. Richardson's voice, and now it was not a friendly, pleasant emotion, but rather upsetting. The voice was hard as flint and cold as ice. Jimmy Dougherty still stared at him in silent hostility.

"What is your reaction?" asked the *News* man.

"No," said Mr. Richardson.

"I don't think you should be hasty in your judgment. It's a fine opportunity and excellent pay. I may say a good deal more than most men earn for such a job. You see, the *News* is the top paper in this part of the State and we want to keep it so. You'd better think it over. We don't demand an answer right now. You could think it over and let us know."

"It wouldn't be necessary," said Mr. Richardson, "the answer would still be 'No.'"

Old Dougherty answered him, "I suppose you realize," he said, "that the *Daily Shield and Banner* is actually bankrupt—if the creditors saw fit they could throw Mrs. McLeod into the bankruptcy court tomorrow."

"Yes, I understand the financial situation. I've gone into it thoroughly. I think if we keep on as we're going we may pull out of it all right."

"And you still want to stay with the *Daily Shield and Banner*?"

"Yes."

"May we ask why?" asked Mr. Hirsh.

"Because I like my job."

"I suppose money doesn't mean anything."

"Sure, it means something . . . only I'm not worried about that."

Then suddenly Jimmy Dougherty stopped staring and spoke up. There was rage in his voice, "Who in hell are you, anyway? And what are you doing here? Who sent you?"

Mr. Richardson grinned, "I'm a newspaperman. I'm trying to put the *Daily Shield and Banner* on its feet. And nobody sent me. I just came."

Then Old Dougherty, afraid that Jimmy in his anger might give the show away, said in a smooth voice, "You'd better think it over, Mr. Richardson. We don't want to hurry you. Think it over, and if you change your mind give us the answer later."

"I can do that right now. The answer is 'No.'"

"You seem very sure about it," said Mr. Hirsh smoothly.

"I am."

A change came into Old Dougherty's manner. The suaveness went out of it, and the timbre took on an edge of hardness. "Then you're going to fight us?" He glared at Mr. Richardson, but Mr. Richardson wasn't to be caught.

He said, "I don't know that I'd call it fighting you. The *Daily Shield and Banner* has to make its way. I don't see that it means a fight. There's room for three papers in this town and the *Chronicle* doesn't really count." He rose and picked up his hat. "There doesn't seem to be anything more to be said. I thank you, gentlemen, for the offer but I'm just not interested."

Mr. Hirsh smiled sardonically behind the shiny glasses, "There's only one more thing to be said. When you're in the gutter again, Mr. Richardson, you'd better not come to the *News* to look for a job."

[115]

"Not a chance," said Mr. Richardson. "Good morning, gentlemen." And without another word he turned and went out.

When he had gone the four men sat for a moment in silence. Then Old Dougherty said, "That's what I call a smooth proposition."

The bald, nervous editor said, "There's certainly something fishy about him."

Old Dougherty put his feet on the floor and swung around in his swivel chair. "Well, boys, I guess there's nothing left to do but clean up the *Daily Shield and Banner*. I hate to throw old Mrs. McLeod into the street but it's the only thing to be done."

"She's asking for it," said Mr. Hirsh from behind his shiny glasses.

Jimmy didn't say anything. He rose, and without a word left the room.

41

Late the same afternoon the typist finished her job on The Book and left the huge heap of typescript in triplicate piled high on Mrs. McLeod's desk. She left a bill too for fifty-six dollars which took the edge off Mrs. McLeod's pleasure at the sight of the job. She didn't know how she was going to pay it, but when Mr. Richardson came in, he took it up and simply said, "I'll see that this goes through. I'll take it up with Myrtle."

"But Myrtle hasn't got any money. We can't use the subscription money for that with all the other things that have to be paid."

"You leave it to me," he said. He had, Mrs. McLeod noticed, been growing more and more masterful of late, and she liked masterful men. She liked men who said, "Leave it to me." For thirty years she had been waiting for someone to say that to her and it had never been said since J. E. died until now.

Then he said, "I'm going to take home a copy to read. I've only read the first two chapters."

"I'm afraid," said Mrs. McLeod, "it's not much good. It's too long and boring."

"We may have to cut it a bit for publication," said Mr. Richardson, "but it's just what we want."

As he was about to leave she said timidly, "I'm scared about Old Dougherty and his gang. They might do anything."

"I'm not afraid of that. I'm lying low until the third."

"And it isn't only that," said Mrs. McLeod. "There's the question of Jane." He looked puzzled, "What question?"

"Jane and Jimmy."

"What does that mean?"

"He was her beau. I guess he still is."

She regarded Mr. Richardson for a moment in silence, as if speculating as to how much she dared tell him. Then she said, "I guess you're really one of us so that I can tell you." She looked shy and then said, "You see, Jane's really in love with him. She tries to pretend even to herself that she isn't, but she is. I know all the signs in a woman. That's one thing that doesn't change with the times." Again she hesitated, and after a second she said timidly, "Sometimes I think I ought to give up the whole idea of the crusade if it means breaking up everything between them. You see, when I first had the idea I didn't realize how serious it was between them." She smiled shyly, "Don't think I'm soft and silly . . . but people being in love always frightens me. There's something wonderful about it . . . and touching."

While she was speaking Mr. Richardson's grave young face grew more and more serious. When she had finished he waited a moment to see whether the halting speech would continue. Then he said, "I understand what you mean, only I'm afraid it can't very well be stopped now . . . all we've done and all the promises we've made . . . not after I've been to see Bill Swain. And besides, the others mean to fight us, anyway. They said as much this morning. They made all sorts of threats."

"What kind of threats?"

"About putting us into bankruptcy. I don't suppose they'd stop at anything."

"Was Jimmy there?" asked Mrs. McLeod with unexpected shrewdness.

"Yes, he was."

"Did he make threats?"

"No, he didn't. He just glared at me. He acted as if he hated me more than any of the others."

Mrs. McLeod made a clucking sound, "That was on account of Jane."

Mr. Richardson took up his hat. He said, "Well, I must say I wish I'd known all this sooner. I'd have stayed in jail and gone on with my job there."

"You mustn't take it like that." Then after a second or two, she sighed and said, "I guess we'll have to go through with it. I don't know why everything is always so difficult."

"Maybe you'd better put it up to Jane. But I don't see how even that is going to get us anywhere. It's too late now."

"Why don't you speak to her? She's impressed by you."

He laughed. "Not as much as you think, I'm afraid." Then he made a whistling sound with his lips. "My God!" he said, "I've just thought of something."

"What?"

"I told her about him being thrown out of the El Dorado. I told her

[117]

everything—about his being drunk and out with that tart—everything—about his sending his love. I thought she'd think it was a good joke. I hadn't any idea. Now I see why she acted like that at the movies."

So he had done it for her. He told her everything. "Maybe," said Mrs. McLeod, "that'll fix it. Maybe that'll be enough to do the trick."

"I doubt it," said Mr. Richardson.

42

It hadn't fixed it. The information had only made Jane miserable and filled her with doubts . . . doubt upon doubt about everything. If Jimmy behaved like that it was better, she told herself, to know it now before it was too late. If that was the kind of man he was, he'd only make her miserable as a husband. She no longer pretended now, she knew that she loved him enough to want to marry him in spite of everything. But what if he had drunk too much and gone out with Fern to the El Dorado because he was miserable and unhappy over their quarrel? What if he felt things as deeply as that? Then she would have lost everything by chucking him. But how, she asked herself, was she to know? And Mr. Richardson? Why had he told her? Was it because he guessed how she felt about Jimmy and told her on purpose to kill her feeling? Was he as bad as that? Was that why he had tried to hold her hand afterward in the darkness of the Palace Theatre? Was he falling in love with her or just trying to make her? But in spite of her wanting to believe that was the reason, she couldn't really believe it. In spite of his puzzling detachment and his persistent blindness to her charms, in spite even of her vacillating dislike for him, she knew he wasn't like that. He might be a Yankee and cold-blooded but there wasn't a hint of anything mean in him.

So she was thoroughly miserable, so miserable that even the excitement of new work made it all no better. She could have solved everything by going to Jimmy and having a talk with him, but that was no more in her nature than it was in Jimmy's. It was pride that kept them both mute, the harsh, bitter, foolish, defeating pride of youth, which with years and experience softens and melts and fades away. How could she, a McLeod, risk humiliation at the hands of a Dougherty? What if, when she went to him, he said he had gotten drunk and gone out with Fern because he wanted to, because he was fed up with her and her kind of respectable girl? What if he said he never wanted to see her again? No, such things were not to be risked, even if for the rest of her life she ate her heart out for him.

So she went on tormenting herself with miserable doubts. She made decisions and immediately unmade them. And at last, because she could find no other way to at least the shadow of peace, she told herself that she would let the annual barbecue and home-coming decide it. If he sent word that he wanted her to go with him, if he was fine enough to overlook her meanness, she would humble her pride and pretend that there had never been any quarrel. There were moments when she felt willing even to desert Aunt Vinnie and abandon the crusade. If he did not ask her again, then she was finished with him.

That night when she returned to McLeod's Folly she had a glass of milk and a piece of Aida's coconut cake in the kitchen and went to bed early so that she would not have to see either Aunt Vinnie or Mr. Richardson. On the hall table there was as usual the letter with the Boston postmark. She took it up and examined it curiously. Mr. Richardson, it seemed, received letters from only one person in all the world. Try as she would she couldn't make out for certain whether the handwriting was that of a man or a woman. The writing paper was thinnish and looked expensive. As she held it under the light she discovered that the inner lining of the envelope had been by some chance folded back so that you were able with some effort to read a few words through the thin paper. For a second she listened to make certain there was no one near her in the big house. Then cautiously she held it just beneath the light and was able to make out four or five words. "Dear Jack, I haven't heard . . ." and the rest was covered by the opaque lining paper.

For a moment she had wild ideas of steaming open the letter and reading it. For a moment she even thought, "If he's deceiving us, I've a right to know the truth."

Dear Jack . . . and he said his name was Thomas.

Then quickly, as if the letter burned her fingers, she threw it on the hall table and ran up the stairs. A McLeod, even at a pinch, couldn't do things like that.

But it made Mr. Richardson seem more mysterious and interesting than ever.

Mrs. McLeod and Mr. Richardson had supper together, and afterward Mrs. McLeod went off to have a conference with Gashouse Mary, leaving him to spend the evening in the library working at his book on labor conditions.

Left alone, he had intended to read two or three chapters of The Book and then go to work, but the evening did not work out in this fashion. In one of J. E.'s huge, worn leather chairs he seated himself with the typescript, a pipe and a whisky and soda. When he had finished two chapters his hands, despite his will, took a third chapter off the table beside him, and when that was finished a fourth and then a fifth and then another. After a long time, when at last he glanced at his watch, it was already a quarter past eleven. For a moment he sat still and thoughtful, and then, abandoning his work altogether for the evening, he went on reading.

At a little before midnight the house door opened and after a moment there was the sound of Mrs. McLeod's footsteps as she climbed the huge stairway. Then there was only silence in the big house, and Mr. Richardson took up the typescript again. He read and read, chapter after chapter, until, feeling stiff and a little chilled, he rose and stretched himself and looked at his watch. It was half-past two and there were still four more chapters to be read.

After pouring another drink, he seated himself again and went on reading. It was a quarter past four in the morning when he finished at last the huge pile of typescript. With a feeling of awe he put down the last page, turned out the light and went to bed.

43

He did not appear at breakfast the next morning, not this time because he had already eaten and gone to the office, but because he had been guilty of Jane's lazy trick. Wakened at seven-thirty by the alarm clock, he had turned it off, rolled over and gone back to sleep. And Aida did not waken him because she thought he worked very hard and should be given a chance to lie in bed late now and then. It was ten o'clock when she climbed the stairs with a tray of hot waffles and coffee and bacon and eggs. It was the first time since J. E. McLeod died that anyone in McLeod's Folly had had breakfast in bed, but Aida was fond of Mr. Richardson. He had become her pet.

Meanwhile, as Mrs. McLeod and Jane walked to the office, Mrs. McLeod screwed up her courage and presently, at the very last moment when they were actually crossing the Square, she managed to say, "Dear, there's something I've got to ask you."

Jane looked suspicious and even hostile. "What?" she asked abruptly.

"It's about Jimmy Dougherty. Will the crusade mean anything to your affairs?" She couldn't think how to put the question discreetly, and now she knew she had bungled it.

Craftily Jane asked, "I don't know what you mean."

"I mean if you don't want to have a campaign in the paper against his father . . . we might still be able to call it off."

"I don't see why it should make any difference to me."

"I thought you were fond of him . . . that's all."

"I haven't spoken to him for weeks."

They were crossing the street now, almost at the door of the *Daily Shield and Banner*. Jane said suddenly, "And I wish you wouldn't mention him to me again. I'm sick of it . . . everybody throwing him up to me—you and Willie and Aida and even Mr. Richardson."

"I never mentioned his name before," said Mrs. McLeod.

"Well, you might just as well. You're always thinking about him and me. And I don't give a damn what happens to him."

Then it was all right. Jane said she didn't care, but she wished that Jane hadn't been so violent about not caring.

44

It was nearly eleven o'clock when Mr. Richardson appeared in the office and it was Willie, refreshed from the Bourbon bottle, who greeted him. There was a ring of satisfaction in his voice at having found a sinner like himself in the great and perfect, the punctual and efficient Mr. Richardson.

"Well," he said. "Had a late night, last night?"

"Yes," said Mr. Richardson, "I overslept."

Mr. Richardson went straight to the cubbyhole and faced Mrs. McLeod as ashamed as any schoolboy. "I don't know what happened to me except I stayed up late reading your book."

"You deserve a good sleep now and then."

Instead of going away at once he sat down. His face became very serious and he said, "Mrs. McLeod, I must talk to you about that book."

For a moment she thought he meant to scold her and timidly she said, "I hope it's all right."

"It's all right, Mrs. McLeod. It's swell. It's just what we want for the paper. It'll bring in a lot of new subscriptions." He took off his glasses, always a sign of great seriousness, and continued, "But it isn't that. Something ought to be done about that book. Books like that aren't lying around waiting to be picked up."

"What do you mean?"

"I mean you ought to find a publisher for it. I mean that it's no ordinary book. It's a great book. It's the kind of book all America is waiting for."

"I never thought of finding a publisher. I wouldn't know how to go about it."

He said, "Will you leave that to me?"

"You've got so much to do already."

"I've got a friend in New York who's an agent. I'll send it to him and he can take care of the whole thing."

Suddenly she began to cry. The tears came in spite of anything she could do to stop them, rolling idiotically down her worn, wrinkled face. They were tears of relief and delight, of weariness and relaxation. She was a woman who was meant by God to be cherished and protected and looked after, and since the death of J. E. nobody had ever cherished her or taken the least trouble; instead they had come to her with all their troubles.

In a shamed and choking voice she said, "I don't know why you take so much trouble about me."

The tears made Mr. Richardson uncomfortable. He was stirring in his chair as if he had what Aida called "a misery."

"You've been pretty good to me, too," he said. Then, rising, he put one hand on her thin shoulder and said, "You leave it to me. I'll send it off today," and left her alone to have a good cry.

45

All that week and next, new subscribers added their names to the swelling list, and belowstairs Myrtle Ferguson, in her cage, recorded them, cashed the checks and put the cash into the old-fashioned till. With each new sub- scription a little more of the defeated sourness seemed to drain away from Myrtle. To Mrs. McLeod the change seemed nothing short of miraculous. The very lines, worn into Myrtle's face by years of disappointment, boredom and defeat, seemed to soften and melt away. The old high collars and jabots disappeared completely and she took to wearing turquoise earrings, and then one morning Myrtle appeared, to the astonishment of the whole office, with her hair cut short and a permanent wave which was still in the first stage and made her look more like a Zulu queen than the cashier of the sober *Daily Shield and Banner*.

Part of the reason for the change in Myrtle came from the transformation in Willie's character. He no longer got thoroughly drunk over the week end, and his Saturday nights he no longer spent at the El Dorado and in Franklin Street pouring his quarters into Bourbon and his nickels into the slots of Mamie Furnoy's and Estelle Laverne's mechanical pianos. He even trimmed his drooping, tobacco-stained mustache and bought a new suit at "Every Day a Bargain" Frendlich's. As to cut there was not much change over his old sagging costumes, but the material was a noisy-checked stuff, to which he added one morning, with a certain self-conscious embarrass- ment, a red bow tie. To crown all he bought himself a brown derby hat, and after that the rejuvenation was complete, and he felt himself once more the lady-killing Southern gentleman he had been in his youth. On the Saturday night before the crusade began, he took Myrtle to dinner at the Beauregard Hotel and afterward to see *Romeo and Juliet* at the Palace.

It was the gossip column which had turned the trick. It was good and its success was recognized at once in Plattesville. It made him a personage. No longer was he a dreary old man who had to cadge for news; people who liked to see their names in print looked him up and telephoned him to give him items of personal interest. The column, alone, he knew, was responsible for a good many of the new subscribers. His self-respect was restored and it worked magic on his character. In his new checked suit he now entered saloons and poolrooms with a swagger.

And the son of Aida's cousin Athena brought in once a week a page devoted to the births, deaths, parties, fish fries and revival meetings in Darkietown. He was a shy high-yaller boy who wrote poetry. When he showed one or two verses to Mr. Richardson, the managing editor told him they were good and bought two or three pieces to publish in the *Daily Shield and Banner*, paying Athena's son five dollars apiece for the poems right out of his own pocket. And he told the boy to bring him some more and maybe he, Mr. Richardson, could get them published in magazines in the East.

But perhaps the greatest change in the office was experienced by the telephone. For years it had hardly worked at all, and now it rarely stopped ringing from nine in the morning until six at night. The one old-fashioned instrument on the end of the table which held the files, rang so much that at last an official of the telephone company called on Mrs. McLeod and persuaded her to install not one but two more instruments, one in her cubbyhole and one on Mr. Richardson's desk. He was even willing to give her reduced rates because the installation would save an immense amount of work and confusion at the exchange, which was often forced to make the same call over and over again because the *Daily Shield and Banner* line was always busy.

And then one by one the advertisements began to come in and the revenue to rise and the week before the crusade began, Mrs. McLeod, with the aid of Myrtle and Mr. Richardson, went over the books and found herself solvent for the first time in ten years—not only solvent, but there was money to pay bills and salaries and two dollars and forty-five cents balance on the right side; that is, if one didn't count the thousands of dollars of debts and the mortgages.

There was a good deal of difficulty and arguing on the subject of Mr. Richardson's salary. He insisted that he could only accept thirty dollars a week as an ordinary reporter because she had engaged him as nothing more than that, but she declared in turn that he should be paid twice as much because he was really managing editor and without him the renaissance of the *Daily Shield and Banner* would never have occurred.

He finally said to her, "What kind of a woman are you, anyway? Just as soon as you become solvent you want to throw the paper right back into bankruptcy."

Mrs. McLeod laughed, "And you? First you want to stay in jail and then you don't want to be paid."

In the end he won by saying that when the paper was well on its feet, he would accept what she considered a proper salary. And during the talk both of them pretended that he meant to stay on forever on the *Daily Shield and Banner.*

The conference evidently troubled Mr. Richardson, for late that afternoon he asked Jane to come out with him for a cup of tea at Mrs. Dacey's Old Virginia Tea Shoppe, and there he said to her, "We've got to make plans for when I go away."

Jane, startled, looked at him. "You're not going away now, are you?"

"No, but I'm going away when my job is finished. I've got to go back East one of these days."

She listened to him apathetically as if a part of her mind were elsewhere, so that he had to talk twice as hard as he had meant to in order to put over his points.

Presently he said, "You were enthusiastic in the beginning. What's the matter with you now? What's happened?"

He hoped, perhaps, that she would be frank and tell him about Jimmy Dougherty, but she said nothing about the Doughertys or the crusade. She only said, "There's nothing the matter with me."

He said, "Some day I've got to leave you to carry on. You've got to be managing editor. Maybe, if the paper's doing well and can afford it, I can send you some young fellow with experience from the East. But in the meanwhile I want to teach you everything you ought to know."

She looked at him shrewdly, and then suddenly turned away and said, "I wish you could teach me some common sense."

He laughed. "You seem to have plenty."

"I haven't any at all. If only I had a little that you could spare."

"What do you mean by that?"

"I mean, I wish I could take things as calmly as you do. You never get excited. You never lose your head. You've always got everything under control." Again she looked away from him and then blurted out, "Sometimes I think you must be inhuman."

"Do *you* want to be inhuman?"

"Yes," she said quickly, "it makes life so much easier."

Smiling, he said, "The nicest thing about you is that you're so damned human. You lose your temper one minute and are all smiles the next. One minute you're bored and the next you're enthusiastic, and you're romantic and full of feeling." He lighted a cigarette and then said, "I wish I could be more like that. Having common sense doesn't get you anywhere in the long run. It doesn't get you much fun."

Suddenly it occurred to her that they were having an intimate talk. They were talking about each other, and it was very pleasant, and Mr. Richardson had never seemed so attractive. But she hated being told she was romantic and full of feeling.

In the next moment he killed it all by saying, "I'm no good at soul-searching. I don't know how. I hate talking about myself but I can tell you this—that you can't always tell by the outside what's going on inside."

She wanted to ask him what he meant by that, but she didn't because his mocking remark about "soul-searching" had withered the intimacy at its very source. It made her feel young again and silly. She said, "We'd better go back and take a look at the paper. It must be off the press by now." And rising, she put out her cigarette and started for the door. But she was aware that he had done something to her. She really liked him for the first time. She had a feeling that she wanted to help him. How, she did not know. How could you help anyone as self-sufficient as Mr. Richardson?

And then as they were walking toward the Square she saw out of the corner of her eye an olive-green roadster stopped in the middle of the street by a traffic light and in it Jimmy Dougherty. She wanted to call out to him, but dared not risk it. Out of the corner of her eye she saw that he was looking at them, and thought, "Damn it, why is it he always sees me when I'm with Mr. Richardson?"

If she had been alone he might have called out to her. Now he'd think that there was something up between her and the newcomer; and she knew how silly he could be when he was jealous. She thought, "There goes my chance of going to the barbecue. There goes everything. It's all over. Maybe I'm well out of it." But she still went on hoping. She hoped up to the very eve of the crusade.

The traffic light changed and the roadster shot forward, grazing a baby carriage, and as they reached the other side of the street, Mr. Richardson said, "Don't you think we might relax and call each other by our first names? It's silly going on as Mr. Richardson and Miss Baldwin. May I call you Jane? Everybody calls me Tom. I'd like it if you'd call me that too."

"I suppose," said Jane slyly, "Tom is as good a name as any other."

He looked at her suddenly, sharply, but the expression of her face was perfectly blank and noncommittal.

Then he said, "All right, we'll be Tom and Jane. It's much cozier."

"I didn't think that coziness mattered much to you."

He laughed, a little ruefully, "It does matter," he said. "It matters like hell!"

46

It was Mr. Richardson who changed the date for the opening salvo. It had been set for the third, the day after his parole was finished, a gesture almost of nose-thumbing which made Mrs. McLeod chuckle. But a week before, he came to her and said, "I've had a better idea."

"Yes, what?"

"Well, the Dougherty-Democratic barbecue is set for the sixth, isn't it?"

"Yes."

"Well, why not open the crusade the evening of the fifth?"

She thought for a moment, "The paper wouldn't reach the county subscribers till the next day."

"We've got most of the county on our side. It's the city that matters."

"Maybe you're right," she said. "You always are." And when she thought it over she saw that it was an excellent idea.

Two days before the barbecue and home-coming, Mr. Richardson announced on the editorial page that the *Daily Shield and Banner*, beginning on the fifth of the month, would begin a new feature—a novel by Lavinia McLeod based on the history of Plattesville. It would be a regular daily feature and of great interest not only to the older generation which shared the memories of Mrs. McLeod, but to the younger one which knew nothing of the rigor, the hardship, the color and the glories of the old life. The announcement was shrewdly worded; it was calculated to throw a little of the fear of God into the *Daily News* and the Dougherty gang, to give them suspicions without facts of what was to follow, but nothing definite enough to work upon.

All the day of the fifth the *Daily Shield and Banner* office vibrated with suppressed excitement. It wasn't any longer possible to keep the crusade a secret. Alf Lyman on the linotype made the keys jump and stutter with his astonishment over the copy he was setting. Old Zimmerman twice swallowed tobacco juice in his excitement over the headlines he was ordered to set up. Belowstairs, Myrtle jittered and shook her turquoise earrings and looked secretive when people came to her cage to pay in money. Willie had an extra drink or two out of the bottom drawer to steady him and keep up his courage, and in the middle of the afternoon, he said to Mrs. McLeod, "All hell is gonna break loose in this cow town, Vinnie."

As for Mrs. McLeod herself, her heart thumped all day with a mixture of excitement and perturbation. She had never in her life attacked anyone and now she was attacking the most powerful gang Plattesville had ever known. It terrified her and made her ashamed, as if in some way she had committed a crime and might be arrested.

Only Mr. Richardson went about his work calmly and deliberately, as if nothing unusual was happening, and only Jane noticed the look in the gray-blue eyes, a look of excitement, almost of fire, and remembered suddenly what he had said in the tearoom, "You can't always tell by the outside what's going on inside." As the day wore on she found herself watching him

[126]

fascinated, wondering how he could care so profoundly about something which was happening in a town he had never seen until a little more than two months earlier. She had no talent for abstract things and she could neither divine, nor have believed if she had been capable of divining it, how much Mr. Richardson cared about Good and Evil.

The sight of him gave a little lift to a day which for her was not exciting but grew more and more dreary as the hope of hearing from Jimmy slowly died. In her heart she knew now that he would look upon the crusade as a blow at himself, no matter how much the attack made by the paper was directed at his father, and he would see it as a plot concocted by herself and Mr. Richardson. It was too late to do anything now, even if Aunt Vinnie and Mr. Richardson were willing to call everything off at the last minute. Nevertheless, at five o'clock there was still a faint pale ghost of hope in her heart that Jimmy would call her up and say he expected her to go to the barbecue with him.

But at five-fifteen, when Myrtle appeared from belowstairs bearing triumphantly the first damp copies of the first crusade number, Jane's heart was hardened. He hadn't sent her any word: so, she told herself, it meant that he was finished with her. He had never really cared for her at all, and he had no desire to make it up. She had been deceiving herself all along; she had made herself believe that they loved each other, but she had been a fool. The sight of the newspapers, still damp with printers' ink and carried at arm's length by Myrtle, so as not to soil her shirtwaist, seemed to her suddenly a kind of symbol. It was finished, and here in the *Daily Shield and Banner* was Mr. Richardson's attack on Old Dougherty. That, at least, was final. The newsboys by now were on the street. The crusade had opened. And everything was finished between her and Jimmy. There was something terrible in the sight of the damp print.

Stiffening her lip, she went over with the rest of them—Aunt Vinnie and Mr. Richardson, Myrtle and Willie Ferguson and old Zimmerman to examine the *Daily Shield and Banner*.

The ordinary news had for them no interest. It was the editorial page and the page opposite.

At the top of the editorial page appeared a streamer headline, reading: "What are the citizens of Plattesville going to do about it?" and just beneath it Mr. Richardson's editorial began. It opened with a general statement of the situation, calling attention to the fact that because the citizens of Plattesville had done nothing about their government, it had steadily grown worse and worse until it had become a stench in the nostrils and a disgrace to the whole Southwest. The *Daily Shield and Banner*, continued the editorial, had been conducting an investigation, and it meant to bring to light in a series of articles all the corruption which had been imposed on the taxpayers of one of the finest cities in the whole of the United States. The *Daily Shield and Banner* called upon the honest citizens of Plattesville to organize and fight. The newspaper would give them every possible aid. What was needed was a new and independent Democratic organization.

Beneath the opening salvo appeared a series of paragraphs each with a subhead. They read: "What About the Graft on Prison Labor—The New Courthouse Roof—The Hillyard Street-Lighting System—The New Water Works—The West Side Sewage Deal—Franklin Street?"

On the page opposite appeared the opening installment of Lavinia McLeod's novel called "The Good Old Days." It looked handsome and imposing, and all the time Mrs. McLeod was engaged in reading the opening crusade article, her eye, despite anything she could do, kept wandering to the page opposite for a glance at the name LAVINIA McLEOD set in bold type at the top of the page. At last she was an author. For a moment, selfishly, she thought, that fact was more important to her than the crusade.

The taciturn old Zimmerman suddenly grinned and said with a smack of tobacco-stained lips, "Well, I guess that'll fix 'em."

It was Willie Ferguson who answered him.

"It ain't over yet. The fightin's only begun and Plattesville always raised the fightinest set of bastards in the whole Southwest."

In Mrs. McLeod's eyes there was a look of wonder as she regarded Mr. Richardson. He didn't seem to be impressed or even excited but was peering at the page through his steel-rimmed spectacles. Jane was watching him too, admiring but hating him at the same time because he was so clever and so efficient.

Mrs. McLeod, in a weak voice, asked, "How did you find all this stuff, all the details, I mean?"

Mr. Richardson looked up as if surprised, and said, "Well, you told me a lot and Gashouse Mary told me plenty more, and the State boss had a couple of men on the job I didn't even tell you about. And I've heard plenty just nosing about on my own. All I had to do was check and organize the stuff."

Then the door opened and a messenger boy came in. They all turned toward him expectantly as if the telegram he carried were the first result of the crusade. He looked at them all and said, "Miss Jane Baldwin?"

"It's for me," said Jane and signed for it.

In turn, the others transferred their interest from the departing messenger boy to Jane. As she opened the telegram her hand trembled. She read it through while they all watched her. Then to turn their eyes away from her she said, in an odd choking voice, "It's nothing," and crumpled the telegram in her hand. All but Mrs. McLeod turned back again to the newspaper. She watched Jane take up her hat and start for the door.

She wanted to be sympathetic. She followed her out of the door and said, "Not bad news?"

"No," said Jane. And as she passed her, she said, "Please leave me alone, I have to go out." And then Mrs. McLeod knew that the telegram was from Jimmy Dougherty.

47

Her face wet with tears, Jane ran down the stairs and across the Square. She had reached the Soldiers' and Sailors' Memorial Fountain before she stopped running and seated herself on a bench. The crumpled telegram was still in her hand, and after a moment she opened it and read it again. It said simply, "I didn't want to, but I had to give in. Will you make it up and go to the barbecue with me? Love. Jimmy."

At the moment she did not know what she felt. She thought, "He can't have seen the paper yet," and then with a catch of hope, she thought, "Maybe he has seen it and wants to tell me he doesn't mind." Then she looked down at the telegram and the address of the sender and she felt suddenly sick. It hadn't been sent from the office in the Dougherty Block. It was sent from Millersville, and at once she knew that of course he wouldn't be at the office but at Millersville making arrangements for the barbecue. And so he didn't know yet . . . he couldn't know because he couldn't have seen the paper. He couldn't know of the dreadful attack. . . .

Near by, through her misery she heard a newsboy shouting, "*Daily Shield and Banner!* Special edition! Read the Big Graft Exposay!"

A little later she rose and walked to the other side of the Square to the telegraph office. There in a kind of nightmare she wrote out a telegram:

"Everything is made up but it is too late now."

The telegraph form was stained with tears and she thought, "If only he saw them he'd understand," but you couldn't send tear stains by telegram.

48

At the same time at the office of the *Daily News*, behind locked doors, a conference was taking place. Mr. Hirsh, the business manager, the thin worried editor, and Old Dougherty sat round the heavy mahogany table of Mr. Hirsh's office. On the table lay two copies, still damp, of the *Daily Shield and Banner*. Behind his shiny glasses Mr. Hirsh's pink face wore an expression like that of an alarmed guinea pig. The face of the thin and bilious editor, Mr. Winterbottom, was corrugated by wrinkles, and on the tough brow of Old Dougherty there were beads of sweat which he kept wiping away with a huge white handkerchief.

Hirsh said, "Well, they've pulled a fast one—springing it now before we were ready for them."

The editor, in a mild voice, said, "If you remember, Mr. Dougherty, I told you some time ago that you were headed for trouble."

Dougherty sweated, "A hell of a lot of good that does me now. What we've got to do is shut them up before it's too late." Mr. Hirsh, in a mild voice, said, "When is that bastard's parole up?"

Dougherty said, "We can't do anything there. It was up five days ago. We've got to bring the creditors down on them and snuff out the lousy sheet."

"That takes a lot of time. They can get in a lot of dirty work before we can shut 'em down. I wanted to set the wheels moving last week but you wouldn't let me."

"There was a reason," said Old Dougherty.

"What?" asked the worried editor.

"Jimmy didn't want to do it."

"Why not?" asked Mr. Hirsh.

Old Dougherty coughed nervously as if ashamed of being sentimental, "Well, the truth is, the boy has been kind of off his feed on account of that Baldwin girl—old Mrs. McLeod's niece."

The thin editor said, "Well, it's going to cost us plenty now."

The alarmed guinea-pig look went out of Mr. Hirsh's face and in its place came the expression of a shrewd rat. "It ain't as bad as you think," he said, "I've got a little dirty work on my own. I've sent a letter or two and I checked up on the mortgages on the paper itself and the old woman's house. It isn't going to take as much time as you thought."

Suddenly Old Dougherty exploded, "What the hell did you do that for against my orders? I'm boss around here and don't forget it."

Oddly enough, although the lines in the face of the nervous editor became anguished and taut, the face of Mr. Hirsh, the guinea pig, didn't seem very frightened, perhaps because in a long and unsavory career he had dealt too many times with men like Old Dougherty. After all, he had been engaged to work on the *News* because he knew a thing or two.

Quietly he said, "Maybe you'd rather go to the State Penitentiary than smash a lousy old sheet like the *Daily Shield and Banner*?"

"Who's going to the penitentiary? They haven't got anything on me."

But Mr. Hirsh was persistent. Quietly, laying his finger on the *Daily Shield and Banner*, he said, "Have you read that carefully? Don't imagine they've shot all the ammunition they've got just trying to find the range."

Old Dougherty began to bluster. "Listen, Hirsh," he said, "I've been in this town longer than you. I know the politics of the place. They haven't got a thing on me."

Mr. Hirsh very quietly folded up his copy of the *Daily Shield and Banner*. "Okay. But you'd better take my advice. Think it over and let me know later tonight. But don't forget that there are other guys besides yourself who can do a little framing."

"What do you mean?"

"Well, I don't suppose you're the only man with a little influence in State politics."

Old Dougherty snorted. Then he said, "That goddamned picnic is tomorrow!" He smacked his thigh, and a gleam of something like admiration came into his eye. "That bastard Richardson," he said, "is pretty smart—choosing the night before the barbecue to unload his garbage! We ought to have offered him a couple of thousand a month to come over to us. It woulda been worth it."

Mr. Hirsh said, "He wouldn't have come if you'd offered him a coupla million a month."

"Why not?" asked Old Dougherty.

"Because he's that kind of guy. I've seen 'em before. Only once or twice—but they're tough . . . about the toughest thing there is. They can't be bought. They're crazy—that kind. Money don't interest 'em."

49

When W. M. Dougherty finally left the office of the *Daily News* for his own house, Mr. Hirsh, the business manager of the *Daily News*, and Mr. Winterbottom, the managing editor, continued the conference over beer and sandwiches.

For Mr. Hirsh, the job on the *Daily News* represented merely a phase of time marking. To him the *News*, even Plattesville and its politics were smalltime stuff. The job served several purposes. Disguised as Mr. Hirsh in a more or less remote part of the Southwest, it made him comparatively safe from pursuit by the officers of the law who had made it uncomfortable for him to remain in Illinois or Indiana. It would, until the charges against him could be fixed, remain extremely uncomfortable for him to return to these States for several more years, and beyond that the Federal government had several questions it wanted to ask of Mr. Hirsh.

Old Dougherty knew about the charges. As a matter of record, he and Mr. Hirsh were, if not old friends, old acquaintances. Mr. Hirsh's name was not Hirsh but Sulzberger, and the two of them had met long ago at a Democratic National Convention. As a business manager, Mr. Hirsh was not brilliant, but he had other qualities which to W. M. Dougherty were valuable. He knew everything about dirty politics; he was experienced in strong-arm methods, and he could, if necessary, summon a troop of gunmen at a moment's notice. It was Mr. Hirsh's mugs who had twice wrecked Gashouse Mary's El Dorado when Mary objected to paying tribute to the Dougherty gang.

Mr. Hirsh did not in the least resemble his reputation with his pink cheeks and shiny pince-nez, his girlish mouth and his immaculate pudgy little hands; he was more like a fussy, middle-aged bachelor Sunday-school teacher than a killer, but he liked pulling the legs off flies, and only the janitor of the *Daily News* office knew that he was responsible for the fire which six months earlier had wrecked the room where the newsprint paper was kept. Mr. Hirsh had, it seemed, one night poured gasoline over a live rat in one of the janitor's traps and turned it loose after putting a match to it. The rat immediately took refuge in the room where the paper was stored. The knowledge of this fact had caused two rises in the salary of the janitor since the incident, rises of which no one save Mr. Hirsh knew anything at all.

As for Mr. Winterbottom, the editor, he was a tired and discouraged man. For thirty-seven years he had labored as a newspaperman in middle-sized towns in the Southwest, and now at fifty-five he was making thirty-five hundred dollars a year with which to support his harassed and nagging wife and four of the seven children who still remained beneath his roof. And although he had the title of managing editor, he managed nothing whatever; so far as prestige or authority was concerned, he might just as well have been the janitor. If, as rarely occurred, he was permitted to write an editorial, the range of his writing was confined to the weather or the county fair or some other innocuous subject upon which it was impossible to be indiscreet. For Old Dougherty thought him a fool, and had no use for him save to translate into passable English the ungrammatical, misspelled editorials which he himself wrote out each night in the library of the big Tudor house.

Unlike Mr. Hirsh, Mr. Winterbottom looked exactly what he was. He had a foolish, discouraged sheep face and a lanky body which appeared to be all angles and joints. He was as untidy as a trollop's washstand, and he wore black sleeve guards to save laundry bills. Twice in his thirty years of marriage he had begotten twins by his ill-natured wife. Behind the exterior, which was like an unpainted house on the wrong side of the railway tracks, Mr. Winterbottom was a mass of grudges. He had a number of large vague grudges against fate and life, and he had grudges against his wife and what, in the wisdom of advancing age, now appeared to him to be his unnecessary children. He had grudges against Old Dougherty and against Jimmy for being young and good looking and for enjoying all the forbidden fruits which his Methodism had prevented him from enjoying at Jimmy's age. And most of all he had a grudge against Mr. Hirsh. Mr. Hirsh was not only a newcomer, but he had a great deal of authority in the *News* office and in the Dougherty machine. In his nasty way, he lorded it over the other members of the *News* staff. There were even times, Mr. Winterbottom told his wife, when you'd have thought old W. M. was afraid of Mr. Hirsh. He hated Mr. Hirsh.

Mr. Hirsh did not hate Mr. Winterbottom. He simply held him in contempt.

So while the two of them sat over their sandwiches and beer, there was not much conversation. The conference, both of them knew, was a mockery, and Mr. Hirsh was making no effort to pretend that it was anything else, an attitude which did nothing toward appeasing Mr. Winterbottom. But if they did not speak, they both did a lot of thinking.

On his side of the copy desk, Mr. Hirsh was thinking, "The old man is going to get into plenty of trouble if he don't watch his step. The trouble is that he's a smalltime politician. He ain't up-to-date . . . and the situation is just right for Swain to take him for a ride."

He didn't know exactly how deep and complicated the old man's trickery and dishonesty had been, but he divined that it was probably a good deal worse than W. M. had ever let him or anyone else know. And the old man was tired too. It wasn't as if he was ready for a fight. And letting this affair between his son and that Baldwin girl count for anything! In crooked politics you had to be ruthless even if it meant doing in your own mother. Girl or no girl, the *Daily Shield and Banner* would have to be smashed before it was too late, and that fresh guy Richardson would have to be fixed too, one way or another.

Mr. Hirsh raised the glass of beer to his rosebud lips, and when he put the glass down again he smacked his lips, not in satisfaction over the beer but over the prospect of fixing Mr. Richardson. He didn't care for Mr. Richardson. He hadn't liked his manner the day he came to Old Dougherty's office . . . too cocky, too fresh for a guy of his age. And he didn't like Mr. Richardson because Mr. Richardson was normal and healthy. Mr. Hirsh didn't like anybody who was healthy, but he specially disliked Mr. Richardson's square jaw and gray-blue eyes. And old W. M. didn't appreciate how dangerous a guy like that could be. There was no stopping that kind of guy once they got started.

"It was the same kind of district attorney that chased me out of Indiana," he thought. "If somebody had bumped him off, I wouldn't be hidin' away out here in this cow town."

No, Mr. Richardson would certainly have to be "fixed" if he went on with this campaign. Why, he might even get nosy about Mr. Hirsh and make life very uncomfortable for him. In the meanwhile they could get to work making trouble about mortgages and advertising and things like that. Mr. Hirsh could send for a couple of the boys to come down and do a job. Bill the Gyp, and Little Hermie, he thought, would be the best pair. They worked all right together and they both looked respectable. They could dress up to look like Rotary Club members and nobody would notice them in a place like Plattesville.

"I'll write. tonight when I get home," thought Mr. Hirsh.

He wasn't a big clumsy spider like Old Dougherty. He was small and plausible, and, looking like a pansy Sunday-school teacher, all the more deadly.

Opposite him Mr. Winterbottom sat, peering fretfully from under his shaggy eyebrows. He had indigestion already from swallowing bits of hamburger sandwiches whole and he was thinking spitefully, "If he don't look out, the old man is goin' to get caught this time. They can get plenty on him—plenty. And this guy Hirsh. Who is he, anyway? Where'd he come from? What was he before? Maybe they'll get him too."

And in Mr. Winterbottom's narrow head ideas began to hatch. He thought, "I know enough myself to send old W. M. to jail. All I need to do is to open my trap about half a dozen little deals that aren't so pretty. I got all the facts too. That'd pay him back for treatin' me like an office boy all these years. I could fix him." And for a long time he sat there, a sandwich poised in his hand, staring out of the window into the Square, imagining the whole story of Old Dougherty's defeat and humiliation. He saw himself testifying on the witness stand. He saw Old Dougherty coming to him, pleading with him, attempting to bribe him to keep quiet. And then Mr. Winterbottom, the worm, would face him and say, "No, you asked for it. You can't treat people the way you treated me for ten years and get away with it. Now you've got to take what's comin' to you."

Suddenly he laughed aloud with satisfaction at the picture of Old Dougherty's humiliation. The sound echoed hollowly through the empty office. Mr. Hirsh jumped and asked, "What's the matter with you? What's so funny?"

"Nothing," said Mr. Winterbottom, "I was just thinking of a story." And the laugh died in him at the sight of Mr. Hirsh's pink sinister face. He could never turn on old W. M. and send him to jail because he'd lose his job and at his age he wouldn't very likely get another, never at thirty-five hundred a year. And he had to think of the missus and the four brats that were still at home living off him.

50

It was half-past nine when Old Dougherty arrived from the *News* office at the huge Tudor house in the Plattesville suburbs. The sight of the house, dreary and empty and dark save for the light in the hall, made him feel suddenly tired and old. He had hoped that Jimmy would be back from

Millersville. It was Jimmy he needed to see, Jimmy more than any other person on earth. Inside, he found a cold supper set out for him by Ella, the only servant who lived in the big house. Beside it there was a note from her saying that she had waited for him until eight-thirty and then gone to the movies.

For a second the misspelled note in illiterate handwriting filled him with fury. He thought, "I suppose she's seen that goddamned paper and thinks she can get away with what she wants now." But almost at once he saw that such reasoning was beyond the powers of Ella's mulatto intelligence and capacity for reflection. He thought, "I've got to keep my head. If my nerves go, I'm finished."

While he ate the cold supper he realized for the first time in his life that he was really tired and, save for the prospect of a fight, he was bored. He didn't want any more money. It was only power that he wanted—power that included not only Plattesville, but the State and perhaps after that power in national politics. He was sixty-one and that wasn't old. He might even end his career by being a senator in Washington; that would fix all these people who were attacking him. He wanted the power Bill Swain now had in the State party, and then suddenly, the thought occurred to him that perhaps Bill Swain had divined his ambition and discovered one or two of his tricks and was behind the crusade, more responsible for it than old Mrs. McLeod and that bastard Richardson. Maybe they were only stooges. Maybe the mysterious Mr. Richardson had been sent there in the beginning by Bill Swain.

He couldn't quite believe that Richardson was as smart as he appeared to be. No newspaperman picked off the street and jailed as a vagrant could be as smart as Richardson seemed to be. If he'd been that smart—smart enough to uncover all the uncomfortable details he had hinted at in the *Daily Shield and Banner,* he'd have a good job somewhere in Chicago, St. Louis or Kansas City. No, he decided, there was something fishy about the whole thing. And the sense of fishiness made him feel still more nervous and uncertain.

It was Jimmy he wanted—Jimmy to talk to—Jimmy to quiet his uneasiness —Jimmy with his optimism and rampant good health and his grin. He couldn't imagine what Jimmy could be doing in Millersville after nine o'clock.

When he had finished the cold snack he went into the empty library, took off his shoes, lay on the sofa and set himself to do some figuring. But his mind didn't work properly. A part of it kept listening to the sound of every motor that passed. He found himself rising up on the sofa, expecting each car to turn in at the drive and deliver Jimmy at the door. And presently it occurred to the old man that Jimmy was the only thing he had in the world on which he could count, to whom he could turn in trouble. Hirsh, Winterbottom, the magistrates, the police chief, even the Mayor himself would double-cross him if things went wrong; they'd turn and run for Bill Swain's camp waving the white flag, but he could always count on Jimmy.

Suddenly he sat up and poured himself a drink and half-aloud he said, "Get hold of yourself, W. M. Nothing's going to happen. You've got every local judge in your pocket. Don't lose your head."

Like a mangy old lion he shook himself and got up heavily. Then he went to the window and stayed there for a long time watching the lights of the cars that went past. One passed and then two and three and then two racing each other, but none of them turned in at the drive. And terrified he suddenly thought, "Maybe something's happened to him. Maybe he's had an accident. He always drives like a damned fool—hell bent for leather."

But quickly he told himself that if anything had happened to Jimmy he would have been notified, because everybody in the county knew Jimmy and the olive-green car. "You damned fool!" he told himself, "you're behaving like an old woman!" And again he thought, "If only that lousy barbecue was a week off instead of tomorrow." And then he thought, "Maybe feeling the way he does about that Baldwin girl, he's done something crazy." But that, he told himself, wasn't like Jimmy. Jimmy was too healthy to do anything like that.

At last it occurred to him that he was doing no good fuming at the window. He had meant to spend the evening planning how to fight the *Daily Shield and Banner* attack, and up to now he had done nothing whatever. He took another drink to steady himself and lay down on the sofa once more to work. But it was no good.

Eleven o'clock passed, and when he could bear it no longer he went to the telephone and called up the Lakeside Inn at Millersville, but Ira Miller only told him that Jimmy had left there a little after six o'clock. Then he called the Elks' Club and Hennessey's saloon, disguising his voice so that no one would suspect that on the other end of the wire was W. M. Dougherty, behaving like an hysterical old woman. But neither place had any news of him. And at last, swallowing his pride, he called the El Dorado. It was nearly midnight, and in his anxiety he forgot to disguise his voice, so that the barman who answered said almost at once, "Hello, Mr. Dougherty," which infuriated the old man.

The barman said that Jimmy had been there, but had left about ten minutes earlier. The news brought such relief to the old man that he did not even resent it when the barman said with veiled insolence, "Yes, I guess you'll want to be seeing him tonight."

He had left the telephone and was returning to the library when he heard a car coming up the drive. His impulse was to go to the door, but he was ashamed of his anxiety and instead he returned to the sofa to lie down. He was just settling himself, when there came from the drive the sound of a violent crash followed by silence, and springing up again, the old man hurried to the porte-cochere door and switched on the light.

Outside, halfway into the garage, he saw Jimmy's olive-green roadster. The splintered doors of the garage leaned against the smashed hood. Unsteadily Jimmy climbed out. At the sight of the light and his father, he grinned sheepishly and said, "I guess I must have forgot about the doors."

Then as the old man descended the steps he discovered that Jimmy wasn't alone. Behind him, climbing out of the car was the figure of a woman with platinum blond hair, wearing a red fox fur. She, too, moved a little unsteadily. Her figure was vaguely familiar to the old man.

As they came toward him Jimmy said, "This is Fern Hedges. I brought her to have a drink. Fern and I are going to be married."

When he heard the name, a kind of apoplectic fury seized the old man. For a moment he couldn't speak at all but only made stuttering sounds. Then suddenly he burst out.

"You're not gonna marry her!" Then he shouted at Fern. "And you're never gonna set foot in this house. You're gonna clear out right now. Scram! Beat it!"

Fern, sobered a little by the spectacle of Old Dougherty's fury, looked to Jimmy for support, but he too found no words.

To Jimmy the old man said, "You must be crazy."

Then Fern found her tongue. "That's right. Call me names. Abuse me. I mighta known what kind of reception I'd get. Like father like son. Just a coupla shanty Irish." Her voice took on a wild shrill quality and she shouted, "I guess you won't be so smart when the *Daily Shield and Banner* gets through with you both. I guess you're gonna get showed up. Let me tell you, I wouldn't marry your lousy son." Then before starting away down the drive, she flung a parting shot, "I wouldn't think of marrying the son of a jail bird!"

Apoplexy seized Old Dougherty once more. Stuttering he shouted after her, "Get out, you dirty whore!" which only brought a fresh torrent of abuse thrown over Fern Hedges's shoulder as she made her unsteady way down the drive. At the sound of her screams windows opened in the houses next door and across the street.

For two or three minutes, the old man, breathing heavily, stood regarding his son. Then he said, "Come on in the house. Every bastard in the neighborhood's listening."

In the library he said to Jimmy, "Sit down!"

Jimmy sat down and threw the copy of the *Daily Shield and Banner* from his pocket on the table.

Still he said nothing, and presently Old Dougherty asked, "What's got into you? Are you crazy?"

[137]

Jimmy covered his face with his hands. "I don't know," he said.

"A nice time to act like this—with the barbecue tomorrow."

"I'll be all right in the morning. I never have a hang-over."

The father lighted a cigar and presently he said, "Well, it looks like your girl on the *Daily Shield and Banner* double-crossed you."

But Jimmy didn't answer anything.

"Is that what's the matter with you?"

Still there wasn't any answer. Jimmy just sat there, his face covered with his hands.

Old Dougherty shifted his cigar to the other side of his mouth. "It's a hell of a way to act. Haven't you got any guts?"

"I've got guts enough."

"It's no good acting like a damned romantic Irishman—a shanty Irishman at that. That lousy whore was right. You're acting like a shanty Irishman."

Again Jimmy didn't answer him, and for a moment the old man was shaken. He'd never seen Jimmy like this.

"You've seen the *Daily Shield and Banner*?"

"Yes."

"Well, you know we've got a fight ahead of us."

"Sure, I know that."

"Well, are you gonna chuck me?"

"Of course I'm not gonna chuck you."

"Well, you act like it—going to Gashouse Mary's to get drunk. Gashouse Mary's of all places!"

Still Jimmy remained silent. Again the cigar shifted from one side of the old man's mouth to the other.

He said, "Listen to me, kid."

"I'm listening."

"Maybe I haven't paid enough attention to you. Maybe we oughta have talked more together, but I don't have to tell you what a busy guy I am." His voice grew soft. He was frightened now.

"No," said Jimmy.

"I'm gonna tell you something I've never told you before. You see, kid, you've always had everything. When I was your age I was walking the streets lookin' for a job. And before that I was a kid who came over steerage on a cattle boat with my old man and woman from Ireland in a famine year. I didn't have anything to start with, and after I got married I wanted plenty—for your mother's sake and after you were born, for your sake too. I wasn't as good as your mother. I always knew you couldn't make a silk purse out of a sow's ear—anything more than I was—just shanty Irish. But I'm as smart as the next fella, and I wanted to have things for you and the old girl. I wanted to show people. I wanted the Doughertys to have money and be somebody, and then just when I got the money, she died. I guess that was kind of hard on you too—harder than it was on me. I've done a lot of things that weren't what you'd call okay, but I did it because I wanted to get ahead—so you wouldn't have to do 'em. I didn't do 'em so that you could get drunk and tell the whole town you were gonna marry a cheap tart. It ain't right, what you're doin'. It ain't right to me and it certainly ain't right to yourself—you, a kid that's got everything."

Without looking up, Jimmy said, "I was never gonna marry Fern. It was just kind of a joke. I guess I was a little nuts tonight."

"I want you to get married to a nice girl with a good family and have a lot of nice kids. You're young and strong. You're the kind that ought to have a lot of kids, and if you marry the right girl, by the time the kids come along I guess the bad Dougherty will be kinda bred out of the stock. Get me?"

"Yeah."

"I'd like you to get married to somebody like that nice healthy Baldwin girl. I hoped it was gonna come off."

"Well, it won't now. Tonight's fixed that."

"I didn't know you felt like that about her. You've had plenty of girls, but none of 'em seemed to matter."

"They didn't."

"Why didn't you tell me? I'd have fixed it somehow." He was silent for a moment. "I'd even have given up the whole works and cleared out if it would have given you what you wanted."

"It wasn't as easy as that."

"What did you squabble about in the first place?"

Jimmy didn't answer him, and he said, "Was it because you tried to make her?"

"No. It wasn't like that. I didn't want it like that."

"Go on. Tell me what it was. Maybe I could fix it."

"Never mind. Forget it."

The old man looked at him for a long time, and then slowly a curious expression of shrewdness came into his face. At the same time it was the expression of a small boy who wants to hide something. In a low voice, he asked, "Was it something that had to do with me?" There was only silence, and presently Old Dougherty said, "I get you. I guess money isn't everything. I oughta thought about other things too, I guess. Sometimes you musta been ashamed of me."

"I wasn't ever ashamed of you."

The old man did something he had never done before in all his life. He rose heavily and went over and put his hand on the shoulder of his son. He said, "I got it. I see the spot you've been in. And now you can't go back on your old man. You know, you can if you want to, if it'll help you out of the jam. You can do what you like. I'll understand."

For the first time Jimmy looked up at him. The Irish blue eyes were bluer than ever because there was moisture in them. Fiercely, he said, "What do you think I am?"

"Listen," said Old Dougherty, "I can't run now. I'd run if it would help you, but it's too late now. I've gotta fight. You get me, don't you?"

"Yes."

"A week ago before that damned sheet came out, we could have called it all off. But it's too late now. I've gotta fight because I've never run away yet. And I've gotta fight . . . you might as well know how bad it is. Maybe I've got to fight to keep from going to jail."

The speech sobered Jimmy completely. Looking up again he said, "Is it as bad as that?"

"If they've got enough dope on me and Bill Swain wants to frame me."

"I didn't know. I always sorta took things for granted."

"There's a lot of things I never told you—I guess because I was ashamed of 'em." He patted Jimmy on the back and said, "You'd better get to bed now. Sleep it off, and tomorrow we've got to put on a bold face at the barbecue—tomorrow of all times. Maybe it'll come out all right."

So Jimmy left him and climbed the stairs to bed. When he undressed he took out of his pocket the crumpled telegram and read it again—"Everything is made up but it's too late now." With an exaggerated, tipsy carefulness he smoothed the bit of paper, folded it carefully and put it away between the pages of a copy of *Gulliver's Travels* given him by his mother long ago when he was a small boy. He had an idea that some day he might want it.

51

At the *Daily Shield and Banner* office there was a meeting in progress until late into the night. It had begun when Mr. Simpson, the Baptist minister, telephoned at six o'clock to ask if he might have an interview with Mrs. McLeod. He had, he said in a somewhat unctuous voice, seen the *Daily Shield and Banner* and marked its appeal to the upright and God-fearing citizens of Plattesville. He would like to make up a reform committee to help in the fight.

Then Jim Newman called up from his undertaking establishment to say, "Bravo! It's a great editorial. If you're gonna be there a while I'll come over. What about calling up Sam Henderson and some of the boys and telling 'em to drive in?"

"Wait a minute," said Mrs. McLeod. And calling Mr. Richardson she told him what Jim Newman proposed and asked what she should tell him. "It's your show," she said, "you've got to decide."

"Tell them to come in," said Mr. Richardson. "It's always better to strike while the iron is hot."

So Jim Newman promised to bring some of the county boys, not Hal Pierce because he couldn't make it with his old-fashioned buckboard and pintos, but the others he promised would come.

Then about seven, Gashouse Mary rang up. "Swell!" she said on the telephone. "Hot stuff! That hit 'em right between the eyes." And when Mrs. McLeod told her about the impromptu meeting, she said, "I'll be up about ten o'clock when I get the place started. Will you still be there?"

"I guess maybe we'll be here most of the night," said Mrs. McLeod. There was a note of hysterical triumph in her voice. The excitement of battle was in her now. Her heart was beating like a trip hammer and her thin veined hands were shaking.

And there were other calls of congratulations, one or two anonymous ones of abuse which frightened Mrs. McLeod, but her fright she forgot quickly in the excitement. Nothing had happened to her like this since the old days when J. E. was alive and a force in politics. The lines went out of her face and a new look came into her eyes. It was like giving a party—a party which was a wonderful success.

By ten o'clock the office was crowded—so crowded that Mr. Richardson's orderly mind found it very difficult to achieve anything approaching organization. The crowd rather startled Mrs. McLeod and Mr. Richardson and Willie and Myrtle Ferguson; they had all expected a response but nothing like this gathering. And the mixture was an odd one including the Baptist and Methodist clergymen and several of their supporters, Jim Newman, fat and perspiring, with his legion of old timers from the county, Mrs. Mabel Urquahart Jenkins and three members of the Women's Municipal Improvement Committee, and last of all, and a little startling to some of the reformers, Gashouse Mary, wearing a red velvet suit, a hat with a plume and a white fox fur.

Once the door opened and she came in it was impossible not to notice her and utterly impossible to ignore her. The effect of the entrance was tremendous, and when Mrs. Mabel Urquahart Jenkins sidled up to Mrs. McLeod and whispered, "What is that woman doing here?" Mrs. McLeod said, "Don't you worry about her. She's one of our biggest supporters. She's got the whole river front organization."

Then Mary disappeared into the back room with Jim Newman and some of the old timers to have a drink out of Willie Ferguson's bottle of Bourbon. While they were gone, Mr. Richardson sent out for sandwiches and coffee, and his calm face took on a worried look as if he had found himself already faced with all the difficulties of a reform movement, as if he found it impossible to reconcile the presence on one committee of people as varied as the two clergymen, the powerful Mrs. Mabel Urquahart Jenkins and her stalwart female supporters, Jim Newman and his county cohorts and, worst of all, Gashouse Mary.

It was Gashouse Mary herself who solved the difficulty. When she returned from the printer's room well fortified by Willie's Bourbon, she took Mr. Richardson into a corner.

Glancing around the room she said, "Pretty good, ain't it? Never thought we'd get a response like this. And there'll be a lot more tomorrow."

"There must have been a lot of people ready to fight Old Dougherty."

"Yeah, there are, only there wasn't anybody with the guts to start the fight. But the real reason is that this county hasn't had a good political fight in twenty years. It was achin' for one. I know this country . . . there's nothing they like better. Look at their faces."

Mr. Richardson looked. Every face was flushed and excited. There was an enthusiasm everywhere. Jim Newman suddenly called across the room to Mrs. McLeod. "Like the old days, ain't it, Vinnie?"

In the corner Gashouse Mary said to Mr. Richardson, "And I don't want to put no spoke in the wheel. Don't put me on no committee or you'll be losin' all the pious rats and we need their votes. I'll go on workin' quiet, but just leave me out of it. Leave me be the power behind the throne."

So with a relieved face, Mr. Richardson at last returned to the long table and pounded on it to bring the room to order. Then he made one of his elegant speeches and suggested they elect a committee. As a stranger, he modestly suggested that the nominations be made by a committee consisting of Mrs. McLeod, the Baptist minister, Mrs. Mabel Urquahart Jenkins, Sam Henderson and Jim Newman. Those five withdrew into Mrs. McLeod's cubbyhole, and in a little while returned with ten names which were unanimously accepted. Others, Mr. Simpson, the Baptist minister, suggested, could be called later on as the God-fearing citizens of the county rose to support the crusade.

Then, having made arrangements for a public meeting the next day at the Baptist Church, the party broke up, leaving behind only the *Daily Shield and Banner* staff, Jim Newman and Gashouse Mary to shake hands and have a drink on the success of the opening salvo of the attack.

It was two o'clock when the party finally broke up with Gashouse Mary saying she must get back to the El Dorado. As she left, she turned in the doorway and said, "I forgot to tell you that Jimmy Dougherty was at the El Dorado again with that tart Fern Hedges. He was stinking and telling everyone he was going to marry her."

[142]

When she had gone Mr. Richardson said suddenly, "But where's Jane? She ought to have been here."

52

Jane was at home in her room in McLeod's Folly. About the time that the rally broke up in the *Daily Shield and Banner* office, she fell asleep worn out by the waves of anger and heartbreak which had swept over her since the moment she sent the telegram.

She had come straight home and gone to her room, and when Aida came up to tell her that supper was on the table and that Mrs. McLeod and Mr. Richardson hadn't yet returned, Jane replied that very likely they weren't coming back and that she herself wanted nothing to eat. And when Aida insisted that she have a bite of something to eat, she grew angry and called through the door to Aida to go away and leave her in peace.

On receipt of this message Aida stood for a moment before the locked door in silence. Once she started to speak but before any words came out, closed her big mouth suddenly and turning away, went down the stairs.

Aida was angry, more angry than she had been since the day fifteen years earlier when Sam had run off to Memphis with that high-yaller girl who had the fancy name of Maisie Dangerfield. She was angry about a great many things—angry at Old Dougherty and his party, angry because the excitement of the *Daily Shield and Banner's* rebirth had upset the household and made meals irregular, most of all angry at Jimmy Dougherty for making uppity Miss Jane so miserable. But the final prod to her anger was the thought of the excellent supper she had cooked, sitting downstairs in the kitchen with nobody to eat it.

Anger, genuine fierce anger, was a rare emotion with Aida. She sulked often enough and she had "miseries," but she hadn't really been angry since Sam's elopement. Now, after fifteen years, she was wild and her anger was monumental and spectacular.

Downstairs in the kitchen, she put the whole of the supper she had cooked on two trays and carried them downstairs to the three tramps who occupied the furnace room, telling them when they had finished to put the trays at the top of the cellar steps. Then she went upstairs again, put on her hat and coat, locked all the doors, bolted the windows and went out. Only Jane, weeping in her room and the tramps seated around the packing case in the furnace room, gorging tomato soup, roast chicken and chocolate cake, remained to occupy McLeod's Folly.

As she went down the path between the bedraggled syringas she thought, "That'll fix 'em. When they come back they won't find nobody in the house and nothin' to eat. That'll learn 'em. Never callin' up or nothin'."

Closing the gate behind her she set out straight for Darkietown. She hadn't been there in a long time, but she knew just where she wanted to go . . . to Joe's Place. There she would find corn liquor and music and good company. And most of all she'd hear a lot of gossip and news, the kind of gossip and news you could only get in Joe's Place, the kind of news that Mrs. McLeod and Mr. Richardson and even Willie Ferguson could never uncover. Because in Joe's Place gathered the cream of Darkietown. As soon as the sun had well set, the cream gathered there, out of kitchens and shops and laundries from all over Plattesville, and with them they brought news about how Mr. and Mrs. McGuire had quarreled and Mrs. McGuire had hit him with a cocktail shaker and how Mr. Campbell was running after Mrs. Barry and how Mrs. Barry's daughter Esther had been all night at a tourist camp with the Jenkinson boy. In Joe's Place they knew practically everything that went on in the houses of the rich and respectable in the upper part of town.

Joe was a big café-au-lait buck of forty-five, and at sight of Aida he gave a cheer and a signal to the banjo, trombone players and the drummer, and Aida made her entrance to a fanfare fit for the entrance of a star circus performer. Joe knew Aida, and he knew she never came in except to celebrate. She was a lot nearer to the good old days than most of Joe's customers, and she knew a lot of plantation songs and dances that the rest of them had never heard or had forgotten. When Aida came Joe never allowed her to pay for her drinks, because she was worth plenty of money as an entertainer.

Tonight when Joe greeted her, he saw that she was mad, and that meant that she was going to get going and give a fine performance. There was a berserk look in her eyes, and at sight of her the whole tempo of Joe's Place went up and that meant that there would be a record amount of drinking, and that when at last the dawn came up and the last customer had departed, the till would be full. The news of Aida's arrival sped from mouth to mouth in Darkietown, and presently the low-ceilinged smoky room was so full that you couldn't have squeezed one more dark face into the place. So the overflow audience stood at the open window, and Joe and Joe's wife and three café-au-lait daughters passed drinks out the window to them.

It took a lot of drinks to get Aida under way. The berserk mood clung, and for a time the corn liquor only made her anger the more sultry. It wasn't till Joe himself began paying her elaborate compliments and offered to do an old-fashioned buck and wing with her, that the look of sullen fury faded from her face.

The white teeth showed for a moment in a grin and she said, "You all can't do no real buck and wing, Joe Jackson. You're nothin' but a kid. You all doan know nothin' about it."

Then Joe made some crack about her sex appeal and she let out a bellow of Rabelaisian laughter, but it took two more stiff drinks to get her on her feet. When she got there on her feet in a space cleared in the middle of the floor before the banjo player, she lifted her skirts and with a yell went into a dance that none of the younger ones could equal for intricacy and speed.

When she had finished the buck and wing and got her breath and had another drink she sang for them an old plantation song called, "When the Cotton is a-poppin'." The crowd outside the window kept getting bigger and bigger, and Joe and his family kept passing more and more drinks over the heads of the enraptured audience. Altogether, it was a night such as Joe's Place seldom knew. And presently Aida forgot her anger altogether and danced again and sang more songs. She was enjoying herself, but in the back of her mind something rankled, some dark little demon which wouldn't be chased away by banjo music and corn liquor. Now and then, right in the middle of the music, Aida would remember that there was something on her mind that she had to get settled. Like a shadow the knowledge of it would cross her wild enjoyment, and she would try to reach out and capture the demon and identify him.

It wasn't until a little after midnight when one of the musicians from the El Dorado, drawn by the news that Aida was in Joe's Place, came over to have a drink, that she remembered what the demon was which wouldn't leave her alone. While she was drinking with him, he said, "Old man Dougherty's son is at the El Dorado. He's drunk and tellin' everybody he's gonna marry that whore Fern Hedges."

Then she knew. She had come out to enjoy herself, but she'd come out too to get something on Jimmy Dougherty so she could go back and tell Miss Jane and show her what kind of poor trash he was so that she wouldn't go on eatin' her heart out about him.

And now she had it . . . just what she wanted. Jimmy Dougherty was delivered into her hands. Dimly, through all the haze of music and corn liquor she felt a single compulsion. She must get on her feet and go straight home and tell Miss Jane. Then Miss Jane would know what kind of poor white trash the Doughertys were . . . his goin' around and tellin' everybody he was gonna marry a whore like Fern Hedges.

In the middle of a drink, she rose unsteadily to her feet and said, "Ah'se goin' home."

Joe stepped in front of her and said in a wheedling voice, "Not yet, sister. We ain't had enough singin' and dancin'."

But Aida was determined. Quietly, but with an awful firmness, she took up a beer bottle from the table at her side. Holding it high above her head she said once more with an awful firmness, "Ah'se goin' home."

There was a murmur of protest and Joe tried again to argue with her, but she only repeated, "Ah'se goin' home," and took two steps forward. This time Joe, remembering the old story of what Aida had done to her husband Sam when the high-yaller girl Maisie Dangerfield left him and he came home, stepped aside. The music stopped, and the banjo player stood up craning his neck for a better view; the crowd drew aside making a little pathway, and Aida, still carrying the beer bottle, went toward the doorway surrounded by an aura of authority and dignity.

But at the very door, she halted and unsteadily, helped by one or two of those standing near the doorway, she climbed on a chair. Still holding the bottle high above her head she cried out to the sea of dark faces, "And we gotta clear that poor white trash Dougherty outta this town. You all got to vote against him. You all ought to be ashamed to let Plattesville be run by white trash that belongs in shanty town."

The speech was greeted by cheers and cries of "Sure, Aida! Sure!"—"Clear 'em out"—"Sure, we'll clear 'em out if you all come back and dance."

But the mood for dancing was gone from Aida, gone before the power of an obsession. She had to straighten out Miss Jane's life. She had to tell her what kind of fellow Jimmy Dougherty was.

So unsteadily, amid cheers, she got down from the chair, left Joe's Place and set out for McLeod's Folly. As she walked, she kept muttering to herself, "Ah'll fix him. The poor white trash! Ah'll fix him! He won't humble no McLeod no more with his poor white trash ways."

Unsteadily, she opened the gate and unsteadily she climbed the steps to the high front porch. Fumbling, she put the key in the lock and opened the door and entered the dark hallway. In her haste and her singleness of purpose she did not even trouble to remove the key or close the door. Weaving a little, she made her way up the huge broad stairway and went straight to the door of Jane's room. Then, planting her big feet firmly, she pounded on the door with the beer bottle.

After a moment the frightened voice of Jane called out, "What's the matter? Who's there?" And Aida answered, "It's only me. Don't you be scared, honey. I just waked you up to tell you what kind of bastard that Jimmy Dougherty is. He's drunk down at Gashouse Mary's place tellin' all the white trash in Plattesville he's gonna marry that Fern Hedges."

Then for a moment Aida was silent, standing with the beer bottle poised, awaiting an answer. But the only answer was the sound of sobbing and Aida said, "You go to sleep, honey. Doan you trouble your poor little pretty haid about no Dougherty."

The sobbing continued, and presently Aida, muttering and feeling suddenly sleepy, turned away and made an uncertain progress down the stairs. With each step the drowsiness increased. Near the bottom of the stairs she let the beer bottle fall. It rolled down the steps before her. At last, when she had reached the hall itself she felt unwilling to let go of the rail until she found a fresh support, and looking drowsily about she chose the coatrack made in the form of a tree trunk with bears climbing up it. It was three or four steps away and this distance she managed without falling, but as she seized the rack for support the whole thing toppled and fell, Aida with it. She made one feeble effort to regain her feet and then, overcome with sleep, gave it up and lay back. In a moment she was soundly sleeping on her back, covered by a mass of hats and raincoats, her mouth open a little way, snoring happily in the dim knowledge that she had fixed Mr. Dougherty and done a good deed. Now maybe Miss Jane would forget about Jimmy Dougherty and marry that nice Mr. Richardson and keep the *Daily Shield and Banner* in the family.

When Mr. Richardson and Mrs. McLeod came in about half-past two, they found her thus, snoring quietly. It took them nearly half an hour to get her out from under the coats, on her feet and into bed.

53

At Millersville the next day the annual Democratic barbecue and picnic took place as usual. There were fifteen barrels of beer consumed, and three steers and ten sheep roasted over piles of red-hot coals prepared a whole day in advance by cousin Ira Miller's hired man. There were prizes given for the biggest fish caught and the greatest number of fish caught in the deep sapphire blue lake, and a bathing beauty contest and a baby contest, and there was music from loud-speakers scattered here and there among the trees of the cottonwood grove.

Outwardly, the affair was a great success. Children got lost, one fell in the lake and was rescued, four or five henchmen who came, armed with their own corn liquor, passed out and were left sleeping in the shade until it was time to go home, two women had a hair-pulling match and fourteen young ladies, after retiring into the bushes with admirers, returned "engaged" for the time being. It was, outwardly, the same as all the other barbecues that had taken place since Old Dougherty held the first one, more than ten years earlier. But in the heart of Old Dougherty, there was a difference.

As he walked about kissing babies and passing out cigars and slapping backs and paying compliments to bathing beauties, his heart wasn't somehow in the business. In the kisses, the backslaps, the compliments, there wasn't the old, almost mechanical enthusiasm. He went through all the motions, but inside himself there was a hollow feeling. The whole performance, which he had always before enjoyed with such gusto, didn't give him any pleasure. It seemed to him that the crowd was enjoying itself, but that there was a difference, and the difference, it seemed, had to do with him. He fancied that whenever he joined a new group under the cottonwood trees, all the people in it fell silent and embarrassed, and that when he had passed out cigars and kissed the babies and made plenty of bad jokes, they didn't seem as pleased or laugh as heartily as they had done in other years. And once or twice when he had left a little circle of picnickers, he found himself turning as he walked away to see whether they were putting their heads together to talk about him and the *Daily Shield and Banner* attack. Always inside him there was a voice saying, "Look out! Watch your step! If things go wrong, they'll all desert you. They'll even turn on you."

Between groups, between backslaps, he kept trying to reassure himself. "There's nothing to be scared of," he'd keep telling himself. "They haven't got anything on you. Even Bill Swain can't do anything. His own books ain't clear. He wouldn't dare do nothing."

But this voice wasn't as convincing as the other one. Somehow, it rang as hollow as his insides felt. And just as he had himself about persuaded that there wasn't anything to be worried about, he'd come to another little group under the trees or someone would speak to him and he'd have to become cheerful and backslapping again, and each time this happened he felt a little more tired and a little more empty. But the thing that troubled him most was how much the *Daily Shield and Banner* outfit knew and who this guy Richardson was. That was a guy who knew his stuff too well to be just a tramp reporter.

And whenever he thought of Mr. Winterbottom and Mr. Hirsh he was troubled, for very different reasons. Mr. Winterbottom was just a broken reed and no help to anybody at a time like this. He was nothing but a stooge and a stooge who didn't like his boss. Hirsh was another kettle of fish, worse because he was dangerous and unpredictable. There were times when Hirsh got fresh, so fresh you'd think he was the one who owned the *Daily News*. He might do something rash that would make a hell of a lot of trouble. Old Dougherty knew plenty about him and suspected that there was plenty more he didn't know. Hirsh was bigtime stuff. Maybe he wouldn't understand that you could get away with stuff in Chicago that wouldn't wash up in a middle-sized town like Plattesville.

And then, right in the middle of his worries, Old Dougherty would have to pass out a cigar or make a joke or slap somebody's back, or kiss a smelly baby.

And Jimmy. Whenever the old man caught a glimpse of him, it seemed to him that Jimmy was a stranger. He wasn't the Jimmy who usually went about, radiant, healthy, good-looking, followed by half a dozen girls, making everybody laugh wherever he showed up. This Jimmy looked gray and wilted. His heart wasn't in his job. Watching him during the afternoon, Old Dougherty kept thinking, "The damned fool! And he said he never had a hang-over." Whenever Jimmy grinned it was like the grin of a pair

[148]

of false teeth. When he shook hands it was like shaking hands with a wax dummy.

Twice during the afternoon Old Dougherty with Mr. Hirsh and Mr. Winterbottom retired to a room in Cousin Ira's hotel to discuss what course they were to take in replying to the opening article of the *Daily Shield and Banner's* campaign, but they came to no conclusion whatever because Mr. Hirsh's methods were inclined to be unorthodox, not to say strong-arm, and in Mr. Winterbottom whatever there had been of originality had long since been destroyed by Old Dougherty's steam-rollering. And each time, before they were able to get down to business, Ira Miller came with a message that Old Dougherty was wanted at once in the grove to present a prize. So at last, late in the afternoon, Mr. Hirsh and Mr. Winterbottom left together to return to the *News* office to confer again in an attempt to devise some plan which would meet with the approval of the old man.

Jimmy and Old Dougherty only left Millersville at seven o'clock when the only picnickers who remained were two middle-aged drunks deserted by disgusted wives. They were still sleeping peacefully at the far end of the grove.

Although father and son rode side by side all the way back to Plattesville, neither of them talked much. Jimmy's head ached, and when he tried to speak his throat felt paralyzed, and anyway he didn't give a damn about whether the picnic was a success or not or about what plan they were to adopt to meet the *Daily Shield and Banner's* attack. He couldn't think of anything except Jane Baldwin and the fact that he had never felt about any girl the way he felt about her. Wildly he kept asking himself, "What the hell do politics matter anyway? Who cares anything about running a town like Plattesville?"

Because he was by nature the healthiest of young animals the hang-over filled him with despair. He drove wildly, as he always did, and once or twice when the car jolted into a rut he thought, "There's something awful the matter with me. I'm going to die." And then almost immediately he thought, "I could scram from this town. Jane and I could clear out from the whole lot." But almost at once he saw that such a plan was impossible. Very likely she would never talk to him, let alone run off with him. And there was pride to be considered as well. He, a Dougherty, would ask no favors of a McLeod. It wasn't only pride which troubled him but Irish pride, the toughest, stiffest, most unnecessary pride in the world. And anyway, he couldn't double-cross the old man.

Suddenly he groaned aloud, and Old Dougherty asked, "What's the matter; you sick?"

"No. Nothing's the matter."

The old man didn't ask any more questions because he was worrying over his own problems and still trying to convince himself that nobody had anything on him, and that Mr. Hirsh wasn't just a dangerous racketeer and Winterbottom wasn't a complete and useless nincompoop.

Presently he said, "A pity it had to be cloudy today."

"Yeah," said Jimmy. "It was a damned shame."

The odd thing was that there hadn't been a vestige of a cloud in the sky throughout the whole day.

54

It was after eight o'clock when they finally arrived at the *News* office to find Mr. Hirsh and Mr. Winterbottom still waiting for them. They sat on opposite sides of the office, their backs to each other, each studying a copy of the *Daily Shield and Banner*. With a snort, Old Dougherty observed that, so far as he could see, very little conferring had taken place.

Gathered about the conference table none of them underestimated either the toughness of the task which confronted them or the cleverness of Mr. Richardson. Paragraph by paragraph, sentence by sentence, word by word, Old Dougherty, Mr. Hirsh and Mr. Winterbottom examined the full-page editorial. Jimmy took part, but with listlessness.

To their astonishment they discovered that not once in the whole editorial, covering an entire page, had a name been mentioned—either the name of Old Dougherty, or Jimmy, or Mr. Hirsh, or Magistrate Flynn or the Chief of Police Harry Bingham. Mr. Richardson had simply made grave and outright accusations of graft and corruption appealing to the consciences and honesty of the good citizens of Plattesville, and calling upon them to fix the responsibility upon the guilty parties. "It was not," he wrote, "for the *Daily Shield and Banner* to name the criminals. The citizens of Plattesville knew them only too well."

Such tactics confused the group about the conference table in the office of the *Daily News*. They could not defend Old Dougherty, the Mayor, the magistrate and the police chief without, at the same time, accusing them.

For three hours they argued, Old Dougherty holding the balance between the recklessness of the guinea pig Mr. Hirsh and the timorousness of the disarranged Mr. Winterbottom. Jimmy contributed no more than an occasional "Yes" or "No," and uttered the only words of wisdom during the entire conference when he said, "If you want my opinion, you'll ignore the whole damn thing." But he had neither the energy nor the spirit to push his idea and they took no notice of it.

At the end of the three hours they had framed a personal attack upon Mr. Richardson and secondarily upon Mrs. McLeod. When the editorial was finished they left it for Mr. Winterbottom to put into passable English.

In it they called Mr. Richardson a crank and an upstart stranger who had come to Plattesville to meddle and stir up trouble among its honest and peaceful citizens. It referred to what it called his "criminal record," pointing out that he had come to Plattesville as a vagrant and been arrested and convicted. He had, the *Daily News* continued, been kindly released on parole and had repaid the kindness of Police Magistrate Flynn and the citizens of Plattesville by attacking them and accusing them of corruption and vice. Mrs. McLeod, the *Daily News* treated as an elderly and kindly half-wit who had been victimized by an adventurer. They made no mention of Old Dougherty himself because they dared not without fixing the attack of the *Daily Shield and Banner* directly upon him.

It was, all in all, a feeble reply, and it was very bad tactics, for it gave Mr. Richardson, now warmed to battle, a chance on the following day to write one of his most elegant replies. Yes, he wrote, the managing editor of the *Daily Shield and Banner* had been counted as a vagrant simply because he had come to Plattesville out of luck and broke and looking for a job. Instead of acting as the Good Samaritan had acted in the Bible, the city administration had seized him, thrown him into jail and prosecuted him. It had meant to make him work in what was virtually a chain gang in order that the gangsters of Plattesville could collect from its citizens the pay roll which should have gone to Plattesville citizens out of jobs and needing the work. Then he launched into an account of the sufferings of workless honest men so moving and so eloquent, that Mrs. McLeod, reading it in proofs in the office, had burst into tears. At the end there was only a brief and dignified reference to Mrs. McLeod, "One of our oldest, best-known and best-loved citizens. Her character, her intelligence, her charm, her love of Plattesville and the county all place her in an impregnable position beyond all attack."

It was a great success, the editorial. It sold hundreds of papers and moved the soft-hearted to tears at the sufferings and mistreatment of honest men who came to Plattesville looking for work. For days afterward the gang of convicted vagrants which dug ditches and removed the garbage of Plattesville was troubled at its work by the kind glances and smiles and even gifts of chocolate and cigarettes bestowed on them indiscriminately— tramps, bums and honest workmen alike—by sentimental and soft-hearted Plattesville women. And Plattesville really loved Lavinia McLeod. It didn't like her attacked even by implication.

And the novel was having a great success. It wasn't until three days after the appearance of the first installment that Old Dougherty realized the subtlety of Mr. Richardson in placing "The Good Old Days" on the page opposite the editorial attacks. On the left hand one read of the existing decay and corruption, and on the page opposite, one read the history of the town, of the struggles of its earliest citizens to found a community where liberty, honesty, justice and charity should have a great place. In Mrs. McLeod's narrative there was a stirring account of the founding and activities of the first committees of vigilantes who brought to order the gamblers, the confidence queens, the bad men at the moment of the land rush. Tacitly, quietly, the juxtaposition of the two pages said, "What we need in Plattesville is a committee of vigilantes. What we need is a thorough cleaning up."

Suddenly the *Daily Shield and Banner* became the interesting paper of Plattesville. Nearly everyone bought it to learn the latest revelations and read the latest installment of "The Good Old Days."

It sold in bundles, and because everybody in Plattesville and the county took to reading it, advertisers came in in numbers so great that within a fortnight after the opening salvo of the crusade, two pages had to be added to every edition.

Across the Square in the office of the *Daily News*, Mr. Hirsh and the nervous editor and Old Dougherty held conference after conference, always with a division of opinion which only served to block and confuse every solution and every possible answer to the attacks which kept coming day after day like the fast punches of an expert boxer, giving them no time to gain their breath. Mr. Winterbottom developed a bad case of jitters and was for writing page after page of wordy editorials in reply, but Old Dougherty told him rudely that no one would even trouble to read them. Mr. Hirsh continued to propose out of his past, gangster methods of suppressing the *Daily Shield and Banner*. Once Old Dougherty would have agreed to these without a quiver. He would have put sand in the bearings of the *Daily Shield and Banner's* press or even consented to dynamiting or setting fire to the funny little old red-brick building which housed that hated journal; but now he was held back, not checked so much by his own conscience as by the spectacle of Jimmy's face growing leaner and more unhappy every day, and by the spectacle of his drinking. For the sake of Jimmy, he couldn't any longer use such methods, and there were Jimmy's as yet nonexistent children to be considered, the Doughertys of the future who wouldn't be like himself, racketeers and grafters, but gentlemen worthy of living in that huge Tudor house far out on Fleming Avenue.

Sometimes Jimmy came to the conferences, but more often than not he found an excuse for not appearing, and when he did appear, he only sat there glumly, offering no suggestions and only speaking to suppress some outrageous proposal of Mr. Hirsh, the guinea pig.

55

In Plattesville the hot sun of the Southwest rose and set the same as usual. There were cloudy days and bright ones and people went about their work as usual. But behind the weather and underneath the daily routine there was a difference. Beneath the surface there were excitement and a new curiosity and suspicions and nervousness. Citizens with a taste for reforming began to join the committee and organize meetings; others, with less active consciences, suddenly suspected that if things were changed in the city and county administration, the taxes might be less. And a great many of the old timers became interested because they discerned the prospect of a good fight.

Once or twice Old Dougherty was hooted at by boys in the street, and once when he passed a gang of convicted vagrants riding on top of a truck loaded with ashes and garbage, he was greeted by ironic cheers. His face turned bright red with anger, and for a moment his head whirled with dizziness and he thought, "I'm going to have a stroke. That's what I'm going to have." And it was all the worse because there wasn't anything he could do. If he came down on the prisoners in revenge, the *Daily Shield and Banner* would discover it and write fresh attacks.

And then the *Daily Shield and Banner* announced that one month before the Democratic primaries, the Reform and Fusion party would hold a monster parade, a torchlight procession such as had once taken place in reconstruction days when Plattesville was Plattesville. The primaries were still a good month away, but there should be, said the *Daily Shield and Banner*, plenty of time to organize. Mr. Richardson was playing up "The Good Old Days," and when Old Dougherty read that particular editorial, he swore long and loudly. He saw what they were trying to do; they meant to show him up as an outsider, a newcomer who had come to Plattesville to introduce graft and corruption.

In his own party he began to discover signs of restlessness and disloyalty. Handshakes were less cordial; the old sycophantic note began to disappear from the voices of those to whom he had given jobs or assigned some petty graft. Once or twice he noticed that men who once had treated him as if he were a king turned aside or left when he entered Hennessey's saloon. These signs did not fill him with despair; they enraged him and brought on again and again that feeling that he was about to have a stroke. And at last Gashouse Mary met him one day just as he was leaving Hennessey's place. This time, instead of pretending as she had always done that she did not see him, she came up to him and said, "Good morning, Mr. Dougherty. How's things?"

He tried not to betray his anger but managed to grin and say, "Okay. How are they with you?"

"Couldn't be better. I see quite a lot of your son nowadays."

His face went suddenly crimson and he said, "I told him not to go near your joint."

Gashouse Mary seemed untroubled. She only said, "Well, boys will be boys, and I suppose he's grown up now. It's pretty hard to tell a grown-up man what to do." She held out her hand and, startled, he took it and gave it a halfhearted flabby shake. "I'll be running along now," she said, "I'm pretty busy these days. Good-by."

And pertly she turned and started off up the street. Old Dougherty, looking after her, still speechless, felt a sudden desire to laugh. In his heart he had always liked Gashouse Mary, recognizing her as someone like himself who had always made war on society. He had suspected for a long time that she was helping that nincompoop Richardson, with all the knowledge of the underworld that had come to her out of years spent in St. Louis and Memphis and Natchez and New Orleans. For a long time he had suspected that she was providing Richardson with choice information and details, and now he knew it. He knew it by the flirt of her skirt as she walked, by the pertness of the plume in her picture hat. And he wanted to laugh because he couldn't help admiring the old girl. It was wonderful to be as spry as that at her age.

Like a lot of others, she thought she had him down. His big jaw set firmly and half-aloud he said, "I'm not through yet. I'll show the old bitch. I'll show all of 'em."

56

Late one afternoon, Mr. Richardson came into Mrs. McLeod's cubbyhole, shut the door after him, and sat down. Before he spoke he took off his glasses and looked at her.

"There are a couple of things on my mind," he said.

"Yes?"

"This is the first," he said, and passed a telegram to her.

She was growing a little weary of the crusade. The constant excitement, the constant attacking, had somehow worn her down, and there were moments now when she thought, "I'm too old to have started something like this. I wish it was over and finished. It's too much for me." And the weariness made her nervous and at times even afraid, as if it were herself and not Old Dougherty who was the guilty one. So when she took the telegram she was frightened.

With a faint twinkle in his gray-blue eyes he watched her as she read it. Twice she read it through, her hand trembling. Then she looked at him and said, "It's true, isn't it? I mean, it isn't a joke?"

"No, it isn't a joke."

"But twenty-five hundred dollars. That's impossible."

"That's just what I wired back."

She looked puzzled and asked, "You mean you told them you thought it must be a mistake?"

"Yes, if a publisher offers you twenty-five hundred advance, you'll get five thousand, so all I wired back was 'Not enough.' Mrs. McLeod, that's a great book. And I know what I'm talking about. The whole country is just waiting for that book."

She looked alarmed, "But I can't refuse twenty-five hundred dollars. I haven't the right to." Tears came into her eyes. "Now I may not get anything and you don't know how I need it."

Mr. Richardson leaned forward and patted her knee. "You leave that to me," he said. "If the first publisher who saw it thought that it was worth twenty-five hundred advance, believe me, you'll get a lot more. I'm awfully glad because it proves that The Book was as good as I thought it was."

She began to cry and said, "It can't be true. I'm sure it's a joke. It's a mean joke being played on me by somebody."

"No, it's not a joke."

"You don't know how badly I need that money. I didn't tell you because I didn't want to worry you, but the bank won't renew the first and second mortgages on McLeod's Folly."

"What bank?"

"The . . . County Bank."

The gray-blue eyes grew hard. "Old Dougherty's bank, isn't it?"

"Yes."

"I thought they'd be trying something like that."

"And they're coming down on me for the paper bill. Unless it's paid they won't deliver any more newsprint."

"They've been busy," said Mr. Richardson, "haven't they?" For a second time since she knew him she saw the veins stand out in his throat. For a second time she saw the pencil he held in his hand snap in two. Then he said, "Well, there's more than one way of killing a hog. We've got to go ahead with it now."

"With what?"

"We've got to come out in the open. We've got to take the next step. We've got to demand an investigation and an indictment. We've got all the dope we need. We can send Old Dougherty to jail for twenty years and that pip-squeak gangster Hirsh along with him. Bill Swain is ready to push the thing to the end. Even the local judge won't be able to let off the gang."

Suddenly Mrs. McLeod grew excited, "No, no. We can't do that. We can't go that far."

"Why not?"

"On account of Jane."

"What's that got to do with it?"

"It might end up by Jimmy going to jail too."

The rage of Mr. Richardson seemed to grow less violent. "No," he said, "I don't think we need worry about that. There isn't any evidence of Jimmy being mixed up in it. I think the old man has kept him out of all the dirty work. So far as I can see that's the only decent thing about him."

"But even if Jimmy wasn't mixed up . . . Old Dougherty is his father."

"So what?"

"It would mean that the grandfather of Jane's children was a jailbird."

"Oh!" said Mr. Richardson. "You've got a long way ahead of me . . . a couple of generations ahead of me." He fell silent and put on his glasses again.

Mrs. McLeod was trembling now. She'd forgotten the news of The Book. She'd forgotten the success of their campaign and the rising circulation of the *Daily Shield and Banner*. She said, timidly, conscious that she was being a little foolish, "I don't want to hurt anybody. I didn't know when we started this campaign that it would mean prison and ugly things like that. Sometimes I wish I'd never thought of it. Sometimes I wish . . ." She halted abruptly and her wrinkled face grew red.

Mr. Richardson grinned, "I know. You wish you'd never got me out of jail and given me a job."

"No, of course not. I don't mean that. Only . . ."

"That's the trouble with this reform business," said Mr. Richardson, "it all gets so mixed up."

"And there's Harry Bingham and his eight children. I don't want to get him in trouble."

Mr. Richardson swore quietly to himself. Then he said, "Now, sit down, Mrs. McLeod, let's talk this out." She sat down and he said, "Now, listen to me. You're up against a gang of crooks. They wouldn't spare you if they had you in the same spot. They're going to fight, and even if you stopped the campaign right now it wouldn't stop them. They're after our skins, and we've got to fight whether we want to or not. Look at them! They're calling in the mortgages. They're making trouble with the paper company. They'll do worse than that before they're through."

"I know," she said weakly. "Only it's so hard . . . to think of sending people to prison. Prison is so awful."

"They asked for it," said Mr. Richardson. "They've been asking for it for years, and now they're getting it, they can't take it."

Mrs. McLeod suddenly looked guilty. "I guess I've got to confess something."

"What?"

"I wrote a letter to Jimmy Dougherty."

"For heaven's sake, what for?"

[156]

With a great effort, her face crimson, Mrs. McLeod said, "I wrote and told him that Jane was in love with him and that she didn't have anything to do with the crusade and couldn't help it, and that when it was all blown over they ought to be friends again." For a second she was silent, struggling to go on with her confession. "It was worse than that, I told him that we wouldn't do anything really serious on account of him and Jane."

"Oh, my God!" said Mr. Richardson and began to laugh. He laughed and laughed until Mrs. McLeod began to be a little alarmed. Then, still a little breathless, he said, "There's nobody like you . . . nobody in the world."

"Were you laughing at me? I don't see what's so funny."

"No, not at you exactly. Maybe you're right. Maybe it's always better to be human. Only, don't you see, Jimmy'll take the letter right to his father and they'll have the laugh on us." His face grew suddenly serious. "You see, we can't stop it now. The whole State organization is mixed up in it."

"I wish we could."

"Did you tell Jane what you did?"

"Heaven's sake, no. I wouldn't dare. She'd kill me."

"How do you know she wanted you to do such a thing?"

"I didn't have to be told. Look at the girl."

"She does look kinda peaked, as Willie would say."

"And wild horses would never get the reason out of her. She just goes on saying she doesn't care if she never sees Jimmy Dougherty again. She says if she met him on the street she wouldn't speak to him. It's that damned McLeod pride."

"You don't seem to have much of it," said Mr. Richardson.

Mrs. McLeod grinned, "I once had a lot, but I've learned plenty. I'm an old woman. I've learned that sometimes pride can be your worst enemy. Sometimes it can spoil your whole life."

"You're the top," said Mr. Richardson. "You beat everything for getting things mixed up."

Suddenly Mr. Richardson grew serious, "How much is the mortgage?" he asked.

"It's for ten thousand dollars—a first mortgage on McLeod's Folly. And there's interest too—interest for two years." For a moment her eyes grew damp and he thought she was going to cry. "That's why I need that twenty-five hundred dollars so badly. It would help a little."

"Not enough," said Mr. Richardson. "Is there anything you can mortgage to meet it?"

"Everything's been mortgaged. There isn't any margin left."

For a time he was silent. Then he said, "I'll go and talk to them."

"It won't do any good, especially now after all that's happened."

"I wish I'd known about this before."

"I never thought they'd do anything like this."

And again he was silent before her great innocence. At last he said, "Who shall I see at the bank?"

"The president is Elmer Hoskins. I guess he'd be the best."

"Thanks, I'll have a talk with him. Forget about it for the moment. I think maybe I can fix it."

This time she could not stop the tears. They flooded down her face despite every effort to stop them. Sobbing, she said, "I don't see why you bother about me. You're so good to me. I'm such a muddled old fool."

Embarrassed, he bent down and put a strong arm about her thin shoulders.

"It's because I'm fond of you and I think you a wise and wonderful creature."

And after a little pause, the square angle of his jaw grew sharp and he added, "And because I'd like to give those bastards a good licking. . . ."

57

It was true that Jane looked peaked. Each day she grew a little more pale. She did her work, but listlessly, without the interest she had shown before the crusade began. And now, suddenly, the worst sign of all, the thing which had alarmed Aunt Vinnie more than anything else—she seemed to grow reconciled to the fact that everything was finished between her and Jimmy Dougherty. She even became amiable in a gentle way with Mr. Richardson and was no longer quarrelsome with old Willie Ferguson. She began to have what Mrs. McLeod called to herself "that old maid look" of resignation, almost of peace, that she had seen so often on the faces of aging spinsters of her own generation who had, when young, been disappointed in love. Mrs. McLeod knew that look; it was an awful thing in the face of a girl as young and pretty as Jane. She tried to tell herself that this sort of thing never happened any more, but she was not convinced, not with Jane's face there in front of her all the time, more listless, more gentle, more anemic every day. She had always thought Jane incapable of love in the sense she herself and a few of her generation had known it; Jane, she had always believed, was a modern young woman and love didn't make much difference to modern women. And yet, here was Jane's face, always in front of her, at breakfast in the morning, all day in the office, at home at supper in the evening, always with that patient, resigned "old maid look" in it. For Jane didn't even go out to the movies any more, even when Mr. Richardson asked her once or twice.

"It is," thought Mrs. McLeod, a little thrilled like the hopeless romantic she was, "just like the story of Romeo and Juliet."

And perhaps that was how the idea of playing Friar Lawrence and writing the letter had come to her.

The effect of the letter upon Jimmy wasn't exactly what Mrs. McLeod had expected, nor did he use it as Mr. Richardson had feared. When he read it his spirits rose and, then almost at once, fell again. Knowing his Jane he saw at once that Mrs. McLeod must have written it on her own, without Jane's knowing anything about it. It was just another of those crazy things Mrs. McLeod was always doing. And anyway, even if what Mrs. McLeod wrote was true, he couldn't desert his father now and go over to Jane, not now when the old man had his back to the wall and was looking more and more tired and ill each day. There was, Jimmy saw, no way out but to call off the whole crusade, and that he knew, better than Mrs. McLeod or Mr. Richardson, was now beyond possibility. The ball had started rolling, and nothing would be able to stop fanatics like the Reverend Mr. Simpson and Mrs. Mabel Urquahart Jenkins and people like Gashouse Mary who were out to revenge themselves. And Bill Swain who, after years, had found his chance to "get" his rival. You might call off Mrs. McLeod and even perhaps that fellow Richardson who, Jimmy suspected in his heart, wasn't a bad fellow. But the others . . . no, there wasn't any hope. He might have gone to his father and taken him at his word and asked him to give up the fight and go away, out of Plattesville, out of the State forever; but he couldn't do that either. It would be as bad as going over to the enemy.

And he was genuinely afraid now of Richardson. If Jane had given him up for good, she might get fond of Richardson, working there in the same office with him every day.

He didn't even answer the letter and he didn't show it to his father or any of the others. He simply tore it up and threw it into the wastepaper basket and went out to Hennessey's saloon to get a drink and play some billiards to get his mind off the whole thing. He told himself that it was all finished, and that he had got what he deserved for ever going around with a nice girl like Jane Baldwin, and getting caught by her. Maybe, he thought gloomily, he *was* shanty Irish. Maybe Fern Hedges *was* his kind of girl.

58

In the Flats along the river Gashouse Mary continued her campaign, growing perhaps a little too bold. Everyone—the longshoremen, the people who lived in shacks in the flood districts, the negroes, the urchins—knew her. Wherever she went her progress was marked by greetings and jokes and sometimes by cheers. For Gashouse Mary was a born politician of the old school. At Christmas she sent out fifty baskets full of food into the poor quarter and had a free soup kitchen running all day at the El Dorado dance hall. She helped out discouraged families with small loans and once or twice had saved a home from the clutches of the voracious banks. She had done all this out of the generosity of her heart and the ageless vitality which made her, even as an old woman, the best of company. And she did it because she was well off and hadn't a soul in the world to whom she might leave her money. Despite her talent for politics, she had kept clear of them since establishing herself in Plattesville—until Mr. Richardson and the *Daily Shield and Banner* began their campaign. Then she plunged, and all her kindness, all her generosity, all her full-bloodedness had its reward. The district along the water front, the region of the down-trodden, was suddenly hers. Even the organization of Old Dougherty availed nothing against her power. Old Dougherty could even pay men five dollars apiece to vote for him but most of them would, she knew, take the money, go to the polls and vote against him, if she told them to. They *knew* Gashouse Mary. She belonged to the good old days, and she had been among them for years. Even in her velvet suit and picture hat she never put on airs; she could exchange rough stories and swear with the worst of them; she was one of them, not like Old Dougherty, one of themselves, who had risen in the world and turned to exploiting them; she had lived too long in the midst of squalor and vice and misery not to be eternally human. And they knew, every man, woman and child throughout the dreary district, that they could count on her.

It was neither a taste for politics nor the zeal of a reformer which moved her now. She was, she knew, in moments which exasperated her, old and sometimes tired, too tired to battle against anything as strong as the Dougherty organization. She was moved rather by a liking for battle and a desire for revenge but, as the campaign progressed, she was moved more and more by her fondness for Mr. Richardson.

He came to see her a couple of times a week, to pick up bits of information and check up on the progress of her part of the campaign. Sometimes they sat at Gashouse Mary's table in the corner of the dance hall near the bar, but more often they retired to the parlor where they sat drinking beer served by Aida's cousin, Minnie. And while they sat there they talked of a great many things other than business, of Mrs. McLeod and her gentleness, of the old days, of glorious episodes in the past of Mary, of the misery of the river-front district and what was to be done about it.

"Nothing," Gashouse Mary said. "The Lord was right. The poor ye have ever with ye. There's nothing to do but make 'em as little miserable as possible."

And while they sat there Gashouse Mary with half her mind, that part of it which when she was young devoted itself to affairs of the heart, would appraise Mr. Richardson and regret that she was sixty-eight instead of thirty. She liked his clear healthy skin and the clearness of his eye, and that look he always had of having just emerged from the bath. And she liked the broad, powerful shoulders and the warmth that came into his voice when he grew indignant about Old Dougherty and the exploitation of the poor and unfortunate.

"What a fine figure of a man," she would think with that part of her mind which had always given itself over to what she called "amoor." "What I could have made of him if I'd only met him thirty or forty years ago."

She kept seeing him in the funny clothes of fifty years earlier, in the Plattesville of her childhood, heading a committee of vigilantes, a revolver strapped on each hip. With a mustache he would have looked remarkably like J. E. McLeod. But there wasn't anything to be done about all that now—nothing except to mother him and help him all she could.

Sometimes she asked him about his own life, but she got no further than she had on that first occasion. And once she tried to "pump" him about his feeling toward Jane. To which he responded, "I like her. She's a funny little thing, but I've got a girl."

"Where?"

"In the East."

"The kind of girl you're gonna marry?" knowing he very likely wouldn't have any other kind.

"Yes."

"When?"

"When I get through here and Mrs. McLeod doesn't need me any more."

Then one night after Mr. Richardson had taken up his hat and said, "I've got to go back to work now," they went through the passage into the El Dorado dance hall, and as they entered, Gashouse Mary stopped in the doorway and stood staring at two strangers standing at the bar. Turning back, Mr. Richardson waited for her and asked, "What's the matter?"

She moved out of the doorway and said, "I just thought I saw somebody I knew."

"Somebody important?" and by "important" she knew he meant someone involved in the campaign on Old Dougherty's side.

She seated herself at the table and said, "Maybe I was wrong. It's just a face I thought I knew." Then out of the side of her mouth she said, "Sit down and have a beer."

"I've got to go now."

In a fierce voice, filled with authority, she said again, "Sit down and have a beer. Don't look in that direction."

Then Mr. Richardson understood and said, "Okay!" and sat down.

They had a beer, and Gashouse Mary said suddenly, "Who's Mr. Hirsh?"

"I don't know. Mr. Hirsh, I guess."

"No, he ain't."

They were silent, drinking beer for a time. Then she said, "Do you know any of the Federal men—G-men, I mean?"

"No, why?"

"It might be a good idea to have them look into Mr. Hirsh."

A great light dawned in Mr. Richardson's brain. Until now he hadn't given any special thought to Mr. Hirsh, except to dislike him after that interview weeks before in the office of Old Dougherty when they had offered him a job. There was decidedly something slimy about Mr. Hirsh, and something sinister as well about the pink cheeks, the too soft hair, the tiny cruel mouth. Mr. Hirsh wasn't just a roughneck like Old Dougherty; about Mr. Hirsh there was something sinister. He saw him, suddenly, very clearly.

"Why did you ask that?" he said to Mary.

"Just a hunch."

Then as he finished his beer and lighted a cigarette, she said again, talking out of the side of her mouth, making a whistling noise through her false teeth, "When you go out of here, turn and go along the side of the dance hall till you get to the passage between it and my house. Go in there and you'll find a cellar door. Hide there and in a little while I'll come over and let you into the house."

"What for?"

"Do as I say."

"Okay."

Casually, Mr. Richardson rose and went out the front door of the El Dorado. Outside, slipping into the shadow, he followed Gashouse Mary's directions, and in a moment he found himself, feeling sheepish, pressed flat against the cellar door. A moment or two passed and then he heard the door of the dance hall opening, and in the shadow he peeped over the edge of the areaway and saw two men in the glare of the bright lights of the electric sign. They walked to the edge of the sidewalk and stood there for a moment, looking to right and left, with an air of indecision, talking together. He could not hear what they said, and in a moment they turned and hurried up the street toward the town in the direction he would have taken.

At the same moment from behind him, he heard the sound of a key turning in the lock and the low voice of Gashouse Mary coming between her false teeth. "Come in quick. I was right."

Inside she led him up the cellar steps back into the parlor.

By the glare of the big chandelier he saw a new light in Mary's face. She said, "Get out of here quick, before they double back."

[162]

"Who?"

"Those two mugs that followed you out. And go home by the back way through Alamo Avenue, and when you get there don't take the front path through those bushes. Go in by the stable. Is it unlocked?"

"I don't know."

"If it isn't, break a window or climb over the fence."

Mr. Richardson lighted a cigarette and asked, "What's all the mystery about?"

"Never mind. I've got a hunch." She took him by the arm. "I'm putting you out the kitchen door. And tomorrow buy yourself a gat."

He went, following her directions, and broke a window in the deserted stables of McLeod's Folly and entered the house by the cellar door, waking Aida in her room beside the kitchen. Clad in a kimono covered with enormous flowers and terrified, she unlocked the inside door when she recognized the voice.

"What's the matter?" she asked. "What you all comin' in this door for?"

"Never mind," he said, "I was just trying to get home without seeing somebody I didn't want to talk to." He placed his hands on her shoulders and said, "Don't tell Mrs. McLeod anything about it."

Aida looked at him showing the whites of her eyes. Then she asked, "What you all been up to?"

"I haven't been up to anything. You go back to bed and get some sleep."

This time she didn't answer him. She only relocked the door and muttering to herself thrust out her big enormous lower lip. By now he knew her well enough to know that she was hurt and indignant. The thrust-out lower lip was a prelude to a "misery." She was angry not because he had wakened her but because he had denied her his confidence.

59

A little while after Mr. Richardson left Gashouse Mary's, just as she had returned to her table, a fight broke out in the corner of the room beyond the jazz band. Nobody seemed to have started it, but when Jake, the chucker-out, sprang into the middle of it, swinging his great chimpanzee arms, it only spread until half the clients of the establishment were involved. Bottles and glasses flew across the room smashing windows and lights. The jazz band and the hostesses made for the door in a body and suddenly the room was filled with police. They arrested Gashouse Mary and one of the bartenders, and the rest of the crowd were driven from the room, all save four men Gashouse Mary had never seen before.

They put her and the bartender into the patrol wagon, and as it drove off she heard behind her the sound of breaking mirrors and bottles and the smashing of shattered furniture. Grinding her false teeth together, she began to swear. This time they were wrecking the place deliberately. There wouldn't be a stick of furniture left. But somehow Gashouse Mary didn't mind the wreckage. It wasn't the thought of that which made her swear. Her blood was up now. They could burn her house to the ground, but in the end she'd beat them. And in the midst of the fight a bit of knowledge had come to her as if sent by God. She knew suddenly who the men were—one of the two who had stood at the bar and afterward gone out to follow Mr. Richardson. Out of the past, the knowledge had come to her. It was Pugface Mahoney. He had dyed his hair and grown a mustache, but it was Pugface Mahoney just the same. She couldn't forget that bashed-in face, the hulking shoulders and the little pig eyes.

She thought, "I'll fix him. Only I've got to see Mr. Richardson. They'll probably try to keep me from seeing him. It won't do any good telling this gang of police about him. He's been hired—he and that other mug—by the Dougherty gang . . . probably he was brought to town by Hirsh, the little rat. Mebbe Old Dougherty doesn't even know anything about it."

It wasn't like Old Dougherty to bring gunmen into a fight like this. She didn't care anything about how much they smashed up the El Dorado. Swaying from side to side in the patrol wagon, she was relishing her knowledge that the Dougherty outfit had made a false move. You could get away with gunmen in a tough Chicago ward but not in a place like Plattesville. The people of Plattesville, even Dougherty's henchmen, wouldn't stand for it. It was probably that Mr. Hirsh who was responsible. And who in hell was Mr. Hirsh? Gashouse Mary had never seen him before he came to Plattesville, but she didn't like the smell of him.

In the morning they charged her with maintaining a public nuisance and held her for trial at twenty-five hundred dollars' bail, and old Flynn wouldn't let her use the El Dorado or her own house as security. Old Dougherty had seen to that. They meant to clap her in jail and keep her there so she couldn't go on taking votes away from him in the district along the water front. She didn't mind the visit to the jail. It wasn't the first time she had been there and, as she reflected with a decent sense of philosophy, it gave her a rest and time to make fresh plans against Old Dougherty and his gang. The only thing which troubled her was how to protect Mr. Richardson against Pugface Mahoney and his sinister accomplice.

She did manage to talk to Harvey Bingham, the police chief. To him she said, "What kind of a town is this getting to be when you bring in hired killers from St. Louis?"

Harvey said he didn't know what she was talking about and she believed him because Harvey wasn't very bright and no good at all at pretending. So she told him about Pugface Mahoney and gave a light sketch of his sinister and bloody history. When she had finished Harvey looked worried and scratched his head and said, "I don't know how a couple of guys like that got into Plattesville without my knowing it. We keep a pretty close check-up."

"Sure," said Gashouse Mary, "on tramps. But these guys ain't tramps. They're dangerous. You can pass on the word to your boss that if they pull off anything, he's finished. I'm an old timer here and I know what the people of the county are like. They'll stand for a lot of things but not for imported killers."

Harvey Bingham locked her in and went away still scratching his head in bewilderment. He didn't like what old Mary had just told him. Fun was fun, but you could run a good thing into the ground. And he had a wife and eight children to think about, and the thought of the killers in Plattesville made the hair that remained on his bald head rise on end.

60

In the morning Mr. Richardson was up early and out of the house before Mrs. McLeod and Jane had their breakfast. He didn't even wait for the postman on the chance of getting a letter with the Boston postmark.

At breakfast Aida had a "misery" and moaned a good deal, but this time Mrs. McLeod wasn't able to cure it because she didn't possess the means; she didn't know anything about Mr. Richardson's midnight return by the cellar stairs. She did notice, however, that Aida's "misery" had a new quality in it which puzzled her. Between moans Aida had an air of mystery and secret triumph. When at last breakfast was finished Mrs. McLeod said, "Aida, what on earth has got into you this morning?"

Aida answered stubbornly, "Nothin'. Ah got a misery."

"Shall I send for a doctor?"

"It ain't nothin' a doctor can cure."

Then Mrs. McLeod, losing patience, said, "Like as not it's the result of what happened the other night."

At this thrust the dark Aida would have blushed if she had been able. Nobody in the household had mentioned her going amok. Mrs. McLeod and Mr. Richardson had simply put her to bed and the next morning behaved as if nothing had happened.

"It ain't got nothin' to do with that." Then she turned suddenly and said darkly, "I doan know what's come over this house." And resentfully she added, "I guess it must be that crazy Mr. Richardson, I ain't never see anybody like him."

[165]

61

Meanwhile Mr. Richardson had gone to the office of the *Daily Shield and Banner*, where he set the paper on its way for the day. Then he wrote a note to Mrs. McLeod saying he had several things to do and might not return until noon. When he had left this on her desk in the cubbyhole he went out, and crossing the Square, entered the office of the First National Bank of Plattesville. The office was only just open and the cashier hadn't yet arrived, so he had to wait for a few moments, impatiently smoking and tapping his foot. While he sat there the office boy and the scrub woman had a conversation which slowly penetrated his consciousness.

The charwoman said with a rich Polish accent, "Well, they got Gashouse Mary last night."

The office boy said, "How?"

"A lotta bums broke up the place and they took her off to jail."

"What for?"

"For maintainin' a public nuisance." She wrung out her mop and added, "What's a public nuisance?"

"I guess it's what you call makin' trouble."

"She never made no trouble."

"Where is she now?"

"In jail."

"It's a lousy shame."

Slowly the conversation had filtered its way through the cloud of thoughts and plans that occupied the crusader's brain of Mr. Richardson. Now, suddenly, he listened to every syllable, thinking, "By God, they're a tougher lot than I thought." But the knowledge that there were a couple of mobsters in town probably looking for himself, and that the Dougherty crowd had framed Gashouse Mary, gave him pleasure. Those things meant that they were scared—scared of him and the *Daily Shield and Banner*, and the Reform Committee and the votes which, somehow or other, Gashouse Mary could control. It was the first definite sign that they were on the run. Like Gashouse Mary, he suspected Mr. Hirsh rather than Old Dougherty. And while he sat listening a new idea came to him.

Then the cashier came out to receive him, a thing which he had not expected. He was a plump little man with horn-rimmed spectacles. He said, "Glad to see you, Mr. Richardson. The telegram came all right. I've got the money. How would you like it?"

"Twelve thousand in thousand dollar notes and the rest in hundreds."

"The weather we're having! Just sit down, I'll have it for you in a moment. A great job you're doing with the *Daily Shield and Banner*. You must seem like a godsend to Mrs. McLeod."

"It wasn't God that sent me, she picked me up out of jail."

The cashier laughed with a shade of nervousness in his voice. "Yes," he said, "I heard all about that story. Ha! Ha!"

Then the cashier handed him the money in an envelope and he thrust it into his inside pocket.

"Thanks," said Mr. Richardson.

"That's all right. It's a pleasure. Any time we can oblige you. By the way, I've joined the Reform Legion. About everybody here in the office belongs."

"That's fine. Thanks again."

Then he went out thinking what a difference fifteen thousand dollars telegraphed from the First National Bank of New York City could make in the attitude of a bank cashier in a small town. Four months ago, if he had walked in as Mrs. McLeod found him beside the Soldiers' and Sailors' Memorial Fountain, he'd probably have been thrown out.

From the bank he went directly to the telegraph office and there he wrote one telegram to the headquarters of the Federal police in Omaha. It read: "Have hot tip on bad proposition. Communicate T. R. Richardson, *Daily Shield and Banner,* Plattesville." But the name signed to it was not "T. R. Richardson."

A second telegram he addressed to the Canadian-American Paper Corporation. It simply read: "Guarantee unlimited credit Lavinia McLeod, Plattesville *Daily Shield and Banner.*" Again it was signed by the name, half of which Jane had read through the damaged envelope with the Boston postmark. As he left the telegraph office the square jaw was a little squarer and the steel gray-blue eyes a little more steely.

Crossing the Square he went directly to the Ranchers' Bank in the Dougherty Block where after ten minutes' wait he was received by the president, with a good deal less warmth than the cashier of the First National had shown him. The interview didn't last very long. Mr. Richardson took the envelope containing fifteen thousand dollars in cash and laid it on the mahogany table, and in a little while he left the office with the mortgage of McLeod's Folly and something over three thousand dollars in his pocket.

From the Ranchers' Bank he went to the office of C. M. Landon, attorney-at-law. Mr. Landon was a lean, cadaverous and pious man, not the type which Mr. Richardson liked, but he was a smart lawyer and he was a member of the Reform Committee, and both these things, Mr. Richardson had need of at the moment.

For half an hour they talked together, Mr. Richardson explaining what had happened to Gashouse Mary and how they must get her out at once. Mr. C. M. Landon, who was, as well as being a smart lawyer, an elder in the First

[167]

Baptist Church, did not approve of Mary and wasn't sure that she and the town wouldn't both be better off if she stayed in jail. It took nearly twenty minutes to persuade him, but in the end he took down his hat and led by Mr. Richardson went to the magistrate's court.

62

Old Flynn, the magistrate, wasn't pleased at the sight of Mr. Richardson and the Baptist lawyer. From the moment he saw them come in quietly and sit down at the back of the courtroom, he couldn't keep his mind on the cases which came before him. In the mind of the magistrate the two were not simply a pair of citizens come to watch the proceedings of the court; they were birds of evil omen. And because he, like the rest of the Dougherty gang, was a little scared, they made him nervous. He had, it must be said, quite a lot on his conscience, and the presence of the leader of the crusade and one of the Reform Committee did not bring peace to his mind.

Worst of all there was the business of Gashouse Mary's bail. He was aware that he had overstepped legal bounds in denying Mary the right to furnish bail for herself, and he knew that C. M. Landon, however pious he might be, was a good lawyer and hard as the calloused sole of a stevedore's bare foot. People like that pair in the back of the courtroom upset him. Crooks he knew you could always deal with; a crook always had a price. But these two cranks! Fanatics, like madmen, were unpredictable. "Goddam it!" he thought, "why did I ever listen to Vinnie McLeod and let that bastard out on parole?" In the end, he had himself been responsible for the crusade which had upset the whole town and now threatened to wreck the machine they had built up so carefully, the machine which was so profitable to all of them. If he hadn't been a damned fool, that fellow Richardson would have been emptying garbage cans instead of stirring up trouble. It wasn't as if W. M. hadn't thrown it in his face twenty times since that opening salvo of the *Daily Shield and Banner*.

"Dismissed," he heard himself saying to the stevedore arraigned before him. "Next case."

And it boded no good that C. M. Landon himself had come to get Gashouse Mary out of jail. It meant that the whole town, good and bad elements, were uniting against the gang. Gashouse Mary and the Baptist elder were strange bedfellows.

And he was troubled too by the bit of news Harvey Bingham had told him just before he opened court . . . that there were a couple of gunmen in town. Who had brought them to town old Flynn didn't know, but he had a pretty fair idea.

[168]

As the last case was disposed of, he saw Mr. Richardson and C. M. Landon rise and come toward him. He knew what they were going to say and they said it.

Richardson, taking out two one-thousand- and five hundred-dollar bills, laid them before him and said, "We've come to bail out Mary."

There wasn't anything to be done but accept the bail and go through the formalities as if there was nothing unusual about the case. When they had been concluded, Elder Landon, with a look of an uncompromising Old Testament prophet, said in a voice of ice, "We might as well tell you that if Mary is convicted, the case will be appealed. If necessary, it will go to the Supreme Court of the United States."

And old Flynn, who for years had been bullying helpless and unfortunate prisoners, took it meekly. He only said, "The law must take its course."

"See that it does," said Elder Landon. "This case is going to be an issue." Then he and Mr. Richardson said, "Good morning," and walked out of the court, leaving a troubled magistrate wondering what they had up their sleeves that made them so sure of themselves.

63

No sooner had the doors of the city prison closed behind Gashouse Mary than she told Mr. Richardson and C. M. Landon all about Pugface Mahoney and his traveling mate. She knew pretty nearly everything there was to know about a mobster with a long record in river towns, and she spared no detail in the account she gave to Mr. Richardson and the startled Baptist elder.

When she had finished, his face was white and set. "It's an outrage!" he said in his icy voice. "Bringing gangsters to Plattesville. Something has got to be done about it."

"Go and see the chief of police," said Mr. Richardson. And away went Mr. Landon to the police station, his lean legs flying, the tails of his Prince Albert flapping about his bony knees.

Back in the office of the *Daily Shield and Banner*, Mr. Richardson went into Mrs. McLeod's cubbyhole, closed the door and handed her the canceled mortgage.

Her astonishment was so great that she could only stand there with the mortgage in her thin trembling hand, saying, "What's this?"

"It's the mortgage," said Mr. Richardson, "it's canceled."

"But how?" she asked.

"Never mind. I took care of it."

"But how?" Bewilderment blurred her features. "How could you do that?"

[169]

"Never mind," said Mr. Richardson, "I'll explain it all later. I've got plenty to write just now." And he left her standing there with the mortgage.

When he had gone, she examined it carefully, not that she would know anything about such things but because, mechanically, it seemed the thing to do. So far as she could see the mortgage was canceled: she was free of it, and suddenly for an instant, she felt happy and light as air, like a drowning woman from whose neck a millstone had been removed. And then the happiness left her, succeeded by alarm—alarm, oddly enough, over no threat nor any evil that was being done her, but over the magical quality of Mr. Richardson's intercession in the stream of her humdrum life. Who was he really? Why should he do so much for her? How dared she, a McLeod, accept so much from a stranger? Was she right to accept it? What would J. E. have said?

But when a little later he came into the cubbyhole and she said to him, "I can't allow you to go on doing things for me—things like this mortgage," he only replied, "We haven't time to argue about things like that now. And don't be too sure that I'm doing it for you. I'm doing it for myself too. Let it go at that. Maybe some day you'll understand."

His young face was very stern and for the first time there was a shadow of impatience in his voice. It seemed to her that he was almost cross, and she felt suddenly very feminine and helpless and bewildered.

Then he said, "You needn't worry about the paper bill, I've fixed that too." He touched her shoulder, gently, with an affection that surprised her. "Don't you worry. Just get on with your work. The Torchlight Procession Committee is meeting here as soon as the paper's gone to press, and I've got plenty to do before then."

She didn't know about Pugface Mahoney and his friend until Myrtle Ferguson came up about five o'clock bearing the first copy of the current edition. There, on the front page, with great headlines was the whole story— THUGS IMPORTED INTO PLATTESVILLE. LATEST NOVELTY INTRODUCED BY CORRUPT ELEMENT.

The story was admirably written. It related the destruction of the El Dorado dance pavilion, the arrest and charges against Gashouse Mary, and the presence in the dance hall of two well-known gangsters, both disguised but recognized none the less by witnesses who had known them before. It even gave their names—Pugface Mahoney and Little Hermie alias Herman Rizzio. The last name was a guess, a shrewd and lucky one on the part of Gashouse Mary: she knew the pair had worked together before in New Orleans and Memphis. The police, continued the article, had been warned of the presence of the killers in Plattesville, but they had not been found, and no great coöperation, the *Daily Shield and Banner* pointed out, was to be expected from a police force so dominated by the corrupt element in Plattesville. Until now, Mr. Richardson wrote, Plattesville had been free of the underworld element: it seemed that the enemies of law and order were prepared to stop at nothing. The presence of Pugface Mahoney and Little Hermie was an insult to every citizen of Plattesville.

As Mrs. McLeod read the story, cold thrills of terror ran up and down her spine. To Mr. Richardson she said, "Why didn't you tell me?"

"I didn't want to worry you."

"Now I won't be able to sleep a wink."

"They won't bother you."

"It isn't myself I'm thinking about. It's you."

"Don't worry about that. I've been through this before."

"You ought to have a bodyguard."

Mr. Richardson grinned, "It's not as bad as that." He patted her shoulder. "I can take care of myself."

But when he left the cubbyhole he found a bodyguard waiting for him. He stood in the doorway, his hat in his hand, rocking back and forth a little on his feet, his huge hands hanging down to his knees, for all the world like an orang-utan. It was Jake—Gashouse Mary's chucker-out.

The bouncer, grinning, handed Mr. Richardson a note written on Gashouse Mary's blue and gold stationery. It simply said that she was sending Jake as a bodyguard. She had instructed him to go everywhere with Mr. Richardson, even to McLeod's Folly to sleep outside his bedroom door.

"You can count on Jake," she wrote. "He's got a gat and he's pretty quick on the draw. I've told him never to leave your side and as he's not quite bright you won't be able to shake him even if you want to. But don't try to with those two bastards in town. I know what I'm talking about."

Grinning, Mr. Richardson tore up the note and said to Jake, "Here, sit down here." And Jake, with his great hands holding his cap between his knees, sat down grinning. From that moment he never left Mr. Richardson's side. When he rose from his desk, Jake rose too. When he went into the composing room or downstairs to see Myrtle, Jake went with him. He went even to the lavatory to wait outside like a faithful bloodhound.

From his corner, Willie Ferguson regarded Jake with awe and considered getting himself a bodyguard. For a long time Willie had been growing more and more nervous, and now the news that there were gunmen in the town made him resort more and more frequently to the bottom drawer for the bottled strength and courage which had never failed him. And Jane, from her desk, looked on, excited and a little impressed by the growing importance of the stranger, Mr. Richardson, a little thrilled by the presence of the gorilla Jake who had come up out of the exciting life along the river front about which she knew nothing at all.

64

At six o'clock, the editorial room began to fill up with the members of the Torchlight Procession Committee. The Reverend Mr. Simpson was there and Elder C. M. Landon, grim as ever and a little more triumphant, and Mrs. Mabel Urquahart Jenkins, and Jim Newman and several of the boys and Gashouse Mary, and Aida's cousin, Athena's boy, the poet, with Joe from Joe's Place. It was an impressive gathering because it included representatives from almost every element in Plattesville, and it was evident that half the committee—people like Joe of Joe's Place and Gashouse Mary and Jim Newman and the boys—were there not so much out of a desire to make Plattesville a moral paradise as because they had had enough of the rule of Old Dougherty and his gang.

The crusade, clearly, was taking care of itself. It was sweeping along now on its own impetus. It had perhaps gotten out of hand and was reaching a state beyond control. It was the kind of thing which couldn't have happened in the East. What Gashouse Mary said in the beginning was true: Plattesville and Calamos County liked a political fight and a good political fight had been long overdue.

65

At about the same hour, a troubled group assembled in the office of the *Daily News*. Old Dougherty was there, and Police Magistrate Flynn, and Harvey Bingham, and Mr. Winterbottom, and Mr. Hirsh, and a handful of less important members of the gang. Only Jimmy Dougherty was absent.

The group had been brought together by the story in the *Daily Shield and Banner* of the presence in town of Pugface Mahoney and Little Hermie, for Old Dougherty, with his old political shrewdness, had seen at once the damage that story did to his position. It was one more step in Richardson's campaign to make him seem an outsider, a crook who had come to prey upon the people of Plattesville, who imported gangster methods into a quiet, respectable city of the Southwest.

The only trouble was that nobody at the conference had seen the two killers, and nobody seemed to be able to lay hands on them.

Harvey Bingham, trembling a little, and accompanied by two fellow policemen, had spent the day searching dives, brothels and cheap hotels, pounding on doors with a drawn pistol in hand, only to discover when the doors were opened, familiar bad characters of Plattesville whom he already knew all too well. Old Flynn was noncommittal: he hadn't seen the gangsters, but he was too hardened and experienced to believe that things did not exist simply because he had not seen them. Old Dougherty himself was puzzled, like a bull which has been played by bullfighters too long. He chewed a cigar and glared and rolled his big grizzled head from side to side. The thing—the whole goddamned crusade—was getting out of hand. He had never believed it could happen. He hadn't believed that the West and the East could be so different, that the people of Plattesville would behave so differently from the people of South Boston or Chicago.

The timid Mr. Winterbottom was simply terrified, and Mr. Hirsh, the guinea pig, wore his rat expression and said that it was his opinion that the whole story had been made up by the *Daily Shield and Banner* and that there wasn't any such persons as Pugface Mahoney and Little Hermie.

At this Old Dougherty grumbled and roared and said, "If they are here I don't see who brought them here or what they're doing." Then irritably he turned to Harvey Bingham and old Flynn, "It's up to you to find 'em and run 'em out of town. Their bein' here ain't doin' us any good." He had a suspicion who had brought them to Plattesville and moved by that suspicion he glanced at Mr. Hirsh; but the little pale blue rat's eyes set in the pink face betrayed nothing whatever.

For a long time they talked round and round in circles, getting nowhere. Old Dougherty kept looking at his watch, wondering why Jimmy hadn't turned up yet, wishing he were there to help—not that he had been of much use lately, moping around as if he washed his hands of the whole affair—he just wanted to have him there in the room. It made him feel less lonely. And the old man was troubled because of a bit of news that had come to him by long-distance telephone from the State capital. It came from one of his henchmen, the district representative, who had been doing some investigating of his own. He had found out a lot of things, not very pleasant things, but the worst was that Bill Swain and his gang were planning to make the Plattesville investigation a State affair. They were going to place the whole thing beyond the reach of the judges over whom Old Dougherty had control. They were going to make it a criminal affair. That was another reason why Old Dougherty didn't like the mysterious presence of Pugface Mahoney and Little Hermie in Plattesville.

And while he sat reflecting grimly on the development of the crusade in the last few hours and listening with only half his mind to the whinings of Mr. Winterbottom, the door suddenly opened and Jimmy came in. It didn't open normally and simply, the door; it was flung open. And the Jimmy who came in wasn't the moping, listless Jimmy of the past three or four weeks; it was a Jimmy whose good-looking face was flushed, whose blue eyes shot fire. Slamming the door behind him, he said, "What are those two gangsters doing in Plattesville?"

For a moment there was silence and then Old Dougherty answered, "We don't know. That's what we want to find out."

[173]

"Well, the other outfit didn't bring them here."

Mr. Hirsh, the rat-faced, said smoothly, "How d'you know they didn't? Gashouse Mary seems to know about 'em."

Jimmy turned to him and pounded on the table. "Because I've just been talking to Gashouse Mary. I've got a damned good idea who brought them here. And they're gonna scram. Goddamned quick!" He threatened Mr. Hirsh across the table. "Get me? They're gonna scram!" Then turning to the others he said, "I'm going to fight. I'm ready to fight now. But I'm not going to have guys like that fighting on my side. It's cost us plenty already. That kind of thing can lick us." Again he turned to Hirsh and asked, "Where are they now?"

Blandly Mr. Hirsh replied, "I don't know. I don't know anything about them."

"Well, you'd better find out." To Harvey Bingham he said, "You'd better shake your tail too. And you're going to send a couple of cops to guard the *Daily Shield and Banner* office as long as those two rats are in town."

Mr. Hirsh said sweetly, "I don't know what I can do about it. I don't know anything about them."

Leaning back in his chair Old Dougherty watched Jimmy with a new light in his eye. This was *his* Jimmy. This was a real Dougherty with Irish fight in him. The listlessness and despair went suddenly out of him.

Then Jimmy turned to the old man and said, "Come on, let's get out of here and make some sense." To the others he said, "And you'd better get busy running those two mugs out of town."

It was what Old Dougherty had wanted. He'd known all along that the cards were stacked against him in the fight and he knew that nearly every move they had made had been stupid and ill-timed, but somehow he hadn't been able to pull himself up and think and fight with any sense or spirit. Perhaps he'd had power for too long, or perhaps he was getting old. And now Jimmy had smashed open the door, come into the room and saved the day— a Jimmy who was reborn, a Jimmy who was what he'd always hoped Jimmy would be. Quietly he rose and followed Jimmy out the door, leaving behind them the chief of police, the police magistrate and Mr. Winterbottom bewildered and shaken, and Mr. Hirsh, the rat-faced, feeling smug and sure of himself, much too sure to be safe.

In the hallway outside Old Dougherty put a delighted arm about Jimmy's shoulder and said, "What's got into you, boy?"

Jimmy lighted a cigarette and threw away the match with a gesture of violence. "I'm sick of you being the goat for a lot of half-wits and small-town crooks," he said. "We're going to fight now, but not the way that shrimp Winterbottom and that crook Hirsh fight. Plattesville's a good town and it's our town too as much as anybody else's. I've lived here all my life. There's no reason why there shouldn't be a good strong Democratic organization but not the kind of a one that guys like Hirsh and old Flynn want. You can't get away with Hirsh's methods in a town like this. Come on, you and I are going to eat out at Millersville and make some sense."

Chuckling, the old man followed his son down the stairs. As they got into the car and Jimmy drove off, Jimmy said, "And that was a dumb idea, shaking down Gashouse Mary and breaking up her joint. Who the hell had that idea?"

"It was old Flynn," said his father.

"Better drop him overboard. We've got to change all our tactics and take up a new line. We've got to get rid of old Flynn and that bastard Hirsh and maybe even that nitwit, Winterbottom."

"That's what I've been waiting for," said Old Dougherty, "and you're the boy to do it." There was a grin on his face, a grin of delight at the change in Jimmy. He didn't even mind the seventy miles an hour the olive-green roadster was making along the Millersville Pike. But in his heart he wasn't at all sure that the change in tactics wouldn't come too late. He wasn't at all sure that the jig wasn't already up. But he betrayed not so much as a hint of this to Jimmy. He couldn't throw cold water on the boy's fighting spirit now.

66

It might not have been too late for the leopard to change his spots; throwing overboard old Flynn and Hirsh might have made a difference because the personal following of Old Dougherty was big enough in the town and all of Plattesville liked Jimmy Dougherty: it might even have been that Bill Swain would have changed his course and called off his plan to bring criminal charges against Old Dougherty. Indeed, the whole story might have been different but for what happened during the next twenty-four hours.

Mr. Richardson worked late at the office that night, long after Mrs. McLeod and Jane and Willie had left. Save for himself and Jake, the whole place was empty, the rattling linotype in the back room and the rumbling press belowstairs silent now that the day's work was finished. He wrote a letter to Bill Swain and one to the agent in New York who was handling Mrs. McLeod's book and one to the Canadian-American Paper Company confirming his telegram of the early morning. And all the while just beside him at his elbow sat Jake, the bodyguard, his face as empty as a vacuum, fashioning toys out of bits of cardboard and paper clips with his giant chimpanzee's hands, the big old-fashioned six-shooter beside him on the corner of Jane's desk.

When he had finished writing his letters Mr. Richardson went to work

[175]

fashioning fresh editorials, making notes, outlining new angles of attack for the following day. The *Daily Shield and Banner* would appear three or four hours before the Torchlight Parade and that particular issue must be good and strong in order to rally the whole town to the procession.

He had been working for about an hour when there was a knock at the door and he turned and said "Come in." At the sound of the knock, Jake dropped his toys, picked up the six-shooter and covered the door. It opened slowly and there came into the room, not Pugface Mahoney and Little Hermie, but a middle-aged woman neither of them had ever seen before.

She was a raw-boned female, with a tired gray skin, a hard mouth and a grim expression about the eyes. She wore a suit of black that was worn and shiny with a moth-eaten collar of skunk fur. At sight of them she said to Jake, "Put down that gun," and as Mr. Richardson rose she came toward him and said, "I suppose you're Mr. Richardson?"

"Yes."

"So you're the young man who's stirred up so much trouble?"

Mr. Richardson grinned and said, "I suppose."

"Well, I'm Mrs. Homer Winterbottom, wife of the editor of the *News*." They shook hands and Mr. Richardson said, "Won't you sit down, Mrs. Winterbottom?" and to Jake he said, "Put away that gun—out of sight, Jake."

As she sat down he divined that despite the weather-beaten warhorse exterior, Mrs. Winterbottom was nervous about something. There was an odd shyness about her and as she sat down she clasped the big hands covered with shabby gloves tightly together over the shabby handbag she carried.

Then she said, "I suppose you're surprised to see me here?"

"I'm pleased to see you," said Mr. Richardson.

"Are we alone?" She looked nervously over her shoulder and then at Jake.

"You needn't worry about Jake."

"I'd rather have him go away. What I want to say is very private."

Mr. Richardson grinned. "All right," and turning to Jake, he said, "You go and keep guard outside the door, Jake. Somebody might come up the stairs and into the room before we knew it. If you're at the top of the stairs you can pot them right off."

Shaking his head, Jake rose clumsily and obeyed him, and when the door had shut behind him, Mrs. Winterbottom drew her chair nearer to Mr. Richardson and after a preliminary gulp, said, "It's about the *News* and W. M. Dougherty. I've got a lot I want to tell you. Maybe you think it's funny—me coming here to double-cross the old man—but it isn't. He's been starving Homer and me and the children for nearly ten years now, and he treats Homer like he was dirt under his feet. And Homer's a good editor.

He's smart and able, but W. M. Dougherty has ruined him. He hasn't got any future left."

She waited to see what Mr. Richardson would say, but he couldn't, it seemed, think of anything better to say than, "I didn't know anything about that. I couldn't very well know."

"Nobody could. Nobody does," said Mrs. Winterbottom, clasping the worn handbag with greater passion. "Everybody thinks that Homer has a good job and I ought to be thankful . . . nobody knows how W. M. has underpaid Homer and tortured him . . . yes, tortured him for years. Homer is a sensitive man. Tonight he came home down in the mouth, discouraged, and said he guessed he'd have to quit because he couldn't stand it any longer. It's worse than it used to be on account of that man Hirsh. Ever since he's come into the *News* office he's tortured Homer too." She paused and looked down at her handbag and Mr. Richardson saw that it was because there were tears in her eyes. "We've got eight children we've got to think about. A newspaperman oughn't to have any children at all."

Then she looked at him again as if wondering whether she dared to go on. Suddenly she plunged, "I've got a lot of information for you and tips about more information. There's a lot of stuff W. M. couldn't keep Homer from knowing about, so I just sat down tonight when Homer went out and wrote it all down." She opened her handbag and took out a paper covered with big emotional writing. "Homer doesn't know I'm here. He doesn't know anything about it. And I don't want anybody to know."

"Of course not," said Mr. Richardson, "I'll never tell anybody. You can trust me."

"Maybe it'll help you and Bill Swain. It's about time this place got cleaned up. And I guess Homer and me won't be any worse off, now that Homer's made up his mind to quit."

Mr. Richardson waited, looking embarrassed, and she said, "I know all about the scandal of the Halstead Street sewer, and about the shakedown of those houses on Franklin Street and plenty more. Old W. M. made Homer help him sometimes with his dirty work. And there's plenty more— enough to send old W. M. to jail."

Then she laid the papers on the table and while Mr. Richardson listened and made notes rapidly, she poured out all she knew of the workings of the Dougherty machine in Plattesville. The account came out in a torrent, driven by the pressure of ten years of resentment and suffering. A good deal of it Mr. Richardson already knew, but there was a lot more that he didn't know. The difficulty was to bring order out of the flood of memories, hints and accusations. A dozen times he had to stop her to ask, "When did that happen?" or "Who was in on that?"

As she talked the grimness went out of her face. It was as if the outpouring came as a relief, as if the passion and resentment of years had finally shattered the dam which held them in and brought release at last. At the end of an hour she finished, saying abruptly, "That's all. If I think of anything else I'll let you know, somehow."

"Thank you, Mrs. Winterbottom," said Mr. Richardson. "What you've told me is very valuable."

"You can use it all. Only you mustn't tell where it came from."

"You can trust me."

She rose, timid once more but at the same time aggressive, and said, "I'll go now. I've got to be home before Homer gets there. He went out to Hennessey's saloon and I guess he'll get himself pretty drunk. I didn't mind tonight. He had a good bust coming to him."

He got up and went with her as far as the top of the stairs, where Jake stood slouched against the wall. He watched her descend and watched her peer into the Square cautiously before stepping into the light. Then he turned and said, "Well, Jake, I guess we'll go home now," and returning to the office he gathered up the notes, put them into a dispatch case, turned out the lights and locking the door, set off across the Square with Jake at his heels like a faithful Great Dane.

67

The shaggy lilacs and syringas bordering the path that led up to McLeod's Folly made an ideal ambush. And Mr. Richardson and Jake were potentially perfect victims for an ambush, the one absorbed profoundly in his plans for the crisis of the campaign, the other slouching along at his side like some friendly jungle animal. Jake wasn't exactly an intellectual companion nor had he any genius for stimulating conversation, so on the way from the *Daily Shield and Banner* office to McLeod's Folly they walked side by side in silence.

Once Mr. Richardson said, "You might as well go home and sleep in your own bed, Jake. Nothing's going to happen to me." But Jake was not to be persuaded. "Mis' McGovern told me I was to stick to you like flypaper," he said, "and that's the way I'm gonna stick."

When they turned in at the rickety gate, Jake, moved by some animal instinct, drew his six-shooter out of its holster and held it ready. The sight of the old-fashioned revolver shining in the light from the street lamp caused Mr. Richardson to hesitate for an instant; perhaps the thought occurred to him that after all it might have been wiser to come in by the window of the deserted stable and the cellar door. Then he laughed and said, "Come on, Jake."

Jake advanced first, boldly, with the six-shooter held in front of him.

Mr. Richardson followed, the grin on his face hidden by the darkness. As they reached the bottom of the high steps leading up to the door Mr. Richardson laughed and said, "You see, Jake. There wasn't any danger."

But at the same moment came the muffled roar made by a modern—a very modern—gun. Mr. Richardson's hat flew off his head, and as if the impetus of the bullet had carried him forward, he shot up the steps and into the house. At the same moment Jake ducked and took refuge in an angle of the high stoop and from there he waited for a moment watching the flash which came from the bushes as the sawed-off shot-gun, or rather both the shot-guns, fired in the direction of Mr. Richardson's heels. Then carefully he pointed his old cannon at the spot in the lilacs where the flashes appeared. Five times he fired carefully and deliberately and at the fourth shot there was a yell followed by silence. The sixth shot Jake kept in reserve.

For perhaps three minutes there was silence and then, emerging cautiously, he reached the foot of the steps and dashed into the house. Inside in the hall Mr. Richardson was seated on the settee, looking a little dazed and wiping the blood from his head with a handkerchief. Mrs. McLeod, in an old dressing gown, her hair hanging about her tired face, stood over him crying and wringing her hands and saying, "I knew it would happen. I knew it would happen. Are you all right?"

"I'm all right," said Mr. Richardson, "it's nothing."

Then, wailing, Aida appeared and Mrs. McLeod said, "Go fetch some hot water and cloths."

Jane wasn't there because she was already on the telephone calling the police, a Jane suddenly full of decision, in whom all the fighting blood of the McLeods had suddenly been roused. When she got through to the police station, she said in a voice filled with authority, "Get a couple of police up to McLeod's Folly right away! And no damned nonsense either! A man's been shot and there's gangsters on the place!"

When she returned to the hall she found Mrs. McLeod and Aida bending over Mr. Richardson, dabbing nervously at the spot where the slug which had taken his hat off had cut the scalp. She saw at once that her Aunt Vinnie's hand was too unsteady to be of any use and that Aida wasn't much good as she only kept on howling and wailing, so she said, "Here, let me do it," and taking the bowl of water from Aida and the cloth from Mrs. McLeod she said to Aida, "Go and get the iodine out of the bathroom and bring the whisky."

68

By the time the police arrived Mr. Richardson was on his feet again, his head bound up in a bit of torn sheet, none the worse save for a slight headache. It was Mrs. McLeod who had given way. Lying back in one of J. E.'s leather chairs, she was having Bourbon poured between her colorless lips by Jane. Aida wasn't moaning any more. She had pulled herself together and was in a good jungle rage, not one of her sulking rages, but a wild one which found an outlet and a relief at the moment Jake opened the door upon Harvey Bingham and two policemen. At sight of them she cried, "A fine set of police you all is . . . lettin' a man like Mr. Richardson get shot at! A fine set of lazy tramps!"

Nobody could get in a word until her beloved Mr. Richardson bade her be quiet. She would do anything Mr. Richardson said, especially now when it was Mr. Richardson, the martyr, his head inclosed in a blood-stained bandage who spoke. She stopped shrieking but did not remain altogether silent. From a point behind Mrs. McLeod's chair she continued to grumble and mutter, glowering at Harvey Bingham like a voodoo witch.

As for Mr. Bingham, the chief of police, he looked sleepy, bewildered and scared. Vaguely, he was aware that all this was going to react upon him, the whole weight of it would come on his head, not only the disapproval of the whole town but the fury of Old Dougherty and Jimmy as well because he hadn't caught the two gunmen and he hadn't sent a couple of policemen to guard Mr. Richardson and the *Daily Shield and Banner* office. Standing there, upset by the spectacle of Mrs. McLeod's hysteria and Aida's witchlike muttering, Police Chief Bingham knew that in this affair there had to be a goat, and he knew too that he was it. Nothing could save him now: he had lost out with both sides. And the spectacle of the smart Mr. Richardson with his head wound about with a bandage so big that he seemed to be wearing a turban, only increased his alarm. The grin on Mr. Richardson's face made his blood run cold.

There wasn't anything to do now but to put on an air of authority, and when Harvey Bingham assumed authority he became pompous. His face bright red with alarm and confusion, he drew himself up and said to the two policemen, "Go and search the bushes. I'll take charge of the investigating here."

The two policemen—one of them had gloated over Mr. Richardson on that day, long ago, when he was arrested—appeared to have no great desire to "search the bushes." One of them suggested that it would be much easier to search the bushes by daylight, but this did him no good because Police Chief Bingham had what was left of his face to save. Turning on his uneasy subordinate, the easy-going Harvey Bingham became the incarnation of Scotland Yard, of G-men, of the French Sûreté Générale: in a voice of thunder he said, "You heard my orders! Search the bushes!" And the two policemen, overwhelmed by the dramatic spectacle of their chief's sudden transformation, left the room with drooping spirits. At the door, Jake with his six-shooter joined them.

When they had gone, the pomp went out of the Chief. He could take out his uneasiness and ill-temper on his subordinates, but with the others in the room such tactics were no good, and he knew it. So turning to Mrs. McLeod, he said, "I'm sorry, Vinnie, that this happened. We've been looking all day for those two guys."

It was Jane who answered him, a Jane still fiery and filled with McLeod spirit. "Plattesville's come to a pretty pass," she said, "when a citizen can't even be safe in his own dooryard."

"Oh, we'll catch them all right, Miss Baldwin. Don't you worry. We've telephoned to every town for a hundred miles around to be on the lookout for them."

This time Aida answered him, "And Mr. Richardson mighta been dead and cold by now. It's pretty smart to lock the barn after the horses is all stolen."

Ignoring her, the Chief took out a notebook and pencil and addressed Mr. Richardson, "Now, Mr. Richardson, tell me how it happened."

So Mr. Richardson told them the story, which was simple enough, but before he had finished, Jake appeared in the doorway of the library. The six-shooter was stuck in his belt and he walked into the room with a swagger, swinging his apelike arms. His big mouth was spread to twice its size in a grin which showed his big irregular teeth.

They turned to look at him and he said, "Well, I got one of 'em."

"What do you mean, Jake?" asked Mr. Richardson.

"I got him right through the haid. They're a-carryin' him in here now."

By the time they had left the library and entered the hall, the two policemen were coming through the front door carrying between them the unconscious form of the man they had found in the tangled lilacs and syringa bushes. They laid the man on the floor of the hall. One of the policemen took off his cap, wiped the sweat from his forehead, and then ran his handkerchief round the circumference of the leather band inside his cap.

"Where's the telephone?" he said. "I gotta get an ambulance."

Aida, still muttering, led him to the telephone, and when she returned Mr. Richardson was on his knees beside the unconscious gunman.

"He isn't dead yet, but you can't tell how bad the wound is. Can't do anything about it until a doctor comes." Then he looked at Police Chief Bingham and said, "I guess if he gets well and can talk, your friend Mr. Hirsh'll have to clear out of Plattesville."

For a moment the police chief stared at him, and then in a slow-witted gaze a light appeared and he said, "That's funny. I never thought about

[181]

that. I never thought about it bein' Hirsh at the bottom of the thing." And on the good-natured, easy-going mouth appeared the shadow of a grin.

Aida slapped Jake on the back and said, "You're a right smart shooter, Jake. It musta been the Angel of de Lawd that pointed that gun for you." And once again the wide, shag-toothed prideful grin appeared on Jake's face.

Then the door opened and Gashouse Mary came in. She was dressed only in high-heeled slippers, a hat and a nightgown with a purple coat thrown over it, and at sight of the little group in the hall she looked straight at Mr. Richardson and said, "You all right? You ain't hurt much?"

"No," said Mr. Richardson, "I'm not hurt at all."

"Minnie heard about it at Joe's Place. I put on a coat and came right up here." Then she looked down at the unconscious form of the gunman and said, "That's him all right . . . Pugface Mahoney . . . dyeing his hair and mustache couldn't change that mug." Then she asked, "Who got him?"

"It was Jake," said Mr. Richardson, and Mary threw her arms about Jake and kissed him on one cheek and said, "God bless you, Jake!" Then turning to Harvey Bingham she said, "A fine chief of police you are . . . arresting me and letting things like that cokey Pugface run loose in Plattesville." With the toe of one slipper she touched the leg of the unconscious gunman and said to Jake, "Too bad you didn't kill him."

"No," said Mr. Richardson, "he can talk plenty when he comes round."

The ambulance arrived and the unconscious Pugface was borne away, followed by the two policemen and the chief of police. He was glad to escape the temper of Jane, the scorn of Gashouse Mary, the imprecations of Aida and the gentle look of reproach in the eyes of old Mrs. McLeod. But he felt a little relieved—that guy Richardson had given him a little clue. Dully, he divined that Richardson was right. It must have been Hirsh that brought these two gunmen to Plattesville. Now, maybe he wouldn't be made the goat after all—at any rate, not the whole goat.

The intern who came with the ambulance unwound the yards of bandage that encircled Mr. Richardson's head, and while Aida, Gashouse Mary and Mrs. McLeod leaned over him with murmurs of concern, had a quick glance at the wound. He said it wasn't anything at all, just to put iodine on it, and the yards of bandage weren't necessary. A bit of cotton and a couple of strips of adhesive tape would serve just as well.

When the intern had gone, Aida said, "I'll make you all some cocoa." But Mr. Richardson said he thought they all deserved something stronger than cocoa and told Aida to go and get the Bourbon and some ice water.

"We'll all have a drink and then get some sleep. Tomorrow is going to be a big day," he said.

"And how!" said Mary. She was triumphant now, for her political sense, like that of Mr. Richardson, understood the full significance of what had happened.

While Aida brought the Bourbon Mrs. McLeod began to cry gently and said, "If I'd ever dreamed of all the trouble it's caused, I'd never have had the crusade."

Mr. Richardson took her hand and patted it. "Don't you worry, it's coming along fine. What happened to me isn't anything. I'd be willing to be shot up a lot worse than I am. It would be worth it. And I guess my gunman friend, even if he died, wouldn't be a great loss to anybody."

"You said it," said Gashouse Mary.

Then Aida appeared and they all drank to the success of the crusade. To Mr. Richardson and Gashouse Mary victory seemed very near. Mr. Richardson, still trying to reassure Mrs. McLeod, said, "We've got them where we want them now. They'll be fighting among themselves now. They'll try to make the chief of police the goat and he'll turn on Hirsh." He slapped his leg. "Wait'll you see tomorrow's paper."

Then Gashouse Mary bade them good night, and when Mr. Richardson suggested that Jake should see her safely home, she said, "No, I've got a taxi waitin' for me. Jake's gonna stay here and look after you all." And turning to Jake she said, "You can sleep on the hall settee and if that other swine turns up you can plug him too." Waving her hand in a gesture of farewell, she added, "We've got 'em where we want 'em now," and gathering the coat over her pink nightgown, she went out the door and down the worn steps of McLeod's Folly between the ancient ragged lilacs and syringas.

Jane was the first up the big stairway. She went silently and without even troubling to say good night to the others, because she did not dare to speak lest she should burst into tears. The emotion which swept her, like one of the tornado winds which sometimes came down from the hills beyond Millersville and buried Plattesville in dust, was compounded partly of rage and partly of bitter sorrow. Even the rage was not simple; it was directed at Jimmy Dougherty and at herself for ever having liked him or believed in him, and the bitter sorrow arose from the knowledge that Jimmy had made a fool of her.

She had believed in him in spite of everything. She had ignored Aida's hint that you couldn't touch pitch without being defiled. She had held out in the face of Aunt Vinnie's obvious sorrow over her attachment. She had refused, even when her pride had been hurt by the story about Fern Hedges, to believe anything against him. She had fought against the influence of all the others, against her own better sense, against her own McLeod pride, and all it had brought her was humiliation and disillusionment. Because now she couldn't any longer deceive herself; she couldn't any longer pretend that the Doughertys weren't as black as they were painted.

They had brought gunmen to town to shoot Mr. Richardson. There wasn't any doubt about that. Mr. Richardson was sitting downstairs with a bandage on his head and in the hospital was a real gunman with a bullet through his head. But for luck, Mr. Richardson would be dead now, and after that perhaps they'd have shot poor muddled Aunt Vinnie or tipsy Willie Ferguson or even herself.

In her own room she turned up the light, sat down in an armchair and lighted a cigarette. She couldn't undress or clean her teeth or do anything until she got things straightened out in her mind, because she wasn't sure yet that the whole thing wasn't a nightmare and that she wouldn't wake up and find that it wasn't true at all, that none of it had ever happened.

Things like that couldn't happen in a nice place like Plattesville. Even Old Dougherty couldn't plan such things, and certainly not Jimmy—not the Jimmy whose grin was so pleasant and so devastatingly innocent and disarming, not the Jimmy who had taken her to Millersville and to supper so many times. But it was true. At last, after three cigarettes, she couldn't hope any longer that she'd waken and find that the whole thing was a nightmare. And presently she knew what she would do—the only thing she could do to save her self-respect, her pride, to make it possible to go on living. She had to write Jimmy a letter and tell him exactly what she thought.

So when she had undressed, thinking all the time what she would say so as not to make a bigger fool of herself, she put on a wrapper and sat down at her desk.

She wanted to address him as "Dear Mr. Dougherty," but that she knew would sound silly. It might even make him laugh. "Dear Sir" was even worse. For a long time she searched in vain for some mode of address that would convey her feeling of coldness, her disgust and a sense of finality, but everything she tried sounded silly, and in the end she was forced to address him as "Dear Jimmy." Nothing else was possible.

Once she began writing she wrote rapidly in a big sprawling emotional handwriting that seemed out of all proportion with her diminutive size. She wrote:

Dear Jimmy—I only want to write to say that I never want to hear your name mentioned again. If, by chance, we should ever meet on the street I'd take it as a great favor to me if you'd turn into a doorway so that I wouldn't have to look at you. That's the way I feel. A snake or a rat would disgust me much less than the sight of you or your father. After what has happened tonight you both ought to be ridden out of town on a rail. That's what happened to people like you in the days when my uncle J. E. was alive. I count every hour I ever spent with you as worse than lost.

Jane Baldwin.

Once she read the letter through wondering whether she could improve it and taking up the pen, she added a line beneath her signature. "Until now my heart wasn't in the crusade. I never worked for it because of you, but now that I know what you are, I shan't rest until you're driven out of Plattesville."

Placing it in an envelope she addressed it and then put out the lights and got into bed, but for a long time she lay awake suffering from hurt pride, and from the awful knowledge that all the others had been right and that there was nothing left but to admit it. In her misery, there was one consolation: she felt free, free as she had been when she first came back from college to Plattesville.

She was finished with Jimmy Dougherty, and she knew now that even the faint flicker of interest she had felt for Mr. Richardson was nothing at all. She had seen him, his head bleeding, having just escaped death and felt nothing whatever, none of the emotion which clearly had swept Aunt Vinnie and Gashouse Mary and Aida off their feet. They might be in love with their precious, cold-blooded reformer, but she was not. On the contrary, she felt a kind of hatred for him, a little like the hatred of him felt by old Flynn and Old Dougherty. If he had never come to Plattesville everything would have been peaceful and very likely she'd be seeing Jimmy. Everything would have been different. As she finally fell asleep, her last conscious, hazy thought was, "Why in hell did Aunt Vinnie ever get him out of jail?"

69

Heat came with the sunrise on the morning of the Torchlight Procession, good, old-fashioned, dusty heat of the sort which had swept the plains of the Southwest since the beginning of time. Along Franklin Street and the river front, negro stevedores collapsed to sleep in the shadow of the big warehouses. On Main Street, citizens chose to walk on the shady side of the street, and even there the heat reflected from the pavement and the buildings opposite beat like a weight upon their heads. In the office of the *Daily Shield and Banner* the new electric fans buzzed and whirred, stirring the hot air into a semblance of life. Old Jim Newman said he hadn't remembered such a spell of heat in fifty years.

It was good, old-fashioned heat like that which had left horses and children dying on the plains in the days of the land rush, but in spite of it, the sense of excitement continued to grow in Plattesville. In spite of it the Reform Committee worked all day, panting and sweating, collecting banners and costumes, rallying dubious enthusiasts, organizing the different sections of "the monster parade and demonstration" which was to take place in the evening. The preachers of the Methodist and Baptist Churches, Gashouse Mary, Mrs. Mabel Urquahart Jenkins, Willie Ferguson, Jim Newman and scores of others equally ill-assorted, worked and sweated as if there were no differences of background, education and morals among them.

The news of the attack made by imported gunmen upon Mr. Richardson in the very front yard of McLeod's Folly spread from mouth to mouth with a speed that was astounding. Jake, usually as silent as a mute, went from saloon to saloon drinking and telling the story of his exploit until at two in the afternoon, overcome by liquor and the sense of his success, he lay down on the floor of the back room in Hennessey's and went to sleep. The interns and nurses at the hospital spread the story, and the two policemen who had accompanied Harvey Bingham couldn't resist, despite orders to the contrary, telling their wives. And as the story spread the wave of disgust and anger and fear rose and spread through all of Plattesville and the county to the very edge of the hills.

Honest citizens asked themselves what Plattesville was coming to. It occurred to them that they were no longer safe in their own houses if hired killers were to be brought into town. Before Homer Winterbottom left for the *News* office his shrewish wife confronted him triumphantly, saying, "You'll be the next. They'll be getting you for knowing too much." A remark which did nothing to stiffen the backbone of her worried, timorous husband.

Every half-hour Mr. Richardson, the scratch on his head covered with a bit of adhesive tape, telephoned the City Hospital to discover whether Pugface Mahoney had recovered consciousness and could talk, but the answer was always the same: he was still unconscious, he might die from Jake's lucky shot, but he was tough and very likely would pull through. But it was clear that Mr. Richardson wanted him to talk now, that very day. Mr. Richardson, despite the heat, became a veritable engine of energy. In his shirt sleeves he sat at his desk writing editorials, answering the telephone, calling the hospital and the Reform Committee headquarters and the police station. It was as if the whole crusade were suddenly placed on his broad shoulders, as if he realized that the crucial moment in the whole campaign was at hand and must not be bungled.

Jane, still angry and hurt, watched him with astonishment, thinking suddenly that it must have been Yankees like him who had started the Abolition Movement, and organized the Underground Railroad and made the Civil War. She couldn't believe that even a McLeod, even J. E. himself, had ever in such terrible heat displayed such a passion for right against wrong. In fact the spectacle of Mr. Richardson terrified her.

It wasn't only the heat which made Jane herself practically useless all that long day. It was the fact too that she felt empty and drained and bitter, as if nothing in the world mattered any longer or ever again would be of the least importance to her. The letter to Jimmy she had sent by a messenger to make certain that he received it while the fires of indignation still seared her soul. The letter was gone and everything was finished. There was nothing left to do but sit in the heat and stare dully at her desk. She didn't even go out to lunch: she hadn't any appetite and could not summon energy enough to get out of her chair and leave the office.

At three o'clock, she felt a flicker of interest when Harvey Bingham himself called from the police station to say they'd caught the other gunman at a place called Walkers Ford. But Little Hermie couldn't tell them anything either. In fact, he would never talk again. When they stopped him, he had tried to shoot his way out, and the local sheriff had finished him off with a pretty long-distance shot through the head from an old army Winchester. Mr. Richardson's only comment was brief. He said, "Why in hell did they kill him? He's no good to us dead."

When poor Mrs. McLeod heard the news she retired to her cubbyhole and relieved her feelings by a good cry. Since the moment she had come down the stairs of McLeod's Folly to find Mr. Richardson in the hall with blood streaming down his face, she had been as useless as if she had been paralyzed. She couldn't, it seemed to her, think straight about anything: she couldn't give an order, even to Aida. In the middle of the night she had wakened and then lain awake until the hot dawn filled the room with light. The whole thing, she thought, had gotten beyond her. Once, long ago, when she was young, she might have had the courage and the energy to go through with the fight to the end, but now she was tired and frightened. It seemed to her, in her fretful mood, that it was all her fault for ever having had a wild, crazy dream about cleaning up Plattesville. She didn't even know what a crusade like this one could mean. She thought, "I'm too old. I'm too tired." Gashouse Mary's place wrecked: Jane made miserable with every prospect of becoming an old maid: Mr. Richardson nearly killed and a man in the hospital with a bullet in him from Jake's gun, and a hundred other violences, bitternesses and quarrels. Mr. Richardson didn't seem to mind at all. There he was now, outside in the office, working like a beaver, as if Plattesville had meant as much to him as it meant to her, as if Plattesville had been his home, as if he had been a McLeod. She thought again, "I'm nothing but an old fool. I haven't the strength to go on with what I've begun. I'm nothing but an old fool."

It was so odd, too, when all she wanted was to make Plattesville a nice clean town where everybody would be prosperous and kindly and happy and love each other.

70

Up until the moment of going to press, Mr. Richardson went on working like a beaver, having new ideas, changing the make-up of the paper, writing new and fierce headlines. The moment had come . . . the moment to crush Evil and make Good triumphant forever in Plattesville: this edition of the Plattesville *Daily Shield and Banner* had to be supreme, to surpass even the reforming blasts put out long ago by J. E. McLeod and his father. It was to be a historic issue, preserved by citizens to show their grandchildren. No loophole must be left open. Attack! Attack! Attack!

At four o'clock the paper went to press. And as the last lot of copy was borne off by old Zimmerman, he relaxed and had a drink with bewildered Willie Ferguson.

And then came fresh disaster.

While they were still drinking, the door of the stairway opened and Jacobi, the pressman, came into the room. Beneath smudges of ink his face was white, and in one hand he held a bar of metal that had once been a tire iron. It was bent nearly double.

Shaking it at them, he said, "Well, this is their latest!"

"What's their latest?" asked Mr. Richardson.

Jacobi waved the tire iron. "Somebody must have got into the pressroom last night and stuck that in the works of the press. When we started it the tire iron damned near tore out the insides of the press."

Richardson, white in the face, said, "Can't we do anything?"

"Nothing," said Jacobi. "The press is all ripped up. It's wrecked."

"The swine!" said Willie Ferguson.

For a moment Mr. Richardson was silent. Then inspiration came. "We've got a hand press, haven't we?"

"Sure."

"Well, we'll get out a special edition on the hand press . . . just a single page. We'll give it away in the streets."

"It'll take a hell of a long time to run off a newspaper on the hand press."

"We'll all work at it," said Mr. Richardson. "They've tried to fix us. We'll show 'em. We'll turn it into a weapon. We'll fix 'em. I'll write a burning hot story of what's been done and Zimmerman can set it up and we'll have it on the streets before the parade begins. It was just what we needed . . . something like this. It couldn't be better . . . tell Zimmerman to come here."

Quickly he went to his desk, and after a pause of a moment or two began furiously typing the copy for the hand press. Old Zimmerman, chewing his tobacco, came back and forth between the composing and editorial rooms, setting up the type almost as fast as Mr. Richardson turned out the copy.

In half an hour, it was done. In twenty minutes more the hand press was at work, rolling off the special and historical copy of the *Daily Shield and Banner*. The boys who delivered the *Daily Shield and Banner* were summoned and found other boys to aid them in distributing the edition free everywhere in the city, along the water front, down Main Street, in the suburbs, telling all Plattesville the story of the plot against the *Daily Shield and Banner* on the eve of the Great Torchlight Parade.

The others in the office took turns at the hand press, even Jane, whose eyes took on a faint twinkle of life and of admiration for this fresh exhibition of energy on the part of Mr. Richardson.

A little after seven a messenger brought a letter to Jane and without a word she disappeared with it into the washroom. She knew the handwriting. Her hand shook as she tore it open to read it.

It said:

Dear Jane: You can believe what you damned well please. I can't change that. But I didn't know anything about those gunmen or my father either. May God strike me dead if I'm not telling the truth. It must have been Hirsh's doing. Anyway he's out, but that doesn't mean the fight is finished.

Jimmy.

As she read it she heard the cries of the newsboys shouting the edition run off on the hand press, and as she folded the note and put it into her handbag she knew somehow that in spite of anything Jimmy or his father could do, the fight *was* finished, and suddenly she was happy because she *believed* what Jimmy had written. She knew Jimmy. He was Irish and he was superstitious. He wouldn't take any chances about calling upon God to strike him dead.

71

At seven-thirty the Great Torchlight Procession had already begun to form in a large field belonging to Elder Landon on the outskirts of the town not far from the Dougherty mansion on Fleming Avenue. The Reverend Mr. Simpson and Elder Landon took charge assisted by Mrs. Mabel Urquahart Jenkins. All three wore across their fronts large white ribbons inscribed with the word MARSHAL in gold letters. Theirs was not an easy task because there were, milling about in the field, several hundred marchers—some in the costume of old-time cowhands, some dressed in white as angels of purity, some in ordinary clothes wearing sandwich boards inscribed with the legends "Clean Up Plattesville" and "Down with Dougherty and His Gang." Others carried gasoline torches and banners. Mixed among them, adding to the confusion, were fifty or sixty boys of all ages come to see the fun, accompanied by dogs of every race, breed and description, which kept up a din of barking and desultory combat. On the outskirts of the mob, three hot-dog stands, one run by an Italian and two by Greeks, had set up a thriving business.

For nearly an hour the three marshals labored to bring order out of the confusion, and in the end, baffled, they summoned the aid of Jim Newman, who unhitched one of his black hearse horses and climbed on its back to ride in and out among the marchers. In the end it was Jim, with the help of a stentorian voice bestowed on him by nature and a megaphone made of brown paper borrowed from one of the Greek hot-dog men, who transformed the milling mob into a column in which each marcher found his proper place.

At a quarter to nine, torches flaming, banners upraised, the procession started on its way toward the center of the town and the public square.

At the head rode the Reverend Mr. Simpson, mounted with a certain amount of disquietude on an old snowy-backed white horse and wearing a costume assembled out of his long career as a "joiner" of many lodges which made him look like a cross between General Robert E. Lee and a British admiral. Directly behind him marched the Millersville town band complete save for the players of the tuba and the piccolo, both of whom held county jobs for which they were indebted to the Dougherty organization. Behind the band came a battalion of Baptist ladies dressed all in white as angels and singing, "Onward Christian Soldiers, Marching as to War" to the accompaniment of the Millersville band, and close on their heels a delegation from the Plattesville Federation of Women's Clubs led by Mrs. Mabel Urquahart Jenkins, clad all in white with a large red cross sewn on the front of her costume just beneath her marshal's insignia. Half the club women carried gasoline torches and the other half large banners bearing such legends as, "What About the Courthouse Roof?"—"Franklin Street Must Be Closed Up"—"Citizens of Plattesville, Raise Your Heads Again and Vote Against Dougherty"—"Who Got the Money for the Elm Street Sewer?"

The third battalion of marchers was badly placed, having got off in the wrong order during the confusion of getting the procession under way. It consisted of a water-front delegation, recruited and organized by Gashouse Mary, made up of stevedores, loafers, roustabouts and patrons of the El Dorado dance hall. It carried more torches and more banners which read variously, "Be Fair to the Working Man"—"Why Should We Work for Old Dougherty?"—"Make Plattesville Fit for Honest Workers"—"What About the Water Works Contract?" Half this battalion was a little drunk and all of it slouched along in a disorderly fashion, singing ribald and bawdy songs against the sound of "Onward Christian Soldiers," played by the Millersville band and sung by the angels one battalion in front of them. Just ahead of the leading club women, Mrs. Mabel Urquahart Jenkins grew red with fury and indignation, but it was too late now to alter the position in the procession of the various battalions and she had to march on, her ears confronted by a strange cacophony blend of "Onward Christian Soldiers" and "The St. James' Infirmary Blues." It wasn't until they neared the center of the town that it occurred to Mrs. Mabel Urquahart Jenkins that the stevedore battalion followed close on her heels, not perhaps through any error but by the design of Jim Newman himself.

Behind the stevedores, again perhaps a little too near them, came another contingent of angels in white, this time Methodist angels, headed by the Reverend Mr. Burwash on another white plow horse. And then the Silver Cornet band of the Foresters' Lodge and then a straggling contingent of mixed citizens who, at the last moment, joined the parade because it looked like a good party. These too carried banners and torches. Behind them marched the local troops of Boy and Girl Scouts, and last of all came a delegation from the county headed by Jim Newman, the chairman, who was too fat to ride a horse all the way and was drawn by his own two black hearse horses in an open victoria resurrected from some forgotten rotting stable. Few of the county contingent were under fifty and some of them were in the seventies. They rode cow ponies and wore old chaps, ten-gallon hats and high-heeled boots that had not been seen in the county for fifteen years. Some of them were dressed as Indians, and all of them kept up a yelping and hallooing that was highly disconcerting to the vocal efforts of the Methodist angels just in front. The old cattlemen had gotten out of hand, and flasks of Bourbon were passing back and forth from one pinto pony to another. Sam Henderson was on one of his piebalds, and Hal Pierce brought up the rear with a special attraction which Mr. Richardson and the Committee had not thought of.

From an old suit of Jim Newman they had contrived an effigy stuffed with straw and labeled in enormous letters *W. M. Dougherty.* To this they had attached a lariat, and as they rode they dragged it after them in the dust of the summer evening, giving it every now and then a sudden jerk to the accompaniment of wild "Yahoos."

Along the whole length of the procession ran newsboys passing out free copies of the historic hand-press edition of the *Daily Shield and Banner* retailing the iniquitous details of the attack upon Mr. Richardson and the wrecking of the *Daily Shield and Banner* press.

The procession passed through the principal streets and at last swung into Main Street headed for the Square. Here most of the crowd had gathered, and it greeted the Baptist angels headed by the Reverend Mr. Simpson with shouts and cheers which reached a crescendo as the old cattlemen, their ponies rearing and plunging with fear at the torches and war cries of the riders, brought up the rear.

As the procession passed the office of the *Daily Shield and Banner,* the marchers looked up to the windows where the staff stood in the lighted windows—Mr. Richardson, a grin on his face and Mrs. McLeod, trembling, with tears in her eyes, in the front. As the procession passed, the Reverend Mr. Simpson, the Reverend Mr. Burwash and Mrs. Mabel Urquahart Jenkins all gave smart military salutes. The angels burst afresh into "Onward Christian Soldiers," the river-front workers cheered and sang "Hinky-Dinky Parley-vous," and the old cattlemen "Yahooed" louder than ever. None of them noticed that they were saluting and cheering not only Mr. Richardson and Mrs. McLeod but Gashouse Mary, Aida and her cousin Athena's son, as well. For Gashouse Mary was there, discreetly in the background, enjoying herself enormously. She had a drink of Bourbon with Willie Ferguson, slapped him on the back, to the disapproval of his wife, Myrtle, and said, "I guess this'll fix 'em."

And Willie said, "Plattesville ain't had so much fun since the land rush."

Only Jane didn't seem to enjoy it. After a time she retired to the back of the editorial room and pretended to be interested in the *New York Times*.

In her heart she was frightened. For a long time now, for four or five days, she had been aware of the rising feeling in the town and tonight she was suddenly terrified. What terrified her she did not know except that she felt a sick horror of the parade and the strange foreboding terror of the mob spirit there was in it. She was afraid suddenly for Jimmy and hoped that he had gone to Millersville or some place out of Plattesville till the procession was over. That was what they should have done . . . both Jimmy and his father. But in her heart she knew they hadn't done it. The Doughertys were Irish. They liked a fight. They weren't going to take anything lying down. Behind the *New York Times* she found herself murmuring a prayer that Jimmy wouldn't show himself in the street tonight.

72

The Doughertys hadn't gone to Millersville or anywhere else. In the darkened windows of the *Daily News* office they were watching the procession. Old Dougherty was silent, alarmed to the depths of his soul for the first time. He hadn't expected the demonstration to be a success. He had boasted that it would fizzle out into nothing. But it was being a great success. There was no denying it. And it was being cheered by the townspeople, by people he had thought loyal to him, by people for whom he had done favors.

Behind him, Mr. Hirsh, the guinea pig, was glum and silent. His gangster's coup with the tire iron had been a failure all round. It had drawn the abuse of Old Dougherty who told him he was out of a job, and Jimmy who threatened to beat him up, and Richardson had turned the disaster into victory. Behind them all Mr. Winterbottom was trembling, like a member of the court of Louis Sixteenth before the spectacle of a revolutionary mob. In the darkness no one spoke, and as the tail of the procession passed on its first tour of the Square, with the effigy of Old Dougherty dragging behind the old cattlemen in the dust, Jimmy Dougherty turned and went toward the door.

Old Dougherty noticed the departure and called out after him, "Where are you going?"

"Never mind where I'm going."

"Don't make a damned fool of yourself. Don't go down on the street. It ain't safe."

But the only answer was the sound of the door being slammed. The old man got heavily to his feet and started after his son, but by the time he reached the bottom of the stairs, Jimmy had vanished into the crowd and Old Dougherty turned back. He didn't want very much to face the crowd in the street. A woman, one of the girls from Estelle Laverne's house, caught a glimpse of his face in the shadows and shouted, "Beat it, ugly mug!"

Meanwhile Jimmy was pushing his way through the crowd across the street and the little park, toward the office of the *Daily Shield and Banner*.

For half an hour he had been standing in the window in the shadow behind his father. He had watched the Baptist and Methodist angels go past and the club women headed by Mabel Urquahart Jenkins, and the water-front delegation and the old cattlemen. He had read by the light of the torches the insulting legends on the banners they carried. And slowly rage had taken possession of him, a wild, burning Irish rage which seemed like a fire inside him. And then at the very end the effigy of W. M. Dougherty dragged in the dust behind the old cattlemen to the accompaniment of wild "Yahoos" had been too much to bear. Suddenly for him the whole world turned red and he was filled with a passionate desire to kill Richardson, who had caused all the trouble and taken his girl away from him.

Now as he ran across the Square he was recognized here and there by individuals in the excited crowd, but before there was time to address a word to him, he was gone. Pushing his way through the cheering crowd beneath the windows of the *Daily Shield and Banner*, he ran up the stairs to the editorial room.

There, at the window, with their backs to him, stood the people who had made all the revolution in Plattesville, the people who were responsible for the insults to the old man . . . all of them but Jane. He saw in a flash that she wasn't there. All the others were standing looking down at the cheering marchers in the Torchlight Procession.

Crossing the room he went directly to Richardson and taking him by the shoulder turned him round and shouted, "Now, you son of a bitch, come out and fight fair!"

For a moment, a little dazed, Mr. Richardson looked at him. Then the odd, hard look came into his eyes. Quietly, he took off his coat and said, "Sure, come on outside," and led the way toward the door.

By this time Mrs. McLeod had become aware of what was happening and began to cry out, "Mr. Richardson, don't go! Don't go! Oh, what are we going to do?".

Willie Ferguson looked bewildered but Gashouse Mary said, "Don't you worry! I'll go with 'em to see there's fair play! I'll look after him! Don't you worry!"

Then Jane dashed out of her corner calling, "Jimmy! Jimmy! Tom! Tom!" and followed them down the stairs.

Aida, who had been in Mrs. McLeod's cubbyhole watching the parade with her cousin Athena's boy, came out and cried, "Where are they all goin'? What's all the rumpus?"

But Jimmy and Mr. Richardson had long since disappeared with Jane and Gashouse Mary following them, and Mrs. McLeod was left behind weeping and wringing her hands, to be comforted by Willie and Myrtle Ferguson and old Zimmerman.

Through the startled marchers, Mr. Richardson and Jimmy Dougherty crossed the street and ran into the Square. There by the Soldiers' and Sailors' Monument they put up their hands and the fight began.

It was a magnificent fight. Jimmy was Irish and a born fighter and the broad shoulders of Mr. Richardson had not been given him by God for nothing. They went at each other like a couple of young rams, and in a second there was a circle round them made up of the tougher element of the town, men and women from the river front and girls from Franklin Street who had been given the evening out to watch the procession because everybody in Plattesville was watching the procession anyway and Franklin Street was certain to be empty.

In the crowd which filled the street Jane and Gashouse Mary lost sight of the two fighters, and for a good five minutes wandered about searching until the encouraging shouts of the little circle watching the combat guided them toward the Soldiers' and Sailors' Memorial Fountain. There in the dim light they caught sight of the two figures, hammering each other doggedly. The advantage was on neither side. Both faces were equally bloody, the shirts of both fighters half-torn from their backs. Around them the crowd kept increasing while Gashouse Mary, who had arrived first, kept shouting, "Stand back! Give 'em room! Stand back!"

Then suddenly Jane was in the midst of the circle pushing between the two men and crying out, "Stop! Stop! Leave him alone! Leave him alone!"

For a moment it was impossible to know which fighter she was addressing and which fighter she wished to be left in peace. And then suddenly it was apparent, for she was beating Mr. Richardson on his bare chest with both her fists, still crying, "Stop! Stop! Leave him alone!" and the fight was suddenly stopped, and in the sudden silence the crowd heard her shouting at Mr. Richardson, "It's all your fault! It wouldn't have happened . . . any of it . . . if you hadn't come here!"

Then with her handkerchief she began to wipe the blood from the face of Jimmy Dougherty. Until now some of the crowd had been taking sides, jeering Jimmy, but the spectacle of Mrs. McLeod's niece coming to his aid silenced them and there was no sound save a dull murmuring that increased as others joined the circle. Then Gashouse Mary, with something of the old strength she had known when she was her own chucker-out, shoved people out of the way, and in her red velvet suit and plumed hat, went to the aid of Mr. Richardson.

At the same time without any warning three policemen came through the crowd, surrounded Mr. Richardson and said, "You're under arrest!"

This was too much for Gashouse Mary and she turned on them with a fine flow of barroom language. But Mr. Richardson stopped her and wiping the blood out of his eyes, said, "Listen to me! Let them go ahead and arrest me."

"Are you crazy?" asked Gashouse Mary.

"I haven't been yet, have I?" asked Mr. Richardson, his swollen lips showing a painful grin. To the policemen he said, "I'll come along with you. What's the charge?"

"Disturbin' the peace and loiterin'," said one of the policemen.

"And what about *him*?" shouted Gashouse Mary, pointing to Jimmy Dougherty, who was attempting in embarrassment to escape the ministrations of Jane. "It was *him* that started it."

"Shut up," said Mr. Richardson. And turning to the policemen, he said with the air of a Christian martyr, "Come on. Take me away," and himself led the way in the direction of the county jail.

But restraint was now beyond Gashouse Mary. In her red velvet suit she climbed across the recumbent allegorical figure of War that ornamented the base of the Soldiers' and Sailors' Memorial. When she reached the figures of Peace and Abundance, she clung to them and began to make a speech.

"Citizens of Plattesville," she said. "Are we gonna stand for this racket any longer? Are we gonna go on witnessin' this tyranny and corruption? Are we gonna stand for the vicious persecution of an honest man like Mr. Richardson?"

Loud cries of "No! No!" arose from the river-front workers, the ladies from Franklin Street and a great many honest and stalwart citizens who had joined the growing crowd.

[195]

"What we need," cried Gashouse Mary, "is what Plattesville ain't seen in fifty years! What we need is a good jail delivery! Who's goin' with me to the jail to rescue Mr. Richardson?"

A wild cheer rose from the crowd.

"Come on. Let's take him away from the police. Come on! We're gonna rescue Mr. Richardson."

Gashouse Mary scrambled down from the figure of Abundance across the prostrate figure of War, and the whole crowd began to move toward the county jail, a wild mob, a mob from the Southwest, suddenly revitalized, suddenly become what a mob had once been in the half-wild cattle country. It was bent now, not upon lynching a crooked gambler, but on rescuing its hero. It swept across the Square and into the street where it was joined by members of the procession which was breaking up in front of the courthouse. By the time it reached the jail, Methodist and Baptist angels, Boy Scouts, ladies from Franklin Street, old cattlemen, club women, river workers, all led by Gashouse Mary, were moving together, shoulder to shoulder toward the jail.

73

Again the Dougherty gang had been wrong. This time the blunder had been that of Harvey Bingham, the chief of police, and old Flynn, the police magistrate. They had acted on the suggestion made long ago by Mr. Hirsh, the guinea pig, that if they could get anything, even the slightest thing, on Mr. Richardson they were to lock him up at once; in jail he could be kept safe and helpless. But that suggestion had been weeks earlier, and tonight, if Mr. Hirsh hadn't been cowering in the darkened upper room of the *Daily News* office, he would have sent them word not to touch Mr. Richardson even if he committed mayhem and murder. Since the incident of the tire iron he knew that tonight was the last time in the world to arrest the public hero. But neither Mr. Hirsh nor Old Dougherty was anywhere near the scene of the fight, and the police chief, who had been watching the procession from the Square and was not very bright, saw his chance and acted upon it.

Now, inside the jail, with the windows shuttered and the doors locked, he wished he hadn't been so impetuous. He was at heart a mild, lazy man who disliked trouble and he had never been confronted before with trouble in such quantities. Outside the jail, the angels, the Boy Scouts, the cattlemen, the ladies from Franklin Street were milling about with torches, shouting for him to open up the jail and deliver to them their hero. Peeping through a crack in the steel shutters he watched the mob for a time. The dying light of the expiring torches gave it a singularly ferocious aspect.

Behind him in the jail office, his prisoner, still clad only in his trousers and the fragments of a torn shirt, grinned and wiped the blood from his face. Suddenly the police chief turned and said, "If you'll come with me, I'll let you out through the coalhole at the back."

The grin on the prisoner's face broadened. "I don't want to go," he said.

"What do you mean?"

"I like it here. It's quiet."

This upset the chief of police. Now that he had his prisoner, he was afraid of him. He couldn't make out this fellow Richardson. He was smarter than Old Dougherty, smarter than Hirsh, smarter than old Flynn, smarter than anybody in the town. Now, suddenly, it occurred to Harvey Bingham that the whole thing might be a trick, that Richardson had plotted to get himself arrested simply to make fools of all of them one more time.

He peeped through the shutter once more and this time he discovered that the mob, encouraged by Gashouse Mary, had got a steel girder from somewhere and were carrying it forward to batter down the door of the jail. Cattlemen, angels, Boy Scouts, even the Reverend Burwash and the Reverend Simpson were lending hands. Mary, her hat now well back on the elaborate coiffure, was shouting, "Come on, boys! We'll have the door down in a jiffy."

The police chief began to feel a little sick, and turning, he said, "Come on, be a good guy and go out through the coalhole."

"No," said Mr. Richardson stubbornly, "I don't want to."

Before the Chief could speak again there was a resounding crash as the steel girder struck the door. Then another crash and then another and another, and Harvey Bingham, who wasn't a newcomer in the county but came of the old stock, began to remember what a Plattesville mob could be like.

Between crashes he said again, "I'll give you one more chance."

"No," said Mr. Richardson, "I'm gonna stay right here."

"Well," said the Chief, "I'm scramming through the coalhole."

Then a final crash and the steel door of the jail gave way, but before the crowd burst in, the police chief and three policemen had disappeared into the cellar to escape through the coalhole into Market Street.

Mr. Richardson, bruised, bloody and half-naked, was waiting in the office of the police chief to receive Gashouse Mary and her cohorts.

74

Meanwhile, in another part of the Square a similar escape had taken place by a similar back exit. The nervous Mr. Winterbottom, Old Dougherty and Mr. Hirsh fled down the back stairs of the *Daily News* building, across a yard filled with rubbish and ash cans, alarming on their way two courting cats. When they had climbed a fence and reached the alley Mr. Hirsh disappeared into the shadows. At the corner, Mr. Winterbottom looked at Old Dougherty, hesitated for a moment, and then said, "Well, good night!"

"Good night," growled Old Dougherty, and they went their separate ways.

Mr. Hirsh, clinging to the safety of shadows, made his way to the kitchen entrance of the Beauregard Hotel. Luckily for him the whole of Plattesville was by now in the Square by the jail and the streets were deserted. Once inside the hotel he went quickly to his room and packed a suitcase. In half an hour he was hiding in the washroom of the depot waiting for the twelve-twenty-one to take him to St. Louis.

He remained in the washroom until he heard the distant whistle of the twelve-twenty-one. Taking up his suitcase, he opened the door and walked out straight into the arms of two hard-looking men. One of them pinioned his arms and the other said, "Good evening, Mr. Sulzberger. Sorry to spoil your getaway."

Mr. Hirsh looked suddenly like a cornered rat. The lipless mouth tightened, the eyes grew beady.

"What's the matter? Let go of me. My name isn't Sulzberger and I've got to catch a train."

"You're catching it all right," said the hard-faced man who held his arms. "Only you ain't travelin' alone. You've got company."

"What have you got on me?"

"Plenty," said the other hard-faced man.

Mr. Hirsh relaxed suddenly and said, "Let go of me. I'll go along with you."

As they climbed on the train, he said mildly, "How did you know where I was?"

"A little bird told us."

Mr. Richardson had taken a gamble with his telegram. Gashouse Mary had said, "Hirsh smells bad," and she had been right.

75

At the moment the police appeared the crowd forgot at once the extraordinary spectacle of Mrs. McLeod's niece administering first aid to the son of Old Dougherty. It was Gashouse Mary, clinging to the bronze figure of Abundance, who took the center of the stage, and Jimmy Dougherty, his Irish rage abated a little now, felt a sudden desire to slip away and disappear. Quietly, with Jane following him, he made his way from the monument toward the bandstand. There in the shadow they were entirely alone, for the crowd, led by Mary, was already on its way to the jail.

In silence the two of them stood there, Jane still working to staunch the flow of blood from his cut lip with a piece of his torn shirt. Up to now, because of the excitement, the whole incident had struck neither of them as extraordinary, but suddenly, with the Square grown empty and silent, they were left alone and the sense of aloneness made them both feel awkward and shy.

Jimmy said, "I'm all right."

"Sure?"

Then there was a long silence.

They were friends again and yet not friends. The old sense of intimacy had raised its head once more only to find itself confronted by pride. By instinct they were, all at once, nearer to each other than they had ever been, with that intimacy which belongs to couples long married who have been through much together. But, outwardly, they were no closer to each other than before the fight. Nothing had been solved. Indeed the situation was, if possible, worse than before, what with Mr. Richardson carted off to jail and the crusade more bitter than ever.

Jimmy looked at her and said coldly, "Well, I guess you'd better go back to the office now."

"Yes, I suppose so." Her voice too sounded detached and indifferent.

"I'll be going back to the *News*."

"Good night," said Jane.

"Good night."

Then because she could think of nothing to say which would not sound silly, she turned and walked back once more across the empty Square toward the office of the *Daily Shield and Banner*. In the distance she could hear the cries of the crowd and presently the crashing sound of steel against steel as Gashouse Mary's supporters attacked the door of the jail. The sounds were terrifying like the sounds she remembered vaguely out of her childhood when there was a lynching at Millersville and she was wakened in the middle of the night and, terrified, lay listening in her crib until daylight.

She thought, "I ought to go back and tell him to clear out . . . to go off somewhere out of the way until the row is over. The old man ought to clear out too. A mob like that might do anything."

And, turning back, she ran, unashamed now because the Square was quite empty and there was no one to witness her folly, but by the time she had reached the grandstand, Jimmy had already disappeared. She went as far as the office of the *Daily News* only to find the building in darkness. Frightened, she pounded on the door and called out, making wild hysterical sounds that echoed in the doorways of the empty silent Square, but to her cries there was no answer.

76

From the window of the *Daily Shield and Banner* office Mrs. McLeod and Aida witnessed the procession returning from the jail. They were alone because everyone else in the building had followed the mob. Mrs. McLeod would have gone too but Aida became suddenly powerful and blocked her way, saying, "You all ain't goin' a step out in that street, Mis' McLeod. You're too old to get yourself mixed up with a lot of white trash."

So they had waited, alarmed and puzzled for a time by the distant sounds of the great jail delivery. And then presently the wave of sound began to draw nearer and up the street they saw the mob returning toward the *Daily Shield and Banner* office. The angels and doxies and cattlemen still carried dying, smoky torches and in the middle of them, borne on the shoulders of three or four old cattlemen, appeared the figure of Mr. Richardson clad now only in trousers.

Full of excitement, Aida leaned out of the window and shouted, "Come on, you all! Come on!" And aside to Mrs. McLeod she said, "What'd I tell you, Mis' McLeod, about that boy when he first come to the house? Nobody can lick him. He's too smart."

In front of the *Daily Shield and Banner* office the mob halted, cheering and singing, and Mr. Richardson slipped down from the shoulders of the cattlemen and made his way to the stairway. Then Gashouse Mary climbed a hydrant and propped up by three or four of her own river-side delegation, she shouted, "Three cheers for Vinnie McLeod!" And the mob roared its admiration. Once more the tears came into the eyes of Mrs. McLeod, and then the office behind her was filled by a confusion of friends and admirers . . . all the committee and Mr. Richardson, who had thrown his coat over his shirtless torso, and Gashouse Mary and Mr. Simpson and Mr. Burwash and scores of other crusaders.

Willie Ferguson got the Bourbon out of the bottom drawer and passed it around and everybody drank out of the bottle and when it gave out old Jim Newman sent Aida's cousin Athena's boy to Hennessey's place to buy more.

Raising the bottle high above his head, an excited, rejuvenated Willie cried out, "Well, I guess we showed 'em who's runnin' Plattesville. Three cheers for Mr. Richardson."

77

About one o'clock the party in the office began to break up and the celebrating mob outside to disperse and go home to bed, and at last no one remained but Mrs. McLeod and Mr. Richardson sitting in chairs on opposite sides of the office. Mrs. McLeod said, "We'd better go home so I can put a piece of raw steak on that eye. It's going to be awful in the morning."

"I'm not worrying about that. I'd like to know what's become of Jane."

"I guess maybe she's gone home to bed. In the excitement I must have forgotten all about her."

He didn't tell her about the scene by the Soldiers' and Sailors' Memorial Fountain, when Jane had attacked him, beating his chest with her bare fists.

"It was a little hard on her . . . the whole thing," said Mr. Richardson.

Then suddenly, almost with a jerk, Mrs. McLeod got up out of her chair and said, "I forgot . . . there was a telegram for you!" And she went into the office and returned with a telegram. Mr. Richardson tore it open and read it and then with a grin handed it to her.

She read: "Publishers offer five thousand advance. Shall I go ahead with sale of picture rights?"

Mrs. McLeod sank into a chair.

"What did I tell you?" asked Mr. Richardson.

In a weak voice she said, "I don't know. I feel kind of dizzy. I don't know whether I'm coming or going."

"Better have some of this," said Mr. Richardson, and poured her a drink of Bourbon in a paper cup.

Then in the doorway appeared the figure of Jane. It was a slightly bedraggled, completely shamefaced figure, which seemed somehow to have shrunk during the excitement of the evening. For a moment she stood in the doorway very pale, hesitating, as if uncertain whether she should come into the room or turn and flee. Mrs. McLeod and Mr. Richardson looked toward her expectantly and for a moment there was a strained silence.

Then Jane in a funny, humbled voice said, "I'm sorry. I apologize. I guess I must have lost my head. I'm awfully ashamed."

"Forget it," said Mr. Richardson. "I never enjoyed a beating more."

"What's the matter?" asked Mrs. McLeod. "Jimmy Dougherty didn't lick you, did he?"

"No, he didn't," said Mr. Richardson. "It was Jane who tried to beat me up."

78

They were tired now, all three of them, from the excitement and the primitive emotions aroused by the events of the last twenty-four hours. They were so tired that all the way home in the taxicab summoned by Mr. Richardson, they rode in silence, each one lost in his own thoughts and problems. In one corner of the taxi old Mrs. McLeod was lost in wonder over what had happened, at the strange succession of events which in so short a time had changed her whole life and precipitated her into a struggle the violence of which she had never suspected. The fear, the regrets, were almost stilled now, for she had had her moment, her big moment when Gashouse Mary had climbed on to the fire hydrant and called for three cheers for Vinnie McLeod and the whole crowd had joined in with a wild enthusiasm. In the darkness, she was smiling, without knowing it, over what had happened and over the extraordinary news about The Book. One thing would have made her happiness complete and that was the knowledge, the assurance, that J. E. knew what had happened—that she had not only saved the *Daily Shield and Banner* but had made it again the fighting newspaper it had been in the old days.

Beside her, Jane, exhausted, lay back limply, faintly aware that Mr. Richardson, whom a little while before she had attacked tooth and nail, was sitting there, very close to her, grinning to himself in the darkness. Out of the corner of her eye she saw him grinning as the light from the street lamps flashed across his face. The sight of the grin angered and humiliated her because in her heart she knew he wasn't only grinning over the success of the evening but over the spectacle of herself, of the memory of her flying at his big muscular figure like a wildcat. And he was grinning because she had given the show away, because in the excitement of the moment she had shown all too well how she felt about Jimmy Dougherty, because she, Jane Baldwin, who thought herself so sophisticated and intellectual, had behaved after all like any immigrant factory girl. And she was angry too because she knew that sooner or later she would have to explain to him about the attack, and why she had lost her head, if for no other reason than simply to stifle that horrid grin.

In his corner, Mr. Richardson simply went on grinning.

At last when they reached McLeod's Folly, and Mrs. McLeod had left them standing alone in the big hall while she went to speak to Aida, Jane pulled herself together and with a great effort said, "I'm sorry for being such a silly fool."

Spitefully he grinned again and said, "Don't even think about it."

"Anyway," she said, "thanks for fighting over me. I appreciate it."

At this Mr. Richardson's maddening grin only broadened. One eye was by now almost swollen shut and there were three long scratches on the side of his face which she hadn't noticed before. His appearance with nothing but his coat over his naked torso was so tough and battered that but for her anger at the grin she would have laughed.

"I wasn't fighting over you," he said. "What made you think I was?"

Then the sagging bedraggled figure of Jane straightened a little and a light came into the eye, a light which made her seem a little more like the normal Jane and she said, "Then what were you fighting for?"

"Well, because Jimmy Dougherty seemed to want to fight and he was so earnest about it I didn't want to disappoint him. And then, secondly," he continued, in a voice mild but ironic, a little as if he were addressing one of the Thursday conferences, "I was fighting over a principle." He must have caught the look of surprise in her face for he pushed his point further home, "No, I'm afraid you didn't have much to do with it. I know that women always like everything to be personal but I'm afraid this was a very abstract fight on a lofty idealistic plane."

Jane sat down suddenly, all the coyness gone out of her. "I think you're horrible," she said. "A horrible, nasty cold-blooded Yankee."

Mr. Richardson went on, "I don't say that I mightn't have gone for you at one time in a big way, except for two things . . . one, we couldn't make a worse combination, and two, I've got a girl already. She's the one who writes me a letter every day."

"Oh!" said Jane.

Weariness was beginning to overcome them both. To show that she was utterly indifferent to him Jane took off her hat and turned to the mirror, pretending to be absorbed in arranging her hair. But over her shoulder in the mirror she still saw the reflection of his battered, mocking face. With a half-hearted burst of indignation she asked, "Then why did you make me believe you were interested in me?"

"I didn't," said Mr. Richardson.

"You tried to hold my hand in the movies."

"I told you it didn't mean anything. I was just kind of lonely."

"Well, anyway, I think it's all disgusting."

"And I'll tell you something else," said Mr. Richardson. "You'd better come to your senses or you're going to lose Jimmy Dougherty. Any man gets tired of tantrums after a while."

"I've never been out of my senses and I don't give a damn if I never see Jimmy Dougherty again."

Once again the wicked glint came into Mr. Richardson's eyes. "No," he said. "You can't get away with that now. You tried to before and didn't get away with it and now you can't, not after you beat me up." He turned the collar of his coat over his bare chest with sudden exaggerated modesty and said, "I'll be black and blue for a week."

Jane only said again, "I think you're horrible," and began to cry.

"You mustn't do that," said Mr. Richardson and put one hand on her shoulder. Savagely she shook it off, "I'm only crying," she said, "because I'm so tired."

"I didn't think it was for any other reason," said Mr. Richardson. Then

[203]

unexpectedly, she turned and asked, "What's she like—that girl, I mean. Is she like me?"

Mr. Richardson laughed. "No," he said. "She couldn't be more different." A twinkle came into his eye. "She's a reformer like me. She's got a lot of common sense."

"No reformer," said Jane, "has got any common sense."

Again Mr. Richardson laughed. "Maybe you're right," he said. "Maybe that's why reformers are reformers."

And then from the kitchen door across the darkened dining room came the booming voice of Aida, "If you all doan come along, your cocoa's gonna be all scummy."

79

In the morning they all slept late since there would only be a hand-press edition entirely written by Mr. Richardson and that could be got out after lunch. At eleven o'clock Mrs. McLeod answered the telephone and heard a voice which sounded vaguely familiar. It said, "Good morning."

"Good morning."

"This is W. M. Dougherty speaking."

"Oh!" said Mrs. McLeod, and for a second she was assailed again by a cloud of nameless terrors . . . that he meant to have her arrested for the jail delivery, that he meant to tell her she was bankrupt, that he meant to sue her for libel, or that he was merely calling to say that he was having her murdered. Collecting herself, she said in a shaking voice, "Yes . . . what is it? What can I do for you?"

"I'd like to have a talk with you. When can I see you?"

She heard herself saying, "Oh, any time . . . any time."

"Right away?"

"That'll be all right."

"I'd like to see you alone."

"I guess that would be all right."

"I don't want to come to your office and I guess you don't want to come to mine."

"Why don't you come here . . . to McLeod's Folly? Then nobody would see us."

"Okay," said the voice of W. M. Dougherty. "I'll come right over."

No sooner had she replaced the receiver than she was assailed by fresh doubts and terrors. She shouldn't have told him that she would see him alone. He might only be going to terrorize her or make a fool of her once more. She had a wild feeling that once they were alone in a room together, he could force her to do as he pleased, to call off the crusade, to leave

[204]

town, even to sell the *Daily Shield and Banner* to him. Quickly she washed her face and did her hair and went to knock on Mr. Richardson's door. She knocked again and again but no one answered and when she pushed open the door she found the room empty.

Then all at once the need to find him became hysterical and imperative and she hurried down the stairs to the kitchen. But Aida didn't know anything about him except that he had eaten a hearty breakfast and gone out an hour earlier.

"He must be at the office," said Mrs. McLeod, but when she telephoned Myrtle Ferguson, Myrtle said he hadn't come in at all. In a panic she thought, "Maybe he's gone for a walk and will come back. Anyway I've got to get dressed. I can't see W. M. Dougherty like this." And while she dressed she kept saying to herself, "I mustn't lose my head. I mustn't lose my head." And all the time she kept repeating the formula she kept saying to herself, "Oh, why should Mr. Richardson be away when I need him most?"

And then the door bell rang, fiercely, aggressively, and for a second she thought she was going to faint.

It was Aida who opened the door, and at sight of Mr. Dougherty her chocolate face turned yellow and she thought, "He's found out about those men in the cellar and he's comin' arrest us all."

But he didn't seem very fierce. He said, "I've got an appointment to see Mrs. McLeod."

"Come right in . . . come right in," said Aida. "Come right on into the liberry." And she took him into J. E. McLeod's library, crowded and crammed with old leather-bound books, so unlike the library in the huge Tudor house in Fleming Avenue. The sight of so many books frightened him a little. Books were one of the few things in the world that filled him with awe.

With her heart in her throat Mrs. McLeod descended the stairs and pushed open the library door. There he was, sitting in one of the worn old leather chairs, huge and formidable. (What was she going to say? What was she going to do?) But for the first time in her experience he rose when she came into the room, and as he came toward her, she saw that he didn't seem as red-faced and bullying as the monster which had been haunting her consciousness ever since the telephone call. He looked tired and worn and he was embarrassed.

He said, "I guess you were kind of surprised when I called you up this morning?"

"Yes," said Mrs. McLeod, as coldly as possible. "What is it I can do for you? Won't you sit down?"

"Many thanks," said Mr. Dougherty and seated himself again. "I just wanted to have a talk with you . . . to see if we couldn't patch things up."

And suddenly, miraculously, she wasn't afraid any more, and she knew that she wasn't going to be fooled. Perhaps it was the memory of the cheer beneath the window on the night before, or the five thousand dollar advance from the publishers, or the feeling that after all, whatever happened, Mr. Richardson was there behind her, to fight and set things straight and look after her. So with a new dignity she said, "What exactly do you mean by patching things up?"

He lighted a cigar before he answered her. Then he said, "Well, you see, it's like this. I kind of thought we might come to some sort of compromise about the whole thing."

It was clear that every word he spoke brought him a kind of suffering. It wasn't that he had never before made a political bargain, for he had made plenty of them, but they had always been made on his own terms, and now he—the invincible W. M. Dougherty—was proposing the bargain, not to someone or some group stronger than himself but to a woman, and an elderly, muddle-headed woman, into the bargain.

Opposite him, Mrs. McLeod sat on the edge of her chair, suddenly filled with fresh alarms because she really didn't know anything about politics or how you made bargains. She was afraid that she'd accept anything he offered. She thought, "I mustn't say yes or no. I must remember to say 'I'll think it over.'" So aloud she said, "Perhaps you'd better explain exactly what you propose."

It was a wonderful feeling to be talking down to W. M. Dougherty. She remembered all those occasions when she had called at his office seeking news and been patronized and sent away feeling that she had been laughed at as an eccentric old fool. It was all changed now on account of Mr. Richardson. He was there behind her whenever she needed to call on him, supporting her all the time as if he had been her own son, the kind of son she had always dreamed of.

W. M. puffed for a moment on his cigar, then swung one heavy leg over the other and said in confidential tones, "I'll tell you something, Mrs. McLeod, I've always liked and admired you. I don't think you're a very smart woman but I think you're an understanding one, so I'm gonna tell you something." Again for a moment he paused reflectively and at last he said, "It all goes back a long way to when I was a kid six years old and first landed in this country. Until I was six years old I had never had enough to eat and the year I was six my old man picked up and came to America because there weren't even any potatoes in the garden patch in County Galway. In America I had enough to eat for the first time. The old man and the old woman and us seven kids all lived in two rooms in a tenement in South Boston." His face brightened a little and he said, "That's where I learned politics . . . in South Boston. You can learn everything there is to learn about 'em right there. I ain't learned a damned thing since then." He took the cigar out of his mouth and said, "Have you got a lot of time, because I want to tell you quite a long story?"

"Yes," said Mrs. McLeod, "I've got plenty of time. We can't get out the paper because the press is smashed."

At this he scowled and said, "Well, I'll tell you something. I didn't know anything about that but I have a good guess who done it and he's lost his job. But that wasn't what I wanted to tell you." He coughed and became embarrassed. "I don't know why I'm tellin' you all this. I never told it to anybody but Jimmy."

"Go on," said Mrs. McLeod, beginning to feel a little embarrassed. In J. E.'s big worn leather chair, Old Dougherty was squirming and writhing as if the effort of confiding in her brought him actual physical pain.

"Do go on," she repeated helpfully.

He went on. He told her all the story he had told Jimmy on the night Jimmy got drunk and brought Fern Hedges home with him. He told her about his marriage, and his wife's death and his ambitions for Jimmy to be an "honest-to-God gentleman," about how he had neglected Jimmy to make more money so Jimmy could live like a gentleman.

"I guess I've done some pretty dirty things now and again," he said, "but I've tried to keep Jimmy out of 'em. Most of it he never knew anything about till the *Daily Shield and Banner* put it all in print. It was kind of a shock to him. I guess it upset him quite a lot. He wasn't himself for a long time . . . but he wouldn't go back on the old man. That was pretty good of him. I guess if he'd been a good politician he would have gone back on me, but he hasn't got any talent for politics. He's too hot-headed and full of high falutin' ideas. He's like his mother that way. I guess Jimmy has had a pretty tough time these last coupla months . . . what with the *Daily Shield and Banner* campaign and eatin' his heart out about that pert niece of yours."

"Oh," said Mrs. McLeod with a new interest, "has he been eatin' his heart out. . . . I mean . . . really?"

"You ought to know that boy as well as I do. He's been made sick by the whole thing. He musta lost twenty pounds."

The tears came suddenly into Mrs. McLeod's eyes. For a long time, while she listened to the crude story of his rise in the world, they had been waiting just beneath the tired old eyelids, and now at the spectacle of Jimmy's suffering they overflowed. But at the same time she kept thinking, "I mustn't make a fool of myself again. He's talking like this to get something out of me and in spite of everything I'm going to get all worked

[207]

up and say 'Yes.'" But even saying that to herself didn't succeed in stopping the tears.

"You see," W. M. went on, "I've decided I haven't got any right to go on making the boy miserable. I'm sixty-five years old and I've had my fun—plenty of it. I've got to give him a chance. It ain't because I'm tired or licked and haven't got any more fight left in me. Don't you think that for a minute, even. I guess I'll have fight left when I'm ninety. It's on account of him. If it wasn't for him, I'd fight till I ran your paper out of business. You see, if I clear out now and call it a day, then he's free. Now I'll tell you what I propose to do. I've had a hankering for a long time for some fishin' and horseshoe throwin'. I'm going away tomorrow down to Daytona and I'm gonna stay there for some time . . . maybe for always. The Democratic machine can go to hell so far as I'm concerned. And that'll leave the town open to you and your Reverend Mr. Burwash and Mr. Richardson and Gashouse Mary."

Opposite him Mrs. McLeod sat farther forward on the edge of her chair feeling that her heart was going to burst. Victory! Victory! What she'd been dreaming about for years had come true!

"It's mostly on account of Jimmy," he was saying. "If I clear out, then he and your niece Jane could get together. And if I go to Daytona he won't have to go on being ashamed of me."

"Oh, no," said Mrs. McLeod. "I'm sure he isn't ashamed of you."

"Oh, yes he is. And it's natural too. If I was in his place I'd be ashamed of me too. He can't help it. Anyway he can come now and then to Daytona to see me and maybe she'll come with him. She's a nice little thing . . . kind of sweet in spite of bein' so uppity." He crushed out the end of his cigar against the brass of the jardiniere beside him and said, "No, all I want is a promise from you people that if I clear out and keep out of Plattesville politics, you'll lay off the whole thing. Stop the charges, indictments, everything."

For a moment Mrs. McLeod was silent. He was putting it up to her now and she had to answer. She wanted to say, "Sure, we'll call everything off." Then there would be peace and quiet again and an end to all this hating, and Jimmy and Jane could see each other again and Jane could be happy. It was fear of Mr. Richardson which stopped her, fear of what he would say, fear of making a fool of herself again in his eyes. So she said, "I think it'll be all right, only I'll have to talk to Mr. Richardson first." She tried her best to look shrewd but the effort only resulted in her looking as if she were making faces.

"That fellow Richardson," said Old Dougherty, "ought to go into politics. He oughta run for something."

"Yes," said Mrs. McLeod, a little smugly as if she had invented Mr. Richardson. "He's pretty smart."

"There's one thing I'd like to know," said Old Dougherty.

"What?" asked Mrs. McLeod.

"Who is he and where did he come from?"

"He's a newspaperman. He comes from New York."

"What was he doin' here out of a job, getting picked up for vagrancy?"

"He wasn't out of a job. He was working," said Mrs. McLeod.

W. M. Dougherty looked astonished. "Working? At what?"

"At a book. He was writing a book about how badly men out of work were treated."

Old Dougherty pondered this remarkable statement for a moment. Then his shrewd eyes narrowed and his lips curled in an expression of scorn. "I see," he said, "one of them radicals."

"I guess so," said Mrs. McLeod.

"He's crazy all right—crazy as a bedbug, but he's a damned good newspaperman."

W. M. rose and took up his hat. "I won't keep you any longer," he said, "only I want you to understand one thing. I'm goin' away on account of Jimmy. Nobody's got anything on me. If it wasn't for Jimmy I'd stay and lick you yet."

"I understand."

He started toward the door and then stopped. "The only thing I'm afraid of is that it's too late to patch things up between the boy and that niece of yours. He's got a hell of a lot of pride and I guess she has too."

"She has," said Mrs. McLeod.

He looked at her doubtfully, almost humbly. "You wouldn't object to 'em marryin', would you?" he asked.

"No," said Mrs. McLeod, "I wouldn't object." At the moment it was what she wanted most. She wanted to see that resigned "old maid look" leave Jane's pretty face, and she knew there was only one way of accomplishing the change.

He even grew a little more humble. "You mean you'd be willing to work for it?"

"Yes."

"I didn't know," he said. "Things being the way they are." For a moment he turned his hat round and round in his big thick hands. "It's kind of like my own story . . . I mean the story of me and Jimmy's mother. Her family thought I wasn't good enough for her. They was lace-curtain Irish and I was only shanty Irish."

"I see," said Mrs. McLeod. A McLeod marrying a Dougherty was something she had never dreamed of a few months ago, but a good deal

[209]

had happened since then. Plattesville and the county weren't what they used to be. Times had changed. And somehow, she didn't quite know how, Mr. Richardson had taught her a lot.

Awkwardly W. M. Dougherty held out his hand. "Well, good-by, Mrs. McLeod," he said. "I've enjoyed talkin' with you. As I said, you always seemed to me an understandin' kind of woman."

Once again the tears welled up, this time only because she was so happy that everything was turning out so well. She always wanted everybody to be happy and to love everybody else. And now everybody was going to be happy and even Old Dougherty was going to be happy, fishing and throwing horseshoes. She even felt herself liking him, and thought, "I suppose you like anybody, even the devil, if you get to know him well enough." And never again would she have to enter W. M. Dougherty's office and sit there and be patronized as if she were an old fool.

At the front door he shook hands again and said, "Well, I'll be saying good-by."

"Come in again some time," said Mrs. McLeod.

"Thanks. I guess I won't be around for a long time."

At the foot of the steps of McLeod's Folly he turned and said, "I just wanted to tell you that shindig last night was the best show Plattesville's seen since I laid eyes on the town."

When he had gone, she turned back into the house to find Aida waiting for her in the hallway.

"What dat old devil want?" asked Aida.

"He's going away. He's through," said Mrs. McLeod. "Don't ask me any more now. I've got to go and tell Jane."

But Jane didn't receive the news with joy as she had expected. She was in her own room sitting by the window, listlessly, with that resigned "old maid look" in her eyes. When she had been told, all she said was, "It's nothing but a trick. Anyway it's too late now."

80

But it wasn't a trick. W. M. Dougherty was licked and nobody knew it better than W. M. Dougherty himself. In the pocket of his trousers there was a rumpled special delivery letter which read simply and briefly: "Better scram while the scramming is good." It was signed "Bill Swain." But you couldn't let the enemy know about things like that. You had to make 'em believe you'd quit because you wanted to.

As he passed out of the rickety front gate of McLeod's Folly, he shook his head in a puzzled way like an old tired lion. He couldn't see how it had happened. He couldn't see how he had been licked so quickly. Even his organization, that machine he had built up so carefully on the model he had studied for so long in South Boston, had collapsed into pieces.

"Mebbe," he thought, "this is a different country from Boston. Mebbe there ain't enough Irish here. Mebbe there's some kind of spirit I never got the right line on." But in the end, it was that smart guy, Richardson, who had licked him. He was a hell of a smart guy, even if he was one of those dumb radicals.

He walked to his office by a roundabout way through alleys and back-streets, because he wasn't very eager to meet people in the street. Nowadays, when he met people they either pretended not to see him or they just nodded to him without saying anything. He knew what that meant. Nobody had to tell him. He'd been in politics long enough to know.

As he walked he forgot presently the sting of defeat, and after a time he didn't even see the citizens he passed, but only the golden sands of Daytona and a bar with plenty of Bourbon, and he heard the clank of horseshoes striking each other as they fell in the yellow Florida dust.

81

At the very moment W. M. Dougherty and Mrs. McLeod had their interview Jimmy and Mr. Richardson sat at each end of the long table in the office of W. M. Dougherty and Son, Contractors. They were fully dressed now but clothes could not conceal altogether the ravages of the heroic battle of the night before. Jimmy's left eye was swollen shut and his lip cut and patched with adhesive tape and Mr. Richardson's right eye was thoroughly blackened and his jaw swollen as if he were suffering from a toothache. Before them on the table stood a bottle of Bourbon and two glasses.

Mr. Richardson raised his glass. "Well," he said, "anyway, let's drink to it."

When he had come in twenty minutes earlier Jimmy Dougherty had opened the door himself and with his one good eye, glared at him, a little in resentment and a great deal in suspicion and astonishment.

He said coldly, "Good morning," and Mr. Richardson answered, "Good morning," and asked, "Could I speak to you for a moment about something important?"

"Yes," said Jimmy, "if it's important enough."

He remained standing and didn't ask Mr. Richardson to sit down, but Mr. Richardson took the matter into his own hands, sat down and said, "I think we can talk better sitting." So there wasn't anything left for Jimmy to do but sit down.

Then Mr. Richardson said, "Now let's get two or three things straight.

First, I haven't got anything against you . . . in a personal way, I mean. From what I hear of you I think you must be a pretty good sort."

"Thanks," said Jimmy.

"And in the second place Jane never had anything to do with the crusade. She never played any part in it and she didn't double-cross you."

"I knew that."

"How?"

"She's not that kind of a girl."

"And in the third place, I was never on the make for Jane. I almost was—once or twice—but nothing came of it. Anyway, I don't think she'd have any of that."

Jimmy looked at him without saying anything, but in the one open blue eye there was an expression of bewilderment. After a moment, he said, "Did she send you here?"

"No, she doesn't know anything about it. She'd raise hell if she knew."

"Why?"

"Because she'd say it wasn't any of my business and it isn't. I only came to get things straightened out. I felt sort of responsible for a lot of mis-understanding. Jane couldn't say it herself . . . she's got too much pride."

"Yes, I guess she has. I guess that's the whole trouble between us."

"When the truce is over the fight can begin again, only don't think that Jane is mixed up in it or double-crossing you or anything."

"I did think that—sometimes—until last night."

Mr. Richardson grinned. "Yes, she made everything pretty clear last night. She's got an awful punch for a little thing her size." He puffed for a moment at his cigarette and then said, "Of course I hope I'm acting on the right supposition. You do want to marry Jane, don't you? I'm not making a damned fool of myself for nothing?"

"What did you think I wanted to do? What did you think the fight was about?"

A little taken aback, Mr. Richardson said, "Well, I was never quite sure."

"I don't see why you're so damned interested. You've done everything you could to break it up."

"I didn't know anything about it. And when I found out, it was too late to stop things even if I wanted to. But that doesn't matter now. The point is to fix things up."

"I guess I can take care of that for myself."

A grin appeared on Mr. Richardson's battered face, a grin of irresistible friendliness and warmth, a grin which had a heightened effect and value because it appeared on the face of one who was not, like Jimmy, prodigal with his grins.

"Listen," he said, "I'm not trying to interfere or be superior or any other damned thing. I like you and Jane and I want you to get together. I'm doing this for my own sake because it'll make me feel good inside . . . that's the only reason people ever do things like this. Jane's been off her feed for weeks." He lighted a cigarette and said, "If I were you I'd go and see Jane right away, this morning, and I'd get into that shiny new roadster of yours and take her right off and marry her before sundown. A couple like you has got a sociological value to the nation. You're good stock. You ought to have twenty children for the good of the State. That's what we need . . . more and more children from the sturdy, respectable middle classes."

"Why don't you start a campaign in the *Daily Shield and Banner?*" asked Jimmy.

"That's a good idea . . . when we get the press repaired." He stood up. "I've got to get back to the office now."

Jimmy got to his feet, slowly, still filled with suspicion.

"Have a drink?" he suggested.

"I can't think of anything I'd like better."

He fetched a bottle of Bourbon, a little resentful that Richardson seemed to consider the crusade finished and the battle won. He poured out two drinks and Richardson said, "Well, anyway, let's drink to it and to a large family."

"Leave that out of it," said Jimmy. They raised their glasses and Richardson said, "Jane has a lot of high falutin' ideas. If I were you I wouldn't take any notice of 'em. What she wants is to be subdued. She's longing for a good subduing."

"Do you mind not telling me about my own girl?"

And then the door opened and Old Dougherty himself came in, or at least stepped across the threshold, for so great was his astonishment at the sight he beheld that he got no farther. There, before his unbelieving eyes, were Jimmy and Richardson himself, drinking together. The blood rushed into his head and again for a moment he feared he was about to have a stroke. His son and Richardson, both battered and bruised, drinking together, apparently in a friendly way. The sight surpassed anything he could have imagined two days ago . . . it surpassed even the spectacle of his own grudging surrender to Mrs. McLeod. He heard Mr. Richardson saying, "Here's to matrimony."

Then Jimmy noticed him and said, "Come in. We were talking about fishing. Come in and have a drink."

Letting go of the door knob Old Dougherty said, "I guess I need a drink . . . a good strong one."

82

When Old Dougherty had gone and Jane had been told of the victory, Mrs. McLeod had to tell Aida everything that had happened while the two of them had been shut in the library. She was eager to hurry to the office and tell Myrtle and Willie and old Zimmerman and all the rest, but she knew that if Aida's curiosity wasn't satisfied Aida would have a "misery" and go about complaining all day, dragging one foot after another. Hurriedly, she told the story, omitting a good deal, but it wasn't any good because Aida suspected her of hurrying and kept asking, "Why?" and "When?" and "How?" in the most tiresome manner. And then when she had at last satisfied Aida, Aida asked, "And what about Mis' Jane? Is she finished with that Jimmy?"

"I don't know," said Mrs. McLeod.

"It's a shame, Mis' McLeod, her carryin' on about him."

Then Mrs. McLeod was thoughtful for a moment. Then she said, "You've been in love, haven't you, Aida?"

"Yes," said Aida wistfully. "A powerful long time ago."

"Why did you marry Sam?"

"Because I was in love with him. I was crazy about that man."

"And he was nothing but a no-good river nigger?"

"That's right, Mis' McLeod, but he was a special river nigger."

"Well, Jimmy Dougherty is a special Irishman. You leave Miss Jane alone."

"All right, Mis' McLeod, ah'll think about it. You kinda put it in a different way."

Then Aida left her, shaking her grizzled old head thoughtfully as she rolled back into the kitchen, and Mrs. McLeod, jamming her old hat on her head, hurried off to the office.

And there she found a fresh surprise. Myrtle Ferguson was upstairs waiting for her. She came forward with a look of wonder and astonishment in her eyes, holding stiffly in front of her, a card. She said, "There's a gentleman to see you. This is him," and for a moment Mrs. McLeod's heart was stopped again by the expression of awe and mystery on Myrtle's face. She thought wildly, "Maybe it's a Federal officer." Then she took the card and read:

JOHN M. BURNHAM

The New York Register.	*The Chicago Journal.*
The New York Recorder.	*The Detroit Gazette.*
The Boston News.	*The San Francisco Review.*

The Kansas City Globe.

When Mrs. McLeod looked up, Myrtle said, her eyes still round with wonder, "He must be the Burnham-Leslie Chain."

"What do you suppose he wants here?"

"Maybe he's come to buy the *Daily Shield and Banner*. Maybe he's heard about all we've been doing."

"Maybe," said Mrs. McLeod. "Tell him to come right up. We can't keep a man like that waiting."

Excitement took possession of Mrs. McLeod. For a moment she felt completely dizzy and thought of asking Willie Ferguson for a taste of Bourbon. But there wasn't time for that. She had to put her desk in order. What would a man like John M. Burnham think of her as an editor if he saw her desk in such a mess? Hurriedly she opened drawers and threw papers into them willy-nilly. With her handkerchief she dusted the top of the desk, even spitting on it to remove the stain of ink where three days ago she had overturned the inkwell. Hurriedly she tried to put her unruly hair in order and set her collar and blouse right, and then the door opened and Myrtle Ferguson in a voice still strange with awe said, "This is Mrs. McLeod, Mr. Burnham."

Mrs. McLeod made a wild effort to pull herself together and gain control of her voice.

"Good morning," she said. "Won't you sit down?"

"Thank you."

With her woman's eye, she considered Mr. Burnham. He was a good-looking, well set-up man about fifty-five. It was, she decided, a nice face, a strong face with a big jaw and firm chin and clear gray-blue eyes.

There was a moment's awkward pause and then the great Mr. Burnham said, "I was in St. Louis so I thought I'd just run down and say hello to my son."

"Yes," said Mrs. McLeod, bewildered but unwilling to make a fool of herself.

"I hadn't heard from him for some time. You see, we had a difference of opinion, partly about politics and partly about how to run a newspaper. He decided to go off on his own for a while. I guess you've found out that he's pretty radical . . . practically red, in fact."

For a moment Mrs. McLeod felt that she was going mad. For a moment she even suspected that she was already mad and that everything which had happened during the last few months had simply been an hallucination. She had to say something, and she couldn't go on pretending that she knew what he was talking about without getting herself into a hole and making a complete fool of herself.

So she said, "I don't know what you're talking about. I'm afraid I don't know your son. I don't know anyone called Burnham."

Mr. Burnham looked at her with astonishment. Then he said, "This is the office of a newspaper called the *Plattesville Daily Shield and Banner,* isn't it?"

"Yes."

"Well, that's where my son has been working."

"I'm afraid there's some mistake. There isn't anyone on our staff by that name."

Mr. Burnham didn't answer her at once. He thrust his hand into his pocket, brought out a telegram and gave it to her, saying, "That's from him; I received it day before yesterday."

She read the telegram:

"Come and see what I've done. Look me up newspaper called Shield and Banner Plattesville. Jack."

Mrs. McLeod handed it back to him.

"I can't imagine what it means. We've got a young man here who's been with us some time, but his name is Richardson."

Mr. Burnham's gray-blue eyes narrowed. "What does he look like?"

"Well," began Mrs. McLeod. "He's quite nice looking, blondish, with gray-blue eyes, a hard worker. . . ." Then through her own words came to her a sudden flash of understanding. Mr. Richardson looked like Mr. Burnham, exactly as Mr. Burnham must have looked at his age before he had begun collecting all that big chain of newspapers. No wonder Mr. Richardson knew everything there was to know about newspapers. For a second she stared at Mr. Burnham and then she said, "I guess maybe Mr. Richardson might be your son working under another name."

Mr. Burnham grinned, "That sounds like him. He does things like that," he said. "Tell me, is he any good?"

So Mrs. McLeod told him. She had been wanting for a long time to tell someone what she thought of Mr. Richardson, but there had never been anyone to whom she might talk, and now she had her chance, a big chance, to tell everything. She told Mr. Burnham how she had found him in jail, of his unwillingness to come out, of how he first built up the newspaper and then launched the crusade, about how he had got The Book published, about how Pugface Mahoney and Little Hermie had taken a pot shot at him, about the Torchlight Procession and the heroic fight with Jimmy Dougherty in the park beside the Soldiers' and Sailors' Monument, about the jail delivery, about Gashouse Mary and the influence of Bill Swain, and the final triumph which ended with the withdrawal of Old Dougherty to Daytona.

"He ought to be in politics," she said. "Even Old Dougherty says so."

Mr. Burnham, it was easy to see, was pleased. He grinned. He chuckled over the story of the fight and the jail delivery. He said, "He's a good boy. He's got plenty of energy and spirit, only he's stubborn. I guess he's just a born reformer. Maybe he'll get over it as he grows older."

"He's awful good at it," said Mrs. McLeod. "I thought he must know a lot about newspapers. He seemed to know pretty nearly everything."

"He does. He's been working around newspapers ever since he was a kid, only he isn't satisfied with being a first-rate newspaperman. He's always wanting to reform the world. He'd be a lot better off if he stuck to his job."

And then Mr. Richardson, battered, bruised and bandaged, came in.

83

Jane was halfway down the path bordered by the ragged syringas and lilacs, hurrying to the office when she heard the voice of Aida calling, "Mis' Jane! Mis' Jane! Telephone for you!"

The sound of Aida's voice startled her and for a moment even frightened her, not because it was the first time the voice had ever summoned her to the telephone but because there was a queer sound to it, a note that was unfamiliar. For a week or more Jane had been aware of many things, subtleties which in her happier, more bumptious days, she had never perceived. It was as if her perceptions had been sharpened mysteriously by her unhappiness: the creak of a chair, the slamming of a door, the sound of a motor horn late at night, sometimes set her nerves on edge. It all went with what Aida called "her peaked look" and what to Mrs. McLeod was the "old maid look." Now as she passed Aida she looked at her sharply and even with suspicion, but the only response was a white-toothed grin.

The telephone was an old-fashioned affair attached to the wall beneath the great stairway, and when she answered it she expected to hear either the voice of Aunt Vinnie or of Mr. Richardson, chiding her perhaps for being so late at the office. Instead she heard a voice that was unmistakable, saying, "Is that you, Jane?"

For a second she felt that she was going to faint and grasped the table beside her to keep from falling. Summoning all her strength, she managed to ask, "Yes, who is it?" as if she did not already know perfectly well.

"You know who it is," said the voice.

"Yes . . . yes, I do." But suddenly her happiness made her shy so that she couldn't think of anything to say except things which her pride would not allow her to say. She wasn't even able to show him that everything was all right, that she wasn't angry or resentful or suspicious any more, that at that moment nothing in the world was of any importance

[217]

save having him back again . . . neither family, nor pride, nor the crusade, nor even self-respect.

"I guess you've heard the news," said the voice.

"Yes, Jimmy."

"Will you have dinner with me tonight?"

"Yes." She wanted to cry out. She wanted to say so much more, but all she could say was "yes" timidly like a schoolgirl.

"We'd better go to Millersville. It's the middle of the week. There won't be any crowd."

"Yes."

"I'll pick you up at home about five o'clock."

"All right."

Then there was a moment's silence and the voice—that familiar voice, so Irish, so beguiling, so dangerous—came to her again.

"What's the matter? You aren't still sore at me?"

"No, Jimmy." And then she managed with a great effort to humble her pride and say, "I won't ever be disagreeable again."

And then the voice again, a voice which in its warmth, its urgency, was as beautiful as the plumage of a courting bird of Paradise.

"That's a good kid. I don't know whether I can wait."

"Good-by, Jimmy." She had to say good-by quickly, before she began to cry. She could feel the tears coming on. "Good-by," she said again in a whisper.

"Good-by, sweetheart."

And then she slipped into the chair beside the telephone and began to cry as she had never cried before in all her life. The tears were strange, voluptuous tears, tears of hysterical happiness, which seemed to refresh her and give her strength. And from behind the door where she had been listening all the time, appeared the figure of Aida saying, "What's the matter, honey? Ain't got bad news?"

"No," said Jane, hysterically. "No . . . no."

Aida gave her a friendly pat on the back and said, "Ah'll go fetch you all some whisky."

When she returned the sobbing had died away a little, and while Jane drank the whisky, Aida said something very odd, "Ah guess you all ain't a little girl no more. Ah guess you all got some sense now. Ah guess you all is a grown-up woman lak Aida and you aunt, Mis' McLeod."

84

Well before five o'clock the olive-green roadster was at the door and Jimmy with his swollen eye and cut lip was bounding up the high steps three at a time. On the night before, in the half-light of the Square, in the confusion of the fight with his face all bloody and bruised, Jane had noticed how thin he was and how pale. Now the sight of him made her want to cry, but it made her want to laugh too because his woebegone appearance told her that he too had been suffering the way she had been.

Then for a second after he reached the top of the steps, they were both struck dumb by shyness. There had been only one way of ending that dash up the path and the high steps, and that would have been for him to take her in his arms and kiss her; but they couldn't do that right there in broad daylight on the front porch of McLeod's Folly with people going past on the sidewalk and Aida undoubtedly concealed behind the window curtains in the parlor.

Abruptly, Jimmy broke the silence by saying, "Are you all ready?"

She gave a little nervous laugh, "Don't I look as if I was ready?"

"Well, let's go."

They drove wildly, the way only Jimmy drove, out of the town, past Doughertys' house, past the familiar pretentious houses and gardens of Fleming Avenue, through Shantytown just beyond, but to both of them the whole scene that raced past them was a new world, different, illumined by a kind of radiance it had never known before. They never spoke at all, and at last when they were a good ten miles out into the open country, Jimmy drove to the side of the road and stopped the car. There should have been a wood or a flowery bosquet, but on that huge plain there was not a tree save the scraggy cottonwoods which grew far off near the ranch houses.

There in the midst of vastness, alone save for the big soft round eyes of the short-horn cattle beyond the wire fence, he took her in his arms, kissed her and held her close for a long time. At last, with both of them a little pale and shaken, he said, "I guess maybe we'd better get along to Millersville before anything happens."

It was a different ride from the last one, months ago when they had quarreled and Jimmy had stopped the car and threatened to return to Plattesville. They talked now about the crusade, about Mr. Richardson, about The Book, about the jail delivery, even about the imminent departure of Jimmy's father, not seriously but as if the whole thing had been a huge joke. It did not matter now, any of it. Jane was guilty of giggling, something she had never before done in her whole life. But underneath she kept thinking, "Maybe what happened was all to the good. I've got some sense now. I know what matters and what doesn't. I'll never be disagreeable again. Help me, God, never to be disagreeable again no matter what Jimmy does . . . now I know what I want. It's frightening to be so happy." And now and then she would glance sidewise at Jimmy to make sure he was still there and she wasn't dreaming.

And she thought, "Maybe after all it was a good thing that Mr. Richardson came along and stirred everything up."

As they climbed the ridge which led down on the other side to the little sapphire lake beside Cousin Ira's hotel, Jimmy said, "That Richardson fellow is a pretty good guy."

She laughed, "You were jealous of him, weren't you?"

"Yes, I was jealous as hell."

"You needn't have been. He's just a machine. He isn't even human. He's just a reformer."

"I'll bet you did try flirting with him."

"Yes, but only because I wanted to make you jealous."

"Well, you did."

85

It was "Mr. Richardson" who suggested the dinner party to celebrate the reconciliation and the engagement of Jimmy Dougherty and Jane Baldwin. He proposed giving it himself at the Beauregard Hotel, but Mrs. McLeod put up strenuous objections.

"We couldn't do that," she said, "on account of Aida. She'd never get over it if we didn't let her cook the dinner. She can get in her cousin Athena to wait on table. We always used to have Athena in the days when we had people in. She worked in St. Louis once in a rich brewer's family and she knows all about serving."

They put their heads together and made out the list. There would be the great Mr. Burnham of the Burnham-Leslie newspapers and Willie and Myrtle Ferguson and Jim Newman and Jane's mother and father.

"And what about W. M. Dougherty?" asked Mr. Richardson.

"But he's already gone," said Mrs. McLeod. "He went to Daytona the day after the Torchlight Procession." For a moment she hesitated and then said, "But there's somebody else I'd like to have."

"Who?" asked Mr. Richardson.

"Gashouse Mary."

"Of course, we'll have her."

For two whole days Aida, aided by Athena who shared her cousin's bed for two nights, labored over the banquet. It was a grand affair, with cream of tomato soup, trout from Cousin Ira's hatchery cooked in oatmeal, Maryland fried chicken, new peas, mashed potatoes which were a poem, sweet corn, salad, lemon ice cream and chocolate cake.

On the day of the feast Aida beamed and bustled. In this there was nothing unusual: the prospect of feeding large quantities of people always raised Aida's spirits. It was something else in her manner which roused the suspicions of Mrs. McLeod. For thirty years they had been mistress and servant: for thirty years they had been friends: for thirty years they had known each other intimately: and Mrs. McLeod knew all the signs displayed by Aida when she had a secret. They were signs almost as violent as those which indicated one of Aida's "miseries." All day she went about smiling slyly, chuckling and even talking to herself. From noon onward on the day of the banquet, Mrs. McLeod was aware that Aida had "something up her sleeve."

It was no use questioning her. When Aida had a secret or a surprise to spring, wild horses could not drag a hint of it from her. What it could be this time, Mrs. McLeod had not the faintest idea. The suspicions crystallized, however, when at seven o'clock she went in to look at the table and found that Athena had laid one place too many. When she summoned Aida and questioned her, Aida put on what Mrs. McLeod called her "canary swallowing" look and said, "Ah guess Athena's made a mistake. She's kind of dumb—Athena," and herself took off the extra cover. But when Mrs. McLeod by chance returned to the dining room a little later, the extra plate was there on the table once more, and she divined that someone was coming as a surprise. She didn't speak of the matter again, but cudgeling her brain with all her might, she could not imagine who the surprise might be.

Mrs. McLeod took an hour off during the afternoon to have her hair waved for the first time in years. She wore her best foulard, and when at last she was ready and stood before the mirror of the huge walnut bureau in her bedroom, she was herself astonished at how neat and collected she looked. She even looked young, younger than she had looked in ten years. It was as if the last two or three days had wiped out scores of tiny, weary wrinkles. As she stood there she heard Mr. Richardson come out of his room and go down the big stairway and out of the house. From her window she saw him go down the path between the lilacs and turn toward Main Street.

"Where on earth can he be going," she wondered, "at this hour? It's only half an hour till dinnertime."

She got no further with her speculation, for the car bringing Jane's parents from the ranch drove up and she had to go downstairs to greet them.

A little while later Jim Newman arrived, and then Jane came downstairs to see about the cocktails, and then Mr. Burnham appeared, and presently Gashouse Mary arrived in a taxicab, dressed in a bright green, summer evening dress with a white fox fur about her shoulders. She wore combs studded with brilliants in her elaborate coiffure, and on her bosom and wrists and in her ears her whole parure of garnets. And then Willie

Ferguson in a hired dinner coat which hung on him like a tent, and Myrtle Ferguson in a blue foulard dress came in. And after them Jimmy arrived, his face still a bit battered but with lips no longer swollen and spread now in a grin, half-sheepish, half-delighted.

Jane distributed cocktails and the party began to liven up. Mr. Burnham and Gashouse Mary took a liking to each other, and he led her on to telling stories of life in dance halls and bars along the river. Once, twice, three times, Mrs. McLeod went anxiously to the window for some sign of Mr. Richardson but there was none. The fourth time she was rewarded.

Coming up the steps was Mr. Richardson and with him was Aida's surprise—a strange woman. Mrs. McLeod had only a glimpse of her, but she knew at once by her dress that she didn't come from Plattesville.

A moment later Mr. Richardson was in the room, saying, "I want to introduce my fiancée—Prudence Higginson."

She was a tall girl and was dressed in a tweed suit and flat-heeled shoes. And she wore a soft, rather mannish shirt with a neck-tie and horn-rimmed spectacles. Her dark hair she wore long and done in a "bun" at the back of her head. You couldn't tell whether she was pretty or plain; but you could tell that she was intellectual. She wasn't shy. She shook hands with everyone and said she hoped that they weren't late, but that her train had only just come in and there wasn't time to change her clothes even if she'd brought any clothes. Jack's telegram, she said, had left her with only forty minutes to catch the train from Boston for the West.

Jane, standing next to Jimmy, so close that their fingers touched, felt a little lift in her heart. She knew she was looking pretty, prettier than she had ever looked in her life before. She thought, "If that's his type, I see why he didn't fall for me," and then again, "If that's the way common sense makes you look, I'm glad I haven't got any." But they seemed to like each other—Miss Prudence Higginson and Mr. Richardson—in their Yankee way.

Then Miss Higginson, in a very polite, well-bred way, asked Jane, "When is the wedding to be?"

For a moment Jane hesitated and Jimmy, grinning, prodded her and said, "Go on. Tell 'em."

"It's been already," said Jane. "Cousin Ira married us in Millersville the day after the Torchlight Procession."

"We got married before anything else happened," said Jimmy.

When the sensation had died down, everybody kissed the bride, and Jane's mother cried a little, and then everybody drank to the newly married couple, and then Mr. Richardson raised his glass and said, "Now let's drink to Mrs. McLeod, who cleaned up Plattesville"; and while they raised their glasses and drank, she stood there confused and red and happy with tears in her eyes. With a lump in her throat she managed to say, "It wasn't me, it was Mr. Richardson."

Mr. Richardson laughed, "I couldn't have done anything if you hadn't got me out of jail." Then he drew out of his pocket a fat envelope and said, "Here's the contract for The Book," and turning to Miss Higginson he said, "Mrs. McLeod's written a book. The first publisher that read it took it. It's called *McLeod's Folly*." He looked at Mrs. McLeod and between them there passed a swift look of understanding. "I think it's an awfully good title," Mr. Richardson added.

Then the voice of Athena interrupted. "Mis' McLeod," she said. "You all is served in the dining room."

As Mrs. McLeod with the great Mr. Burnham of the Burnham-Leslie Chain led the way to dinner, she had a quick glimpse of Aida's figure as she scuttled away in the direction of the kitchen. She had been there all the time, hiding behind the plush curtains since the moment Mr. Richardson arrived bringing his surprise.

II

The Hand of God

BUT for the house on the point at Salasso I would never have known the Onspenskis, and not knowing them I would never have noticed their names among the survivors of the disaster which happened to the liner *Philippe Auguste* on its way home from China. Indeed, I would never have known their story at all, for they were never first-rate swindlers whose names appeared in the headlines but only middle-sized ones, who rarely pulled off a *grand coup*, and without knowing them we might have passed over their exploits even without remarking them.

It was a lovely house built in the style of the country with a low sweeping roof of faded and clumsy red tiles on which heavy stones had been laid to keep the wild winter winds of the Bay of Biscay from tearing them loose. I never saw it in winter but I know that while I lived in it the autumn storms were sometimes so violent that one had to close the heavy shutters on the seaward side to prevent the panes from being blown in. The house had big windows with shutters which opened on to small balconies where there were boxes of petunias and ivy geraniums and convolvulus trailing downward in a cloud of blossoms. Inside on the second floor there was a marvelous big room where one ate and sometimes sat over coffee in the evening, looking out over the mountains and the sea, at the moment when the Bay of Biscay turned a deeper and deeper purple until at last sea and sky came together and there were only the stars and the little circlet of lights marking the distant harbor of Saint Christophe to show where one ended and the other began.

One knows at once whether a house has been built with love and whether it has been lived in with love. Sometimes I have come to a house to spend a month or a season and found myself staying on for years or returning to it again and again because there was something about it which I had been seeking, sometimes without knowing it at all. Usually for all of us, it is peace which we seek, and of all things in life the hardest to find is peace. One needs peace to return to. One knows at once when there is peace in a house.

It was a very old house and the date of its building, 1657, was cut in stone over the doorway. In it generation after generation had been born and died. From it young Basques had gone off to places like Brooklyn and Buenos Ayres to make their fortunes and to return at last to die between the mountains and the sea. The house had peace and dignity and beauty and age.

I came upon it one day by accident while I was walking with the dogs on the moor above the sea, aimlessly and happily because there was so much of solitude and beauty all about me. Behind me rose the whole vast barrier of the Pyrenees, the high distant mountains blue and purple and rocky, the nearer ones melted away into soft mounds of green bracken with little goat paths cast over them like spider webs. Under foot there was purple heather in bloom and a froth of wild flowers, and before me there was the sea and the little harbor, with its blue and green fishing boats. The heather scented the air and suddenly there, a little before me in the small hollow which concealed and protected it, stood the house.

It was like a magic house which had come up out of the earth. I could not remember having seen it before, and after a moment's reflection I understood why. It stood in a small depression of the moor and was so covered with vines that unless one came upon it by chance one never saw it at all. But there was magic about it as I found out later, for although you could not see the house from the highroad or the distant town of Saint Chistophe des Eaux, once you were inside it you had a view which seemed to take in all creation—mountains, sea and sky.

A big garden surrounded it, all inclosed by a hedge of tamarisks which on the day I found it was all in bloom and covered with pink feathery flowers. It was a low friendly hedge. The passers-by, and they were few, might peep through it or look over it by standing on tiptoe. And there, in the midst of the garden, sat the house, close to the earth, bound to it by bonds of clematis and roses and the lovely sky-blue morning glory which is so difficult to grow elsewhere and which grows so easily in that country. At one end of the garden there was a little orchard where vegetables grew beneath the fruit trees, and at the other end, away from the sea, there was a little walled inclosure filled with roses where it was always warm and sheltered.

Beneath the house on the harbor side, the ground sloped away steeply to the tiny village of Salasso so that it seemed one could step out of the garden on to the roofs of the houses. There were no summer people in Salasso, but only fishermen and their families, handsome dark fishermen, who set out with the tides to come home knee-deep in silver sardines and anchovies. At the end of the village protecting it from the sea lay the great ruin of a Roman fort, and just inside it, sheltered by its ancient rocks, lay a little beach, white and slender like a young moon, with here and there a red rock to break its monotony.

But best of all the house was solitary. On its jutting little plateau, inclosed in its friendly garden, it stood in a world of its own, high above the sea with the wall of mountains sheltering it from unfriendly north winds. It was difficult even to find the way to it, for the only road by which a motor might enter was a narrow, partly overgrown lane, sunk between thick walls of briers and eglantine, which came across the moor from the highroad a mile away—the highroad where Hispanos and Rolls-Royces whizzed backward and forward between San Sebastián and Biarritz all day and all night; and the entrance to the lane was so hidden in a grove of ancient druid oaks that strangers with an adventurous spirit passed it by without even entering. After I lived there I found it was easy to be rid of the people with expensive motors who pressed you for permission to "come and have a look at your little paradise." One only had to tell them to take the first turning after the bridge. Usually they drove past without seeing it at all and if they saw it they only believed that so narrow and tangled a lane could have nothing more impressive than a cow pasture at its flowery end. And so those unworthy of that small paradise seldom entered it.

2

The moment I saw the house I knew it had been lived in by someone who loved it, and happily, I thought, "This is my house. I am the successor to the man who loved it."

The shutters were up and it had the sad look which friendly houses have when they are closed and abandoned. In this case the owner who had loved it was dead only a few months before I discovered it, and his widow could not live there; she was a very old lady and the sea air was bad for her health. And so it was for rent. She would not sell it because she had been happy there and some day, when she felt death coming on, she hoped to return there to die.

"It is a place," she wrote me, "which grows about the heart."

And so, for all too short a time it became mine, and for five summers I lived in it from the beginning of May until the frosts came and turned the bracken brown and the shepherds set fire to the hills so that in the spring the fresh young grass might grow thick for the sheep and goats.

Houses, like people, have personalities, and like the personalities of people they are partly molded by all that has happened to them. There are houses which are cold and empty, houses which are malicious, others which are friendly, others dignified and some, perhaps the best of all, are disheveled and merry. The moment you came into that house, out of the hot sunshine into the cool of its big tiled entrance hall, you were aware of its personality, and the longer you stayed there, the more you knew that this was a house in which charming people had lived, people who were simple and knew the things in life which had value and those which had not. One divined its peculiar warm quality, without reflecting, in the chairs and the very texture of the wall, in the cracks which had never been repaired because the owner had not the heart to outrage the house by tearing aside the garments of flowers and vines to violate its nakedness with fresh plaster and cement.

The owner too was there, although he had been dead for a long time. The fishermen in the little village below loved him in life and they loved him in death. They never spoke of him by his family name but only as "Monsieur André." When first I came to the house they regarded me with suspicion and when I met them in the single street of the little village they would address me with a cold *"Bon jour."* The Basques, a singularly honest and dignified people, are suspicious of you until you have proved yourself. It was only at the end of the second year that they came to be friendly, slowly, at first one and then another and another. Only then did I discover that they had looked upon me as a usurper who had no right in the house of Monsieur André. When they saw how I kept the garden and that I changed nothing, only striving to keep the place as it had always been and never bringing to it any of that noisy vulgar world which had spoiled all the rest of the lovely coast, they began to accept me as the rightful or at least the appropriate heir.

And they talked to me about Monsieur André—how he had come to them nearly forty years before as a young man to buy the place when old Etcheverria died and how he let the widow of old Etcheverria live on for nothing in the little house at the end of the garden until she went to join her husband. He had broken no traditions, changed nothing. The Etcheverria family had lived in the house since it was built in 1657 and had owned the land since the time the Romans built the now desolate fortress, but the coming of Monsieur André had changed nothing.

"That," the fishermen said, "was right. Monsieur André belonged there. He had the feeling of the place. God looks after such things."

The people of the village were religious, but it was impossible to say where their Christianity ended and their paganism began, for the Church in its wisdom had compromised with a stubborn people by accepting a blend of the two things. Most of them believed in spells and charms and some of them who had never been away from the village in their lives talked of nymphs and sprites who lived in the groves of oak trees which dotted the countryside. There were witches among the village folk, whose craft had come down through nearly two thousand years from the days before the Romans had penetrated their rocky country. In June, at the beginning of summer, there was a fete in the village which lasted for three days. They burned a young oak tree or a pile of faggots to which the priest himself set fire, coming out of the tiny church at the head of a procession of awkward fisher

[227]

boys bearing candles and piping in treble voices. On the second day there was a wooden bull carried on the shoulders of two men, which capered through the crowd, spouting harmless fireworks, to go up at last in a blaze of Roman candles, rockets and Catherine wheels. On the third day they danced and drank, and on all three they made love.

For the rest of the year they were a hard-working, moral people, but for the three days which marked the beginning of summer, during that ancient festival of fertility, they cast aside restraint and became pagans. For them the Druids were still only a little way off, no farther than the grove of oaks at the entrance to the lane, where they had worshiped and held sacrifices two thousand years before. In that lost corner the line of tradition had never been broken. The fishermen were content with their hard spare lives. They wanted only to be left in peace. And Monsieur André had not disturbed them. Although he was dead they still spoke of him as if he were alive. If the Onspenskis had not come he would have lived on forever among them in his house and garden just above their roof tops, and presently he would have become a legend and after a longer time he would perhaps have become a local saint, perhaps Saint André des Falaises. That is the way such things came about in that country.

I heard about Monsieur André from the Baron as well. The Baron was a little old man who was land poor and lived with his sister in a huge decaying château at the top of one of the low foothills between the house and the highroad. He it was who owned the moor and he it was who for fifty years had been the protector of the village and the house, for he had refused to sell a hectare of his land when bit by bit the whole coast came to be ruined. During the boom days of the twenties he could have got any price for it, but he preferred to keep that last corner of his world as he had always known it.

He was a small man, very dainty in build, with a kind of shabby elegance that was touching. When I first knew him he was seventy years old and his sister Mademoiselle Fernande was only a little younger. They lived alone the year round in the big château with only one servant, and I never saw the inside of it for I was never invited there. After a little while I learned that it was not through lack of friendliness. No one had been invited inside its walls for nearly thirty years. The fishermen said it was because there was no furniture; bit by bit, for years they had been selling it secretly to keep their land. The Baron was rather dry and shriveled and his wit had the same quality. There was about him the innocence of an elderly professor; he was one of those who are born to remain innocent in spite of everything. The fishermen, when I came to know them better, told me that in the village he had two sons and a daughter, and fourteen grandchildren descended from the days when he had been young. Perhaps it was these bonds of flesh and blood, sprung from the bacchanalian revels of the annual fete, marking the beginning of summer, which made him doubly the protector of that little corner of the world. I suspect that there was an unspoken understanding between him and the village people.

He spent most of his time among them and long ago when he was younger, he and his friend Monsieur André would go out in their boats with them, far out into the Bay of Biscay. His sister Mademoiselle Fernande shared his love for the village and the moors. She too had a passion for fishing and most of their days in good weather were spent in fishing from the crumbling jetties of the Roman fort. After I came and began fishing with a rod and reel among the rocks in the churning water on the sea side of the jetties, a new passion came into her life. Armed with rod and reel, barefooted with a knee-length khaki skirt, the old lady would join me in clambering over the rocks, fighting the surf as stoutly as any young man. Sometimes I was alarmed lest a wave should toss her against the rocks and break her limbs, but she seemed indestructible. When she was overturned by a boisterous wave she only shouted with laughter, picked herself up and set about casting once more.

The Baron was a scholar. All his life he had lived among the shepherds and fishermen, and he had collected and written down their legends, their spells, their superstitions, and in the end he had come to believe in them himself. If you mocked at them he would grow very still and serious and concerned and say, "But there *is* a power in them. You shouldn't mock. I know. I have seen things happen. You see, this is an immensely old country. We are still very near to the remote past." But he would rarely go deeper than that into the subject. Although we came to be friends, I think he always regarded me as an outsider, not to be trusted with the secrets he knew. Mademoiselle Fernande too believed the dark sinister stories, even more profoundly I think than her brother.

From the Baron and the fishermen I came presently to know all about Monsieur André. They told me that he had died in the house one summer evening in the great room on the second floor, propped up in a chair so that he might look out for the last time on that beloved view of the mountains and the sea. For forty years he had lived part of every year in the house. He was a lawyer whose work was in Paris but he never stayed in Paris when it was possible to escape to Salasso. "This is a very ancient country," the Baron said. "He may have lived here before and loved it and so always wanted to return."

But Monsieur André was much more than a mere lawyer, for he had loved music and played the piano and he was an expert gardener and a good cook and a wit and for him, as for the Baron and Mademoiselle Fernande, there were neither kings nor beggars but only men and women. In his old

[229]

age he liked fishing from the jetties and making water colors of the houses in the village and of the brown village children.

In the village the fishermen said, "He is one of those whom God blesses by giving the secret of a rich life. God must have loved him." They did not mean that God had given him money, for Monsieur André had never had more than he needed to live upon simply and to keep his wife in comfort when he was dead. They meant that for him life had always been, until that moment when he died in the room overlooking the sea, rich and full. He loved so many people and so many things.

Sometimes in the quiet of the evening and sometimes in the heat of the day, you were aware of the presence of Monsieur André in the house and in the garden. There were the roses and the plum trees which he had grafted and planted and the flat stones he had laid down from the doorway to the little gate in the hedge of tamarisk and the funny little water colors made with such intricate pains adorning the walls, and in the cupboard in the hall there were his fishing rods, where he had put them away neatly for the last time years ago. Sometimes while walking in the garden in the evening with the sound of the sea at the foot of the cliffs in your ears, you were certain that he was walking there beside you, as pleased as anything that you loved the place and the garden. There were moments when I was almost certain that he touched my elbow gently, calling my notice to a spectacular rose or a fine ripe red plum. And again late at night when everyone but myself had gone to bed and I lay on the balcony looking up at the stars and listening to the sound of chains rattling about the fishing boats below, I knew that he was there beside me enjoying the peace, drinking it in, savoring it, as I was doing.

I do not believe or disbelieve in ghosts but I do have faith in the presence of the past and the sense of being and continuity which lies in old houses and gardens. Monsieur André was a friendly presence and I know that he came very near to speaking to me. Perhaps it was that in that corner, so ancient and so undefiled and full of peace, the presence found it simple and easy to speak to me. Perhaps it knew that I was grateful.

3

For five summers we lived there, my wife, my children and the dogs, between the mountains and the sea. The children ran about half-naked and brown, in and out of the sea, catching hermit crabs and little red fish among the red rocks. They never had enough of it—that corner where man lived at peace with his fellow men, a life which was simple and good. There was not, I think, in all that village a man who lived to pile up money or would descend to cheating his neighbor. At the end we came to think of it as the Last Paradise.

And then one day a cablegram from America finished it all. We had to go home, perhaps for years, perhaps forever. We left in October after the garden and house had been put in order for the winter and Monsieur André's fishing rods and reels had been well polished and oiled and neatly put away in the cupboard in the hall. We left at night so that we should not be tempted to look back and see the house for the last time across the wide bay on our way to the station in Saint Christophe. There on the station platform we found the Baron and Mademoiselle Fernande, looking very odd and stiff in the worn old-fashioned clothes which they thought dignified and suitable for seeing us off. Mademoiselle Fernande wore a jacket with high sleeves which must have been made in the nineties and carried in her hand a little bunch of heather which she gave us "to remember them by."

It was a clear moonlight night when the distant high mountains seemed very near. Just on the opposite side of the canal, and on the station platform an old Basque sang "Ay-ay-ay." On the train I could not look at my wife for I knew that there were tears in her eyes and that if I looked at her I too would weep. The youngest child looked out from her berth and said, "When are we coming back to Salasso?"

"Some day," I replied.

"Next summer?"

"Some day."

But we never came back because the Onspenskis were there before us.

4

I prospered in America and when four years had passed, I knew that we could go back, and in the middle of the winter I wrote to my friend Dalambure for news of the house. I meant either to rent it or to buy it, no matter what it cost me.

Dalambure lived on the coast but he never belonged properly to Salasso, and on the rare occasions when he came to the house, he brought with him a certain restlessness and discontent. I was always vaguely disturbed and angry when he came because he seemed unaware of the beauty and peace of the place. I was always like a gardener who, showing a visitor through his garden, is rewarded only by politeness and stupid insincere remarks. Except for the disturbing quality which he brought to the place, I was fond of him. Away from Salasso, in a city street, in a café with a drink and a pile of newspapers, he was quick and witty and cynical and intelligent.

He wrote bitter books and inflammatory articles for the Paris newspapers, but he spent as much time as possible on the coast, though as far as I could see for no other reason than because he was born there, for he seemed completely unaware of its beauties or its character. In time I had a letter from him, full of political gossip and the details of the great Dumesnil scandal. A bank had failed, ruining thousands of modest depositors, and the scandal penetrated like a sinister growth to the very heart of the French government.

"It was," he wrote, "an affair as despicable and sordid as possible and most of the men involved are of the lowest sort. But what can one expect in depraved times like these when greed and fear lie at the root of everything? I doubt if any of the criminals will be brought to justice by man although I still have hope that God will not overlook them, for they are guilty of the blackest of all sins—that of preying upon their fellow men." His letter was largely an echo of some flaming article he had written for a Paris newspaper. From it, I knew that he was launched again on one of his famous crusades, but this foreign scandal neither touched nor interested me very profoundly. I wanted news of the house and Monsieur André, the Baron, Mademoiselle Fernande, the village, all that paradise to which one might escape from a sordid, weary and depressing world.

Of this then he merely wrote, "I have been to look at the house at Salasso. The old lady died three years ago and it has been sold to some people called Onspenski. It is much changed. I don't think you'd like it any more."

"Even if it has been sold," I thought, "I can buy it back and undo the changes." The memory of it had grown about my spirit as the old vines had grown over the house.

The children asked, "Are we going to Salasso? Can we go bathing and shrimping and fishing there? You promised us you'd go back to Salasso." And I answered, "Yes, somehow or other, we'll arrange it."

As soon as we landed I went off to the coast to stay with Dalambure and see what might be done. On the train I wakened early in the morning and, looking out, saw that we were in the mountains going through a little green valley where the hillsides were checkered with little patches of maize and potatoes and pasture land. Inside me the old excitement returned. It was as if I were returning home after having been away for a long time. I could not go back to sleep and I fell to speculating whether it was possible to have lived many lives and to have kept some dim memory of them. Otherwise, how could one explain the feeling one sometimes had on seeing for the first time a new country? Here on this coast I was always at home, although I was in a foreign country where no one spoke my language. I had never felt a stranger even among the fishermen. I had known this country the moment I saw it, as my very own. I had lived here once, long ago in some other life.

The train slipped down and down through valley after valley and suddenly in a blaze of sunlight I found the sea, without which life for me becomes after a time petty and tiresome.

[232]

Dalambure was there to meet me and we had a late breakfast on his balcony above the canal.

He was a man of middle age, nervous and thin and energetic, with a body which seemed burned out; but in his eyes the fire was still alive. They were large and dark, almost his only claim to beauty, and at times they would blaze with the light of fury and indignation. He was a man who had little sense of *things*, and very little sentiment. There was very little warmth in him and he had almost no sensual contact with life. He was very nearly all brain and so he was always alone. He traveled light with no wife, no children, no baggage. He fancied himself a cynic, and so he was until the questions of justice and humanity raised their heads; then the dark eyes would blaze and the spirit of a crusader would take possession of him. In spite of himself and his intelligence, he was by nature an idealist and something of a reformer. He was a powerful man in France for he had a wicked, biting pen whose molten outpourings were read by friend and enemy alike.

Dalambure's house was as perfect a reflection of himself as Monsieur André's was of him. It was rather a gaunt house, plain and undistinguished, which by accident had a picturesque view of the canal and the harbor, although I am certain that Dalambure had never noticed the view and would have been quite as content if there had been only a blank wall opposite him. It was furnished with the necessities of life and nothing in it had any charm or personality. For him a chair was merely something to sit on and a bed a construction which made it possible to lie down and sleep. He had no idea whether his furniture was ugly or beautiful or whether any piece of it possessed any character, any past or any associations. His concern was wholly with ideas and so to him my obsession for the house of Monsieur André was merely absurd and foolish.

When Dalambure died, he would never live on in the house and garden he had created. He would simply vanish into thin air together with his ideas. If he survived at all, it would be in a few cold pages of print, unread because the issues which they concerned were dead with him. He was a tormented man with no sense whatever of how rich life might be. He saw the man at the next table in the café, his neighbor or greengrocer, and the Baron and Mademoiselle Fernande not as individuals and human but like most reformers, all lumped together into a single great abstraction which he called "Humanity." He was not like Monsieur André and the old Baron one of those "beloved of God."

At breakfast we had vile coffee full of chicory, some stalish rolls and marmalade out of a pot. When we had finished, I said, "What about the people who have bought the house?"

He grinned and the mocking cynical look damped the fire of his fine eyes. "They're coming for lunch," he said. "You can see for yourself. We're on very good terms at present. They're trying to bribe me and I'm pretending that I'm willing but am not satisfied with their offers."

"Bribe you?" I said. "What do they want of you?"

"Plenty," he said, and grinned again. "You see, it's like this. Onspenski—that's the name. There are two of them. Onspenski and his wife. You see, they're mixed up in the Dumesnil scandal. He's one of the guiltiest. He not only swindled the poor investors but some of his fellow crooks as well. I don't know whether he or she is the crookedest and the smartest. I should say he had the brains and she is the force behind him, but anyway there are a lot of people fighting to hush up the investigation, and my friends the Onspenskis are two of the most interested. I'm fighting to bring the whole thing into the light." The cynical look went out of his eyes and the fire returned. "And I mean to do it. They're trying to buy me off from writing the articles I've been doing. I'm about to start on the Onspenskis themselves. They think they can buy anything with money so I'm letting them hang themselves. I'm letting them think that I feel the way they do—that money is the only important thing in the world. I'm letting them think that until I've got everything I want and then I'll explain that I'm not interested in money and thank them for the little story they've given me. You can only fight fire with fire."

"Have they ever been in your house?" I asked.

"Yes."

"Then I should think they'd see that money and luxury don't mean much to you."

Dalambure laughed. "My dear fellow," he said, "they're not writers like you. They're thinking of nothing but money. That's why crooks usually come a cropper in the end. The longer they work the narrower they get. In the end they can't see *around* things."

"Why are they called Onspenski?"

"That's not his real name. I know all about that, too. I've been finding out things."

"Are they French?"

"I'm not sure. He speaks with an accent—Russian, I should think. She must have lived in Paris most of her life. When she gets excited she shows it and talks like a concierge. But it doesn't matter where they were born or what country they came from. They haven't any nationality at all. They aren't attached to anything or anybody—not even to each other, I'd wager, if it came to a pinch." He chuckled. "Maybe they'll amuse you. Perhaps you'll like them."

I knew that the last remark was a shot fired at random in my direction. Often he had accused me of being too gregarious, of liking people too easily, or at least of suffering the presence and acquaintance of scoundrels and bores merely because I liked picking their brains and using them as

[234]

material. The odd thing about Dalambure was that while he loved humanity in the abstract he detested it individually. He loved the forest and hated the trees. In his idealism no man ever was perfect enough. Even his friends had to suffer criticism, if indeed he had any friends. His peculiar humanitarianism made him utterly lonely. I, who knew him very well, never had the faintest idea of his life when we were not together. Whether he had ever been married, whether he had mistresses, who his other friends were, I never knew. That was one of the things which made it so difficult when one or two men tried honestly to discover how it was he died. No one knew anything about him except his cook Marie Thérèse and she only knew that he rose and ate and went to bed at certain hours.

In reply I grinned and said, "Maybe they will amuse me. I've never found anyone as bad as you paint them."

"Some day you will. I think the Onspenskis will give you the chance."

"You won't take people as a whole."

"No. Some qualities are so bad that they can poison or destroy all the rest of a character. The trouble is that you're never really forced to associate with evil people. You never know them except in a casual way. They happen to be my business. Some day you'll see."

Beneath the speech and in the intelligent twinkle of his dark eyes, I discovered an amazing satisfaction and certainty. He was almost sunny about it, as if he found a kind of vindicatory pleasure in the vileness of mankind, and I was aware suddenly why it was that he had no intimates. Even I, sitting there opposite him, was no friend in the human sense, but only a specimen in his laboratory, like the Onspenskis with whom he was experimenting over the matter of a bribe. Doubtless toward me as a microscopic organism he had a little warmer feeling than for the Onspenskis; otherwise there was not much difference.

It was a fine bright morning and all the while we sat talking I kept thinking of how lovely the house at Salasso must look and how pleasant it would be to have a swim and lie naked in the sea behind the red rocks of the little beach, and when we had finished breakfast I proposed setting out at once on foot for the village.

But Dalambure stopped me. "No, I wouldn't go out there if I were you—not until you've met the Onspenskis. If they saw you poking about they'd become suspicious and that might spoil your chances of getting back the house. They have a lot to be suspicious about just now. And besides it might make them think you want it as much as you do, and that's something you must never let them know, or they'll make it cost you your last penny. Take my advice. They're coming to lunch. Wait until the afternoon."

So I yielded to his cynical arguments and spent the morning with him in the town of Saint Christophe. It was a dullish morning. We sat at his favorite café and read all the French newspapers and Dalambure waved his arms and denounced the evil ways of the world. A dozen or so of acquaintances passed by the table with a word of greeting or sat with us for a moment. On the whole they seemed pleasant, dull fellows, but at their approach, I observed that Dalambure always withdrew inside himself. It was like a turtle drawing in its head. He had no real contact with any of these men and desired none. You felt that in his heart he found none of them worthy, and it occurred to me that there was something immensely aloof, almost Jehovah-like about him.

"Perhaps," I thought, "he is not human but merely an instrument of God for punishing the evil ways of mankind." But it was a very lonely business, being an instrument of God.

The little square before the café was flooded with sunlight and the plane trees cast blue-black shadows across our table. It was still too early in the year for the descent of those regiments of tourists and idlers which had come to infest the coast, bringing devastation in one hand and fantastic prosperity in the other, and so the square was pleasant and empty except for the townspeople, the fishermen, and now and then a soldier.

5

It was their voices I was aware of first of all. I heard them quarreling as they arrived below the balcony of Dalambure's house in a large and very smart roadster painted yellow with *aubergine* trimmings. I do not know what they were quarreling about but as the motor stopped I heard her voice, rather coarse and throaty, abusing him, and then his occasional reply, in a lower voice. She was using good Rabelaisian words straight from the gutters of Paris, and one had the impression that behind them there was a woman who suffered from blasted nerves and was tortured by perpetual anxiety, not one of those "favored by God." Suddenly he made a retort spoken rapidly and viciously which silenced her. I do not know what it was and I dared not betray my presence on the balcony by peering over the edge. I have a horror of overhearing scenes in which two people exhibit themselves naked and shameless, and at that moment, even though I had never seen the Onspenskis and as yet they meant nothing whatever to me, I suffered a sudden feeling of sickness and retreated into the sitting room. Perhaps, I thought, that is why Dalambure is really contemptuous of me, because I run away from unpleasantness and unpleasant people.

Dalambure himself brought them into the sitting room and introduced them, walking a little behind with a mildly contemptuous expression on his thin face. It was as if he were holding them at arm's length like a scientist presenting a pair of exotic animals which have a very bad smell.

The man was the more subtle and more perfectly concealed of the two. He was small and slightly built and nondescript in appearance, like any small middle-aged clerk in a bank. He was growing bald and his hair was simply hair-colored. He wore white flannel trousers and white buckskin shoes and a blue yachting jacket with gold buttons. His clothes were expensive and smart, but too new, as the clothes of most Latin men nearly always are, and there was something grotesque in the sight of a bank clerk dressed as the owner of a fashionable yacht. His eyes were his only point of distinction. They were small and dark and very bright, and crafty rather than intelligent. When he was introduced he gave me a quick glance and then looked away out of the window, as if absorbed by the beauty of the view which Dalambure had never seen. But it occurred to me that he did not see it either and that he really never saw anything because his consciousness was always turned inward, absorbed in the swift and complicated and evil things which were always going on inside the small, slightly bald head. But he had awareness, which came to him one might have said, through the skin rather than through his eyes. He was aware, I know, of myself, of his wife, of Dalambure. I was not at all sure that he was unaware even of the *insides* of all of us. His left arm he carried in a sling and the side of his face was covered with scratches which were almost healed.

The woman was quite different. She was three or four inches taller than her husband and had an inclination to be fat. This she had endeavored to restrain by corseting and I suppose by occasional dieting and cures, although this must have been difficult, for greed and sensuality were written in every line of her face and curve of her body. Actually she presented the illusion of an outline which was fashionably slim, but the illusion was a failure. She was inclined to bulge, and beyond that you were aware without thinking of it of the woman God and nature and glands had meant her to be. You *saw* her as fat. The impression surrounded her as if a dotted line had been drawn about her figure, indicating the true contour of curves and billows. She too was fashionably dressed in expensive clothes which had come from the smartest of dressmakers, but as with the man, the clothes made no difference. One had the impression of a cook who had gone out on her day off in a costume borrowed from her fashionable mistress. Madame Onspenski must have been a blonde for her skin was fair and her eyes were a peculiar shade of pale blue. The exact color of her hair it was impossible to divine for it was dyed a garish shade of gold.

They were a pair such as one sees often enough in expensive hotels, casinos and watering places, pretentious and assertive, yet arriving nowhere in the world to which they aspire. Gotten up in all the trappings of people of the world, they still remain what they are. You see them dining alone or occasionally with a pair like themselves and now and then with a man or a woman belonging to a different world, and then you know that there is some evil work afoot, blackmail or swindling or sometimes even murder.

6

Perhaps because it is my business to notice things about people, I noticed small details about the Onspenskis, among them, that she was greedy and that he ate like a man whose stomach is delicate and whose nerves torture him. The food was what one might have expected of Dalambure—the food of a man who was insensible to cooking and ate merely because it was necessary to eat in order to keep alive. It was cooked by an old woman called Marie Thérèse who came from the village of Salasso to work in Saint Christophe in summer.

She was wrinkled and bent but her hair was black with the black of dye, streaked and purple at the ends. By profession she was not a cook at all, but a witch, and no one who cared in the least about food would have kept her for longer than a meal or two. But she had been with Dalambure for seven years and had come to look upon him as her charge. Perhaps there was in her feeling for him something of gratitude because he never complained of her cooking and kept her on.

When she saw me, her wrinkled face crumpled into a smile and she said, "Ah, my friend, I'm glad you're back. Perhaps you can change things at Salasso?"

When I asked what needed changing, she shrugged her shoulders and said, "You will see for yourself. Everything is different. Now when you walk down to the port, your neighbor passing you on the opposite side of the dike looks at you and wishes you ill."

She was very good herself at ill-wishing and with some families in Salasso she was the object of fear and awe. When a catch was poor or a goat died they blamed it on Marie Thérèse; yet when anyone, whether friend or enemy, in Salasso fell ill, he sent for the old woman. She tried spells but she also had a whole pharmacopoeia of her own which included such things as dock and rhubarb leaves and poultices of nettles. She was a hereditary witch and her secrets had been passed on to her down the dim corridors of a hundred generations. She herself did not know their origin but I think it likely that she was descended from one of those Druid priestesses who had dominated the people and performed their offices in the oak grove near the Baron's castle long before the Romans came over the mountains from Spain.

She was one of those who was aware of good and evil, and although for years I tried to discover how it was that she could divine the internal spirit of a stranger, she was never able to tell me, save to say simply, "I don't know. It just comes over me. I feel it. I am always right." And she always was. In

[238]

her long life she had predicted personal disasters. Scientifically, I suppose, she was able to do this by means of a keen instinct joined with a genius for observation. Her black beady eyes rarely missed the smallest gesture or intonation which might be significant.

She believed profoundly in the presence of Monsieur André in the old house and the garden and asserted flatly that she had met him walking at night on the dike or in the ruins of the old Roman fort. "I did not see him," she said, "but he was there. He was even carrying his fishing rod as he always used to do. He walked along beside me for a long time and we talked to each other without speaking at all. He was a happy presence. He was glad when you came to live in the house. He is not happy now. He is wandering in the village."

And now while she passed the *potage garbure* and the tough octopus cooked in its own juice, she bristled. She hated the Onspenskis and it seemed to me that she was also frightened of them, and I had never before seen the indomitable old woman frightened of anyone. When she served them she stood at arms' length from the table as if they had some disease which might be acquired by contact.

Madame Onspenski made what she considered polite and worldly conversation. She talked of "the season" and the coming speedboat races and the new casino as if she were an important figure in relation to all of them—something which she was not. Presently when she had overplayed her game I divined that she really knew no one on the coast and had no part in its life. It was all swank and nonsense. Onspenski scarcely spoke at all. He was the cleverer of the two and might have gotten on in a worldly way had he been alone, but she queered his game. I think he knew what she was doing and was, not perhaps ashamed of her but annoyed with her for being such a transparent fool.

When the meat was brought in she had to cut it for him because his left arm was useless in its sling. I wondered how he had come by the injuries which were nearly healed. Now she had an excuse to tell the story.

She told it while preparing his food for him.

It had happened on the road from Paris to Saint Christophe two weeks earlier. Onspenski was driving the car with Madame Onspenski sitting beside him and the chauffeur in the rumble seat. Above Saint Christophe there is a pass over the mountains which bears the name of the Devil's Footprint. Some ancient legend has it that the Devil made the depression one night when he stumbled and in a rage kicked the mountain. In the pass the road is narrow and winds up the side of the bare mountain, and on one side there is a drop which ranges from a few yards to two thousand feet. In the highest part of the pass the accident occurred.

"*Figurez-vous,*" said Madame Onspenski, "the steering gear snapped and the car went sideways right through the wall at the side of the road. I thought 'This is the end of the Onspenskis' and then I didn't remember anything, until I found myself halfway out of the car door with nothing below me but two thousand feet of space. I was so dizzy I didn't dare to move. And then I thought of my jewel case and pulled myself back into the car. The chauffeur was crushed under it and there was blood all over everything. Alexei had his arm broken and his face scratched but otherwise he was all right. But the chauffeur was dead—killed right off, just like that," and with her knife she crushed one of the peas on the plate to show how he had been smashed. "It was a miracle. Everybody said so. It was one chance in a thousand that we didn't fall all the way down right into the river. The car caught on a small rock. They pulled us both up with ropes, but to get the chauffeur's body they had to pry the car loose and let it fall all the way down the mountain."

And then she gave a chuckle of satisfaction, "But after all, we had luck. Alexei wasn't hurt much and we'll get the insurance for the car and a nice fat sum besides from the automobile manufacturers. There wasn't any doubt of what caused the accident. Imagine an expensive car like that being made with a flaw in it. They'll have to pay us for that, all right!" She chuckled again.

There was something triumphant and awful in her manner as if she felt herself immune from all the misfortunes of ordinary people; as if she were aware of some special protection. While she talked I discovered the figure of Marie Thérèse standing in the doorway, listening to the talk. Twice I saw her cross herself and make the sign against the evil eye. Then she went on with the serving, still keeping at arms' length from the other guests.

Onspenski scarcely talked at all, yet you felt his presence far more strongly than that of the woman who was so dominating and noisy. He was always there, watching. He was a watcher, a little like a snake, silent and observant, awaiting his chance to strike. That perhaps was his way of working. That perhaps was how he had swindled not only simple people but fellow crooks as well. He was the brains and she was the force of the combination. When he felt scruples or fear or distrust, she bullied him into action. It was one of those combinations in which one was essential to the other. They were two parts of a whole which fitted together. And the more I saw them the more I knew that it would cost me trouble and much money to recover Monsieur André's house and garden, for his wandering presence and for myself.

When we had had our coffee, Dalambure said quietly to me, "Go and have your after-lunch nap. We have business to discuss." And his dark eyes twinkled for a second.

But before I left Madame Onspenski said, "You must come out to tea with us and see what we've done with the house. I hear that you lived there before us so I suppose you'll be interested."

I thanked her and said that I should like to come out that very afternoon. For a moment she hesitated and then said, "Yes, do come. Alexei won't be there, but you can come another time when he is." And as she spoke, I caught the briefest shadow of a glance exchanged between them.

When I wakened it was nearly four o'clock and Dalambure was standing in the doorway with a grin on his face, a cigarette hanging from one corner of his tired mouth.

"Good sleep?" he asked.

"Yes, I dreamt of your friend, Madame Onspenski."

"Bad dream?"

"No, I can't remember now except that she was in the room, over there by the window."

"It must have been a dream. She was never out of my sight."

I sat up and lighted a cigarette, "Anything settled?"

"No, I asked too much." He was silent for a moment. "I think she's going to try seduction next, like a female crook in a melodrama."

I laughed.

"Don't laugh," he said. "She showed every sign of it. But I found out one thing. I have a suspicion things aren't going well. He's nervous. I may get a letter from Paris by the afternoon train. Then I'll know."

I looked at him for a time in silence, and it occurred to me suddenly that after all, in the matter of human relationships he was a child, without experience. He was enjoying the affair of the Onspenskis as a child enjoys a game. He never thought of me or the house at all. He meant to bring the Onspenskis to jail.

"Do you think it's a safe game you're playing?" I asked.

"What do you mean by safe?"

"If bribery fails, there's only one other way to stop you."

He laughed. "They'll never try that. They're cowards."

"Rats fight when cornered."

He threw his cigarette out of the window into the canal. "Run along," he said, "to your tea party. I fancy Madame Onspenski will outdo herself because you're a friend of mine."

I took the white road along the sea under the dunes, past the graveyard and the old grove of oaks and without passing through the village I came to the foot of the goat path leading up from the beach. But the goat path wasn't there. In its place was a clumsy stairway of concrete and the goat path up which the children and dogs had scrambled so many times was overgrown with weeds. The stairway was like a scar on the face of the rocky hill. I climbed up and up, because the path was impassable. At the

[241]

top I found the sea spread out in the brilliant sunlight on one side and on the other the distant mountains which were blurred by the haze of late spring heat.

But something awful had happened. The hedge of tamarisk was gone, the hedge which had been covered with feathery flowers on the day I first stumbled upon the house, and in its place was a high wall of concrete. No longer could you peep over the hedge into the friendly garden. For a moment I was tempted to turn back without even entering the garden at all, and then I thought, "Perhaps the inside isn't changed. After all, I *could* pull down the wall."

In place of the rickety old slatted gate, there was a solid gate of oak, painted red, and when I pulled the bell, it was answered by a fierce sound of barking. I waited and then rang again and again, and when at last it was opened, I understood the delay. Madame Onspenski had been sitting all the while on the terrace in front of the door but instead of opening the gate herself in a friendly way as Monsieur André would have done, she had waited for a servant to come from some part of the house or garden. A lady, she thought, did not open her own gate. With her on the terrace was sitting a man, dressed in the uniform of a commandant of the French Navy. The dogs which had barked had been shut up.

The house was no longer there, or rather the old house had been so changed that it was difficult any longer to recognize it. The shutters were gone and the old wooden balconies and the flower boxes. The Onspenskis had made it *moderne*. It would have been more merciful to have pulled it down altogether than to have violated the old walls with wide sheets of glass and harsh window frames of steel. On the terrace surrounding Madame Onspenski and her other guest was a strange conglomeration of bright-colored furniture bought at some Paris department store as "smart." I wanted to run away but now it was impossible, for Madame Onspenski had risen and was coming forward to greet me with that artificial graciousness which it seemed she put on and took off as if it were an old coat.

The conversation during tea was not very interesting and for what there was Madame Onspenski made herself responsible. The Naval officer was not made happy by my presence and so he sulked. He was a little dark man with a rather stupid good-looking face and a chunky air of virility. He was, I should say, the sort who took up with the first woman he met on coming into port. At Saint Christophe his woman was Madame Onspenski. It was clear as day that he was impatient for me to go away and I had the feeling that I had upset everything by arriving at exactly the wrong moment. Also it was clear that they had known each other for a long time, for they addressed each other by their small names and had an air of intimacy and understanding which is born only of the long association of lover and mistress. His name was Bessantin and his boat lay anchored in the middle of the bay a couple of miles off. I wondered how Onspenski looked upon the affair and then remembered the glance I had intercepted between them. It was very likely that he knew all about it.

For myself I was too sick to feel like talking much, least of all to a woman I did not like and a man whose only feeling for me was that he wished me out of sight so that he might have what he wanted from the woman. From time to time while I drank my whisky and soda I discovered other barbarities committed by the Onspenskis. The fruit trees grafted by Monsieur André had been cut down and the neat box-bordered kitchen garden destroyed to make place for an ugly red tennis court. The rose garden had vanished to make way for an absurd summerhouse. But worst of all, the view was gone. From the garden one could see neither the mountains nor the sea. They had changed the garden from an open friendly place from which one might see the heads of one's neighbors as they passed along the hedge into a prison, barren and bleak. Now, sitting in the garden was like sitting in the recreation yard of a prison.

When tea was finished, Madame Onspenski asked me if I should like to see the changes in the interior of the house but I had had enough and said I would see them on some other occasion. She seemed proud of what she had done and in no hurry to have me leave, but that may have been part of the game she was playing with the Naval officer. She was neither young nor fascinating, and it was difficult to see why he should have felt any desire for her, but men of his physical type, leading the life he led, sometimes develop strong tastes in women.

I took my hat and stick and bade them good afternoon, but Madame Onspenski insisted on going as far as the gate with me. I wanted to walk home over the moors and so I went to the back gate. As I opened it she said, "I hope you like what we've done. We've made it quite modern."

I looked at her, wondering that there were people in the world of so little taste and sensibility, and then I said, "Madame, you have murdered a house!"

To this she responded with a loud peal of laughter. "Oh!" she said, "you *are* a joker! I must remember to tell Alexei that."

The gate closed and that was the last time I ever saw her.

From the gate I walked along the little sunken lane which led up to the moors and as I walked I kept thinking of Monsieur André and what had become of him. He could no longer stay in that garden. It was impossible to think of his presence in the evening inside that fortress guarded by dogs. Perhaps Marie Thérèse was right. Perhaps he was wandering in the village and in the ancient fort, homeless, his tiny paradise destroyed.

And then I came to the top of the little rise in the lane where the moors stretched away toward the blue mountains with the Baron's ill-kempt old castle in the foreground; but even there the blight had struck. They were scarred with ugly new roads scraped out of the soft purple heather and scattered over them stood perhaps fifty new villas. They were built of brick and concrete and were of monstrous designs made to order not even by an architect but by a contractor. A half-dozen of them were finished and ready to be occupied, but the others were all in various stages of construction, some without windows, others without even roofs. And the odd thing was that although the season was only a month away when they might be rented, there was no sign of any effort being made to complete them. There was not a workman in sight and already the weeds had taken possession of the roadways. The finished villas stood as empty as the unfinished ones and all of them had that gaunt look of houses which had never been finished and occupied and were already beginning to fall into ruin. They were dying without ever having lived.

7

Dalambure was standing on the balcony waiting for me with a grin on his face. When I joined him there, he asked, "Well, did you like the changes made by our friends?"

"You might have prepared me a little."

"I couldn't. You wouldn't have believed me."

"It seems a pity that God permits such people to live."

"That," said Dalambure, "is one of the many mysteries which make me doubt the existence of God."

Marie Thérèse brought us apéritifs, and I saw that she was full of curiosity and had a desire to talk to me but dared not in front of Dalambure. I gave her a glance which said, "We'll have a talk later," and she understood it perfectly and went away satisfied.

"Are the villas their work too?" I asked.

"Yes."

"How did they get the land away from the Baron?"

He looked away from me toward the harbor and I saw again in his eyes that old hatred and contempt for man as an individual. "That was easy enough. The whole place was loaded with mortgages. The old man and his sister have been selling chairs and tables for years to pay the interest and keep their land. When the Onspenskis found the place and thought it was a good speculation, they simply got hold of some of the mortgages and squeezed him out. They thought they'd take advantage of the Baron. I have a suspicion they may have been caught."

"Is he still here?"

"He kept the château. That's all there is left. They didn't want that. It's a white elephant. The old man has been ill, I hear. He might like to see you."

I told him about the commandant who had been so rudely impatient for me to go.

"Ah, Bessantin. That's an old story. It's been going on for three years."

"Onspenski knows of it, I'm sure."

"I'm sure he does."

"Blackmail?"

"Nothing so simple as that. I shouldn't be surprised if Bessantin ended his days in Guiana on the island."

"What are they up to?"

"I don't know. That's one of the things I'm trying to find out."

He seemed so good-humored that I thought he must have had news of some sort, and after a little time I found that I was right. He took his time but presently he said, "I had a letter from Paris this afternoon. It's true. They are hard up for money. My price is really too big for them. Something seems to have slipped up. That's why the villas never were finished. It's just possible that someone higher up in the scandal has been blackmailing them."

"Maybe there is a God after all."

He laughed, "No, they'll wiggle out some way or other. It isn't the first time they've been in a hole. I found out who they are too. He was born in Odessa. His father was a Roumanian. She is a Belgian. She came to Paris as a child. That explains her accent. He has been in prison twice and once in a lunatic asylum."

"I suppose that's why he's so quiet."

"The lunacy was a trick. It should have been prison instead. But there's a reckoning ahead. About a month from now there will be trouble. Maybe I can help along God a little in this justice business."

"That won't bring back the house nor rid the moors of those God-forsaken villas."

He grinned. "You're too attached to *things*. If you liked ideas better, you would be happier. Nobody can steal ideas from you. Nobody can destroy them the way the Onspenskis have destroyed Salasso." Then his fine eyes contracted to little black points. "I should like to see them roasting nicely in hell."

I was spared Marie Thérèse's awful cooking that evening for we dined in the restaurant on the square and afterward went to the Casino. I had no chance to keep my promised appointment with the old witch. After midnight when I returned she had not gone to bed and when Dalambure had retired and I was reading in my room, she came to the door and knocked, asking if she might speak to me. In an old flowered wrapper with her dyed hair in curl papers, Marie Thérèse looked more than ever the witch. Her wrinkled face had an expression of anxiety and malice as she stood, with an air of deprecation, just inside the door, still holding the handle.

"You have seen the place, Monsieur?" she asked.

"Yes."

"They have brought evil to Salasso. It was so quiet before."

"I haven't been in the village."

"You wouldn't know it. It's full of the evil they brought with them." For a moment she was silent and then asked, "Will you do something if I ask?"

I smiled, "I can't make promises without knowing."

"It's about Monsieur Dalambure. Tell him to let them alone. They're evil people."

"Don't you want them punished?"

"It's not for him to do. He's not strong enough. Only God can punish them. The devil is on their side." Then suddenly she was angry. "Don't smile, I know about these things. God meant to kill them when that accident happened, but the devil saved them. It was the hand of God which broke the thing it steered by. Don't smile. I know about these things. Monsieur Dalambure isn't strong enough to be God."

I wasn't smiling now. She was so earnest and so tragic and intense that one believed for a moment that she did "know about these things."

"I promise, but it will do no good."

She seemed relieved but she chattered on for a time about good and evil and God and Monsieur André. She said that the Onspenskis built the wall and kept dogs inside because they were afraid. "People like that are always afraid." They liked the house, she said, because it was so near to the frontier. They could escape if necessary into Spain on a moment's notice.

At last she left me, but when I put out the light, I could not sleep. My mind was awake and I was aware of the spell of that dark beautiful country. From my window I could see the mountains in the moonlight, the distant ones blue and cold, the nearer ones stained here and there with dark patches made by the ancient oak forests, still inhabited, the shepherds said, by dryads and tree spirits. In the darkness I came again to believe as I had done when I lived in Monsieur André's house that all things were possible and that nothing was astonishing. There was good and there was evil in the world and why should these elements not manifest themselves in people? Why should not evil be a tangible force unseen but known by its effect, like electricity? These two strangers, coming suddenly into that quiet world, had poisoned it and defeated the good kindly powers of the dead Monsieur André and the living Baron.

[246]

8

My train left at nine o'clock the following night. Dalambure asked me to stay on but I had no desire to stay or ever to see Salasso again, which indeed I never did. It was too much like the pain of looking upon the body of one you have loved. It was over and finished. There remained only my visit to the Baron.

The château was surrounded by a wall and partly hidden from the road by the trees of the ragged park. Once, long ago, before the façade of the house, there had been a garden of rare plants, exotic to that part of the world, but with no one to care for it, it had fallen into ruin and decay. On that last morning, looking up the abandoned driveway, I had the feeling that with the passing of the château and the park a whole era of civilization and good living had come to an end. Once the owners of this house had lived off their land, quiet simple folk, gentle and unpretentious. But that was all finished now. What Dalambure said had truth in it—that those who got on in this modern world were like the Onspenskis, those who gathered about to feast on the corpse, without scruples, very often even without nationality, the greedy, the money-changers, the ghouls. You could not envy them. You could only feel contempt. Through the trees as I walked, I had a view of the moors scarred by the new roads and violated by the gaunt half-finished empty villas.

At the door I pulled a rusty bell handle and from some far-off part of the château there was a ghostly answering jangle; but no one came. Again I rang and then a third time and presently I heard the sound of footsteps coming down the big stone-paved hallway.

It was Mademoiselle Fernande herself who opened the gate, and for a moment she did not recognize me. She, herself, was terribly changed. It was natural that she should have looked older, but there was a deadness and melancholy in her face and manner. The old spirit which had led the old lady barefoot across the rocks through the surf with her fishing rod was gone. She smiled but it was worse than if she had not smiled at all. And she invited me to come in, a thing which she had never done before. She was glad to see me.

The hall was absolutely empty of furniture, a big ugly hall built in the wrong period with a clumsy chandelier of glass, but the salon into which she led me had a certain romantic style and there were still some furnishings in it—two chairs, a sofa, a pair of tables and a screen. They remained, I understood at a glance, because they had no value. They were all of the Second Empire, pretentious and vulgar and ugly, just as the furniture of our times is spare and mean and without character. The good furniture, the inherited pieces, had gone long ago in order to keep the land, and now the land was gone with the furniture.

Mademoiselle Fernande seated herself in one of the chairs, sitting upright a little on the edge like a young girl of a middle-class French family receiving her first caller. As a child she had been trained thus and now as an old woman, receiving one in her house for the first time, the manner returned to her. She smiled but she was sad. She asked politely after my wife and children and even the Aberdeen terriers. One of them was dead, having left sons and daughters. That bit pleased her and for a moment she seemed jolly again. But it was impossible to picture this tired old woman ever again climbing over the rocks barefooted to fish for *meunier*. She was, in spite of her stiff prim carriage, limp, defeated and tired, a woman who had finished with life.

"It was good of you to call so soon," she said.

"I'm only here for two days and I didn't want to go away without seeing you and your brother."

For a moment the ghost of surprise came into her face. "Didn't you know?" she asked.

"Know what?"

"My brother is dead. He only died last night."

"Oh!" For a moment I could think of nothing to say. These two people more than twice my age, of another world and another blood, strangers, had been very near to me. People I knew had died, relations and friends and acquaintances, yet very few of them had gone away leaving me with a sensation of sorrow and genuine loss. I was suddenly aware that these two old people had meant something special to me. I had never thought of it until that moment. There was no one who could fill the small niche which the Baron had occupied, no one ever again who would be as Mademoiselle Fernande had been in her old khaki skirt and sweater laughing and swearing, when the surf swept round a rock and struck her full on. That would never happen again for she too in a way was already dead. Their going left a hole which nothing would fill, until I myself was dead.

"I'm so sorry," I said, "I didn't know."

"It was the land," she said. "After they took the land away from us he never went out any more. He kept all the curtains drawn on that side of the house. You see the land never belonged to anyone but our family— never. And when they took it away it made him feel useless and weak. And now he's dead." She spoke dully, without resentment or hatred, and when she had finished there was a silence as if she had meant to add that she too would soon be gone.

"Would you like to see him?" she asked.

I dislike looking upon dead people, but I was aware that she was old-fashioned and that it would please her. She led the way through the empty hall and up the big stairway to a room with a view of the mountains. It too was empty of furniture save for a great bed and two chairs which were occupied by two nuns who did not stop their prayers to look up as we came in. The old man was dressed in shabby old-fashioned evening clothes which he had not worn for perhaps thirty years. I had always thought of him as pleasant and kindly but never as handsome. Now in death he was beautiful and one saw in his face that he had had a good life and been a friend to his neighbors. Like his old comrade Monsieur André there had been neither kings nor beggars for him, but only men. I said a prayer for him and we went out.

At the door Mademoiselle Fernande took my hand. "He would be glad to know that you came. He often spoke of you—especially after they came and destroyed Monsieur André's house." Again there was a silence and I understood what she was thinking—that this would be the last time we should ever meet. She did not ask me if I meant to come back to Salasso. She *knew* that for me as well as for herself, it was finished.

As I walked along the roadway to the big gates, the whole bay was spread out below me and on the clear blue surface a single boat moved. It was a launch coming from the destroyer to the tiny harbor of Salasso—Commandant Bessantin, bestial and full of lust, going to his mistress, Madame Onspenski.

I left by the night train and Dalambure went with me to the station. He was still in high spirits. His investigation was going well. We had a drink together and he promised to meet me in a month in Paris. As the train pulled out his tall, lonely figure was the only one on the platform save for the porters. When I leaned out of the window to bid him good-by he grinned, but it was a grin without good humor, a cold grin which had nothing to do with me. He was thinking of his ideas and of the task he had set himself, pleased that it was going so well.

"You'll be seeing all of us before long," he said, "me and the Onspenskis. I'll be coming to Paris when they're arrested."

But he was wrong. Within the month he was dead and all the papers which he had collected to finish off the Onspenskis were never found, not so much as a scrap of them. And most of the evidence I imagine he had kept in his head.

9

There were fine eulogies of Dalambure and his work in the Paris news-papers. His friends praised him with sincerity and his enemies because even in death he was a dangerous man to have attacked. The papers said

[249]

that he had died of ptomaine poisoning, suddenly, alone in his grim characterless house while his one servant was at market. In that theory there was a certain bitter humor; it would have been so easy to die of poisoning from the cooking of Marie Thérèse. But I knew and I fancy a great many others knew that he did not die in that way. I remembered the visit of Marie Thérèse to my room long after midnight when she stood, holding to the door handle, saying, "It's not for him to punish them. He's not strong enough. Monsieur Dalambure is not strong enough to be God."

The exposure of the Onspenskis and the others in the great Dumesnil scandal died with Dalambure. In the reform papers there was talk of an investigation of his death but nothing came of it in the end. They buried him in the cemetery of Saint Christophe which was the one place he had ever loved, and when I examined myself I found that oddly I did not miss him at all. His going left no hole as the death of the Baron had done. God had not loved him as he had loved the others.

The only echo of the case came when Marie Thérèse was arrested. For weeks she had gone about Saint Christophe and Salasso saying openly that the Onspenskis had poisoned Dalambure to be rid of him and his knowledge. It was the Onspenskis who had her arrested at last on a charge of slander, and they did their best to bring against her an accusation of having poisoned her master, something which with all their crooked spidery inclinations they might easily have done. That would have been the ultimate refinement of their power for evil. But the magistrate, an upright and intelligent man, saved her by finding that she was not malicious and evil but merely a harmless old woman who was not quite sane and could not be held responsible for the gossip she spread. The accusation against her turned the whole of Salasso against the Onspenskis, so that it was impossible to find anyone to work for them and they were left more than ever alone in the prison which they had made of Monsieur André's house and garden.

At the end of the summer they left and never returned there. The half-finished villas fell slowly into decay and the poor house itself had a succession of fly-by-night tenants until it was bought at last by a Greek syndicate which turned it into a restaurant and house of assignation. And one night in November after the shepherds had begun to burn the dead bracken from the hills Mademoiselle Fernande died alone in the château.

10

And so the story might have ended, the story of how the Onspenskis brought the blight of evil to one of the last pleasant corners of Europe. For me Salasso and Saint Christophe was finished but in my heart I still felt the need of vengeance. I wanted to know the end of the Onspenskis.

[250]

I wanted to know whether Marie Thérèse was right when she said that in the end the Hand of God would reach out and crush them.

Their name one encountered from time to time during the years that followed. It was an unusual name and I learned to pick it out almost at once from among dozens of others in a newspaper. I found it in papers in London and Berlin and Paris, nearly always concerned with the account of some new financial scheme. Now and then it appeared in the list of names of those visiting Venice or Biarritz or Deauville, spots where they might ply their trade profitably; and at once I could see the pair dressed for roles which they were never permitted to play, moving among people who ignored them, lonely perhaps without knowing it, trying always for money and even for distinction which would never be theirs because they could not work honestly either for the one or the other.

I do not think that, in spite of their swindles, they were ever very rich. There was always blackmail to be paid and fellow crooks and corrupt politicians to be appeased and several times at least their ventures failed and left them bankrupt, but no matter what their fortunes were they always bluffed and always they seemed to find new victims. They belonged to these times when one day a man is fabulously rich and the next he finds himself with nothing but debts, and no more than honorable people were they able to escape the seethings and surgings of economics in a day of depressions. It was the world crisis which ruined them at Salasso where they had gambled on wrecking the place to make a fortune. They had come too late and one day there were no more rich English or Americans or Argentines or Spanish on the whole coast and the bottom dropped out of everything. So they simply walked off and left it, leaving the money-lenders to gather what they could from the half-finished villas and the ruined house and the defiled moor.

Year after year their names kept bobbing up in the stormy times, like bits of cork in a wild surf. You could read that they were now in this country, now in that one, always themselves without nationality casting a blight wherever they appeared.

And then four years after I had had tea with Madame Onspenski and the French commandant, I discovered the clue to their affair. There was at that moment one of the spy scares which regularly afflict European countries, when there is an uproar and a scandal and names and accusations are hurled and in the end only the stupid and those without influence are caught. They make dull reading and rarely are they like the romantic stories of spies one reads of in fiction. The spies of reality, or at least the ones that are caught, seem always to be gentle retired professors or chambermaids or old maids in need of money. I would not have troubled to read this particular scandal save for the sight of a name in headlines, this time not the name of Onspenski but of the dark little Commandant Bessantin who had wished me in Hades the day I went to tea. He hanged himself in a brothel in Havre a little time before the police came to arrest him on suspicion of having sold naval secrets to the Germans. And suddenly years after it had happened I understood the glance which I had caught passing between the Onspenskis in poor Dalambure's dining room. Even that had had nothing to do with anything so human as a love affair: it had had to do with money.

Somehow her name never came into the case and it was not for me, a foreigner, to turn informer and make an accusation which, however certain of it I might be, I could not possibly prove. If Dalambure had been alive he would no doubt have charged into the fray, but I had no desire to play at being God.

II

The *Philippe Auguste* was a liner de luxe, small, but beautifully and expensively made to sail between Hong Kong and Europe, touching at the Straits and Colombo and Port Said. She was a costly boat not alone because of all the chromium plate, the modern paintings and the silks which had gone into her construction, but also because there had never been any need of her. She was born out of the idiocy of competition between nations and steamship companies, by one line to spite another. She was the fastest ship in the Orient trade, but even when she made a successful voyage she did so only at the expense of her sister ships. Like the Onspenskis, the *Philippe Auguste* was a product of these times, one of the brilliant ideas of giant businessmen who had a reputation for being at once clever and sound; and she was a millstone about the neck of the company which owned her. More than that she had always had bad luck. At her launching two workmen had been crushed to death. Once she went aground in the Malay Straits. In the Red Sea she cut a big Arab dhow clean in half and again while in the harbor at Marseilles she had caught fire mysteriously and lost half her beautiful insides. The men who had built her as a spite ship came to regard her as a monster.

But in the end it was always the government who paid for the folly, out of the subsidy which came from the pockets of taxpayers and went, a large part of it, into the pockets of the businessmen. It was only when a wave of reform washed over the government and the subsidy was cut in half that the men who had built the *Philippe Auguste* began to feel alarm. Among them there were two or three who felt that perhaps it was better if she were done away with altogether, under circumstances of course, by which there could be no doubt as to the validity of the insurance.

And so a few months after the subsidy had been cut, the *Philippe Auguste* burned and sank in the Red Sea almost within sight of Aden. It had been well planned to take place at a season when the weather was fine and there was small chance of passengers drowning or dying of exposure in the open boats; but the ship had a full list of passengers and something went wrong and forty-two passengers were drowned or burned to death. Among them were twenty-eight women and seven children. Most of them were French and English returning home on leave from the Orient.

No amount of investigating ever fixed a cause for the disaster. According to the survivors the fire seemed to break out all at once in a dozen different places. It happened at eight in the morning when the first early risers were coming into the dining saloon for breakfast. A great many passengers, not yet dressed, had not even time to put on their clothes, and escaped clad only in pyjamas and dressing gowns.

All sorts of strange stories were brought out at the inquiry, one that the ship had been threatened with destruction many times by Chinese opium dealers who claimed they were charged too much by certain of the ship's officers for smuggling drugs into Europe. The directors of the company hinted that she had been set on fire by men in the employ of the rival line whose competition was so costly. There were stories of time bombs and phosphorus bombs but nothing whatever was proved save that by some means or other the ship had been deliberately fired. In the end the pious commission in charge of the inquiry gave out the opinion that the disaster was probably the work of communists, and for this it may have been that the members received a reward, collected in the end from the taxpayer. Only the insurance companies dared to hint that the ship had been burned by the company itself and for this hint they were censured in court and threatened with suits for slander and libel and in the end they paid. I think the directors of the company knew by that time that they were safe, for the only people besides themselves who knew the truth were dead. One fact never came out at all during the investigation. It was the fact that the Onspenskis were on board. Again the Hand of God had stretched out toward them.

They had escaped in a small boat, comfortably and calmly among the first of the passengers. As if they had been provided with some foreknowledge of the disaster they appeared fully dressed on deck almost at the moment of the alarm, he carrying two motion picture cameras and a case full of films and Madame Onspenski with her furs and jewels. Their lifeboat was the first one clear of the ship and for three hours while the *Philippe Auguste* burned like a furnace, the boat containing the Onspenskis had circled about her until at last with her cargo of burned bodies the liner slipped out of sight. The boat managed to pick up five people struggling in the water but in these rescues the Onspenskis played no part for they were busy all the time with his two motion picture cameras photographing the dying ship, the wretched people who jumped overboard and those who were struggling in the water. (It was the more exciting as a spectacle because the sharks appeared a couple of hours before the boat sank.) When one film was finished he handed the camera to Madame Onspenski who had already charged the other with film; and so they missed nothing. It was a beautiful clear day with brilliant sunlight. The burning ship was painted white and altogether the conditions were perfect for photography. From time to time Madame Onspenski urged the crew of the boat to go nearer to the ship so that they might make pictures which were more detailed.

It was late afternoon when the boat containing the Onspenskis was picked up by a passing ship bound for Aden. There the rescued were landed and taken to the grim hotel which stands a little way from the port; but when the party arrived at the hotel the Onspenskis were not with them. They had simply vanished.

In the same boat there had been a Dutch banker hurrying home from the Orient to save his bank from disaster and a young Englishman on his way to see his wife who was dying in Bournemouth. They it was who discovered whither the Onspenskis had vanished for when they went to the flying field to engage a plane to take them to London and Amsterdam, there was no plane because the only one available had set out for Europe half an hour earlier bearing a certain Monsieur and Madame Onspenski. There had been room in it for three more passengers but Monsieur and Madame Onspenski had chartered the whole plane on the guarantee that it would leave immediately. They had, it seemed, some excellent photographs of the *Philippe Auguste* disaster and they were in great haste to reach Paris and sell them at once before there was any competition. The sooner they sold them the better the price would be.

Their plane landed and refueled the next morning at Istanbul. It left there about eleven o'clock, soaring up and up until it disappeared in the clouds bound for Italy and Paris. The next day passed and the next and there was no news of it. It was as if it had climbed into the clouds and simply vanished.

In a café in Tunis I picked up the *Petit Parisien* one morning to read that a certain Monsieur and Madame Onspenski together with a plane and the pilot had been lost. It was believed that the plane had fallen into the Adriatic. One paper, for which Dalambure had written long ago, remarked that the unsavory Onspenskis had escaped from one disaster only to lose their lives in another. I closed the paper thinking, "The Hand of God has struck them down at last. Now I shall never see their names again."

But I was wrong.

In the middle of Italy in the widest part of the Apennines there is a great expanse of country which is savage and marshy and uninhabited. Wild boars live there and a few packs of wolves, which during hard winters come out of the region and attack cattle and even children in the neighboring villages. Under the winter rains the marshes become impassable for man and only the wolves with their soft pads can cross them. Sometimes even a wolf is caught and sucked down into their muddy depths. But in summer the marshes dry out and the earth becomes firm enough to bear the weight of a man, and then it is, late in August, that the peasants organize great drives to kill the wolves which plague them during the winter. They kill them in great numbers. In October the rains begin and once more the marshes become impassable and the wolves are safe for another year.

It was the wolf hunters who found what was left of the bodies. The plane, torn, smashed, rusted and half-buried in the quicksand, was their first discovery. Inside crushed beneath the motor, they found what was left of the pilot who must have been killed immediately. It was a boy of fourteen who found Madame Onspenski. All that remained were bits of torn clothing, bones and a few wisps of dyed yellow hair. The skeleton was buried to the waist in the mud which in winter must have been like thick soup. She had died thus in an upright position. She could not have been badly injured by the crash of the plane for none of the bones were broken and she had managed to struggle through the mud for a distance of nearly a hundred yards before the quicksand slowly sucked her down.

Another hundred yards beyond her skeleton they found the torn clothing and the bones of the sly little Onspenski himself. He too had been caught in the mire and about him on the now firm earth lay scattered two motion picture cameras, a box containing films, now rotting and ruined, and a despatch case filled with papers on which the writing was illegible. (It is sad to speculate how much evil might have been uncovered if one could have read those papers.) All these things had belonged to him, but these things were not all. Beside the skeleton there lay a woman's handbag with more than four thousand francs in it and a woman's jewel case filled with jewels.

Knowing the Onspenskis it was easy to reconstruct the story. The woman's greed had done for her at last. Weighing twice as much as her "husband" she had been the first to sink into the quicksand and there he had left her, struggling, in the knowledge that she was already as good as dead, first taking from her her money and her jewels. There must, I think, have been a struggle and curses and a scene between them which dimmed all the other countless scenes which had taken place in their long knavish association, a scene infernal in its evil.

And so he had left her there to die only to be caught himself a little further on in the awful devouring slimy mud. He was light and spidery and he might have escaped save for the weight of the cameras and the jewel case and the papers, but in the end the obsession of greed was too strong in him too, and he sank carrying his possessions with him.

The wolves had picked their bones clean. It may have been that while they struggled there, floundering hopelessly in the quicksand, they heard the howls of the animals coming nearer and nearer. It was impossible to know whether they were alive or dead when the wolves attacked.

I thought again of Monsieur André and the Baron and old Mademoiselle Fernande and Marie Thérèse and the commandant who had hanged himself in Havre and all the other victims I had known—there were countless others, the old men and women ruined in their swindles, the men, women, and children who had died when the *Philippe Auguste* was burned—but I thought most of Dalambure, lean, tall, with the fire in his eyes and the look of contempt about his mouth whenever he spoke of the Onspenskis. In the end justice had been done. If they had escaped the Hand of God a dozen times, it had fallen at last with an awful vengeance.

I put down my paper, finished my drink and went inside the hotel to the writing room. There I wrote a letter to old Marie Thérèse telling her the whole story. I knew she could not read but her granddaughter would read it to her and she would go about from house to house in Saint Christophe and Salasso spreading the tale of God's vengeance, and I knew that in not one house would she find a soul with pity for the Onspenskis or sorrow that the hand of God had reached the Onspenskis at last. As I wrote there echoed in my ear something which poor Dalambure had said long ago, "They aren't attached to anything or anybody—not even to each other, I'd wager, if it came to a pinch."

III

New York Legend

THE old house is gone now, destroyed, slain, annihilated in the way of old houses in New York which disappear without leaving a legend. In its place is a monstrous new apartment house, as typical of its day as the old brownstone structure with its neo-Georgian façade was characteristic of the latter half of the nineteenth century. They pulled it down only a couple of years ago but already, as is the way in New York, the old house is forgotten.

When you pass the cold modern entrance to the great building which now stands on the corner, you have to think hard for a moment to remember what had been there only a little time before. I can remember, for in my childhood and youth, I used to go there very often, but I'll wager that your average New Yorker, even a New Yorker familiar with Murray Hill, could not tell you that only a little while ago there stood on that corner in the very center of the district a big house which, unless you studied it carefully, seemed to be nondescript, characterless—almost, you might say, self-effacing, like a timid old maid who dresses in a conventional, colorless fashion in order not to attract notice.

It sometimes behaved like a house in which someone lived—a house where there were deaths, births and funerals. One had the impression that behind its big old-fashioned mahogany doors people moved about, eating, sleeping, making love. It was boarded up in the summer, but in winter the shutters were taken down and at the windows behind draperies of faded green brocade, patched lace curtains, newly washed, appeared. In the spring there were even flowers in the window boxes on the first floor.

It had all the appearance of a living house but it was dead. If you spent a day watching it, the only person you would have seen leaving it was an old gentleman, obviously English and obviously a manservant, who would come out from the areaway during the afternoon, returning in about an hour bearing a package or two. You might see a grocer's boy leave packages. Otherwise, there was no sign of life.

Year by year, one tall building after another crowded into the blocks

[257]

near by, but the old house took no notice of them. Among the shadows which each year grew longer and longer, it continued to exist, dignified and aloof, like a superior old dowager who refuses to follow the fashion and dresses in the period which suited her best.

If you had continued your watch far into the night you would have seen another old gentleman, tall and slim and fragile, come out of the servants' entrance after midnight and walk twice round the block. Then he would return, and letting himself in with his latchkey, he would disappear once more.

There *was* life in the house but it was a kind of life in death. It had been like that for nearly forty years. My cousin lived there. I doubt if any of you have ever heard his name, although if you were old enough and had lived in certain fashionable circles in New York you would have known it well enough, for it was a name known everywhere in the Mauve Decade and a name which was flashy and even notorious a generation earlier.

When my cousin's wife died, he came back from the funeral and never went out again in the world which once he had loved so well. I remember the date of the funeral because Elena was buried three days after the Hotel Windsor fire.

2

In my childhood, the house was exactly what the house of a rich buccaneer banker should have been, for Michael Denning belonged to the age of Robber Barons—the New York of Jim Fisk and Jay Gould and Commodore Vanderbilt. He made his millions ruthlessly, unscrupulously and, by the standards of today, criminally. When I knew him in his old age he was a big man and vigorous still, with a white chin beard and congress boots, a loud voice and the domineering manner of a money-maker. In his way he was, I suppose, a kind of monster.

The same type exists today, but no longer is it free to bully and swindle and rob. The world and New York have changed a good deal—in some ways for the better; in other ways for the worse. I've seen a good deal of the change in progress, and the story of old Michael Denning's son Ogden is a story of change. He was born at the wrong time. He should, I think, have been born sixty years earlier or into this modern world. As it was, he fell between the two epochs, into a world which was sly and vulgar, false and provincial.

Old Michael was married for years to a plain, common, barren woman who ran his house like a Hessian trooper, berating the servants and quarreling with tradesmen. He had married her when he was a young man and poor, having chosen a strapping, vigorous woman who turned gradually into a termagant. It did not matter much to him, for in his earlier years he was too busy making and losing one fortune after another.

He would have liked children but she bore him none, and after a time he saw less and less of her, amusing himself elsewhere with girls he met through that lady-killer, Jim Fisk, and girls from the French opera and Koster and Bial's. He had a large appetite and a large capacity and in the face of such extravagant competition, his wife grew gradually more and more eccentric. Living in a house which the newspapers said cost half a million, she would go out in the morning to Third Avenue with a basket over her arm to do her own marketing.

The house was a sensation at the time it was built. I think the old robber wanted it not because he enjoyed a big luxurious house or even for show, but because it was a way of spending some of the millions with which he was surfeited at the time. In any case, it was left entirely to the architect and the furnishers, and in the end they delivered to him a solid monstrosity of black walnut, red plush, marble and statuary.

He and his wife moved into it and gave a great reception to which all New York was invited. They asked people they knew and people they didn't know. It was a kind of huge gesture in the style of the period and of Michael Denning himself—to show that he had arrived and to demonstrate his power. But it did not work out that way. He must have been puzzled when he found that, for all his power as a money-maker, there was one side of New York he could not dominate. None of the people he did not know came to the party, and a good many of those he did know failed to show up.

It must have been a strange sight—old Denning and his grenadier wife, dressed in their best, standing in the big ballroom waiting to receive guests who never came. A good many accepted the invitations and then failed to appear at the last moment. The only ones who came were Denning's pals, some rather déclassé women, and men who dared not offend him, accompanied by their flurried and indignant wives. There was food and champagne for three times as many people as appeared.

After midnight, old Denning stood on a chair in the ballroom and announced in his bull-like voice: "If there are still any stuffed monkeys here, they'd better go home now because the rest of us are going to have fun!" A few drifted away, and then, indeed, the fun began.

In rage and indignation the old boy had sent out to the French opera and to Koster and Bial's for singing and dancing acts. A whole new orchestra appeared, and by morning the party had turned into a party after his own heart—champagne and coryphées and singing and dancing. It was a famous scandal and a howling success. In the middle of the evening, the dragon wife went upstairs, packed her trunks and left the house, never to enter it again.

Whether the two ever met again I do not know, but a few years later she died. Why Michael Denning, who made his first entrance into New York City as a boy of eighteen driving cattle to market, should have wanted to give a fashionable party I do not know. From all evidence, one would have said that nothing could have interested him less. Heaven knows his real life was full enough, with his money-making, his girls and his champagne. But apparently even this great robber baron had an Achilles' heel, and the Achilles' heel was "society."

For a long time afterward he took no notice of the people who had snubbed him save to keep watch and when the occasion arose to ruin one of them here and another there. He was accountable, I think, for the ruin of fifteen or twenty families of importance. One day they would be living in a fine house receiving and entertaining and the next they would be on the streets. Sometimes it was known openly that Denning was responsible, but more often the ruin occurred mysteriously.

After a time the responsibility for half the failures in New York was attributed to the buccaneer who had been snubbed. There was a time when old families trembled at the mention of his name—families who had not even troubled to answer the invitations to his notorious ball and reception. That was back in the sixties and seventies. Those who had snubbed him must have felt as did those Romans who were on the proscription lists of Sulla.

Old Denning was in his middle fifties when his hard-faced wife died. He was a big vigorous man but as sixty approached, something which appeared to be the Hereafter and turned out not to be seemed to trouble him. To the astonishment of the congregation he came on Sunday to the Church of the Ascension, and after that he never missed a Sunday.

The whole tempo of his life grew slower and more steady. He gave money to charities and heaped gifts on the destitute families of the parish. He even interested himself personally in the work and paid visits to tenements and squatters' shacks. That was how he met my aunt Sarah.

My aunt Sarah was a tall, rather frail woman who at the time she met Michael Denning was thirty-one and already resigned to the status of old maid for the rest of her life, a status as rigid, as fixed in its code of behavior in the New York of that day, as that of a Hindu widow. She had had a love tragedy, and so for the rest of her life there was, in the opinion fashionable in that day, nothing for her to do but devote herself to church work or sit quietly at home.

She was a handsome woman, so intensely feminine that in these days she would perhaps have been called kittenish. At that time, she was the ideal of womankind—pretty, shy, timid and frail and given to fainting now and then ever since her "decline." She went into a decline at the age of twenty-two when her fiance, a young fellow named Hubert Standish, was drowned before her eyes at Newport. After that she never went out again.

But it was not only the "decline" which shut in my aunt Sarah. Her family were among those who had not come to old Michael Denning's party; worse than that, her parents, who were my grandparents, had looked upon the invitation as an insult and never even troubled to answer it. On their part it was, I think, less snobbery than moral indignation. They were not themselves very rich, but they had enough money to live comfortably and well, and their position in the provincial society which centered about Washington Square was unassailable.

My grandfather was a lawyer, and his business was looking after the estates of old families like his own. It was a small life they led—Victorian, provincial and walled about by principle and prejudice and pride. My grandfather objected to Michael Denning not because he was a rather vulgar self-made man who had millions, but because he had made those millions in an unscrupulous fashion. It was that which Aunt Sarah's father could not forgive him. He would never see him or meet him on the same level as that upon which he met honest businessmen. And so one morning he wakened to find he was a ruined man.

It was an intricate business which must have taken Michael Denning hours of detailed work to plan, for my grandfather's money was invested in a number of things. But the buccaneer managed it. Mysteriously, fantastically, my grandfather's investments turned into nothing at all, and he was left with his wife and two daughters to live on what he earned. And presently even that began to dwindle in the wake of his ruin and a whispering campaign which spread the rumor that he was a poor businessman, foolish and untrustworthy, perhaps not quite honest.

People began to withdraw their estates from his care and presently he had to give up his house and take his wife and his two daughters to live in a flat in Tenth Street over a drug store. Their position was still good but they had no money. Michael Denning had done his work thoroughly.

At the time the old rascal began attending the Church of the Ascension clad in respectable sheep's clothing, my aunt Sarah was the poverty-stricken old-maid daughter of a ruined man. She was resigned to her lot, as genteel women were in those days; I think it quite possible that at thirty-one she had even begun to find the kind of morbid pleasure which some women find in martyrdom. Her life was over! Fate had treated her shamefully, taking first her handsome lover and then her fortune. And everyone—her friends, her relatives, the congregation of her church—held the same belief.

I do not know what methods old Michael used in his courtship of my aunt Sarah. I have heard stories about them, and I knew both of them well enough to imagine a great part of the story. When I knew old Michael, he was already nearly seventy. I was only fifteen or sixteen when he died of a stroke, but the memory of him is one of the clearest I have. He was one of those unforgettable people who stamp themselves upon one's memory by sheer force of vitality and animal charm.

At seventy-odd, he was like a vigorous man of fifty, and at fifty-seven, he must have seemed to Aunt Sarah like an attractive man of forty. Even as an old man, he had personality and magnetism. His figure was that of a man of middle age accustomed to hard exercise, yet he never in all his life took any planned exercise. He rose early and walked to his office, not for exercise, but because he liked it.

He dissipated but dissipation seemed to have no effect on his powerful body save to keep off excess fat. It was impossible for him to do without women, and there were always plenty of them in his life, but he never became a roué and the ardent fire never died out.

I think his appeal for Aunt Sarah on that first day when they met in a Ninth Avenue tenement must have been purely physical. And it must have been a strange scene—that first meeting between the shabby, timid little woman believing her life was over at thirty-one, and the strapping, vigorous, middle-aged man who had ruined her father. Their son Ogden told me that she said of that meeting. "The first thing I thought was, 'Why, he isn't a bit the way people say.'" In that admission there was weakness, and from that moment she was lost.

I have no doubt that Michael Denning knew exactly how to play his game. He knew the thing to say and exactly how to say it, using his big husky voice as an instrument with which to charm. Her first impulse, she told her son long afterward, was to run away, but somehow she could not, and by that, of course, she meant that she did not want to. In any case, she did not run away, and after they had visited the other poor families in the tenement, he insisted on driving her home in his closed brougham.

"No one will see you," he said.

Probably she blushed, and being unworldly and confused, yielded because she did not know what else to do, and also because she wanted to yield. She insisted on only one thing—that he stop the brougham and let her descend two blocks from her house so that her father should never know. It was winter and already dark, and no one saw her scuttling away from the temptation of *liking* this middle-aged man who she had been taught to believe was an ogre.

He made no attempt to suggest another meeting. He simply got down and helped her out and bade her good night. It was all very formal save for one thing. Her hoop skirts caught in the narrow door of the brougham so that she pitched forward and for a moment he held her in his arms, suspended in mid-air, until the coachman freed her. It was unladylike and embarrassing, but it was funny, and my aunt Sarah never lacked a sense of humor. For all her blushes, she must have laughed.

When she returned to the flat over the drug store in Tenth Street she behaved as if nothing had happened, but after she had gone to bed she lay awake for hours until her sister, who was my mother and shared the bed, complained of her restlessness. My mother told me long afterward that she thought her sister Sarah must be ill because until that night she had always slept quietly and soundly. But in the morning there was no sign of illness. There was color in her cheeks and a light in her eyes the family had not seen there since before her fiance was drowned.

It must have been an extraordinary night for a woman who had believed her life finished—lying there puzzled and a little frightened by the knowledge that at last something had happened to her. I don't imagine she knew quite what it was, or if she did know, she refused to admit it even to herself.

I have an idea that some of that first emotion had to do as much with her drowned lover as with Michael Denning. They must have been a good deal alike in a physical way, possessing the same physique and vitality and the same sort of good looks and animal charm. Of the two, Michael Denning was probably the more intelligent.

It was not Denning who made the next move; he was, I think, too wise and experienced for that. For days, perhaps for weeks, he did not see her again save in church on Sundays, when he appeared, dressed soberly, sitting in his pew in the midst of a congregation of people most of whom did not speak to him. And even then he did not bow to her. Instead of bowing, he did something far more clever. He knew perhaps that she would look toward him in spite of anything she could do, and he waited, watching her, until she stole a glance, and then he simply smiled at her, more with his eyes than with his mouth (it was a trick he had), showing her that they had a secret of which no one in the world save his coachman even had a suspicion.

And then one day they met again as if by accident in the same tenement. (It was not by accident because he had kept a man to watch all her movements and discovered that she made her visits neatly, on schedule, and that she visited this particular tenement on Thursdays.) Again they visited all the families, and again after dark she drove off with him in the brougham and he let her down two blocks from the flat over the drug store. Only this time she did not pretend she did not want to drive with him.

But when she got down she was careful this time that her hoop skirts should not trap her, because she had suffered so bitterly ever since it had happened before. Day after day she had felt his big muscular arms encircling her and holding her firmly while the coachman freed her skirts. For days she had been aware of the faint scent of good tobacco and expensive Eau de Cologne that came from his clothes. For days she had suffered from thoughts which no genteel woman of her day was supposed to have.

In a novel I suppose Michael Denning would have seduced her and left her ruined with an illegitimate child as his final act of vengeance against her father; but it was not like that. Denning, for all his skulduggery as a businessman, was not that bad. There was a certain grandeur about him, and as with all greatness, simplicity accompanied it—a simplicity that at times was almost childlike. I think that probably Aunt Sarah was suspicious of his intentions, but I think, too, that she could not have saved herself however base they might have been.

What he wanted was something at once grander and more naïve than mere seduction. Certainly no one suspected at the time. People attributed his sudden change and his interest in good works to all sorts of things—repentance, social ambition, fear of the Hereafter—but none of the guesses was right.

Certainly he was not repentant. With regard to his own buccaneering I once heard him say, "All businessmen are crooked. You can't touch pitch without being defiled. Some men are more clever than others and do things in a big way. Nobody notices the little fellow. That's why no man in business can ever be a gentleman in the strictest sense of the word. That's why this New York 'society' is so ridiculous. Its very foundations are laid by a lot of crooked businessmen pretending to be gentlemen."

And it certainly wasn't fear of the Hereafter, because on that subject he had a clear philosophy, which was, "Live as hard and fast as you can because this is the only life you're sure of."

It might have been social ambition save that it was on a much grander scale. He did not want to be invited to parties. He wanted nothing for himself. The truth was that he had plenty of money—millions and millions—and now that he was beginning to be old, he wanted to found a dynasty. He wanted the name of Denning to go on and on in New York and in America. But nobody suspected this until he was dead.

I think his choice of Aunt Sarah was an accident. He was, to be sure, on the lookout for a suitable woman to marry—a woman not so young as to make him appear ridiculous and not so old as to be useless for bearing children. He wanted, too, someone of good stock with the kind of background he himself had not known as the son of a poor farmer in upstate New York, or as a successful man with a grenadier wife and a troupe of ballet girls on the side. My aunt Sarah was all these things, and what was most important of all, he fell in love with her. It wasn't only that she was pretty and feminine and soft, but there was, too, something in the circumstances of their meetings that attracted him. He was sentimental, and the sight of my aunt Sarah bending over the bed of a sick child in a tenement finished him.

And then before long he discovered, I think, what no one else had known —that in respectable, provincial New York society he had found a passionate woman, a mate worthy of himself. As an old man, he used sometimes to look at his wife, covered with jewels, her fine eyes flashing, and laugh loudly (in company where he dared) and say, "Look at Sally. She thought she was finished with life. She hadn't even begun to know how glorious it could be."

Meanwhile, their courtship went on secretly. How they managed to keep it secret in that tight little world is a mystery; perhaps they succeeded because it was carried on in the closed brougham and on the backstairs landings of tenements. The old coachman was discreet. He had been with Denning for twenty years and rarely a day passed without the necessity for discretion on his part. And then one day Michael said to my aunt, "We are going to be married."

At first she cried and protested, knowing all the time that the whole thing was as much her fault as his. All the time she had gone about in the dark clothes of a deaconess visiting the poor, she had been flirting and desperately in love. After what I suppose was called a "pretty scene" in those days, she yielded and agreed. They were not to tell any of her family. They would be married and go away one night to Charleston.

It was spring and the magnolias and azaleas were in bloom. Denning knew Charleston; he had been there during the war. He could keep the news of the license an absolute secret. She could write her family a note.

I have that note in my possession. It is written in violet ink in a hand surprisingly firm for a lady who had always been led to believe that she was weak and helpless and a victim of fate. It is old and yellow now, but there is still passion and determination in it. It read:

Dear Father:

Please do not think that I have lost my mind or that I am inventing a preposterous lie. Do not be alarmed when I do not come home tonight. I will have gone on my wedding journey. I am marrying Michael Denning. No, I am not insane. Perhaps I should have told you earlier but I was afraid of scenes, and I meant to do it anyway—for the last four or five weeks—the moment he asked me.

I suppose you will want to know where on earth I met him. Well, it was while we were both visiting the poor. We met in the tenements. There, now none of you —Mother or Susan or you—will expire from curiosity.

He is not at all as you think. I am in love with him and willing to trust myself in his care for the rest of my life. I suppose you will want to disown me. I shall be sorry but I mean to cleave to Mr. Denning. I've no doubt that we shall all make it up in time. We are going to Charleston and then to New Orleans and expect to be back in June.

With much love to you all,

Your devoted and unworthy daughter,
Sarah.

The last phrase was, I am sure, written with humor.

The marriage was a sensation in New York. The spectacle of Michael Denning marrying the daughter of one of his victims was something not to be seen twice in a lifetime.

In June, they returned from their wedding journey. My aunt Sarah sent her mother a note saying that she had returned, that she was completely happy, and that she had but to send word for her to come at once to the flat in Tenth Street. She sent a fabulous basket of hothouse fruit with the note and wrote that for the next two weeks she would be at the vast brownstone house which Michael had built in the days when he was married to the grenadier. After that she would be at Newport, where she would spend the summer in the house which Michael had bought for her.

That first summer at Newport wasn't very successful. At first people didn't come near the Dennings—at least no one who didn't *have* to come because of Michael Denning's power—but before the summer was over some of Aunt Sarah's old friends came to call. The Sarah they saw was a changed woman—no longer dressed in drab gray and black, but wearing the most expensive clothes and looking pretty and dashing and happy.

It was clear that Michael Denning had found the woman he had been looking for all his life, and that he meant to devote the rest of his life to her. I don't think she minded not going out and not seeing people. I don't think she even minded the fact that she had had no sign of forgiveness from her own family. She was happy in a way that few women of her world knew. She had a wild, reckless lover who was not a "gentleman."

When they came back to town in the autumn, the world began to open up for them. People came to the house, and sometimes they went out to dinner. It was not so hard as it would have been twenty years earlier because New York was changing. There were growing pains in evidence on all sides—new streets and new buildings; new people seen about at balls and receptions; people like Mrs. Manson Mingott building new houses far uptown in the Fifties. The little provincial New York of Washington Square was breaking up, leaving behind lovely old houses and families who could not keep up with the change, to be forgotten in the obscurity of side streets, to live alone for two or three generations until they disappeared, leaving no trace save old Dutch and English names in the nostalgic pages of Valentine's *Manual*.

The race was now to the rich and flamboyant. Men with not a tenth of Michael Denning's good looks and physical charm were becoming first respectable and then fashionable. Aunt Sarah helped a great deal. With her background and her husband's money, it was inevitable that Michael Denning should fix the background for a dynasty.

And the dynasty was under way. During those first months Sarah always had an excuse for not going out and not receiving. She had become pregnant at once and nine months after her marriage she gave birth to a son—a son who was endowed from that moment with the responsibility of a great fortune, and as an only son, the responsibility of carrying on Michael Denning's dynasty; for when he was born his mother nearly died, and when she had recovered she learned that she would never have any more children.

The son was named Ogden, the family name of Michael Denning's mother. He was my cousin and born two months after me. We were destined to know an intimacy unusual even between cousins, and for the last forty years of his life I was the only person he spoke to outside of his lawyer and his servant.

3

What I have told you is, in spite of being a story itself, in a way only a prelude to the story. I have told it in detail because it is of great importance in the story of Ogden Denning and Elena. Ogden was born, needless to say, with a certain heritage, a certain physical endowment, and as they would say nowadays, in the world so distantly related to the world of Michael Denning and Aunt Sarah, with a certain gland control which would have determined his character in any age and any time, but his story would, I think, have been quite different if the story of his parents and the time in which they lived had been different.

Their story is important, too, because there was something profoundly American in them both and because the story of Michael Denning and his son Ogden is the story of so many Americans of his time. For me the story of Michael Denning did not end with his death but with the death of his son nearly fifty years later, for Ogden Denning in reality existed only as a part of his father's career. Ogden Denning was called into existence by the will of Michael Denning, and until he died, his whole life was determined by the will of an old man long dead.

He was born—Ogden—with the seed of death already in him, a throwback perhaps to some ancestor who had neither his father's vigor nor his mother's will. As a little boy, he was not strong and he had a natural timidity which increased with pampering, for old Michael Denning, who was now over sixty, worshiped the child with the adoration of an elderly parent, and always in the back of his mind was the thought that his son must be a "gentleman."

He never could have been anything else, and I think the old man knew it and was at times saddened by the knowledge. He knew, old Denning, almost everything there was to know about living. He had begun in poverty and hardship. He had made his own success.

In his heart he always had a contempt for men who lived off inherited income, trembling each time there was a panic with the fear that suddenly it might vanish leaving them helpless. He himself had been ruined and penniless a half-dozen times, but in his tough old heart was the knowledge that he could always build another fortune. He was never afraid.

And now he knew his son would be one of those soft men who *inherited* money, and lived in terror of losing it. His son would never know what it was to be poor. I think the old man understood even in his day that there was some necessity, profound and urgent, in every good American to make his own success. Inherited success seemed to ruin young men.

But in spite of all that secret knowledge, he went on making his son into a "gentleman," preparing him for that world of the nineties which was just beginning to flower and for which in his heart the old man had only contempt. Everything was against the boy—his wealth; his elderly father; the whole world into which he was born. For it was no longer the little old provincial New York where a few buccaneers went their spectacular ways; it was an awkward adolescent New York in which the sons and grandsons of the old buccaneers were trying to create a world in imitation of Europe, in which they attempted to take the place (one might have said) of princes whose families had existed before the crusades.

They did not know how to do it, and so what they managed to create was a society more like a circus than anything else—a world which was an imitation made for show, cheap, without cultivation, vulgar and founded almost entirely upon great wealth. They built themselves Gothic and Renaissance châteaux in the midst of a great city, without so much as a leaf or a twig anywhere near to provide an illusion of open country. In a way, they were trying to do what old Michael himself sought to do in another way. They tried to buy background.

Old Michael Denning knew that the good old buccaneering days were drawing to a close and that a too early decadence had set in. Being far more intelligent than most of his contemporaries, he saw the secret of the New York that was to come—the New York which made and destroyed families in a generation or two, and made and destroyed men overnight. And so when his son was fifteen he made plans to send him to the Far West. He bought a ranch and built a house, and told the boy that when he was eighteen he would go to Wyoming to stay until he was of age.

But it never happened. It might have saved Ogden, although I think the decadence was born in him, a very part of him. It was Aunt Sarah who prevented it. She had what she wanted now—money, and a great house, and a husband whom she loved.

I think she made no open opposition to the plan for sending her son to the West, but in her heart she was determined that it should never happen. She was, I think, quite as determined about this as she had been about marrying Michael Denning. She, too, wanted her son to be a gentleman, not in the eternal sense as the old man had seen it, but in the fashionable sense of the day. But the plan never came to an issue, for one morning when she went into her husband's room she found him dead.

He had a fashionable funeral to which nearly everyone came, for with the help of Aunt Sarah he had turned the trick; he had made himself not only fashionable but respectable. He had founded a dynasty and left a great fortune to his wife and son. His old enemies, a good many of them turned respectable now like himself, sat on the stiff gold chairs and heard the rector of the Church of the Ascension deliver a sermon praising him. I went to the funeral. I was sixteen years old at the time and I remember it clearly. It was magnificent. Even my grandparents were there, for they had long since forgiven Aunt Sarah and the old man. They had a comfortable house on Sixteenth Street and a country place up the Hudson, bought for them by the rogue who had first ruined them and then married their daughter.

He left them enough money to live well for the rest of their lives. My mother, too, had a legacy and even my great-uncle William had a gift.

My great-uncle William enters the story much later, but in the last years of Michael Denning's life he had come to be a great friend of the old man. Uncle William was my grandfather's brother, although he was the age of my mother and my aunt Sarah. He was the godfather of my cousin Ogden and the black sheep of the family, and the old man liked him because he had never behaved as he should and had lived riotously. He wanted Uncle William to be sure of enough money to go on having a good time for the rest of his life.

When the old buccaneer died, his son Ogden was nearly sixteen years old, and as different from his father at the same age as it was possible to be. At sixteen, Michael Denning had made his own living, working on a farm. At eighteen, he had come to New York driving cattle. At twenty-one, he was married to a woman whom he thought he loved and perhaps did love—a woman as hard as he was.

At sixteen, his son had horses of his own, a valet, a sailing yacht, and he had been to the most expensive and fashionable schools. Perhaps such a background created impressions which were not altogether true—that Ogden was insufferable, a snob and a waster. He was really none of these things. He was a tall, awkward, shy boy (his father had never known what shyness was, not even when he came to New York as an upstate country boy). Ogden was pale and gentle, and people liked him. He had a charm which came to him from his mother rather than from old Denning. There was nothing boisterous about him. You scarcely knew when he entered a room, but presently you were aware of something pleasant and warm and even a little fantastic. He was good-looking, with pale skin and reddish-brown wavy hair, eyes that were bright blue and like his father's save that they lacked the light of the old man's fierce vitality.

He rode well and swam and sailed a boat but he did these things only to

[269]

please his father, who believed they were things a "gentleman" should do. He was solitary by nature, and what he really liked was poetry and pictures. I know that by the time he was fifteen he had already begun to suffer from the horrors his mother had installed in the great house when she took possession of it—the bad pictures, the horrible tapestries, the inhuman furniture, the palms and the bric-a-brac.

It was an epoch with the worst taste the world has ever known, and in the New York into which Ogden was born, it was especially crowded with horrors. He divined how bad it all was in a day when everyone around him believed it to be all there was of beauty and good taste. He should have lived a generation earlier or a generation later. In either time he would have found himself; but in the New York of the Mauve Decade he was alone.

I liked him. I liked him for the simplicity which had survived in him, somehow, in spite of every force working against it. I liked him, too, for his quiet fidelity. He was slow in coming to know people, but once he accepted them, he had a doglike loyalty. As I think of him now, it seems to me that he was like a setter dog, quiet and gentle and full of trust. When he loved someone, he could believe no ill against him.

The lusty quality of the old man shocked and terrified him in spite of everything he could do. He adored his mother. To him she was, I think, everything that was beautiful and perfect. The passion which had been in both his parents was translated in Ogden into something else. It was there, but muted and controlled and not a little morbid. There was in him none of their recklessness.

He never saw the ranch in Wyoming, although he owned it until the day he died. After his father's funeral, my aunt Sarah decided that she had had enough of New York and would close the house and go to London. She was full of vigor and spirit. She still wanted fun, and I am sure that nothing would have pleased old Michael Denning more than to know that, instead of turning her back on life when he died, she had gone on enjoying herself. She and Ogden stayed in Europe for the next seven years, until she was killed.

To this day I do not know whether Ogden liked the life he led over there. They stayed with dukes and bankers, and Aunt Sarah entertained a good deal. In summer they had a palace in Venice and a part of each winter they spent on the Riviera.

Sometimes I think that perhaps he would have liked Wyoming better. Certainly if he had gone to Wyoming his life would have been different. Certainly his mother would not have been killed, and he never would have met Elena, and certainly he would not have been so lonely in America.

During all those seven years I saw him only twice. Toward the end of the period, while he was spending his life between Venice, London and the

Riviera, I had already gone to work in my father's brokerage office. He never entered my life again until he brought Elena back as his bride.

4

When I was nineteen, my parents sent me to make the grand tour. They believed that the education of no young man was complete unless he had seen Paris, the Tower of Pisa, the Sistine Chapel and the ruins of Ancient Rome. They gave me plenty of money, and dutifully, like a good son, I visited all the places they had indicated for me. But I hate looking at spectacular sights. I have always liked a small intimate landscape with little gardens and humble cottages far more than all the palaces and mountains in the world; and so I hurried at top speed through Rome, Florence and the hill towns of Italy in order to have enough time left before I returned to college to make a walking tour through the Black Forest.

I came to Bavaria early in September and set out alone, because the boy with whom I had meant to make the trip had to return to America at the last moment. The weather was superb, and the world I discovered was an enchanted one. For me it was like a lost paradise—like an enchanting country in which I had lived in some other life and to which I had now returned. It seemed to me that I knew it all—the hills; the pine forests which filled the air with their scent all through the heat of the day; the swift cool little streams and waterfalls; even the tiny gentians and campanulas that starred the grassy banks.

Setting out from Munich, I walked deeper and deeper into the mountains, farther and farther away from cities and show into a quiet, lovely forgotten world. In the early morning when I set out the mist would still be lingering like veils of gauze far down among the black trunks of the tall pines. By noon it would be burned away, and I would stop for beer and lunch at some tiny inn hidden among the pines.

Now and then I would meet a fellow walker, some sturdy Bavarian boy in *Lederhosen* with bare knees. When it grew hot we would swim in a lake or stand under a waterfall with the icy *Schneewasser* tumbling over our naked bodies like champagne. It was one of those times in one's life when it is good simply to be alive, to have a strong body, to feel the sun and the rain, and smell the scent of pine woods.

And in the midst of the Black Forest I fell in love for the first and only time in all my life with a girl to whom I did not speak save to call a friendly *"Grüss' Gott"* in passing.

It happened in a tiny watering place called Bad Münster. No one I know has ever heard of it, and now when I think of it, it sometimes seems to me that it was a kind of Never-Never Land which never existed at all but was

[271]

born out of the enchantment of the *Schwarzwald*, the legendary home of gnomes and trolls and goddesses. Sometimes late at night at the moment between wakefulness and sleep I wonder whether the girl was real or only a kind of wood witch. Sometimes I doubt whether she herself and everything that happened after I saw her were not simply an illusion, from which I will one day awaken.

The tiny place had a tiny casino at the edge of a torrent which ran down from among the pines through the very center of the town. There were a half-dozen little villas with gardens filled at that season with dahlias and Michaelmas daisies, and in all the windows there were boxes and pots of pink geraniums and petunias. It lay in a valley and one came upon it suddenly, neat and pretty like a charming doll's village.

The people who lived in the hotel and the little village were butchers and bakers and little shopkeepers who could not afford places like Carlsbad and Bad Nauheim and Marienbad.

When I saw it, I thought, "I'll stay here for three or four days and rest." I had only four days left before I had to take the train to Hamburg to sail, for I had to be back at college before the end of the month. I stayed ten days and was two weeks late for the opening of school. I would have stayed longer if she had stayed, too; perhaps forever.

The hotel was built around three sides of a garden which ran to the edge of the little river, and I found a room there with a balcony overlooking the courtyard and the waterfall. In the evening an orchestra played in the garden and people sat around tables listening and eating sandwiches and drinking beer. They were simple, friendly people, and they had a lot of curiosity about Americans and about me in particular. Most of them had relatives who had migrated to America and lived in Milwaukee and St. Louis and Cincinnati. It was hard to make them believe how different those great cities were from this enchanted village in the forest.

On the third morning, the day before I planned to leave, I wakened and went to my balcony to have coffee and rolls. It was a morning like any other morning, the air crisp and bright, with the sun streaming through the mist that still hung in the pines, and the sound of the waterfall heard above the singing of the kitchen maid on the terrace beneath the balcony. Yet it was not the same, because *she* was there on the balcony just opposite having coffee and rolls with a man. They were really too good to be believable. It was as if the little hotel were the setting for a comic opera, and now the hero and heroine had arrived. She was dressed in a gingham dress with puffed sleeves which left her arms bare, and she could not have been more than nineteen or twenty years old. Her hair was red-gold and was done in little curls all over her head, and the clear morning sun shining on it gave her a kind of halo. The man with her was dressed for walking in *Lederhosen* and bare knees and a gingham shirt open at the throat. He was dark with a long, aristocratic face and black eyes.

It struck me at once that these two were different from the others in this hotel and village. I could see them plainly, although I could not hear their voices. And then suddenly she laughed, tossing back her head. It was a delicious sound, in which there was a reckless gayety, and when she laughed I knew with a sudden adolescent envy that she was in love. The man leaned across the table and kissed her, and then they saw me and she laughed again.

I did not see them again until early in the evening when the first chill had begun to slip down from the pine forest all around. They came into the garden and had some beer and then disappeared again into their room. They sat only a little way off from me, the girl facing me so that I could glance at her now and then without being noticed. She was lovely to look at but she had something beyond beauty, some exciting quality which attracted me.

The man held a light for her cigarette, and I felt a sudden twinge of jealousy which I told myself at once was absurd. The evening light faded until it was so dark that I could not have seen her face save for the warm light which came through the open doors of the dining room, where the stodgy guests of the hotel were gathering for dinner. There were pretty girls among them but they were heavy and giggly—*Backfisch*, all of them. This woman was something else. The pair rose suddenly and went into the hotel. Then it was that I saw she was tall and that she moved magnificently.

I suppose that I was ripe to fall in love and that I would have been attracted by any lovely woman. Yet there was something different about this. I was to know for the rest of my life how different it was. Now, as an old man, I believe profoundly that a man can fall in love with one woman who remains forever more desirable than any other he has ever seen.

In the morning I wakened and hurried through my bath and dressing, peeping now and then through the shutters to see if she had come to the balcony for her breakfast, but I saw nothing of her. I breakfasted and still she did not appear, and when I inquired of the chambermaid, she told me that they had already gone into the forest. From then on, I had the chambermaid call me at dawn so that I should not miss seeing her. When I asked the chambermaid who they were, she said, "They are Herr and Frau Doktor Müller." I was young, but I knew the world well enough to know that such a couple were never "Herr and Frau Doktor Müller."

I did even more preposterous things, like trying to discover which direction they had taken in order to follow them. For four days I wandered through the forest paths, and on the fifth I did encounter them on the edge of the stream far below the hotel. They had finished their lunch, and the dark man lay asleep with his head in the girl's lap. I was aware that I was an intruder and that I was a fool and that nothing could change the situation and that

[273]

there was no hope of ever coming any nearer to her than I was at that very instant.

I prepared to turn and run, but at the same time, as if aware that she was being watched, she turned and looked at me and I was forced to continue along the path past her as if I had come upon them by accident instead of after a four-day search. She looked at me and smiled, and then put her finger to her lips. It was a frank and charming smile and I felt my face grow hot and my heart begin to pound, but somehow I managed to get past her without seeming too great a fool.

The torment was not confined to the day. At night I could not sleep but lay tossing, thinking of her and her lover in the room across the courtyard. I tried to imagine myself in his place, and I kept seeing her white teeth and dark eyes and the tiny red-gold curls that covered her head. I knew that I should go away, and each night I planned to leave but in the morning I could not go.

I tried to draw the plump manager and his buxom wife into conversation about the pair, but with his broken English and my bad German we never got very far. When I asked where the couple came from he said, "Vienna," and that was all, although he looked at me with a humorous glint in his eye as if he knew what was the matter with me.

I saw them a half-dozen times within the next few days but the only time we spoke was when we passed once on the street and with a mocking smile, as if she, too, knew what was the matter with me, she said, *"Grüss' Gott,"* like a peasant. When we had passed I turned to look after her, for I found pleasure even in the way she walked, and as I turned she turned too and gave me a smile. My heart leaped, and I thought, "To live with a woman like that! No, love couldn't be that wonderful!" I loved her recklessness and her humor and her coquetry.

And then one evening when I came in from the forest they had gone. When I asked the innkeeper where, he said, "To Munich, but they are not stopping there. They are going back to Austria." For a wild moment I thought of trying to follow them. Perhaps I should find her alone; but what should I do if I did find her thus? What could I say that would not be ridiculous? What could a shy, green American boy mean to a Continental woman like her?

I had missed my boat and was already late. All night I lay awake, and in the morning I left. When I had paid my bill, the innkeeper said, "And now I will tell you about Herr and Frau Doktor Müller. You are an American and you are going home, so it will not matter, only you must promise to tell no one in this town."

I promised, and he said, "He is the Prince of Hohenheim—the heir to the principality. The woman I do not know; perhaps her name *is* Müller. I used to work in the kitchen of the great castle there. That is why he came here."

I think he told me the secret partly because he was humorously sorry for me and partly because he thought his little hotel in that forgotten part of the Black Forest would gain *réclame*. Perhaps I would go back and tell rich Americans that princes went to the Gasthof Eckermann in Bad Münster.

I walked to the nearest town on the railroad and went to Munich but I found no trace of them. Then I picked up my baggage and went to Hamburg to sail back again to the drab reality of America, feeling sick and romantic in the belief that I would never again see the girl who had looked up at me and smiled with her finger to her lips there in that enchanted forest.

5

I did not forget her. I returned on a German boat, and I found myself questioning everyone about Hohenheim in a vague hope of finding out who the girl might be. I was curious, too, about the man. Beyond all dispute he was attractive, handsome, dashing—one of those whom one might call the Blessed, since God, it seemed, had given him everything. In the dark, handsome, sensual face there was intelligence as well as beauty.

I did find out a good deal, partly from books and partly from fellow passengers. Hohenheim was an independent principality, not large, but rich and singularly beautiful, which lay between Germany and Austria. The ruling prince was an old man, and his heir was a nephew just over thirty, gallant, distinguished, handsome. He was the one who had been in Bad Münster. One of my fellow passengers, a brewer from Munich, told me that he was famous for his conquests both of women and of horses. I could discover nothing at all about the girl.

When I arrived in New York, both my father and mother, dressed in mourning, met me at the dock. My mother was weeping. A week before, while I was at sea, my aunt Sarah, Ogden's mother, had been killed in a collision between trains on the Swiss-French frontier at Vallorbe. Ogden, who was with her, had suffered a broken arm.

"Otherwise," my father said, "he is all right."

I remember that the speech shocked me, although I could not at the moment have told you why, save that I knew, perhaps better than they, his singular, almost morbid devotion to his mother. Now, with the help of Freud and all the new psychology which has long since become commonplace, I can explain it to myself, but then I only knew that this was a terrible tragedy, far worse than the loss of a mother to a son like me or to any normal man.

The odd thing was that when they told me the news I had a sudden quick vision of Aunt Sarah as I knew her after old Michael had given life to her. I saw her—grand, humorous, frivolous and spirited—and in the same moment it occurred to me for the first time that there was a curious subtle likeness between her and the girl I had seen in the Black Forest.

I returned to college, and from time to time I had letters from Ogden which were no different from the letters I had always had, describing his travels, the people he met, a room, a wedding, a painting which had roused his enthusiasm. It was only from friends returning from Europe who had seen him there that we heard of his reaction to his mother's death. It was not what I would have expected. Judging from his habits and character, one would have thought that he would hide himself away somewhere to grieve in solitude. Instead, he had cut loose for the first time in his life and was living high.

Perhaps it was some heritage from his father that suddenly came to the surface, but I think it much more likely that it was desperation and a grief which was beyond the solace of solitude.

I envied him. I thought, "If I had the money to do all that, I could probably forget that girl." She still troubled me, deep inside. She was there all the time, and she would reappear suddenly at the most inopportune moments to spoil whatever fun I might be having. If I became attracted by a pretty girl of my own class I would find myself, in the very midst of my admiration, comparing the brightness of her hair and the color of her eyes with those of the girl I had seen in Bad Münster. But most of all it was the smile—that smile she had given me when she raised her finger to her lips to keep me from disturbing the sleep of the dark man who lay with his head in her lap.

And then one day, nearly three years after Ogden's mother was killed, he sent me a note from the big brownstone house in New York. He had returned without letting anyone know. He was married. He wanted me to come and dine that night to meet his wife.

I went, wondering whom he could have married without the news leaking out, for he was an important person, both as the son of old Michael Denning and as one of the richest of the spectacular young men of his time, and so he was known to newspapermen in London and Paris as well as New York. He received me in the long drawing room opening into the hall, still decorated in the hideous style of the times.

He looked older, thinner and paler, and there was something foreign about him which at first put a constraint on both of us. We had seen each other only two or three times in years, and during all that time we had been drifting farther and farther apart, he into Continental ways of thought and living, and I, through college and my father's brokerage office, into ways which were not American, perhaps, but exaggeratedly New York. We had cocktails together, and he said shyly, "My wife is late; she's likely to be late. I think you'll like her." He did not say it with irritation but almost with pride, as if he were so much in love with her that she not only had a right to be as late as she chose but that every other woman would do well to imitate her.

"Who was she?" I asked bluntly.

"An Austrian," he said. "I'll tell you about her after you've met her."

I stood with my back to the doorway opposite the great marble stairway, but in front of me there was, in those days, one of those vast mirrors which the New York of the Mauve Decade deemed elegant. Idly I stood watching the stairway, when suddenly she appeared, coming slowly down it, one hand resting on the marble rail.

I think it was that gesture which first roused a train of recognition. There was something young in it, something eternally young and at the same time sensuous, as if she loved the *feel* of the smooth white marble. And then suddenly I *saw*. Some betraying look must have come into my eyes, for my cousin turned at the same time and over his face came a look of adoration.

Coming slowly down the stairs was the girl I had seen smiling at me beside the torrent in the Black Forest.

6

Any other woman I would not have recognized in surroundings and in clothes so different, but her I would have known anywhere. She was dressed splendidly now, and she wore the superb collar of pearls which old Michael had given my aunt Sarah when he married her. Her radiant hair she still wore in the same fashion, done in little curls all over her small head.

I turned from the mirror sharply in order to see, not the reflection but the reality, and I remember that my heart beat wildly and that I felt a sudden wild sensation of soaring flight. A great many things happened all at once. Beyond the desire I felt (because there was something about her which always roused a great deal more than mere sentimental love), I thought again, "This is witchcraft. It can't be true," and then, "She does look like Aunt Sarah, only a million times more radiant and beautiful. That is why he married her."

And then she was in that hideous room, and we were moving toward her. She smiled, and I thought with wild hope, "Perhaps she'll remember me." But she did not. She came toward me as toward a stranger, holding out her hand, a white hand on which there were no rings, and suddenly I felt sick at the knowledge that the awkward boy who had followed her and her lover in the Black Forest had made no impression at all. I was aware that there was a subtle change in her, as if a veil had come over her brightness.

Where in the forest she had been like that gay, flashing torrent, she was still now, like a deep pool.

And then Ogden said, "This is my cousin William and my best friend in the world," and in a flash I hated him, for by making that speech he had bound my hands and made me helpless.

7

There was, I remember, an excellent dinner of the kind Ogden took pleasure in giving—carefully thought out, studiously presented, with all sorts of things out of season. It was a dinner of the period when eating was eating. Although the three of us dined alone, there were ten courses with five kinds of wine, interrupted in the middle with Roman punch to refresh us and give us strength to go on. I do not remember any of the conversation, save that it was stilted and awkward, until Ogden began talking about some baroque doors he had bought in Vienna, and then he became enthusiastic and talked for nearly half an hour.

"I am going to do over the whole house," he said. "That is much more amusing than building a new one. Anyway, I like the structure of this one. I don't want to live 'way uptown. Elena and I bought a great many things in Vienna and Salzburg and Innsbruck—all baroque," he added enthusiastically.

I knew very little of the baroque style, for in those pseudo-Gothic days, it was considered overblown and vulgar. Indeed, in the circles we knew in New York no one spoke of it, if indeed there was anyone save architects who had ever heard of it. Neither Elena nor I was much interested, and in any case it would have been impossible for me even to pretend an interest with her sitting at the end of the long table, looking more beautiful in the gown of silver brocade than she had ever looked before.

The gown left her shoulders bare and showed rather more of the white firm breasts than was considered proper in the New York of that day. I was a little shocked and thought, "She must not wear gowns like that. She must not show that to all the men in New York," unaware then, as I now am not, that I was not so much shocked as jealous. It was as if she belonged to me, and even Ogden had no right to her.

After dinner, Ogden and I did not remain in the dining room, half stupefied with food and drink, while the ladies—in this case Elena alone—went into the drawing room. We went with her. The rest of the evening passed, for me at least, in a kind of nightmare-paradise in which I was filled with delight at having found her again and having her near me and tormented by the knowledge that she was still as far removed from me as she had been in those days in the Black Forest.

She did not talk much and it struck me again and again how different she was from the laughing girl in the gingham dress. She spoke rarely but she had a lovely voice—low, a little hoarse—and she spoke with a faint accent that was irresistible. The stillness was still on her.

I thought, "Perhaps she is bored already," for I knew that Ogden could be a bore, especially when he got on to one of his hobbies; but slowly I came to understand that the stillness came of something more profound than boredom. "Perhaps," I thought, "it is only because she is a woman now and no longer a girl." And I kept thinking of the dark lover with the black eyes and the sensuous mouth who was so obviously not interested in *things*, but in living and in love.

That was what she needed, not a man like Ogden—precious, pale, handsome and curiously *dead*. What she wanted was life, and Ogden, I knew more at that time by instinct than by knowledge, could never bring her what she had need of. Ogden's character, his physique, his tastes—everything was against it. He would make a poor, fumbling lover.

And then presently she rose and said, "I will sing for you," and she went to the piano and seated herself and sang three or four songs in German in a lovely fresh voice that was like the girl I had known in the Black Forest and not at all like this grand *femme du monde* wearing my aunt Sarah's pearls, and when she had finished she rose and said, "I think I'll go to bed now. I'm still very tired from the voyage."

She said good night, shaking hands in the Continental fashion, and although I hoped again for some sign of recognition there was none. She did not remember me at all. We walked with her as far as the marble stairway, and as she turned to go upward, she looked at me suddenly. It was not more than a glance, yet it was charged mysteriously with appraisal and with—yes, I think—even then with invitation. She said, "I hope we shall see a lot of you, William," and went on up the stairs.

Silently we both stood waiting until she had disappeared. I did not speak, and Ogden said, "Yes, she is fascinating. She will be a sensation in New York." It was as if he were speaking not of a woman but of a magnificent picture or a piece of furniture. It was a *very* Ogden remark. He *wanted* her to be admired and himself to be envied.

When she had gone, we went into the library for whisky and another cigar. It had not been changed since the death of old Michael and it was an ugly, heavy room, all mahogany and black leather, and the books were mostly lawbooks. Even the porcelain cuspidor which the old man clung to, in the privacy of his own room, was still there, half hidden beneath the great mahogany desk.

At sight of it, Ogden said, "I don't know why they've kept that thing here all this time," and with his foot he pushed it out into the center of the

[279]

floor and rang for the butler. When the man came, he said, "Take that thing away and smash it. I never want to see it again."

The gesture fascinated me. It was a kind of symbol—the smashing of that cuspidor—and in Ogden's way of doing it there was an exaggerated emotion. It was not simply an order. It was an irritated command. The king is dead! Long live the king! It was as if the humble cuspidor were a scepter. But it was only the beginning of what Ogden meant to do. It was the first sign of the madness which later seemed to take complete possession of him.

The thought of smashing the cuspidor gave me a pang; it was so much a symbol of the old man's vigor and commonness, wit and charm. And I could not help thinking of the delight which the sight of his son's beautiful wife would have given old Michael.

When the butler had gone, I looked at Ogden and said, "Well, are you going to tell me about your wife?"

If I had been a simple man, or a fool, or a man not in love, I would have said, "I've seen her before." But I did not. I thought it better not to speak of that meeting three years before. I told myself that this was because I did not know how much he meant to tell me or even how much he knew of her past, and I did not want to embarrass him; but this was not true. I did it out of craftiness, because already I *knew* somehow that the marriage would be unhappy, and that in the end I might win her for myself.

The long deceit had its beginning on that very first night. What I did then was the result more of animal instinct than of reason and planning.

At first he did not answer my question, and then, looking at me sharply, he said, "I want to tell you. I feel a necessity for telling someone, but you must never repeat a word of it."

"Of course not," I said. "Why should I? You can trust me above anyone on earth." And it was quite true. I was no gossip, and I had no desire to repeat the story. What I wanted was to know my ground so that I should make no clumsy mistakes.

8

I understood why he wanted no one to know the story. Aside from the scandalous side of it, the tale was so fantastically romantic that it was vulgar, and that element, I suspect, Ogden hated more than the scandal.

The whole thing began during the period when Ogden was drinking and running about with actresses and demimondaines. He told me all about that. "I never lived with any of them. I couldn't. They were always so hard and common. But it amused me and helped me to forget my mother's death."

Although he did not say it, I knew that, like many weak men, he had paraded all these women before the world in order to make it believe that he was a devil with women. It is almost an axiom that the man with attraction for women works quietly and discreetly. He has no need to show off.

He had taken a villa at Nice where he lived quietly enough, sleeping most of the day in order to stay up all night in the restaurants and casinos. One night about eleven when he was playing in Monte Carlo, he felt suddenly tired and bored and ordered a fiacre to drive him back to the villa in Nice. It was a cold night but beautiful and clear, with the stars shining like diamonds above the Mediterranean. Wrapped in a blanket, he drove peacefully along, watching the lights in the villas below the Corniche Drive. And as he drove the feeling of satiation with the whole noisy life he had been leading grew stronger and stronger until he reached the decision of returning to America.

When the fiacre had reached that part of the Corniche Drive just before Nice where the road crosses high above a deep ravine, he ordered the driver to stop while he got out and walked. The view below was magnificent, with the lights from Villefranche in the distance and the moon painting the Mediterranean with silver. He stood for a long time looking down across the ravine toward the open sea and presently he heard someone sobbing.

Following the edge of the road, he walked toward the sound until in the moonlight he saw the figure of a woman lying among the rocks by the roadside. Kneeling down, he bent over her and raised her up. She did not resist but at first she could make no answer to his questions for sobbing. At last she said, "Please go away and leave me in peace." But he refused to go, and presently he said, "Tell me where you live and I'll drive you there." But she only said, "Don't bother about me. I don't live anywhere. I'm finished. Please go away."

At length he persuaded her to sit up, and in the moonlight, out of the shadow of the rocks, he saw that she was beautiful.

He said, "If you won't tell me where you live, let me take you to my villa tonight, and tomorrow when you are feeling better you can go away. I shan't trouble you and I shan't even ask you questions."

He argued for a long time and in the end she yielded, partly, I think, because she was so tired and partly because she really did not care what happened to her. And so he drove her to his villa.

The villa was large and the servants were French and came with the house, and in that world they were startled by nothing. Ogden said he felt they rather disapproved of him until the night he returned bringing Elena with him. From then on their attitude changed and they were all kindness and understanding. Once inside the house, he saw that she was, in spite of her weeping and her soiled clothes, more beautiful than he had believed—and something more than beautiful. He was aware of a kind of dazzling quality he had not seen in other women.

He wakened one of the maids and had broth and fruit brought to her, and she was put to bed in a room remote from his own. She never spoke at all save to answer yes or no to his questioning of what she wanted to eat and drink. There was something wild about her, like a wild bird brought into a house and caged.

In the morning the maid wakened him to say that the young lady was very ill and did not seem to know where she was. It was the beginning of a long illness which upset Ogden's plans for returning to America. The doctors of that day called it brain fever, and for more than three weeks they did not know whether the girl would live or die.

The odd thing was that no one on the whole coast seemed to have missed her. There were no inquiries registered with the police, and when the doctors insisted that they must know her name in order to protect themselves, Ogden hired detectives. After three days they returned with the news that she was a Frau Doktor Müller, an Austrian, who was registered at a small *pension* in Monte Carlo. The proprietress, an Italian woman, had not been alarmed by the disappearance of her guest, as Frau Doktor Müller had left her luggage and gone off almost at once, saying that she would return in a few days. They found her passport, which seemed to bear out the story, and Ogden had her luggage brought to his house.

Most men, I suppose, would have sent her off to a hospital or a clinic, but Ogden was a romantic always, and the situation appealed to his whole inclination to live by fantasy rather than by reality and common sense, and so he kept her at the villa, providing the best care possible to give her. Without it, I suppose, she might have died; but in the end, three weeks after he had found her, she opened her eyes one morning and returned to life.

At first she was terrified, and then, when the doctors would allow it, she asked to see her benefactor. He came in and sat beside the bed, looking, I suppose, more reassuring than most men would have done under the circumstances. Her own instinct must have told her after a little while that she had nothing to fear from him. He explained who he was. He even told her, painstakingly, how rich he was—that he could not spend his income, and that she need not worry about the expense. Then, surprisingly, she said that she herself was well off and that she wanted him to keep an accounting so that she might pay him back. But on the first day she gave no hint of why she had been alone sobbing among the rocks by the side of the Corniche Road.

She grew stronger in the days that followed, almost, Ogden thought, in spite of herself because she showed no desire to live. She seemed to be wrapped in a thick veil of indifference. Sometimes, even while they were talking together, she would seem to slip away from him to some great distance.

Slowly he fell in love with her, seeing her there day after day on the

[282]

terrace above the Mediterranean, frail in the beginning as if she were still hypnotized by staring too long into the eyes of death, and then with the color returning slowly to her face as her magnificent body and vitality forced her to live. He fell in love with her in his own way, not as you or I might have and certainly not as that lover I had seen at Bad Münster would have, but slowly and profoundly as he might have fallen in love with an antique statue. To him she was something very precious, which should be cherished.

Ogden suffered from sensibility of the kind that is like nerves exposed in the skin. His charm for others and his greatest weakness from the point of view of himself was, I think, the fact that he always put himself in the place of the other person. This gave him a kind of remoteness which as he grew older engulfed him in loneliness. When he talked to you, you sometimes had an impression that he was not talking to you at all, but to himself— that he was so sensitive throughout the conversation he was constantly substituting himself for you and asking you nothing, saying nothing that could possibly be painful or embarrassing; and so he kept you at a great distance, despite himself. Because of this he asked the girl no questions at all and she told him nothing, until one day nearly six weeks after he found her beside the road, when he said to her, "Where are you planning to go when you leave here?"

She answered him with indifference, "I don't know."

"Why not go home to your family and friends?" He was searching when he asked that question, feeling his way without coming directly to the point.

"I have no home and my friends are lost—long ago." She spoke dully, still in that same trance which had permitted her to remain on and on in his villa.

At last he found courage to speak. He told me that not only was he in love with her, but that marrying her seemed indicated by fate. It was a solution for him. It would sober his own life, restless and without direction since the death of his mother. The odd thing was that the element of the girl's resemblance to his mother and the influence of that fact on his own emotions never occurred to him consciously.

He said to her timidly, "Why don't you marry me?"

She did not answer him at once, and he told her modestly all the things he could offer her—the houses, the jewels, the money, never mentioning himself at all. She looked at him for a long time in silence, and I know that she must have been using her instinct, as any wise woman always does. I think her instinct told her: "This is a kind and charming man, weak and full of good will, who will never trouble you much."

I know the look, that gay, half-mocking glance of appraisal which she would give a man in whom she was interested—the look she had given me at the bottom of the marble stairs. I think she knew, too, that she was the kind of woman for whom a life spent in solitude meant nothing.

For the first time she laughed and said, "Why not?"

Ogden told her he was aware that she was not in love with him but that in the end he could make her happy, never suspecting then—in fact, he never did discover—how much it took to make her happy.

That night she came downstairs to dinner for the first time. They had champagne to celebrate the occasion, and after dinner she said, "You are taking a great gamble, marrying a woman about whom you know nothing." And Ogden, suddenly playing the romantic again, made the speech which such a remark called for: "I know all about you. I know all I want to know."

But she was not content. "No," she said, "I must tell you everything that led up to your finding me on the side of the road. I shan't marry you unless you listen, because you ought to know. Then, whatever happens, you can never reproach me with having deceived you." And she told him about the man I had seen her with in the Black Forest.

9

She was the daughter of a professor, coming from a family which had always devoted itself to music, the law and the arts, and when she was fifteen she was left an orphan and went to live with two aunts who had a little house in Semmering. It was not a gay life, and the aunts were both spinsters who were rigid in their thoughts, their habits, their morality. She had little fun save in summer when she went on walking tours, sometimes in the Tyrol, sometimes in the Salzkammergut. They did not object to that, because she always went with friends who were accompanied by the father of one of the girls.

But even on these tours she was aware of a restraint which took the edge off her fun. Even as a child she was aware, I think, of something deep inside her which made her different from the girls who were content to marry boys with whom they had grown up and settle down for the rest of their lives to children, beer, waltzes and coffee with whipped cream. Women like her seem to happen, sports of nature, without rhyme and reason, without regard to heredity, in any country and in any society. Perhaps, in her case, her nature was born of the mixture of wild Hungarian blood with that of the gentle, sentimental Viennese; for her mother was a Hungarian from Budapest.

On the walking tours she would sometimes escape, overcome by the dullness of her companions, and go high up in the mountains alone. Perhaps it was not their dullness which annoyed her so much as their incapacity to understand that surging unhappiness deep inside her which none of them shared. She herself did not understand it; it was only that she *knew* in some inner part of her young soul that life was never so fine and so exciting as it could be. The only relief she knew was to escape into the mountains. When she returned home in the evening after a day of climbing, the storminess had gone out of her, and there was peace in her soul for a little time.

Then one day when she was twenty she was climbing not far from Innsbruck when she came on a man hobbling painfully toward her through the pines. He was, she thought, the most beautiful man she had ever seen. He was tall and dark, with black eyes. He had fallen and sprained his ankle. His hand was cut, and the side of his dark face was badly scratched.

She spoke to him and they sat down beside a stream while she took from her rucksack the bandages she always had there. With her big peasant's handkerchief she bathed the cut on his hand and bound it up; and she helped him to bandage the twisted ankle, and when the wounds were all dressed, they shared her lunch together beside the stream. She told him about herself, and he told her that he was a young Doktor Müller from Munich on his holiday. He too had a passion for climbing mountains.

I am inclined to believe that if one has the romantic temperament romantic things happen. Certainly I have never known them to happen to dull conventional people. On that sunny day above Innsbruck, if Elena had been like the other girls in the party with her, she would no doubt have aided the handsome stranger, but when it was done she would have said, "Good day, sir," and marched primly down the mountain alone to return to Semmering and marry a respectable citizen. If the stranger had been what he said, plain Herr Doktor Müller of Munich, he would no doubt have accompanied Elena down the mountain, bade her good-by, written to her spinster aunts in Semmering, finally come on a visit and taken her back at last as Frau Doktor Müller.

Like Elena, he had gone mountain climbing to escape a life he hated as thoroughly as she hated the life in Semmering with the spinster aunts, and he had gone alone, hoping, like Elena, that something wonderful would happen. It was not the first time he had gone off like that, alone, in search of love and adventure, but until now he had never found what he sought. Being a romantic, he went on forever hoping.

When they had finished their lunch, they had come to know each other very well. Elena told him about the dullness of her life and about her dreams and ambitions, and he told her a long and ingenious story, wholly false, of his student's life in Munich. At last, late in the afternoon, they reached the foot of the mountain, Elena helping him over the rough places, and before he left her he called at the little *Gasthaus* where she was staying to present himself to the middle-aged gentleman whom the aunts had trusted to look after her.

Elena left with the others the next morning, knowing perhaps in her heart that she had not seen the last of Herr Doktor Müller; and sure enough, on the next day he turned up in the village where her party was staying.

He followed them along the valley and over mountains. There never was, I suppose, any barrier between them either of shyness or convention or fear. Elena managed to meet him secretly in the forest or at some little *Gasthaus* on the edge of a lake or a stream. They had been in love from the first moment they saw each other, and now they admitted it. Sometimes in the evening he came and brought a guitar and sang for the little party like any bourgeois Bavarian suitor. The deception amused them both.

But the game of hide-and-seek up the long valley above Innsbruck came finally to an end. The young man was troubled, yet he was so much in love that there was no saving himself or the girl. The day before she was to go back to Semmering, he told her the truth—that he was not Herr Doktor Müller but a prince, and the only heir to the principality over which his uncle ruled.

10

In a way, Elena was born out of her time as much as Ogden. If it had been a generation earlier, she would perhaps have become a morganatic wife or at least a mistress with a recognized position. If it had happened a generation later, after the war, he would have said, "To hell with it!" and married her; but it happened in a world which was uncertain and crumbling, a world in which royalty and even the aristocracy had begun to be aware of the perils threatening them, and so in decadence had become more rigid than in times when their position was more certain.

He told her the truth—that he could never marry her, that there was no heir to the principality save himself and that one day he would be forced to marry and produce heirs of his own. The time, he said, was not far off because his uncle was seventy and insisting that the succession should be assured before he died. You might say that he should have chucked everything and married her, but that is unjust to him, for you must remember that Hohenheim had been governed and cared for by his family for five hundred years. He told her all this, but at the moment nothing mattered to either of them save the fact that they were in love.

So she never went back to Semmering. The evening before the rest of the party were to return, she left a note behind and took the night train across the border into Bavaria with Herr Doktor Müller. She wrote a note to the spinster aunts trying to explain to them what had happened but it was beyond their understanding, and they wrote to her only to tell her that she was disowned and they never wished to see or hear from her again. It was the last time she ever heard from them, and she never again saw Semmering or any of the little party who had gone with her into the Tyrol. That was what she had meant when she said, "I have no home and my friends are lost—long ago."

She did not mind, I suppose. He took a small flat for her in Munich and she went on with her music, living quietly, almost secretly, never seeing anyone save "Herr Doktor Müller," who only came to the flat after dark. They never went out in Munich, but when he could get away from Hohenheim, they went off together into some remote place where no one would recognize him. That was how they came to that little town where I saw them on the balcony one morning.

Thus they lived year after year, Elena asking nothing of life save music and love and her dark good-looking Herr Müller. One year passed and then another and another, and the prince still managed to evade his promise to marry and settle down to breeding a family. But each year it grew more difficult, and each year the pressure became stronger. They never spoke of it to each other but the dread of that final moment was always there.

At length there was pressure not only from the old uncle—the ruling prince—but from the ministers, and there was trouble, too, among the people who had caught the infection of Socialism from neighboring states. It grew steadily worse until one day he gave his final promise. But he demanded a two-month holiday before he presented himself to the Princess of Saxe-Coburg who had grown impatient and humiliated waiting for him year after year.

He took Elena to Monte Carlo, and there they lived together for the first time openly—a wild, reckless life which was clouded always by the knowledge that each day, each hour, each minute was precious. Time slipped away like quicksilver until the morning of the last day arrived. They had agreed that they were never to speak of the parting but to treat it as though he were leaving on a short journey, and they had agreed, too, that once they were parted each was to behave as if the other had died.

In the end, it was Elena who kept her word and Toni who broke his.

She said good-by to him in the midst of all the flurry and gayety of the Café de Paris, and when he had gone, she went back again to the villa and, taking her trunks, left in a fiacre for the *pension* kept by the Italian woman. When she had paid a week's *pension* in advance, she drove off again in the same fiacre, after telling the proprietress she would return in a day or two.

The fiacre took her along the Corniche Road as far as the deep ravine just above Nice, and there she paid the driver and dismissed him, saying that she meant to go the rest of the way on foot. When he had gone, she walked along the barrier to the place which she had selected to throw herself over.

[287]

It was a magnificent starlit night, and when it came to the point of climbing over the wall to jump into the ravine, she found that she could not do it.

Alone, frightened and ashamed of her own cowardice, she threw herself down among the rocks beside the road. It was there that Ogden found her.

II

When he had finished, he looked at me with a faint smile in his eyes, as if he would apologize for the vulgar melodrama of the story.

"You see," he said, "why I do not want the story to get about. I am saying simply that she is the daughter of a Viennese professor who is dead. That's all that is necessary."

Again for a moment I had the brotherly impulse to say that I had seen her once long ago in the Black Forest, but again something deep inside me told me that it was wiser to keep silent. That craftiness and deceit which an illicit love can raise in any man told me that it was better not to betray any interest in her whatever.

It was long after midnight when I left, knowing in my jealous heart that the moment I had gone he would go up the marble stairs to take his place at her side.

I did not sleep at all that night, and two days later I went away on my holiday, not willingly, for my only desire in life was to see her again, but because it seemed the only thing to do. I did not escape; her image went with me as it always had, only more vivid now and more changeable and fascinating since I had seen her in the role of a fashionable woman who was the wife of my cousin.

When I returned, I found that they had taken an apartment in the Waldorf-Astoria, which was only a five-minute walk from the big house, and that the house itself was already being torn apart to make the changes Ogden had planned. The whole inside, every trace, every memory of the house old Michael Denning had built was being destroyed. All that remained was the façade and the curving marble stairway.

The architect who did the job was an obscure little man whom no one had heard of in that day. Where Ogden had found him I do not know, but he passed over all the fashionable architects who built the monstrosities of the nineties, to find this eccentric little man who shared his own ideas of beauty and his own worship of the baroque style. Between them they took a house which was a horror filled with cubbyholes, heavy mahogany, gilt bamboo and verdure tapestry and made it into an Austrian baroque palace with a Georgian façade.

Ogden did it, I think, partly to please his adored Elena, but partly too because he really suffered from the ugliness of the old house. This new palace, all cream and yellow and peach color and gold, was, he felt, his real background. It was one of those strange things which happen in America—that the son of the buccaneer Michael Denning should find his background in a decadent style of seventeenth-century Austria.

So far as the world was concerned, whatever old Michael Denning had done was always "news." His vitality, his recklessness, the breadth of his gestures made it so. And now his son became "news." Both his wife and his new house were sensations in the New York of that day. When the house was finished Ogden gave a fabulous ball to which the guests were invited in the costumes of seventeenth-century Austria so that he might have the satisfaction of seeing the picture complete and of living, for one night at least, in an age which he hated less than the one in which he found himself.

It was the first time New York society had seen the inside of the house. Old Michael's son avenged the snub the old man had received from the New York of his day. Everyone in the New York of Ogden's day came to the party and there were intrigues on the part of those who were not invited in order to get there. The party, the publicity, the sensation were all in a way triumphs for old Michael Denning; yet in the triumphs there was something dead, for the whole party, and indeed Ogden's whole position in the life of America, was rootless and decadent and without meaning.

12

The ball served, but only incidentally, I think, in the mind of Ogden, to launch Elena. He believed, it is true, that she must be launched extravagantly like no ordinary woman. She had already made a small sensation, and after the ball she could have had what she liked from fashionable New York.

There were women who held out against her, pooh-poohing the extravagant opinions of her beauty and her charm, but they would have been helpless had she chosen to take up the challenge. The men, save for a handful of fops, would have been her slaves. There were perhaps other women in that world who were as beautiful but not one had her charm or her quality of smoldering brilliance. And she was a foreigner and exotic, and there was always about her an aura of mystery and indifference.

She could have had what she liked, but she turned her back on everything that was offered her. After one winter season she took the measure of that world into which Ogden had brought her, and by her standards she found it all pompous and childish and dull. She told me afterward that she found it a pretentious and empty world filled with people who spent their lives playing at living without ever having lived at all. There was nothing in it to rouse her from that lethargy which I felt in her the evening I met her as Ogden's wife.

[289]

For their second summer they went to Newport, although Ogden was already bored with America and longing to return to Europe, where he felt so much more at home. I think that in her heart she was afraid to go back and that she meant never to return. Toward the end of that summer she seemed to come to life, not as her old buoyant self, but hysterically, as someone frantic and desperate. She was rude to the women who could have helped her, rude even to women who meant only to be kind and generous to her, and when she came back to town I discovered that she had almost managed to cut herself off completely from the world which had come to Ogden's ball.

13

Nevertheless, she went out a great deal more, only it was nearly always with people who were considered déclassé and rather scandalous—divorcées and women who openly had lovers. For a little time I was alarmed, thinking that perhaps after all I had been deceived and that she was only an ordinary wanton at heart. I thought, "Maybe she is just like those women—no better, no worse." Once I dared to reproach her about her company but she only laughed at me.

Among them was a gay young woman named Kate Blakeley who had always been wild. She came from a good family and she had as much money as she needed to be completely independent, and long ago as a school girl she had chucked her reputation over the moon and gone out for a good time.

She was a small dark woman with lively black eyes and hearty laugh and a ribald sense of humor. She was utterly reckless, and her recklessness seemed to have a fascination for Elena. They became inseparable companions.

Ogden did not seem to mind the milieu Elena had chosen. Fashionable New York bored him as much as it bored Elena, and he was, I think, glad to be free of it. I think it did not matter to him what Elena did or whom she saw so long as she belonged to him; so long as he could show her to the world as the finest item in his great collection of beautiful things. He allowed her a good deal of freedom, and she never abused it by showing more attention to any one man than to another.

There were moments, nevertheless, when Ogden had terrible outbursts of jealousy and made scenes and accused her of infidelity. But these outbursts only seemed to be symptoms of madness, for once they were past he would fall on his knees and beg her to forgive him and promise never to repeat them. She accepted the scenes with a curious calm and indifference, and always forgave him, out of pity. He went on remaking the house, adding a new door or new furniture to this room or that. He was busy all day long, and at night he and Elena dined alone or with some of her fast friends.

At first I saw little of either of them, for I avoided seeing her because it only meant torture for me afterward. Ogden was always pressing me to dine with them or to go to the theater. Three times out of four I managed to make an excuse and escape going, but the fourth time it was necessary to go in order that the situation should not become noticeable. And then one night I discovered why it was that Ogden pressed me to see more of Elena. It was because he thought that she was safe with me.

That was bad enough, but on the same night I found myself alone for a moment with Elena, and she said, "Why do you always try to avoid coming here? Is it because you hate me?"

She looked at me with that same appraising, tantalizing look she had given me on the first evening as she turned to go up the stairs, and again it threw me into happiness, despair and confusion. I made some excuse about how hard I was working, but she only swept that aside disdainfully.

"What are you afraid of?" she asked. "I don't like to think," she added, "that I have broken up a lifelong friendship between two cousins."

Perhaps at that moment I should have come out into the open. I know now that I should have succeeded, for afterward she told me that that was what she had hoped. Perhaps I should have done so if Ogden had not returned at that very moment. I think she had suspected all along that I was in love with her, but at that moment she *knew* for the first time. When Ogden appeared, I turned scarlet and confused, filled with the knowledge that in my heart I no longer had any scruples and that I was willing to betray him at the first opportunity.

Three days later, I went to pay my weekly visit to poor old Uncle William, who was living now on the last of the money left him by old Michael Denning, in the Windsor Hotel. He was only sixty-five but he appeared much older. Unlike Michael Denning, he had lacked the physique and the vitality to survive his wild living. He could scarcely walk any longer, and Ogden and I made it a point of duty to visit him regularly, bringing him news.

Nothing gave him so much pleasure as Ogden's arrival accompanied by Elena. At the sight of her beauty the old rake would sit up in his wheel chair and become almost young again. He adored her.

I do not know why he chose to live at the Windsor Hotel; it was neither smart nor amusing nor cheap, although it did have about it a veiled air of rakishness. Despite the fact that most of its permanent tenants were middle-aged and elderly men and women, respectable and nondescript, one felt that "things went on there." On the ground floor there was a bar much frequented by stockbrokers and financiers and racing men. Except for Uncle William, I knew no one who lived in the hotel.

[291]

That afternoon, I remember, the old gentleman felt rather well and made one or two ribald jokes about Ogden, hinting that he was unworthy to fill the shoes of lover to such a magnificent creature as Elena.

"The old man—old Michael might have done it," he said, "even in his sixties. But not Ogden, with his la-di-da ways."

I left him at last and stepped out into Forty-sixth Street to walk home. At the door I ran into Kate Blakeley, looking dashing and smart and wicked in a fur hat with a dotted veil. Once I had nearly fallen in love with her, but in the midst of my interest, the image of Elena had come between us and spoiled everything by making Kate seem a cheap little adventuress. Kate was good-hearted and never lacked suitors, so she forgave my sudden cooling off and we remained good friends.

She, too, was bound downtown, and together we walked along Fifth Avenue through the falling snow. I don't remember what we talked about save that she asked me whether I was dining that night with Ogden and Elena. When I told her I was not, she asked pertly, "What's the matter? I never see you there any more. Have you quarreled with Ogden?"

The question made me suspicious and put me on my guard, for I knew that Kate, like most women who lead free and easy lives, are forever doing missionary work, trying to lead others into the same paths. So I simply said, "No."

"Which means that it is none of my business," she said, with a laugh. "Well, anyway, it's too bad. I don't know what's come over you lately. You used to be good fun but you've been impossible for a long time."

"All right," I said, "but let's talk about somebody else."

"Elena, for instance?" she said.

"Elena? Yes. Why not?"

"She's not very happy, you know."

"I know very little about her state of mind."

"You could help by showing up more often."

I said that I thought she never noticed whether I was there or not, and when I said it, I did my damnedest not to let my voice betray the faintest emotion.

"Oh, yes, she does," said Kate. "You know as well as I do that she isn't in the least in love with Ogden. I don't deny that she is fond of him, but sometimes she gets bored, and then it helps to have congenial friends about."

I gathered my courage and asked, "What do you mean by that?"

Kate laughed. "I don't mean anything, except that she's doing her best to stick by the fort, and I think you might help her by showing up now and then. Otherwise, I don't think she can hold out much longer."

I asked her if Elena had said anything to make her believe she was unhappy, and Kate said that they'd never discussed the subject but that it didn't require second sight to see that she was.

She said, "You'd better come tonight, all the same," and with that she pertly bade me good night and turned into the Waldorf.

The rest of the way I walked alone, disturbed and excited by what Kate had said, wondering whether it was Elena who had asked her to speak to me. By the time I reached my own doorstep I had made a decision.

I went to Ogden's house that night to dinner.

There were twenty people there, mostly belonging to Kate's set—actresses, divorcées, racing men and men about town. There was a freedom, an abandon, a recklessness about the company and the conversation which seemed oddly out of place against the delicate background of the house, and somehow Ogden with his preciosity and Elena with her serenity seemed strange in such a background. I had the impression of an unhappy household which had brought in this strange company because it was distracting, and so made the household forget its unhappiness.

I should not perhaps have been aware of it save for Kate's conversation. In the midst of all the noise and laughter Ogden and Elena, with that strange "stillness" on her, seemed aloof. The drinking, the questionable jokes, seemed to go on all about them without touching them at all. Elena sat almost opposite to me, for she always seated her tables in the Continental way with the hostess at the side.

As usual, I found myself watching her as discreetly as possible, and two or three times she caught me watching her and then something miraculous happened which had not happened before. In the exchange of glances there was a sudden understanding. She managed, somehow, to convey to me both the profundity of her unhappiness and the knowledge that I was in love with her. I had the feeling that she was very near to desperation and that beneath her serenity hysteria was welling up.

Watching Ogden, with no shame in my heart, I thought, "Now is my chance, only I must play the game so that he will never suspect." If his adoration of Elena had been the passion of a normal man, I should have been less fearful and less cautious, but there was in it something morbid and there was always that strange abnormal sensitiveness which made him divine things other people could not know. But on the other hand, I knew that he trusted me. And that was a great advantage.

After dinner Ogden ordered a big baize-covered table to be put up in the room which had been Michael Denning's library, and the party settled itself there to a game of *chemin de fer*. Not only had the china cuspidor been destroyed, the whole room with its huge books and monstrous mahogany-and-leather furniture had ceased to exist. It had walls of peach color now, elaborately carved and gilded, with upholstery of silver and green.

It was a lovely room but unreal and removed from life, and more like a boudoir than a study. In it old Michael would have been like a bull in a china shop. It occurred to me again that Ogden had come slowly to hate the very memory of his father, and that he had chosen to destroy and remake this house rather than build a new one simply to demonstrate to himself his power to destroy what Michael had created.

14

Elena said she would prefer not to play, and after we had watched a round or two I asked her if she would sing for me as she had done on that first evening three years before.

So we went into the drawing room and she sang for me again. She was dressed in black velvet and looked pale. Like most fascinating women, she was extremely changeable and there were moments when she appeared almost plain. Tonight, she was an Elena I had never seen before, beautiful as always, but in a different fashion, melancholy and strange.

When she had sung five or six songs, she suddenly let her hands fall into her lap and sat very still. She had come to wear more and more jewels, and the idea came to me that perhaps she wore them as a distraction from her unhappiness. She was a woman who should never have worn them. On her they seemed vulgar and barbaric.

There was a long peaceful silence, and then all at once I plunged. I do not know how I came to choose that moment, but suddenly I found myself saying the words. I said, "Do you remember Bad Münster?"

She turned quickly and looked at me with an expression almost of terror in her eyes. A shiver went through her and in a low voice she asked, "What do you know about Bad Münster?"

"It was there I saw you for the first time. Look at me and then think of Bad Münster and the little river and see if you can't remember."

She was silent for a moment, regarding me sadly, and then she said, "No, I don't remember you, but then you see I went to Bad Münster so many times. Besides, I didn't notice other people much then. I really never saw them."

"Do you remember a boy who came upon you one day by the side of the river? You were sitting in the sunlight and he was asleep with his head in your lap and you smiled and put your finger to your lips so that I shouldn't waken him."

Almost at once I knew that I had made a false step. I do not know why I spoke of Toni as "he," anonymously, save that it seemed to me that although I had never met him I knew him too well to use his title, and I felt that it was presumptuous to call him Toni. An expression of pain came into her eyes and suddenly she was weeping, but she managed to control herself enough to say, "Why, yes, I do remember now—a good-looking boy about nineteen or twenty. Was that you?"

"Yes, I fell in love with you almost on sight." And then, quietly, I came and sat on the end of the bench beside her. "You see, I'm in love with you still. That's why I've come here so rarely. It made me suffer too much."

She looked at me in astonishment. "Until lately I thought you hated me," she said with a kind of wonder. "It always made me so sad because I thought you were so nice and so understanding and so alive. I always wanted to be friends, ever since that first night. Sometimes I've been very nearly in love with you."

She had a frankness, or perhaps it was merely a simplicity, which I never found in any other woman, and the simplicity and directness had more power than the wiles and coquetry of any other woman I have ever met.

"You see," she continued, "sometimes I've been so lonely. I wanted to find somebody who was alive and natural and honest. I don't mean alive the way Kate is alive, but something quite different. It isn't life with Kate. It's a kind of illness that makes her go on and on until some day she'll smash up. She's got what I call the New York disease."

It was odd how discerning she was, seeing something which I had never seen before. Perhaps, as a foreigner, it was easier for her. Afterward, when Kate did go to pieces, I knew she was right. In those days Kate and her little crowd were almost the only ones affected by the "New York" disease. But it spread and spread, until nowadays there aren't many New Yorkers who have escaped it—that disease which gives you no rest, driving you to seek sensations, filling your veins with restlessness and your nerves with a horror of ever being alone. It is a disease which seems to infect the very air of Manhattan. Elena never had it, even for a day.

I took her hand and kissed it, and then, aware suddenly that I was being a fool, I sat up very straight, listening. I did not mind any longer being a cad and making love to my cousin's wife in his own house. I did not mind taking advantage of his blind foolish trust in me. I was already far beyond such artificialities as the standards of a gentleman. I was simply a lover, willing to use any ruse or any weapon I could find.

She knew that I had suddenly become cautious, and with a shadow of contempt in her voice, she said, "You needn't mind Ogden. He won't come in. He loves gambling too well. He'll stay there until the last card is played. That's why he puts up with those people—because he can gamble with them." She looked at me slyly, and then said, "If you're afraid, we can go to my sitting room upstairs."

I did not know exactly what she meant, for I did not know then the full depths of her directness and simplicity, nor that prudishness or hypocrisy had nothing to do with her. I did not answer her, and so left the decision to her. She rose, and once again I kissed her hand. She must have known from the kiss how I was suffering; I think that it infected her somehow with something of my own blind passion.

15

She said, "You're trembling. I never knew you felt like that." It was odd, but I was aware of pity in her voice.

I followed her up the stairs.

It was an insane thing to do in Ogden's own house, but I never thought of that, and the thought of discovery never occurred to her, or if it occurred to her, she was by that time so unhappy that she no longer cared what happened. If the punishment had been death by flaying or by fire I do not think I could have stopped myself, and looking back now on that evening, I would have no desire to do so, for if one turns away from life there is no value in living.

What she had said was true. Ogden never left the green-baize table and we were alone together for nearly two hours, but it was like a lifetime compressed into one breathless and incredible moment. I told her everything about myself and we talked of Bad Münster a little stiffly, without ever speaking of Toni, and we made plans as to how we were to go on deceiving Ogden. She was discreet, I think, only because she did not want to hurt him.

"He has been very good and generous to me, and he has so little in life— nothing but books and furniture and old doors." And she added, "You reproached me for taking Kate as a friend. She's the one to help us, don't you see? Kate will always lie and give me an excuse to get away."

For a moment I was again struck by a doubt. I wondered whether she had not chosen Kate and her friends long ago because some day they might be useful; but I said nothing.

"You could have had me almost at once," she said. "It would have been easy. I was so unhappy."

So I had lost all those precious hours and minutes and months trying to be an honorable fool. Suddenly the ecstasy was drained out of me, and I felt depressed and tired. I rose from her side and walked across the room to stand looking out of the window.

After a long silence she said, "I know. You are reproaching yourself. You needn't. You haven't betrayed Ogden."

I turned from the window in wonder and asked, "Why? How?"

"Because we have never lived together. He has never so much as touched me." And suddenly it all became clear. I understood everything—Ogden's strange behavior, his liking for exhibiting her; his growing hatred of his father and his desire to destroy his memory. I should have known it all along if I had not been a fool.

I left her then and went down to the party in the library, where I took a hand in the game. I told them that Elena had a headache and had retired, and at the news Ogden scarcely looked up from the game. We played until daylight, and after I came to the table Ogden won steadily, and I lost far more than I could afford, but I did not care. I scarcely knew what I was doing and doubled my stakes like a drunken man again and again.

Once Kate looked at me with a sharp twinkle in her black eyes. "You must have drunk a good deal to make you so reckless." I was drunk, it is true, but drunk with ecstasy. Kate *knew*, perhaps. Certainly she suspected. But even that did not matter.

16

From that night began a long story of deceit and double-dealing, in the process of which my whole character became so changed that when I look back upon it, it is impossible for me to recognize myself. By nature I was a conventional, honorable fellow. But I found myself stealing my cousin's wife, and in order to succeed in the theft I lived a lie day in and day out.

Success in business, success in life itself no longer meant anything to me. My family scarcely saw me. I no longer troubled to call on poor half-paralyzed Uncle William, shut up in his rooms in the Windsor Hotel. I never went to the club. But I did go to the big brownstone house more and more often, refusing only when it was necessary to cover up what was going on, and Ogden seemed pleased that he and I were back again on the old basis of intimacy which we had known as boys.

Elena played her role better than I, for she had a control which never allowed her to betray herself by the slightest intonation. And all the time both of us were afraid, not of being discovered so much as of the effect that discovery would have upon Ogden's eccentric, unbalanced character.

We saw each other a part of every day without Ogden's even suspecting. In the beginning I was insatiable and begrudged every second she spent in the company of others. I took a small flat in West Thirty-fourth Street, not more than ten blocks from the brownstone house, and in a district where no one lived who was known to either of us. There we met, sometimes in the afternoon, now and then in the evening, and once, at a risk, we spent a whole week-end there together. Elena herself did the cooking and seemed again like the girl I had seen in the Black Forest.

For these meetings Kate was invaluable to us, for by now she was in on the secret and delighted that Elena had proved after all no better than herself. If Ogden inquired of Elena where she was going, she always replied that she had a rendezvous with Kate.

My passion might have burned itself out, save that somehow I was never able to possess Elena completely, and so the game was never finished. Some part of her escaped me, and of this I was aware even in our most intimate moments together. I knew that there was something which she withheld, something which would have made our love perfect, which I was never able to reach. Once or twice I tried to discover why she kept up that strange reserve, but she only laughed and then grew sad and said that I wanted more from her than any woman was able to give.

Again and again I proposed that we chuck everything and run away together, letting Ogden go his own way. There were times when I grew sick with deceit and longed to cut ourselves free from it once and for all. Each time I saw Ogden, I felt remorse. But she would never agree to an elopement.

She would say, "Aren't we well off as we are? If we ran off it would ruin you, and knowing Ogden, I know he would never divorce me. What could we live on? You haven't enough to go on forever living in Capri or Florence or Monte Carlo. It isn't as if Ogden were really my husband and I had to submit to him."

She never told me, as she had told Ogden, that she had a small fortune settled on her by Toni so that he'd never have to think she was in poverty. She did not, I think, ever want to marry me, because in her heart she was always hoping that Toni would come back. Ogden did not matter, but being married to me would have been different. Sometimes, too, a suspicion came to me which now I am certain was the truth. She loved me in a way; of that there can be no doubt. But she never loved me passionately, with all her being, as I loved her.

17

I think she loved me because in the past, even as a stranger, I had been distantly a part of all the happiness she had known in that little watering place in the Black Forest. In a way, I was a symbol, a substitute for Toni; being a passionate woman, she had to have someone whom she could love. She was happier now that we were living together almost as man and wife, but the old Elena I had watched from a distance never returned. The "stillness" enveloped her always.

The odd thing was that as time went on Ogden's passion for her seemed to increase, stimulated perhaps by the knowledge that I now admired her openly. At the same time, his hatred of his father seemed to approach the borders of madness. It was not only the old jealousy which he had had of his mother's devotion to old Michael Denning; in his impotence he hated the whole legend of his father's wild life.

At length he even asked Elena to return to him the pearls and the other jewels which Michael Denning had given his mother, telling her that they had become old-fashioned or were not splendid enough for her. He replaced them with much finer jewels, and the originals he had taken from their settings and sold one by one. The jewels were the last remaining concrete vestige of the old man's existence, and after they were gone I think Ogden felt free.

Autumn turned to winter and winter to spring, and then suddenly, inexplicably, something happened to Elena. It was as if she had closed a door shutting me out. The first news I had of the change came one afternoon when I had a message from her by way of Kate saying that she could not meet me as usual at the flat because she was ill. I called at the house before dinner but she sent word down that she felt too ill to see anyone.

For two days I did not see her at all, and on the third day she came down the marble stairs looking lovelier than I had ever seen her. The "stillness" was gone, and in its place was a kind of radiance, yet when she spoke to me she seemed changed, aloof and cold. She begged me not to ask her to make a rendezvous until she felt less ill. She did not look in the least ill, and I complimented her on the color in her cheeks and the brightness in her eyes, but she said they came from fever.

I talked to her as rashly as I dared, for in my heart, without knowing why, I was terrified. I knew suddenly that now she had escaped me altogether. Even the part which belonged to me, she had withdrawn. The woman who sat there talking to me wasn't the Elena I knew. It was some other person. It was Elena bewitched and changed. Nothing I could say, no eloquence, no pleading changed her, and presently when Ogden appeared she made an excuse to escape and went up to her room. It was the last time I ever saw her.

I sent extravagant baskets of flowers and fruits, which seemed to please Ogden, and on the next evening when I called at the house, he said she was feeling better and had gone to Red Bank for two or three days to stay with Kate, who had opened her house there. It seemed odd to me that Kate had not asked me, too, but with a sinking heart I decided that she had not invited me because Elena had asked her not to.

I had a cocktail with Ogden and refused dinner, saying I had an engagement, because I could not dine there alone with him when my heart was soaked in misery. When I left, I went straight to the Waldorf bar and began to drink. By four in the morning I was drunker than I have ever been in all my life, and instead of going home, I went to the flat in West Thirty-fourth Street. I do not know how I managed to reach there alone, but I do remem-

[299]

ber that on climbing the stairs a wild hope rose in my heart that when I turned the key in the door and opened it I should find her there.

But the flat was dark and empty. I fell on the bed fully dressed, and presently I was asleep. It was evening of the next day when I wakened, and my first thought was that I must see Ogden at once and discover whether he had any news of her. It was horrible to waken there for the first time alone.

I dressed as quickly as possible and went out to have a cup of coffee in a restaurant near Broadway. It was there I had the first news of the Windsor fire. Everyone was talking about it. The waitress brought me a newspaper, and I read it for myself. There had been a number of people killed, some by the fire and some by jumping from the windows.

I thought at once of Great-uncle William, tied to his wheel chair. He lived on the seventh floor, and save for a miracle there could have been no chance of his escaping. For a moment I forgot even Elena and my own unhappiness. I thought, "Ogden will know. I must go to Ogden." I hailed a hansom cab and drove as fast as possible to the brownstone house.

There in the hall I found Ogden pacing up and down on the edge of hysteria. His face was ashen and his long lean hands were trembling.

He cried out, "Where have you been? I've been trying everywhere to find you—at home, at the office, everywhere. They told me you didn't come in at all last night."

For a moment I thought that at last he suspected me and that this was the cause of the agitation. I said, "I was out on the town. I was drunk. That's why I didn't come home."

He looked at me with disgust, as if his fastidiousness had been outraged by the thought of me intoxicated, perhaps spending the night with some showgirl I had picked up. It was a curious look of revelation which showed me how infinitely remote from all living he had become, how completely and inhumanly he had been absorbed by "things."

I asked, "What has happened to Uncle William?"

"That's it! That's it!" he cried. "It's horrible. He's dead, and they insist I must go to the morgue to identify him. I can't do it alone. I can't face it. You'll have to go with me."

"I'll go myself, alone, if you like."

But he would not have that, either. He was in the grip of some obsession that it was his duty to go.

After the first shock, the news of Uncle William's death did not much affect me. He was an old man and chronically ill and bored and unhappy, and if he had not died horribly, death was probably a merciful release. And in my heart I was suffering at that moment what seemed worse to me than any death.

I wanted to know whether Ogden had had news of Elena and when she was coming back from Red Bank, so I said casually, "Have you told Elena?"

"No," he said. "I didn't want to upset her. She's gone to Red Bank for a rest."

"She'll see it in the papers. That will be worse." And suddenly an idea came to me. "I'll do it," I said. "Let me telegraph."

"All right. You do it."

He had already rung for his hat and coat. I was excited again, for now at least I had an excuse to communicate with her. Somehow I would manage to let her know that I was thinking of her, tenderly, day and night.

Together we set out in his carriage for the morgue, and on the way I stopped at a telegraph office, where I spent ten minutes of uncertainty and unhappiness trying to compose a telegram which would convey to her my misery without annoying her. At last I wrote: *Uncle William desperately ill. Am yours always and forever.*

It was short. When she saw the papers she would guess the truth. And it was not compromising. She would *know.* In my heart I think I knew that although she would understand the limitless things I had tried to say in five words, it was likely that she no longer cared very much.

We drove the rest of the way in silence, Ogden still shaking with nerves, and I thinking of Elena. Once or twice he spoke of the fire. It had been a strange inexplicable conflagration, breaking out with terrible swiftness in the late afternoon, and lasting only a little while. Some of the people who had leaped from the windows might have been saved if they had kept their heads. Most of the victims died of suffocation.

18

At the morgue there was an enormous crowd. Those who had come to identify relatives or friends were admitted one by one. To the very end I tried to persuade Ogden to let me go in alone, but his determination had now become a kind of madness. He kept saying that he must "face it."

Once inside, I begged the intern in charge to let us first see the bodies of those who had died of suffocation; that would be less horrible for Ogden than having to see those who had died from burns or from having leaped from the windows. I doubted that Uncle William had jumped. All the victims found above the third floor had been suffocated. Luckily, those in charge had already thought of all this, and the bodies of the burned and mutilated were kept apart.

The bodies lay on slabs in a long row, each covered with a sheet, and we followed the attendant as he moved from one slab to another, raising each sheet for a second that we might see the faces. Most of the dead were middle-aged and elderly people who had been living at the Windsor in retirement.

We had come nearly to the end of the line when the attendant lifted the sheet from the face of a young and handsome man. He was dark, and the pallor of death had given a sculptural quality to his face. I glanced at it quickly, meaning to go on to the next, but I was arrested by something, and suddenly I felt an actual physical pain at the pit of my stomach.

It was a strange unearthly experience, one of those things which happen so quickly that one seems to have lived through the same moment before in some other life. This was the face of a man whom I had seen but a few times and had never met, and yet in a way I had loved him because he had been young and happy and in love. I knew in that single terrifying moment that I had loved him in spite of my own jealousy. And in the same second I knew the whole story. I knew what the end of it would be. I knew everything. The man on the slab was Toni!

I did not speak. I think I did not even breathe. The attendant had covered the face again and was drawing the sheet from the body on the next slab. He need not have troubled, for I knew already what lay beneath the sheet. I felt a sudden wild impulse to cry out, "Don't! Don't!" But it was too late. He had drawn the sheet away, and there before us, looking serene and lovely, lay Elena.

The shock seemed to clear my head, and the first thing of which I was aware was Ogden. I knew that I should have to keep control of myself. I could betray nothing. It was I who must support Ogden. I suppose acts of heroism are accomplished like that, automatically. You act, and think afterward.

I looked at him, and his face had gone whiter than those of the dead people on the slabs. He did not speak. He simply stood staring, as if fascinated, long after the attendant had covered her lovely face once more. I took his arm in a fierce grip and forced him into life and motion, compelling him to walk beside me, hypnotized and trembling, until we had finished what we came for. Two slabs farther on we found the body of Uncle William.

In the room beyond, I led Ogden to a chair, and as he collapsed into it, he said, "She must have been calling on Uncle William," and then he fainted and slipped out of the chair on to the floor. In my heart I knew he did not believe what he said. He never believed it, though he tried to for the rest of his life.

19

At home in the brownstone house he collapsed again, and so in the end it was I who had to make all the arrangements for the burials of Elena and poor old Uncle William. It was I who had to see the reporters and concoct a long fantastic story of Elena's devotion to Uncle William, in order to explain her presence in the hotel.

The newspapers vulgarized the story, making her an angel who met her death while on an errand of mercy. For days and weeks afterward there were photographs and stories in the paper of her beauty and her fabulous jewels.

The body of Toni was left on its slab, alone and unclaimed, long after Elena was buried, until it was identified at last by the proprietor of an obscure Broadway hotel who claimed it as the body of a man who had disappeared mysteriously from his establishment. He was registered there as Gerhardt Eckermann of Freiburg, Germany. A long time afterward I realized that the name Toni had taken was that of the fat little man who owned the hotel in Bad Münster. He had taken every precaution, abandoning even the name of Müller. There was no one in New York save myself who knew who he really was.

It would have been the romantic thing if the lovers had been buried side by side, but that wasn't possible. It was impossible for me to admit that I knew him, but with the utmost discretion I saw to it that he had good burial in a quiet corner of Greenlawn Cemetery. There was plenty of money for it. In the hotel safe there was more than two thousand dollars belonging to him without anyone to claim it. The police tried to trace him but got nowhere.

I think that all the duties and responsibilities I had thrust upon me in those first few days were good for me; they kept me distracted and numbed the pain. It was only afterward that the agony began and I went to pieces. It was only then that I came to understand not only that Elena was gone forever, but that what I had suspected long before was true: she had loved me only because in some way I had become to her a part of all the happiness she had known in the Black Forest. In me she had tried, wildly perhaps and vainly, to regain what she had believed was lost forever. The moment Toni reappeared she forgot the existence of myself, of Ogden, of everyone in the world save him.

In his own country there was no alarm at first over his disappearance, because he had gone off in the same way many times before both as a young man and as husband of the Saxe-Coburg princess, to return after a fortnight or two. But this time the fortnight became a month and then two months, and presently they began a search for him. They succeeded in tracing him as far as Paris, where he seemed to have vanished.

For years the search continued until there was no longer any hope of finding him. He had done his duty. There were two small sons by the dull Saxe-Coburg princess, and so the succession was assured. He had kept his promise in a world of standards and conventions which was collapsing, and his sacrifice was all wasted, for in 1918 Hohenheim ceased to exist, and there was no need for an heir.

During the thirty-odd years which followed his disappearance, various impostors appeared from time to time claiming to be the lost ruler of Hohenheim, but each time their claims failed. I alone knew that he lay in a corner of Greenlawn Cemetery beneath a stone marked simply "Gerhardt Eckermann."

When Ogden came home from the funeral, he would see no one but me. I thought for a time that the collapse and the melancholy which settled upon him would pass and that he would return again to life, or at least that he would recover again his old interest in "things," but as the months passed, he grew more solitary and eccentric.

At the end of two years he dismissed all the servants save the man who had been with him since he was eighteen. He had the main door of the big house locked, and after that he went in and out by the servants' entrance after nightfall. He saw no one but me, whom he sent for from time to time in order that we might talk about Elena. I alone could console him, and for me there was no consolation, save from Kate who alone knew our secret, and as the years went by I lost her, too, for her life grew steadily wilder and more disorderly until at last she died of drugs and drink.

The lovely baroque house grew untidy, and on the occasions when I went there to see Ogden we dined in the library where they had played *chemin de fer*, the two of us alone, waited on by the single manservant, who grew old along with his master. We talked of Elena but never after that day at the morgue did we speak of the Windsor fire.

Ogden must have wondered who the man was whom she met there, for among the other dead there was no one whom he had ever seen. There is just a chance that he did know, an even slimmer chance that he knew the whole story. If that is true, he was a nobler man than I had ever believed him to be.

For nearly forty years I dined with him thus many times a year, and when we talked of Elena it was not of the dead Elena but of the living one, so alive, so beautiful, so reckless and mysterious. I, too, if my lips had not been sealed, would have talked of her faithful heart, of the fidelity which survived even her own pitiful efforts to make a life for herself once she believed she would never again see Toni, which survived even the pitiful inadequacy of her love for me. But of all this I could not speak to Ogden.

In all the years I went there I never saw any room but the library. When Ogden died and the other rooms were opened, the furniture was found covered with dust and the lovely baroque ceilings festooned with cobwebs.

He added not one penny to the fortune Michael Denning had made so ruthlessly. Worse than that, he allowed the millions to dribble away until when he died there was nothing left. It may have been that he found pleasure in the destruction of the very fortune itself. He had failed at everything in life, but he was a "gentleman." Michael Denning had succeeded in making him that.

Now that I am old and all passion is spent, it seems to me that there was a kind of Greek quality in the whole story, as if the Furies themselves had been present throughout. Old Michael's plan of founding a dynasty came to a barren end within one generation, as if there was a curse on the fortune he had piled up so recklessly.

As for Elena, I think that she was one of those women who are born destined to a tragic end. The gods had given her too much of beauty, of intelligence, of passion—too much of life itself. Such bright creatures are too resplendent for this shoddy earth of ours. In the end she brought tragedy not only to herself but to all those concerned in her story: to Toni, who had defied the gods and tried to deny his very nature; to poor impotent Ogden for his presumption in marrying so dazzling a creature; to myself for loving her and betraying my cousin and best friend.

When Ogden died, the house was sold and pulled down to make way for a glittering grown-up New York whose very existence he had continued to deny until the end; but the city, long before his death, had forgotten that he existed; it had nearly forgotten that there was ever such a buccaneer as Michael Denning. When the furniture, the doors, the marble stairway came to be sold, the sum they brought totaled more than the poor remnant of Michael Denning's great fortune, for the baroque style had become fashionable. The contents of those dreadful houses owned by the people who had mocked Ogden's taste had long since been thrown on the dust heap or sent to ornament the servants' hall belowstairs. One footstool from Ogden's house was worth more than all the bric-a-brac, the bad tapestries and the fake Italian Renaissance.

Now that it is all over there is only one thing in the whole story that I should have liked to see for myself, and that is the moment when Elena, in the brownstone house so barren of life, found among her letters one addressed in the handwriting she knew so well and loved so profoundly—the letter which told her that Toni had broken his word and come back after all. I should have liked to see that "stillness" leave her and the life rush back into the beautiful body and face when she knew that she was no longer a lonely foreigner, lost and forgotten in New York. I should have liked to see once more that look which was on her face the day I came upon them in the forest when she raised her finger to her lips.

Now that all the suffering is finished, I am glad that he came back. I am grateful for the ecstasy which it brought her for a little time before she died. That is how much I loved her.

[305]

The brownstone house is gone now and already forgotten, but perhaps when you pass that corner again you will remember that it once stood there, and perhaps you will give a thought to the people who once lived in it—to old Michael Denning and my aunt Sarah, to Elena and poor Ogden, and perhaps even to me. All that remains of it is the marble stairway. At the sale it was bought by the architect who did the great hotel which stands there now, and when you enter the hotel and go down to the bar for a drink you will be walking down the same stairway up which Elena moved on that night when we were alone while the others played *chemin de fer* in the room belowstairs.

IV

The Girl Who Knew Everybody

SHE was neither a pretty girl nor a plain one. She had an attractive face, bright and full of intelligence, and blue eyes which looked at you with immense interest and curiosity the first time she saw you, so that you in turn were interested and because your vanity was touched, you liked her and wanted to go on with the adventure.

Her name was Mary Carlin and I saw her for the first time seated on a stool before the bar of the Palace Hotel in St. Moritz. It was in one of the big seasons when everyone had money or thought he had money and everyone was spending it. As Toto Rossi said, "*Every*body was there," and by the way he said it, you knew he meant "*every*body who was *any*body" in Toto's scheme of things. And to understand Toto's scheme of life you had to know Toto.

He was the son of one of the myriad Italian counts and his mother had been Miss Winegartner of Newark with an enormous fortune made partly out of copper and partly out of brewing. She gave birth to Toto and then in despair at the life in which she found herself—a millionairess with her freedom and all her rights vested by Italian law in the silly little man who was her husband—she gave up the struggle and simply fell into leading the depraved life for which her husband had set her so detailed an example. But Toto remained and as he grew up, he was dragged about with her from hotel to hotel and watering place to watering place, practically a witness to the countless liaisons which the Countess Rossi, nee Miss Elline Winegartner, conducted with a lavish hand. His father faded out of the picture and saw him once or twice a year.

Toto was nothing much to begin with but what there was of good in him never had a chance. At twenty-four he was simply a continental bar fly, much more Italian than American, dressed much too carefully with elaborate double-breasted waistcoats and jackets which were cut too tight at the waist. But he knew everybody and was "frightfully amusing" and went everywhere, and by that he meant that he frequented all the expensive hotels in season and that he knew everyone of the troupe which went in turn from hotel to hotel always in season, from Deauville to the Lido, to Biarritz, to Morocco or Algeria, to St. Moritz, to London, to Paris and back again to Deauville to begin all over again. He had a generous allowance but it was by no means enough for him, and he augmented it by charging a price for introducing climbers who sought an entrance into the squirrel cage. He got them invitations to parties and saw that they spent enough money on their own parties to make it worth the while of "everybody who was anybody" to accept their invitations. Either the climbers failed after the first attempt or became initiated into the world of "everybody who was anybody."

2

It was Toto, dark, sallow, dissipated, with sleek hair and shaped waist, who introduced me to Mary. She was then, I think, in the middle of her career. She must have been about twenty-seven or eight, slender, with blond hair and a lovely complexion, and dressed superbly in the smartest, most expensive clothes it was possible to find. That night on the bar stool she wore a gown of peach-colored crêpe de Chine.

The look of interest in her eyes when I came toward her with Toto was so intense that I, like all the others, wanted to know her at once, talk to her and spend the whole evening in her company. As I crossed the floor, I thought, "Thank God, here is someone who is young and fresh, someone with enthusiasm in whom I shall perhaps find some fun." Among the others who were anybody, there were plenty who were young, younger even than Mary herself, but like Toto who was only twenty-four, they were as old and as tired as time itself, and save when they were not malicious or witty at the expense of a friend, were almost as deadly.

"Oh," she said, when she heard my name, "I've been longing to meet you for years. I love your books . . . all of them."

I thanked her, the only answer one can make to that statement which always leaves the conversation in mid-air.

"Have a cocktail with us?"

Toto excused himself. "I'll see you later," he said. He went to join a fat woman in *pince-nez* and a beaded gown, and a short little man with a plump stomach who might have been the keeper of an American speakeasy.

"Who are they?" I asked, looking after Toto.

"That's Mr. and Mrs. Hagedorn," she said. "He's the new American minister to one of those funny Balkan countries. He made his money partly out of glass and partly out of backing the cinemas. He gave a lot of money to the Republican party, so he's an ambassador now."

"Oh."

"They've got lots of money. They're entertaining in a big way." She laughed, "I don't mean they're amusing. I mean they're spending money for other people's entertainment. Why don't you come along? They're giving a party tonight."

"I don't know them. They've never heard of me."

Again she laughed. "That's all right. They've never heard of most of the people here. They'll be delighted. They want to know everybody. Go with me. I want some new company. I'm sick of always sitting between two of the same ten men."

"All right, if you'll have another cocktail on me."

We had another cocktail and while I talked to her, I kept watching her, in the way of writers, thinking that she must be very rich indeed, for not only were her clothes expensive but she wore a half-dozen diamond bracelets and a diamond pendant set with a big emerald.

Over her cocktail glass she looked at me and laughed, "You're all tanned. You must have been skiing."

I smiled, "That's what I came here for."

By now it was nearly eight o'clock and the bar was filling up with everybody who was anybody. There were a half-dozen members of dethroned royal families, innumerable poverty-stricken counts and dukes and princes, two great Paris dressmakers, one or two racing men, a fashionable photographer and his excellency Mr. Hagedorn and the Ambassadress who sat with her full bosom resting on the marble top of one of the tables, a dozen gigolos of different nationalities, and a dozen middle-aged and aging women, all hard, all dressed with extreme smartness, all fautlessly made up, waved and talking with animation, three or four women who, in less liberal days, would have been known simply as cocottes.

As the room filled up Mary Carlin gave me less and less of her attention. The restless blue eyes wandered this way and that. She kept bowing and people kept coming up to speak to her. Some of them I knew. Some of them I did not. Once when I asked her a question she could not answer at all for she had not been listening.

I grinned and said, "You seem to know everybody."

"Yes, pretty nearly." She slipped down from the bar stool and said, "I must go and fix it up with the Ambassadress."

She crossed the room to the table where the Hagedorns sat, buying cocktails for everyone who came to their table. They were near enough for me to hear some of the conversation. At sight of Mary, Mrs. Hagedorn's large fleshy face beamed with pleasure.

Mary put her arm about the plump shoulders of the Ambassadress and said, "How are you, darling? I haven't seen you all day."

Then their voices lowered and I saw Mrs. Hagedorn look toward me and then turn away quickly. I knew it was all right. I had a name which some-times appeared in the newspapers. I was of the second class because the name appeared respectably. If it had appeared scandalously I should have been of the first class, and I was by no means rich enough to make up for my sad penchant for respectability.

Then Mary led me over to Mrs. Hagedorn. To my astonishment the Ambassadress got to her feet, and held out her hand beaming at me through the shining *pince-nez.*

"I'm afraid you don't remember me."

I fell into lies at once. "Yes, of course. I've known you all along." Desper-ately I waited for a clue. She gave it to me.

"I haven't seen you since you lectured in Zenith. Let's see, that must have been five years ago. I was the one who brought you there. I was chairman of the program committee."

Mary interrupted us. "I'll just run into the dining room," she said, "and change the places. You can trust me, darling. I know everybody and who gets on with who."

The Ambassadress bridled. "She's just like a daughter to me. She's the sweetest girl. I don't know what we'd have done without her here. She's just arranged everything. Have another cocktail?"

"No thanks. And please do sit down."

She sat down and pursing her lips a little she said, "I only worry about whom she may marry. She's running about with Toto now. He's a nice boy but not for a husband."

"No, certainly not."

"I don't approve of these foreign marriages, even if I am an ambassa-dress."

"They don't seem to turn out well," I answered, making conversation.

"Don't repeat what I've said because Toto would never forgive me."

She liked saying Toto's name. She liked the bowing and smiling at passers-by. She liked saying Mary Carlin was like a daughter to her. I think she knew her glory was short and that after the next election she would return to live in Zenith. It wasn't a pretty spectacle. She wanted to know every-body who was anybody, and they were only using her for what she was worth. That night she had brought a jazz band and two singers with good Zenith money all the way from Paris, just to entertain them.

At dinner I sat next to Mary Carlin and on the other side sat a countess whose name I never heard distinctly. She was a tall, gaunt, sour woman who had once been a beauty. She did not seem inclined to talk but only regarded me as she regarded the rest of the room, with a bitter expression of dis-illusionment.

So I talked to Mary Carlin.

She told me she came from Indiana and that she was rich. Her money came from an uncle who had made it out of a factory which confected felt hats. During dinner she forgot herself for a little while and the restless look went out of her blue eyes. She listened to me and she herself talked. Perhaps she was interested because we talked about Mary Carlin.

I asked her where she lived and what she did all the year round.

She said that she lived Nowhere in Particular, or rather that she had a small flat in Paris and the rest of the time traveled about living in hotels.

"Doesn't the life bore you after a while?"

"No. It's fun. There's always people about and parties."

"You seem to know everybody."

"No, not quite."

And then she made a cynical remark, odd for anyone so young. "We all belong to two classes," she said, "those who give parties and those who go to them. The ones who give them have to have the money and the ones who go have to work. They have to be amusing."

I grinned, "And which lot do you belong to?"

"I belong to the lot who give parties. I'm not clever or amusing."

"What would happen if you lost your money?"

"I'd be down and out."

I tried a few words with the countess but nothing came of it and I turned back to Mary. She saw I was interested in her and she gave me all her attention. I could, I think, have asked her anything. I think she fancied she was being intellectual and the idea excited and amused her for the moment.

"Don't you ever think about getting married?"

For a moment she didn't answer. Then she said, "Yes, sometimes. But there's no hurry. There's plenty of time."

"How old are you?"

"I'm twenty-seven."

"If a nice man came along wouldn't you marry him?"

"No—not yet. I'm having too much fun."

I looked about the table at the tired faces, the sallow faces, the bitter faces, the bored faces. "I don't think there's much chance of a nice man coming along out of this party."

"Besides," she said, "the marriages I've seen haven't turned out so hot."

And just then a nice fellow came through the doorway. You knew he was nice as soon as you saw him because in his tanned face and blue eyes, there was nothing bored, bitter or dissipated. He was tall and blond and looked as if he were good on skiis or at steering a bob or at doing almost anything. He had a look of race and of honesty. The sight of him among all the others was a shock.

In the middle of a sentence Mary saw him and stopped talking. I saw the old restless look come into her eyes and I divined that here was someone who attracted her.

"Who is that?" she asked.

"I've not the faintest idea."

From then on our conversation was ruined, for she could not rest until she had found out who the stranger was. All the intimacy was gone. She turned to her dinner companion and asked the people who sat opposite but no one knew him, and slowly I divined another fact, that she was not interested in him for himself or because he was attractive, but because he was the only person in the room she did not know. It might have been amusing to have attempted a flirtation on my own side, but now I knew it was no longer possible. It seemed to me suddenly that she was not a woman at all but a kind of machine.

The stranger was an acquaintance of Mrs. Hagedorn. I could see him making apologies for being late. She made a place for him beside her. He did not dine. He merely sat there talking to her now and then. The Ambassadress bridled and shook her carefully waved head.

Suddenly I felt tired and bored and unbearably sleepy from a day spent in the open. We rose from the table to go into the ballroom for the music and the performers. I saw Mary Carlin go straight to the Ambassadress and I saw her being introduced to the stranger. She had forgotten me utterly. She knew me well enough now to bow to me wherever we met in the world and to ask me to parties. For the moment at least that was all the interest she had. It was not very flattering.

I went to bed.

3

In the days that followed I met the stranger. He turned out to be an Englishman, Wemyss by name. He was an engineer and had been in South America, building railroads. We met at the top of the Cresta Run and from then on saw a good deal of each other, for he had lived alone or among Indians and negroes for so long that he felt shy and restless in the fashionable crowd that haunted the bars and the rinks.

The odd thing was that when he was not seeing me he was always with Mary Carlin. I do not know what drew him to her unless it was the attraction of opposites for he was rather a taciturn, solitary fellow and Mary chattered a great deal and was always surrounded by crowds. Perhaps he found some attraction in the struggle to separate her from the people who always surrounded her. He spoke of her now and then and frequently I saw them together always surrounded by the Totos and the Mimis and the Pipis.

The Ambassadress and her husband returned to their Balkan post since it was necessary for him to put in an appearance now and then, and for a time there was no one in the place but Mary Carlin rich enough to give parties as big as those given by the Hagedorns.

Then one morning Wemyss said to me, "Do you know Mary Carlin well?"

"So-so," I said. "We call each other by our first names."

"She's an odd girl," he said. "She's never alone."

I laughed, "No, that's true. She knows everybody."

He looked at me with his frank blue eyes, a little puzzled and suddenly I understood that he was in love with her and would have nothing said against her. He thought that I was laughing at her.

"She oughtn't to be running around with all these people."

"She likes it, apparently."

Then naïvely he said, "I'd like to get her away from them. She's too nice a girl to make a mess of her life."

"I don't think she's really involved in any way. There isn't any sort of a mess. Sex doesn't concern any of them very much . . . at least not straight-forward sex."

His eyes narrowed and he said, "I didn't mean that, there can be worse things than that. There's such a thing as frittering away one's existence. That's the worst sin one can be guilty of."

It was, I suppose, a priggish speech, and yet under the circumstances and in the surroundings, it seemed profoundly true.

"She's much too nice a girl. There's something fine in her."

Abruptly I said, "Are you interested in her as much as that?"

"Yes, I am. Only I'd like to see her alone just for a moment now and then. I'd like really to talk to her, but it's never possible. As soon as I begin two or three people interrupt us and she forgets all about me and what we were saying." He lighted a cigarette and looked off over the mountains, "Do you think you could help me?"

I laughed, "Of course. How?"

"Help me with a plot to get her alone for a little time. I'm not bad at making love. If I could get her alone I think I could make her listen to me."

"If you can think of a plan I'll help you."

That night he came to me with a plan. I was to say that I was giving a party at the inn and invite her. I was to bring her myself and once we arrived we would find him there and I was to make an excuse and escape, leaving them alone together.

I agreed, partly out of friendship for Wemyss and partly because I had come to see what he had divined—that there *was* something good in Mary Carlin. There were fine qualities. They could be saved if some nice young man would carry her off and marry her, saved out of the fathomless depths of utter triviality and banality. Since I had come to know her better, she seemed to me a nice girl who had lost her head.

I asked her to a small party at the inn and she accepted. Wemyss was happy. It was odd to see a man so much in love. I think he was a genuine romantic, the kind of man who falls in love blindly, once and never again. And he had a faint Messiah complex: he was determined to save Mary. He had lived to the age of thirty-four without ever having had his heart touched and now he had fallen in love with a girl whom he scarcely knew and had never spoken to except in crowds. With a man like that a girl can do as she pleases. Any woman is lucky to find a husband of that sort. They happen once in a lifetime and they are devoted forever. In all the world, he was the one man to save her. The nice man had come along.

Wemyss and I skied and bobbed and once or twice we took Mary Carlin on the bob, and always she arrived bringing two or three people with her. But he was content in the knowledge that on Thursday he would meet her alone at the inn.

And then the blow fell. At four on the afternoon of the rendezvous we came in from skiing and I found a note from Mary Carlin.

It read, "Sorry, darling, but I can't dine tonight. I looked for you everywhere and had to leave without explaining. I'm going to Paris tonight on the Engadine express. Alice and Reggie are throwing a big party at the Ritz."

I had no idea who Alice and Reggie were. Mary Carlin always called everyone by his first name and most of the time I never knew whom she was speaking of.

I had to break the news to Wemyss. I did it as gently as possible. His blue eyes darkened, and he said, "Well, that means I go to Paris in the morning."

4

Two days later my own holiday came to an end and I went to Paris to sail for New York. I did not have Wemyss' address and it never occurred to me to look up Mary Carlin at the Ritz. I understood perfectly my own relationship to her. I might not see her again for five or ten years but wherever I saw her, she would come across the room and greet me as an old friend and say, "Hello, Jimmy. Where *have* you been all this time?" and then introduce me to Alices, Reggies and Totos. So I did not discover whether Wemyss had been able to find her alone or whether he had proposed to her.

But six months later I met Mary Carlin's aunt. It was in Cordova, Indiana that it happened, in the little town where Mary had been born and lived all her life until as an orphan of twenty-two she came into the money left by her uncle. I was lecturing in the Town Hall and after it was over a score of women came out into the reception room to shake hands with the noted author. Among them was a plump little woman with a jolly face. She waited until all the others had passed along the line.

Then she came forward and said, "I'm Mrs. Carlin. I heard from my niece that she met you last winter."

"Oh, yes. Of course, Mary Carlin. I saw her in St. Moritz."

"And how is she?"

"She was fine, enjoying herself."

"Yes, I gather from her letters that she's having a wonderful time, meeting all the most celebrated people, ambassadors and dukes and everything. I don't hear from her very often nowadays. When she first went over, she used to write regularly, but now I only hear now and then. You see, in a way, I'm a kind of a mother to her. She lived with me from the time she was seventeen after her poor mother died."

"Yes. She told me something about that."

"It's funny. She seems to like Europe. The first time she went over she only stayed six months, but this last time, she went over for six months and she's never come home. That was more than three years ago."

As I watched Mrs. Carlin I began to discover the clue to what Wemyss meant when he said, "She's too nice a girl to get mixed up with all this set." I began to see that beneath the restlessness and the fine clothes of Mary Carlin there lay hidden somewhere the elements of this jolly, cozy, little woman who stood talking to me. Mrs. Carlin was provincial and all that was unsmart, but she had honest blue eyes and a friendliness that never could be found in the world of everybody who was anybody. In every line of her face, in the very tone of her voice, in her smile was written the story of all the happiness of a woman who had found her place in life and filled it with success. She was a little dazzled by Mary Carlin's accounts of her brilliant life, just as Mary herself was a little dazzled.

"I hope she's not going it too hard," said Mrs. Carlin, "she always liked a good time. I've never been to Europe, but I'm thinking about going over to see Mary. My husband and I are thinking about a vacation."

My first swift impulse was to discourage the idea. It was impossible to imagine Mrs. Carlin visiting Mary in a hotel surrounded by Totos and Alices and Reggies. Out of all that world, only Wemyss seemed appropriate. I thought he would understand Mrs. Carlin and appreciate her and that they would like each other. But it was none of my business.

"Well," said Mrs. Carlin, "I'm certainly glad to have seen you. I'll write to Mary about seeing you. When you see her again, tell her not to go it too hard." She bridled a little. "You know what I'd really like to see? I'd like to see Mary married and with a family. She's that kind of a girl."

Suddenly I realized that if her aunt did make that trip to Europe and saw Mary Carlin, she would not know her at all.

5

I saw Mary Carlin the next time in the bar at the Hotel Royale in Biarritz. The bar is perched on a rock above the beach and one can sit there in the sun or shade as one prefers, drinking and watching the naked bathers on the beach below. It is a place frequented by everybody who is anybody.

At first I did not recognize her. I saw Toto, looking exactly the same as when I had last seen him, sallow, dissipated and ageless. Only this time he was wearing a purple and white striped dressing gown and a pair of bathing trunks. He saw me and crossed over and then I heard a woman's voice cry out, "Hello! Jimmy, where *have* you been all this time?" I turned and saw Mary Carlin coming toward me.

I knew her at once, more by the sound of her voice than by her appearance, for she had changed a good deal. She was still smartly dressed in the newest of hats and gowns, but something had gone out of her, something which I think must have been the flush of first youth. She was no longer a girl. She was about thirty then, and if one had wanted to argue about it, she really did not look more than thirty. Her skin was smooth. Her throat was thinner than it had been, her eyes more brilliant and there were hard little lines at the corners of her pretty mouth. I thought, "Across that face is the shadow of the old maid." But it was none of these things which made her seem a well-preserved woman of middle age. The thing lay in the too careful and too brilliant make-up she had put on as a protection, as if she herself already felt that she was beginning to grow gaunt and rattly, and in a nervousness which made itself felt all about her. And in her voice there was a faint hint of nervous shrillness.

She took us back to her table and we pushed chairs in among a circle of Argentines, dukes and dressmakers, clad in peignoirs and bathing trunks. I felt suddenly and thoroughly out of the picture. People kept coming and going from the table, greeting Mary Carlin and passing on. All the talk was of Mimi or Reggie or Alice. There was nothing for me to say for I had no idea who Alice or Mimi or Reggie were. And Mary Carlin had less time for me now than she had had when we met in St. Moritz. She wanted to have me there at the table with her but after that her interest ceased. I had the impression that she would have liked one large table at which everyone in the bar was seated drinking the drinks she paid for. She wanted me there but she had no time for me. There were so many other people.

At last when I rose to go, she called across the table, "Come along to dinner tonight, Jimmie. I'm throwing a party at the Reserve in Ciboure. Dinner's at half past ten. I must see more of you. There's so much I want to talk about."

Her voice was shrill. She seemed to me a person who was going faster and faster.

And as I turned I saw Wemyss coming through the door. He was as glad to see me as I was to see him. He looked a little older but still healthy and vigorous and honest. We made a rendezvous for the late afternoon and then he went into the bar to Mary Carlin's table.

Toto walked back with me to my hotel.

"What's Wemyss doing here?" I asked.

"Mary Carlin. He follows her every place."

"So the devotion has lasted."

"It's got to be a famous story. He never went back to South America. He's stayed in England. His father died. He's Sir Arthur Wemyss now."

I grinned cynically, "Maybe she'll marry him now."

"No," said Toto seriously, "I don't think that interests her. I don't think it would interest her if he was King George, except as somebody to invite to dinner so that she could say, 'Yes, King George dined with me last night.' She's a funny girl. I don't think you'd find her in any country but the United States."

"Why?"

"She's not interested in men as such. I don't think she's even been the tiniest bit in love with anyone. She likes parties and knowing everybody, and she's willing to pay for it."

"She looks much older than she ought."

"It's no wonder," said Toto. "She always stays up till the last cat is hung and then she gets up early in the morning for fear of missing somebody or something. When she's in Biarritz she's worrying all the time for fear there's something she's missing at the Lido. She keeps going faster and faster. She can't even find time to go back to America on a visit. And you can't go on doing all that all the time without some help from the outside. She's taken to drinking a good deal. I think too she takes stuff to make her sleep. The story is that she's lost a lot of her money too."

"If she'd only marry Wemyss he could save her."

"Maybe."

"Why do you say maybe?"

"Maybe it's too late."

"He's a romantic sap, hanging around like that all this time."

Toto grinned cynically, "I think the affair has taken on the proportions of a missionary adventure. He's as British as she is American."

"Why does she keep him hanging about?"

Again Toto grinned, "Because, I suppose, she has the horrors sometimes and then she thinks she might want to marry him some day, and have him look after her."

I saw her again that night, but no more intimately than I had seen her in the morning. We greeted each other and exchanged a few remarks and then the crowd swallowed her up. At dinner she had a grand duke on her right and a dressmaker on her left. Across the table I watched her and I saw what Toto meant. She kept going faster and faster. She was talking so much that she bored both the duke and the dressmaker. Watching her I wondered where it would end and it seemed to me that it could only end in complete bedlam. I thought of Mrs. Carlin back in Cordova, Indiana, and used her as a measuring rod. I saw that there was very little left which was nice in Mary Carlin. She had grown hard and thin and brittle. It was impossible to think of her any longer as the niece of the plump little woman. I wondered whether Mary Carlin had stopped writing altogether to her aunt.

6

I went away the next day and I never saw Mary Carlin again. In the months that followed I read about her in the continental papers, the *Daily Mail, The Chicago Tribune, The Paris Herald*. She was always giving parties and attending parties, always in the smartest resort at the smartest season. I went to America and when I returned I discovered that a strange thing had happened. Mary Carlin's name had disappeared from the newspapers. It was as if she had suddenly disappeared. I thought, "Perhaps, after all, she has married Wemyss or she has gone back to America." But in the back of my mind there lurked always a less healthy suspicion. She had been going faster and faster . . . When I thought of her, it was, oddly enough, as I had seen her that first time in the bar at St. Moritz, young and gay and enjoying herself.

In August I found myself in Paris. It was hot and dusty, the one month of the year when Paris is at its worst. One afternoon I was reading, clad in dressing gown, when the telephone rang and Toto's voice came over the wire.

"I read in the papers you were in town."

It seemed odd that the fashionable Toto should be in Paris in the one month when it was deserted like a plague-stricken city by everybody who was anybody. The next minute he made his apologies for being there.

"I had to come to Paris on account of business. Can I see you for a moment? Something awful has happened."

"Of course. What is it?"

"I don't know whether I can tell you over the telephone."

"I'd better know."

"Mary Carlin has committed suicide. That's all I can tell you now. I'll be right over."

He arrived in a high state of Latin excitement.

"I want you to go with me to the hotel and help fix things up. I'm no good at such things."

We went downstairs and hailed a taxi. "To the Ritz," I said to the driver.

"No," said Toto, "to the Hotel de Portugal, rue Bonaparte." Then as we climbed in he said, "She hasn't been at the Ritz for more than a year now. She couldn't afford it. She's been living in a scrubby hotel on the left Bank."

"Couldn't afford it?"

"No."

Then he told me what had happened. As her life whirled faster and faster, Mary Carlin spent more and more money. It cost a great deal of money when you weren't especially clever and amusing because then you had to give all the parties. And she was not, apparently, as rich as people thought her. And presently she began drawing on her capital and to save that she began to speculate desperately, for she had to have money to go on as she had been living, entertaining people and knowing everybody and being everywhere in season. And slowly the money she had began to ooze away, now in a steady stream, now in large lumps. She ran into debt and sold the diamonds I had seen her wearing. And then came the great crash in the American stock market and nothing remained. Then it was she went to the people she knew, the countless people she had entertained and looked upon as friends. She tried to borrow money but the clever ones had none and the dull rich ones turned a cold shoulder to her. She couldn't give parties any longer and people found it unpleasant to invite someone to dinner who would ask for a loan. She wanted enough to go into the stock market again, but the most she ever got was a gift of a few hundred francs or lira here or there, enough to carry her along from day to day.

"The last time I saw her," said Toto, "was at Easter. I met her walking alone in the Bois. I heard nothing of her since then till this morning when her maid came to my flat.

"The maid wasn't any longer with her because Mary Carlin could no longer afford a maid, but the maid liked her and kept in touch with her and sometimes came in to press her clothes for a few francs.

"So," concluded Toto, "when this happened, the proprietor sent someone to tell the maid and she came to me."

He had been drinking. His nerves were on edge and he began to cry.

The taxicab stopped before a simple little hotel and we went in. The proprietor met us, wringing his hands. Nothing like this had ever happened before in his hotel and would we get the body out as soon as possible.

"I've sent for an undertaker. I've arranged all that," said Toto. And I thought suddenly that after all there was something commendable about Toto.

The undertaker was already there, waiting for a hearse to take the body away. He greeted us in the hall and asked whether we would like to see the body. I refused and we entered the little cupboard which Mary Carlin had taken as a sitting room to receive the friends who never came. The maid was there, a big dark Provençal woman, who kept crying and drying her eyes. She had collected all the clothes and on a table a little pile of telegrams and letters. She thought we had better take possession of them. I took them saying I would send them to her aunt in Indiana. Toto did not even know that the aunt existed.

There were three or four telegrams, all from the people she had once entertained saying that they were away, here or there in some fashionable place, and would see her when they returned. There was a letter from her aunt in Indiana telling the gossip of the little town of Cordova. It sounded strange and remote from everything which had been Mary Carlin's life and I wondered if Mary Carlin had had any interest any longer in any of the people her aunt wrote about. Probably she had skimmed through the letter scarcely reading it. At the end Mrs. Carlin reproached her for not having written in six months.

At the bottom of the little pile lay a gray envelope. As I turned it over I read engraved on the back, Marshcote, Hampshire, and something told me that it was from Wemyss.

I opened and read it.

Dear Madame:

Your telegram addressed to Sir Arthur Wemyss arrived this morning and I have forwarded it to him by post. I regret to say that he is now on his way to East Africa, following his marriage of a week ago, and it is impossible to count upon its reaching him short of three weeks.

Hoping that the delay will not cause you too great inconvenience, I am

Yours respectfully,
Martha Davis,
Secretary to Sir Arthur Wemyss

I gave it to Toto to read.

"So in the end," I said, "she sent for him."

I looked at the postmark. It must have arrived the night before, just before she went to sleep after the glass of veronal.

Toto put down the letter and looked toward the door behind which Mary Carlin lay dead. His lip curled a little.

"She was never even in love. She never even had an affair," said Toto, "she died an old maid . . . a virgin." And into that word the gigolo put the full force of Latin contempt. "She never had time to live."

Then after a little pause he added, "The girl who knew everybody and nobody at all."

The undertaker's men came into the room and we went quickly out.

That night I had a telegram from Toto. He had been called away suddenly to the Riviera. In the end I paid the undertaker's bill. I, who had only met Mary Carlin a few times in hotel bars.

V

Bitter Lotus[1]

IN THE beginning Tom Dantry came to Nivandrum by accident. When he went aboard the *Vivandière* at Penang he did not even know whither she was bound. He had been for nine months in the Malay States and he was sick of the place, with that sickness and boredom which had overcome him again and again in one place after another in half the countries of the world. And he had come aboard quite drunk, as sick of himself as of the States, thinking, "I'm nothing but a damned bloody useless neurotic. I might just as well shoot myself and be done with it." But at the last moment, instead of shooting himself, he had come aboard the *Vivandière*—he did not know why he chose her, save that she was French and a little untidy and unlikely to turn up at any big prosperous ports where he would meet people he knew and have to drink all day and half the night in clubs and bars and meet women of his own class, or something near to it, which was worse.

If you asked him why he was a damned neurotic he could not have told you. He had thought about it a good deal, until presently, after several years, his whole character had changed. In the beginning he had been what is called an extravert, rushing about frantically, seeking to devour fun and excitement and life in great gulps, and by now, when he came drunk on board the *Vivandière*, he had reached that point where he thought no longer of the world in relation to himself, but only of himself in relation to the world. And that, he knew, for he was an intelligent fellow, made him a bore. And there were moments when he felt not only that he was a bore to others, but to himself, which was far worse. Bored with himself, he had begun lately to drink, not moderately as an occasional celebration as he had always done, but earnestly and steadily, to get away from himself, for he had no longer any faith in a change of scene. Suddenly one night in an awful moment of lucidity, he had discovered that ever since the war he had been going from place to place, not from any genuine restlessness or even

[1] "*Bitter Lotus* is a technical experiment—that of taking three characters from *The Rains Came* and allowing them to work out their destinies in a different story and a fresh background."

from curiosity, but only to escape from himself. And wherever he arrived he always found himself.

At that time he was thirty-four, which is not a great age, and he might have begun a wholly new life, save that he had no desire to begin again. There was, he knew, something dead inside him, something which had been dead ever since they had dug him out of a mine hole in Flanders at the age of nineteen, given him the Victoria Cross, and invalided him out of the war for good. But by the time they dug him out, he had had enough of living—too much of it—and now, when he looked back on the rescue, he knew that in his heart he had been sorry when he found himself alive once more in a London hospital. It was as if his spirit had already accepted death and resented being dragged back to life.

He did not regard this theory of his own futility as an excuse. He merely accepted it as a possible explanation. He had hated the war. He hated the killing and the danger and the insanity of the whole spectacle. He had been out of it forever, and then they played him the dirty trick of bringing him back to life in a world which from that moment on disgusted him. He knew now that all the fun he had had, all the reckless, vicious living, had not been fun at all, but only hysteria, the hysteria of a man trying to get back what had been taken from him as a boy. And he had been cursed, too, with enough money to live well, and with friends, too many friends, and with good looks and education and charm, so that he had never been forced to face a cold world and take himself by the scruff of the neck and work in an orderly fashion.

"No character," he would say to himself. "Now at thirty-four, I suppose you could say that I have no character, not that that means anything either. Hell!"

He hated self-pity. He hated thinking about himself, but neither thing was he ever wholly able to escape. And while he had been running away from himself, he had been looking desperately for something which might have been peace or stability or faith, and was perhaps a mixture of all three. You would never have known or even suspected, as you sat drinking with him in some bar in the Far East, what went on inside the good-looking, well-shaped head. He never bored you with it. All his talk was trivial and noncommittal, like the talk of any remittance man. He saved all his despair for the moments when he was alone, and he hated those moments; that was one of the reasons why he was so often mixed up with women and never in love with any of them. Women liked him; they even fell in love with him all too easily, and so the game was easy enough; the difficult part was in escaping. There always came a time when he had to run away because that was the easiest way out. He had never been in love since he was twenty-two, and he was still in love with the same woman, although he had not seen her for ten years and she couldn't possibly be the same woman any longer.

When he came aboard the *Vivandière* at Penang, he was running away again, this time from a woman who lived in the hotel, whose husband's business took him round and round the Malay States, the Dutch East Indies and Indo-China. He did not blame her, and he knew that in her heart she loved her husband more than himself, but he had had enough. So he got drunk in the Runnymede Bar after writing a note to say that it was finished and that she would never see him again, and came aboard.

The captain was a Breton, small with ruddy cheeks, black hair and bright blue eyes—a man who knew his way about in the world. When he saw Dantry, he thought, "This fellow is all right," and took him aboard even though he was drunk. He even kept the *Vivandière* in port another few hours to make the necessary alterations in the ship's papers. He was not a soft man, but there was something in the look of Dantry which affected him. He had a feeling that Dantry was the sort of man who shouldn't be as drunk as he was, a man perhaps who was on the downgrade for reasons which the captain himself could not fathom, a man whom he felt inclined to help. He was not a soft man, but men much harder than he had felt the same way about Tom Dantry's easy-going charm. Even drunk, Dantry was not offensive like most men. Neither was he pathetic as many drunken men can be. The captain liked him. He felt that for reasons he could not quite understand the presence of this odd passenger would make the long voyage home more pleasant for everyone on the ship from himself to the meanest of the stokers.

And so it proved. The presence of Tom Dantry, drunk or sober, always made the world seem a brighter, cheerier place. For he had been born one of the blessed whose vitality and good looks and charm have a way of making the world seem to the less fortunate a brighter and more agreeable place.

When he went aboard he knew nothing of the ports at which the ship might touch, save that in the end it was bound for St. Nazaire, and that meant France and Europe and home where he did not want to go. He would, he told himself, leave the ship at some port on the way back—if necessary the last port east of Aden—for he was sick of Europe. To him it seemed that Europe was dying, and dying or not, the spectacle was unpleasant and disgusting, like that of a man stricken with plague. The East was better. He felt no desire to do his small part in helping his own world to recover, for in his heart he felt that it was time for it to die. Better die than go on making a hideous spectacle of itself. He did not much care where he left the ship so long as it was not in Europe.

The next morning, as the ship left the lovely harbor of Penang, he rose from his berth and inquired the route of the ship. It was, he learned, bound for the Andaman Islands, for the Cocorandos, for Nivandrum, Aden, Port

Said and St. Nazaire. He had, it seemed, chosen without knowing it a ship which touched only the most obscure ports, a ship which, at the moment, suited him to perfection.

"And Nivandrum?" he asked of the little Breton captain. "What is Nivandrum?"

"It is the port where we load copra and spices," he said. "It used to be one of the great ports of the East . . . two hundred years ago. It is a dead place now. One can't even enter the harbor. The ship has to anchor off the Great Bar."

The Andaman Islands, he found, were dreadful and barren, inhabited by convicts and aborigines, and the Cocorandos were lovely but an old story, so as the ship approached Nivandrum he felt no very great curiosity. He had heard too many times of the charm of this island or that one, only to find them nearly all the same in the end, beautiful, banal and monotonous. He was not even impressed by the statement of the hard little Breton that it was a lovely spot with *un caractère tout à fait spécial*, different from obvious places like Bali and Penang and Tahiti. He liked the captain and he liked the untidy little *Vivandière*, and for seven weeks he was happier than he had been for a long time, perhaps because there were no women in that world to trouble him and nothing familiar to arouse memories or regrets. He would, he thought, stay aboard the ship as far as Aden and there find another boat bound East again. It would not be a bad way to spend one's life, always at sea, always free from the complications in which he found himself entangled the moment he went ashore.

It never occurred to him that when he reached Nivandrum he would leave the ship with the intention of remaining there forever.

2

Long ago in the seventeenth and eighteenth centuries it had been the richest port of all the coast. From Nivandrum were shipped the cargoes of silk and cardamom, cinnamon and pepper, which brought fabulous prices in far-off Europe. In those days it had belonged in turn to the Portuguese and the Dutch, and they had built houses there and churches, and first the Jesuits and Carmelites had come and after them the Dutch Protestant missionaries, and the governors and the traders had built themselves fine houses and lived in a style they could never have known at home. And then slowly the great river which carried down the earth of the vast burning red plateau that lay inland beyond the mountains, piled up a great barrier of mud and sand at the harbor's mouth and Nivandrum died, slowly strangled by the Great Bar, for no great trading ships could cross it, and for most of the year it was unsafe for ships to anchor outside in the open sea.

One by one the traders and the missionaries left and the trade moved far to the north and the south to more favored ports, and presently Nivandrum reverted to the people of the coast and there were no more Europeans and no more ships. The great houses remained—beautiful houses in the baroque style, executed by local workmen and painted shades of pale green and pink, yellow and blue. For a time the people of Nivandrum, on the principle of squatters' right, tried living in them, but in the end they went back to living in their own clean, small houses made of bamboo and thatched with the fronds of coconut palms, and the houses were left to ghosts and cobwebs, belonging to no one, claimed by no one, until the greedy old Ranee laid claim to them. They had no value, for there were no tenants, but she had a way of claiming anything which lay about loose.

During the winter season, when the great ocean was still, two or three ships like the *Vivandière* called for bits and pieces of cargo, copra and spices, coconut matting and cheap brass ware, anchoring outside to be loaded by the *wallum* boats which could cross the Great Bar at high tide. There was a broken-down, narrow-gauge railway which ran from the cities beyond the high plateau down the mountains to the stifled port, but no one ever came by it. Only two Europeans lived in Nivandrum, one a Cockney called Carleton, who managed to scrape a living from his coconut palms and by a little trading, and a Dane called Rasmussen, who ran the Grand Oriental Hotel, whose only clients were Mees Opp, the State doctor, an occasional half-caste commercial traveler and the officers and the crews of the occasional tramps which called at the dead city during the winter season.

Vaguely Dantry knew that the whole coast was beautiful, a coast which somehow had been overlooked in the admiration of the sick West for Bali and the South Seas, and as the *Vivandière* cast her anchor outside the Great Bar, he could see the beauty of the distant blue mountains covered by rain-drenched jungles; but it was not until the ship's boat with himself and the captain had pitched across the Great Bar and entered the narrow mouth of the harbor between all the fishing nets, that he became aware of the extraordinary melancholy quality of the place. Slowly, as the boat advanced, the harbor opened up before him, its seven islands and the mainland covered by groves of coconut palms with the pale gleam of the deserted old Dutch and Portuguese houses showing between the trunks of the trees. The lovely *wallum* boats, with the nostalgic look of China about their bows, moved back and forth across the water, some propelled by half-naked boatmen, others driven slowly like ships in a dream by the breeze from the jungle-covered mountains that filled their great sails of torn coconut fiber cloth. The water beneath the boat was green and clear. The little Breton captain had, he saw almost at once, been right. The place had *un caractère tout à fait spécial*; a ghostly quality. The pale baroque houses, deserted and empty, among the coconut palms of the islands were like houses in a dream.

Beneath the hand of the captain the boat steered toward a small island in the center of the harbor with an old house painted pale pink set in a garden of coconut and betel palms, crotons, bougainvillea and jacqueranda.

"First," said the captain, "we have a drink at Rasmussen's." He grinned, *"Voilà, le Grand Hotel Oriental."*

"That old house?" asked Dantry.

"Yes."

It was the loveliest hotel he had ever seen.

Rasmussen, the captain told him, was a Dane who had run away from his ship in Colombo twenty years ago. He was married to a woman of the country who was cook of the Grand Oriental Hotel.

"Not bad," he said. "She is a good cook . . . for curries. A handsome woman but a bad face . . . might poison you if she didn't like you."

Rasmussen himself greeted them. He was fishing from the small pier because there was nothing else to do, a small solid chunk of a man about fifty, with a ragged mustache and very bright blue eyes, clad in canvas trousers and singlet. Pulling in his lines, he led them up the path beneath the coconut palms into what had once been the hall of the old house.

It had a vaulted roof, and in one corner a magnificent baroque stairway, and it was cool and damp. Now it was rigged up as a café and restaurant with a half-dozen cheap tables, a gramophone with a gigantic horn and an old-fashioned wireless set fed by batteries. At each end of the hall there was a great open archway which framed a lovely view, on the one side of the harbor entrance, and on the other of nearer islands and the distant mountains.

Inside the hall Dantry remained silent, watchful, like a cat. It was as if he were holding his breath, as if he had crossed his fingers, lest all this might suddenly vanish. He was thinking, "Perhaps this is the place. Perhaps I have found it at last. The place I have been looking for ever since I ran away from England."

The interior of the hall was clean. The cups and glasses shone. Rasmussen drank brandy and coffee with them and gossiped with the captain in broken French. When the captain asked, "Well, what is the news? What has happened since last year?" Rasmussen grinned and said, "Nothing. Nothing at all," and then added. "Oh, yes. Sandy Carleton's wife is having another kid."

"How many does that make?" asked the captain.

"An even dozen."

"A fertile climate."

They drank for a little time in silence, lazily, and then a bright look came into the eye of the cocky little Breton captain, and he said, "And that girl of his . . . the oldest one . . . she must be a woman by now."

"She's eighteen," said Rasmussen.

The Breton captain turned to Dantry with the look in his bright blue eyes of a Frenchman who is a connoisseur of women. "There's a beauty," he said. "In Marseilles or Paris she could have what she liked."

But Dantry scarcely heard him. He was still caught, as if hypnotized by the beauty of the scene framed by the great doorway, and as the Breton captain spoke, he became aware of Rasmussen's wife, Léah, who was serving them. She was, he calculated, perhaps forty or more, not fat, but on the contrary, tall and very straight with a handsome figure and fine dark eyes. There was a pride in her walk and carriage. She was still handsome; young, she must have been very beautiful. But he saw what the Breton captain meant when he said that she might poison you if she didn't like you. The eyes were set too near together and the nose was too long. And she had a way of studying you when you were unaware of it.

Still silent and watchful, he looked out of the doorway again at the harbor where the *wallum* boats were moving past with the naked boatmen standing one in the bow, one in the stern, like gondoliers in Venice, and he thought, "The people are all beautiful here. Why has no one discovered this place? Why has it not been named 'the Venice of the East,' and ruined?" Then he remembered that it was safe because there was no way of getting there, no way at least luxurious enough for the sort of people who spoiled such places. And he still kept his fingers crossed against the discovery of the serpent which might contaminate this paradise.

And then, as he sat there drinking and feeling at peace and almost happy, one of the *wallum* boats drew up at the landing and a woman climbed out from beneath the little hut of thatched palm leaves on its deck and stepped from the boat to the little landing stage. He noticed her at once, not because she was beautiful but because of her extraordinary appearance and of some special quality he could not quite define. She was tall and heavy and ugly and she was dressed in a business-like suit of very clean white drill, with a grotesque hat of straw upon which she had lavished the only gesture of femininity in the whole costume; it was covered with faded artificial flowers and carried a bedraggled bow of faded mauve ribbon. She gave two small bags to one of the boatmen and came up the path between the jacquerandas and bougainvillea toward the Grand Oriental Hotel. As she came nearer he saw that not only was she fat and ugly and walked with difficulty because of her huge weight; her skin was of that peculiar muddy color which sometimes goes with a half-caste and her eyes were blue, an extraordinary clear blue, and in one of them there was a squint. At sight of her the proprietor, Rasmussen, rose quickly from the table and went forward to greet her, and when she saw him she smiled, and with the smile the ugliness seemed to

[328]

flow away from her. The smile illumined the whole face and made you forget the clumsy body and the grotesque costume.

Once inside the room she seated herself heavily near the door, glanced at Dantry and the Breton captain, and had a huge glass of beer. While she drank it, seated grotesquely in profile against the extraordinary beauty of the picture framed by the doorway, Dantry, who had a taste for young and pretty women, studied this ugly, middle-aged one. He did not quite know why, save that she was so extraordinary in appearance and that her manner was different from most half-caste women. There was something authoritative, even commanding, about her, and he saw that the ugly face was a good face, just as the handsome face of Rasmussen's wife was an evil one.

Then, when she had finished the beer, she crossed the room and heavily climbed the lovely baroque stairway to disappear somewhere in the upper reaches of the vast and beautiful old house.

When she had gone, Dantry said to Rasmussen, "Who is that woman?" and the hotel proprietor, smiling, said, "That is Mees Opp."

"Everybody who comes here knows her," said the captain. *"Elle est presque une légende le long de la côte.* She is a doctor. She comes here twice a year to look after the health of the people. She has a kind of hospital inland at the capital. Now and then she gets some money for it . . . God knows how . . . out of the old Ranee. Tomorrow they'll come here from all parts of the islands and the lagoons to see her . . . even those who believe in witch doctors and charms, because they know that somehow the powders Mees Opp gives them work better than the other things."

When the captain had finished drinking and prepared to leave for the harbormaster's office, Dantry said, "I'll stay here for the day. I suppose I can hire a boat to explore with."

"Yes," said Rasmussen. "My boys will take you out."

To the captain he said, "Send a boat for me about seven."

He spoke not as a stray passenger on a tramp steamer making a request, but as if he were giving a command. The captain showed no resentment. He did not even look up from his coffee. He had been right about this Monsieur Dantry; he was good-looking and gentle and charming, but he was sick, not the captain had divined, with any sickness of the strong wiry body, but with some sickness of the mind and spirit. Being a Frenchman and a Breton he understood about things like that. There was something about this man with his good looks and dark unhappy eyes that made you want to do favors for him.

So the captain said, *"Bien sûr,"* and left him behind at the Grand Oriental Hotel. It was after he had gone that Dantry, going into the garden to stretch his long legs, saw the house.

It stood on an island so near to the edge of the water that one could land directly at the foot of the large outside stairway which led down from the upper floor—a big house with a Dutch baroque façade and a long wide balcony with arched windows opening on to it. The moldy pale yellow walls caught the mottled sunlight that fell through the trees. That it was empty and deserted was evident; the windows were barren of glass and the main door stood ajar. While he watched a flock of brilliant green parrots flew out of one of the windows. Taking up his glasses, he looked through them and made out with little difficulty the big cool rooms which had lain empty and undisturbed for more than a hundred years, but what he saw through the glasses was not a ruined empty house of extraordinary beauty, but a house, reclaimed, restored and livable, with himself moving about on the island, gardening, fishing, reading, painting, thinking undisturbed, at peace at last.

When he had gone back into the hotel, he said to Rasmussen, "Who owns· that house?"

"Nobody in particular," answered the Dane. "At least nobody knows who."

"If I wanted to buy it how would I go about it?"

Rasmussen regarded him with an expression of doubt and wonder. He had made his estimate of Dantry, an estimate which was not very different from that made by the Breton captain. This was a man who knew the world. He wasn't a beachcomber and he wasn't a remittance man. What could he possibly want with a half-wrecked old house on an island in a ghost town like Nivandrum?

"Yes," Dantry repeated, "I might want to buy it."

Rasmussen laughed. "Well, if you're really serious, I guess you could buy it from the old Ranee. She'd sell anything for a few rupees, even herself, if anyone wanted her."

Dantry turned to look at it again, thinking how extraordinary it was that the house was exactly what he had dreamed of for years past, ever since Alix had married Simpson and he had left London forever. He had seen the house many times in his imagination, or one very like it, but only now, after more than ten years, had he found it.

"If you get me a boat and some sandwiches," he said, "I'll go off exploring."

All the afternoon, even through the heat, poled by the two boys whom Rasmussen had sent him, he drifted in a *wallum* boat among the islands along lagoons, past rice fields, up blind inlets, and everywhere the boat drifted he found the same still beauty filled with peace, and the same handsome, peaceful, forgotten people. It was a peace which to him in his bitterness was better than the peace of a primitive country uncontaminated by the touch of the white man; it was the peace of a country which had conquered the white man and been given back again to its own people. It was the great river which had vanquished the invaders—the river which in a half-primitive way the people of the country, even the traditional Christians, still worshiped, because it was the great river which had choked the lovely harbor and kept out the great ships of the shopkeeping Europeans.

And as he drifted, he kept thinking, "This is the perfect place." But the wisdom of experience kept telling him, "There is no perfect place. There is always something wrong. What can it be here?"

But when he returned and talked to Rasmussen, he could discover from him no hint of any serpent in this Eden. For Rasmussen, the place was perfect. He had, he said, come upon it by chance when he had run away from his ship hundreds of miles from Nivandrum, twenty years before, and he asked for no better life than he found here in the dead city with the choked harbor.

So when the boat of the *Vivandière* called for him in the evening at the moment when the sun seemed to linger on the horizon and the fishing boats came rushing in like birds across the Great Bar, he sent it away again with a request that it should return with all his luggage.

He was afraid to return himself for fear that once he stepped upon the deck of the stolid little ship, common sense or perhaps weakness and indecision might return to claim him, and the port of Nivandrum with its melancholy beauty would vanish, lost forever. He meant to stay here for the rest of his life, for in his heart he knew suddenly that this was the place for which he had been searching.

That night, after his luggage had been landed and the *Vivandière* slipped over the horizon bound for Port Said and Europe, he had dinner in the big room alone, with Mees Opp in the far corner opposite him. Rasmussen waited on the two of them, serving the food which his wife Léah cooked, stopping now and then and seating himself with the greatest informality to chat, now with Mees Opp, now with Dantry. When they had finished eating and he was having brandy and coffee, still watching the beauty of the harbor framed by the great doorway, a canoe appeared presently on the water between the hotel and the light and fires of the nearest island. It came up to the landing stage, and presently on the path in the glow of light from the great hall there appeared the figure of a young girl. For a moment, as she reached the doorway, she stood, a little blinded by the light, looking about the room. Then she saw Mees Opp and quickly crossed the room close by the table where Dantry sat, apparently without noticing him, but so close that he saw she was a beauty, even among these island people who seemed to him a race of gods and goddesses. For a second he felt a sudden rush of predatory excitement, but almost at once he said to himself, "No. None of that. In that direction lies ruin! It's always that which spoils everything."

The girl had a fair skin, the color, thought Dantry, of pale gold, was dressed in a simple clean white sari and she walked with the grace of a woman who had never known heels and was accustomed to carrying burdens on her head. But her eyes were the most extraordinary. They were enormous and dark and soft like the eyes of a doe. And suddenly he knew that as she had passed his table she had not looked at him at all because she was shy. Even the presence of a stranger in this forgotten world had not tempted her. The knowledge touched him—that there could still be in the world a woman like that.

At Mees Opp's table, she spoke for a moment with the big ugly half-caste woman, and then Mees Opp rose and, climbing the stairs heavily, descended in a moment wearing the grotesque hat and carrying the smaller of her two bags, and the two women, the one so huge and coarse and ugly, the other so fragile and lovely, went out together. In a moment Dantry saw the canoe moving away again against the lights of the nearest island toward the mainland.

When Rasmussen came in again, he said, "Who was the young girl?" and Rasmussen said, "That's Sandy's oldest girl. Sandy's the only other white man in Nivandrum. He's English, too. His name is Carleton. The girl came to fetch Mees Opp because her mother is having a baby. Good luck, I call it, that it came along while Mees Opp was here. . . ."

When Dantry had finished his brandy, he went out again in the *wallum* boat, drifting aimlessly among the islands where the fires threw a glow far in among the palms. It was long after midnight when he returned and went to bed at last in the *chambre de luxe*, a room with a turkey-red carpet, a paraffin lamp, and a huge Victorian bed of teakwood ornamented with bits of mother-of-pearl and draped with folds of white mosquito netting. At peace, he fell asleep almost as soon as he had drawn in and fastened the netting over the vast, ugly bed.

3

After their strange guest had gone to bed in one of the rooms overlooking the moonlit harbor, Rasmussen's woman, Léah, looked at her husband and said in her own tongue, "What for does he want to come and live in a place like this . . . a fine gentleman like him? He's not like you and Sandy Carleton."

Long ago Léah had been suspected of being a witch, and in the dead town there were people who still believed that she had the evil eye and the power of cursing an enemy and withering all his life. That was how she had come to take up with Rasmussen in the beginning—because, despite her fine looks, most of the men in Nivandrum were afraid of her. Rasmussen did not mind the witchcraft nonsense. He had been a sailor, he was a Scandinavian and he knew a fine woman, witch or not, when he saw one, and in the twenty years he had lived with her he had been troubled by no evil manifestations of her fine black eyes.

Now he grinned at her, and it was a smug grin. He had no desire to be a fine gentleman like this Dantry; he knew he was quite well off, perhaps far better off than the unhappy stranger. His own eyes were clear and blue, not clouded and full of misery like Dantry's. His was a life which suited him to the ground, a far better life than he would ever have known in his over-crowded homeland.

He said, "Maybe he wants a life like mine and Sandy's. It's not such a bad life."

Léah only shook her dark head and went on putting out the kerosene lights.

"Maybe he's done something he's ashamed of. Maybe he had to get out of his white man's country and hide. I guess he won't stay long. Anyway, I wish he hadn't come."

"Why?" asked Rasmussen.

"Because I don't like him."

"Why? He's good-looking. He's a gentleman. He has nice manners. He's got an honest face—a nice face."

For a moment Léah was puzzled. It wasn't easy for her to analyze her own feelings, and it was even more difficult to express them in a simple language which had no words for tortured, complicated analysis. At last she said, "There's something not nice about him."

"Rubbish."

But she persisted. "It's something inside him . . ." She hesitated for a moment—"Like a maggot."

He regarded her for a moment in surprise. Perhaps three or four times before in their lives together she had expressed an opinion like this suddenly and vehemently, and as he watched her he was remembering these occasions and remembering too that each time she had been right. But like Cassandra, no one had ever believed her prophecies. Now and then he did feel a sudden inexplicable awe at her shrewdness, and there were times when he felt that there was something deep within her, something almost animal, a vision undistorted, unblurred by civilization, some skill like that of the primitive trackers in the high jungles which permitted her to see true. But now, as ever, he would grant her nothing, for she was a proud woman who was sometimes arrogant and always likely to get out of hand.

So he merely repeated "Rubbish!" again and rose to go upstairs to his bed, up the beautiful winding stairway built long ago for a Captain Mynheer van der Burgh of the Dutch factory, a stairway that was like the stairways in the King's palace back in Denmark. And it belonged to Rasmussen—his own—and to no king.

As he reached the turn in the stairway she spoke again. She was standing just below him, holding the last lamp in her hand, and as she looked up at him he could not help thinking now, even after twenty years, how lucky he was to have such a fine woman.

She said, "So long as the Bar is there to block the harbor we will be happy in Nivandrum. When they take away the Great Bar, we will be unhappy again. There will be tragedy and suffering as there was before the river brought down the Bar to protect us."

There was a kind of beauty and dignity in her speech as well as in her attitude, standing there, a prophetess, with the shabby kerosene lamp in her hand, which Rasmussen had never noticed before. For a moment he was a little afraid of her—not of her body, which was the body of his woman, but of something inside her. He was so afraid that he laughed and said, "If they took away the Great Bar, my fortune would be made. The Grand Oriental Hotel would be one of the biggest hotels in the East."

She put out the light and in the darkness he heard her saying, "And do you think that would make you happier?"

4

In the morning, a little after eight o'clock, Dantry wakened to the sound of murmuring and chattering beneath his window. For a moment he did not remember where he was or that the *Vivandière* had sailed and he was left behind to settle in Nivandrum, and live there for the rest of his life. And then presently through the netting he observed the details of the *chambre de luxe* of the Grand Oriental Hotel, the monstrous bed, the turkey-red carpet, the pitcher and washstand of hand-painted china, the chromos on the wall—all assembled by Rasmussen in the idea that they were luxurious and "tasty." Outside, the murmuring and chattering continued, and at last, lazily, for he was by nature sensual and luxurious, he rose, and throwing a dressing gown about him, for he had long ago learned to sleep naked in the heat of the East, he went to the window and looked out.

There, just underneath, were assembled more than a hundred people who were ill with one disease or another—crooked, maimed, sallow, shaking with fever, a dozen or more clearly suffering from elephantiasis. There were old women and children, old men, and young women about to have babies. Patiently chattering among themselves, comparing symptoms and telling stories, they waited their turns to go into the little, half-ruined summerhouse where the huge ugly Mees Opp sat at a table examining them in turn. Before her on the table lay thermometers, medicines, bandages—all neatly laid out in the most scientific order. At the landing stage near by there were thirty or forty *wallum* boats and canoes lashed together until each patient, examined and satisfied and dosed, was finished with Mees Opp and ready to depart in his own conveyance.

The sight of so many sick people early in the morning did not cheer him, but he stood there for a time fascinated, watching Mees Opp go through the business cheerfully and efficiently, and as he watched he became aware that it was not only that she gave them medicines which were mixtures of chemicals and herbs, but another kind of medicine which probably did them quite as much good, for each one of them seemed to leave her presence in good-humor and full of confidence. They even exchanged jokes in passing with those whose turn to be dosed had not yet come, and presently, after watching for a long time, the spectacle, instead of depressing him, put him into a strange good-humor. Instead of finding the sight of so much sickness, of so many human ills, so much misery, utterly repulsive, he found it rather warming and touching. And that he saw was because of Mees Opp and her confident, jolly manner. Coming to see Mees Opp twice a year was, he began to understand from the behavior of the patients, a kind of festival and holiday. Invalids, both imaginary and real, could talk about their symptoms, and in Mees Opp they would always find a sympathetic listener, ready with some joke which they understood.

When he had had a shower with dipper and *chattee*, he dressed and went downstairs to breakfast, and from his table in the great hall he was still able to watch the clinic in progress, until, about eleven o'clock as the heat rose, all the suffering had been cared for and had gone away, leaving Mees Opp to pack up her belongings in the ruined little summerhouse.

Rasmussen said to him seriously, "She is a great help in the State. If ever you're really ill you can rely on her. She's a good doctor."

"How did she ever come here?"

"I don't know. She's been here for thirty years . . . since before I came . . . not here but up at the capital."

"How old is she?"

"She must be fifty-five."

Then Mees Opp came in carrying her two little bags, and ordered another large glass of beer, and Dantry said to Rasmussen, "Will you let me meet her? I'd like her to lunch with me."

"You can meet her," said Rasmussen, "but she won't be here for lunch. She's going away at once. She's got to visit three villages before sundown."

So he was introduced to her almost at the moment she was leaving and they exchanged a few polite remarks, which led to nothing at all, but he made the discovery that she was both intelligent and frank and he thought, "She will be interesting to talk to. She must have had some extraordinary experiences," but when he asked her when she would be coming to Nivandrum again, she said, "In six months. You see I'm only able to get here twice a year . . . sometimes not as often as that."

He and Rasmussen walked with her as far as the landing stage and stood there looking after her until the *wallum* boat which carried her had disappeared behind the nearest island.

"Sandy Carleton's new baby is a girl," said Rasmussen, almost as if Dantry had lived in Nivandrum for ten years instead of a single night. Then suddenly, "Do you like shooting?"

"Yes. When there's nothing else to do."

"Sandy is a great *shikari*. And there's wonderful shooting up there in the hills. No better in the world," and he made a gesture toward the blue mountains covered with rain-drenched jungle. And Dantry thought, "It's all better than I had hoped. It's so easy. I am going to be happy here at last."

5

Sandy Carleton was a fat little man, one of those extraordinary fat little men who seem more agile and full of vitality than many men of half their weight. On the mainland a mile or two from Dantry's island, he had a kind of compound filled with small palm-thatched houses that had been put up one after another as his ever-growing family increased. Like Rasmussen he had come to Nivandrum to escape a seafaring life and settle down, and like Rasmussen he had quickly taken a Christian woman from among the people of the islands. After three children had been born he married her, for he knew by that time that he had found the place he had been searching for, and that he would never leave it. His wife, unlike Rasmussen's sterile Léah, had proved unbelievably fertile, and now at forty-eight there were times when he found himself a little hard put to provide plenty of food and the rudiments of clothing for them; but he was never downhearted, because he knew that he was far better off than he would ever have been in Camden Town, and that his children, even though they lived on rice and coconut milk and went naked, had a better life than any children he might have bred in the slums of London.

He knew, too, that they were healthier, more beautiful children than he could ever have had at home by the Cockney girl he had jilted long ago. He liked children; he did not mind how many his wife bore him, and his children were both handsome and healthy. Some of them were dark, and some of them almost as fair as himself. The loveliest of all was Maria, his second child, whose older brother, Silas, went to work for Dantry when his house was finished at last, and he left the Grand Oriental Hotel and took to living in it.

Sandy did not mind his son going to work as a servant; on the contrary, it seemed to him a solution of Silas's problem, especially as he was going to work for Dantry, who, by the time the home was finished, had become a friend, almost an intimate friend after the shooting trip he had made with Sandy into the high mountains. The plump little Cockney was a good *shikari*.

He knew at once that Dantry was a "gentleman." With his English instinct he knew that it had taken dozens of generations to produce a man like him, and he respected him for it. He was glad to let his half-caste son work for Dantry, because Dantry, being a gentleman, would treat him well and teach him a great many things which only a "gentleman" could teach him, things which, whatever happened to Silas later in life, would be useful to him. Dantry would make him into a good servant and a great deal more. Perhaps—who knew—Rasmussen might die one day and then Silas could take over the Grand Oriental Hotel.

About his children and their future Sandy was a realist, and he did all that was possible to keep them from having the ideas above their station which ruined the lives of so many others of mixed blood. Their place, he knew, was in Nivandrum. They belonged with their mother's people and not with his own, and in that, he decided, thinking of his own undernourished, overworked childhood, they were very lucky, far luckier than they would ever know.

Sometimes he talked with Dantry about the problem while the two of them sat by a fire of coconut husks in Sandy's compound, in the evenings when Dantry left his house because he could no longer bear being alone with himself.

One evening, not long after they had come back from the shooting expedition, he said to Dantry, "What about women? Are you going on living without them?"

Dantry grinned, showing his fine strong teeth and said, "I don't know."

"I don't suppose you're used to doing without them."

That made Dantry laugh. He said, "No, but I'm not sorry to give them a rest for a time."

This time Sandy grinned, "Oh, so it's like that."

"No, it's not like that . . . at least not altogether. It's true that I've only met one woman I ever wanted to marry—one woman who seemed to fit. You know what I mean . . . a woman you felt suited you and would go on suiting you forever. But that was a long time ago. I haven't seen her for years."

"Why didn't you marry her?"

"She married someone else . . . a bounder who had millions."

Sandy's Cockney face wrinkled into a look of shrewdness. "If she was that kind," he said, "if you'll pardon me for saying so . . . she wouldn't have suited you for long."

For a moment Dantry remained silent and thoughtful, and watching him in the firelight, even Sandy, who was not much given to admiration for masculine beauty, noticed the beauty of his friend's head, its fineness and look of race. It was a head that was over-bred. It was almost too fine.

Then Dantry frowned, as if he were alone, as if Sandy weren't there at all. "It wasn't like that. It was my fault too. We were both foolish." Then he smiled again, as if he were alone, almost as if he were talking to himself. "But rather nice, attractive young people for all that—as young people went in London after the war. Which isn't saying a great deal."

"Have you seen her since?"

"Once . . . in the distance, in a hotel in New York. She was with her husband."

The romantic in Sandy led him on. He'd never seen a cinema and he had no novels to read, and so Dantry had to take the place of such things. "Had she changed?" he asked.

"I really couldn't say. I didn't speak to her. It was bad enough just seeing her across a big room. She looked the same except a little . . . well . . . harder."

"Yes," said Sandy, "I suppose that would be true." He relighted his pipe and said, "Well, I left behind a girl called Sarah Jane in London, but there wasn't anything very special about her. I reckon she didn't miss me. She got married, my old mother wrote me, less than a year after I sailed the last time." He puffed at his pipe for a moment and then said, "I can't complain. I got the mother of all these fine brats instead. I never objected much to color and she's suited me well enough . . . no trouble at all."

He looked sharply at Dantry, who was staring into the fire, and after a moment he said, "There are worse solutions than one of these local girls."

"Yes, sometimes I've thought about that. Sometimes in the night I can't help thinking about it, only it's complicated."

"Not as complicated as you think," said Sandy, and then quietly, "I know what you're thinking about . . . the kids."

"Yes . . . and a lot of other things. I'm not very simple."

"I see how it's different for you. You've probably got ties and home responsibilities." It was a feeler on Sandy's part, just a thrust to see what he could discover of his friend's mysterious past.

"None that I need observe," said Dantry.

"Well, anyway it's different. . . . You having a troupe of half-caste kids and me having 'em. You being a gentleman makes a difference."

"It shouldn't," said Dantry.

"But it does," said Sandy. "I can't quite explain what I mean."

Dantry didn't answer him, so Sandy went on talking. "When I came here, I left everything behind. It wasn't very hard because there wasn't much to leave, and what I did leave I didn't like much, just a lot of memories of being overworked and half-starved. It wasn't the same with you."

"One can have a lot of other memories," said Dantry, "that are different perhaps, but just as bad. I'm sick of Europe."

"Still, it ain't the same with you."

"No, I suppose it isn't."

Sandy gave a great laugh. "To hear me talk you'd think I was a bloody pimp." Suddenly he grew shy. "It's hard to explain what I'm driving at, only I'd like to get everything fixed up for you. Rasmussen and I would both sort of like to see you stay on here . . . for good. It makes for company and, as you might say, it raises the tone of the community. If you had a woman, you wouldn't get restless."

"Thanks," said Dantry, and the sharp angle of his jaw grew harder. "Anyway I'm staying here . . . harem or no harem."

"That's good," said Sandy. "We'll have some good times. I haven't taken you fishing yet . . . with a torch and a spear. That's real sport. We won't talk about the ladies no more. It's always kind of a disturbing subject, but if ever I can help, just pass along the word. They all like me here pretty well. Most of 'em would do a favor for a friend of mine, especially as any girl here would leave home and parents any time for a good-looking fellow like you, with a big house and a gramophone and a piano."

"Right," said Dantry, "and now I'll go along to my lonely bed."

And then as he rose to leave, he noticed suddenly that Sandy Carleton's eldest girl, Maria, was standing in the doorway, and that at sight of him she sprang away shyly and disappeared. It was not the first time he had suspected her of watching him. He started to speak to Sandy, to say, "Tell your daughter she need not be afraid of me," but after the conversation he thought that it might sound odd, and so he held his tongue.

As he drove the canoe ahead toward his island he turned once to look back toward the compound, and caught a glimpse of the plump Sandy tending his fishing lines on the pier—the lines which would bring him tomorrow's food for that huge happy family of his, and suddenly he felt a sensation of warmth about his heart which surprised him because it had been so many years since he had felt like that about anyone. And he thought, "Perhaps it's going to be all right. Perhaps I *am* being born again. If only I can get all the way back."

At home in the bed in the big upper room which overlooked the harbor, with a brandy and soda by his side, he lay awake for a long time thinking of the conversation which had taken place by the fire in Sandy's compound, and out of all the talk he remembered one phrase of Sandy's, "I guess you haven't really given up the other life."

Sandy wasn't a brilliant fellow, but he had the shrewdness both of the Cockney and the sailor, and without thinking of it, it seemed to Dantry that he had put his finger on the thing that troubled him most. It was true in a way that he had really given up the other life. Here in this house with its pleasant furniture, its chintzes and Kashmiri rugs, with the gramophone and piano, with the books and papers from the West, he wasn't living like Sandy and Rasmussen. In a way it was an artificial life, apart from the life of Nivandrum. And just a little drunk for the first time since he had left the *Vivandière*, he grinned and thought, "Perhaps it's the same thing over again. Perhaps I'm trying to eat my cake and have it too. Perhaps I'm not willing to give up anything." And then he thought, "Perhaps it's only because the house is all finished now and I haven't enough to do."

Maybe that was why the restlessness had returned to him; maybe that was why in spite of himself he was thinking about women again. Then he poured himself another brandy and soda, drank it and went through the pages of a six-weeks-old *Times*, and by that time sleep took possession of him, and he was happy again and at peace, listening through his sleep to the distant sound of drums and flutes that came from among the islands.

6

It was time now for Mees Opp's visit, and the house was finished at last.

From the moment he left the *Vivandière* and began to occupy himself with the idea, he had felt changed and charged again with interest and energy. With each new chair, with each tile and pane of glass, he came to love the old house a little more, until presently, thinking about it, he came to see that the house was a kind of symbol of his own existence—a house, abandoned, empty, filled with memories, falling into ruin, which was being restored, refitted and made human and livable once more; and during those months he succeeded in losing himself in the house and in the landscape of Nivandrum itself—that awful self from which he had been running away for so long, the self he hated for its treachery, its selfishness, its despair and cowardliness, for all those qualities which men like Rasmussen and Sandy never saw in him, because they were simple, innocent men, and because they liked him.

It was only when the work was nearly finished and he had left Rasmussen's hotel to live in the house that there were moments when the self returned—moments when there was no more work and he was bored, when he could not read one more word of the books which arrived from London, nor listen to one more of the gramophone records sent him from New York, when in the heat he could not even bear the thought of fishing. For a time he tried teaching Silas to cook European dishes. The boy was willing and clever, but after a time Dantry grew bored with the idea. He played the piano and went fishing, and called on Rasmussen and Sandy, but still there were hours in the day . . . long hours . . . when there was nothing to do but think, and now that the house was finished he found that he always thought about the past and the world he had left behind him, not with regret, but because the life in Nivandrum somehow lacked reality and because the past, being more real to him, was always there, waiting.

The evenings were the worst, at that moment when the sun sinking into the Indian Ocean seemed to hang for a moment on the horizon and the fishing boats rushed in across the Great Bar to reach the harbor before night came down. Then for a moment the earth seemed to suspend all motion. The breeze from the land died away before the breeze arose from the sea. The air was still and hot, and then as the sun slipped below the horizon, the jackals came out in the foothills behind Nivandrum and their ghostly howling echoed back and forth across the lagoons and canals behind the harbor. All about, everywhere, in the still warm air there was that evening smell of woodsmoke and spices, jasmine and mangrove swamps, all blended together in a smell which was Nivandrum itself. At that hour the drums began, the sound drifting across the still waters as the night fell, and against the sound of the drums the thin thread of music from a flute or two. The music went on and on every night until long after midnight, nostalgic, restless, raising old longings for a life that was better than any life could possibly be, bringing back the memories of the old house where he had spent his childhood, and beyond that, farther back, strange, almost atavistic memories of things which had been dreamed. The sound ate into the soul. Then it was that he thought again of Alix, and dreamed sometimes of what life might have been if they had not been fools and had gone on loving each other. And her ghost came back to him, making him think how perfect she would have been here in this lovely house, how she would have loved this place and this life. If he had not been a fool and lost her, there would never have been any other woman.

"But she was a fool too," he thought bitterly. "We were both fools. We had everything between us—everything that humans could ask—and we threw it all away."

And then he would forget her, hearing the sound of the drums which had never ceased. He had only not heard them because he himself had gone away from Nivandrum, far away. He was in a London night club just after the war and saw her coming in the door, saw her for the first time, lovely, dazzling, fresh, with that look of innocence which she seemed to keep through everything. Or he was in that house by the sea and the morning light was coming through the faded chintz curtains and she was there beside him, and they were both young and reckless and in love. And he would try to imagine what she was now and he was afraid, because he knew himself and what he had once been. And in the end, he would laugh at himself and think, "I'm behaving like a bloody fool in a melodrama. If we meet again we shall probably loathe each other—or worse, we shall bore each other."

The sound of the drums would come back and then he would remember what the old Dutchman Tobias had said in Sumatra listening to the drums. "If a man listened long enough he'd commit murder or suicide."

It was the most beautiful moment of the day, and in it he should have found peace, save that it was the one moment of the day when he felt utterly alone and friendless, when even Rasmussen and Sandy seemed strangers to him. There were times when the sound of the jackals howling filled him with a sense of terror of the dead town and all the wild country beyond, of the people who were so friendly and yet so strange to him, of the lovely choked harbor and jungle-covered mountains beyond. It was a nameless, indescribable fear—the fear of a man who is lost and doomed, trapped and shut within the prison of his own character and destiny. The prophetess Léah never saw him at such moments; had she seen him she would have been triumphant.

And then slowly it seemed to him that he was beginning to discover what was wrong. It was not Nivandrum but himself, again that self which clung to him like a shadow. He was trying, too, to lead the life of a sophisticated, worldly man in a place that was primitive and simple and even wild, and so in a way he isolated himself in spirit even from men of his own race like Rasmussen and Sandy. They were happy, it seemed to him, as happy as Adam had been in Eden before the Fall, because they had left all Europe behind them. They belonged to this country; he did not belong, and perhaps never could belong.

So he began presently to believe that he had been wrong in thinking that he might make a life for himself in Nivandrum on the old terms. He began to believe, what he already knew but refused to admit, that he was wrong in thinking that he could do without women, that he, of all men, sensual and self-indulgent, and spoiled, could live like a hermit.

Yet he did not want a woman as Sandy and Rasmussen had their women— a part of their very lives. Sandy's wife going on breeding and breeding, Rasmussen's superior, dominating, a little sinister. And presently it occurred to him that in this country you might have a woman on your own terms, have her when you wanted her, to quiet your spirit and your restless desire to kill the loneliness, to entertain and amuse you, to fill those hours of the day which were haunted by ghosts. You could send her away when she was not wanted. She would not poison your whole life with scenes and hysterics, reproaches and jealousy, in the way that women in the West had a way of doing. You could, perhaps, effect a compromise, a wonderful, hedonist compromise between the old life and the new, by which you took everything you wanted and gave only what it was easy and convenient to give.

And so he began to look at the women of Nivandrum in a new way, not as creatures to be avoided, but creatures to be studied in cold blood as an expert studies bloodstock cattle to discover the finest, the fairest, the most docile. He was already looking at them in this fashion when Sandy Carleton spoke to him about the need of a woman in his life, and by that time he had, against his conscious will, almost without knowing it, made his choice.

It was Sandy's own daughter, Maria.

For a long time, ever since she had passed his table so shyly when she had come to fetch Mees Opp, he had been interested in the girl; but it was not until he had that sudden glimpse of her in the firelit doorway of Sandy's compound that he knew for the first time that she was the one. It was her shyness which caught him. The other girls in Nivandrum were bold enough, showing off their charms, waiting for him at the pier on the mainland, ambitious, coquettish and puzzled that he seemed never even to notice them. Maria he had never seen at all save in the shadows or vaguely through a tangle of bougainvillea.

Twice before that night he had seen her in his own garden, distantly on occasions when she came to see her brother Silas, and then one day, not long after his talk with Sandy, as he was reading on the balcony with a glass of brandy beside him, he became aware slowly that he was being watched by someone or something.

For a long time his nerves had been jumpy, and in odd moments he had suffered from an abnormal awareness of things which usually he would not have noticed, and to make himself more insensitive he had taken again to drinking, and now as he sat reading and drinking, he refused to give in to his nerves, to turn and discover who or what it was that kept staring at him and annoying him. For five minutes, for ten, he sat there trying to keep his attention on the book, but the words only grew blurred before his eyes, and the sense of what was printed on its pages escaped him completely. When at last the feeling of being watched became unbearable, he turned his head suddenly, quickly, but only quickly enough to catch a flying glimpse of a white *sari* disappearing among the crotons.

The experience both annoyed and pleased him. He was annoyed at the impertinence of the girl, and his vanity was pleased by her interest. Then suddenly he laughed, thinking, "I suppose if I were to play my proper role, if I were to behave the way men do in novels about the East, I would rush after her and carry her back into the house."

His instinct told him that this was the thing to have done, but his sense

[343]

of the ridiculous held him back. Even here in Nivandrum he could not quite see himself in such a role, at least not without feeling comic and self-conscious. He was, he knew, no cave man and not altogether a scoundrel. His methods had always been more subtle, partly because it was rare enough that he had found the pursuit on his side, and partly because, out of long experience, subtlety in the pursuit added pleasure to the conquest and the consummation. And so, his will paralyzed, he did nothing, and in a little while he had a distant view of a figure all in white, paddling across the harbor toward Sandy's compound.

After that his interest in the girl began slowly to attain the proportions of an obsession, so that at odd moments throughout the day, when he was reading or fishing and eating his solitary lunch he would find himself thinking of her, seeing her, speculating about her. And then after a while in the evenings he began to drink more than ever, so that at the nostalgic hour between twilight and dark he was too muddled to care.

It was not easy. He did not want to marry the girl; he had no thought of it; and he did not want to seduce the daughter of a friend. There were times when he thought of making an open declaration to Sandy, of proposing to take her for as long as it suited him, with a settlement which would be more money than anyone in Nivandrum had ever heard of, and which he himself would not miss at all. That he had never really spoken to the girl did not help the obsession; instead it seemed to make it worse. After a time, he thought, "If I see her clearly, if I talk to her, I may forget her. It may kill the damned thing."

So after that he kept watch to discover when she came to the island to see her brother. He found himself, standing like a fool in the upper part of the house watching for her. Two days passed and then three, and at last on the fourth day he saw her through the fronds of the coconut palms coming in a dugout across the open water between the mainland and the island. He tried the glasses, but the palms spoiled his vision and so he came no nearer to her.

It was in the cookhouse he found her, helping Silas to prepare the lunch. He came down quickly and trapped her there in a corner so that she could not escape. At sight of him she stood up quickly, like a servant, and turned a little away from him. She was dressed in a white *sari*, the ceremonial *sari* of the country, with a tiny wreath of jasmine flowers about the knot of smooth, shining hair at the back of her small head. She had turned away from him quickly, but not quickly enough, for he had seen in the hot light of midday that she was more beautiful than he had imagined.

For a moment he was silent and then he said, "Please sit down," aware that he was trembling a little and that his face was as scarlet as that of a schoolboy at his first party . . . his face, the face of Tom Dantry, whom no woman had been able to confuse since he was a boy of fifteen.

Then he said, "I suppose you are Maria," and with her eyes still cast down she said in a low voice, "Yes, *sahib*."

"You must come to the island often . . . as often as you like." He looked again at her dress and asked, "Is there a festival today?" The girl still looking away, answered, "No, *sahib*."

Then he turned suddenly and left the cookhouse because he could not think how he might go on with the conversation. For a long time he sat on the terrace feeling like a fool, unable to discover why this shy half-wild girl had upset him so profoundly, and in a little while he saw her in her canoe moving again across the shining blue water toward her father's compound. He knew now what she looked like; it had not made it better, but worse.

That night when he went to play cribbage with Rasmussen, he got so drunk that Rasmussen had to bring him home. When Rasmussen returned to the Grand Oriental Hotel, Léah was waiting. She said nothing at all. She merely looked at her husband, but the brilliant evil eyes said triumphantly, "You see, it has begun."

7

For nearly three weeks he waited, thinking now one thing now another, but never acting. He drank more than he had ever drunk in his life, not only on account of the queer unholy passion for the girl, but because he hated himself. One day he would be for going straight to Sandy, even for marrying the girl if necessary, and the next the idea would go from him completely in the belief that if he once took up with her it would be the first chapter of a story that would be monstrously like the story of a thousand other white men. First he would take to wearing a *sarong*, and then he would be drunk all day, and after a time there would be opium, and finally one day he would die, forgotten and regretted by no one. He hated all that. Sandy was right. It was different for Sandy and Rasmussen; with them such a thing was easy and simple and natural.

Again and again he thought, "If only I were like Sandy or Rasmussen." But he wasn't.

He had not meant it to be like this. He had meant to find peace in Nivandrum. There would be peace for a little time with Maria and drink and opium, but that was not the peace he had been seeking.

And he was ashamed, too, that a girl to whom he had spoken scarcely a half-dozen words should have aroused a desire so profound and enduring. For by now, he knew that the feeling he had for the girl was no simple thing. It was like nothing he had ever experienced before, so violent, so agonizing that in sober moments, it seemed to him a retribution for all the philandering he had done before he came to Nivandrum. He was suffering now, he knew, as that hysterical woman in the hotel at Penang had suffered when he ran away from her. He was caught now as he had caught others not once or twice but many times. He did not pretend that it was love that he felt for the girl. How could you feel love for a girl to whom you had scarcely spoken, whom you barely knew, a girl who was half-savage and could barely read or write?

"Perhaps," he thought, "I am growing old. Perhaps it is the senile passion of an old man for a young virgin," and that thought made him feel sick, for he was a man to whom youth had been everything, the bright youth of one who had good looks and charm and riches and freedom.

Then one day when reading on the terrace he came across a paragraph which it seemed to him had been written for himself. Twice he read it through.

It read:

"Dans la damnation le feu est la moindre chose; le supplice propre au damné est le progrès infini dans le vice et dans le crime, l'âme s'endurcissant, se dépravant toujours s'enfonçant nécessairement dans le mal de minute en progression géometrique pendant l'éternité."

When both Rasmussen and Sandy suggested that he was drinking too much for a climate like Nivandrum, he only said, "It's all right. It'll pass. It's just a temporary business."

But Léah *knew* and at last she told Rasmussen. "It's Maria," she said, "Sandy's girl. That's what the matter with him."

"He's hardly seen her," said Rasmussen, but Léah, instead of answering him, shrugged her shoulders.

"How do you know?" he asked her.

"I know," said Léah.

"Well, why doesn't he have her and be done with it?"

"A man like him. He's too grand for any of us." And there was a fine scorn in her voice.

"He needn't marry her. Sandy wouldn't mind, if he was good to her."

"It's not that," said Léah. "He's afraid of himself . . . he's not thinking about Sandy or Maria. He's haunted."

"Haunted?" asked Rasmussen.

"Yes, haunted by himself. Most men who take to drink are haunted." And as she put out the lights, she said, "You'll see."

When Rasmussen climbed the baroque stairway to his bed, Léah did not follow him. Instead, she put out all the lights but one, and when she had gone above to listen outside her husband's door and make certain that he was asleep, she went out and unfastened a canoe from the landing stage, climbed in and set out in the direction of Sandy's compound. She did not go to the compound itself but to an island farther on, surrounded by mangrove swamps and hidden away in one of the inlets. She found her way easily enough by the brilliant light of the moon, for she had known every island and every inlet since childhood. When she had circled part way the round island, she came to a break in the mangroves, and driving the canoe into it with the force of a strong boatman she ran its nose firmly into the thick mud on the shore beside a dugout which already lay moored there. Then pushing her way through the jungle she came at last to a little clearing before a ruined hut, and there in the moonlight she found Maria waiting for her.

At sight of her the girl sprang up timidly and came toward her without speaking, but Léah said, "It is working. He was drunk again tonight."

Then, while Maria listened in silence, Léah seated herself cross-legged facing the moon and recited a long prayer, addressed not to the moon but to the River God, who had closed up the harbor and driven away the white men Léah hated. When she had finished she remained for a time in a kind of trance, the girl watching her, shivering a little with fear. Then at last she opened her eyes and looked at Maria. She said, "You must go to him. He is a coward. He is afraid. He is haunted. It is for you to act now." Then she gave the girl a charm, and Maria went away again, alone through the thick jungle to the break in the mangroves, where she climbed into the dugout and set off in the direction of Sandy's compound.

When Maria had gone, Léah went into the hut, and from among the rubbish which littered the floor she took out an image, carved crudely from the soft red stone of the high mountains. It was squat, obscene, the crude representation of the River God who brought fertility and confounded the white man, killing his profits, and protecting from him all the wide, great valley that ran inland toward the high plateau. The squat little figure was caked with the blood of many sacrifices.

Alone, in the moonlight that streamed through the door, she prostrated herself before the image and began to address it in a whining, singsong tone, promising it that she would protect the harbor, that she would do away with white men who came there to remove the Great Bar and bring their ships once more among the islands. When she had finished she rose and went behind the hut, where a she-goat and two kids were tethered. Taking one of them, she carried it back into the hut, struggling and bleating, and when she had taken a knife from among the rubbish, she cut its throat and held it above the image until it was dead and there was no more blood in it.

In the Grand Oriental Hotel, Rasmussen wakened about two in the morning and turning over found that Léah was not beside him in the vast double bed. The discovery did not alarm him, because it had happened before so many times. Once each month at the time of the new moon, she would go away in the middle of the night, whither he did not know, and he did not much care so long as she was a good bed companion and cooked well, and her witchcraft left him in peace and comfort.

The next night Dantry came sober to the Grand Oriental Hotel. He looked neat and pale and he did not drink at all. Most of the evening he was silent, and in her corner Léah, with an air of demureness, did the embroidery the nuns had taught her to do long ago in the days when there was still a convent in Nivandrum, and while she embroidered, she watched with a look of sinister triumph in her brilliant black eyes.

At midnight he rose and said to Rasmussen, "Good night and good-by. I'm going away tomorrow by the morning train."

"When'll you be coming back?"

"I'm not coming back."

Rasmussen regarded him in silence, tongue-tied and shy and a little emotional because he liked Dantry so much.

"If you and Sandy want the things in the house, divide them up between you."

Then Rasmussen managed to say, "It's pretty sudden. We were used to you. We'll miss you. It won't be the same."

"I'll write to you. Perhaps sometimes . . . in a year or so . . . I'll come back and pay you a visit."

"Why are you going?"

"I can't tell you. I always have to go. I've been going now for years, wherever I've been. I can't stand it any longer."

He turned and said, "Good-by, Léah."

She rose and came forward from her corner, putting down her work to shake his hand, but she did it only for Rasmussen's sake. There was no emotion in her farewell. She liked Dantry no better than she had liked him on that first day more than a year before. She said, "Good-by, Mr. Dantry."

Then he put his arm about Rasmussen's square thick shoulders and said, "You've been good to me. I envy you. Thank you." And he went off suddenly down the path under the coconut palms he had loved so much.

When he had gone Rasmussen made a rueful attempt to laugh and said to Léah, "Well?" This time she was going to be wrong. Dantry was going away and nothing had happened.

"It's a good riddance," she said. "If he goes."

"What do you mean by that?"

"I mean *if* he goes."

Then she put out the lights and followed him up the stairs.

[348]

When they had gone to bed and were lying in the darkness with only the sound of the drums to break the stillness, he could not sleep—he, Rasmussen, who always slept like a log. And he could not sleep because he kept thinking of Dantry. Now that he had gone, Rasmussen found that he was not sorry. It was odd, but suddenly he did not miss him. Indeed, lying there between sleep and wakefulness, he found it difficult to remember what he was like. He could not even recall his face. It was as if he had never come to Nivandrum at all. He had given nothing at all and left nothing behind. He was, it seemed to the hotel proprietor, lying sleepless in the heat, not even a friend.

Puzzled, the simple Rasmussen thought, "I'm going crazy."

Beside him Léah slept content. She had not meant to drive the stranger from the island. What she sought was something worse than that. She had promised the River God to destroy him.

8

Paddling the dugout back through the darkness, peace came to Dantry once more for the first time in weeks, the peace which never endured, the terrible, deceptive, illusory peace which always came when he was running away, because in his heart he always believed that the next place would be all right, that in the next place life would be endurable.

For a little while he allowed the canoe to drift and sat quite still looking up at the stars which in the soft, black night of Nivandrum seemed to hang down out of the sky like lanterns. In the distance from the islands all around came the sound of the eternal drums and the thin thread of sound from the flutes. Everywhere among the palms gleamed little fires of coconut husk, and about each fire there was, he knew, a little cluster of people gossiping, singing, beating drums, at home, happy and friendly. But he belonged to none of them. Even when he went to Sandy's the little group about the fire would break up at once and wander off to some other compound leaving the two of them alone. And the girl Maria was always the first to vanish into the shadows.

No, he did not belong here in this loveliest and most peaceful of places. And he was running away again. Well, this time would be the last. There could be no others. He had tried nearly all the places and always they were the same. Since running away did no good, he would go back to Europe or to America, and try to lose himself there. He would go to Colombo and take the first boat home.

It was a good feeling . . . to have made a decision, to be leaving Nivandrum and that house which he had for a little time loved so much. It was good to be making a clean break, to be going away, taking nothing with him but a few clothes. It was a little like being reborn, save that it had all happened so many times before. For a moment, in this new sense of triumph, he loved Nivandrum, now that he was leaving, as much as he had loved it on that first morning when he sat with Rasmussen and the Breton captain in the great vaulted room in the Grand Oriental Hotel. Then slowly he dipped his paddle again into the warm clear water, and at each thrust of the paddle the water sprang up and glittered and sparkled in the darkness in a thousand phosphorescent colors.

"All that color, all that beauty," he thought, "is born of decay—the decay of a million tiny bodies, the death of billions of tiny lives," and he wondered suddenly if from another planet like the moon, the whole earth appeared phosphorescent.

Half-drifting, the canoe came at last against the foot of the great stairway from which long ago priests and warriors, rich merchants and adventurers had stepped into the boats that took them across the once bustling harbor. When he had made fast the canoe, he stood for a moment listening again to the distant sound of the drums and to the sound of the lapping water which always brought him a certain peace. "Water," he thought, "whatever else happens I shall never live away from the sound of water." And as he turned to climb the steps in the house he discovered an extraordinary thing. For the first time since he had lived in the house he returned to find a light in his bedroom. He had given orders long ago to Silas that there was never to be a light because it attracted insects.

Quickly he climbed the great stairway, and as he reached the top he discovered that not only was there a light in the room, but someone sitting there—a woman in European clothes wearing a great picture hat covered with flowers. She sat by the light with her back to the door, looking at the pictures in one of the illustrated London papers which were always on his bedside table, barometers of his own occasional nostalgia for England in which he always found photographs of old friends and acquaintances, out of that other life which was now so far away. They were all going slightly middle-aged now, and pictures of their children had begun to appear in their places. His own pictures, *his* children's pictures, might have been in them, but they were not. He had begun life like all those others, with even greater chances. . . .

While he stood there, cautious, tempted to turn and escape before the woman became aware of his presence, the memory of a half-dozen women out of the years just past went through his brain, the woman left behind in Penang, the Russian woman in Shanghai, the wife of the French planter in Indo-China, that odd English girl in Calcutta. Which one of them had followed him all the way to Nivandrum and how had she got here? There had been no boat, and the first of the bi-weekly trains arrived only the next morning. It was perhaps the Russian woman. She was romantic and over-emotional and was given to wearing large hats covered with flowers.

Then the excitement stirred in his blood, the old excitement which had never brought him anything but complications and troubles, and he knew that it was impossible to go away without discovering who the woman was, and he knew too, that if he stayed, the venture was almost certain to end in scenes and complications and perhaps tragedy. As he moved the woman heard the sound of his footsteps, and springing up as if terrified she turned toward him and he saw that it was none of the women out of his past, that it was no European woman at all, but Maria herself, and his heart gave a sudden leap.

She was trembling and leaned on the table as if she were going to faint, and suddenly he saw that the extraordinary hat was not a European hat at all, but simply an old hat of coconut fiber such as the women wore when working in the rice fields, and that the flowers which adorned it were not artificial ones, but real clusters of jasmine and bignonia, bougainvillea and jacqueranda. She must have seen a hat like it in one of the illustrated papers at some moment when she had come to see Silas and he himself was absent from the house . . . she must have come alone to his bedroom when he was not there . . . she had copied it from the picture of some dowdy woman opening a bazaar. The effect was charming, naïve and a little comic, like the European dress of cheap cotton which she must have made with her own hands, laboriously. She must have dressed like this for his sake.

And then he noticed another thing. The whole of the great Spanish bed had been strewn with flowers. They lay everywhere, trumpet flowers, jasmine, bougainvillea, even on the floor about the bed, their thick perfume filling the room, flowers which she herself had gathered out of the exuberant abundance of the islands.

At the sight of all the flowers and Maria, shy and frightened in the absurd frock and hat, a lump came into his throat and he could not tell whether he meant to laugh or to cry. It was a curious emotion and he did not deceive himself. He was weeping for himself . . . that anything so simple and so lovely should have happened to him after so many years of disillusionment and despair.

It was the girl who spoke first. In a low voice, scarcely more than a whisper, she said, with a kind of simple dignity, "*Sahib,* I have come to you."

He smiled, a smile which women liked because in spite of everything, of all his selfishness and falseness and treachery, it was at the moment it happened, a real smile full of tenderness and emotion. Then he moved toward her and put his arm about her so that in her terrible shyness she would not have to go on looking at him, and when he touched her she began to cry like a frightened child. For a long time, in silence, he held her close to him,

[351]

and with her young body, trembling, pressed against his, he saw suddenly that in spite of everything, in spite of his own misery and indecision, there had been a meaning in his coming to Nivandrum. There had been a reason why on that first morning he had been compelled to stay, without even going back to the *Vivandière*, to bid the ship farewell. This was something which had happened to few men, for it was as if, shedding all that tired and cynical world of his youth and young manhood, he had fallen into Eden. If nothing again ever happened to him, it would not matter. . . .

At last he held the girl at arm's length and looking at her, said, "I like you better in your *sari*."

The girl smiled and said in her odd, funny English, "I thought you didn't like my *saris*. I dressed like this because I thought you would like it. I thought it would help you."

The expression "help you," was a kind of revelation. He thought, "Then she knew all the time how I felt. She thought I was afraid. She knew it."

She repeated, "I thought it would please you. I'm sorry."

"You are a good girl," he said quite simply. "I love you."

"I love you too. You're not ashamed of me?"

"No, I'm not ashamed of you. And you mustn't call me *sahib*."

"What shall I call you?"

He had meant to say simply, "Tom," but something would not let him and he found himself saying, "Dantry."

Then he put out the light, and for a long time there was only the sound of the lapping water and the distant thumping of the drums dying out one by one as the moon slipped down into the sea and silence crept in among the islands.

When the broken-down, narrow-gauge train left the next day for the burning plateau and the great cities beyond, it went without him, and when Rasmussen heard that he had not gone, he said nothing, even to Léah. He remembered her saying, "*If* he goes," and again he was a little terrified of her.

9

He did not leave the next day or the next or the next and slowly, in the animal charm of days and nights with Maria, Nivandrum, with its island and backwaters and ancient houses and mountains came to be what he had dreamed on that first morning long ago when he came ashore. In it he found forgetfulness and a kind of peace the existence of which he had never known or even suspected until now. It was a peace in which all the memories, the remorse, the regrets of another life faded until at last they no longer had any existence. It was like a dream produced by certain drugs. And now and then, at rare moments when he awoke for a moment and tried desperately to see himself, he thought, "It is killed. It is dead. I have escaped at last."

There was nothing save Maria and the sun and the moon, the stars, the water and the mountains. Not even Sandy made any difficulties, for when Dantry went to see him, ashamed and filled with a desire to make amends, he found that the fat little Cockney was pleased. At first this astonished him, but when Sandy talked to him he understood.

"It is perfect now," Sandy said. "Now you won't go away. You'll stay. And Maria is happy and so I am happy. You'll be good to her. It is better for her than taking a fisherman for a husband. Perhaps some day you will want to marry her, but even that doesn't make much difference here. Even if you were married to her it wouldn't mean that you'd stay here. You could always run away. It's a good life. You'll never find a better one. It's better than Europe."

It was, Dantry thought, much much better than Europe. It was better than anything he had ever known, now that he had lost himself, that self born and bred and educated in another world. He began to forget even the existence of Europe, reminded of it only by the bundles of London news-papers and the illustrated weeklies which went unopened for days, and the gramophone records from New York which sounded strange and yet extraor-dinarily like the music of the drums at night among the islands. He began to wear a *sarong*, and sometimes on days when he went fishing with Maria beyond the Great Bar he did not even wear a *sarong*, but only a loin cloth, and presently he became the same color as the café-au-lait fishermen, burned by the sun and the sea spray. But he did not begin to take drugs and even the desire to drink left him, for there was now no reason to stifle conscience and memory.

But Maria still called him "Dantry," and she never came to the island to live in the house. She still lived with her brothers and sisters in Sandy's compound and came to him only when he sent for her. And so he managed to keep what he liked of his old life intact, a thing apart from her and Sandy and Rasmussen—all the music and the books and the life of the spirit, all the things which none of them, he believed, could ever comprehend.

Thus, he thought, he might preserve his dignity. Thus he might save himself from the degeneration which overtook other white men who tried what he was doing. It was, he knew, a wise plan, but also it was a plan which at moments he knew was a little less than human, moments when Maria was unhappy because there was a whole part of him which he ex-cluded from her passionate, self-sacrificing, worshipful love. He knew, too, that Maria was shamed before all Nivandrum because he did not take her into his fine house with the piano and the gramophone, but kept her outside like a concubine. It was not that she complained or even betrayed her unhappiness by her looks or manner. He was her Lord whom she worshiped and his word was law.

And so he found a way at last into that world for which in his soul he had been forever searching; a world in which he would be given everything and he need give only what he saw fit.

One year passed and then two and then three, with nothing to interrupt the selfish perfection of his existence, nothing to disturb the days spent partly in sport, partly with reading and amusement, partly with Maria, and presently the old life, all of Europe, everything of the past, faded into insignificance. He had found what he wanted. It would, he believed, go on forever. Even the memory of Alix, and all the bitter regrets associated with her, returned to him less frequently. He had, he sometimes thought, cheated Fate itself. He was not drinking any more. He did not take drugs. He had cheated the classic legend of the white man in the East.

There were not even any children, any "eight anna products," to destroy his pleasure and fill him with remorse. That this filled Maria with shame and regret did not at first occur to him, and when it did occur he did not allow the knowledge to trouble him, any more than he allowed her unhappiness at living always in Sandy's compound to trouble him. It was not that she ever complained or deliberately made him aware of her unhappiness as a western woman would have done, and so, after a time, he found it easy to be insensible to her unhappiness. He did not love her, but he was fond of her and he was kind to her, so long as the kindness cost him nothing. And at last the thought came to him that he might as well marry her, since he meant never again to leave Nivandrum, and it would bring her a new dignity of position which would compensate for her unhappiness over her apparent barrenness and her exclusion from his house. Marriage would give her face among the people of the islands and it would cost him nothing.

So the marriage was arranged and took place in the Syrian Christian church by a rite which was half pagan and half a part of the ancient ceremony of the Church of Antioch, a ceremony which he found charming in a literary way; and afterward Sandy gave a great feast, to which half the people of the islands were invited. Mees Opp was there, for Maria had arranged that the ceremony be held during one of the brief visits of the woman doctor. The doctor saw her hundreds of patients during the morning and attended the ceremony and feast in the afternoon, drinking vast quantities of beer and making jokes with everyone save the bridegroom.

It was an odd thing that he had never got on with Mees Opp. Again and again he had tried to become friendly with her. It seemed such an easy thing to do; she was so friendly with all the natives. But nothing had come of it save a few polite speeches. There was something disturbing about her; there were even moments when he felt that she was as unfriendly toward him as the witch Léah. It was as if somehow in all their contacts, in every conversation, she left him "outside," as if she existed in another world into which he could not enter, almost it seemed that he was a little boy and she herself was as old as Time.

But at the feast even the detachment of Mees Opp did not trouble him. He was aware of her presence, full of kindliness and good humor, beloved by all the people; that there was neither real friendship nor real enmity between them did not disturb him, for he was happy now in a new way, because at the wedding feast he found that the people of the islands accepted him for the first time as one of them, as they had long ago accepted Rasmussen and Sandy. He ate and drank with them, seated on the sand. When he returned to his own island with Maria, their canoe was escorted by dozens of canoes and *wallum* boats filled with friends and neighbors.

That night, with Maria at his side, a married man, he lay awake for a long time and he thought, "At last it is all right. At last I have lost the past. At last I belong here."

But in the morning Maria went back to live again as before at her father's compound, and she still called him not "Tom" but "Dantry." Again he had cheated circumstance and Fate. He had become one of the island people and he had kept his dignity. He had taken what he wanted and gave only what cost him nothing. He was neither a beachcomber nor a remittance man. And that night he did not send for Maria, but went instead to play cribbage at the Grand Oriental Hotel with Rasmussen.

Only Léah had not come to the wedding. Pretending illness, she stayed away, and when Rasmussen chided her she said, "I am sick. I have a bad head. Why should I go? What good this marriage? Inside his heart he hasn't changed. He's got a use for us all. That's all. His heart is the same evil heart."

"Evil?" said Rasmussen. "There's no evil in him."

"He is one who brings unhappiness."

"Rot!" said Rasmussen. "He wishes evil to nobody."

"People can make great evil without wishing it. Sometimes the worst evil is made like that. They can make evil just by being what they are."

She hated him worse now than when he had first come to Nivandrum, because somehow he had outwitted her and undone her spells. He wore a *sarong* and had a native woman, but somehow he had not taken to drink or to drugs. He had not become degraded. She had hoped, and even planned, that by this time he would be a drunkard, living in squalor, his character gone, his end in sight. Léah had a strange feeling that he had cheated her and the River God, that he had charms of his own that were stronger than hers.

So on the night after the wedding, when Dantry came to play cribbage, Rasmussen almost at once caught her making desperate signs and incantations

[355]

behind Dantry's back, but he could not stop her because at that moment he had just told Dantry that Lord and Lady Groton with a secretary, a valet, an *ayah* and four servants were on their way to stay at the Grand Oriental Hotel, and the news had produced an extraordinary effect upon his friend.

Before he had finished speaking Dantry looked suddenly very strange and said, "Lord Groton! You're sure that's the name? Lord Groton? It can't be. He's in Europe. There must be some mistake."

"It's typewritten in the letter," said Rasmussen. "It's from his secretary; Eric Lansbury is the secretary's name. There can't be any mistake. Look!"

He passed the letter to Dantry and Dantry read it through not once, but twice without speaking, and the curious hard, mirthless grin changed the look of his whole face. He said, almost as if to himself, "Why is he coming here? Why is he bringing his wife to a place like this? It must be a dirty business of some kind."

Rasmussen, watching Léah, a little uneasy now about what she might do, saw that she too had noticed the change in Dantry, had forgotten her incantations and was now watching him. Her dark eyes had become small, and their gaze concentrated as if they were not watching the body of Dantry but looking inside him at his soul.

The letter was short and direct and written on Government House paper. It merely said that Lord and Lady Groton were coming to Nivandrum for a short stay, and that their party would need at least four bedrooms and plenty of servants' quarters. The secretary wished to point out that Lord Groton and especially Lady Groton were accustomed to the best and most luxurious hotels and that it would be appreciated and the proprietor would be rewarded properly if the rooms were as clean and as comfortable as possible. It also requested especially good food, and at the end there was a postscript which read, "In case there is a good *shikari* in the vicinity, Lord Groton would be interested in some shooting. Lady Groton is interested in native dancing and would appreciate it if you could arrange to have an exhibition by some local dancers."

There was an arrogance in the letter which angered Dantry as he read it. Particularly there was arrogance in the postscript which assumed that the world existed only to provide Lord and Lady Groton with luxury and entertainment. The word "native" brought a sudden flush to his face for now it struck suddenly home. It also made him see and understand the secretary as clearly as if he had come into the room himself—an echo of the world he had nearly forgotten.

"It ain't any Ritz," said Rasmussen, "but it's clean and Léah makes good curries." Then he noticed Dantry's face again and said, "You know them?"

For a moment Dantry was silent, thinking, and then he said, "No, I don't know them. Perhaps they are just coming for the shooting."

[356]

"Sandy hasn't heard from them," said Rasmussen. "Nobody ever comes here for the shooting. If they were coming for that they'd go to the hills to Rankotah. They sound like swells."

"They are," said Dantry. "Perhaps the last swells in Europe."

This appeared to frighten Rasmussen. "Maybe," he said, "they'd be more comfortable staying with you. You'd know what they like."

Dantry laughed, a rather nasty laugh. "Oh, no, I'm not entertaining distinguished visitors. Anyway, why should I cut you out of a small fortune? Clean them, Rasmussen. They're rich as Croesus."

Rasmussen put away the letter and they began to play cribbage, but Dantry played badly and there were moments when he seemed not to know what he was doing, and a little before eleven in the middle of the game he pushed back his chair and said suddenly, "It's no good. I'm too tired, I can't keep my mind on the game."

When he had gone Rasmussen said to Léah. "He seems upset by the news. You'd think he'd be glad people like that . . . people of his own class . . . were coming to Nivandrum."

"Yes," said Léah, "he was never tired like that before." And set about putting out the lights.

Rasmussen put out his pipe. "Maybe," he said, "this swell is coming because they're going to do something at last about opening up the harbor again."

Léah did not answer him. When he had gone upstairs she went quickly out of the hotel to the landing stage, unfastened a canoe and set out for the island with the ruined hut and the image of her god.

10

Halfway across the lagoon in his canoe, Dantry knew that his peace had come to an end. If Groton was coming to Nivandrum it could only mean the destruction of the place. And that she should be coming with him was unbelievable, now after nearly fifteen years, when he had thought himself free of her forever, when at last he had found peace. It was unbelievable, he kept telling himself; it couldn't be happening. She couldn't have heard that he was here and have come because of that. Perhaps she was divorced from Groton and this was a new wife, a strange woman who was coming with him. But that couldn't have been or he would have heard of it long before now in *The Times* or the *Telegraph* or one of the illustrated papers. People like them couldn't keep out of the newspapers.

Hysterically he thought, "I'll go away. I'll take Sandy and go up to the hills until they're gone again. I won't see her. I won't talk to her." And once more he thought, aloud now, speaking the words in a kind of wonder, "It's not possible. Such things don't happen. I'll go away. I'll go away."

[357]

But when he was a little more calm, he saw that the whole thing was more than possible. There weren't many places left in the world to be exploited, and forgotten Nivandrum was one of them; Groton, the great exploiter, the great destroyer, must have got wind of it.

All that night he lay awake tossing in the heat until the last sound of the drums had died away, until the jackals ceased their howling, until at last the sun came up behind the high blue mountains, for all the old memories of her had claimed him again with a terrible force he had never experienced before, and he saw suddenly that all his life in Nivandrum had been nothing, only a bitter negation in which there had been no reality, a kind of makeshift, a drug. But most of all he was afraid, of what he did not know, but he thought, "I should not have boasted that I had cheated Fate." He kept repeating, half-aloud now, "I'll run away. I won't see her. I won't," but all the time he knew that he would see her, that it was the thing he wanted most in the world, the only thing. Nothing had changed the old desire.

II

Two hundred miles inland the narrow-gauge train bearing Lord and Lady Groton moved across the burning plateau toward the high mountains which sheltered Nivandrum from the heat of the interior and kept the rains from the southeast for the narrow strip of wet green coast. There were in the train seven third-class carriages filled with farmers and shopkeepers, pilgrims and *sadhus* and men who simply wandered from one part of the country to another, picking up a living where they could. They were all packed together, some on seats, some on the floors, the children perched on the laps of the adults. The carriages, baked by the sun and the heat which rose from the rocks and scorched barren red earth, were like ovens, the smell of them was staggering. There were two luggage vans, one containing the usual articles of commerce, and the other nothing but the trunks and hat and boot boxes of Lord and Lady Groton and their suite. Ahead, near the engine, where the smell of the rest of the train would not reach them, were three first-class carriages which had been converted into private cars. Here traveled Lord and Lady Groton with Lord Groton's secretary and valet, and the *ayah* who replaced Lady Groton's maid, Harris, left behind with malaria, and four bearers.

In one of these three carriages Lord Groton lay on the bed, half-naked, drinking brandy and soda, with a great packet of papers spread across his barrel chest. Now and then he shuffled the papers about and added a figure here or took away another there, but all the shuffling and jotting brought no order to them. In the heat his brain whirled round and round inside the hard, massive head; the brandy and soda sent up his blood pressure and made his face even more purple and apoplectic than it usually was. It was a large, fleshy face which, unlike most fat faces, was unpleasant and ill-humored, perhaps because of the thin, almost lipless mouth and the square hard angle of the jaw. It was a face upon which was written by the age of fifty-four the whole of his career—not a very nice career, in which ruthlessness and cunning, dishonesty and even cruelty had played large parts—from the time he had left a day school in Birmingham, plain Albert Simpson, son of a small building contractor, to this moment when, as the rich and powerful Lord Groton, one of the kings of the West, he rode in a miserable carriage on a second-rate, narrow-gauge railway across one of the hottest and dustiest plains in the world.

Although the sun had set long ago, the heat of the day still clung to the carriage, so that the metal was hot to the touch and the very sheets of the bed seemed to be filled with heat. The dust crept in everywhere, red, silky, hot dust, fine as powdered talc; it came in beneath the doors, through the ventilators and even through the fine screening that covered the windows. It lay in a film over everything, a film which on the floor was an inch thick, stirred into movement by the current of the fans. It lay on the sheets and covered his face and half-naked hairy body. It turned the papers on his chest all soiled and gritty, so that the movement of one bit of paper against another set his teeth on edge. It fell on the melting block of ice in the basin on the floor and turned quickly into a thin trickle of red mud that was like blood.

It was not the heat, he told himself, which muddled his brain. Damn it! What was heat to Albert Simpson, who, as a young man, had sold cutlery and cheap watches and clocks all over the Sudan, Malaya and India? And it wasn't the brandy, he told himself. What was brandy to Groton, who had drunk as much as he wanted all his life without any harm?

Tortured, with the taste of the awful red dust in his mouth, he told himself that at fifty-four he was still young, as strong, as healthy as ever. He kept telling himself over and over again to still the small, gnawing suspicion that he was no longer young and was a little ill. Illness was something he had never known and he could not tolerate even a suspicion of it. But in spite of anything he could do, in spite of repeating assurances, of making a vast effort which seemed to burst his head, the small terror remained and the papers grew more and more muddled, and the figures out of which he meant to wring new wealth and fresh power, only danced and grew blurred before his bloodshot eyes.

The truth was that Lord Groton was no longer the bull-like young Albert Simpson who had flourished in the gridiron heat of the Sudan, and that alcohol had begun to devour him. In the beginning he had drunk without evil effects, and then presently he had drunk because his brain only functioned when saturated with fumes of alcohol, and now it had got beyond that; the alcohol, instead of helping him, only muddled his head. For thirty-two years he had worked like a dynamo; now, far from home, from his great house in Sussex and the beautiful house in Hill Street, the mechanics of the dynamo had begun to rattle and squeak.

Presently, when he could bear it no longer, he pounded on the wall of the carriage and shouted, "Bates! Bates!" and in a moment the door opened in a whirl of dust and his valet came in.

He was a thin little man with a narrow, undernourished face and high cheekbones, and a skin that seemed forever damp. His eyes were of no color at all. At sight of him his lordship pulled himself up in bed and shouted, "Where's Lansbury?"

Without raising his voice, without changing the expression of his face, Bates answered him, "Asleep, sir, I should think."

This seemed to enrage his lordship. "Asleep!" he shouted. "Damn it, why is he sleeping? *I* can't sleep. Tell him to come here."

"Very good, sir."

"And tell one of those black devils to bring more ice for the basin."

"Very good, sir."

Bates withdrew and delivered his various messages with calm. He had been with Lord Groton for twelve years, which was four years longer than any servant, or secretary, or partner or employee had ever been with his lordship, because either Lord Groton dismissed or betrayed them or they left, their nerves shattered, their self-respect destroyed. But all the shouting and abuse did not disturb Bates, because as insulation against it he had for his lordship a fine thin coating of pure, distilled hatred. And he regarded himself as a machine, and there were moments when he found himself feeling superior to his master, moments when he betrayed him without being discovered. He had made a neat little fortune by accepting bribes, and he was a secret member of the Communist party and hoped for the day when men like his lordship could be stood against a wall and be shot in cold blood. Sometimes Bates thought about this, imagining the scene and picturing himself as the Communist who gave the order to fire. It would be, he thought, like exterminating a plague-carrying rat.

For Bates, like most ignorant men and fanatics, had a single-track mind. Already he had laid aside quite a fund during the twelve years of his service, and within a year he would have enough on which to live for the rest of his life, in a semidetached villa, with a small garden, in the suburbs of his native town of Manchester. When the last necessary shilling had clinked into his postal savings account, he would pack his bag and walk out of his lordship's service without so much as giving notice. His lordship would ring the bell and bellow for Bates, and Bates would simply not appear; it was a scene which in imagination provided Bates with a great deal of pleasure—his lordship preparing for a large capitalistic banquet and at the last moment no one to dress him. He regretted that he would not be there to witness it. In the meanwhile he both pleased and exasperated his lordship, simply because he was a machine. He pleased because as a machine he was absolutely efficient, and he exasperated because as a machine he was beyond being hurt or humiliated.

The secretary, Mr. Lansbury, came in when he had put on a dressing gown with a scarf to match tied neatly under his rather weak chin. He was a pink-cheeked, good-looking young man, whose whole appearance, even in pyjamas and dressing gown, cried out, "Eton, Oxford, and the best clubs." As a secretary, he was conscientious and uninspired; he would not have kept his place for fourteen months if he had not been efficient. He had been engaged because his father was a gentleman, and being very hard up, had begged Lord Groton to take him on; the kindly old gentleman had been made to beg, with tears in his eyes, before Lord Groton agreed. The boy had been kept on because he was Eton and Oxford and the best clubs and a great many other things which Lord Groton was not and never could be, and because the boy was overbred and sensitive and could be made to suffer, and because Lord Groton had been born Albert Simpson and educated at the Laburnum Road Grammar School and the University of Hard Knocks.

Now Groton bellowed at Lansbury, "How can you sleep in this heat?"

Flushing the young man answered, "Sorry, sir. It must have been because I was exhausted from all the difficulty over the luggage."

The older man grunted and shuffled the papers, gritty with dust. "Well, I've got a lot of work to do and I can't make head or tail of your reports. Sit down."

Lansbury, still flushed and trembling a little, sat down in the chair beside the bed, and together they went over the papers and figures while Lord Groton forced the aching head of the boy to do the work of two heads, one of them muddled and a little drunk. He drank more and more brandy to wash the burning dust from his throat. There was nothing wrong with the reports; they were neat and efficient, but Groton's brain was unable to grasp their significance.

Two hours later, when poor Lansbury's patient explanations had failed to make the figures any clearer, Lord Groton put up the papers, sent the secretary away and for half an hour experienced genuine terror for the first time in all his life. He was afraid that he was breaking up at last, and that now, when he needed them most to pull off a coup against the man he hated most in the world, his strength and energy were failing him.

For that was the reason he, the great Lord Groton, was bound on a second-rate, narrow-gauge, upcountry train, through the heat of the Great Plateau. He must get there first and look over the ground and buy or lease everything that was loose before Hugo Deakin even suspected what was happening. The tip that brought him to Nivandrum had cost a fabulous sum, enough money to have ruined the character and conscience of at least three government servants, who otherwise would have been honest and conscientious. "Every man," he was accustomed to say, "has his price," but the price of these three government servants had been out of all reason. He had paid them each enough to found a fortune and leave their children provided for when they died. He had very likely ruined them, and it had cost him more than anything in the world, except his own wife. The money did not really matter, for he was so rich that from day to day he did not know whether he was a million pounds to this side or that. It was the principle of the thing. He hated being done. If he succeeded, the price was worth it, for he wanted to humble, to outwit a younger man, as ruthless as himself, who the world said was more clever, who was slowly passing him on the way to the utmost heights of money and power. He, Groton, had to beat out Lord Deakin and own Nivandrum and the burning plateau above it before Deakin ever discovered there was oil in the burning desert, and that the government meant to clear the silted channel of the harbor and make of Nivandrum once more a living city and a bustling port. And he had to go to Nivandrum to see for himself, lest something be wrong and he make a fool of himself. Because he pitied any man who trusted him he himself had never trusted any man.

When the moment of terror had passed, he chuckled in anticipation of his triumph, of the articles in the papers about his victory over Deakin—that damned clever Deakin—and the talk that would go about the city. Again he would be the admiration and envy of all the little men who hoped that one day they, too, might be Grotons or Deakins. And then he chuckled at the knowledge that the world thought he was at this moment upcountry in Burma, shooting—Burma, where there wasn't another drop of oil or a teak tree or a laborer left to be exploited! And all the time here he was slipping across the hot plateau on his way to a forgotten place called Nivandrum. He had no idea of what Nivandrum was like nor what the Grand Oriental Hotel would be, but it did not matter to him who, long ago, as plain Albert Simpson, had slept in dock sheds and native huts and eaten lizards and flying foxes.

And then when the terror had passed, he thought of his wife in the second carriage behind—damn it, there was no corridor on the train—and decided he would go to her when the train stopped at the next station. He had need of her just now; there was something about her, a calmness, a certainty which always restored his weakened confidence. He thought of himself always as a man of hard common sense, but there were moments when it seemed to him that he was simply a giddy fool in comparison with her. And lately she had come to be a kind of obsession with him, as she had been long ago in the

[362]

beginning, when he had snatched her out of the brilliant life she was leading in London. "Brilliant" was a word he liked; his wife, to him, was brilliant, despite her aloofness, or perhaps because of it, and the life she had led then was "brilliant." The fact that he, a dull businessman, had been able to snatch her out of a brilliant life filled with clever, fashionable, fascinating people left him, after nearly fifteen years, still a little breathless with astonishment.

Lately she had become once more infinitely desirable, as if that period when he "had grown used to her," had never existed. He could not see that she had changed at all save that she seemed to have grown finer and more delicate, like a steel knife which has been worn fine by much polishing and sharpening, and that now instead of withdrawing from him she accepted him, not with pleasure perhaps, but at least with indifference. If he loved anything or anyone in the world it was his wife, and he loved her, although he had never quite thought it out, for the same reasons that made him hate poor Lansbury—because she was everything that he was not and could never be. Unlike Lansbury, she belonged to him; she was a possession in which he took great pride as he took pride in his horses. Whenever they entered a great restaurant or a drawing-room he was aware that her beauty, and her air of distinction created a mild sensation, and the knowledge always filled him with a wild surge of pride. Lansbury could escape, but she *belonged* to him. Yet about her he had bad spells of terror, when it seemed to him that for all his pride in her, she had never belonged to him at all, not even in the moments when he embraced her; that no matter how much money he poured upon her, she had always managed somehow to elude him. But the knowledge did not dampen his ardor; on the contrary it seemed to kindle it, so that now, at fifty-four, it was stronger than ever.

But he thought, too, "Perhaps I feel like this about her again because I am growing old or because I am going to die." And quickly he told himself, "But that is nonsense. I'm in the prime of life. I have never been stronger." It was not a nice spectacle for himself or anyone else—the spectacle of Lord Groton facing the possibility of the grave, to which he could take neither his fortune, nor his power, nor his wife.

12

At the first station after Bates had left his lordship, he got down, and, pushing his way through the crowd on the platform, he knocked at the door of Lady Groton's carriage, calling out, "It's Bates, me lady. Is there anything you want?"

The *ayah* opened the door and Lady Groton called out, "Come in, Bates." She was lying back in the silken sheets with which she always traveled, and as he came in she put down the book she had been trying to read. It struck him how miraculously cool she appeared—the only one of the whole party who did not seem hot, red-faced, dusty and disheveled. She seemed utterly undisturbed either by the heat or by the screaming that went on outside the carriage, as cool, as calm as if she were lying in the luxury of her own bedroom in Hill Street. And he thought, as he was forever thinking each time he saw her, how pretty she was, and how ageless and what a look of race she had. He did not think of her as a man might think of a desirable woman; that would have been disrespectful, and, in any case, it was not in his nature. He thought of her rather in the abstract, as an authority on Chinese art might consider a wonderfully fine Ming vase, of her fineness of bone, the clearness and easy straightforward gaze of her blue eyes, the somewhat faded gold of her hair and the perfect, almost insolent beauty of the gesture with which she raised the cigarette to her scarlet lips. Above all, he liked her perfect and undisturbed, undisturbable elegance.

He liked, too, the way she spoke to him and even to that strange, dark, half-savage woman, the *ayah*, whom she had known for only two days. He liked to think of the generations, the centuries which had gone into her look of race, the quality of her voice and her manner, for in spite of his communist leanings, he liked ladies and gentlemen. Once the thing he referred to as "Boorjoy" civilization was destroyed, there would be no more room for them, but while it lasted he liked having them about. It gave him pleasure to see that she was luxuriously comfortable. He made it a point to see to it that the gilding of the frame which inclosed her should never become chipped or tarnished.

"I thought," he said, very respectfully, "that with 'Arris away you might want a little attention."

She smiled and gave him one of her warning looks—a look which seemed to say, "We understand each other. We both know his lordship and what a scoundrel he is." Aloud she said, "You might find one of the boys and tell him to fetch some more ice. And bring me a brandy and water—plain Evian water with no ice in it."

"Very good, my lady."

"Cold, Bates, but no ice in it."

He withdrew, and while he was preparing the brandy and water he continued to think about Lady Groton. She still fascinated him, after twelve years, because there was always something mysterious and unpredictable about her. He knew, if not everything about her, a great deal, much more than she imagined he knew, just as he knew vastly more about his lordship than his master ever guessed . . . enough, indeed, to have sent him to jail unless he bought himself off the way very rich crooks had a way of doing under the "Boorjoy" régime.

[364]

He knew about her flirtations and friendships and he suspected her infidelities, but he had never spoken of these things to anyone, not even to 'Arris, her maid, because somehow he had always felt a desire to protect and shield her, not only against others, but against her own husband, and sometimes, in her folly and unhappiness, against herself. It was always puzzling to him, when he "studied" the question, why she had ever married Lord Groton in the first place, and he had never been able to find out why she had done it, beyond a hint or two dropped by old 'Arris, lying ill now in the hospital in Madras. Old 'Arris had been with her since she was a little girl, and once or twice 'Arris had dropped a hint or two about the past . . . that she had married Groton because she and her father were swamped with debt. And that there had been another man, long ago, at the time of the marriage, a man who was her own age, attractive, handsome, well-bred like herself. But that, Bates gathered, had gone badly because both of them were too high-spirited. They had quarreled and he had gone away from London, and so far as 'Arris knew, he had never come back. Sometimes, it seemed to Bates that 'er ladyship was the victim of a vast indifference, born of her unhappiness, that she no longer cared what she did or what happened to her. It was a pity, too, he thought, as he mixed the brandy and water, when she was so pretty and nice, and such a lady, and so many men would have liked making her happy. If she had never been unfaithful to Groton, thought Bates, it was a great pity. A woman like her needed love and protection, not just money, which was all Groton gave her—in vast, staggering quantities.

13

When the train pulled out of the station, Lady Groton, because it was too hot to sleep, went on trying to read her book. It could not be said that she actually *read*; she looked at the words, and now and then an idea, not always a very sound idea, it seemed to her, transmitted itself from the pages into her brain. It was a book called *The Colour Problem of the Empire*, and was written by a Cambridge professor who had never been farther from England than Étretat, where he had once spent a rainy week-end. There was no gainsaying the dullness of the book, and even to her untrained but keen intelligence, it seemed singularly vain and inept.

She had bought the book in Port Said, along with many others of the same sort, because she wanted to know about the countries whither she was bound with her husband, but beyond facts and statistics and somewhat moldy theories, she had found nothing in them to help her, and since her arrival three months earlier, she had learned very little at first hand, for it had been, it seemed to her, quite impossible to establish any contact with the people who lived in those countries. It seemed to her that she had spent all her time at pompous dinners and receptions, which had no reality, and that she was forever surrounded by her own countrymen, who were as ignorant of the country as herself, people whom at home she would have avoided like a plague. She had come to the East not because of devotion to Lord Groton, but because she had hoped that something would happen to her, something tremendous, which would excite and stimulate her and make of life something more than a succession of days to be got through. And nothing had happened, nothing whatever.

Now, hopelessly bored by the book, she fell to watching the *ayah*, and suddenly she felt a fierce desire to establish some contact with the woman, not as mistress and servant, but as woman to woman. In her heart she knew, out of her long experience as a *femme galante*, that neither race, nor color, nor creed, nor social station made people different from each other. She knew, as she knew so many things by instinct, that she and the *ayah* in the corner were both women and that in the tests of passion or disaster they were alike, and the rest was mere nonsense, a kind of veneered prejudice laid upon the surface of dull and stupid people by false education. That much, at least, her "badness" and unhappiness had taught her. That much nearer to reality she had been brought by it.

The *ayah* had no interest for her as a maidservant. She was stupid, untrained and more of a nuisance than a help to her, but as a woman, a fellow human, she was a subject of passionate interest. What was her life? What did she think? Had she a husband or a lover? With what bright hopes had she started life? Had all the *ayah's* life, like her own, been one long process of disillusionment?

So presently she lighted another cigarette and fell to studying the woman who squatted at the far end of the carriage, fascinated a little by the mystery and the strangeness that separated them, a mystery and a strangeness which had been imposed upon them by other minds, by stupid traditions. "My world is dying," she thought, "it is dead already. Perhaps the whole of Europe, the whole of the West is dying. That woman and her people are healthy. They have a past, but it is so remote that it has ceased to count as reality. Our past is still too near for us to have a future. We have to die before we can be reborn and we are not yet quite dead."

The woman was not ugly. She must, Lady Groton thought, be about her own age, thirty-seven or eight. She looked older. "She is not lucky like me in that way. I look no age at all. I might be anything you'd want to call me. I am not very changeable. I have bought all that security with the thousands of pounds I have spent on dressmakers and hairdressers and *masseuses*. She can't buy such things, but she is healthier than me and in her soul not so tired." The woman must have had many experiences. She wore a *sari* of some dark purple cloth, with a great many silver bangles, and set in the side of her nose was a single brilliant.

Presently Lady Groton said, "Laksmi."

The *ayah* rose at once, all her silver bangles jangling, and Lady Groton said, "No, I don't want anything. Don't stand. I just wanted to talk to you."

Shyly the woman squatted again, waiting.

"Are you married, Laksmi?"

"Yes, *memsahib*, twice."

"How twice? I thought widows could not remarry in your country."

The woman smiled, a humorous, almost malicious smile, as if she had outwitted someone who had meant to do her harm. "I got converted. I got a Christian. I got a divorce from my first husband. He was bad mans."

"How was he bad?"

"He beat me and ran after other women and took the money I earned."

"And your second husband?"

A relaxed, almost sultry look of pleasure came over the *ayah's* dark face and Lady Groton thought, "She's in love with him—lucky girl."

"Very good man, *memsahib*," said the *ayah*. "Very handsome man. Mahratta. *Chuprassi* at Government House."

"Does he mind your working like this?"

The woman grinned. "Don't go with any *memsahib* . . . just now and then with *burra memsahibs* like you, to please Governor's lady. I make money, too. Save money. Going to buy land in his village."

"And your husband . . . he's Christian, too?"

She laughed. "No. Bad Hindu. Mahrattas all bad Hindus. Too wild. Like me bad Christian. Never go church or temple." She grinned and this time the grin had no shyness in it, but a kind of friendliness, as if she were saying, "Me just like *memsahib*. Know *memsahib* has good heart. Temple church not matter when peoples have good hearts."

"Tell me all about your life," said Lady Groton. She had forgotten the cigarette and was listening now, charmed by the humorous, mischievous quality of the woman. *The Colour Problem of the Empire* had long since slipped to the floor to lie there, forever forgotten, even the next morning when they left the train.

The *ayah* began to talk, no longer shy now, but pleased to gossip with another woman. She said she came of a low caste and was born in a village on the great burning plateau, and was married when she was thirteen to a man she had never seen before. For ten years she endured being his wife, and then the handsome *chuprassi* came along, and the last child she had wasn't her husband's but the *chuprassi's*. Her husband and the *chuprassi* quarreled over her (and again her face lighted with pleasure and became suddenly beautiful) and the *chuprassi* won, and then he told her about becoming a Christian

[367]

and getting divorced and so she did. She went on and on, embroidering the story in her pidgin English with sly touches of humor and wit so that Lady Groton was amused and charmed and forgot all about the heat, and when she had finished, she fell abruptly silent and sat watching Lady Groton with dark, shining eyes. Waiting, it was as if she said, respectfully, "And now, *memsahib*, what about your life?"

But that couldn't be. "My life," thought Lady Groton, "would probably shock her. Her story is perfectly natural and simple." So she said, "It's a very interesting story, Laksmi . . . not so different from the stories of a great many ladies in my country."

Then the train drew into another station and the deafening noise began, made by the vendors of pineapples and sweets and Mohammedan and Hindu drinking water. Lady Groton said, "I won't need you any more to-night. In the morning wake me at the first station after it is light. I want to see the country."

The *ayah* rose and smiling, salaamed with another tinkling of bracelets and anklets and withdrew. When she had gone Lady Groton felt more cheerful, for it seemed to her that this was the first time she had had a human conversation in three months, a conversation which was not either official mouthings or simply a wordy grovel at her feet because she was the rich wife of Lord Groton and a goddaughter of the old Queen. She felt much less alone in this vast and terrifying country. It had all been extremely dull and boring, as if she were wrapped round with cotton wool to protect her and keep her from knowing the truth about anything. The *ayah* had made her feel human.

Then suddenly she felt an emotion of regret, almost of self-pity, which was like a physical pain. She, the rich Lady Groton, wife of one of the most powerful men in the West, felt a sudden envy of this humble native woman, to whom life was so exciting and satisfactory. And she thought, "If I had married Tom my life would never have been like this. I wouldn't have been so rich, but whatever we did would have been exciting. I would have been happy like that woman."

But it was far too late for regrets now. She did not even know what had become of poor Tom, so charming, so full of life and naïveté and excitement about living. And with a little stab at the heart she remembered herself, indeed saw herself suddenly as if she were another person, as a girl just after the war. She saw again the cottage near the sea with the faded chintz and herself—such a nice young girl, too—and Tom muddling together with inexpert hands to prepare the breakfast. What had happened to Tom? What had all those years done to him? Was he bored, too, and tired and utterly fed up?

In the middle of the reverie she became aware presently of something outside the window of her carriage, something which was large and white and bulky, standing quite near among all the vendors of pineapples and water and rice cakes, and as her gaze focused itself, she saw the figure of a very big and ugly woman dressed in a plain suit of white drill and wearing a large straw hat covered with ribbon and flowers, faded by the dreadful sun of the country. There was something extraordinary about the figure, some permanent, eternal static quality, like that of a monument, which held her attention. The woman carried two small handbags and stood very quietly in the midst of all the pushing and shouting of the crowd. The face was rather flat and broad and the skin muddy, but even by the lights of the station platform, Lady Groton saw that the eyes were extraordinarily blue and alive with intelligence. In one of them there was a cast.

And then the Eurasian stationmaster came up to her and bowing elaborately he said, "I've found a place for you, Mees Opp," and the big woman moved away toward the third-class carriages, those dreadful, hot, reeking carriages filled with beggars and *sadhus* and native women and babies. And all at once she felt a wild desire to step out of the carriage and go and find this strange, big, ugly woman and talk to her as she had just talked to the *ayah*, Laksmi, to find out what she was like, and what sort of life she had. She even felt a half-hysterical desire to be a friend of hers, a little perhaps, because it would help her to break out of that world of enchantment surrounded by wealth and luxury and dull people, in which she lived, isolated in a way from all reality.

Then even above the clamor on the station platform, she heard the voice of her husband shouting at Lansbury, and she thought, "He's got poor Lansbury in there torturing him because he can't sleep. When he's finished with him, he'll come in here to annoy me with his attentions."

She thought of him with a slight shudder, for his loutish clumsiness; but the shudder did not endure; she had grown used to him long ago, so that his embraces no longer troubled her much.

Presently she put out the light and lay back on the silken pillow waiting, and with her pale gold hair and her blue eyes she was, even at thirty-seven, like a lovely child. At the next station, she knew, he would come in and wake her.

14

The *ayah* came faithfully to rouse her soon after dawn, saying, "Very pretty country, *memsahib* . . . all green, not dry like my country." And the look of friendliness was still in the woman's dark eyes while she poured the tea.

When she looked out of the window she discovered that the narrow-gauge train was winding back and forth down the steep mountains toward the sea, and it seemed to her that after the high, burning plains she must have died in the night and was now waking in Paradise. The air was still warm, but after the burning dryness of the plain it seemed fresh and cool. Here there were no burning rocks and baked red soil, but only green everywhere—the thick, lush green of mountain jungle still glittering, where the long rays of the sun struck it, with the drops of an early morning shower. And the air was filled, not with dust, but with the rich odor of growing life and the scent of flowers and spices and rich, damp decay. It was green and damp like the England she loved, the England to which she always returned, her heart full of contentment. As with most sensual people there was in her some secret, mysterious affiliation with dampness and water, so that in deserts and hot, dry places she became frightened and a little mad.

Below the train, the damp valleys still lay in deep blue shadows, and as she watched the enchanting scene, forgetting even her tea, she thought, "I was right to come out here after all. Perhaps I shall be comfortable and at peace in this place," and she experienced an odd sensation of having returned home, to a place which she knew very well. She forgot suddenly all the heat and dust and boredom of the past week, and even the tipsy, messy visit of her husband the night before. But she did not consider whether she would be happy, for happiness had long since ceased to play any great part in her existence. "At any rate," she thought, "it will be a half-savage, primitive place, and at least there will be some fun in that."

And then the train came round a bold thrust of the mountains and below her suddenly outspread like a glorious map lay the whole harbor of Nivandrum, dotted with its seven islands covered with coconut palms, set like a jewel in the maze of lagoons and canals inside the reefs and bars along the coast that sheltered the harbor from the storms of the Indian Ocean. Beyond the mouth of the choked harbor the fishing boats, their great ragged sails filled by the morning breeze that came from the mountains, were rushing like a flock of swallows across the great bar and the line of foam which marked it.

For a moment she did not breathe lest the scene suddenly vanish like something she had dreamed, and leave her once more in the heat and dust of the horrible plain. In her weary spirit peace and excitement were born side by side. And then, like a sudden pain, the thought of Lord Groton returned to her. She thought of him vaguely, not as a man but as if he were something detached, which hung over her and all this lovely country like a black unspeakable menace. He was on this same train coming down the green mountains toward this lovely harbor, like a bird of prey. He would destroy all this. For the sake of money and more for the sake of power, he would build ugly piers and oil tanks and sheds roofed with corrugated iron, and the lovely green water would soon be covered with oil, and the fish and the sea birds would die, and the simple people would become corrupt and diseased, and he would be proud of his small, spiteful victory over a rival as vulturine as himself.

At the foot of the mountains the train came to flat ground and ran for a time between rice fields, and green islets, and there for the first time she saw the people of the lovely coast, poling the *wallum* boats or working up to their waists in the water of the flooded rice fields, nearly as naked as Adam and Eve had been long ago in another paradise; and the sight of them brought to her a new interest and a new vitality as the sight of beautiful people always did. They were not small and thin and tough like the people of the hot plains, but tall, with rounded arms and legs and muscles beneath a smooth skin the color of pale café au lait.

And while she watched them as they turned smiling from their work to regard the train, a strange thought came to her, "I could do it. He would never need to know. It would even all sorts of old scores. It would be so easy to send a cable to Deakin about what he is up to. I could tip off his bribery. I could make a scandal that would rock London and ruin a whole government. But more important than all, it might save this lovely place from desecration for a few more years."

Then the train crossed a little causeway and halted unexpectedly beside a small, ramshackle station, and hastily she rose to dress herself and arrange her hair and remove the last vestiges of the dust of the hateful plains. By the time she had finished she heard the husky voice of her husband and the rather piping voice of poor Lansbury giving orders to the servants. When she got down she found that the train, like a caterpillar lopped in two, had lost half its length during the night. There were only the first-class carriages in which the party had come, and one broken-down, third-class carriage, out of which came an old woman and a child. And she felt a thrill of delight that Nivandrum was a dead city to which no one came, that it remained forgotten, secret, lovely.

At the same time she saw coming toward her a short, grizzled man with bright blue eyes wearing a white yachting cap with the label, "Grand Oriental Hotel," in gold letters just above the peak. The sight gave her a sudden pang of disappointment, that here in Nivandrum you should be received exactly as if you were arriving in Cannes by the Blue Train. She guessed that the man was the proprietor and she thought shrewdly, "He looks well fed and good natured and contented. The hotel should be all right." But she could not know that Rasmussen's cap was simply a bit of swank made in Colombo, which he had reason to wear not more than once or twice in a year, when some rare and eccentric visitor came to Nivandrum by train.

Rasmussen took them in his own boat, poled by two boys, children of the people she had seen from the train in the fields and on the little boats, tall, straight boys, who wore nothing but a little cloth about their waists. There was no disappointment for her, neither in the lovely boat with its carved prow and stern nor in the look of the islands, with the pale old baroque houses set among the coconut palms. She had not expected these houses, pale green and yellow and pink, deserted and empty, and at the sight of them she thought as Tom Dantry had thought five years earlier, "I must have one of them." It did not matter if she had to return to that other weary world in the West; it did not matter if she should die without ever seeing the house again. If she had a house in Nivandrum—one of those pale, ghostly houses surrounded by water—it would bring her peace. She would always think that something of her remained here among the green islands. In the midst of great deadly dinner parties she could suddenly think, "I always have that house in Nivandrum," and she would feel cool and young again. And almost at once she remembered that her husband had come here for only one reason—to destroy Nivandrum, to turn these houses into store-rooms for cheap cutlery and cotton and oil.

All the way she was silent, sitting just inside the palm-thatched roof of the boat, so that her eyes might drink in every beauty. She was very silent. Even when Groton said in his husky voice, "Pretty place, isn't it?" she only replied, "Yes, but too picturesque," because if he knew how she felt about it, he would be jealous of the place—he was as fantastic as that—and would hurry through his work and go away. If she remained indifferent, he would take his time. She might even induce him to go shooting in the mountains. She wanted to stay; it seemed to her at that moment that she would not mind staying here forever, doing nothing, the rest of the world forgotten.

When the boat suddenly came alongside Rasmussen's pier, she felt yet another happy shock of surprise. She had dreaded the "Great Oriental Hotel," thinking it might be some awful structure like the railway hotels one saw everywhere in the East.

"Here we are," said Rasmussen, hopping on to the dock, and at sight of the hotel, she wanted to cry out with delight, for it was one of the loveliest of the ghostly old houses, brought back to life, set on its own small island with a lovely garden surrounding it. But again she held her peace, lest her husband discover her secret delight and spoil everything.

Inside the great cool hall, where Dantry came sometimes to play cribbage with Rasmussen, she asked for a gin and tonic, and sat at one of the tables alone, while her husband bustled and snorted about, seeing rooms, making plans for boats, giving abrupt orders with poor Lansbury, pale and perspiring, at his heels. She sat looking out of the wide-arched door at the harbor with the little boats moving back and forth, and suddenly a strange thought came to her. It was in reality less a thought than a sensation, for by habit she thought through her senses, by her instinct. It occurred to her suddenly that she was happy, and happiness meant peace. It was as if she had come to the end of a journey which had gone on for days and months and years. And then her husband was standing beside her, red-faced and sweating.

He was saying, "It's all right. The rooms aren't bad at all. No plumbing, but they're big and cool and comfortable." He was, she saw, groveling and apologetic, afraid that the simple comfort of the place was not good enough for her.

She scarcely heard him, thinking that it did not matter what the rooms were like, and then, pulling herself together, she said, "I'm glad," and she saw for the first time that he looked ill. His face was purple and there seemed to be a film over the cold blue eyes. She thought, with a sudden leap of the heart, "Perhaps he is going to die. Then everything will fail and the place will be saved, and I can stay here and have a house and come back to it when I like. I can even come here when I am an old woman and there is nothing left."

Her instinct was right again, for death was there in Nivandrum, waiting for him, but not the quiet, swift death for which her heart cried out—the death that would be better for him as well as for herself.

15

The coming of Lord Groton's party brought more excitement to Nivandrum than the annual arrivals of the ships, and all during the afternoon and early evening of the first day, boats and canoes circled round the Grand Oriental Hotel and its tiny island, a little way off the shore, their occupants eager for a glimpse of the great lord from the West, or some of his party. If they attempted to land or came too near, Léah rushed out from the kitchen and ordered them away, and they obeyed her because even the least superstitious of the lot were afraid of her evil reputation. A few did manage to come ashore on the pretext of business with Rasmussen, offering for sale cucumbers and gourds, chickens and passion fruit and mangosteens, and from the window of her bedroom Lady Groton watched them come and go, amused by the color of the spectacle and pleased that her presence should have excited so much interest. In the room itself, the *ayah* came and went, bringing bits of gossip and information collected belowstairs, about Nivandrum, unpacking, chatting, excited by all the new sights and by the greenness and beauty of a place so different from her own country. Her shyness was all gone now. Since the hot night on the train she felt that the *burra memsahib* was her friend. She talked to the men and women who came selling things, with difficulty because their language was so different from her own, and told them fantastic and exaggerated reports of the wealth and importance and beauty of her mistress. "A woman of milk and gold," she told them, "beautiful as the moon in its first quarter." By evening her stories had penetrated up and down the lagoon and even to the more remote islands.

The sightseers were treated to a view of Lord Groton himself, in shorts and shirt made by a Hanover Square tailor, bustling about red-faced and perspiring, making arrangements for boats and boatmen and studying the harbor through his glasses, and they had glimpses of the fair-haired, pink-cheeked secretary, whose clothes were of a cut even smarter than those of his lordship, and they saw Bates still dressed in the discreet, dark clothes he wore in cold, damp London, apparently unmoved by the heat, pale, and suffering as always from low blood pressure; but they had no glimpse of Lady Groton, and so by evening she had already become a kind of legend created largely by the *ayah*, Laksmi . . . a lovely princess of great fragility, who appeared only after the sun had gone down into the sea.

In the evening, when Lord Groton came in to dress for dinner, he entered his wife's room while she was dressing.

He seemed in a good mood and said, "Not a bad place, really, quite comfortable, and the food's a lot better than some we've been treated to."

She saw that he was thinking of staying on for a time and needed only a little encouragement, so she said, "It's hot."

"Better than the heat of the plains. Of course, if you can't stand it, we'll leave as soon as I've had a look around."

She smiled. "Oh, it's not as bad as that. I think it's a good deal more pleasant than most places we've been. At least there aren't any bores here to sit next to at dinner. I have books. I shouldn't mind staying awhile."

"It's a long way from Cannes and the yacht."

"The lunch wasn't bad. The curry was excellent."

She knew, as she made up her face with infinite skill and taste, that he was watching her. In the mottled glass of the cheap dressing table she could watch his face while pretending to concentrate upon her own, and she noticed that he was watching her with that queer, concentrated, hungry look with which he had watched her long ago, when they were first married, a look which always set her teeth on edge, not so much from distaste as from sheer boredom—that any man could be at the same time so worshipful, so full of desire and so deadly uninteresting. And she hated being stared at as if he were trying to get beneath the smooth, perfect surface in order to discover what she really was . . . she, who did not really know herself from hour to hour, from minute to minute.

She was thinking, "If I could only get him to go away for a time, I might be able to rest and enjoy this place." So aloud she said, very casually, "The

[374]

proprietor tells me that there is excellent shooting in the hills . . . tiger, panther, sambur and bison and the Lord knows what else."

"He told me."

"And there's a first-class *shikari* . . . a Cockney called Sandy who has been out here for twenty years. Quite a character, I believe."

Suspiciously he said, "Would *you* like to go shooting?"

"You know how I detest 'characters.'"

Then for a time he was silent, suspicious and jealous, still trying ponderously to discover what was really going on inside her head. Was she trying to be rid of him? There couldn't be any man in the offing but Lansbury, and he could fix that by taking Lansbury with him. Anyway, that was ridiculous. She couldn't be interested in a pink-cheeked boy with an Oxford accent, who wasn't dry yet behind the ears.

"I shouldn't mind being left here," she said, leaning forward and putting rouge on her lips. (Perhaps if I am left alone here, something might happen to me. Something exciting. There's nothing to be afraid of. Nothing could happen to me that would be unbearable, and anything is better than this awful dullness.)

Aloud she said, "Anyway, it's lovely and cool as soon as the sun goes down. A breeze comes up from the sea. The proprietor says the nights are always cool." She turned and asked, "What are your plans for tomorrow?"

"I'm going off early down the lagoons. I want to discover the lay of the land. If I only had a launch I could do the whole thing in a few hours. I should have ordered a launch to meet me here."

She smiled. "And have someone tip off Hugo Deakin?"

He laughed, amused and pleased again at the fast one he was pulling over on Deakin. "I could have had it ordered in a false name. Anyway, we haven't any launch, so I shall have to be away overnight . . . for only one night. You won't mind, will you?"

"No, of course not."

He watched her more sharply now and said, "I shall have to take Lansbury with me. That'll mean you'll be left with only Bates, except the natives and this Rasmussen I know nothing about."

She rose and turning, looked at her reflection in the spotted glass, thinking how well she looked and how young. On the burning plain and in the great, steaming cities, she had looked haggard and tired.

"What should I be afraid of?" she asked. "What could happen to me?"

"What do you mean by that?"

"Nothing." (You fool, if you'd only go away, something *might* happen to me.)

"No, I suppose there isn't any danger. Bates will look after you. He'd give up his life if necessary to protect anything belonging to me." And he laughed in a smug way which made a shudder of hatred run up and down her spine.

She thought, "How can a man be so shrewd about money and such a fool about people! Bates would protect *me* if I wanted protection, but he wouldn't protect anything else belonging to you. He hates you. You're a fool not to have discovered it before now." And aloud she said, "Don't worry about me. I think I'm going to like this place very much, so take your time about your work. It's as good as a cure. Perhaps we shan't have to go to Freiburg this summer after a week or two here. Anyway, you might tell Lansbury to get me a boat of my own and a couple of boatmen so that I could go about seeing things."

"It's been done. The boat will be here every morning at nine to await your orders."

Then there was a knock on the door and when Lady Groton said, "Come in," Bates thrust his head in the door and said, "Me lord, the bath is ready. I had quite a little trouble getting them to understand that you like lots of hot water."

A little while later they sat opposite each other at a table in the great vaulted hall eating a dinner of soup and prawns and curry, salad, vegetable drumsticks and a pudding—an excellent dinner, for Rasmussen, wisely or not, had repeated to Léah what Dantry had said, "Clean them. They're as rich as Croesus," and Léah meant to keep them there, plucking them, as long as possible.

The old-fashioned wireless supplied a sputtering concert of café music from the Hotel des Indes in Batavia, and Rasmussen, his porter's cap exchanged for an ill-fitting suit of white drill, served them, retiring discreetly after each course to a little distance according to the instructions of *The Waiter's Guide and Instructor*.

"If only we had ice," said Lord Groton, "it would be perfect."

She looked at him and again she saw the queer glazed look in the cold blue eyes, and after a moment's calculation, she said, "Lucky they haven't. You'd drink a lot more. And you shouldn't drink so much in this climate." (Now he'll take two or three extra drinks just to show me that Albert Simpson, Lord Groton, the Superman, can drink as much as he likes without any harm; and his blood pressure will go up again.)

"Rubbish," said Lord Groton, and asked Rasmussen to bring him more soda for another drink.

When dinner was finished, he said, "I've ordered the boat. There's a new moon. We might take a little turn about the harbor before going to bed."

(To make me feel romantic, I suppose.)

"Yes, it would be lovely. I'll go and fetch my coat."

Half-drifting, the boat carried them as the tide rose, among the seven islands. It seemed to her that at night the place was even more beautiful than it had seemed in the early morning light, with the new moon above the palm trees and the distant sound of the drums and the dusky bodies of the boatmen shining a little in the pale light. But when Lord Groton said, "Almost as beautiful as Venice," she answered, her nerves on edge, her whole spirit hungry, "Almost as banal."

And then as they drifted back across the channel between the Grand Oriental Hotel and the nearest island, she heard above the faint rhythm of the drums, the sound of European music, played on a piano, quite a good piano. It came across the water, faintly and in snatches, but clearly enough for her to recognize it as one of the Chopin nocturnes, and she thought, "What perfect music for a night and a place like this!"

"Listen!" she said to Lord Groton.

"Yes, what?" He was a little annoyed at being interrupted while planning a spot to build the oil tanks. They would have to be near deep water but isolated on account of the insurance rates. Tomorrow he would go over the charts with Lansbury, while they were on their way down the lagoons.

"Music."

"Oh, that!"

"It must be a European," and she tried to keep the excitement out of her voice.

"It's a wireless."

(You fool, I know the difference. It's coming from that house over there . . . the one opposite the hotel with the beautiful stairway down to the water. What a lovely house!)

"It's probably coming all the way from Madras or Singapore."

Then through the great arched windows of the house she discovered the evidence of her rightness. There *was* someone playing a piano, a man, but he was not a European. He was naked to the waist, and by the dim light from the old-fashioned lamps his skin seemed very dark, but he was playing Chopin and playing it not too badly; there could be no mistake about that. It was very odd. She wanted to tell the boatman to alter the course of the boat and go nearer to the house, but she did not know the language, and almost immediately she was thankful that she had not spoken, for that would have made Albert suspicious of the house and the musician.

Turning a little, she kept watching the house until the boat had passed it and she could no longer see the man playing Chopin.

"Perhaps," she thought, "something is going to happen to me after all."

When they had returned to the hotel, she made an excuse to stay behind in the hall, and to Rasmussen, who was waiting for them, she said, "Who lives in that house on the next island . . . the one with the great stairway?"

Rasmussen made a great effort to collect himself, for he was a simple, truthful man to whom lying was not easy. After an extra breath or two, he said, "A rich half-caste, madam. He's a little daft. He never leaves the island." That was what Dantry had told him to say.

"Does he play the piano?"

Rasmussen stammered, "Oh, yes, yes. He plays the piano."

"Funny that a half-caste should own a piano and be playing European music."

Again Rasmussen choked. This time he had to improvise. "But he was educated in Europe, madam."

"Thank you. Good night."

As she started up the stairs, Rasmussen recovered himself a little and said, speaking out of *The Waiter's Guide and Instructor*. "I beg your pardon, madam, but I've engaged some dancers. They can come tomorrow night if you like."

"That will be all right."

"Lord Groton won't be here."

"That doesn't matter. He wouldn't be interested." And she turned and went up the stairs, leaving Rasmussen confounded and a little angry because she seemed always so abrupt and so casual. It had been a long time since he had seen a woman like her. When he thought about her, carefully and laboriously, he could not remember ever having known any woman quite like her. For a moment he was sorry that she had ever come to the Grand Oriental Hotel, even if she was rich as Croesus. There was something disturbing about her, something which alarmed him more than he had ever been alarmed by Léah.

Abovestairs in a little while Lord Groton came into her room, but he went again in half an hour, and after he had gone, the wind, having changed a little, brought the sound of the piano fitfully into the bedroom. It came faintly, now vanishing, now returning, always against the dying sound of the drums. Lying in the darkness, striving to hear, she found in it something decadent and corrupt . . . the music of Chopin against the barbaric sound of drums.

In the morning she wakened to a sound of murmuring, a little confused, wondering where she was and how she had come there, and then after a moment she remembered the journey down the lovely mountains and the sight of the harbor after nightfall with the drums and the Chopin and she felt suddenly happy to be alive, consciously happy for the first time for months and years. Beneath the window the murmuring continued and presently, filled with curiosity, she pushed back the nettings, rose and crossed the room to look out. Beneath her window there was a great crowd of people of all ages and sexes, murmuring and talking together, and in a half-ruined little summerhouse before a table filled with medicines, sat the woman in the white drill suit and the extraordinary hat whom she had seen two nights before on the station platform on the dusty plain beyond the mountains. The quality of solidity, of eternity, still marked her, as she sat there, taking temperatures, chatting, making jokes as one after another the patients —old men and women, sick babies, pregnant women, passed before the table. And again the idea came to Lady Groton that she would like to know this big ugly woman.

"She must be staying at this hotel," she thought. "She must be a doctor of some kind. When I go down I will speak to her. She will be able to tell me all about the country."

But by the time she had had a bath, and coped with the blunderings of the *ayah* and made up her face and dressed and gone downstairs, the woman had gone. Rasmussen said, "She's a very busy woman. She has to visit two more villages before sundown."

And again Lady Groton felt regret, why she could not say, but she had an odd feeling that something had passed her by, something the quality of which she could not define. And she thought, "Perhaps she is in my destiny. Perhaps that is why I noticed her." But almost at once she laughed, thinking, "Soon I'll be getting mystical and having my horoscope done and trying to find a *guru*."

17

Tom Dantry had not gone away. In the house on the island he was waiting, in indecision and weakness, trying to find a compromise by which he might still remain and even see her, somehow perhaps from a distance, without ever letting her discover that he was in Nivandrum. All the first day he waited, impatiently, watching the hotel from time to time through his glasses without ever having a glimpse of her. And in the evening when he could not sleep he played the piano until long after midnight, hoping to lose himself and discipline his spirit by the music.

It was extraordinary how the memory of her was still able to disturb him, how he kept seeing her still with an extraordinary vividness and clarity after so many years. It was extraordinary, when he considered it, how there was some fate which had linked them together since the beginning, how it was Groton, her husband, who had separated them in the beginning, who brought them together again now nearly fifteen years later, again to destroy something which he cherished. Groton, it seemed, was meant by God to be his enemy.

And then the next morning he saw her, quite early before the heat had

come up, drifting in a *wallum* boat in the channel which separated the hotel
from his house . . . the boat poled by an old fisherman called Raniji and his
equally decrepit brother-in-law. When he recognized them it struck him as
odd that she should have chosen the oldest and ugliest boatmen in the place
where so many young and handsome fishermen were available. Then he
thought, "Perhaps Groton chose them. He can't really be as bad as that. He
couldn't insult her in that way."

She was half-sitting, half-lying on a pile of coconut mats, dressed all in
white, wearing a broad-rimmed hat of white straw. A dark woman, perhaps
an *ayah* from her dress, squatted near her. At first he could not see her face
because of the hat, and studied her body, clad in the most expensive and
simple of Paris clothes. What she wore, he reflected, must have cost enough to
have supported a whole family in Nivandrum for a year . . . the stockings,
the perfect shoes, the dress, the expensive hat. Then she turned her head, and
with a little leap of the heart he saw again the lovely pure line of her throat
and the oval of her face, and noticed that she had scarcely changed at all.
There was still about her that rather childish look which had always disarmed
him, and in her face the same expression almost of innocence and purity.
He thought, "How has she accomplished it? What has she done in order to
keep herself so intact, so unchanged?" And he saw that she was as desirable
as ever, perhaps more so with the wisdom and the experience which must
have come to her during all those years.

Then the boat disappeared around the end of the island and he was alone
again, and lost. It was done now. He knew that now, having seen her, his
only salvation had been in running away to the hills with Sandy. And it was
too late. He had to see her now. He had to talk to her, to try to find a little
of that thing which long ago they had thrown away so wantonly.

Then the maggot, that maggot which Léah had divined, began to work,
and he thought, "Weakness, it is. If I were strong I would run away—now
—today, and save this good life I have made with so much wisdom and care."
But another voice answered, "You would be a fool to run away now, after
having seen her. You would never again have peace. And why should you
give up pleasure? Pleasure is the only thing of value in life and the memory
of it is the only thing that endures." And he told himself that it was fate, an
extraordinary, unbelievable manifestation of fate, which had brought about
her presence in the hotel there in sight of his own house, and that to resist
fate was only folly. And another voice said, "Fate is nothing but the combination of one's character with the set of circumstances in which one finds oneself.
The seeds of one's fate are there at birth." If only he were simple and honest
like Sandy or Rasmussen. And all day the maggot gnawed, until in order to
have peace he knew there was only one thing to do.

During the day Silas, coming back from the mainland, brought him the gossip that Lord Groton had gone away and would not return for two days, and that tonight the dancers were coming to the hotel to perform for Lady Groton alone in the great hall.

When he had told the news, Silas said, "I have a message from Maria. She wants to know if she shall come to the island tonight?"

For a moment he was silent, and then quickly he said:

"No. Tell her tomorrow, perhaps, but not tonight. I'll send word." It was a habit now, this carrying of messages between Maria and himself. It was as if Dantry were ordering vegetables from the greengrocer.

Then as Silas turned to go, Dantry said, "Take the night off if you like. Go and see your wife."

"Thank you, *sahib*," and Silas went away.

It was all following the old pattern, as if nothing had ever intervened, as if Silas were not a half-caste boy in dead, forgotten Nivandrum, but the man-servant in the flat in Bruton Street long ago. It was as if he no longer had control over his own will or actions, but was being carried along by something stronger than himself.

The day was interminable, and at eight o'clock he began to dress, alone, for Silas had already gone, and when he was all dressed in the black trousers and waistcoat and smart white mess jacket he had not put on for months and years, a new idea came to him and, taking off all his clothes once more, he put on a purple *sarong*, a singlet, a white drill jacket and sandals on his naked feet.

"That is better," he thought, "that will tell her what I have been doing, what has happened to me."

Then he went into the garden and gathered a great bunch of jacqueranda flowers and going down the steps climbed into the canoe, paddled across the channel. It was quite dark now. She could not see him from her window.

In the big hall, Rasmussen in his waiter's costume, a napkin thrown over his arm, was standing beside a table where one place had been laid. At sight of Dantry, a look of astonishment came into the clear blue eyes. Dantry answered the look before Rasmussen was able to speak.

"It's all right. Don't look so alarmed, Rasmussen. I've changed my mind. Put another place at the table."

"But . . ."

"Don't worry. It'll be all right. Do as I say. If it isn't all right, it doesn't matter."

It was the old voice, the voice which the Breton captain was the last to have heard, a voice of authority, and even arrogance, which Rasmussen out of the far past remembered as the voice of those who have been born with every privilege, the voice of the very rich. It was no longer the voice of Dantry, his friend.

While Rasmussen laid the place, Dantry took from the table the scrubby bunch of flowers placed there by Léah, and put the great glowing bouquet of jacqueranda flowers in their stead. After that he fumbled with the old wireless set until he found music that came this time from Raffles Hotel in Singapore. Then he lighted a cigarette and waiting, shaking a little with excitement, not only at the prospect of seeing her again, but of seeing a woman, any woman, elegant, expensive, frivolous, out of the old life. Through the great archway at the end of the room he could hear above the sputtering music from Singapore, the occasional tinkle of music as the musicians who had come to play for the dancers squatted in the garden trying out their instruments. For a moment he listened to them, and then, shutting off the old wireless, he stepped to the door and ordered them to play where they were in the garden until it was time for the dancers to appear.

A little before nine o'clock she came down the stairs, dressed all in white in an evening gown as if she were going to supper at the Savoy. On one arm she wore three wide bracelets of diamonds and emeralds, and when he saw her he thought, "How bored she must be to have taken all that trouble when she is dining alone!" and then he remembered, digging up evidence out of the distant past, that this was exactly what he should have expected of her, with all her love of elegance and jewels.

She moved slowly, watching the wide stairs before her as if she were afraid of tripping. He had her at a disadvantage for she clearly thought herself alone, and because she thought this, he was able to see her as she was, perhaps for the first time; and he had a quick impression of aloofness and pride and self-sufficiency and weariness which was new even to him who had known her so well. And like a revelation the thought came to him that she had remained lovely and uncorrupted by the years because nothing had ever touched her. She was intact, complete, perfect, a work of art produced by a decadent civilization. He thought, "It's odd. It's as if nothing had ever happened to her."

Then halfway down the beautiful stairway, she raised her head to look at the room and saw him. He was standing by the table and he did not move or change the expression of his face. He merely looked at her, inwardly a little amused to see how long it would take before it dawned upon her who he was. Even when she recognized or thought she recognized him, she would not believe that he was here in Nivandrum in the Grand Oriental Hotel. But she was quicker and more clever than he had believed possible. She saw him, dressed in *sarong*, singlet and sandals, and the languid look of indifference quickened into interest, but without changing her manner she came to the end of the stairs and halted, looking at him again, this time frankly and boldly in a queer, near-sighted way for a long time, for nearly a minute, with

[382]

a look which, by its poise and recklessness, made his heart leap with old memories.

Then suddenly she smiled, the old unchanged smile which out of her sleeping vitality somehow reached out, embraced and warmed you. She said, "So you are the half-caste who plays Chopin?" She came a little nearer and said, "Let me look at you. Yes, it is you. It couldn't be anyone else with those large, suffering dark eyes."

He smiled then and came toward her, a little shy, a little uncertain what to do. Deceived a little by the fact that she looked almost the same as when he had last seen her, his impulse was to kiss her, but quickly he knew that he could not do that on account of Rasmussen, who was watching. So he took her hand instead and as he took it he noticed an extraordinary thing. There were tears in her eyes where he had never before seen any tears save those of anger.

"You were a swine to take me like this unawares. You might have sent word. Don't mind if I feel like crying, only something awful has happened just now inside me." She looked at him again and said, "I don't know what I'm doing. Give me a moment." For a second she closed her eyes, then she asked, as if nothing at all had happened, "What are you doing here, dressed like this?"

"I live here. That's my house on the island over there."

She smiled, "Beachcombing?"

"No, I've still plenty of money."

"Oh, a remittance man!"

"Not that either . . . not quite."

"I've always heard that a white man without a job has to be one thing or the other in the East."

"I flatter myself that I've got away with being neither. I've set a new precedent. With Europe as it is I should think it's a precedent which might become very fashionable."

Again she smiled, this time a little cynically, so that he had a sudden glimpse of the hardness that was new to him. "Perhaps," she said. "Anyway, I'd rather have found you here than any person in the world. You know, it's funny, I was thinking about you on the way here."

"Thanks."

"Don't let's do that. Let's not begin again where we left off."

"All right. What about a cocktail? It'll make us feel a little more natural."

"Yes, it *is* what you might call an extraordinary situation."

"Yes, your coming here."

"But extraordinary things rarely happen to ordinary people."

"Thanks again."

"Well, a thing like this wouldn't have happened if we'd been ordinary. An ordinary woman would have let Albert come alone to a place like this and stayed at Government House and played bridge. An ordinary man wouldn't be standing here now in the Grand Oriental Hotel, tanned as dark as a native and dressed in a *sarong*."

"Native is a word I don't like."

"Ah, so now you've got principles!"

"Didn't I always have?"

"Yes, put away in a cupboard where you never used them except to dazzle dull stuffy people. Then you dragged them out."

"Still the sharp tongue."

Then he told Rasmussen to fetch gin and lime juice and himself made gimlets for them to drink. It was better than he had imagined, far better. There was no strangeness. It was, as she had suggested, as if they had taken up where they left off. They must have changed; it was impossible for two people to have spent so many years apart without changing. Yet the core of each of them was the same. They had struck fire at once, and the old excitement which she, of all the women he had known, was the only one to arouse, was there again. He thought, "Sentimental, may be, but we must have been meant for each other, whether for good or evil."

When the first shock of surprise had gone from her, they felt easy and more natural. When he asked her, with an edge of irony in his voice, "Why is the most noble Lord Groton here?" she said, smiling, "It's a secret. I'm not allowed to tell."

"Money to be made, I suppose."

"Yes, if it works out. Don't sneer."

"It couldn't be that there's a plan to open up the harbor?"

"It might be."

"And he's bought the information in advance."

"Don't go on. I shan't tell you anything."

"I think I've guessed it." His face grew serious for a moment. "That means I'll be chased out of here, just when I was settled for life. I suppose he'll pull down my house and put oil tanks in its place." The sharp angle of the jaw hardened. "Well, for once he's met his match. The island is mine. He'll never get it during his life. I think I'm likely to survive him." His voice raised a little. "You can tell him that from me. He took one thing from me. He shan't take another, not for all his money."

Quietly she said, "Let's forget that. Let's not poison the evening by talking about Albert . . . not tonight, anyway. He's poisoned so many evenings for me."

"So I was right. It hasn't got any better. Time didn't make him decent or you indifferent."

She put down her glass. "If you go on talking about Albert, I shall go upstairs and have my dinner in bed. I mean it. Listen!" She was silent for a moment listening to the sound of the music in the garden against the distant sound of the drums. "Why should we spoil that? You haven't learned a thing about living since I last saw you. You never did know how to squeeze the most out of an occasion."

"If you mean living is a business of snatching pleasure and excitement here and there for a moment or two when it is convenient and opportune. . . ."

"I meant nothing of the sort. You can give me another cocktail and take one yourself. If I remember rightly, after a drink or two you always locked your principles in the cupboard and threw away the key."

He made another gimlet and she said, "The trouble is that you're a Utopian."

"Perhaps."

"You'd like to change the whole world, but you never work at it. When it doesn't change itself, you grow sulky."

"Go on. Abuse me."

"Then forget Albert. He needn't matter to us. He's an outsider. He always has been. That's why he had to make so much money. He had to have some sort of compensation, but he knows he's still an outsider, from everyone and everything in the world. He'd give everything he has—all his money, all his power—for five minutes like this with me, or even perhaps with anyone in the world, even with his own valet. There now, that's Albert. Finished! Done! No more speaking of Albert, the great Lord Groton . . . poor Lord Groton, the most futile and pathetic man in the world."

"He has the power to hurt people and ruin their lives."

But she said stubbornly, "No more talk about Albert. Shall we have the dancers now . . . like a turn in a West End restaurant?"

"Yes, if you like. They'll go on dancing forever until you stop them. They do a kind of dance Marathon."

"Let's have them and go on with our dinner. I'm in excellent health and very hungry. The heat agrees with me."

"The British talk a great deal of nonsense about heat and sun. Look at me. Half the time I live like a fisherman. I've never been harder or healthier in my life."

She looked at him slowly, from head to foot, her eyes closed a little with an air of appraisal. "I must say," she said, "it seems to agree with you. I've never seen you look so handsome. And the *sarong* is very becoming. You looked very handsome last night, playing the piano. I got quite excited thinking that you were a stranger and that I might make a new conquest."

"I hate it when you talk like that. It's cheap."

"You're not going to be jealous of yourself? That would be a little too complicated, even for you, my dear."

"I wish to hell that just for once we could be simple. We talk too much."

"And primitive?"

"Yes, primitive as hell."

"Have you been taking lessons here?"

"Yes, I have, and I'd almost learned my lesson and then you turned up. I was right. I meant to run away and not see you. That's what I should have done."

"Yes, that's what you should have done. Perhaps it would have been better for both of us. But what does that matter? We're having fun now and fun isn't lying about waiting to be picked up. I know."

Rasmussen served the cold soup, his blue eyes wider than ever with astonishment, not only because these two seemed to know each other so well, but because the fragments of conversation that he heard were so complicated and puzzling. He strained his ears because each time he went into the kitchen Léah attacked him hungrily, asking what he had overheard, and he was able to tell her nothing. If he told her word for word it would have meant nothing to either of them. And each time he went into the kitchen he was forced to open the door cautiously because Léah was standing behind it, watching through the little grill.

Dantry said to him, "Tell the dancers to begin. We'll watch while we eat."

Then Lady Groton said, "Have your lessons been a success?" and the simple Rasmussen was a little startled by the look in her blue eyes, a look of hungriness and excitement.

"Yes. Quite."

Then the dancers came in and they both turned to watch.

First came the little band—a man who played the drum, a man who played the harmonium, another who played the lute, and a boy with a violin of the country. They squatted on the floor on the opposite side of the great room, gay and brilliant in their gala costumes, like tropical birds, and then abruptly and without ceremony the two dancing girls came in. They were plump and neither of them was young, for they had been retired by the old Ranee and had come back to live in their native Nivandrum, to live well on the money and the jewels they had begun collecting long ago when they first came out of the temple schools in Tanjore. They were dressed now more gaudily than birds of paradise, in gold and silver and brilliant colors with large headdresses made of real flowers, the sight of which brought a sudden pang of memory to Dantry.

Lady Groton, disappointed, said, "But they're not young and they're not beautiful."

"Wait," said Dantry.

Then one of the dancers spoke to him in the local tongue and he answered her and in turn she spoke to the little orchestra, which began to play. Lady

Groton looked at him a little astonished and said, "You're very clever. What did they say?"

"They asked me what Your Highness—they really said 'Her Highness'—would like to see danced. I told them to dance the Kite Dance, and Krishna and the Gopis, and the Legend of Rama and Sita. They take a very long time, each of them. I think you'll have enough before they finish."

The two dancers took their positions, ugly artificial positions they appeared at first, until suddenly by faint quivering gestures they evoked the beauty of all the statues and carvings scattered through the islands of the East. Watching them, it suddenly occurred to Dantry that it was good that they were neither young nor beautiful because youth and beauty would have distracted the attention from the dancing, from the beauty of the archaic patterns thousands of years old, refined now to the point of decadence. There was no longer even a trace of realism in their dancing, nor any compromise made to lust or desire. Each incident, each action, had become thousands of years ago merely a pattern, a filigree, part of a frieze, exquisite in itself and related to nothing else. It was a pure art, pushed to its ultimate refinement beyond which there was nothing but decadence and finally destruction and at last a new beginning.

Dantry, watching Lady Groton, saw presently that she too understood the beauty of the dancing. She had forgotten to drink her coffee. Her cigarette had gone out, and she sat quite still watching. He had been afraid that she would expect something cheap and be disappointed in the dancers and so in turn disappoint him. In a way it was a kind of test. Long ago he was certain that she would have understood, but now, on this night, he had been unsure and a little troubled.

She had not failed him. She had not lost, in all those years, either taste or understanding and now, sitting beside her, he was again acutely aware of her perfection, her breeding and her poise, of her clothes and jewels, her hair, her grace of manner as she sat, leaning back a little, absorbed, listening and watching. And it seemed to him suddenly that he had discovered the very essence of her existence. He thought, "She is one of the last examples of something which will soon be gone from the world because there is no longer any place for it." She was not, like Groton, a kind of crude fungous growth, sprung up overnight out of the confused ordure of his times; she was the product of hundreds of years of leisure, of privilege and responsibility, of intelligence and feeling and education. And now even the civilization, the epoch to which she belonged, was coming to an end, and there was no longer any place for her or for himself for that matter, and both of them were touched by the decay of something which was too old. They were, he feared, both already rotten at the core. And suddenly he had a vision of

Groton himself, the Samson who was pulling down upon them all the whole structure of their times.

Then the Legend of Rama and Sita came to an end and the dancers stood, perspiring but unwearied, in archaic positions, side by side, one foot placed slightly in front of the other at right angles, awaiting orders. Dantry looked at his watch: it was long after midnight and he said to the dancers in their own language, "That is enough. Her Highness thinks you very wonderful, and will see that you get a rich gift. She would, I think, like to see you again." And the dancers, smiling and salaaming, withdrew.

Lady Groton said, "I should like to have seen more."

"No, that's enough. More would be too much. We'll have them another time. Don't try to swallow everything at once."

She looked at him and smiled, "You might do well to follow your own advice." Then they had some brandy and she said, "I think they're wonderful. If I can do that at their age . . . how old are they?"

"Nearly sixty, I should think."

"I wonder what exercises they do?"

"Do you do exercises?"

"Not yet. But I suppose I shall have to think about doing them one of these days." And suddenly a look of terror and anger came into her face. "I can't bear the thought of growing old. If ever I *feel* old I shall kill myself."

"It is worse to *be* old and *feel* young."

"You needn't have said that."

"No, I suppose not. I know well enough what you mean."

"I'll have another brandy. I'm beginning to feel that the time is growing short and there is so much that I have missed."

"You've drunk quite a lot already."

"Why not? Isn't it an occasion to celebrate? That was always the trouble with you. You only got drunk when you were angry or depressed . . . never to enjoy yourself."

So they each had another brandy and Dantry said, "You must come and see my house. It's quite beautiful . . . built by the Dutch when Nivandrum was still a great port, about two hundred years ago."

"I noticed it. I wanted it for myself."

"What could you want it for?"

"To come to when I'm old. It might be a shade better than suicide."

"It's a lot better, believe me. It's a little like being born again."

She looked at him sharply, and then said, "If you had really been born again, you wouldn't be here now sitting at this table with me. You'd have run away to the hills. You'd have fled from me as from a plague."

"Perhaps."

"No perhaps about it. You mustn't go on forever deceiving yourself."

"What's the use of being unpleasant?"

And suddenly he seemed collapsed and tired as if all vitality had been drained from him.

Then they were silent, hearing the sound of the drums as they died away one by one among the islands, and presently she said, "Why shouldn't I come and see your house now? I couldn't possibly sleep if I went to bed now and it's a lovely night."

For a moment he was thoughtful, the maggot working rapidly inside him. He had not meant to make so much progress in one evening. He had meant to keep her at a little distance. He was not even certain now of what it was that he wanted from her.

She said, "It will be more difficult when Albert comes back. He's such a fool."

He answered her without enthusiasm, a little wearily, for he was frightened.

"Yes, I think it's an excellent idea. I'll take you over in my canoe. We can have a drink and I'll bring you back."

She was aware that for some reason he had turned suddenly cold, withdrawing from her in spirit to a great distance, and the knowledge left her puzzled, irritated, uncertain. For the first time it seemed to her that he had changed, that there was in him something new and strange and annoying.

"I shan't embarrass you by coming?" she asked. "You haven't a woman in the house?"

"No, I haven't a woman." He rose suddenly and said, "Shall we go?"

18

Sitting at the table he watched her climb the long stairway, angry and annoyed at himself because suddenly the savor had gone out of the evening and in its place there was a kind of inexplicable dread, why or of what he did not know. In a little while she returned, wearing a long cloak of purple velvet over her white evening gown. When he saw it he said, "That's not a very good slumming costume. You're not going in a Rolls-Royce to the flat in Bruton Street. You'll ruin it. You may even get a soaking."

She smiled. "It doesn't matter. It's an old one."

"A cloak," thought Dantry, "which from the cut and material must have cost at least fifty pounds." Obviously it was neither old nor worn.

To Rasmussen he said, "Lady Groton is going to have a look at my house. She'll be back in half an hour," and Rasmussen, his eyes still a mirror of astonishment, said (out of the *Waiter's Manual*), "Very good, sir," exactly as if Dantry were a stranger to him.

They walked down the narrow path beneath the palm trees to the landing stage and behind them Rasmussen remained, puzzled and still watching them until they had both entered the canoe and Dantry had shoved off from the shore. When he returned to the kitchen, he found it empty, and he discovered after a little while that Léah was outside in the garden in the shadow of the crotons watching the canoe as it was swallowed up slowly by the darkness which separated the two islands. As she turned and came toward him he remembered sharply the prophecy she had made long ago on the first night that Dantry ever came to the island.

When she came near to him, she said, "That Lady Groton is a bad woman," and from her eyes Rasmussen saw that she hated the English-woman as much as she hated Dantry.

Farther down in the garden, hidden away in a little arbor, Bates, still wearing his dark clothes, smoked his pipe and indulged himself in philo-sophical ponderings on the ways of the people who caused revolutions and Communism. All the evening from his hiding place he had watched her ladyship and the stranger through the great arched doorway, wondering who Dantry could possibly be, until at last unable any longer to control his curi-osity he had gone into the kitchen to demean and humble himself by asking for information from the heathen cook. He could not fathom how her lady-ship was able to become as intimate as her whole manner, her face, her voice indicated. He knew the look she had in her face tonight, and he knew what it meant. He knew the change which always came into her voice. It was always like that, as if suddenly she came alive.

As they crossed to the island Dantry's spirits rose again, kindled by the beauty of the evening and the sound of the single drum which remained out of the evening chorus. The others were stilled now and only the one, accompanied by the thin music of a flute, went on and on, drifting toward them from somewhere on the mainland near Sandy's compound, drawing his thoughts against his will toward Maria, a Maria who only three days ago had filled his life and brought him peace and happiness, a Maria who now, since nightfall, had become simply an ordinary native girl in whom he had no special interest.

In front of him, Alix, wrapped in the purple cloak, lay back in the canoe trailing one hand in the water like a child on a boating party, watching the phosphorescence which sprang up whenever her hand touched the surface. She was silent all the way until he said presently, "What are you thinking of?" and she laughed and answered, "I'm thinking how incredible this whole night is."

At the foot of the stairs he brought the canoe to a stop in the shadow of the big, silent, dark house, and, springing ashore, helped her out of it. While he stood making it fast, she waited, looking about her, her head thrown back a little, breathing in the night smells, so familiar to him, of smoke and jasmine, mangrove swamp and spices. She seemed for a moment to have forgotten where she was or that he was near, for when he had finished fastening the canoe and stood up beside her, she did not move or speak.

He said, "Now do you see why I love it so much? Why I never mean to leave here?"

As if coming back from a great distance, she said, "I see." And then, as if pulling herself, with a great effort, back to reality, she said bitterly, "It would be a pity to let Albert destroy all this peace and beauty."

"Isn't there some way to stop him?"

"I don't know. I have an odd feeling that this place will be the end of Albert. I've a feeling that it's stronger even than the great Lord Groton. I'd like to stay on here forever and ever and never again see that other world." And again suddenly the idea of the cable to Hugo Deakin came to her, only how could you send a cable from a place like this?"

He did not answer her, but instead said, "Let's go in and have a drink."

He led her up the great stairway and halfway to the top she said, "Is there no one here? Is the house empty?"

"Yes, I sent away my boy for the night."

"And the house is all open?"

"No one in Nivandrum would steal anything from me."

She gave a harsh laugh. "That'll all be changed if Albert has his way with the place."

In the long room that was half a balcony he lighted the kerosene lamps and went himself to fetch the drinks, and when he returned he found the room empty and Alix outside again on the terrace as if the harbor fascinated her in some way. She was half-sitting, half-lying on the Indian bed covered with skins and cushions, one foot touching the great tiger skin that covered the floor just beside her.

When she took her drink, she said, "I think you're very lucky . . . and wiser than I thought."

"It had come to the point either of suicide or finding a place like this."

"I can understand that."

Then they talked for a little while, almost shyly, of their life together long ago, and of people they had known then and of what had become of them, and presently they fell silent listening to the sound of the single drum from the mainland. She lay back, with her eyes half-closed, relaxed as if the peace of the night had stilled the restlessness of her spirit. The old excitement stole over him, and after a little time he smiled and looked at her and said, "Are you thinking what I'm thinking?"

At the sound of his voice she came suddenly to life again and gave a low excited laugh, "Of course I am, you ninny."

"You're looking very beautiful tonight . . . you're more beautiful than you were then."

[391]

"It's a long way from the farm in Sussex. We've come a long way since then."

"It's as if it were meant to be . . . something about the whole evening —the music, the dancers, the drums."

Again she laughed, almost derisively now. "Yes, it's all very Elinor Glyn."

"Don't do that."

"Even to the tiger skin," she said, kicking the skin with her toe.

He did not answer her and again she laughed. "Yes . . . all very romantic and unhealthy . . . not a good place for Europeans. It heats the blood. It's too provocative and savage and primitive. So what?"

He crossed the terrace to the Indian bed where she lay among the cushions, but as he reached the divan she slipped down from it and stood up, and even in the soft darkness he was aware that her whole mood had changed, that somehow she was different, as if she had become another person, as if it was Lady Groton now who stood suddenly beside him instead of Alix, the old laughing gay Alix he had once known so well.

She said, "No, it's no use trying to begin over again. We can never get back what we threw away. We're no good, either of us."

And then he too changed. He felt himself changing, growing cold, and detached, as he had changed a little while before in the hotel just before they had set out for the island. He did not touch her. He did not even speak, and she said, "I think I'll go back now. Otherwise they will begin to talk."

He fetched her purple cloak, and as he crossed the terrace he was sharply aware of two things—that the solitary drum was no longer being beaten, and that on the water just off the shore, in the shadow of the island, there was a canoe and in it a solitary watcher. But he said nothing of his discovery because he did not want to frighten her. He felt suddenly exhausted and despairing, as if a part of him had died.

19

It was the habit of Bates to regard all hotelkeepers as natural enemies and all hotel servants as worms beneath the contempt of a gentleman's servant, and so when he arrived at the Grand Oriental Hotel, he behaved as usual, looking down his long thin nose at both Rasmussen and Léah; but after twenty-four hours he reached the conviction that the Grand Oriental Hotel was neither a hotel proper nor a country house but a kind of cross between the two set down in "jungly" country in the East. For a little time the discovery upset him, and then slowly it occurred to him that he might like it and that out of such conditions something of excitement and interest might be born. By the middle of the second day he had even begun to unbutton a little, not the black, correct clothing which he wore, but the jacket of his spirit and curiosity.

By nature he was a spectator, not an altogether unmalicious one, who really disliked the human race and held it in contempt, for he was as much a Methodist as a Communist; and because watching, eavesdropping, intriguing was a passion, even a disease with him, he had a way of discovering the most startling and unexpected things about people. He had all the talents of a blackmailer, and inside his narrow head he kept information, gossip and evidence about any number of rich and important people which could have made for him a large fortune; but he really had no desire for a great fortune and would not have known what to do with it, and so he remained an amateur and a philosopher endowed with a never-waning wonder at the folly and viciousness of the rich world in which as a servant, detached and no part of it, he found himself.

He lived, in an odd way, through other people, for he had a lively imagination and an extraordinary power of projecting his own mind and spirit into the laggard bodies of others about him. All this endowed him not only with the powers of a blackmailer but with something of the attitude of a scientist. There were, for example, times when he imagined himself to be Lord Groton and understood perfectly the motives and actions of his master. That was one of the reasons why he held him in a contempt so profound. And there were times when in a mystical way he *became* Lady Groton, and so understood her restlessness, her unhappiness and that shell of artificiality and indifference with which she had as a protection inclosed herself.

Thus Bates led a life in which there were few dull moments, and the only element in the prospect of retirement to a semidetached villa in Manchester which troubled him was the thought of dropping out of the exciting world in which he had spent most of his life as a servant. It would not be very stimulating to project yourself into the body of the greengrocer who lived in villa Number Eighteen or into that of the clerk who dwelt at Number Twenty-two, unless by some lucky chance one of them happened to be a Doctor Crippen or a Mr. Peace. There was always that hope.

In the beginning he had come to Nivandrum somewhat resentfully, expecting a dull time, for, belonging to the pavements, he detested the jungle and all nature no matter how beautiful, and he saw no excitement in the prospect of projecting himself into the body of a fisherman or a boatman. Immediately on arrival he had initiated an investigation into the character of Rasmussen whom he chose as the most likely prospect on the horizon of Nivandrum; but almost at once he had come to a dead end in disappointment. Rasmussen, he discovered quickly, was just a simple fellow, like most honest, working people, not very bright, with no mystery and no vices. He lived a simple life, it was quite clear, performing the natural functions of a working man in his prime, but simply and directly without any of the complications and the perversities which lent tone to fashionable life. And you could get nothing out of Rasmussen because there was nothing there—no gossip, no good tips, no scandals. Rasmussen, Bates divined, even in the face of the most blatant scandal would simply have been unaware of it. He never *saw* anything. He was what Bates, in his private catalogue, marked off as an "empty."

But Rasmussen's wife, Léah, was a different proposition.

He discovered it almost at once, on that first evening when he had difficulty in impressing upon Rasmussen the importance of quantities, vast quantities, of hot water, ready at all hours in case His Lordship wanted a bath; for His Lordship, as Bates knew, was like Lady Macbeth; he had a kind of obsession about washing himself, as if there were inside him something that he felt might be washed away if only he had enough baths. Sometimes, to Bates's annoyance, he had as many as four a day. "Just like Lady Macbeth," Bates used to think.

When he saw Léah for the first time in the kitchen superintending the cooking of the first dinner, his heart leaped, not because of her handsome face (a thing which had never interested him very much and now interested him scarcely at all) but because of the extraordinary eyes, black and opaque and set a little too near together, and the look about the disapproving mouth. He had divined, almost at once, what no one else had ever discovered, that Léah must have European blood, that she must have had a grandfather or a great-grandfather in whose bloodstream coursed the corpuscles of Mrs. Grundy. She was the type, he saw, which not only was aware of *things* but made things happen, not openly and with violence, but subtly. From the way she looked at him, a little coldly and defiantly, he saw that she was the one for him . . . the agitator type. She would have been a good agitator anywhere in the world. She was, he decided, just his kettle of fish.

He succeeded in wresting from her several more kettles of hot water for His Lordship's bath, and by the time this operation had been concluded, he had also succeeded, by tact and a great display of false meekness and subtle flattery, in making at least a sizable break in the wall of her hostility. He had never quite seen himself in the role of flatterer to a "native," but in this case he made a concession. After all, in this out of the way place, where there was no society, and very little civilization, there would be no one to suspect or discover such an awful lapse.

During the next day he made a point of poking his head in the door of the kitchen once or twice to pass the time of day. He was not even above clowning a little, so that by evening he had even succeeded in winning from the grim Léah the shadow of a smile.

So when the canoe bearing Dantry and Lady Groton had left the hotel in the direction of the island, Bates, still smoking his pipe with an air of reflection, had slowly made his way back from the garden to the kitchen of the hotel. He was suffering from excitement and a curiosity so devouring, that it was like a painful malignant disease. Actually the curiosity, at work all the evening while he spied on Her Ladyship and her friend through the great arched doorway, had given him a bad case of indigestion. If he did not discover something about this stranger from the island —this newcomer whom Her Ladyship had seemed to invoke out of thin air—he knew that he would not sleep at all.

Léah was not in the kitchen when he entered it. He waited for a time, and as he was about to give up the chance of seeing her, she was suddenly there behind him without having made a sound.

He remarked at once that she did not glare at him as ferociously as she had done on the occasion of his first invasion. This, he knew, was the technique of many cooks, even in the great houses in the country in England, for he had had experience with cooks, and had practiced the same methods, on the occasions when he discovered that the cook was the only good source of information in a house.

He said, "What about having a beer with me?"

Léah made a sound that was something like a snort, the faintest ghost of a snort, and said, "I never drink beer," as if she belonged to the congregation of Plymouth Brethren.

"What will you have?"

"Maybe having a bit of grenadine."

So Bates told one of the boys to fetch him a beer and a grenadine and water for Missus, and Léah allowed him to pay for them, for as yet Bates was nothing to her but one of Lord Groton's party which was "rich as Croesus," whoever that was.

"Nice place this," said Bates.

"Yes, nice place."

"Beautiful place."

"Yes, beautiful place."

She sat across the room from him at a small table, aloof, watching him suspiciously as she watched all Europeans except Rasmussen and perhaps Sandy.

"Yes, it's a beautiful place," said Bates. But this time as if she felt that Bates needn't have repeated himself she did not trouble to answer and Bates felt strangely ill at ease. He thought that perhaps if he asked a question things might go better so he said, "Ever get much hotter than this?"

"Getting much hotter in monsoon time."

Bates took another sip or two of beer and came to the conclusion that all this preliminary talk, all this warming up so to speak, was getting him nowhere, so he said, speaking very loudly as if Léah were deaf and he wanted to make her understand, "What's the name of the gentleman who came here tonight?"

"Dantry," said Léah, "Mister Dantry."

"European?"

"Yes, Englishman."

"Live here long?"

"Five years."

"Is he a pretty nice chap?"

"Not nice."

"Oh," said Bates, and then after a minute, "What does he do?"

"Doing nothing."

Again Bates took a reflective sip of beer, thinking again that all this was really getting him nowhere, for he might have answered all these questions himself. What he wanted was to get her talking; that was the only way you found out things—by people giving themselves away, saying things that weren't discreet.

Even her saying "not nice" didn't mean a thing, except perhaps that for some purely personal reason she herself did not like him. She seemed neither resentful nor embarrassed, but sat there opposite him drinking her grenadine and staring at him with such boldness and intensity that he began to feel more and more uneasy. Bates, the watcher, had no liking for being watched. He had a feeling that in this cook he had met his match. At last he said, "Family man?"

"Who?"

"This Dantry."

But this was too much for Léah's English. She said, "What you mean—family man?"

"Is he married?"

"Sure, married—three days ago. Big feast."

Bates unconsciously took a long breath and then said, "European woman?"

"No. Half-caste woman."

"Oh," said Bates.

He took another sip of beer wishing that she were drinking beer too, so that she would become more communicative. Then, while he was trying to find some new method of attack, Léah took the offensive.

"What for," she asked, "you want to know about this man?"

"Nothing . . . no reason . . . just interested."

"What for your master come here?"

"Well," thought Bates, "that is a poser." He had no intention of telling why His Lordship was in Nivandrum, so he said, "Don't know. Perhaps he's going shooting."

"What for lying?" asked the woman and Bates thought, "Well, she's got me beat."

"Not lying," said Bates, beginning in spite of himself to talk pidgin.

"Maybe he come to open up harbor."

This rather took Bates's breath away. Trying to collect himself he said, "Not knowing."

But the woman took her answer from his manner and look of surprise. She simply assumed that he had said, "Yes."

"Better going away again. Shaputra stopping him."

"Who's Shaputra?" asked Bates. "Head man?"

"Big River God. He closed harbor. Wants harbor stay closed."

"Hmmm," said Bates, "perhaps you're right."

Then he took out his pipe and filled it slowly, still disconcerted and made uneasy by her stare. Also he was trying to collect himself and discover some way of getting round her, of making her more friendly. "Perhaps," he thought, "direct attack is best." So he said, "I don't want the harbor open either. I like it much better this way."

She did not answer him and so he said abruptly, "Look here. We ought to get along together. No use treating me like a bloody vulture."

Something, perhaps the fact that Bates with his long head and long nose looked a little like a vulture, made her smile. It was a grudging smile, which emerged in spite of her will. But she didn't say anything, and after a little while he said, "You know a lot of things I don't know and I know a lot you don't know. That's right, ain't it?"

"Maybe right."

"Well, I don't like this place and I don't give a damn whether the old man has come here to open the harbor or not. I'd like to be friendly."

"Me friendly," said Léah surprisingly, without changing her expression. "Liking you too. Right at beginning."

"Well, you'd never guess it," said Bates. Then he smiled too and the woman smiled back at him and Bates, suddenly alarmed, thought, "I 'ope she hasn't taken a bloody fancy to me."

"Well, that's fine," he continued. "You tell me what you know and I'll tell you what I know. How about it? A bargain?"

"Bargain," said Léah grinning.

"Have another grenadine?"

"Sure," said Léah.

[397]

This time, in the new-found intimacy, Bates took his beer across the vast kitchen and seated himself at the table beside her, and Léah, as a token of the treaty between them fetched some damp, stale biscuits, for which she made no charge.

"Well," thought Bates, "this is cozier."

"To tell the truth," he said, "the old man *has* come here to see about opening up the harbor, only it's a secret, see? A terrific, terrible secret."

"Woman making trouble," said Léah.

"What woman?"

"Old man's woman."

Bates wagged his head, and said nothing. So she said, "Dantry no good either," and Bates thought, "Anyway she's no fool. Pretty quick she is."

And he said, "Tell me about this man Dantry," and Léah, trusting him a little now, told him about Dantry in her pidgin English, about how he had come there and stayed and taken Maria and at last married her, how he never allowed her to stay in the house but kept her in her father's compound on the mainland. She told him a lot of other things, small things which she had observed and which to an ordinary listener would have meant nothing at all, but to Bates in his role of watcher-amateur blackmailer, meant a great deal, for they helped him to fill in a great many gaps so that by the time Léah had told the story he had a very good and a very accurate picture of Dantry. "Another one of those," he thought, "that makes revolutions and Communism."

When she had finished he did not ask her any more questions, thinking it better to go a little slowly so that she would not become alarmed and suddenly close up the spring he had just tapped with such success.

He said, "Well, well," and filled up his glass with an air of pondering deeply all she had said.

"What about missus?" said Léah.

"Well," said Bates, "that's a whole story in itself."

After he had collected himself, he told her a little, a very little of Lady Groton's wealth, and her success and how she had her pictures in all the papers, and how Lord Groton was one of the richest men in the world.

"Why she marry old pig like master?" asked Léah.

"Don't know," said Bates. "No accounting for tastes."

"Money," said Léah, and a curious look of hatred came into the queer black eyes so that for a moment Bates was startled and thought, "Mebbe she's one of those evil eyes."

Then for a long time they just sat, Bates rather embarrassed, studying the bowl of his pipe as if it were a new and wondrous object he had just seen for the first time, Léah simply staring at him with an opaque black-eyed gaze, which seemed to bore into him like a gimlet into soft wood.

Certainly, thought Bates, the woman had no social graces; she did not know how to keep a conversation afloat. "The watcher watched," thought Bates. "The joke is on me. She's already got out of me what she wanted to know."

The strain came to an end when one of the boys put his head in the door and said, "*Memsahib* coming home," and Bates rose and said, "Well, good night."

"Good night," said Léah.

"Have another grenadine tomorrow night?"

"Sure."

It was all right. He had won. They understood each other.

He reached the big hallway in time to see Her Ladyship returning. She was alone, wrapped in the purple cloak, looking, Bates thought, as if she were about to step into the Rolls and drive off to dinner, her hair perfectly done, her face made up in that masklike perfection which had been fashionable just after the war. But Bates had been with her too long to be deceived. It was not in such things that you discovered what she had been up to; it was in the eyes that you always found an answer.

So as he went toward her, his own back to the light, and said, "Is there anything Your Ladyship wants?" he watched the eyes, and before she had time to answer him, he thought, "Well, she *is* a fast worker."

"Nothing, Bates, except some lime juice and water."

"It's already by the bed, me Lady, in the stone jug. That keeps it cool when there's no ice."

She said, "Thank you, Bates," and went past him up the stairs and he knew that she had not seen him at all but, like a woman drugged, had simply answered a familiar voice which came to her out of a fog.

Behind them beyond the great doorway, Léah, like a ghost, slipped away through the tangle of bougainvillea down to the landing stage to find her canoe. It was necessary now to see the River God quickly, to give him the blood of a goat, to tell him what she had discovered—that the white men were coming to open up his harbor. It was necessary to invoke his aid against their powerful charms, to find some way of defeating them as she meant, in the end, to defeat the charms of Dantry which up to now had been too strong for her. She knew that it would be an intricate and difficult business because the white men were not afraid of her like the people in the islands.

20

On the mat at the door of her room the *ayah* lay asleep, and at the sound of Lady Groton's footstep the woman sprang up, awake in an instant.

Again as through a fog she was aware of the *ayah* and said to her, "Don't trouble, I shan't need you tonight," for she wanted to be alone. When the *ayah* annoyed her by protesting she said, "No, I don't need you," and then, half aloud to herself, a little to the *ayah*, she said, "Once, long ago I dressed and undressed myself and even did my own hair. I'm not as dependent as that. I don't want you. Understand, I don't want you." The woman looked at her, puzzled, as if she had seen her for the first time, and then held the door for Lady Groton, closing it behind her to lie down once more on the mat like a faithful dog.

Inside the room, Alix lighted a cigarette and undressed herself slowly. She had never taken drugs because it had always seemed to her a foolish thing to do, but she thought, "This is what it must be like." There was a softness, a haziness all about her. Even her reflection in the cheap spotted glass came back to her more dimly, more blotched and mottled than usual, so that when she first looked in the glass she had a sudden startled feeling of terror as if she had been dreaming and was really an old woman who had simply imagined all that had happened to her of beauty and romance since that moment when the train, rounding the shoulder of the mountain, had permitted her to look down upon the loveliness of Nivandrum. Once or twice she thought, "No, it can't be. It can't have happened," and then half-undressed she began to cry, silently, the tears rolling down her cheeks. They were neither tears of sorrow nor of regret, but the relaxing luxurious tears of happiness and pleasure touched by melancholy. She had not wept like this, luxuriously, pleasurably, since she was an hysterical schoolgirl.

For a long time she sat there weeping helplessly, and then presently she rose and went to the window and stood there looking out across the water toward Dantry's house. It was dark now save for the light in his room, and presently that too went out, and with a pang she wished that she had not been discreet and come back to the hotel when her heart cried out for her to remain, to stay there always, never to go back again to the old life. Once long ago she would have done it, but now, she knew, it was not herself who brought her back, the reckless self who once gave up everything for him, but the long habit of years, the habit imposed by the world in which she lived, a habit based upon the rule that it does not matter what you do but how you do it, the rule that you must never be found out. And she knew suddenly how changed she was by those years between, how much of weakness, how much of hardness there was in her now.

She thought, "I could go back now," only there was no way of going back unless, like Leander, she swam the channel. And then an awful thought came to her that perhaps he would not want her to come back.

And she remembered how he had changed suddenly in the hotel and looked at her as if she were a stranger. Perhaps he cherished this solitude he had won for himself even more than herself. Men, she knew, were like that.

"It would not matter," she told herself, "if I went back tomorrow and stayed forever, if I never again left here." But immediately she was frightened at the thought that perhaps it was too late now. Perhaps now she would not have the courage to stick it out. For even in moments like this she was honest with herself; she had been born honest and her life had made honesty a necessity if she were to survive.

"I was a fool then, long ago, and perhaps I am still a fool."

At last, aware with a painful suddenness of the stillness of the night, she left the window and finished undressing. Before climbing into the bed she took a double portion of sleeping draught, not because she needed it, but because tonight of all nights she must go to sleep at once in order not to go on thinking. But once in bed, with the net drawn about her and the light out, the draught had no more effect than if it had been water. Her mind, it seemed, was on fire, and thought after thought, regret after regret, bitterness after bitterness, passed through it in turn, tormenting her and aggravating her state of indecision.

For a long time she thought that perhaps it would be better if she went away as quickly as possible, back across the burning plains in that awful train to Government House to sit all day on the veranda playing bridge and mahjong, gossiping and hating all the women she saw. Boring that might be, but it would not be painful, and it would not be dangerous. Then the thought rejected itself because she knew that she would do no such thing. She had always done what she wanted to do, from the very beginning when her father spoiled her and gave her whatever she wanted, although there were times when he put himself deeply into debt in order to give it to her. And now she would again do what she wanted, and she wanted to stay here, to go on and on seeing Tom, night after night, forever, in an effort to get back what they had lost. What she wanted, in her heart, was never again to leave Nivandrum.

She thought, "I wanted something to happen to me, and it has happened. The last thing I ever expected or wanted to happen."

And yet she did want it. She had wanted it all the time in her heart, more than anything in the world. It was the only thing she could possibly have wanted. For she was in love again, as she had been long ago, recklessly, voluptuously in love, as she had never been since that day when Tom had walked out of her life, as both of them had believed, forever. She knew now what it was that she had been searching for all those years. She had wanted that old feeling back again and she had tried to find it here and there, where she might, but she had never found it, and presently she had come to enjoy the endless, restless search; the variety, the perverse curiosity which compelled her to regard every attractive man as a possible lover. She had come to enjoy it so much that in the end it was the only thing which interested her. She had tried now and then to find what Tom alone had been able to give her, but she had never found it. Not one man had made any difference to her. In a way it was as if she were still innocent, save that the scars were there—the scars were there —the scars of dozens of encounters, which ended always in boredom and restlessness and a desire to run away.

Thinking now of all that had happened during the evening, it seemed to her that suddenly she understood his changeableness, the moods of depression and coldness, which came over him as if suddenly he felt a distaste for her. It was the scars which he had seen, those scars which she kept so carefully concealed that no one before had ever discovered them.

"But," she told herself, "he has been no better than I have been." Only, with a man, alas, it was different. In her honesty, she could not deny that. It *was* different. Things like that could leave a man untouched, but they bit into the soul of a woman, because with a woman the emotions, even in the most casual flirtation, were involved—women involved sentiment, the romantic, and sometimes even tenderness. She knew it now, perhaps for the first time, and she was ashamed of her cynicism, of the cheap wit she had used, the cheap gibes she had made at him over principles.

At last the sleeping medicine made her drowsy, and on the verge of sleep, once more in a daze, as she had been on returning from the island, she kept repeating to herself, "I am in love. I am in love. I have never been in love with any other man. I never loved him then as much as I love him now."

There was a new savor in this love, different from the first, almost innocent raptures of long ago, born of what had happened to both of them since then, a savor almost of perversity. As a boy he had been desirable; now he was more so. As a gourmet or the eater of curries demands more and more seasoning and hotter and hotter spices as he eats his way through life, so what she had needed now was not love so much as passion, and he could give it to her, this Tom who was the same Tom with something more. This Tom, hard as iron and half-naked in a *sarong*, burned as dark as any fisherman.

She thought, "Tomorrow I shall see him again. Tomorrow! It does not matter what happens to Albert."

But on the next day she did not see him, for early in the morning before the sleeping draught had worn away, he set out with the fishermen across the Great Bar to escape from her.

He wakened late, and when Silas brought him his tea he did not, as he always did, ask the boy if he had enjoyed his evening out, but scarcely spoke to him, and then only to say that he would need lunch packed to take with him and that he meant to be gone for the day.

After he had been given his orders the boy still remained, passively, as if there were something that he meant to say. It was only a matter of a second, but to Dantry, with his nerves on edge, it seemed that he stood there for a long time, silent with a reproachful expression in his eyes which were so much like the great, gentle eyes of Maria.

Angrily he said, "Well, what is it? What is it you want?" and the boy simply answered, "Nothing, *sahib*," and went away. As his back disappeared through the doorway, Dantry felt a sudden impulse to shout after him, "Tell your bloody sister never to come back, and to take Lady Groton with her. I never want to see any woman again." But he said nothing.

On waking he knew that he did not want to see Alix, for now in cold blood, the intoxication of the night having passed, he saw the whole thing in a new way and was a little terrified by what he saw.

He thought, "We are a couple of fools. I am as bad as she is. What can come of this but misery and catastrophe?" For he did not pretend that this was simply a passing adventure like so many others. It was not even like that strange passion he had felt for Maria in the beginning. It was, he knew, more serious than that, more profound and more lasting. It was like recurrent malaria which attacks its victim when he least expects it. The mere knowledge that he had but to see her again to be in love with her told him how serious it was. For a little time, as he dressed, he hated her for having come again into his life, for he knew now that the peace was gone, that the slow, never-changing, animal contentment of the life he had built up for himself so carefully was gone again forever, exchanged for what he did not know.

With a sense of shock and fright he realized suddenly that he had not thought of Maria since the second when he fancied he saw the canoe in the shadow of the island. Without his knowing or willing it, he understood now that he was tired of her, that he had no desire ever to see her again, and he knew that this was what, in the heart to which he would not listen, he had known from the beginning—that there would come a time when her beauty would no longer be beautiful to him and her devotion would be only something to bore him. It had been true, he knew now for a long time, but he had not recognized or admitted it because it did not seem, in the long peace of monotonous days, to matter very much. Since last night everything was clear. He could think of Maria now only as she was—a pretty, ignorant, half-wild half-caste who no longer held even the faintest interest for him. He thought, "My bad luck is that I've never been thoroughgoing. If I had been, bitter things like Maria wouldn't upset me."

All day he stayed fishing, with no luck, beneath the burning sun above the shoals beyond the Great Bar, but he had not come to fish but to escape from her and from himself, and so the fishing was not a matter of great importance save that a fight with a great fish would have diverted his mind for a time. So he sat in the boat all the day, brooding. By sundown, at the hour the wind changed and the jackals came out and the drums began, he had come again to a plan of action.

He would run away this time, for certain, taking Sandy with him into the hills to remain there until she had gone away, and while he was there he would tell Sandy that he did not want Maria any longer and that he would settle on her a sum which would keep her in luxury by the standards of Nivandrum for the rest of her life. And as usual, having made a decision, he felt suddenly free once more, and as the boat sped homeward, charging across the Bar and into the still water of the lovely harbor, he experienced a wild sense of exhilaration. He even decided that when he came back from the hills he would go away for a time to Shanghai or Hong Kong. It would make a change, and perhaps he had stayed too long in Nivandrum. It was nearly five years now since he had left the place save to go shooting in the hills. He would be free again, free of Maria, and free of Alix, this time forever.

Lest, from the window of her room, she should see him returning, he drove the boat through the inner channels and approached the island from the back, leaving the boat there until it was dark, when Silas brought it round to the landing stage.

When he saw Silas he did not ask for news of what had happened during the day, but the boy again, after waiting for a second, respectfully said, "English lady came to island about five o'clock."

To which Dantry replied, "Very good," and then he said, "Get together my shooting kit. Tomorrow I am going off to the hills," and he fancied that a look of relief and approval came into the eyes of the boy, and he called him back, meaning to tell him that even if Maria was his sister, what went on between Maria and his master was none of his business. But immediately he knew that it was impossible to make such a speech and he said instead, "Bring me the brandy."

And so he knew that his self had returned, the self from which he had at last escaped for all those months and years when Maria had made him happy, for it was not the eyes and voice and manner of Silas which were reproaching him now, but his own self, that spiteful, divided, wavering self, looking back at him from Silas's eyes, speaking to him with Silas's voice.

[404]

By nine o'clock he was quite drunk, and when Silas came to help him dress he told Silas to lay out his European clothes, and hesitatingly, unsteadily, with Silas's aid, he put them on, even to the starched shirt which had long since turned soft and a little yellow from the dampness. Even while he dressed he drank.

And Silas, hovering about, handed him his clothes, brushing off bits of invisible dust, a little embarrassed and a little fascinated by the spectacle of his master rapidly making himself drunk. Through the mist of intoxication, Dantry was aware of the reproachful eyes of Silas, and presently he came to understand that this was nothing new in the manner of the servant. Silas had always watched him thus, with a kind of velvety curiosity, as if he were an exotic animal. Now, aware of it, the watching annoyed him, but no matter how quickly he turned, he was never able to catch the boy staring at him directly. Yet all the time he knew that Silas was watching everything he did, every change of expression on his face. He could feel the eyes of the boy on his back, and slowly he became fascinated by the speculation as to what went on inside the head of the boy.

Then, drunk and irritated, he turned quickly from the mirror, but again the boy was too quick for him and appeared to be absorbed in a spot in the cloth of the dinner jacket he held. Looking at him, Dantry said, "Well, what is it you see? What are you looking at all the time?"

But Silas was not to be caught. His face went cold and opaque and he said, "Nothing, *sahib*, I don't understand."

"You see too bloody much. What is it? Have I changed? Am I different? What are you staring at?"

"Nothing different, *sahib*," replied the boy, and again, "I don't understand."

And then it occurred to him that it was impossible ever to discover what went on inside the head of his servant, and in his drunkenness it seemed to him that all along, all these months and years, he had been deceived not only by Silas but by Maria herself. He did not know what she was thinking. He had never known. Perhaps all of them, even Sandy, had simply found him a convenience, a rich man off whom they might all live. Perhaps they still looked on him as an outsider whom they tolerated for what they could get out of him.

Or again, he thought, Silas might only be interested in the process of a white man getting drunk. Perhaps he was glad or perhaps he was sorry. Or it might be that Silas saw his master as he did not see himself, even in moments of self-reproach . . . as a broken, useless, dissipated man to whom it was worth while being devoted because the place was good and easy and there was money in it. Perhaps he was thinking, "One more European going the way of the others. One more European who will soon be finished and out of the way." For five years they had been together, but he had not the slightest idea what his servant thought of him. And suddenly catching a glimpse of the reflected face of Silas in the mirror before him, he had a quick impression of contempt and even enmity.

He turned quickly and said to Silas, "I won't have any dinner. I am going to Sandy's compound." And then an inspiration came to him. "When I go, put out all the lights." If the house was dark it might not occur to Alix to come over to the island and wait for his return.

On his way to the mainland and Sandy's compound he passed by chance quite close to another boat, the biggest, most important *wallum* boat in the harbor, and in the pale light of the new moon he had recognized, lying on a pile of matting, the bull-like figure of Lord Groton, all in white, returning from the lagoons.

21

During the whole of the morning Lady Groton had waited for Dantry to come to the hotel or for a message asking her to come to the island. A little before lunch she went to her room, and locking the door she took the glasses and watched the island for a long time, but she saw nothing save a servant, a good-looking boy, dressed all in white. Through the great windows she could see into the sitting room and the bedroom, but there was no one there save the boy, who came in once and, seating himself, looked through the copies of the London illustrated magazines which lay on the table. And then when she was about to abandon the watching, she saw a canoe approaching the island from the mainland, and in it the figure of a woman who was young and as nearly as she could make out, pretty. The canoe disappeared behind the house, and the woman in a little while reappeared in the garden where she set about cutting bunches of jacqueranda and trumpet flowers. Then she entered the house and went into Dantry's bedroom, and there she placed the flowers in a vase on the table by the bed and the servant joined her and they talked for a moment and then disappeared again.

For another hour she watched the house through the glasses and presently the woman walked across the garden and disappeared, and a moment later the canoe came out again from behind the house on the way back to the mainland.

She thought, "That is his woman. She has put the flowers there to make him think of her when he comes in. Someone must have seen us last night. Someone must have told her."

Alone, bored and restless, with no appetite, she ate lunch, and then she waited again all through the heat of the early afternoon, thinking of nothing but what had happened the night before and what had happened years ago, of that first night when she had seen him and liked his face for the misery and the intelligence and even the weakness she found in it—the weakness which she did not then recognize—of the days and nights at Tipton Farm when sometimes they had quarreled but most of the time they had been wildly happy.

About five o'clock when she could bear the waiting no longer, she ordered the boat and crossed to the island. At first she found no one and wandered through the house observing many things which she had not noticed in the excitement of the night before, and when at last she came to the bedroom she could see nothing in it but the bunch of flowers thrust tightly into the vase by the side of the bed, for to her it was not simply a vase filled with flowers, but the spirit of that woman who had come and gone without her ever having seen her face clearly. And the flowers, brought there by the woman, became a symbol of the menace which might separate Tom from her for a second time. For a long time she stood regarding the flowers as if fascinated, wondering what the woman was like and whether she had made Tom happy even for a little while. And then a thought came to her, "If I were to take away the flowers, he would never know that she brought them. He would never know that she had been there, and so he would never think of her, but only of me." But she thought too, "No, I can't do anything as cheap as that. I can't behave like a tart."

Yet she did do it. As if hypnotized, she walked to the flowers and took them out of the vase, thinking, "Now I must go quickly before the servant appears," and she felt faintly disgusted with herself, but she did not put the flowers back in the vase. Quickly she made her way out on to the terrace with the Indian bed and the great tiger skin, and quickly she descended the wide stairway, but not quickly enough, for as she reached the bottom, the figure of the servant appeared, hastily buttoning his white jacket. There was nothing now that she could do. She could not throw the flowers away, pretending she had never had them. So she stopped, blushing, waiting for the servant to come up. She, Alix Groton, who never blushed, felt suddenly like a small child caught in a nasty act.

With a great effort she said to the boy, "Tell *sahib* that Lady Groton came."

"Yes, *memsahib*."

She saw that the boy had noticed the flowers and wildly she said, "Tell him that I took the flowers for my room. There are no flowers at the hotel." And at once she knew that what she had said was idiotic, for the boy had only to turn his eyes and see on Rasmussen's island the garden filled with jasmine, jacqueranda, cannas, bignonia, and a hundred other flowers. And she saw by the eyes of the boy that he understood what she had done, and why she had done it. She saw that he knew the story —the whole thing. How he could have known it, she could not imagine.

Quickly she stepped into the boat and gave orders to return to the hotel. She still held the miserable flowers in her hot hand. She could not pitch them overboard with the servant and the boatmen watching. They stayed with her, like the Albatross about the neck of the Ancient Mariner, all the way to Rasmussen's island. Even when she stepped ashore she still had them, hating them now passionately because they had made her ridiculous and cost her her dignity in front of a servant. She carried them all the way to her room and there she flung them on a table and called for the *ayah*.

When the woman came, she said, "Take those and throw them out."

The woman said nothing, but looked at her in an odd way, so that she thought, "Does she too know everything? What sort of a place is this?" And for the first time she was a little frightened, feeling suddenly something of that dread and sense of doom which long ago had sometimes come to Dantry in the evenings when the jackals came out and the drums began.

Through the rest of the evening she waited, sitting by the window, and at dusk she saw the fishing boats returning, each one finding its way home like a bird seeking its nest among the channels and the islands, and presently she heard the jackals begin to call to each other, back and forth among the rice fields on the mainland, but still there was no sign of Tom. Even when it grew dark there was no light in the house. And presently anger took the place of anxiety and her injured vanity cried out, saying, "He has no right to do this to me. He is a coward and a swine." And she thought, "He can wait now forever before I will make any effort to see him. I hate this place. I'll go away on Thursday by the first train and never see him again."

But she did not forget him.

At last a light appeared in the house and she thought, "He has returned and is dressing and will come over in a little while," and all her anger was swallowed up again in anxiety and desire. Then presently the light went out and she thought, "He will be here now in a few minutes," and rising from the seat by the window she went to the dressing table and made up her face again for the fourth time that afternoon, and when she had done that she dressed herself, without the help of the *ayah*, in another gown, and put on more jewels, and all the time she was thinking, "Now there will be a knock at the door. Now Rasmussen will come to say that he is downstairs again, waiting for me." And she saw him again very clearly in the purple *sarong* which made him seem more attractive than he had been even in the old days.

But there was no knock and no Rasmussen, and when she went to the window again the house on the island was still dark and she knew that he was not coming at all, and throwing herself down on the bed she began to weep. She did not know how long she lay there, but presently there was a knock at the door and she started up from the bed half-covering her face with her hands, and said, "Who is it? What is it?" trying to control her voice so that the *ayah* or Rasmussen or whoever it was who stood outside the door should not know that she had been weeping and spread the story among the islands. For an instant she had a sudden hysterical feeling that all those people she had seen from the train and from the *wallum* boat as she drifted among the islands, all those swarming, anonymous half-savage people were all watching and listening.

But it was only Rasmussen, who had come not to say that Tom was downstairs waiting, but to ask if she would have her dinner in her room. She sent him away, saying that she wanted nothing, and then undressed herself and taking a heavy dose of sleeping draught climbed into the bed hoping that she would lose consciousness at once and not waken again for hours, because the waiting and the disappointment had now become unbearable to her, like the violent aching of a tooth.

She tried to read, thinking that it would make her sleep more quickly, but the book she chose meant nothing to her. She could not even see the words on the pages. She was falling asleep at last when again there was a knock at the door, and lying with her eyes closed she tried to take no notice of it, but after the second knock the door opened and into the room, carrying one of the kerosene lamps, came Lord Groton. Opening her eyes a little she recognized the great bulk of his body, filling the whole doorway, and with a shock she realized that during the whole day and the evening she had forgotten him, forgotten that tonight he was coming back. It was as if he had never existed.

As he crossed the room toward her she wanted to cry out, but instead she remained mute, her whole body contracted, her eyes still half-closed, watching him. He was wearing a dressing gown which she hated, and the sight of it set her teeth on edge. She had given it to him long ago at Christmas, thinking that it would please him because it was covered with a design of horses, and she had succeeded only too well. It had been cleaned countless times and was worn shabby, but he would not become separated from it. Whenever she suggested chucking it away, he always told her that it brought him luck. It was covered with horses—horses racing, horses clearing hedges and ditches, horses rearing, horses in full stride at the finishing post. It had come slowly with the passage of years to be a symbol of his visits to her. It had succeeded in the end in making her hate horses so much that she no longer hunted nor went racing.

He did not speak until he came to the bed where, lifting the netting and placing the lamp on the table beside it, he seated himself. His silence made her think, "He has found out. Now there is going to be a row." And she wanted to cry out, "Go away. Please go away just for tonight." But in the next moment she saw from his face that he did not mean to stay. He looked ill and sullen, and at the corners of the heavy jaw there were little knots of hard muscle which always appeared when he meant to make a scene.

He said, "You might have waited for me."

She made a great effort to control herself and said, "I didn't know what hour to expect you and I was very tired. Was the trip a success?"

"In some ways, yes." And then he took out a cigar and lighted it while she watched him, and then he said, "Alix, who is this man Dantry?"

For a second she hesitated, aware even in the haziness that enveloped her, that she must spar for time, to find out how much he knew. The sparring did not require much effort, for she had done it so often that in a way it had become a kind of fixed technique. She said, "An old friend. Why?"

"I was just interested."

"I haven't seen him for nearly fifteen years."

"Was he the boy . . . the Dantry who had the V.C.?"

(So he knows that much. How much more does he know?)

"Yes. Who told you about him?"

"Bates."

The name of Bates made it easier for her. If it was Bates who told him about Dantry, then he had no knowledge but only suspicions. Bates had protected her so many times.

She said, "He turned up here last night. He's been living here for a long time."

In reply he said, "He ought to know a good deal about the place. He ought to be of some use to me."

"I doubt it."

"Why?"

"He wouldn't know the things you're interested in. He's not very practical."

"Is that meant to be a sneer?"

"No . . . no."

She was certain now that he did not know all the story, either of what had happened last night, or many years ago. He was suspicious and he was being disagreeable because the man was Tom Dantry, and men like

[410]

Tom Dantry always gave him a sense of inferiority. He never minded her friendships with sporting men. It was that eternal inverted snobbery of his, that unhealthy hatred of any man born with the things he had never achieved and would never be able to achieve. "That," she thought, "is how the caste system works at home," for suddenly her mind, challenged, was clear, and she felt strong and full of hatred for him, not the physical hatred she usually knew, but a kind of cold dispassionate hatred for him as a symbol of all those men like him, whose lives, whose souls, however dubious their existence, were concerned only with material things.

He was saying, "How friendly are you with him?"

"I used to know him very well. We were friends in London just after the war."

His jaw set a little harder. "Where has he been since then?"

"Wandering about the world. I don't know exactly where."

"By choice?"

"By desire."

"He must be a damned fool."

"I don't think so. He's been trying to straighten himself out."

"What's the matter with him? What has he got to straighten out?"

"A lot of things. What happened to him in the war . . . and his own character. It's not a very interesting story. It would bore you."

The ash from his cigar fell on the pink silk sheets and she wanted to say, "At least you needn't smoke in here," but again she thought, "If I let him do as he pleases, he'll go away sooner." She was feeling drowsy again, and with a conscious effort she raised herself in the bed and sank back among the piled-up pillows, aware that she must keep her wits about her if she was to endure this game and not betray herself.

He said, "One of those damned radicals, I suppose?"

"I suppose you might call it that. Anyway he doesn't fit into the world as it is."

"Why do you always pick up asses like that?"

She laughed, and the laugh was a secret one, against his stupidity. She had no special taste for radicals or intellectuals or any other class of men. She wasn't attracted to men by their ideas or their brains, but by something else, much simpler. "It's comic," she thought, "how a husband is always the last to understand the truth."

She was tired and bored because she had been through these same scenes so many times before. She knew all the questions and all the answers, and at this sort of thing she was much the quicker witted of the two.

He went on bitterly and abusively, about her carelessness in the matter of propriety, about the provocative way she dressed and looked at other men, about a hundred other things. She did not trouble to listen, but now and then she looked at him, and for a time she thought that he had been drinking too much again, but presently she realized that it was not drink which made him look and behave thus. His face, instead of being purple as drink made it, was pale and pasty, and at times it seemed to her that he was making a great effort in order to speak. And then she became aware of her boredom again and the awful dressing gown, and in her drowsiness it seemed to her that the horses had all come to life. They were in dizzy motion, jumping, striding, rearing, plunging.

Because it never did any good, she never lost her temper and never answered back during these long scenes of jealousy, and now it was not Groton who made her angry, but the dressing gown and the silly, rearing, plunging horses. She heard herself saying, "Why do you always pick on men like Tom Dantry? Is it because you hate all gentlemen? Because you know that in a lot of ways they're better than you?"

For a moment he stared at her, his heavy, lipless mouth half open, so astounded that he seemed unable to find words with which to speak. Then he asked, "What do you mean by that?"

"Nothing in particular."

"Well, don't get any silly ideas. I'm proud of being Albert Simpson. I'm proud of having made my own way. I'm proud of everything I've built up. It's more than any of your sickly, down-at-the-heel gentlemen could do."

And again she astonished him by saying, "Yes, that's quite true," and before he could speak, she said, "What is it you want of me, Albert? If you don't like men speaking to your wife, why did you marry me? You should have married a plain suburban respectable woman who wore fancy hats, but not me. Sometimes I think you didn't marry me for any reason save that I was Alix Ainsworth, who was in 'society,' who had a lot of cheap publicity in the illustrated papers. You wanted to show people that you could take what you wanted from the world—that nobody was too good for you. I was a kind of prize and you wanted to show me off. You didn't really want *me*. If I'd been just plain Mary Smith living in Bloomsbury, you wouldn't have looked at me. We've never had the least understanding or sympathy. You just wanted what I, quite by accident, happened to be."

For a long time he regarded the end of his cigar without speaking. She knew what he was doing. He was pulling himself together, counting ten before he spoke, so that he would say nothing which he need ever take back. He was being the shrewd businessman. She had caught him at it now and then when he was talking to other businessmen. But it was in truth that and a great deal more, for suddenly, in his tired, muddled brain, he saw that perhaps for the first time since he had married her he had a chance to learn the truth and his vanity was afraid. For a moment he hesitated, wondering whether it was better to continue in ignorance and doubt as he had done for years, and then, like a man hesitating to dive into icy water, he plunged.

"Why did you marry me?" he asked.

She answered at once. She said, "Because my father and I were stony and had a lot of debts. Because you offered me a big settlement, because I thought it would be wonderful to be colossally rich, and because I was in love with somebody else and was unhappy and really didn't much care who I married." Then for a moment she was silent, thinking, trying her best to be honest, and the effort, the concentration made her look very young, like a naughty child. She said, "I think it was the settlement that did it. That meant that whatever happened I should always be independent. I wouldn't even need your money."

He looked at her for a moment, directly, wearily, understanding for the first time the fathomless indifference of the woman he had married, the hopelessness of ever dominating her or breaking her will. Then silently he rose and crushed out the end of his half-smoked cigar on the table beside the bed, leaving it there, sordid, dead and broken among her own feminine things, the gold and platinum cigarette case, the smelling salts, the prayer book. It was a coarse, brutal gesture, and she thought, "That is what he would like to do to me at this moment, but he's afraid. He's poor, bumptious, awkward Albert Simpson, afraid of the gentry."

He started to speak, but his mouth only opened and closed and then he managed to say, "Good night," and went out of the room, closing the door behind him, leaving her aware that she had at last hurt him who she thought could not be hurt. She had found the vulnerable spot in the first Baron Groton, born plain Albert Simpson in Wilhelmina Crescent, Birmingham, and she was not sorry. It avenged her for many things. Perhaps now he would leave her in peace forever. Anyway, with the settlement she would always have enough money, even if he left her nothing in his will. But she was a little ashamed because she knew that he had been made to suffer because Tom had never appeared. He had paid for what Tom had done to her.

The effect of the sleeping medicine had worn off now and she was dreadfully awake, and excited because she believed now that she would have to remodel her whole life and be free again, but she was able to bring no order to her own thoughts, and presently she rose and lighted a cigarette and took more sleeping medicine, and while she was out of bed she went, despite her pride, to the window again and looked toward the house on the island and found it still dark. It was late, for the drums had begun to die away, slowly, one by one among the islands.

When she was in bed again there was another knock at the door and when she said, "Who is it?" a voice answered, "Bates, me lady."

"Come in."

He came in, respectful, rather shifty in manner and cadaverous in appearance.

"What is it?" she asked.

"Sorry to disturb Your Ladyship, but I think there's something wrong with His Lordship. He's not well."

"What is it, Bates?"

"I've no idea, me lady, but he certainly has a fever. I wanted to take his temperature, but he wouldn't hear of it. You know how he is. He'll never admit it when he's feeling seedy."

"What about a doctor?"

"He wouldn't hear of that either. He said there wouldn't be any good doctors in a place like this." The ghost of a smile appeared on the long face and he added, "He used much stronger language than that, but that was what he meant."

It was as if the shadowy grin had said, "You and I understand the old bastard." It disturbed her, the smile. They might both hate Groton. They both did. But while they were living off him they ought not to admit it to each other. The implications of the smile were too uncomfortable.

For a moment she was silent, thinking of a great many things, and then said, "Thank you, Bates. If he's not better in the morning, I'll try to find a doctor. I can persuade him, I think."

"Thank you, me lady, good night."

"Good night, Bates."

When he had gone, thinking about Bates, she came to the conclusion that he was a bad servant, not because he was inefficient or stupid, but because his spirit was far too independent and his powers of divination far too great. It was not pleasant to have about you a servant who knew your motives and even your very thoughts. "He is probably one of those servants," she thought, "who are involved in lodging-house murders." His manner was one of the utmost professional discretion, and in her own case, Heaven knew, he had given evidence of discretion in practice; yet her instinct told her that he was not to be trusted. The interview left her with a curious sense of distaste, as if somehow he had managed to make her an accomplice to one of his own plots. As if somehow he had involved her in something sordid. He had betrayed himself, save for that single shadow of a grin, neither by glance nor by word, nor even by the intonation of his voice, but she *knew* that he was thinking of Groton's death and finding pleasure in the thought, and that he knew that she too had been thinking of it in the same fashion.

Presently she put out the light again, but she did not sleep for a long time.

The distant sound of the dying drums and the buzzing of insects annoyed her, and for a moment, while she lay between sleep and wakefulness, a hysterical terror of Nivandrum and all the country about it seized her. And then again just as she was falling asleep she had a strange dream in which she was searching for something desperately, but what it was she did not know. She was aware of a terrible anxiety and the necessity of haste, and of wandering through ill-smelling streets and vast dusty fields, and at last through a jungle in which she seemed to *hear* the plants, the trees, the giant ferns, the vines, growing all about her, closing her in. And everywhere there were eyes without faces watching her struggles, and then just as she knew that she was about to find what she was searching for, she wakened screaming, and in the first moment of consciousness she remembered that all the eyes were alike, black and set rather close together. They were the eyes of the woman called Léah, Mrs. Rasmussen, whom she had scarcely noticed, whom she would never have noticed save for the peculiar quality of her eyes.

22

When Dantry arrived at Sandy's compound he found the Cockney with half his family and a half-dozen neighbors seated about the fire. One of them, Sandy's third son, sat with one drum between his knees and another beside him. While the others gossiped and gambled, he thumped at both drums, exploring new rhythms, finding new combinations of sound between the male and female drums. Save for the hands which moved swiftly from one drum to another and back again, he sat quite still, absorbed utterly in his playing. At sight of Dantry coming out of the darkness dressed in European evening clothes, the little party fell silent, so silent that the boy with the drums, aware suddenly that the accompaniment of gossip had ceased, looked up and stopped his playing. Then one by one the family and guests, embarrassed and awkward, stole silently away to join the fire in another compound, and last of all the boy picked up his drums and vanished into the crotons and ragged bougainvillea that grew close about the houses. It was as if a ghost had suddenly appeared, or some creature infected with a nameless and terrible disease. And Dantry thought, "My God, they must all know something is wrong." It was all different again, the way it had been in the beginning.

At last only Sandy was left seated before the fire, smoking his pipe, fatter now than he had been when Dantry first came to the islands, and more placid and solid, more than ever a plump little Cockney Buddha.

As he watched Dantry approach, he saw from his walk that he had been drinking, and then when he saw that Dantry was dressed the way people dressed to dine in restaurants in London, he knew that he must be very drunk, and quietly he thought that it was a great pity after things had gone so well for so long. It was a pity that this should have happened just when the people of the islands were becoming used to him, and beginning to accept him. Now, tonight, at sight of him drunk and dressed as he was, they all ran away again as they had done when he first came to the islands. Sandy knew why they ran away; they were not, by nature, a drinking people, and the sight of drunkenness always offended them a little. It made them feel shy and ashamed as when they saw a mad person. And Dantry had made it worse by putting on all those European clothes. The sight of a European drunk always upset them profoundly; a European, drunk, became either bestial or overfamiliar and embarrassed them, or he became brutal and their enemy. Now Sandy waited, as Dantry came toward him, to see which manifestation the brandy had taken with his son-in-law, and as soon as the firelight struck Dantry's face he knew. It had turned ugly and unfamiliar. It was a strange face which Sandy, his friend, had never seen before, a face that struck him, in his simple way, as a little like the masks which the dancers wore to impersonate the demon in the legend of Rama and Sita.

It disturbed him, but he sat quietly until Dantry had come up to the fire, and then he said, "Hello."

Dantry did not seat himself. It was hardly possible in a dinner jacket to squat by the fire, and the gesture of remaining standing alarmed Sandy a little more. It was as if the gesture, with the clothes, were a kind of silent declaration, as if Dantry had said, "I have gone back to what I was by birth. There is a barrier between us at home, where we both came from, and nothing can change it here. . . ." And the memory of Sandy, traveling back across twenty-five years, roused an obscure impulse to rise to his feet and likewise to stand, not arrogantly, balancing a little drunkenly on two feet like Dantry, but submissively, awaiting orders. But immediately he thought, "All that is past and finished. That is something I shall never do again. This is my world, not his, and he will have to suit himself to me."

Dantry did not answer his greeting, he merely said, "Why did they all run away? Have I got the plague?"

"No," said Sandy quietly. "They were frightened."

"Why were they frightened?"

"Because drinking makes friends into strangers."

"I haven't been drinking."

Then Sandy, very quietly, turned a little hard. It was a manifestation which Dantry had never seen in the plump, good-natured little man, but Sandy was still thinking, "This is my world, not his, and he must neither dominate nor destroy it."

Very gently, Sandy said, "You must have been drinking a great deal more than I guessed, if you think that anyone can't see how drunk you are." And as he spoke a strange thing happened inside him. He knew that he had no respect for this countryman of his, and he knew now that he had never had any respect. In the jungle, shooting, or here at home spearing fish and living a healthy, placid life, he knew that he was a better man than Dantry. Without him Dantry would have no shooting, no fishing, not even a wife, if it came to that. Without him Dantry in Nivandrum would have been lost, a stranger. Until now he had not thought of any of these things, save once or twice when Dantry's treatment of Maria had wounded him. He had overlooked them partly from good nature, partly from natural friendliness. He had been willing to overlook the occasional arrogance of this man who came from a different class and a different world, and was so helpless once he found himself outside of its buttresses and protections. No, Sandy was the better man, and now he knew it. All the money, the background, the education had in reality brought nothing to Dantry, save perhaps disadvantages. In a way, before the world, they had weakened him. Sandy did not mind drinking, but he liked drinking for fun, noisily, wildly, with good nature when there was an occasion to celebrate. He did not like sullen drinkers, who drank in solitude only to give themselves courage and decision or to make them forget their own unhappiness, and now, as if the smoldering, sweet-smelling fire before him were a blinding white light, he knew that this was why Dantry drank; this was why each time he drank, during the five years Sandy had known him, he had grown more and more impossible. He had always drunk not to be gay or to celebrate, but to drown his own misery.

The face of Dantry looking down at him in the light from the fire went suddenly blank as the significance of Sandy's speech made its way into his muddled brain. For a moment he felt a desire to say, "Stand up when you are speaking to me," but almost at once, even in his drunkenness, he knew that under the circumstances such a speech would only echo, ridiculous and grotesque, without response, through the silence of the compound. For a moment he felt ashamed, as a little while before he had felt ashamed and angry as Silas watched him dressing. So he said feebly, "I'm not drunk, not as drunk as that."

"I'll get you a chair," said Sandy, and raising his voice he called toward the main house, "Anthony! Anthony! Bring Sahib Dantry the chair." And a moment later one of Sandy's smaller boys came out, bringing with him a cheap, stiff chair—the only chair in the house, which was never used save when Sandy's wife sat at the elegant sewing machine which Sandy had bought her with money that came from Dantry.

The boy, shyly, awkwardly, placed the chair beside Dantry, glanced at him with fear and then scurried off again into the darkness.

For a moment Dantry stood regarding it, suddenly ill at ease and feeling a little ridiculous, aware now for the first time why in his drunkenness he had dressed himself so pompously. Without thinking, he had dressed himself as if he were going out to dinner in London in a feeble effort to reëstablish his prestige, as if already he were a beachcomber who was forced to *demand* dignity and respect instead of having it given him. He had tried to force something to which he no longer had any right. And now as he stood beside the chair he saw that if he sat on it, that stiff cheap chair, beside the fire in Sandy's compound with Sandy seated on the ground, he would become hopelessly ridiculous. Even now the neighbors and the children were probably hiding among the crotons and bougainvilleas watching him, grinning at one another, stifling their good-natured chuckles. The calmness, even the dignity of that squat little Cockney Buddha sitting cross-legged on the opposite side of the fire, did nothing to help him. It was as if Sandy said, "You have made a fool of yourself. Now get out of it as best you can."

So with a sudden kick, he sent the chair halfway across the compound, and taking off his coat, he threw it on the ground, and after that he tore off his shirt, and at last, naked to the waist, he seated himself on the ground beside the fire opposite Sandy, and Sandy watching him, made no sign save the shadow of a sardonic grin, so faint that in the flickering light of the fire, Dantry could not be certain it had ever existed, crossed his face.

Then he said, "And now," and looked at Sandy, but Sandy said nothing.

He had come meaning to propose a shooting trip, but now, with a sensibility that was partly natural and morbid and partly the result of his intoxicated condition, he saw that this was impossible because something had come between them, something which would mar the whole trip and make it and the relationship between them strained and unnatural. And the silence of Sandy disturbed him, making him believe that all the five years in Nivandrum had been for nothing. It seemed to him that, sitting there half-naked by the fire, clad only in black evening trousers, he was as much a stranger as on the first day he had come to the islands.

When Sandy said nothing, he felt a sudden compulsion to speak, and so when he spoke he was a little hysterical and jumped farther than he had meant to. He said, "I am going away."

This time Sandy answered him. He said, "I think it would be a good idea. I think a change would do you good. You have been here too long without going away. The place is getting you down."

And then again when he spoke, he jumped, driven this time by irritation, farther than he meant, "No, I mean I am going away for good." And this time Sandy said nothing. Once before he had said he was going away, but he had not gone because of Maria. After a silence Dantry said, "I'll make a settlement on Maria. I'll leave her an income that will take care of her forever. I'll be generous."

[418]

"I wasn't thinking about that," said Sandy.

"You've all been much better off since I married Maria."

"No," said Sandy. "Not much better. Not better off at all."

"What do you mean by that?"

"You haven't brought any special happiness. A sewing machine and a few European clothes for the kids ain't happiness."

"There's been a lot more than that."

"Not much. There's been more unhappiness than happiness."

"How?"

"There's Maria."

"Haven't I been good to Maria? Haven't I given her everything?"

"Everything you've given her didn't mean anything. You didn't give her the one thing she wanted." Dantry did not ask, "What was that?" for even in his drunkenness he knew all the things he had refused to give her.

"You mustn't forget," said Sandy quietly, "that Maria is half-European. Even if she wasn't she wouldn't have liked being treated as a convenience."

"You're very fond of Maria, aren't you?" asked Dantry.

"Yes. You see she's my child. That her mother is dark doesn't make any difference. Her mother has been a good wife. She has made a good life for me. She has brought happiness to me and to her children."

For a second Sandy was silent, puffing his pipe and staring into the fire. Then he said, "But I wouldn't ask you to stay. It wouldn't get any better. I thought it might be all right. I had doubts even when you married her, but I still thought it might be all right." Again he paused and quietly, shaking the ashes from his pipe, he refilled it; and said, "And I'll tell you frankly that I hoped it would be all right. I wanted it to be for your sake as much as hers, but now I know it won't be. I was wrong when I thought you might be different. You aren't. It was bad for you and for her and for everybody. Now it's better that you go away and that she forgets you. I can find a good husband for her among the islands who'll care for her and give her the children you were never willing to give her because you were never willing to give up that other world. You never really wanted to be one of us. You wanted to have everything and give nothing."

Then surprisingly he rose and held out his hand and said, "Maybe it isn't your fault. To judge things like that you have to know the whole story. I'll wish you good-by. Don't worry about the settlement. Maria won't need it because money isn't very important here. I hope that some day you'll find a place where you fit."

So Sandy was dismissing him, Sandy, a Cockney sailor who had been his *shikari*, was sending him off. He still remained seated on the ground, feeling awkward and aware that for a second time Sandy had him at a disadvantage. He had meant to come to the compound as the injured party, to accuse Sandy

[419]

and his family and all Nivandrum of putting up with him for the money they got out of him, and somehow Sandy had turned the tables, not because he was more intelligent or clever, but simply because he was right, because both his small plump feet were planted in the earth, in reality. The knowledge sobered him a little and he felt ashamed, and at the same time a fury sprang up inside him and he thought, "It's her fault and Groton's for ever coming here. They've destroyed everything, and now Groton is going to destroy the islands and corrupt all the people with his petrol tanks and docks. God blast them!"

In silence he rose to his feet and took Sandy's hand, and then very quietly he said, "Good-by Sandy," and Sandy said, with an odd embarrassed dignity, "Good-by, sir."

The word "sir" was almost like a blow. For a moment it left him without words. It was as if in that single short word Sandy had ironically condemned everything he was and everything he stood for, all that world from which he had come and from which Sandy had escaped so surely, so triumphantly, and which he himself had never been able to lose. He looked for the irony in Sandy's face, uncertain whether he had spoken thus deliberately or from a habit long dead, but the plump, pleasant face was both calm and expressionless.

There was nothing to do now but take his leave, and how to take it with dignity was a problem. Sandy helped him a little, for he said, suddenly, "And Maria?"

"I think I had better not see her. It would be easier for her."

"Perhaps." And again the faint ghost of a grin drifted across the plump face, but a ghost potent enough to say, "Easier for you. Now you can run away again. You can run away, but your precious self will be waiting for you on the dock in Singapore or Batavia or Shanghai, or wherever it is you land."

Then, because there was nothing else to do, Dantry turned and walked away from Sandy and the little fire, but before he had reached the gate of the compound, he heard Sandy's voice, "You've forgotten your coat and shirt," (Would there be no end to Sandy's power of making him ridiculous?) and he called back, "Throw the damned things in the fire."

Then he was outside the compound where the sardonic eye of little Sandy could no longer follow him, but he was not yet free, for as he approached the little pier there stepped toward him, out of the bamboo, the familiar figure of Maria. The moon gave enough light for him to recognize her at once, and even as she came near to him, enough light for him to see her face and her great dark eyes. She looked very small, and the sight of her caused his heart to contract suddenly, not from fear or from affection, but from pity . . . the pity against which he was never able to arm himself, the pity from which he could never escape save by running away, the pity which lay at the core of all his weakness and indecision so that he had no peace. And there was a kind of wonder, too, in his confused brain, that once the sight of her should have roused him so terribly and that now it roused not the faintest desire.

He stopped at the edge of the pier because there was nothing else to do, and he said nothing. It was Maria who spoke. She merely said, "Dantry," and now the name seemed to him more inappropriate, more shameful than it had ever been. Somehow, he saw, the fact that she should call him "Dantry" instead of "Tom," lay at the root of everything, a kind of symbol. That was why he did not know her at all; why he had never known her; that was the reason he had never known any of them here in the islands. To all of them he had never been either "Mr. Dantry," or "Sahib," or "Mr. Tom," or "Tom," but merely "Dantry," an impersonal appellation which meant nothing at all—neither dignity, respect, friendliness nor intimacy; it only meant that he had tried to take everything they had to give him and to give nothing in return. In a blinding moment of clarity, watching the still, small figure in the moonlight, he saw the whole thing complete for the first time.

He said, as gently as possible, "Yes, Maria?"

"What have I done?"

He could not answer her. How could he? How could he make her understand—a simple, direct child, living in a state of nature when he had never been able to make other women, far older and wiser and more subtle, understand that there came a time when they were all measured against one woman and suddenly became intolerable. So he said, "Nothing, Maria. It isn't what you've done. It's myself."

She looked at him, puzzled, and he felt a sudden impulse to put his hands on her shoulders and try to make her understand, but he was afraid to touch her, lest the gesture should bring back to him all the strange, healthy animal happiness which they had had together and weaken him once more. And he meant to run away; he had to run away.

Yet he had not the courage to tell her that he was going away forever, and that this was the last time she would ever see him. That he could leave for Sandy to do.

"When will you let me come back?" she asked.

And he lied, saying, "I don't know. I'll send word by Silas."

There was a little silence, and Dantry heard the drum beginning again in Sandy's compound and knew now for certain that the rest of Sandy's family, the neighbors, the boy with the drum, had all been waiting, watching from the bushes, until he went away. Now that the man with the plague had gone they would return.

"Dantry," she said softly, "I'll do what you want because it is you I want to be happy."

The speech made him silent and full of shame, because it was a speech he had never made in all his life, not even to Alix long ago. If he had made it then, the whole of life would have been different. He had wanted people to be happy, not for their own sakes, but because their happiness in turn made him happy. When they could not be happy he ran away.

At last he said, "There isn't anything you can do. It's too late now to do anything." And in the fear that she might think he was accusing her, he added, "You see, it isn't your fault, Maria . . . it's the fault of things which happened long ago . . . which have gone on happening for years and years."

He knew that it was impossible for her, whose whole world was the harbor, the islands, ever to understand what he wanted, and for a moment he hated her for loving him. In the end it had always been like that; he had come to hate those who loved him, who somehow in a shadowy way fastened responsibilities upon him, roused his pity and made him miserable. Only Alix had never done this to him, never once. He saw it clearly now for the first time; that was the reason why nothing had ever changed his feeling for her, why he had used her as a standard by which to measure all other women. She loved him, but left him free because she herself was free, in spite of everything; in spite of Groton and the life she had led, she was free always. "Free," he thought. "Shining and free." And suddenly he saw her very clearly in all her beauty, with her childlike face as if she were enveloped in light so that he could not see Maria at all. In all her overbreeding and decadence that one good thing stood forth. She was clear and unmuddled and free. Perhaps it had taken hundreds of years to produce that freedom, just as it had taken hundreds of years to produce the decadence.

Now, half-sober, his mind worked with brilliant alertness so that he seemed to see all things at once, and to understand everything with an understanding that was neither agreeable nor helpful, and so the course he must take became clearer than it had ever been. He must go away and finish himself off before he caused misery to any more people, before he muddled their lives and corrupted their spirits. He could drink himself to death, going from one bar to another back and forth among the islands and the cities of the East. But Alix should finish herself off too, for she had the same curse upon her, only she would never do it because she was wiser and more scornful and harder, and she was free.

For a long time he had stood there, ignoring Maria, his hands pressed against his aching head, covering his eyes as if to shut out the pale light from the virginal new moon—that moon which was new and fresh with all her course still before her. It was the moment of blackest misery he had ever known, and it was Maria who roused him from it by the touch of her hand.

When he took his hands down and looked he found her prostrate before him, her arms about his knees. She was crying quietly and saying, "Dantry, I will do whatever will make you happy . . . because in your heart you are a good man."

He left her there lying on the ground and went quickly to his canoe, not to set out for his own island, but to drift about on the enchanted lagoons and channels. As his canoe disappeared into the mist, another came out from the shadow of the shore and slipped along the glassy water up to Sandy's little pier.

23

When Dantry had gone, Sandy remained sitting by the fire, and presently, one by one, the children and the neighbors reappeared to take their places in the little circle. But Sandy's good humor had gone, and he no longer made the jokes which set them to laughing. Dantry's coat and shirt lay beside him on the ground, and he did not speak of them nor make any joke about them, for he was thinking how he could explain to Maria what Dantry had told him without hurting her too much. He knew well enough that when Dantry had left the compound, Maria must have followed him, but he knew too, for by now he knew his son-in-law all too well, that Dantry would not tell her the truth, but only put her off. He thought again, "There is nothing to be done. The sooner he leaves Nivandrum forever the better. For every day he stays on there will be new tragedy." And he reflected that the only train would not leave until tomorrow in the late afternoon. He was afraid, not of Dantry, but for what Maria might do.

Beside him his third son went on thumping and exploring new rhythms, and one of the old men with a flute presently joined in the music, first setting a theme and then, accompanied by Sandy's boy, playing it over and over again with countless variations. Sometimes the neighbors conversed in low voices, but most of the time they remained silent, for it was as if Dantry had left behind him not only the tangible jacket and shirt, but a kind of shadow which dimmed the fire and made the theme and variations of the old man playing the flute, turn more and more melancholy and sinister.

Sandy stared into the fire, not a merry Buddha now, but a grave one like the Buddhas of the north, until presently he was aware of a murmur all about him and a restless moving, and then raising his eyes he saw that the old man who was playing the flute had stopped and was making with his withered old fingers the sign against the evil eye. There was a look of terror in his wrinkled face, and as Sandy followed the glance he discovered standing silently in the light by the fire, the figure of Léah, Rasmussen's wife. She was dressed in a dark *sari*, so that, in the shadows, you saw only her narrow-

eyed face, so handsome and yet so disturbing, with its expression of malevolence and its implications of evil.

The children ran away and the older people remained, terrified, but afraid
to offend her by leaving. Sandy watching her, thought as he always thought,
"All this evil eye business is nonsense," yet he was obscurely disturbed, less
perhaps by any fear of her magic than by the sense of her subtle malevolence.
She never left Rasmussen's island, she had not been to the compound since
the night long ago when Maria had stolen away to Dantry's island, that
night which was the beginning of all her unhappiness. Now, for the first
time, it occurred to him that Léah perhaps had had something to do with
Maria's behavior.

He made an effort, especially before all the others, to regard her visit as
perfectly usual, and said, "Sit down, Léah." And a little afraid of what she
had to say, he spoke in English, which his neighbors, if they understood at
all, understood but vaguely.

And Léah answered him in English, saying, "No sit down. Coming to
see Maria."

"What for see Maria?" asked Sandy.

"Helping Maria."

"How helping?"

"Telling her how she get her man back."

For a second, sparring for time, Sandy was silent. Then he said, "Maria
still got her man."

Léah smiled. It was an expression which was scarcely a smile, but more
the look of a tired prophetess in a trance. . . . The prophetess, the Cassandra
who always predicted rightly, whom no one ever believed until it was
too late.

"No got her man," she said stubbornly, "Maria knowing it too."

"Maria no want her man," said Sandy stubbornly.

"Maria wanting her man . . . wanting him happy."

For a moment Sandy reflected, thinking, "Perhaps after all she can help
the girl. Perhaps there is something in her hocus-pocus. After all it was Léah
who got Dantry for her in the first place. Perhaps she's interested. Perhaps
she wants to keep him for her. Perhaps I haven't got any right to interfere.
Anyway she can't do any harm." So he said, "Maria inside house. No do
Maria harm."

"What harm?" asked Léah, smiling with benevolence. "Making Maria
happy. Knowing what Maria want."

"All right," said Sandy.

"Thanking," said Léah and moved off into the shadows in the direction
of the main hut. The eyes of the others followed her, still filled with awe.
She walked slowly and with prophetic dignity, and as she disappeared like

a shadow into the door, Sandy felt a sudden impulse to rise and go after her and send her back to Rasmussen's island without her ever seeing Maria, but he did not move. It was only laziness that prevented him, and the fact that he was growing older and that it was not so easy to get up and down as it had once been.

24

At eight o'clock in the morning Lady Groton was roused by a violent knocking at the door and, still befogged by all the sleeping stuff she had taken, wakened with difficulty, to say, "Come in," expecting the door of her bedroom in Hill Street to open and admit Harris. But the door, which very strangely was not at all like the door of her own bedroom, opened and admitted Bates, who seemed as nearly as it was possible for him to be in a state of agitation. Mechanically she said, "What is it, Bates?" and then listened, still trying to discover where she was and why it was so hot and why there was no grate with a fire in it.

His Lordship, so Bates said, had not wakened properly. He appeared to be in what Bates referred to as a "comber," and now that he was no longer able to resist, Bates had managed to take his temperature and found that it was seven degrees above normal.

"I'm afraid, me lady," said Bates, "that he has one of them Eastern fevers."

Then suddenly Bates and the room became clear to her, clear enough for her to think, "You're not afraid at all. You hope he has. You hope it's nothing worse than plague." But pulling herself together with a great effort, she said, "I suppose we should send for a doctor, only I don't know whom to send for or where to send for him."

"I've inquired, me lady, from this man Rasmussen and there isn't any doctor, except a kind of witch doctor." He hesitated for a moment and then said, "I've heard that sometimes they can be quite good. They have all kinds of native remedies for snake bite and things like that."

After a moment of thought, she said, "No, we can't do that. Lord Groton would be furious."

Then Bates said, "This man Rasmussen did say there was a kind of lady doctor—a half-caste or something—that lives in the capital. She is called Mees Opp . . . only the capital is a long way from here and no train."

The name brought up at once the picture of the great, homely woman dressed in white with the hat covered with faded flowers. Lady Groton saw her again as she had seen her outside the carriage window, calm, reassuring, serene, in the midst of the squalling pilgrims and vendors of rice cakes. She saw her again as she had seen her from the window, dosing the long lines of ill and suffering islanders. And suddenly the thought returned to her that this woman was somehow mixed up in her own destiny. It kept returning again and again. But she thought, "I mustn't be an idiot. I must have common sense." So aloud she said, "We might telegraph to Madras or Colombo for a doctor to come by plane."

But Bates saw the error of this. He said, "I went into that, me lady, with this man Rasmussen. There isn't a decent place for a plane to land, and anyway he doubts whether a doctor would come."

"Even if he knew who the patient was?"

Bates smirked. "That's just it, me lady. We can't tell them that. His Lordship strictly forbade sending for a doctor."

"When?"

"Last night, when I was trying to get him to let me take his temperature. He said, 'One thing, Bates, if I fall ill you're not to send for any doctor. I'm a strong man and I'll pull through, but I'm not going to have any doctor messin' around here. That's orders,' he said, 'the strictest orders you ever got, and you're not to let Her Ladyship change them. You're working for me,' he said, 'and not for her.'"

"Why did he say that?"

"I'm not sure, me lady, but you know how he is about doctors. They always make him curse. And then . . ." he hesitated and plunged, "I suppose he doesn't want it to get out why he's here. That's something I'm not supposed to know, but I do."

Again, as on the night before, the shadow of a confidential smirk crossed his face, and again Lady Groton felt a moment of uneasiness. It was terrifying how much Bates knew. She did not mind how much he knew about her so long as they did not admit it to each other. Suddenly she said, "Can one send a telegram from here?"

"No, me lady; I inquired. It has to be sent from the other side of the mountains."

"Do you mean to say there's no telegraph at the station?"

"No, me lady. That's the kind of place it is."

She thought for a moment, wearily and with a great effort, "Then I suppose Mees Opp is the best we can do."

"His Lordship hates doctors," said Bates. "A lady doctor would send his blood pressure up to bursting."

Then suddenly she felt angry, wildly angry, because Albert had put her in this position, alone, isolated in this forgotten place with himself helpless and ill, with no doctors, no nurses, no telegraph, no luxuries, all because he wanted to make more money and have more power. He wanted it so much— this victory over Hugo Deakin—that he was willing to run the risk of dying rather than have the news get out to the world that he was in Nivandrum. He was willing to die rather than let Deakin discover his secret. It was incredible; yet faintly, obscurely, there was something magnificent in such determination and singleness of purpose. That, she supposed, was how men like Albert became rich and powerful. But it was terrifying too, because it was a kind of madness.

She said, "I think it's got beyond what Lord Groton wants. If he's unconscious he can't make a row. I think that brings us back to Mees Opp. How can she get here?"

"By boat, me lady."

"How long will it take?"

"Two or three days."

Again she reflected and then said, "I'll go in and see him and then I'll send a note to Mr. Dantry. He'll be better than anyone under the circumstances. He has lived here for five years. He ought to know."

She thought she heard Bates saying, "Very good, me lady, I think that is the wisest thing," but she could not be quite certain, because deep inside her she kept hearing a voice which said, "It's Mees Opp you need here. She could manage everything. It's Mees Opp you want."

She felt strangely tired and for a moment she thought, "Perhaps I too am going to be ill," but she was aware of Bates standing there watching her and she said, "That's all, Bates; if I need you, I'll send for you."

And as he went out of the room it seemed to her that there was almost a look of glee on his face as if he thought, "Now these fine birds are in hot water. Now they'll know what it means to be poor and without the money for a doctor. Now the bloody old fool is going to be ill and die proper like any ordinary man."

For the first time she was profoundly disturbed by Bates, and she was troubled by his manner of confidence as if somehow he sought, feeling his way, with the greatest diplomacy, an alliance with Albert.

When she had made up her face and arranged her hair and put on a peignoir she seemed less dazed and numbed, although her brain still felt as if incased in cotton wool, and when she raised her hand it was leaden and strange as if it did not belong to her.

It was the first time that she had gone to Groton's room, and when she saw it she was tempted to laugh, not only because of the room itself, but at the thought that Albert had undoubtedly chosen it because it was the largest and most imposing room in Rasmussen's hotel. He lay, grotesquely, in a vast bed of teakwood, ornamented with bits of mother-of-pearl, placed on a square of faded turkey-red carpet, and the sight of him lying half-conscious in the bed (as she had never seen him in all their life together) gave her a sudden shock. It was as if she had never before seen him quite properly, as he was, as if she had never seen how heavy, how gross he could be, for now the spark, the vitality, the energy which had always animated his great bulk and turned mere weight into strength, was absent, and he appeared dull, inert and heavy, the hard line of the brutal jaw gone soft, the muscles of the big face all flaccid.

And then she remembered a little vaguely, as if she had dreamed it, what had happened the night before and the quarrel that had taken place in her bedroom when for a moment she had been vulgar and common; and she was filled with a feeling of shame and a loathing of herself as well, because she had lived for more than fifteen years with this gross mass of flesh that lay on the bed, that again and again she had been able to accept him with indifference. And she thought suddenly of Tom Dantry and how different his body was, how slim and hard and brown, in spite of all his drinking. And she felt a strange desire to weep for herself, for all her mistakes and folly and cold misery. Looking down at Groton, she thought, "Whether he lives or dies it is all finished between us. I shall never live with him again." But now, she wished shamelessly, in her heart, that he would die, for she knew now that so long as he lived and perhaps long after he was dead, she would always see him thus, betrayed by his illness, heavy, gross, purple-faced, with his mouth hanging open a little; and each time that she saw him or thought of him she would remember that she had prostituted her fine slim body for him, not once, but many times.

Leaning over the bed, she knew that Bates from his corner of the room was watching her, darkly curious to see how she would behave, and she knew that she must put up some sort of show which would check forever that dreadful insinuating grin of his, a show which, although it would probably not deceive him, would nevertheless put him in his place.

She said, as if she were a devoted wife, "Albert! Albert! It's Alix," and the dull pale blue eyes opened a little way but only looked into space, far beyond her, without focusing. Then he made a faint grunting sound and again closed his eyes. Again she tried to rouse him, but with no better success, and then to Bates she said, "I'll write a note to Mr. Dantry. You can send it across at once. If we're to send for Mees Opp, we must do it at once, but I want to hear first what Mr. Dantry has to advise. You'd better take it across yourself and wait for an answer."

"Very good, me lady."

"I'll bring it when I've finished," she said, and then went out of the room, leaving Bates content that he was, after all, going to see this Dantry at close range, in his own house, where he could discover all sorts of things about him, what sort of furniture he had, and what sort of servant and how he lived, and whether he was really as much of a gentleman as he appeared.

In her own room she opened her writing case, but when she began the note she found it far from simple to write, because there were other things she wanted besides simple information about Mees Opp or a doctor. She was aware now that he was deliberately avoiding her, and she was a little afraid that if he had not already gone away he might go away during the course of the day, and now, with Albert lying in that awful bed like a sick animal, she could not think of Tom leaving her here alone in this strange hotel with a half-witted proprietor, and Bates becoming more and more difficult. And in her mind there hovered all the while, like a subtle temptation, the thought that after all, whether he lived or died, she might soon be free of Albert, and then she could have Tom perhaps forever. She wasn't so young any more; perhaps it was time to think about settling down for good, forever; and at the thought of being old a little shiver of horror shook her body. And finally, while she struggled, trying to think how she could best accomplish her complicated purpose, the image of Tom returned to her as he had been on that first evening when the dancers came, and she knew that she wanted him more than any man in the world and that there had never been any other man.

Three times she drafted the note and destroyed it, and she might have gone on for half the morning save that time pressed, and she was afraid that if she delayed too long Bates would begin to grow curious and insinuating. It was odd, but slowly she was becoming afraid of Bates, as if he were her own conscience of a spy stationed to watch her.

Then as she began a fourth draft, she thought suddenly, "What a fool I am! I'll not send him a note. I'll go to him myself." For now she saw, she had an excuse, a reason, which would save her vanity and her pride. She could go to him and perhaps manage to keep him here in Nivandrum, near her, at least for a little while longer, because each hour, each minute, seemed precious to her now.

Hastily she tore up the note, and when she had looked at herself in the blotched old glass and arranged her hair a second time and touched her lips with scarlet, she dressed and put on her hat and went down the stairs to order Rasmussen to send for her boatmen.

A little while later Bates, watching from the window of Lord Groton's *chambre de luxe*, saw her cross over to Dantry's island, and he thought, "There is going to be trouble before we've finished."

He was disappointed and a little resentful that he had not been sent himself, for now he would very likely never see the inside of Dantry's house and discover whether he was really as much of a gentleman as he looked. He watched her step ashore and climb the great open stairway and disappear into Dantry's house, and then he went downstairs to fetch gruel for His Lordship. The gruel was not what interested him most, but the opportunity for another chat with that woman Léah.

[429]

25

The train left at noon, but Dantry had been awake since a little after dawn, going through the house for the last time, telling Silas what to pack in one or two rather battered handbags—some shorts, some shirts, some books, the toilet things. As he watched the boy packing, it occurred to him how deeply he had sunk into the life of Nivandrum, how far he had drifted from the civilization of the West. There was scarcely anything material left out of the old life. And now, for the first time, the departure became a reality, and he felt a sudden pang at the thought that very likely he would never again wear a *sarong* and never again go naked save for a loin cloth, fishing beyond the Great Bar. His head ached from sleeplessness and the drinking of the night before and his spirit sagged with shame at the memory of the humiliating scene which had taken place in Sandy's compound. For a moment he thought, "I could still stay and never see her again." But in his heart he knew that such an idea was no good. He would have no peace so long as she was in Nivandrum.

He had had tea and two drinks to put him on his feet, and was standing in the great bedroom overlooking the harbor when he heard someone enter the room, softly, as Silas always entered it, but with a different softness, and turning, he saw Maria standing shyly in the doorway. She was dressed all in white as he had seen her on that day long ago when he surprised her in the cookhouse, and she wore a wreath of jasmine flowers about the knot of her dark hair. Something in the sight of her made him feel not annoyed, but shy and a little ashamed, so he said to her, with softness in his voice, "Come in."

Shyly she came toward him, saying, "I have come to say good-by."

It was a strange scene and he was aware of its strangeness. He was aware that she had come to him full of love, and he knew that in his heart he no longer felt any emotion for her save that of pity. He was not good at acting, and now he felt the imposition by something stronger than himself, something in the situation itself, of the necessity to play a role which he did not feel.

She said, "I will go to the station, if you don't mind. I will help carry your things."

The speech hurt him somehow by its implications of simplicity and devotion, for she made the speech with a childlike sincerity and not as other women, Western women, had done, to save their vanity or to heap coals of fire upon his head. She was not playing the martyr. She had come thus simply because she loved him, because she had wanted to look at him again for the last time, and there was something agonizing in the knowledge that he had to hurt her; it was like hurting a child or a puppy.

He said, "No, of course not. I won't have you carrying my bundles on your head like a farmer's wife," and quite simply she answered, "I would like it if it would please you."

"Sit down, Maria. We can talk while I finish what I have to do." For he saw suddenly that it would be much easier if he made the visit an affair as casual as possible, and that it would be much easier if he found himself occupied while she was there watching him. In that way he would not have to see the look in the great dark eyes, the look of someone who was dying.

She seated herself not on a chair, but shyly on the edge of the great Spanish bed, and as she did so he saw the bed again as it had been on that first night long ago, when it had been covered with jasmine and jacqueranda and bignonia blossoms. The memory gave him a sudden feeling of illness and he thought bitterly, "That too is finished. That went the way of everything else." Some day, when he was an old man, the memory would no longer be like an acute pain, but glowing and beautiful. But for that he would have to wait; it was still too near to cause anything but pain. The girl sitting on the edge of the bed was not the girl he had found in his room that night dressed in a European frock, wearing an old fiber hat covered with real flowers. This was simply a pretty half-caste girl toward whom he felt no emotion whatever. And in a moment of revelation he saw what it was that had caused the whole thing to fail. There had never been anything between them but the bond of their bodies. For her, in her simplicity, that had been beautiful. It had been enough. For men like Rasmussen and Sandy that was enough. But on him, Dantry, rested the complicated curse of civilization, and so after a little time he had grown bored, with a boredom which did not matter until Alix had arrived. The moment he saw her, he had known at once his madness and his error. He had discovered that after all he had not escaped.

The girl sat on the bed quietly, with that stillness which Eastern women have, filled with sadness, yet knowing a kind of resigned happiness that he was still there, that there were still precious minutes, being ticked off with horrible speed by the noisy little clock on the dressing table—moments, seconds, when she could watch him, knowing how much she loved him, how many hours of delight they had had together. Presently she lifted her feet from the floor and sat on them native fashion, covering them with the edge of her white *sari*.

Dantry, too, was aware of the ticking of the clock, but for him each minute, each second, dragged. Occupying himself uselessly with taking things in and out of drawers, he talked to her without looking at her. He told her that he was arranging to send her money so that always at Nivandrum she would be rich. The girl neither protested nor accepted the offer, but only sat there silently, but her silence carried a reproach born, not of her intention, but out of Dantry's own bad conscience, as if the silence said, "I do not want the money, but if it gives you pleasure to give it me, if it makes your mind more peaceful and happy, I will accept it."

It was not easy, the conversation, for she did not feel the European woman's necessity for talk to hide the emotions. She had never talked much. He remembered now that in all the time they had been together she had said very little, and nothing which had ever interested him very profoundly or roused in him a desire to talk. On that side their life together had always been empty. It had endured because whenever he grew bored with her he sent her back to Sandy's compound.

The hands of the clock crawled slowly round the face that had grown rusty from the eternal damp of the lagoons. It seemed to him that it would never reach that point which would permit him with decency to say that he must leave for the train and that she had better go back to the compound. He had run away many times, but never had it been as painful as this. Scenes, hysterics, screams, anything was far better than the simple questioning silence of the tiny figure on the great bed.

He lighted a cigarette and gave it to her and then took one himself and poured himself a glass of whisky. At the same moment he saw standing in the great doorway silhouetted against the brilliant blue of the harbor, the figure of Alix in her white expensive clothes, and he thought, "The bitch! Why should she have come here now?" Then he thought, "Well, here's for it. Now she'll know."

Aloud he said, in as casual a voice as he was able to command, "Hullo! Come in. I was just packing." He thought, "I've been caught . . . this time by two women instead of one," for at the moment he thought only of escape. It seemed to him that he had never felt so tired in all his life.

She came across the threshold and then saw Maria sitting on the edge of the great bed. For a moment she hesitated, and he saw that for once she very nearly lost her self-command. He said, "This is Lady Groton, Maria," and to Alix he said, "This is my wife."

This time she found nothing to say and the color went out of her face. He might not have noticed it, save that the sudden paleness left the subtly placed rouge isolated in two spots of color high on the cheekbones.

Maria slipped to the floor, trembling a little. She did not salaam, as a full-blooded native woman would have done, but stood, a little frightened, clinging with one hand to the end of the painted bed.

Then Alix recovered herself and said, "How do you do?" and Maria bowed and muttered something which he could not understand.

"I seem to have come at an awkward moment," said Alix. "I apologize for having run in without warning, but it couldn't well be helped."

"Sit down," said Dantry. "I can't entertain you for very long. My train leaves in forty-five minutes."

He was aware that there was something comical in the air of politeness between them, something which would not have been comical with any other woman in the world. But with her it was absurd. They knew each other so well that there were times when each knew what the other was thinking, when there was scarcely any necessity for speech.

She did not sit down, and he knew that it was her pride that prevented her. She said, "It's about Albert. He's very ill. I didn't know what to do. I don't know anyone here. I don't know whom to send for."

"How ill?" asked Dantry.

"As ill as it is possible to be. He has a temperature of a hundred and seven."

For a moment, he was silent thinking, "Why not let him die? It would be better for everyone. No one wants him to live . . . not Alix, not the secretary, nor me, nor even the valet. If he died Nivandrum might be saved . . . for a little while anyway." Then he said, "I suppose there's nothing to do but try and get Mees Opp. It's a pity he wasn't taken ill three days ago when she was here. She's back in the capital by now."

"He was ill then, but he wouldn't let anyone do anything about it."

"I don't know whether she will come or not."

"When she hears who it is?"

Tom laughed, a quick rather harsh laugh. "I don't think that would impress her much. The name of the great Lord Groton doesn't mean much out here . . . especially to Mees Opp. She's a singularly simple and human person. To her rajahs and coolies are much the same except that coolies have a greater need for her."

He was aware again, sharply, of the ticking of the clock. The time was growing short. In a little while he would have to go or he would miss the train, and if he missed the train. . . . Now suddenly, with her standing there in front of him, outwardly so utterly calm, he did not want to go, and he knew that in his heart he had never wanted to go. There was something about her self-possession, her quietness, even the hardness which he divined beneath the smooth surface, which gave him a kind of strength. And he knew that in her heart she was suffering as he was suffering. He thought again, "But *she* is honest. Shining and free."

Then Maria did an extraordinary thing, the first positive thing he had ever known her to do. She said, "It is half-past eleven, Dantry. If you do not go now you will miss your train." And he knew that she had divined everything, even if she had not divined it earlier, and that she preferred to let him go out of her life forever than to stay behind with this white woman.

Alix said, "If you must catch your train, go by all means. I shall manage somehow."

He felt the great dark eyes of Maria watching him, but he dared not look at her, for he knew that whatever happened, whatever course he took, she was finished. The clock kept on ticking loudly. He was thinking, "If I stay there is only one end to it all. If I stay she will have to quit Groton and come with me, forever," and then he heard himself saying to Maria without looking at her, "Tell Silas I shall not be going by this train. Perhaps by the train on Saturday; perhaps straight from the capital; I cannot go and leave the *burra sahib* who is very ill."

For a moment Maria stood quite still, silently watching him, and then without a word, she turned and like a servant, went out of the room to obey his order.

When she had gone there was a little silence, and then Alix said, "It is good of you to stay."

"It isn't good of me. I didn't want to go. I only wanted an excuse."

"Then why were you going?"

The speech, he saw, was characteristic of her, of all her honesty and her freedom, of all the strength he found in her. Weakly he said, "Because I thought it best . . . because it seemed the only thing to do."

After a little silence she said, "What is the matter between us, Tom? Why can we never be honest with each other and just a little simple? If only we'd been honest a long while ago, everything would have been different."

He did not answer her, and she turned away from him, saying, "I didn't know it was as bad as that."

"What?"

"That you were married."

He laughed. "I've been married less than a month. I was married the day before the letter came announcing your arrival." Again he laughed. "Oh, it wasn't a new story. We'd been living together for more than three years."

"Do you love her?"

"No, I never loved her."

For a little time she was silent, thinking. Then she said, "No, I don't suppose that's not possible . . . not with a man like you."

He finished his whisky and heard her saying, "Now I suppose we had better talk sense. How am I to send for this woman doctor? How long does it take?"

"It's a good twenty-four hours' hard traveling one way. If she'll come at once, we can be back here day after tomorrow. I'll go for her myself. I doubt if she'd come if we only sent a boy to fetch her. Very likely she'll need some persuading."

[434]

"It's a good deal to ask of you . . . *you* of all people."

"Yes, it is rather." And he laughed again, mirthlessly, at the idea of Alix and himself working to save the life of a man whom neither of them in their hearts wanted to go on living. "But I don't mind. It's all in the day's work."

He turned away from her and said, "You'd better go along now to the hotel and tell Rasmussen to send for Sandy's third boy. He's called Anthony. He can show me the way. I'll come over there as soon as I've changed my clothes and got ready for the journey."

She did not say anything more, but went out of the room and down the stairs to her waiting boat, but she kept remembering all the time what he had said to Maria, "Perhaps I'll go on Saturday or perhaps I'll go straight on from the capital." He couldn't go now. He mustn't go when she had just found him again. As the boat crossed the inlet she thought, "I should have had courage. I should have said to him in spite of everything that we have always loved each other . . . that now we've found each other again we must stay together for always." And then she knew that she had not spoken because of his perverse mood of irony. You could not say things like that no matter how much you wanted to say them when the air was filled with bitter mockery. And there was that girl, his wife. Even after she had gone, she had left something behind, some intangible thing which had made them both feel a little ashamed, something which separated them and left them silent.

And as she walked up the path she thought, "If only I could help him in some way," and strangely enough she thought suddenly of the girl she had seen in his bedroom, so tiny and so young, and she felt sorry for her too, because she would never be able to understand why Tom was so strange and perverse and miserable. She would never understand that power he had of torturing himself and bringing misery to others.

When she left the pier she gave Rasmussen the message and then went to Groton's room, idly, vaguely, because she did not know what she wanted to do. He was alone, still in a kind of coma, breathing heavily, and she saw him now, objectively, coldly, more coldly perhaps than she had ever seen him before in all their life together. He had not stirred when she came in, and now he gave no sign of knowing that she was in the room. The *ayah* had said that she ought not to enter his room until she knew what the illness was; if it were the plague or even cholera, it might be dangerous. But she had no feeling about danger, because deep within her was a consciousness, like that of many soldiers in battle, that nothing would happen to her. And lately she had had the feeling too, a depressing feeling, that it was her fate to go on living, on and on until she had lived the damned thing out to the very end, that this perhaps would be her atonement, because as she grew older, she was at times aware that she had an atonement to make at some time in some place, and that there was no escaping it.

Now in her coldness she felt no desire to leave the room and the spectacle of her husband unconscious on the awful teakwood bed. It even gave her a kind of perverse pleasure to look at him lying thus, helpless, down, beaten for the first time. She had no particular feeling of pity or regret, because she knew so well that neither feeling had ever touched him in all his life.

While she sat there she thought, "There you are—not the great swaggering Lord Groton, boasting and bullying and buying what you want—but just plain, vulgar Albert Simpson, the son of a small building contractor in Birmingham, Albert Simpson, who got beyond himself. You've never done a good or generous deed for anyone unless it brought you profit and glory. And you've ruined men and women who trusted you, for the sake of power and money. Oh, you've given money to charities in large lumps, well advertised in your newspapers, but it never cost you anything. You never missed it, and it made people who didn't know you say you were generous, and it served to whitewash your character and cover up a lot of skulduggery and stifle the criticism of your enemies. You'd betray your own country if it brought you another shilling or another ounce of power. Long ago you sold rifles and shells in underhand ways to the Turks to kill at Gallipoli boys who came from your own country, men better than yourself who went off to their death while you stayed at home to make money out of the tragic needs of your own people and wrote wild leaders in your own papers to keep the war going. And now, only a fortnight ago in Singapore, you wrote a leader to be printed in all the Groton papers that was certain to make ill-feeling and bitterness and cause more wars. It cost you a nice lot to cable it all the way from Singapore—enough for my father and I to have lived on for a couple of months long ago—but it didn't matter because if there was a war you'd get it all back a million times over. You didn't know that I read it before it was sent, but I did.

"There are so many things you don't know about me and what I know of you. Bates and I together could write a biography of you that could put you in jail for the rest of your life or in an asylum for madness, only you'd probably buy your way out. Oh, you're very shrewd—using your newspapers, your steamship lines, your mines, your factories, round and round in an endless chain, turning out profits for yourself at the expense of workmen and shareholders and humanity itself. You've never had a friend you didn't buy. You even bought your own wife, and a bad bargain she was, probably the worst you ever made. What was it that happened to you long ago, perhaps when you were a little child, that made you want all those things for which you sacrificed everything decent? Were you thinking about all this long ago when you were selling cheap cutlery and watches in Malaya? Who hurt you? What put into your head the idea that all this power and all this money were the only things worth having in all the world? What made you think you could buy things in life—things like love and fidelity and respect and breeding? What are you like inside? What must it be like to be *you*? What does it feel like to be so ruthless, so bitter, so alone, hating everybody who does not lick your boots?

"You'll never tell anyone because you don't know yourself how it feels. You've never known. You can't know because you're like a man born with a horrible physical deformity who can never know what it is like to be fine and straight and young and beautiful. Your brain, your soul, must have some horrible deformity which is all the worse because it cannot be seen. You must have been a horrible child—grasping, calculating how to make money even out of your own mother. But it's destroyed you, too. Because you're a finished man, Albert Simpson. The world has finished with you, and you are sick of yourself and tired and worn down by the thing you built up with so much trickery and ambition. You're going to die in a cheap uncomfortable hotel in a horrible bed, and not at your fine house in Hill Street or your great Georgian house in the country. You're going to die in the East of some awful disease and no one will care, not one person in the world, not even your wife or your secretary or your servant. Perhaps your ashes will go home on one of your own boats and perhaps they won't. But you're finished, goddamn you! You'll never leave this lovely place alive, this place which you meant to ruin as you've ruined everything you've touched. You'll never come into my room again to sleep with me like the animal you are. You'll never again shout at servants and inferiors as if they were dogs. You'll never again make me ashamed in public that I ever knew you. You did something horrible to me, to my very soul. Oh, I let you do it because I was tired and didn't care, but you could have helped a little. You might have seen what I needed—oh, so little—to have saved me, because in the beginning I tried to make it go, but you didn't see. You never had time. All you did was to shove money at me.

"Well, you're finished. You're going to die and rot, and in a few years nobody will even remember who you were. You haven't even an heir to leave behind you. I'm glad that vile blood of yours won't go on living because I bore you a child. I'm glad I saw to that. You're finished and nobody cares. Go on, slobber and snore, like the gross animal you are. There were times when you thought you could break my pride and make me as coarse as yourself, but you never did. In the end I've won. Even last night I won when I sent you skulking out of my room. You hadn't any kindness or any sensibility or any morals or any ethics, so nobody could ever touch you but me. I knew you well enough to know where it would hurt, and you made me use my knowledge at last. You forced me to do it. I'm not sorry. I only wish I had been more cruel. Oh, if you only knew how many times I've betrayed you, and never once with a man who wasn't better than yourself—warmer, kinder, more decent, more human, more beautiful. Yes, and every one of them was a better lover than you. People grow to look like what they are, Albert. You were a hog and you've grown to look like a hog, lying there snoring and slobbering in your own spittle. Well, you're going to die. This is the end of you, and the whole world—even the little brats in the streets of Canton and Bombay and Madagascar—will be happier and have a better life because you are dead."

And suddenly she felt a wild desire to cross the room and spit on him, but she did not do it because it occurred to her almost immediately that such a spectacle would only be extremely funny.

"What's happened to me?" she thought. "Perhaps I, too, am going to be ill. I shouldn't be in here, but even if I caught something, what difference would it make? I shouldn't care. Why should I suddenly care so profoundly about Albert's nastiness? Why should I be so hysterical?"

And suddenly she was afraid, not of Albert, of whom she had never been afraid, nor of any illness, but of herself and of that nameless dread which she had felt now and again ever since coming to Nivandrum. Quickly she ran from the room, and in her own room she bolted the door and threw herself on the bed, where she wept for a long time, silently, hysterically, without making a sound, and presently, when the weeping was finished, she lay with her face buried in the pillow, cold again and terrifyingly calm, and after an hour she rose and went to her writing case and wrote a telegram addressed to Lord Deakin in London.

It read: "Groton in Nivandrum on South coast. Oil prospects certain. Buying up railway and water front. Act at once or too late."

It was the only way to save Nivandrum. If Albert and Deakin began fighting over it, the whole thing might end in a deadlock, and neither the one nor the other would be able to ruin the place.

She was very calm now. She knew what she was doing. She thought, "He has double-crossed everyone all his life and now his own wife is double-crossing him."

Then she sent the *ayah* to find Bates, and when Bates came in she was silent for a long time looking at him, searching the pale eyes and the long sallow face, wondering whether she dared do what she meant to do. At last, after Bates had half-divined what was going on in her mind, she said with as much dignity as possible, "Bates, you've always been a good friend to me."

Bates's face remained inscrutable, "Yes, me lady. You've always been able to trust me, I think."

"I want to do something terrible."

Still unmoved, Bates said, "Yes, me lady."

She handed him the message and watched his face while he read it. When he had finished, he looked at her and the slow grin appeared once more, the grin which now sealed their understanding and their alliance and delivered her into his hands for good or for evil. But it did not matter now, for she had a strange feeling that everything was coming to an end.

Again he said, "Yes, me lady."

"Is there any way it can be sent?"

"I think it could be managed."

"Do you understand . . . can you imagine why I am sending it?"

"Yes, me lady."

"Send it then . . . the sooner the better."

"Yes, me lady."

He left her, his face still lighted by a grin that had become almost mystical. Slowly, each step a satisfaction, he made his way down the great stairway and out into the garden. On the way he met Lansbury and when they exchanged good mornings, the pink-faced secretary asked, "Is His Lordship better?" And then in a feudal patronizing way, with a strong Oxford accent, "You look like the cat that swallowed the canary."

"About the same," said Bates; "I was thinking of something else." Bates hated Lansbury, but he never hated him more than at that moment because he was so stupid, so useless, so patronizing.

Down the narrow path he went to the place where the crotons and bougainvillea were thickest, and there, taking out a match, he set fire to the bit of paper, watching it burn until nothing but ashes remained.

He had destroyed the cable not because he disapproved, but because there was no need to do anything about it, for the message had already been sent by himself, with a messenger who had gone, not by train, but down the coast to the capital, and it had been sent in duplicate, one message to London and the other to Deakin's agent in Bombay, so that there could be no delay and no error. Bates knew the ways of businessmen; he had had a long experience and knew what to do. It was not the first time he had received money from Lord Deakin. With what he would be paid for this message he could buy the semidetached villa in Manchester and become a member of the Manchester division of the Communist party. Bates, too, felt that things were drawing to a close.

It was Léah who had helped him, Léah who had produced the runner to take the telegram down the coast, for with all her faith in the River God, she believed in the force of action. Sometimes it was necessary when you had to get things done.

[439]

26

When he had taken off the worn traveling suit and was dressed again in a *sarong*, Dantry crossed over to the Grand Oriental Hotel. At the landing stage he found Lansbury, dressed in white drill trousers, a school blazer and topi, fishing languidly. The secretary regarded him with astonishment, and when he divined that this dark-skinned man dressed in native clothes was a countryman, he said, "Good morning," rather uncomfortably as if Dantry had been a leper, and Dantry, walking up the path thought, "The damned narrow-minded snob! They don't want me here in Nivandrum and now little pip-squeaks like him don't want me back."

Lady Groton sent down word that she was dressing, and while he waited he ordered a brandy and soda.

Rasmussen, still in his preposterous waiter's costume, said "Good morning, sir!" and the word "sir" puzzled and hurt Dantry as it had hurt him on the night before when Sandy used it. He inquired after Dantry's health, not cordially as a friend, but distantly as a waiter making a professional inquiry, and Dantry thought, "So, he's in on it, too! They're all against me!" And then he realized that he must appear openly ridiculous to Rasmussen after he had failed a second time in his announced determination to quit Nivandrum forever. Then the idea of Fate occurred to him again—that there must be some obscure mystical reason for his having come to Nivandrum in the first place, some reason why whenever he tried to leave it something always intervened to prevent his going. Perhaps it was his destiny. Perhaps there was something ahead waiting for him, which he must go through to the very end. And then he thought, "But that's all bloody Eastern nonsense!"

Then Alix came down the stairs, slowly, as she had come down on the first evening, and at sight of her he was at first angry again and then a little shaken. But he told himself, "No, I must go through with this. I must go away forever."

She smiled at him, and when he said abruptly to her without any other greeting, "Have a drink?" she replied, "No, it's much too early for that."

He tried to discover from her face whether she was troubled by Groton's illness, but the face betrayed nothing save a faint weariness which made her seem more attractive to him. When she sat down he said, "What do they think he has?"

"Nobody knows. Here they just call it 'the fever.' I suppose that covers almost everything."

"Everything but elephantiasis and leprosy."

"I don't think it likely he has either of those two things. What might he catch here?"

"It might be cholera or plague or typhus or malaria or half a dozen other things. They're all pretty nasty. From the symptoms it's likely that it's typhoid or malaria; I should think it might be what is called 'black malaria.'"

"Is that bad?"

"Yes."

"Why?"

"Because it attacks the brain."

She was silent for a long time considering what he had told her, thinking, "Perhaps I was a hysterical fool. Perhaps it wasn't necessary to send that telegram." Aloud she said, "Perhaps I had better take things in my own hands and send for a regular physician."

"No. Mees Opp is quite as good as any of them, and she has had a lot more experience than most with this kind of thing."

"I was thinking, too, that a woman doctor might be very annoying to have about."

He glanced at her sharply, wondering what it was she had in mind in making such a speech. He said, "A woman doctor can be more inquisitive, I suppose, but I don't think Mees Opp will be. She's too busy." This remark she did not answer and he asked, "Did you send for the boy?"

"Yes. He should be here any moment."

"He's the best to be had . . . the quickest. He wins all the canoe races."

"Tom."

"Yes."

"What are you going to do?"

"What do you mean?"

"Are you going away . . . straight from the capital?"

"I don't know."

"Will you lunch with me today . . . before you start?"

"No. I'm taking some curry and rice with me. I've got to get underway."

"I shan't be leaving here very soon."

"No, with his Nibs in the present state, I should think not."

"You're being stupid, Tom."

"No, I'm not being stupid. I'm trying to make sense, for once."

"Whenever you were disagreeable you used to call it making sense." He did not answer her and she said, "Is there any special reason? I promise to behave myself."

(Why in God's name couldn't she leave him in peace? Why did she keep stirring him up, prodding the past into life, again and again?)

"No, there's no special reason except that I'm a bloody neurotic and I've got to be alone. I've got the jitters . . . permanently, I think. I've made a mess out of everything I've ever touched."

[441]

"Take another drink."

"No, Jezebel. That's no solution. I drank last night and made a hopeless ass of myself."

"It certainly never makes you more attractive." Again he did not answer her and presently she said, "You've got to be a little kind to me. I can't run away and leave Albert here. I'll have to stay for two or three weeks more. You've got to help me or I'll go crazy in a place like this."

He grinned. "I thought you found it so beautiful?"

"I did, but something has happened to it. Once or twice I've been frightened."

"What do you mean, frightened?"

"It isn't anything I can explain. Just frightened . . . by everything." And as if somehow it made her fear more tangible and concrete she said, "I hate that woman, Mrs. Rasmussen."

"She won't poison you."

"I'm not afraid of that."

"What else could she do?"

"Nothing, I suppose."

"They say she has the evil eye."

Again a silence fell between them and he said presently, "Well, we seem to be getting nowhere." He finished his drink and rose.

She said nothing. She did not accuse him of letting her down. She did not reproach him. She only said, "Shall I ever see you again?"

"Perhaps."

"Have you any books I could borrow? I shall be awfully bored here." (He can't be going away. He can't be leaving me now. If he does, I can't go on living.)

"Send over and take anything you like."

He was aware suddenly of someone crossing the room just beyond the range of his vision and turning, he discovered Léah. She did not speak to them or give any sign of recognition, but he knew that she had been there all the time in the room with them, listening from behind the screen near the wireless where she sat to work at her embroidery.

Alix said, "I thought you loved it here. I thought you meant to die here. Is it my fault?"

"No, not really. But if you hadn't come here, I shouldn't have gone away."

She thought for a moment and then said, "You can come back again when I've gone. It'll be the same as before."

"No, it wouldn't be the same. It wouldn't be any good. It isn't as simple as that. Your being here or not being here wouldn't make any difference."

"Oh, it's like that."

"Yes, that's it. If I'd never seen you again it might have gone on being all right. It was bad luck—your coming here. You were the only person in this world who could have made that difference."

Then Rasmussen appeared with Sandy's boy Anthony. The boy was naked save for a loin cloth and stood respectfully waiting. He was seventeen and he had the great dark eyes of Maria. Even Lady Groton saw the likeness.

Dantry spoke to the boy in his own tongue and then turned to Alix. "He says it's all right. He thinks Mees Opp can be here in three days." When he sent the boy away she said, "The people here are extraordinarily beautiful."

Dantry grinned a sort of bitter half-grin, and said, "Yes, you wouldn't think that boy's father was a Cockney from Camden Town." He stood up and said, "I suppose we should be getting off."

For a long moment she looked at him and then said, holding out her hand, "Good-by and good luck. Very likely we shan't see each other again."

"No, it's not likely."

He took her hand as coldly as he was able and then turned and left her. Feeling sick, he crossed the stone floor, and as he reached the great doorway he heard her voice crying out in a kind of anguish, "Tom!"

In the doorway he halted, "Yes?"

"We haven't said it all."

"No, we haven't said it all."

She came toward him and when she reached his side, she said, "I've been doing a lot of thinking, not just now, but at night when I couldn't sleep. I'll go away with you, Tom. I'll stay with you forever, if that's what you want. I'll stay with you here."

"No, that I can't do."

"It would be all right once Albert is gone."

"No, it wouldn't be all right."

"Why?"

"Because we could never stay here now . . . it's too late for that." He grinned. "You see, in a way, we've been driven out of paradise."

She looked away from him and then said, "Oh, I understand. On account of her . . ."

"On account of her . . . and ourselves . . . what we are . . . what I am."

"And you never even loved her."

"No. Never, not even in the beginning." He put his hands to his head as if the gesture would help to clear his muddled brain, as if she were not there at all and he was talking to himself. "I had to have her. I was searching. . . . I was looking for something."

"I know. I understand." Then impulsively, "I'll go away with you now if you want . . . today . . . now."

[443]

He laughed. "That would be a pretty thing to do . . . worthy of both of us."

"Why not?"

"And let him die and let the world say that we ran off together leaving him to die. Oh, that would be a fine story! That would finish us off properly. It would follow us wherever we went. There wouldn't be a place we could go to. Oh, no, we can't get out of it as easily as that! We should simply hate each other in the end and destroy each other."

"I wouldn't mind even that if we were together."

"No, for a little while, for a week or two it might be all right. And then there would only be hell. A woman doesn't mind things like that as much as a man." Again he put his hands to his head. "No, I've got to think it out. It's a last chance. I can't muddle this too."

"It's the only thing we have left . . . the only thing in the world."

"No, you mustn't talk like that. That hasn't anything to do with it." He took her hand and holding it in both his, kissed it and said in a low voice, "It's the thing I want most in the world. If we'd never lost each other in the beginning we wouldn't be such rotters now."

She said quietly, "Go away then. And while you are gone remember that some day when we're both old and there isn't any longer any savor in life, there will always be an agony in our hearts because one of us was not strong. If you change you can send me a message. I won't say good-by this time . . . even if we never see each other again. But you can remember that I shall always be waiting . . . always."

He turned away without another word and walked to the little landing stage where Sandy's son Anthony was awaiting him, and she remained, standing in the doorway until the canoe had disappeared out of sight among the islands of the blue lagoon.

27

As she climbed the stairs she thought, "Oh, I'm paying for being a fool! I'm paying all right. And I've got a lot more to pay. It isn't finished yet. It'll go on and on and on . . . forever."

As she went toward her own room she heard the voice of Groton shouting angrily and then the voice of Bates trying to calm him, and thinking that Bates could perhaps do nothing with him, she opened the door and went into the room.

He was half out of the bed, delirious, with Bates doing his best to keep him down. He was shouting, "Where is that bastard Dantry? . . . The bloody Communist. The double-crosser . . . trying to steal my wife while I'm done in . . . Where is he? I'll straighten him out. I'll finish him."

Then the pale blue eyes caught sight of his wife and he fell suddenly silent, as if ashamed by the memory of their quarrel the night before. He recognized her for a moment and then began to rave again against Dantry, against her, against Deakin, against everyone in the world who had ever dared to oppose him. Quietly she put both hands on his bulky shoulders and tried to shake him.

"Listen, Albert! Listen to me! He's gone away, do you understand? He's gone away forever. It's all over."

The pale eyes looked at her for a moment wildly and then suddenly the huge body collapsed on the bed and lay there breathing heavily, the face congested and purple.

28

The "hospital" stood in a compound of its own a little way outside the capital, not far from the palace of the old Ranee. In the beginning it had been no more than an abandoned house once occupied by a cousin of the Ranee, but after his death left abandoned to the rats and flying foxes until Mees Opp returned from Edinburgh and, after a long struggle with the avaricious old queen, received permission to use it as a hospital. Now, fifteen years after, on the night that Sandy's son arrived from Nivandrum it had half a dozen "wings" all inclosed by neam and peepul trees.

The original house had never been pretentious—merely an affair of stone walls with a roof of thatch which required constant repairing and was inhabited by rats, lizards and snakes. It was built about a great court with a tank of fresh water in the center, which was a great convenience from Mees Opp's point of view. The "wings" were even less pretentious, for the walls consisted not of stone, but of bamboo, and there were no floors save the beaten earth, but the whole was a remarkable structure considering the circumstances under which Mees Opp labored, as remarkable as the finest of modern hospitals in any city of Europe. For it had been called into being out of nothing by the will of Mees Opp, with no help from the old Ranee, and with the very little capital which had been left her by her Dutch grandfather, and with the pittance she received from time to time from two old Presbyterian ladies whose acquaintance she had made during her studies in Edinburgh. Out of nothing she had created it and on next to nothing she kept it going. She needed no money for herself. And there were times when it became so overcrowded with the ill and the miserable that sheets of tarpaulin were put up beneath the peepul trees to shelter patients for whom there was no place either in the "hospital" or in the "wings." There were sufferers from typhoid and malaria, measles and elephantiasis, and even sometimes from cholera and typhus, from nearly all the ills that affect the human race in the tropics. There were victims of snake bites and women having babies—special cases suffering from deformities or acute anemia who had to be kept beneath the eye of Mees Opp from hour to hour.

Mees Opp did it all, aided by three or four coolies and four native women whom miraculously she had recruited from among the widows and the unmarried, women like herself, unwanted or forgotten. On the edge of the compound near the gate she lived in a little house which consisted of an office, a bedroom and a veranda, which was no more than a thatched roof above the naked earth where three times a week she held a clinic and administered medicine and advice to a long line of ill, suffering and maimed men, women and children.

It was in this tiny pavilion that Dantry found her when he arrived thirty hours after having left Nivandrum. For all that time, without sleep, without stopping even to eat, he and Sandy's boy, Anthony, had paddled through the heat of the day and run along obscure short cuts known only to the boy, until the sun went down into the ocean. In spite of every effort, it had taken them longer than he had expected, for they had lost much time after darkness had fallen finding their way and trying to make themselves understood among people whose dialect was so different from that of Nivandrum. By the time they reached Mees Opp's compound the sun was setting a second time since they had left Alix standing in the great doorway of the Grand Oriental Hotel.

Mees Opp was having her supper when they arrived, seated with another woman, very dark, whom she introduced as Mrs. Badoki. She was dressed no longer in the suit of white drill with the bizarre flowered hat, but wore against the terrible heat a kind of Mother Hubbard wrapper. At sight of Dantry and the boy, she looked up in surprise, not recognizing them at first because of her nearsightedness. Before they had spoken she said, "What is it? Who is ill?" and Dantry answered, "Lord Groton."

She only repeated the name, and Dantry saw that she did not at first remember who Lord Groton was, so he said, "An Englishman who has come to Nivandrum."

Then she remembered the train which she had boarded at that little station high on the burning plateau—the train which, save the few third-class carriages filled with *sadhus* and workmen and farmers, had belonged to the great *burra sahib*, with his secretary, his wife, his servants, his mountains of luggage.

"Yes," she said, "I remember now. I thought it might be Sandy or Maria."

Then quietly she told them to sit down, and the first thing she asked was how long it would take her to get there "not by bullock cart and *wallum* but by canoe." She addressed the question to Anthony, knowing that he could tell her more surely than Dantry. At the same time she clapped her hands, and when a servant appeared she told him to fetch water and toddy, and turning to Dantry she asked, "Have you eaten?"

"No, doctor."

"You had better eat here then. The Magistrate eats early so that he can play polo in the cool of the evening."

"Thank you," said Dantry.

"I suppose you'll be staying with the Magistrate?"

"No, I don't know him. I didn't come prepared for that. If you have a corner here, I would prefer it."

She turned to Mrs. Badoki and said, "Mr. Dantry could stay in the *jobedar's* room." And to Dantry she said, "It isn't very luxurious, but it's clean."

"That will be all right."

He divined that she was puzzled by his presence, wondering why he was there at all when the boy Anthony could have brought the message alone. The servant brought the toddy and water, and when both of them had been served, she told the servant to bring curry for them both, and to Dantry she said, "What is the matter with Lord Groton?"

And Dantry told her of the high fever and the violence of the symptoms. "Of course, I don't know myself, but I should think it was black malaria. There's no typhoid or typhus in Nivandrum."

She was silent for a moment, and Dantry wondered that she did not send Anthony away to eat with the hospital servants. That was what he wanted, in order that he should be able to talk to her alone. The presence of Anthony, with his great dark eyes so like Maria's, embarrassed him. And then he remembered that she was treating him, as he had desired to be treated only a few days earlier, as one of the people. He remembered with a little shock that after all the boy Anthony was his own brother-in-law.

She interrupted his thoughts by saying, "I shan't be able to leave before tomorrow night at the earliest."

"It's a very urgent case, doctor. Lord Groton is a very important man," and again he felt the irony of his making a case for Groton, of trying to persuade her to leave at once to save the life of the man he hated most in the world, perhaps the only man he had ever hated. And almost at once he knew that the big, ugly woman had divined a certain falseness in the tone of what he said.

The servant brought the curries and served him and Anthony at the same table with Mees Opp and Mrs. Badoki, and then he knew that he would have to continue his persuasion there in front of all the others. Quietly he told her of the beginning of Groton's illness, of how perhaps he had been already ill when he arrived in Nivandrum, and she listened, asking him now and then a professional question, expertly, so that his faith in her was greater than it had been before.

At last he said, "That is the only reason I came. I knew you were busy. I know you are always busy. I only came in order to explain to you how important it is that something should be done at once. You understand he is one of the most important men in the British Empire."

"Oh, yes," she said quietly. "I understand that. I remember all about him, perfectly. I give you my word that I am doing everything possible. I cannot leave here before tomorrow evening." Then she rose and said, "If you'll excuse me, I must make the evening round with Mrs. Badoki while it's still light. If there is anything you want simply ask the servant. I shall be free again at half-past eight."

He too rose and remained standing until she had left the little house and crossed the compound with its tank of fresh water. Then he seated himself and tried again to eat, but he was so tired that he had no appetite and, rising, he called the servant and asked to be shown the room where he was to spend the night.

He was too tired to argue Groton's case any further, not only dog-tired in body but weary in spirit, and in his heart he knew that the whole journey had been useless. He knew it from the moment Mees Opp had said, "I cannot leave before tomorrow night."

He had respected her, always, since that first morning when he had looked out of the window and seen her dosing and joking with the long line of suffering humanity beneath the window of the Grand Oriental Hotel, but never until now, when he found her on her own ground in this hospital which she had created out of nothing, had he suspected her sense of authority. It was as if here she were all-important, as if here he and even the great Lord Groton were of no more importance than any coolie. And he thought, lying on the hard Indian bed, in the dying light of the evening, "Perhaps she sees the world in a different way. Perhaps she sees us as we are. Perhaps she thinks us equally useless . . . both Groton and myself."

In a little while Anthony came in to share the room with him, sleeping on the floor on mats which Mrs. Badoki sent in. The boy, less tired than himself, stayed for a moment to inquire if there was anything he wanted and then went out again to talk with the servants, something which he, Dantry, could not do. He could neither talk with the porters nor go to stay with the Magistrate. "Neither flesh, fish, nor fowl," he thought.

Vaguely, he could not quite divine why, the whole trip left him feeling empty and useless and insignificant. It was as if a part of him had died, as if that part of him which he might have respected, was gone now forever. And he thought bitterly, "Well, I have done the honorable thing. I have done my best to bring back a doctor as quickly as possible. I will try again tomorrow, and if I fail and he dies, I cannot blame myself. We have done our best . . . Alix and I."

In his weariness he could not sleep, but lay thinking of Alix left behind in Nivandrum with Groton dying, with only that ass of a secretary and the sinister manservant for company. In a way she had not been left behind at all. She had been with him all the time, throughout the long hours of paddling through the heat of midday, during the dark stumbling journey through the jungle. She had been with him all the time. And for the first time he thought, "Nothing else matters. Nothing but this thing between us. It is something which happens to few people, never to most. It is in a way indestructible." Yet he could see no way out, not because of Groton, or even of Maria, but because of the weight of folly, and selfishness, weakness and self-indulgence that hung over them both. Somewhere in the future they would have to atone. He felt the thing closing in upon him with a sense of indefinable dread.

At last, unable to sleep, he sat up on the edge of the bed, smoking, in a kind of half-conscious state, and he thought of nothing but of her, standing in the great doorway, of her saying, "We haven't said it all, Tom. I'll go away with you now . . . forever . . . wherever you like." The thing was stronger than either of them. His whole body, spent and exhausted, ached with desire.

A knock at the door roused him and pulling himself together he said in the local dialect, "Come in." It was the great figure of Mees Opp which shut out the dim twilight in the doorway. She stood there with an electric torch in her hand saying, "Have you everything you want? Anthony tells me you were planning to go away. So I sent a runner to fetch your suitcases. He told me you'd left them behind with the canoe."

So everything, everyone was against them now. There was no excuse left for returning to Nivandrum.

29

During the rounds with Mrs. Badoki, Mees Opp had gone through the motions of making the regular evening tour of the hospital. She talked to the patients and even made jokes with them . . . all the sufferers from malaria and dysentery and typhoid and horrible skin diseases. But on this occasion she did it all half-mechanically, a part of intelligent mind distracted by the problem of Lord Groton and of this strange man, Dantry, so clever, so brilliant, so unhappy, whose misery she had never been able to touch or to fathom.

She was no longer young. Lately, for the first time in her life, she had been aware of a weakening of that immense vitality and strength which had carried her through the most unbelievable trials and achievements, and now she faced the prospect of the long hot journey back to Nivandrum with a sense of dread. Another woman . . . almost any other woman—would have refused to go; there was no lack of reasons for a refusal to make the trip. And she had no interest in Lord Groton nor any particular desire to save the life of Lord Groton. She had known the West long ago, well enough to know all about Lord Groton and his sort, to understand that they were a scourge in their own world quite as much as in the East. She knew the slums of Glasgow and Leeds and Birmingham, where people lived in a squalor and depravity worse than anything which existed even among the outcaste people of her own world. When she thought of Lord Groton, the idea occurred to her that it might not be a bad plan to let him die there alone in Nivandrum far away from all the luxury and power he had won by exploiting his fellow men. Such a decision might even prove to be a blessing to mankind.

But she was at heart a humble woman, and she felt that this decision was not in her hands but in the hands of God, and because she had spent all her life in helping other people she knew that in the end she could not do this, even to a man like Lord Groton. The habit was too strong. In the end she would have to make the long hot journey.

And then, in the very midst of going through the poorest ward, where there was only earth for a floor and palm thatch for a roof, another idea came to her, an idea which seemed almost miraculous, and she was a little astonished that it had not occurred to her, driven and harassed as she always was, at the very beginning. It was founded upon the twin facts that Lord Groton was fabulously rich and that the "hospital" was miserably poor. If she went to Nivandrum and saved his life, he might give her a huge sum of money, enough money to build real "wings" and put new floors in the main building, enough money to buy a generator for electricity, enough to buy the X-ray machine of which she had dreamed for years. Long ago she had abandoned the idea of ever receiving any help from the old Ranee, and men of Lord Groton's sort never made gifts to obscure, unknown hospitals like that of Mees Opp; they had only made spectacular extravagant gifts to institutions which were big and rich and would attract public attention to the generosity of the donor; they were like the feudal barons who bought absolution for their oppression and evil deeds. Now, in a way, she had one of them in her power; she could almost force him to give her money, not for herself, but for the swarming, suffering, ignorant people of the villages whom she loved so profoundly that she had given her whole life to them.

She was not a religious woman, but for a moment it seemed to her, sitting there in the steaming heat, that God had sent her a sign, that He had delivered into her hands a man who could help her, whether he wished to or not, to establish something that would go on and on after they were both dead, that would help the poor and the miserable and serve to annihilate a little of the world's vast burden of wretchedness.

Mrs. Badoki was a tiny, thin, dark woman, a widow of forty, ugly and unwanted like Mees Opp herself. She came of a low caste and once she had been miserable, but Mees Opp had cured her too, not of any illness of the body but of the illness of defeat and despair of the spirit. For ten years now she had worked in the hospital. She was as clever as she was ugly, and much of what Mees Opp had learned long ago in the medical schools of Edinburgh she had passed on to Mrs. Badoki, so that when she left on her tours through the district there was always someone whom she might leave behind in charge of all the sick and suffering who filled the old houses and thatched huts. It was Mrs. Badoki who accompanied her on the rounds she made of the compound twice daily.

When Mees Opp had said good night to Dantry and closed the door of the *jobedar's* room, Mrs. Badoki said to her, "Who is this white man?" and Mees Opp said, "He has lived in Nivandrum for nearly five years. He is the one who married Sandy Carleton's daughter."

But that was not what the ugly clever little Mrs. Badoki wanted to know. That told her almost nothing. So she said in Hindustani, "I don't mean that. What is he like?"

"Ah?" said Mees Opp, and after a moment's reflection, she said, "He is unhappy. It's hard to explain what he's like if you've never been to Europe. He's got a sickness of the soul which many Europeans have . . . only he's better than the rest. The ones you usually see out here aren't worth saving."

They were crossing the compound now to the ward where the maternity patients were kept, a ward that Mees Opp tried desperately to keep as clean and as modern as possible. She walked in silence for a few paces, until they had passed the tank of fresh water, and then she said, "He could be cured of the sickness . . . but he doesn't want to be. He is like a Hindu who wants to die and won't make a fight. He knows he is sick just as well as I do, but he won't let anyone help him. He has a kind of stubborn pride. He won't let me help him. It's a pity. He could do so much. He could be happy too." And at last she said, "He should never have married Sandy's daughter. He did that, too, because he was ill."

Then they came to the converted old house where the pregnant women were, and Mees Opp suddenly forgot Dantry and said, "Is there any sign yet?"

And Mrs. Badoki said, "No, she hasn't complained."

There was no need to use a name, for the two women knew who "she" was, the wife of a coolie who had been there for three days awaiting her baby.

Mees Opp said, "Was she awake?"

"She was a moment ago."

[451]

"Frightened?"

"She says not, but I think she is. Her mother came to see her. I let her stay."

"That's right. I'll go and talk to her. When I go away you might take her something to make her sleep. There's no use in her being frightened."

"Shall I come with you?"

"No, it might alarm her."

So Mees Opp went into a room where on a cheap bed in the corner lay an abnormally small woman huddled in the heat beneath a single sheet of cheap cotton. On the earth beside her lay an old woman with white hair and a wrinkled face like a bit of old black leather. At sight of Mees Opp she scrambled stiffly to her feet and salaamed, but Mees Opp bade her lie down again, and the old woman squatted beside the bed, looking up at Mees Opp with eyes that were bright with anxiety. On the bed the crippled woman tried to smile shyly at Mees Opp, her face yellow-gray with acute anemia, her big dark eyes dull with fear.

"How do you feel?" asked Mees Opp.

"Not good."

"It will be all right tomorrow. You must trust me."

"Yes, *memsahib*."

"You will have a fine baby."

"Thank you, *memsahib*."

"And Mrs. Badoki will give you something to drink that will make you sleep and forget everything. You must take it. It will do you good."

"Yes, *memsahib*."

"Good night."

"Good night."

The old woman scrambled to her feet again, but this time Mees Opp scarcely noticed her and walked out of the room again into the ward where Mrs. Badoki sat. To Mrs. Badoki she said, "She *is* frightened. Give her something to make her sleep and keep her asleep until after it's over."

Then she went out again into the clear night, and for a long time she walked up and down under the trees because she herself was frightened. Tomorrow or the day after she would have to do an operation which she had never done before. She had seen it done in Edinburgh, and she had read book after book about it since women were always dying in the village because when they were children they had not had enough to eat and were deformed. This woman she had found in the coolie quarter, almost a dwarf, with legs that were twisted and half-paralyzed. And when Mees Opp had persuaded her to come to the "hospital" they discovered that there was no way for her to have her baby. There would be nothing for her but death unless Mees Opp could save her. So now it had to be done. She had to be saved because she believed in Mees Opp—the woman herself, and her husband and her mother and all her relations and the people of her village. They all believed that Mees Opp could work miracles. That was what made it all so terrifying. If she failed, the people of the village would suffer a weakening of faith in her, and she would have to begin all over again to get them to come to her away from the filthy midwives and the witch doctors. She was afraid, now, but if she succeeded it would be easier after that to save the lives of hundreds of women before she herself died.

Presently she went back to the little house to have a few hours' sleep so that her nerves would be steady to make the operation, but she did not sleep. She sat for a long time in the little veranda overlooking the "hospital," dark now save here and there where the dim yellow glow of a paraffin lamp showed beneath the black shadows of the neam and peepul trees. And as she sat there she experienced one of those moments of emotion which had come to her now and then over the long years she had spent here in the wilderness, a moment of satisfaction, of elation, of having conquered life itself.

This thing, this compound, this "hospital" was her own; she had made it out of nothing, or perhaps out of her own sense of defeat in life. For at eighteen Mees Opp had understood that the gods had not been kind to her; they had made her ugly and fat and poor and, worst of all, a half-caste, so that in a way she was forever shut out from both the people whose blood was mixed in her veins. The gods had given her nothing at all save intelligence and health, but those gifts, she knew, were great ones which few of the people about her had been given. And at eighteen she had already known what she must do and what was to be her role in life, and from then on she had gone on stubbornly learning, persistently studying, until somehow at last she had managed to go to Edinburgh and learn what she had to know. She had done what she had been told, again and again, both in the East and the West, was impossible. And now this "hospital," this compound, those clinics held three times a week in the little veranda, were for her love and a husband, children, household, domesticity, everything which she would have liked and which had been denied her. Now she was not sorry any longer that she had missed those other things. She was content with what she had done, and even more content in the knowledge that there was so much more yet to do—enough indeed to keep her occupied all day and all night for the rest of her life until at last she grew old and ill and died and was buried here in the compound which she loved so profoundly. There was all the East swarming, ignorant, ill and suffering—the East which was slowly, painfully being born again in a kind of magnificence like the rising of the sun in the high mountains.

She knew now what she must do. Lord Groton could wait. He might even die, but the coolie woman must be saved. And there was, too, the question of Dantry. She liked him, in spite of everything. He was too good to be lost. She might cure him too as she had cured poor ugly Mrs. Badoki. She knew what the cure was, but she would have to have a little time. Dantry must not go away now, back into that other world from which he had come, the world which had made him sick and despairing. She knew that he was running away, and that if he ran away this time he was certain to be lost. Somehow she must force him to go back with her to Nivandrum.

And then another thought came to her. There was the question of Léah and the mischief she might do, the mischief which she had already done so many times when Mees Opp was not there to stop it. She knew that it was Léah who had sent Maria to Dantry in the first place. It might too be Léah who was responsible for the strange violence of Lord Groton's symptoms.

Tomorrow she would make the operation, and she must make it with a sure hand so that there was no delay, so that she might leave at once, taking Dantry with her.

30

In the morning when Dantry wakened he found the two battered suitcases already by the side of his bed. Anthony had already disappeared from the *jobedar's* room, and Dantry, on the edge of the corded Indian bed, sat for a long time regarding the two worn pieces of luggage as if somehow they were symbols, as if there was some mystical force in them which had the power of making him do what he did not want to do. More than ever it seemed clear to him that Mees Opp had divined most of the story and was intent on sending him away, to Singapore, to Colombo, to Batavia, anywhere outside this world in which he had failed so miserably. The physical weariness had gone now, but the weariness of the spirit still remained, so that he was in a way glad of the presence of the two miserable suitcases, since they forced him to make a decision which he no longer had the force to make. And then the desire for a drink came over him, a frantic, ravening desire which he had never before experienced in all his years of drink. It seemed to him that he would be unable to rise from the bed and wash himself at the tank of fresh water and set about the day without the stimulus of alcohol. And he thought, "This is the end. It has caught up with me at last," and it seemed to him suddenly that not only had the desire for drink caught up with him but that all his life was there, too, weighing down upon him . . . all the hedonism, the selfishness, the evasions, the shameless profit he had made out of his own good looks and charm, out of all the advantages with which circumstances had endowed him in the beginning.

"Now," he thought, "I know what a real beachcomber feels like." He knew that desire suddenly to lose onself in drink, in sensuality, in debauchery; to achieve a kind of oblivion in which nothing was any longer of any importance save plunging deeper and deeper into vice and dissipation, until in the end one destroyed oneself and so there was no longer any misery but only nothingness. And suddenly he was frightened.

The sound of a knock on the door of the room startled him out of his reflections, and he was aware sharply of a neurotic dread of seeing and talking to anyone, even to one of the hospital porters; but something of the compulsion of civilization remained, and he wrapped himself in the *sarong* and said, "Come in."

It was one of the porters, who salaamed and said, "Mees Opp sent me to ask if you would have coffee with her on her veranda."

For a second he hesitated, still filled with the dread of having to talk with anyone, and he was about to send a message saying that he felt too ill, when the boy said, "She wanted to know if the *sahib* would like a drink? She said to say there was only brandy."

Then he answered, "Yes. And say that I will come for coffee in a few minutes."

When the boy had gone, he sat for a time considering with amazement the character of Mees Opp—that she, an old maid, who had never lived in the world, who had never known drunkards nor what it was to want a drink on opening one's eyes in the morning, should have thought of brandy, the one thing which he needed. He thought, "She knows everything," and again the old desire to be friendly with her came to him so strongly that now it seemed that friendliness between them was as necessary to him as the brandy. It was as if he could not go on with the day until he saw her and had some assurance of her respect for him.

When the boy had brought the brandy and he had drunk it, he went to the tank of fresh water and there bathed himself. On the great steps descending into the water were half a dozen women doing their washing, and opposite him, quite naked and shameless, were two *sadhus* who had come into the compound off the red and dusty road. The women stared at him with their great dark eyes, pausing in their work to watch him, a white *sahib*, bathing simply in the tank like one of their own people.

The sun was not yet high and the air was clear and still cool, but in it there was that stillness, almost sinister in quality, which always preceded the breaking of the monsoon, a stillness which once, long ago, had sometimes in the hot nights terrified him. Now he no longer had any fear of it because, like the people of the country, he knew that in a little while the rains would come, the drenching, cleansing rains which set the trees and shrubs and vines growing with a kind of animal vitality; the rains which brought their own damp heat but which also brought a sense of cleanness and a freshness, as if the world, tired and dusty and exhausted, were being reborn.

[455]

He found Mees Opp seated at a plain teakwood table in the little shed which she called her "veranda." She was dressed again in the spotless white drill, but wore no hat, so that he saw for the first time that her hair was thin and straight and mud-colored. There was no beauty about her save the look in the pale china-blue eyes. In front of her were piles of papers and hospital charts, each anchored to the table with lumps of coral or jade or garnet which patients had brought her as offerings. At one end of the table there was a jug of coffee and a painted wooden bowl filled with papayas and melons and pomegranates. She had been reading a copy of *The Times* already six weeks old, and when he saw it he thought, "What a fool I am! Of course she knows who Groton is. She knows all about him."

She greeted him with a remark about the beauty of the morning and poured out his coffee. Then she said quite abruptly, "Are you planning to leave today?" and again he was aware that he had made no decision and had no plans. In his weariness, he wanted simply to stay on and on, drinking and sleeping there on the hard bed in the *jobedar's* room.

But the memory of the battered suitcases forced him to say, "Yes. I was planning to go when you leave for Nivandrum."

"If everything goes well, I shall leave tomorrow about noon."

"In the heat?"

"I cannot go before then, and I must get there as soon as possible. There is no other way."

He lighted a cigarette and then said, "I was hoping that you could leave tonight. You see, there isn't only the question of Lord Groton. His wife is there, too." He hesitated and then went ahead. "She is not much used to the life out here. I think she is frightened."

Mees Opp looked at him and said, "What is she like?" And for a moment he did not answer, because he could not think of any way to describe Alix and her life to a woman like Mees Opp. If he told her about the jewels and the expensive clothes and the luxurious hotels to which she was accustomed it would not give Mees Opp any proper impression of what she was like. Because she was not like that. He had to make her understand about the peculiar honesty, the sense of freedom, the quality of innocence which in spite of everything was so much a part of Alix.

So he said, "She's very hard to describe. She's unhappy. She's had bad luck. She is an admirable woman who has always had the wrong place in life. When you see her perhaps you won't think what I say is true. But it is."

"Why did she come to Nivandrum? She should have stayed behind at Government House."

"Because she is like that. She has always been waiting for something. She has always been searching for something. But in her world she never found it because it doesn't exist there." And then he knew that he was saying too much and that he was speaking with emotion which he had not meant to show, and he was aware that ugly Mees Opp had missed neither the words nor the peculiar emotion which went into them. He had a sudden feeling that he was one of those suffering natives who waited their turn patiently to come before her, be examined and have their illnesses diagnosed.

Mees Opp said, "You must have known her for a long time to know her so well." And he said, "I have known her always, even before I saw her."

She took one of his cigarettes, lighted it and moved one of the lumps of jade which served as paper weights. Then she said, "Where are you going when you leave here?"

"I don't know. I haven't any plans."

"Isn't there anything you want to do . . . any necessity which makes you go here or there?"

He had never thought of it before in that way. He was simply aware that he had had freedom, absolute freedom from every tie, for even Maria had never made any real difference. He had worked and planned for years to achieve that freedom from every tie, from every responsibility, and now Mees Opp made that freedom seem a cheap and sordid thing, something which was even dangerous and sinister.

"No," he said. "There is nothing."

"If there is nothing, you could be a help to me."

He looked at her sharply and asked, "How?"

"You could go back with me to Nivandrum."

His heart gave a sudden leap, but he said in a low voice, "No, that I can't do."

"Is it because of Maria?"

"Yes . . . a little on account of Maria."

"I will talk to Maria. I will make her see." Then she said, "You should never have married Maria."

"No, when I did it, I thought it didn't matter."

She went on persistently, "You could help me. I don't suppose Lord Groton will be an easy patient . . . under the circumstances."

He knew what she meant, without her saying it . . . that a man like Groton would have only contempt for her, both as a woman and a half-caste. He said, "I couldn't be of much help to you there. Lord Groton hates me." And then he realized that without meaning to do it, he had told her everything.

"I didn't mean exactly that. Only you could be of help in a great many ways. Rasmussen and Sandy aren't of much help, not with grand people like that."

Then Mrs. Badoki appeared, coming across the compound from the "maternity ward." As she stepped on to the veranda, Mees Opp said, "Is everything ready?" and when Mrs. Badoki said, "Yes," she rose and said to Dantry, "You must excuse me now. I have to do an operation," and she left him, walking beside Mrs. Badoki through the dust. She was trembling, and she kept saying to herself, "I must not tremble. I must keep my nerve." When she reached the "ward" she found the crippled woman lying on the makeshift operating table. She was not frightened any longer. She lay quite still, breathing quietly.

31

In Nivandrum the heat which heralded the coming of the monsoon came up suddenly, strangely, without the usual warning wind that each day grew a little more moist and hot. Only the trees, the plants and the vines seemed aware of its approach, and for ten days before it arrived they began sending out green new shoots and fresh leaves and extravagant blossoms from trunks which had grown tired and a little weary with the long months of dry sunshine. It was as if each one had been touched by some invisible and miraculous hand; each hedge, each cluster of croton and bougainvillea became thicker and more green. Against the houses and at the edge of the water the bamboos grew feathery with the rush of delicate pale-green new leaves. And then with the changing of the moon, the heat came down in the night like the suffocating blast from the open door of a furnace. Beyond the Great Bar the sea grew ominously still, so that at midday it became a sheet of copper, waveless and burnished beneath the cruel sun; and in the evenings the breeze which always brought freshness from the sea did not rise at all, and quietly, imperceptibly, as the night advanced the heat of darkness became more intolerable than the heat of midday had been. For the first time the fishermen failed to stay out the whole day, but came hurrying in before noon because it was impossible to live beneath that cloudless sky on that sheet of burning metal. They returned, too, in fear of that first great gale which one day would come up suddenly, without warning from the southwest to destroy even the strongest boat before it could slip across the bar into the shelter of the palm-fringed harbor.

Inside the barrier on the still surface of the lagoons and channels, the heat rose from the water, carrying with it an invisible vapor so that the islands and the lovely old houses of pink and blue and yellow seemed from a distance to grow insubstantial and to float without support in the hot still air.

In the middle of the day all life ceased and all Nivandrum, if the heat was not too great even for sleeping, slept. From the window of the Grand Oriental Hotel at noon the houses and islands appeared deserted, a town from which all life had fled. Even Léah, thin, and bred in the heat of that world, fled her kitchen for the coolness of the great stone hall where, wakeful, in one corner, sheltered by the screen of coconut matting, she prepared her vegetables, and when that was finished, did a little sewing. She sat there all through the heat of the day, the only person in all the hotel who remained awake and watching.

Abovestairs, Bates, when no one was about, capitulated at last and sat by Lord Groton's bed in braces without a collar, for his Lordship being unconscious could not see him; nor did the Saxon pinkness of the secretary Lansbury trouble him, for the pinkness had turned to a painful lobster red under the tropical sun, and Lansbury himself never appeared at all save after the sun had gone down, when he came out timorously, soft and wilted like a lettuce in need of water. Once each evening he came to knock on Lord Groton's door, but Bates never admitted him, and before Bates opened the door he always had time to adjust his collar and put on his coat, so that he appeared correctly dressed, impeccable in manner, as if he were still living in the damp fog of Hill Street. The *ayah*, used to the burning heat of the plains, found the dampness of Nivandrum less terrible and, being free all the day, went off in the afternoon to the mainland where she had already found a lover among the fishermen. Of all of them only Bates was able to maintain what he called his "moral." The others, even the correct Lansbury, went to pieces. As the heat, rising from the lagoons, drove the inhabitants indoors and made the houses and islands float in the air, so it altered the minds and the very characters of every European in Nivandrum.

And all the while Lord Groton lay, feverish, in a coma broken now and then by spells of delirium. Bates remained at his side, not so much from devotion to His Lordship as from devotion to his calling, and because the sight of His Lordship, broken, helpless, perhaps dying, like any ordinary man, gave him a subtle satisfaction and pleasure. He even found satisfaction in the idea of keeping His Lordship alive to suffer as long as possible. The illness became in Bates's mind a kind of atonement, and His Lordship had much to atone for. That he should have the opportunity of sitting by to watch the atonement was a privilege and a pleasure of which Bates had never dreamed. And while His Lordship was atoning, his wife was betraying him.

It was not that she betrayed him openly, physically, as she had done before, but in the spirit, which, Bates knew, was far worse. Watching her, the man-servant discovered something he had never believed possible—that Lady Groton was in love. He knew the difference. He had watched her before with other men, but nothing on those occasions had ever touched her. Always she had remained free and intact, and always a little apart. This, Bates saw at once, was a different thing . . . a thing, indeed, which she obviously took the trouble of trying to hide from him. With the departure of that mysterious character Dantry, Bates saw Her Ladyship go to pieces. It was a process of which men like Rasmussen and Lansbury would remain perhaps forever unaware, but Bates understood it and so did Léah, who came to believe that her prayers and sacrifices and incantations had begun to work at last with a power beyond her hopes.

Lady Groton no longer lunched at all, but left the hotel during the cool of the early morning and returned only after the brazen sun had gone down into the sea. Regularly, dutifully, she called at Lord Groton's room twice each day, once in the morning before she left, and once after she returned. But her visits were different now, because she no longer made any attempt to deceive Bates. Since the sending of the telegram she had capitulated. She no longer gave a kind of theatrical performance, pretending in front of Bates that she was a devoted wife and profoundly concerned over the health of her husband. It was as if she said to him, without speaking a word, "I am too tired any longer to pretend. You have known always. In this place that other life, that other world, does not exist."

It seemed to Bates that for the first time in all the years he had known her she had lost that poise, that control, that resignation which had at times seemed to him almost inhuman. And out of the knowledge a new feeling for her was born, a warm feeling of sympathy and affection which astounded the cold-blooded Bates. She was better than he had believed, much better, because now, having given up what Bates thought of as "playing the game," she had become human, a woman such as Bates might have encountered anywhere and not simply in that world of wealth and artificiality which Bates had passed most of his life in watching.

32

Each morning the aged boatmen came for her a little after dawn, and for an hour or two before the heat rose steaming from the lagoons they poled the *wallum* boat here and there, back and forth among the islands, ending the voyage at last at the foot of the great stairway on Dantry's island. There she sent them away to return for her at nightfall. At first after he had gone away she felt only a kind of numbness and despair, and then quickly the numbness passed and in its place came pain, the aching pain of desire and regret and emptiness, for now it seemed to her nothing remained to live for. Before she had seen him again there had not been much, but life had taken care of itself, moving in a round of prescribed and rigid habits and formalities, varied only by the excitement of an adventure; but now all that was broken, and she knew that for as long as she lived she would never again find even the faint excitement which came of flirtations and adventures.

The sight of his house, of his books and bed and chairs seemed to ease the pain a little. She had for the house the feeling of a woman who had once been very happy there with a lover who was long since dead. And she came there too because the hotel with Rasmussen, the eavesdropping Léah, the stupid Lansbury and the knowing Bates, had become intolerable to her, a hideous place, which set her nerves on edge.

The day on the island passed slowly. She tried to read, to play on the piano. She walked in the thin shadow of the coconut palms during the heat of midday. And she drank more than she should have drunk, which in the heat only made her feel ill. It astonished her that the house remained open, with all its doors and windows wide for all the islanders to see, a deserted place where neither theft nor trespass was committed. It was as if it were enchanted, as if something about the place inspired the islanders with a fear and horror. And sometimes it seemed to her, when her nerves were on edge, that she was not alone there in the house, but that it was a haunted place. On the second day she told the boatmen to return for her before sundown, because she was afraid of the shadows and that quick silent nightfall with the howling of the jackals which came down suddenly as if a black curtain had muffled all the earth.

At the hotel she always went quickly to her own room because she was aware that everyone in the place watched her—Léah with the gimlety black eyes, Rasmussen with his blue uncomprehending stare, Lansbury with his idiotic half-feminine giggle. It seemed to her that even the porters and the boatmen followed her everywhere with their eyes, perhaps gloating over her misery, perhaps sorry for her, which was more intolerable, but always curious and aware of her suffering.

Abovestairs she forced herself to go to Groton's room. He still remained unconscious most of the day, and whenever for a little time he opened his eyes and looked about him, he became wild again, cursing and raging against Dantry, so that Bates had difficulty in keeping him in bed, a thing which grew a little easier each day, as the fever made him weaker and weaker. Dantry, it seemed, had become an obsession with him, a fact which Bates regarded, too, as significant, because he had never before been like this; never before had he been very profoundly disturbed by an adventure of his wife; usually he knew nothing about them. But now, suddenly, in his illness, he was filled with a delirious desire to destroy Dantry.

When Bates, trying to reach His Lordship's reason through the mist of his illness, said, "But, Your Lordship, Mr. Dantry has gone away for good. He has gone forever. He is not coming back," Groton would stare at him for a moment and then say, "No, he is coming back. He hasn't gone away," and then he would fall to raving again until from exhaustion he fell back on the teakwood and mother-of-pearl bed, and Bates, watching him, would think, "This is the end of you, all right. It can't go on much longer. Not even a

[461]

bull could survive that fever. You're going where you'll pay for all your deviltry."

And when Lady Groton returned in the evening, Bates said nothing of the attacks, for he did not want to disturb her, and he knew well enough that she understood what was happening. There were moments when even Bates felt sorry for both of them. There was something pitiful in their helplessness, in this place where all their money and all their power brought them nothing, where they were both alone as they had never been alone before.

33

On the fourth day, at Dantry's house, a little after the heat of midday, Lady Groton lay on the Indian bed beneath the awning with her eyes closed. She was saying over and over again to herself, as she had done many times lately, "He will come back. He is on his way now. I can't think of him slowly drinking himself to death, not even knowing where he is. He will come back. He will come back. He must come back."

She lay there, silently, her whole body tense, *willing* him to return. She who was without superstition, who detested mysticism, was willing now to try anything at all. She no longer seemed ridiculous to herself. There were even moments when wildly she considered going to Léah for charms. She was no longer the proud, self-sufficient, overcivilized Lady Groton, but only a woman who was in love for the first and only time in her life. And then, as she lay there in the terrible heat, whispering to herself in a kind of trance, she became aware that someone was watching her. The consciousness of being stared at came over her slowly, forcing its way through the wall of her misery, and presently, opening her eyes, she saw standing over her with a pistol in her hand, Dantry's wife.

The sight of the pistol brought her back to reality with a sudden shock, and she thought first, "It can't be true. A thing like this is too melodramatic to happen to *me*."

The golden skin of the girl had gone quite pale. The revolver she held awkwardly as if her slender wrists were not strong enough for its weight. For a long moment they looked into each other's eyes, and then a strange thing happened. The pistol dropped from Maria's hand and she slipped to her knees, burying her head in her arms on the edge of the Indian bed. She made no sound, but her whole body shook with sobs.

Lady Groton sat up and put one hand on her shoulder and said, with a kind of tragi-comic politeness, "Did you come to talk to me?"

The girl only shook her head, and Lady Groton said, "Shoot me if you like. Perhaps that would be a good way out." And suddenly the girl began to talk, in her halting English, her voice broken by sobs. She spoke with her head still buried in her arms as if she were overcome by shame.

She said, "I meant to kill. I came here to kill you. I was going to kill you and then kill myself . . . but I couldn't, not when I saw you. I didn't know it was like that. I didn't know it hurt you, too." And Lady Groton, clear-headed now, had a sudden vision of how she must have looked, lying there on the bed with her eyes closed, saying over and over again, half-aloud, "He will come back. He must come back." She did not know how long the girl had stood there watching her.

Quietly she put her arm about the girl and lifted her up, but Maria, like a child, still kept her face covered with her arms, and although she sat with docility on the edge of the bed, she would not look at Lady Groton.

She said, "Forgive. I was wrong. What I did was evil. I was crazy. I didn't know."

Sitting there beside the girl, the sense of pity for her returned to Lady Groton. Her own unhappiness seemed less to her now because, in a way, the black misery of the girl was so much blinder and more profound. She herself was strong, strengthened at least by knowledge and understanding. She herself had known Tom always; she knew what he was like inside; she knew what had made him what he was; she knew the sick world out of which he came. This girl, who had never been outside Nivandrum, could not know these things. She had no way of knowing why he acted as he did. She had no way of protecting herself against him.

She heard herself saying, "You must not take it so hard, because he isn't worth it. He is never coming back to you. It is best to forget him." Then, after a little silence, she said again, "I do not say that because I want him. It is finished and he has run away. You must not care for him so much, because he is selfish and weak and spoiled. Do you hear me? Do you understand what I mean?" She found herself speaking carefully and slowly and with exaggerated distinctness, as she would speak to a foreigner or a child, for she was trying honestly to help the girl and make her understand.

Maria said, "Yes, I understand. If only you hadn't come here, he would not have run away."

"Some day he would have gone. Some day he would have been fed up and gone away. You see, he's no good. He's not worth your caring so much."

Then Maria stood up suddenly, and for the first time took her arm from in front of her face. She said, "You mustn't talk of him like that, because he is really a good man. You mustn't try to make me hate him. That is wicked."

"Oh, I love him as much as you do, only I know what he is like. He is not a good man. He is evil because he is weak . . . you understand?"

Then all at once the girl seemed to collapse again and, sobbing, she turned and went down the stairs, running all the way into the garden. And Lady

Groton, still filled with a desire to help her, followed her a little way, but stopped at the head of the stairs, aware that there was nothing she could do, that whatever she said or did, the girl would never believe that she meant good and not evil.

She remained standing at the head of the stairs until the canoe with Maria in it appeared crossing the lagoon toward Sandy's compound. As it disappeared she thought, "Oh, God, I wanted something to happen to me. It has happened." It had happened, but it wasn't finished yet. A little frightened, she returned to the Indian bed, picked up the pistol and placed it among the embroidered cushions. Then she lay down again, and late in the afternoon, because she had scarcely slept for nights, she fell asleep.

34

On the fourth day after the heat began, they traveled all the day from early morning without stopping at noon even to eat . . . Dantry in one canoe, Mees Opp and Anthony in the other. Mees Opp hated the heat, and there were times when it seemed to her that her great bulk was slowly melting away, but her spirit was fortified by the knowledge that she had done the operation and that the coolie woman with a son by her side lay convalescent in the care of Mrs. Badoki. All day, even at noon when the leaves of the trees curled piteously beneath the burning sun, there was in her mind the picture of the crippled woman, no longer terrified, the old mother no longer frightened and the coolie husband childishly delighted by the birth of a son who even the witch doctors and midwives had said could never be born. Mees Opp had accomplished the miracle and the news like fire had gone through the districts, and now they would come to her from all over the State, even from the distant mountain jungles. But best of all, she was no longer afraid. She had done the thing.

In the canoe behind Mees Opp, Dantry paddled through the heat in a kind of daze, scarcely knowing what he was doing or whither he was bound. The rhythmic dip and swing of the paddle brought with it a hypnotic sense of relief. The physical effort, which once would have been torture in the great heat, now seemed almost pleasant and agreeable.

In his weariness he had become like an obedient dog, content in the sacrifice of will for the comfort of being told what to do, for now he had placed himself in the hands of Mees Opp. He would do what she told him to do. Why she wanted him to return to Nivandrum he had been unable to divine— perhaps it was because she really wanted him to help her, perhaps it was because she hoped he would return to Maria. He made no very great attempt to discover her reasons, and certainly she did not betray them by the slightest hint, but it never occurred to him that she regarded him as an ill man and,

[464]

in her compassion for human suffering, could have no rest until she had cured him. Presently he ceased to think at all, but only paddled . . . dip, swing . . . dip, swing . . . driving the light canoe across the glassy surface of the lagoons.

When the sun went down at last the little party was still twenty miles from Nivandrum, but in the darkness and by the aid of the fires and the torches of the fishermen, Sandy's boy Anthony kept his way along the main channel. With the fall of night Mees Opp took on a new vigor, and from time to time she gently urged the boy to fresh efforts, for now that the coolie woman and her child were safe, she thought only of Groton and, knowing Léah, she was afraid.

It was the kind of night which roused to consciousness all her passionate love for this country, which made her know that whatever happened she would never again be content away from the magnificence of the East, which made her know that in spite of her divided blood this was where she belonged. Along the edge of the lagoon the torches of the boys spearing fish were like gigantic fireflies. It was as if she and Anthony and Dantry were in a way making a triumphal advance guarded on both sides by the lights of the village fires. And overhead the heat lightning broke in great sheets of opalescent color, revealing now and then a canoe or a *wallum* boat drifting close beside them in the breathless darkness. And above everything rose the sound of the eternal music of drums and flutes, punctuated by the occasional solitary howl of a jackal. There was a splendor in the scene which she had never found in the West, as if here man was allowed by nature to survive on sufferance alone.

Now and then she would say, "Is it much farther?" for in the darkness she no longer knew the familiar channel. And Sandy's boy Anthony would say, spent and weary, "Only a little farther."

When the little party came within sight of the familiar lights of the Grand Oriental Hotel, some of the apathy flowed away from Dantry, leaving him alive again in the first cool of the evening and conscious for the first time of the complications which were certain to come of his return. Now, suddenly, he dreaded seeing the faces of people like Rasmussen and Léah. He dreaded even the first moment of the encounter with Alix, and so his instinct was to put it all off as long as possible, and pressing forward he brought his canoe abreast of Mees Opp and Anthony, and shouted to her, "I will go to my house first and come to the hotel as soon as I've made myself presentable." And then as they entered the channel between the two islands, he turned away from them and drove his canoe to the foot of the great stairway.

Against the glittering sky the old baroque house stood out solid and black, and at sight of it something of the old pleasure and his love for it returned. He thought, "I might stay here and never leave the island again. That way

I could perhaps escape getting myself into a mess." But he knew that he would not stay forever on the island, for the excitement of Alix had returned suddenly, and in spite of his weariness he was filled with impatience to see her again.

"Now," he thought, "now that I have been fool enough to come back, it doesn't matter what happens."

Taking the electric torch from one of the worn handbags, he swung the two bags ashore and climbed after them to the foot of the stairway. With the aid of the torch he found his way up the stairs. From among the islands the drums had begun again, and in the distance from the mainland came the sound of the jackals, and in his blood the old excitement of the place returned.

The stillness of the house and of the whole tiny island, set down among the sounds of life from the shores near by, was like something tangible, and for a moment he too experienced a sense of the place being haunted. For a moment his weary nerves grew taut with a fear and horror which he could not seize or understand, as if the figure were a ghost he saw or a dead person. Then turning the light full on the bed he saw that the person lying there was Alix. She was not dead, for she was breathing easily and quietly, her head thrown back a little, her face very pale in the yellow light. She looked, in her sleep, like a tired child.

Quietly, his heart thumping, he crossed to the bed and there knelt quietly beside it and laid his head on her breast thinking, "It was meant to be. This could not have happened otherwise." And the last resistance flowed from him like water from a broken dam and he was happy.

For a second, as she wakened at the touch of his hand, she was frightened, and then, suddenly awake, she thought, "It can't be true. It can't be Tom. Such things don't happen." Then without opening her eyes she reached out and touched his head, and feeling the dark strong hair as she had done long ago in the darkness of the little room at Tipton Farm, she thought, "It is Tom. Oh, thank you, God! Thank you for bringing him back to me! I will be good now forever." And slowly she drew his head up to hers, and said softly, "Tom, dear Tom." And the tears began to flow. Then he kissed her, and against the sound of the drums and the jackals the world about them ceased to exist, and it seemed to her that they were enveloped by a great and blinding light.

35

When the canoe arrived at the little landing stage of the Grand Oriental Hotel it was Rasmussen himself who answered the hail of Anthony and came hurrying to meet them . . . a Rasmussen alarmed and made sullen by the heat and the strange sense of muddle which had seemed to envelop the hotel since the moment Lord Groton's party had arrived. Without welcoming Mees Opp, he said abruptly, "I am glad you have come."

Standing on the little pier with her two bags, Mees Opp asked, "How is the patient?"

"The same. He can't stand the fever much longer."

"What have you done for him?"

Rasmussen shrugged his heavy shoulders. "Quinine. Cold water. What we could."

"I could not come sooner."

"I hope it is not too late."

Carrying her bags, Rasmussen led her through the great hall and, as they passed, the head of Léah appeared for a moment in the doorway of the kitchen. She did not greet Mees Opp. She simply stared at her sullenly, with a terrifying expression of hostility in the black eyes. Mees Opp in her haste did not even see her, but followed Rasmussen up the stairs to a room next to that of Lord Groton. Indicating a door, he said rudely, with an odd lack of respect, "He's in there."

"Thanks," said Mees Opp. "I'd like something to eat and drink."

"What would you like?"

"Anything you have."

Then when he had gone she went to the door and knocked, and Bates, relaxed at last in a dressing gown for the night, opened it, and carrying her little bag of medicine, she went in, saying, "I am the doctor, Miss Opp."

Bates, a little astonished by the precipitancy of her entrance and the authority of her manner, said stiffly, "My name is Bates. I am His Lordship's manservant."

For the space of a second they regarded each other with something near to hostility, Bates because he did not fancy welcoming a half-caste woman doctor, and Mees Opp because she was aware of his feeling, and because something in the narrow, pale, long-nosed face put her on her guard. Then she glanced at the teakwood and mother-of-pearl bed, sat down without being asked and said, "Tell me exactly what happened, how it began and how it progressed."

Bates, awed a little by something in the fat woman which he could not quite analyze, remained standing, and told her how His Lordship had seemed ill for two or three days before he had been forced to give in, how he had lain for nearly four days between a coma and delirium, how they had done what they could, trusting to Rasmussen's and Léah's knowledge of local medicines.

Then she asked more intimate questions and said suddenly, "Where is Lady Groton?" and for a moment, to his own astonishment, Bates felt shame, because he saw that Mees Opp would expect the wife to be at the bedside. Clumsily he said, "The heat has been hard on her. She's not used to it, and in the evenings she goes out in the boat for some air. Sometimes in the daytime she goes to a house belonging to an Englishman who is away just now. It's much cooler there than in the hotel."

Without looking at him Mees Opp said, "Yes. Mr. Dantry came back with me." And Bates thought, "Ah, so that's it! That's why she stayed out long after sundown. She knew he was coming back." But it seemed to him, with his new feeling for Her Ladyship, that he must cover her tracks, so he said, quietly, "Her Ladyship will be very glad of that. I think she is very bored here."

"Oh!" She opened the bag which rested on her huge knees and began taking out bottles and thermometers, and presently she said, "When do you expect her back?"

And again Bates felt ashamed, without quite knowing why. He said, "She should have been back two or three hours ago. She's much later than usual." He had not meant to defend Lady Groton; he had not even thought it necessary to defend her to a half-caste woman doctor, but this woman upset him because she ignored all the rules which gave solidity to his world, this woman who clearly was not impressed by Lord Groton, nor even by Lady Groton. She overlooked or ignored his own casual rudeness, and somehow, in some mysterious fashion, her authority and dignity and calmness made him feel small and uneasy and a little ashamed.

"I should like to see her when she comes in. Have you been caring for him?"

"Yes."

"Then you'd better go and have some sleep. I'll take charge. I'll sleep in the next room and come in now and then. How old is the patient?"

"Fifty-four."

"Has he had malaria before?"

"No . . . not for ten years. Before that I don't know."

"Before that it wouldn't matter. Does he drink?"

"Yes."

"Heavily?"

"Yes."

"Well, I'll examine him. From what you say, it seems to me that it's malaria, the bad kind. It certainly isn't enteric. You might stay about in case I want anything."

So Bates remained, watching from the foot of the bed, resentful as a child from whom some cherished privilege had been taken away. This woman, this strange woman, had taken from him in a moment, not only His Lordship but the pleasure he got from watching His Lordship die.

[468]

He watched while she took the pulse and the blood pressure, and then, turning to him, she said, "Tell that woman Léah to fetch some hot water. I want to give him a tepid bath. After you've done that you can go to bed."

He went out without answering her or bidding her good night, aware suddenly that he wanted Lord Groton to die and that now the chances were that he would not die, because this woman was here, because Bates saw at once, with his talent for such things, that this woman knew her business, and she had, what was more important, a devotion to her profession and a talent for it.

In a little while Rasmussen brought her some supper, and then a coolie appeared with jars of hot water, followed by Léah, who came not so much from a desire to help as from curiosity. Mees Opp greeted her. She did not even come into the room, but stood outside peering through the half-opened doorway. Mees Opp told her to go to bed after leaving a boy outside the door, in case she wanted anything during the night.

The curry and rice which Rasmussen brought her she did not touch until Lord Groton had been bathed and given medicines, to bring down his fever. When at last he lay quiet, breathing peacefully for the first time in days, she returned to her own room, and, leaving the door open a little, she sat down to a supper which long since had grown as cold as the heat of Nivandrum permitted. She did not mind the tepid food; she was scarcely aware of what she was eating, but she knew that in the heat she must feed the great bulk of her body, because if the fat ugly body should break down, the spirit would be of no use. For her the body had long since become something almost detached from her, little more than an instrument, a machine which served her and without which she would be useless.

So she did not think of the food, but of Lord Groton and Bates and Rasmussen and the woman Léah and the strange sense of confusion and doom which had struck her at once on arriving at the landing stage. Rasmussen, the only one among them all whom she had known at all well, seemed to her changed, anxious, irritable and nervy. The woman Léah, she scarcely knew, save by reputation, but she did not like the long-nosed, narrow-eyed face which had a way of appearing from behind screens and at half-closed doors. Mees Opp had no belief in the evil eye, but she did believe in the power of atmosphere and environment. It was, she knew, quite possible for a patient to be killed by those about him, neither by blows nor by poison, but by emanations which came very near to the borders of magic. She had known patients in the villages, who should have recovered, to die simply because there was in the tiny world about them an atmosphere of death and a will to death. Now her dark blood told her that there was here, in the Grand Oriental Hotel, an atmosphere which was strained and sinister, something which she could not quite analyze because she still knew too little, but

[469]

which seemed directed toward the helpless, unconscious man on the bed in the next room. There were things she was able to divine which no European doctor would have suspected.

And as she ate she kept seeing the faces, the stolid Rasmussen's, perplexed now and uneasy, and the face of his wife, never seen quite clearly, but from the shelter of the coconut matting screen or the half-closed door. Mees Opp did not like that face, and as she thought about it, thinking of the evil eye and the witchcraft of the villages, a strange thought came to her and she said to herself, "Tomorrow I will tell the woman that I mean to eat myself whatever is brought for the patient."

It was a strange thought. The man was ill, certainly, and quite as certainly the illness was malaria, but it might not be the black malaria, which was rare enough. The violence of the symptoms might come from something else, from something which was being given him by the woman Léah. Cases like this were common enough in the villages, cases of men and women who died violently of an illness which in itself was simple enough. Only the absence of motive perplexed her. Why should the woman Léah want a stranger like Lord Groton, a man who was rich and powerful and could benefit her, to die?

She wondered, too, about the manservant, but to judge him was for her far more difficult. The woman Léah she understood; there was a woman like her in almost every village, who, as she grew old and toothless, became an outcast, but an outcast who kept the whole village paralyzed beneath the spell of terror she was able to impose. But the manservant was different; he came out of a world which Mees Opp, even during her stay in the West, had never seen, for her life there had been confined to classrooms and cheap lodginghouses. Never once had she seen the inside of one of those great houses where the rich of England—the world which kept menservants like Bates—dwelt in a kind of secret luxury. The surroundings, the world of menservants, might be something of which she knew nothing, but a human face was a human face, no matter what the difference of wealth and environment, and the face of Bates, the manservant, Mees Opp decided that she liked little more than the face of Léah. Indeed, by the time she had finished her meal, she disliked it so much that she began to mistrust his devotion.

About the sick man it was difficult to form any judgment beyond the facts which her experience with the human body at once revealed to her—that he was heavy and gross and that he was soaked with alcohol. So long as he remained unconscious and sodden, without that animating spark which invested the body with personality, the rest of him must remain a mystery. Out of the lot it was Lady Groton who interested her most—that the wife should be absent at such a time from the bedside of her husband, that she should have been devoted enough to come with him to a place like Nivandrum and then leave him in his illness to the care of a manservant like this one.

When she had placed the tray with the remnants of her supper outside the door, she put on a kind of Mother Hubbard in coarse white cotton and looked at the clock. To her astonishment it was well after midnight, and she thought, "Perhaps Lady Groton has come in and gone to her room without coming here at all," but after she had combed her hair and taken another look at the sleeping patient, she heard a footstep on the stair, followed in a moment by the sound of a knock on the door of Lord Groton's room. Knowing that Lady Groton would be expecting to find the manservant there, she went herself and opened the door.

Outside stood a tall, slim, blond woman, dressed all in white. She was not what Mees Opp had expected. She had thought to find Lady Groton middle-aged and faded and dowdy and a little eager and anxious, like so many Englishwomen she had seen in the East who were married to important and domineering men, and so for a moment, in the shock of surprise, she could only say, "Won't you come in?"

Her tongue was leaden, but the intuitive mind set in the great body worked rapidly. She did not know what was *chic* and what was not, for such things had never had anything to do with her life, but she did know that the woman in the beautifully cut white clothes had a look of race and a manner of poise and authority. She thought at once, "She is better than I expected. She is better both ways," and for a moment a little stab of envy struck at the great heart of Mees Opp, because in the doorway stood a vision of what, long ago, as a young girl, she had wanted to be more than anything in the world—beautiful and blond and slender. And at the same moment it struck her as very odd that this woman should be the wife of the coarse alcoholic who lay unconscious, snoring faintly, on the teakwood bed. It was all wrong, thought Mees Opp. "The whole thing is wrong."

But by that time Lady Groton had recovered from her astonishment at finding this ugly, great half-caste woman instead of Bates, and she said, "I suppose you are Mees Opp?"

"Yes," said Mees Opp softly. "Come into my room. We can talk there without disturbing him."

So she led the way, and in her own plain room Lady Groton sat down just within the circle of light from the paraffin lamp and now, when Mees Opp saw her more clearly, she wondered that she seemed, in the awful heat, so calm and cool, so utterly free from either discomfort or anxiety. And then, even while they were talking, it seemed to Mees Opp that there was a radiance in the face of the woman, a kind of light which was exciting and brought to her small, childlike face a look that again struck back into thoughts and emotions which had not occurred to Mees Opp for more than thirty years. She thought, trying to keep her mind on what she was saying, "But this woman is in love!" One did not have to know great houses or Paris dressmakers or menservants to know when a woman was in love and that her love was fulfilled. In the villages of the East and in the West End of London, women, Mees Opp knew well, were exactly the same when it came to love.

Lady Groton was saying, even before she asked after her husband, "I hope your journey here wasn't too bad. It was wonderfully kind of you to have come, but the circumstances were a bit exceptional. Perhaps I can explain all the reasons later on . . . before I leave."

"No," said Mees Opp, "I'm used to such weather. I couldn't come sooner. You see, I have a very busy life."

"It was good of you to come at all. Neither of us can ever be grateful enough to you." There was a little silence and then she said, "How do you find him?' '

Shyly Mees Opp smoothed her own stringy mud-colored hair and replied, "I can't say yet. Tomorrow I can tell more. I should think everything would be all right. A great deal depends on your husband's vitality."

"It is immense," said Lady Groton.

"And I can't be sure yet how bad the attack really is. I should say now that it is less bad than it seems. But we shall see."

"If there is anything I can do, you mustn't hesitate to ask me. I mean if there is anything I can do to help *you*. You probably know that there is no question of money."

"No," said Mees Opp. (Perhaps she will help me to get money out of him for the hospital. She seems so nice, so smooth and nice, and so pretty. But why did she stay away from her sick husband until long after midnight?)

Lady Groton opened a gold and platinum cigarette case and offered it to Mees Opp, and Mees Opp, without quite knowing what she was doing, took a cigarette. (She smoked now and then with Mrs. Badoki, who had once lived in Bombay.) Then, as Lady Groton held her tiny onyx and ruby lighter to the cigarette, she said, "It's very late, I know. I stayed out much longer than I expected to. You see, I met Mr. Dantry. I didn't know he was coming back."

Mees Opp, wondering how much she knew, how much of the whole story of Maria, looked at her for a moment in silence and then said, "Yes, I persuaded him to come back. I thought it much better."

Impulsively Lady Groton said, "That was good of you," and then, as if to cover herself she said, "It's been very boring here with no one I knew very well." But in spite of herself the look in her face said to Mees Opp, "Oh, thank you! You are a good woman and kind! Oh, thank you!"

"He's ill himself."

Then the face of Lady Groton grew still and frightened. She said, "How is he—ill?"

"In the spirit," said Mees Opp. "Perhaps he can be cured." And Lady Groton thought, "He is cured now. If you could have seen him tonight . . . how he is changed, how he was like he used to be long ago. If you could only know. . . ." But aloud she said, "I stayed later than I expected because he found an old album of photographs . . . full of old friends and old faces."

"It was all right," said Mees Opp. "The manservant was a great help."

She noticed that at the mention of the photograph album a faint shadow came over the face of Lady Groton and she thought, "Then she did know him before. She knew him long ago," and she felt a sudden envy of this woman younger than herself, not now because she was more beautiful and richer and more lucky, but because of the look in her face. Now she was certain of what had happened on the island and she was a little alarmed, thinking, "Perhaps I was wrong to bring him back," but at the same time another voice said, "You were right. There is so little happiness in the world and so much misery. You have helped two people to happiness at least for a few hours, and that is something."

But Lady Groton was saying, "Oh, Bates. You mustn't mind Bates."

"I didn't mind him."

"Sometimes he's bumptious and impossible." And like a shadow, the memory of the betraying telegram returned to her. For hours now, ever since she had wakened to find Tom there beside her, she had forgotten it.

For a time they both smoked in silence, and then Lady Groton said, "How long do you think it will be before my husband can leave?"

"That's impossible to say. It depends so much on the patient. But he won't be able to leave before a fortnight at the earliest."

"Will it be hotter than this?"

"Sometimes after the monsoon breaks it is hotter. It's steamy, but for part of the day it seems fresher."

Then Lady Groton stood up suddenly and said, "I won't keep you up. You must be very tired. I hope that Rasmussen saw to it that you had a good dinner."

"A very good dinner," said Mees Opp, who had not thought about it one way or another.

Lady Groton held out her hand. "Good night," she said. "Would you like my *ayah* to help you? I've almost no work for her."

"Perhaps," said Mees Opp. "We shall see."

She opened the door for Lady Groton, who smiled at her as she went out, and Mees Opp, with a little stab at the heart, was again aware of the look of radiance.

When the door was closed once more, Mees Opp stopped for a moment in front of the mottled glass on the dressing table and then quickly put out the lamp, but before going to bed, she went to the window, feeling somehow that if she could have a few breaths of air before inclosing herself in the netting, she would be able to sleep. Her heavy body was weary and her feet pained her as they always did during the heat, but her mind was awake with a terrible wakefulness.

It was a little cooler now, although the air was still, and the moon was high in the sky, shedding a pale white light over the channel and the distant island where Lady Groton's "old friend" lived in a house that in the moonlight was no more than a ghost of a house. For a long time Mees Opp leaned on the edge of the window, trying to take the weight of her body off her aching feet, while she breathed the air that smelled faintly of the distant mangrove swamps. She was thinking of Lady Groton and could come to no opinion about her. And then through her thoughts, she saw something moving on the surface of the channel, and fixing her attention, she discovered that the moving thing was a canoe and in it the figure of a woman. It came nearer and nearer, until the palm trees hid it from view. Curious, she waited to see whether it was coming to the hotel pier.

In a little while the moonlight caught the white *sari* of the woman as she came up the path beneath the palms. From the arched doorway below there was still a faint glow from a lamp left burning in the great hall, and Mees Opp waited until the woman came into the area of radiance. Then she saw with surprise that the woman was Léah Rasmussen, and she thought, "What can she be doing out now, a little while before dawn? Where has she been?" And then it occurred to Mees Opp that the woman had perhaps been waiting until the light went out in Mees Opp's room before she returned. "She thinks that I am already in bed where I can't see her return."

A solitary jackal howled somewhere on the mainland, that long-drawn wail which, to Mees Opp, used to it all her life, still seemed like the voice of the dead, and beneath her window the faint light that came through the arched doorway was suddenly extinguished.

36

By the time Lady Groton had reached her own room, the radiance had gone out of her, and after she had stepped over the *ayah* and had closed the door and bolted it, without quite knowing why, she sat for a long time at her dressing table not troubling even to take off her clothes. There was no reason for haste in going to bed. There was nothing to do all day in the heat but sleep, or try to sleep. In a place like Nivandrum one lived only at night during the monsoon. Going without sleep had not seemed to matter much during these past four days. When she thought of it, she realized that she had not had more than four or five hours of sleep a night and yet, even in the terrible heat, she felt well now, alive, even excited. Now, for the first time since she had wakened on the terrace outside Tom's room, the memory of the four days of misery returned to her, but the memory did not matter now; in an odd way it seemed to her that they had only heightened the beauty and the pleasure of what had happened tonight. Now it seemed to her that for the first time in her life she was alive.

It had not been as it had been long ago during those week ends with Tom; then it had been a kind of frenzy, in which two spoiled and headstrong young people had been caught up and swept along, not unwillingly but without understanding what was happening to them. They had been like all the rest of their generation and that was what had broken the thread of their lives and changed everything afterward muddling it, leaving them both unhappy, aimless and despairing.

Now it was all clear for the first time, and she knew, perhaps out of all the experience which had come to her, sometimes pleasantly, more often sordidly, in the years between, the value and the significance of what it was that held them together forever, what it was that had set them both to searching for something which neither of them could ever find, save in each other. And all the time, during all those wasted years, if either of them had had the intelligence or the wisdom or the courage, they could have come together and had what they had had tonight.

For Tom was himself again, what he had been long ago, only nicer and more gentle, and more tender. When she thought of his tenderness, which had never existed long ago, she wanted to cry. It was the tenderness which had made her even in the midst of their happiness and ecstasy, ashamed of herself and all she had been, suddenly, without warning. It was not conscience, nor moral precept, nor even the training of childhood, which had made her ashamed of herself and of him, but the tenderness which she had suddenly felt enveloping her. It was as if they had both become children, as if in some miraculous way they had regained their innocence, as if somehow they had shed the evil, the promiscuity of all those years. It was, she thought, still conscious of her old dislike for sentimentality, like being reborn. It was something she had never dreamed was possible.

Now they would never leave each other. She would stay here until Albert was well enough to leave. She would go on playing shabbily the role of wife, and then she would tell him that it was finished forever, and if he refused to give her a divorce it did not matter. It did not matter whether they were ever received by anyone, or whether no one in the world ever spoke to them again. The only thing of importance was that they never lost each other again; everything else seemed to have slipped away, leaving her with a feeling of freedom and triumph. They might even go away before

Albert was well enough to travel, as soon as it was clear that he would not die. And then the thought of his blood pressure occurred to her; perhaps they would not dare risk telling him until he was quite well for fear the news should bring on a stroke. And again she thought, "Why should he care? Why should he want to keep anyone like me?"

And the thought of the telegram and the betrayal returned to her and she felt suddenly sick, physically sick. Now suddenly she knew that it was the worst thing she had ever done in all her life. Until tonight she had felt revengeful and even triumphant, as if at last she had paid Groton back for all the evil he had done her and the evil he had done so many others who were more helpless, less capable of defending themselves, than she had been. But now it was quite different. For a moment she almost felt sorry for Albert, because he was dying without having lived at all, without ever knowing what she had known tonight and would know for the rest of her life. She felt sorry for him because he was dying now like a machine, without soul or feeling, which, worn out, runs down and stops at last because there is no longer any force to keep it going. With all his shrewdness, with all his calculation, Albert knew nothing about tenderness or love or friendship; he knew nothing about anything. The money he had given her did not soften her. "I have earned that," she thought with bitterness, "as sordidly as any Piccadilly whore. I owe him nothing for that."

The thing was that for the first time Albert seemed human to her. "Perhaps," she thought, "that too is because of the tenderness." She was sorry that he should be so miserable a man. "Perhaps it was not his fault. I have never known what happened to him as a child. He would never speak of his childhood or his brother or his parents. Something must have happened to him to have made him as he is, something which in my world I never knew."

But there was no going back now. She meant not even to give up so much as one evening on the island with Tom, not one moment of those long hot nights together, because tomorrow, even tonight, one of them might die, and they had so much to get back which belonged to them, and which they had thrown away. With astonishment she understood that it wasn't physical desire which drove her now, as it had driven her on that first night when she came down the stairs to find Tom dressed in a *sarong* like a boatman. It was something else, which she had never known before, even in those wild days when they had been together just after the war. It was something that warmed her and made her feel radiant and—once more she blushed that an idea so sentimental should come to her of all people—almost consecrated. It was a feeling which made her weak and astonished.

And all the time she sat there she was aware of Mees Opp, who was not at all what she had expected. She kept seeing the face with extraordinary clearness, the muddy skin and thin hair, the great fat body. It existed for her more clearly than any face, even Tom's, had existed before. Out of her vague memories of Mees Opp on that first day seated at a table in the dilapidated summerhouse, treating the long line of suffering people, she had expected a commonplace, efficient, perhaps groveling half-caste woman, but she had found something else—a woman with character and dignity and with something in her face which she had never seen before in the face of any person she had ever known, something which in a strange way was related to the tenderness and which had the same power of shaking her armor of confidence and making her feel ashamed.

She had not been aware of it at first when she stood in the dimly lighted doorway of Groton's room; at that moment Mees Opp had been little more than a silhouette, with a warm and rather pleasant voice, clad in an absurd cotton nightgown. It was only when they had passed Albert's bed, while she turned her head a little so as not to see him, and had gone into Mees Opp's own room, that she understood the quality of the look in the doctor's face.

She was thankful that she had been gracious in the beginning, although her graciousness did her no credit. She thought, "I was taught all my childhood and early youth to be gracious, because there were not many people I was to meet in life who would be anything but my inferiors, and one had to be gracious to inferiors." Being gracious was the easiest and most natural thing she did. From childhood she had been gracious, at village fairs, at bazaars, at balls. It was so easy—that artificial graciousness—when you were born in security, with health and beauty and prestige, when all the world was waiting and eager to be pleasant in return. There was, she told herself, no credit for her in that. With poor Albert perhaps it had been different; he had never had any graciousness, not even the artificial graciousness that was automatic and easy.

But now, sitting before the dressing table, she was thankful for that early training because, afterward, while she sat by the lamp in Mees Opp's bedroom, the graciousness had ceased to be artificial and had become genuine, born not in tradition and training, but in the heart, and it had brought with it a warm, comforting feeling like stepping into a hot bath on a cold foggy London day.

It was a feeling she had never had before, and how it came to be born she could not discover even now, save that something in the face of Mees Opp made her feel generous, and made her wonder, too, about Mees Opp and what it must be like to be ugly like her and poor and a half-caste. Mees Opp might have minded all those things once, but she did not mind them now; you could tell that from her bearing. If she had minded, if she had thought of her looks and circumstances and been envious, you could have read the dissatisfaction in her face. It was easy enough to do that; all her life she had been reading envy in the faces of other women. In the face of Mees Opp there was no envy, and so, thought Lady Groton, she must have found something which to her was better than beauty or wealth or position, or any of the things she did not have and would never have. Lucky Mees Opp! If she herself did not find something like that there was only misery before her and the horrors of growing thin and wrinkled and tired, and older and older and older until at last she died, glad that the bloody thing was finished. But perhaps she had found it, in Tom and that new tenderness.

Whenever she thought of him her blood ran a little faster and she felt for a moment like a schoolgirl discovering the world for the first time, thinking how wonderful it was and what romantic and incredible things could happen in it. And she felt a little proud, too, that she had won and changed him, that she had been shameless on the morning he went away, when she ran after him to say what her heart had been crying out to say. Because tonight he *was* changed; he had forgotten all his worrying and self-torment, all his weakness and indecision; for a little time she had persuaded him to live in the moment, in the precious moments that were left to them. He had been reckless and gay and tender with her, free of all those barriers which always before had shut him away from her, even when they were in each other's arms.

At last she began slowly to undress, and presently, just as the sky began to turn crimson and gold beyond the high mountains, she fell asleep, feeling somehow clean and redeemed and free, now that everything was settled and there would be no more muddling and no more searching. She fell asleep thinking, "In a little while after I wake, it will be evening again and I shall be able to cross over to the island and be with him alone, no one there but the two of us"—for Dantry, she knew, had sent Silas away for good because the eyes of the boy, which were so like the eyes of Maria, were unbearable to him.

37

On his island Dantry too slept at last, peacefully, luxuriously, as he had not slept since he was a boy, long ago before the war, because he had come at last to the end of things, and coming to the end had brought him release. The monotony, the dreariness of soul which had afflicted him during the long journey back to Nivandrum, vanished in the second he discovered her there asleep on the Indian bed. In that moment something inside the tired head had snapped and suddenly he was free, thinking, "Nothing matters now! Nothing save enjoyment! Nothing save life! Nothing matters for the two of us . . . neither Maria nor Groton nor anyone in the world!"

Afterward nothing existed for them, and the whole world became simply the house and island, bathed in moonlight, where they were together. There was no food in the house so, like Adam and Eve, they went into the garden, and in the moonlight they gathered coconuts and papayas and passion fruit, and then on the terrace they sat by a little table and ate the fruit and drank champagne, drawn up from the bottom of the deep well of sweet water dug long ago by some Dutch or Portuguese trader. It was a little as Tipton Farm had been long ago when they went there as boy and girl to cook their own food and do their own housework. Only then they had sat in the little garden in front of the cottage above the sea instead of on the terrace of this haunted old baroque house, with the sound of drums and jackals in the distance.

Watching her across the table, he had thought, "This is better than anything I had ever dreamed of. It is far better than it was long ago, because now we know everything there is to know of each other, both good and bad. There are no longer any mysteries or any misunderstandings. There is no ambition and no worldliness and no world outside to distract and weary us and fray our nerves. Perhaps in the end we are luckier than most lovers, because now that we have gone such a long way and know so much and are so tired, there is nothing we want from the outside because we know what is there, all of it, too much of it."

And again it struck him that there must always have been some power of destiny which brought him to the island in the beginning, that perhaps all along, each thing that had happened, each misery and disillusionment, had occurred in some mysterious order or succession simply to bring about this unbelievable moment.

They did not talk much, but were content to sit there now and then looking at each other, almost shy and in the glory of their happiness. Once she said, "I am ashamed and afraid," and when he asked, "Why?" she said, "Because we are having what we do not deserve."

Puzzled, he said, "It is you who always reproached me for thoughts like that."

"I know," and without saying it she thought, "perhaps happiness is changing me—the happiness which I never took into account."

He laughed and said, "You're not going to be Thaïs and try to convert me back again?"

"No," and she laughed, too, because the idea was funny and because she was happy.

"Let's not speak of it . . . forget it."

"I promise not to speak of it again."

But there was a little silence, painful and filled with thoughts which went unspoken. They both had the same thoughts and knew it well enough, so

[479]

there was no need of their being uttered. And afterward he brought out the little photograph album which he had kept with him through all his wanderings (her own was gone, lost somewhere in the dusty attics of the great house in Hill Street), and they looked at the pictures of themselves, taken long ago, when as children they had thought themselves so wild and so worldly. There was a picture of herself on a stile and one of him on the top of a hayrick, and one of the two of them on bicycles which must have been taken by some friendly passer-by they had encountered in the Devonshire lanes. Oddly enough they seemed only funny now and did not move her to tears, partly because the boy in the pictures and the girl in very, very short skirts seemed to be photographs of people who were strangers, and partly because they both knew that what they had now, this thing born out of so much seeking and adventure, was better than the thing they had had then.

They talked for a long time making plans as to where they would go when Groton had recovered and had gone from their lives. They planned to find a place like Nivandrum if such another place existed, where they would have a house to return to from journeys. They would travel a great deal to strange and exotic places like Omaha and Toronto and Buenos Aires, in a world newer than the one they knew too well, and in all their talk there was a strange greediness, as if there lay before them too much of joy and delight to be savored before they were old and finished. Now that they had found each other at last there would no longer be any doubts or quarrels or unfaithfulness.

At the hour when the drums had begun to die away, he took her in his arms and they made love again with a satisfaction, a completeness, a kind of voluptuous peace which neither of them had ever known before.

Long after midnight, she said, suddenly, "I should go back now. They'll begin to talk in the hotel."

He laughed. "Don't imagine they haven't been talking ever since you came here that first night."

"Don't talk about that night."

"Why not?"

"I don't like thinking of it."

It wasn't necessary, she knew, to give the reasons, for he knew them as surely as herself—that there had been something neurotic and greedy and perverse about that first encounter, something sordid because they both brought to it ugly, cynical overtones of all the reckless and promiscuous searching they had gone through. It was as if those two people who had met and fallen in love again that first night beneath the stars of Nivandrum were strangers to them now, like the boy and the girl in the faded photographs.

He said, "What does it matter? Why not stay here . . . all the night . . . forever?"

Then she grew serious and a look of pain came over her face and she said, "No, that's what we've always done. We mustn't spoil everything now—just when we've found each other again. We've always ruined everything by being spoiled and greedy. We were too lucky in the beginning. We always thought we could have everything just for the taking."

At last after many false starts they descended the stairway to the water and he took her back across the channel to the hotel, and there on the pier he left her after holding her close to him for a long time in the scented darkness. And as he kissed her for the last time he said, "Some day, some time we shall be free to do as we like. We shall live somewhere where no one will know us or care what we do."

38

All day Mees Opp sat by the bed of Lord Groton and at night she slept lightly in the stifling room adjoining that of Lord Groton, waking every hour, as if there were an alarm clock by her side, to go in and have a look at him. He was quieter now than he had been under Bates's care, for the fever had weakened him, and only twice in the three days before his death did he recover consciousness for a little time and begin to rave against Dantry. Mees Opp, far stronger than Bates, was able to hold him in bed until the moment of raving passed and he fell back again exhausted.

After the first day and the second her patient began to take on the proportions of a crusade. He was better and then worse and then better again, and once he became almost calmly conscious for a time, staring at her out of his pale blue eyes with a look of wonder, and then losing himself once more in fever. It was not easy . . . the fever *and* the heat—but Mees Opp had made up her mind that she would not, she could not, let him die. The decision came from a number of motives, all mixed and none of them very clear. She did not know what sort of man he was, but she did not like the way in which he had been neglected before she came, because Mees Opp believed that you could not neglect even the devil himself if he were ill. After he was well, there would be time enough to send him packing.

And she was determined to defeat the woman Léah, for the more she watched her, the more she talked to her, the more certain she was that Léah *had* been giving him something, some herb or drug which would have been certain to kill him in the end. A second time she caught Léah returning just before dawn, but now the strange nocturnal excursions of the woman did not trouble her because she had taken care to go down to the kitchen herself for

Lord Groton's broths and to taste them all, ostentatiously, in Léah's presence. If Léah were simply going off to some island incantation or to consult a witch doctor, she did not mind; that never killed anyone, least of all a man who was unconscious with fever, a European who could not be touched in his imagination.

But the motive still puzzled her, and the nearest she came to it was a remark made by Léah one night when Mees Opp came to the kitchen for the broth. She asked whether Lord Groton was improving, and when Mees Opp said that the fever was down and that he was a little better each day, Léah said suddenly with an extraordinary intensity, "He is a bad man."

Mees Opp, curious, asked, "Why do you say that?"

"Why does he come here? We were all happy in Nivandrum. What does he want here?"

By now Mees Opp had divined the reasons for Groton's visit, but she only said, "I don't know."

"After him will come other men like him. If he has his way he will send them here and everything will be changed and miserable." And then suddenly she said, "I don't think he will ever leave here." And there came into her brooding face a terrifying look of evil and malice.

"Why do you say that?"

"Because the River God is against him. The River God closed the harbor. He wants it kept closed."

To which Mees Opp only said, "Nonsense," and left the room with the broth.

She was used to talk like this among the women of the villages, and it did not alarm her, so long as she was there to protect her patient. Once he was well, he could protect himself. Once he was well, he would go away. She was not frightened of Léah, but the woman made her uneasy, because she knew that women like Léah were quite capable of lending a hand to the River God in case he did not act quickly enough.

But what troubled her more than Léah was the thought of the moment when Lord Groton would emerge from the coma and ask for his wife, and when she considered what she would do, she knew that she would protect Lady Groton, lying, if necessary, as Bates had done so many times. The ethics of the situation did not trouble her very profoundly, because long ago she had abandoned standards of ethics and morals and come to trust her instinct and her sense of humanity. Long ago she had learned that it is better to be human than to obey any code to the letter, and her instinct told her that of the two it was the wife who must not be betrayed.

She liked Lady Groton; she had liked her from the moment she opened the door and saw her standing in the dim light of the hall. There was something nice about her and easy and there was an honesty too, a way of looking things straight in the face, which Mees Opp liked. She did not pretend that the man on the island was not her lover; she made no excuses and no evasions, and so in her own mind (thought Mees Opp) she must have weighed it all and found her conscience clear. Mees Opp did not pretend to understand the ins and outs of the situation; she was simply willing to bet on Lady Groton.

By the second night they had come to an arrangement. When Lady Groton returned she was to open the door of Mees Opp's room gently, and if Mees Opp happened to be awake she would tell her about her husband's condition. If she were not awake, Lady Groton refused to waken her and waited until morning. In the mornings when she came in they sometimes talked, and Mees Opp was a little astonished to find that a woman like Lady Groton was so interested in her, that she asked so many questions about her past and her hospital and her work, because Lady Groton seemed to her to belong to a world as different from her own as the sun from the moon. But she was not displeased, because if Lady Groton was so interested, then it was quite possible that she would induce her husband to make a rich gift to the hospital.

On the second morning, while they were sitting together in wrappers in Mees Opp's room, Lady Groton said, after a little silence, "I should think you were very happy."

"I don't know," said Mees Opp, "I've never had time to think about it. I suppose I am."

"It must be a wonderful feeling when you save a life or help someone who is suffering."

"It is," said Mees Opp, quite simply. "It's like . . . like . . . ." She felt for words and found none, finishing the sentence limply by saying, "I don't know what it's like."

Lady Groton said nothing more that morning, but went away. Nevertheless, the image of Mees Opp's homely face remained with her all the morning, and before she went to sleep again she thought, "Once Albert is well and this mess is all cleared up I shall give her some of the money Albert settled on me for her hospital. I shan't miss it. I shan't want clothes any more or jewels or any of those things," and then it occurred to her that she was free, really free for the first time in her life; not only of Albert and all his money, but of all those things—the clothes, the jewels, the parties, the yacht, the house in Hill Street—which once she had thought she could not do without. It wasn't only because of what had happened to her and Tom; Mees Opp had something to do with it too, not exactly Mees Opp, perhaps, but the thing she had seen in the face of Mees Opp on that first night.

[483]

39

It was Bates who told her of the arrival of Mr. Clapton. She wakened slowly about five in the afternoon to the sound of a knock, and when she said "Who is it?" Bates answered and came in.

She said, still half-asleep but angry, "I did not tell you to come in," and Bates answered, "I beg your pardon. I misunderstood," but she knew by the sly look on his face that he was lying. He was being insolent, for he permitted her to know by his very expression that he was lying. But she was awake enough to think, "He's presuming too much. I'm free now. He can tell Albert about Tom and all the others for all I care. Perhaps it would clear matters up if he did."

Then he said, "He's here, me lady. I thought you'd like to know."

"Who's here?"

"Clapton is his name, I believe. Lord Deakin's man."

Then she felt suddenly sick. That was why Bates was insolent. She wasn't free after all. He could still blackmail her if he chose. "I should have known Bates wasn't so stupid," she thought. "He knew all along that I didn't mind his telling Albert about Tom or the others, but he does know that I mind about this." And again she knew that the telegram of betrayal was the worst thing she had done in all her life. She hadn't expected results so soon; she had even hoped that they might escape from Nivandrum before an agent of Hugo Deakin put in an appearance.

"He came very quickly," she said, determined not to give herself away to Bates.

"I believe he came by plane to the capital and from there in a launch sent up from the south."

"Has he a launch? I didn't hear it."

"Perhaps you were asleep, me lady. It's noisy enough."

She knew by the expression on his face what he was thinking—that the sound of the launch would be the first thing Groton would hear when he wakened, and that he would know at once what the sound meant. The sound of a launch could kill him and then . . . murder could be accomplished in many ways.

"He was wiser than His Lordship," said Bates.

"How?"

"He's been to the Ranee. He has leased the best of the water front and bought options inland."

"Oh!" Then she said, "But how do you know all this?"

For the fraction of a second Bates did not answer. Then he said, "Oh, just talking. It just came up." There was a shadow of confusion in his face, as if he were commanding it to do something which it could not do. "He was so pleased, I suppose he wanted to tell someone."

"Where is he staying?"

"Here, me lady. There isn't any other place."

She thought for a moment and then said, "What is he like?"

"Rather a common fellow, me lady," and suddenly she felt a wild desire to laugh, hysterically, without restraint. For a desperate second it seemed to her that to laugh thus was the only thing that could save her, and in the same second it seemed to her that they were all mad—Albert with his ambitions, herself and her triviality, Bates and his disloyalty, Tom married to a native woman, even Mees Opp. It was all mad and distorted and without balance, that she should find herself in a room in a place like this, parrying with her husband's manservant, attempting to keep him in his place. A part of her mind kept asking, "How did I get here? What have I done? It was not I who sent that telegram but someone else. None of it is true. Perhaps I have not even seen Tom and gone to him night after night. Perhaps I am mad and have imagined all these things," and she felt a cold sense of terror, but she managed to say, "Thank you, Bates. That's all."

When he had gone, she got out of bed and bathed and began to dress herself quickly, thinking, "I must see this agent, I must talk to him. I must stop him and send him away. Perhaps I can buy him off with my own money, with jewelry I don't want any longer. Perhaps . . . perhaps . . ." For a moment her thoughts scrambled wildly, melodramatically, "Perhaps if I let him sleep with me," but that was too naïve, and anyway now she could not do it. A week ago it could have happened, but not now.

Then almost at once she saw that all this was hysterical. If he had already taken leases and options the thing was not to be undone. Suddenly she was frightened as she had never been frightened before, because never before in all her life had she been trapped.

When she came down the stairs he was sitting in the far end of the big vaulted room, near the doorway, drinking whisky and soda and looking out across the harbor, and she knew the moment she saw the back of his head that it was no good. It was rather square and flat, the fleshy neck burned red by years of sun in the East. It was like the back of Albert's head, which was the part of him she hated most because it seemed to her that there was centered all the stubbornness, the brutality, the lack of sensibility. For years she had avoided looking at the back of Albert's head.

But she meant to talk to him, to discover at least what sort of person he was, and so she crossed the floor as if to go past him into the garden, but as she reached the table he turned and she smiled at him. At once he sprang to his feet and she thought, "He *is* like Albert, only younger. I suppose Albert at his age sprang to his feet in the same way whenever the aristocracy put in an appearance."

She said, "Good afternoon," and Clapton, in an oily way, said, "You're Lady Groton, I suppose."

"Yes," and she felt a sudden wild desire to laugh again at the memory of Bates's speech, "Rather a common fellow, me lady."

"Will you have something with me?"

"With pleasure."

He was bouncing and full of animal vitality, like Albert had been once; on the make, too, as Albert had been. "He's Deakin's man," she thought. "But he thinks it a good idea to be in well all around. His motto very likely is, 'You never can tell what may happen.'" But this was only a sprawling cub, the old lion was tired now, and ill and perhaps dying in the teakwood bed abovestairs.

She ordered gin and tonic and then said, "Well, what do you think of the place?"

"Too hot. You've been here quite awhile, but it doesn't seem to trouble you much."

"No."

He grinned. "I guess we're here for the same reasons."

"Probably you know more about that than I do. You see, I don't know why you're here."

Rasmussen, tired and white in his waiter's costume, brought the gin and tonic and went away again, sour in his manner as if he had had enough of all these strange, disrupting, demanding people and longed again for the simple trade of the sailors who came in winter.

Clapton grinned again and said, "I'm here for the same reasons as your husband."

"Oh!"

"I hear he has been ill. Is he better?"

"A lot."

"He won't be very pleased to find me here."

"No, it will make him very angry. How did you find out he was here?"

Clapton looked at her shrewdly and then said with a certain smugness, "We businessmen have ways of finding out things."

"I know that. I've been married to one for a great many years."

"And a shrewd one, too."

Into the coarse face of the man there came a look of admiration that rather sickened her. She thought, "He can be bought, only I haven't enough money to buy him, not with all my jewelry and the money Albert settled on me, because he's gambling on the future—that some day people will address him too as Your Lordship."

She said, "Are you planning to stay for a long time?" (He might go **away** before Albert recovered consciousness and then I would escape the **worst**.) "I don't know. Until I've done everything I have to do."

His eyes narrowed a little and again she wanted to laugh, thinking, "He believes I'm trying to vamp him to gain information for Albert in the best cinema style." The naïveté of men like Albert and Clapton always astonished her. It was always new and incredible that with all their villainy they were like children. Real villainy, like her betrayal of Albert, was something beyond their imagination, something which to them was unbelievable. And she felt a quick sense of superiority and of contempt for the man. But all this, she knew, was getting her nowhere, and by now she knew that any number of conversations would produce no further progress, because he was on his guard against her, thinking of her in terms of cinema vamps.

Suddenly he said, "Do you know this man Dantry who lives here . . . a kind of English beachcomber?"

She thought, "He knows that I know him. He knows everything," and she said, betraying herself a little by anger, "I know him, but he's not a beachcomber. He's a gentleman living on an income."

"A remittance man then?"

"No, not that either."

Then it occurred to her what he was doing. The tables were turned and he was trying to use *her*. But he had hit on the wrong thing, because she did not mind now who knew that Tom was her lover. It puzzled her that he did not use the telegram against her, but, after all, he might be holding that as a final card.

"He should know a good deal about the place. He ought to be useful, but very likely your husband has thought of that before me."

"No, my husband hasn't even seen him. Anyway, it wouldn't do any good. Mr. Dantry doesn't want the harbor opened. He'd do everything to prevent it."

Clapton's jaw grew sharp with contempt and determination. Then he laughed and said, "A lot of good it will do him. Will you have another drink?"

"No thanks. I'm going out in a moment in the boat to have some air."

"That Cockney Sandy told me the same thing. He said Dantry was a queer bloke and there wasn't any use going to him. He's married to Sandy's daughter, you know."

She felt her face stiffen as she had seen Bates's face stiffen a little while before when it refused to do what he had asked of it. "Yes, I know," she said, and a wild, fantastic idea struck her. Perhaps it was Bates who had done the betrayal before she had had time to do it. Perhaps he had been there all along, manservant to Albert, but in reality a spy for Deakin. It was fantastic, but somehow the idea had a ring of truth about it. It explained other leakages that had happened over a period of years. And Bates's face and manner. And a manservant would be the last to be suspected. Albert had discharged typists and secretaries and even broken with partners, but the leakage had gone on. Again and again he had come into her room to storm about it.

She tried to control her face, to pretend that she was listening to what he was saying, but her brain was on fire with the idea of Bates. Then she heard him saying, "This place is full of gossip," and she thought, "No, you don't catch me that way. You can't blackmail me about that."

"Yes," she said, "most small places are. I don't know really. I haven't had much contact with the people."

"Well, that's part of my business out here. It's one of the reasons I've been able to pull out of things when others failed. I always say, get next to the natives first and the way will be easy. I don't go in much for this color bar thing. It doesn't pay in business out here."

She did not answer him, and then he said, "The latest I heard is that this Dantry has deserted the Cockney's daughter and that she's gone potty."

"That's something I know nothing about."

"Yes, quite off her head. They've been trying native cures. The wife of this fellow Rasmussen has been saying hocus-pocus over her. Seems she is some kind of witch doctor."

"What a lot you find out."

"Well, that's my business." He lighted a cigarette and leaned back in his chair. As if she took this as an excuse to escape, she rose and said, "Thank you for the drink, I must go now," but instead of continuing on her way to the landing stage, she turned and went back again up the stairs, aware that she was hurrying and that she must not hurry because if he noticed it he would think he had perhaps achieved what he wanted. Trying to go slowly and calmly, it seemed to her that she would never reach the top of the open stairway with the lovely wrought-iron rail. But at last she was there at the turn, out of Clapton's sight, still thinking what a loathsome man he was. "There are worse than Albert perhaps, or was Albert really as bad as that when I first married him?"

She was not sure of anything now. It was as if she were changing, as if she were becoming another woman. Was it the heat or the illness or was it Tom, or was she losing her wits or going insane? How had she come to find herself, to whom nothing had ever happened, in so melodramatic a mess? Going along the broad hall she thought again, "I wanted something to happen to me. It's happened all right, with a vengeance!"

At the door of Mees Opp's room she knocked, and then, without waiting for an answer, stepped inside. Mees Opp was there, standing by the window,

[488]

preparing some sort of drink for her patient. She was peering at it through her thick spectacles and stirring it. At the sound of the opening door, she turned and said, "Good afternoon."

"Good afternoon. How is he?"

Mees Opp smiled, a great warm enveloping smile that changed the ugly face and made it almost beautiful. "A great deal better. His fever has gone down a point and a half."

"Is he still delirious?"

"He's sleeping now. When he wakes I think he'll be all right."

"Have you seen Bates?"

"He's in the other room. Some laundry of His Lordship's has just come and he's getting it in order. He said His Lordship wouldn't like it if he wakened and found the room any way but in perfect order."

That was a lie. It was just one of Bates's tricks for poking his nose in where he was no longer wanted.

"Would you ask him to come to my room for a moment?"

"Of course, Lady Groton."

Before she went out the door she took a long last look at Mees Opp. She had turned back to her stirring and peering. There was something calm and eternal about her, nothing mad or fantastic or exaggerated, as there was about everyone else in the hotel, every one of them, even Lansbury, pink, decadent, collapsed and useless in the heat. Mees Opp was sanity. She was solidity. She was genuine virtue. She must not go away. She must stay there even after Albert got well again, until she and Tom could leave Nivandrum together.

While she waited for Bates, she walked up and down the room, thinking all the while, "I must not be hysterical. I must not again do something like sending that foul telegram. I must be calm inside. I must pretend to act a role, as if I were in the cinema, facing down the villain . . . or one of the villains, only there are so many . . . Albert and Clapton and Tom and myself and that woman Léah. There are so many villains. It's all so complicated." And for the first time it occurred to her how loathsome the human race could be, how loathsome she could be and Tom, and so many other people who thought of themselves as nice and attractive.

Then there was a knock on the door and Bates came in, closing the door behind him, his face wearing the blankest of his many expressions. The moment she saw him she thought, "It's true. Now I've got to bluff him. He knows I've talked to Clapton and he's afraid."

She began abruptly by saying, "Bates, did you send the telegram I gave you?"

"Yes, me lady, it went at once. It must have gone at once for Mr. Clapton to have arrived so soon."

[489]

The last sentence he should not have spoken, for it gave her a clue. Very quickly she said, "He arrived so quickly, it occurred to me that you might have sent the telegram before I gave it to you."

The face was still blank, but he did not answer at once. There was a silence of a second, but a silence long enough to make her know that the thrust had struck home. She thought, "I'm enjoying this. It must be fun to play melodrama."

"I don't understand, me lady."

"Mr. Clapton never got it."

"He must have got it, me lady, to be here now. . . ."

Again she tried a shot in the dark, saying, "He got a telegram, but it wasn't my telegram. I've just been talking to him."

She had the upper hand now, and she knew that there would be no more insolence from Bates for the moment. He was attempting to look puzzled, all the cockiness gone out of him.

"I can't understand it, me lady. Perhaps Your Ladyship misunderstood Mr. Clapton."

"He's not very difficult to understand." She thought, "Now I must clinch it. I must make one more shot." So she said, "Do you remember about the South American business and the Mittel Europa Bank affair and one or two other things?"

This time he did not answer her at all for a long time. Then a faint sickly grin spread over the sallow face, a sardonic grin which suddenly made her like him again in spite of all his villainy. Then he said, "I understand, me lady. May I go now?"

"Yes, Bates."

She thought, "That's fixed him. In his heart he's a coward and afraid of Albert. Now I shan't have any more trouble with him."

He went out, closing the door behind him, and outside the door he took out his pocket handkerchief and wiped his forehead. It was not the heat this time, but the strain of trying to make his face do what it did not want to do. He had tried to keep it blank when all the time it wanted to break into a grin of admiration. He said to himself, "You can always tell a lady. Not many women could have done that. If all the rich was like her there wouldn't be no revolutions. There wouldn't need to be any. A thorough-bred is a thoroughbred, no matter where you find them. Only she's the last of her kind. They've gone out of date."

And what made it funnier was the certainty in his heart that she had never for a moment discussed the telegram with Clapton, and if she had, the certainty that Clapton was the last one to give anything away.

Slowly he went back to Lord Groton's bedroom, thinking, "Yes, things

[490]

are drawing to a close. The old man isn't going to die after all, but he's finished, and for him that's worse than being dead."

40

About midnight Lord Groton opened his eyes and *saw* the room for the first time since that evening long ago, years ago it seemed, when he had gone to bed feeling seedy. But when he first looked about he could not make out where he was. In one corner of the room there was a dim light and the room was filled with ugly teakwood furniture, and near the light he made out the bulky figure of a woman all in white standing with her back to him shaking down a thermometer; that made him know that he must be ill. His body felt extraordinarily light, as if it had no substance at all, and the sensation confused him, taking him back a long way, more than thirty years, to the time he had malaria in Samarang. So for a moment he experienced again the precious sensation of youth, mingled with the sound of the drums from the islands, the drums he had first heard, as a boy of twenty-one, one still, hot night in Macassar. And for a moment he felt again that all the world was before him, waiting to be conquered, waiting to deliver into his hands the money and power he meant to have from it. But he was not altogether young because somehow he was someone else looking back on himself. He was himself at twenty-one, but he was himself watching himself—an old man watching a boy. He tried to lift his head, and almost at once the sensation of lightness left him and his whole body seemed leaden, pressing into a bed that was drenched with sweat.

He thought, "Who am I? Where am I?" and for one terrifying moment he thought, "I am dead." For even in his weakness and confusion the terror of death was still haunting and keen. Then clarity came to him for a moment and he thought, "I know who I am. I'm Groton, and Groton can't be dead. Groton couldn't die at fifty-four. I must get this bloody thing straight."

So he opened his eyes and called out, "Who are you?" but the voice was not the voice of Groton but of a man who was weak and old and ill. Nevertheless, it was loud enough to startle the woman in white standing by the light. Turning quickly, she said, "I am the doctor, Mees Opp."

Even in his weakness, the reply made him angry. Why was she trying to take him in? She was the nurse and the nurse couldn't be the doctor and the doctor the nurse, all at the same time. But the word "doctor" made him think of Harley Street and he said, "Where is Sir Sidney?"

"Who is Sir Sidney, sir?"

"Sir Sidney, my physician. Where am I? Where is Bates?"

"You are in Nivandrum, sir," said Mees Opp. "You mustn't talk now. You've been ill."

[491]

"Nivandrum?" The word echoed and then he said, "Is Deakin here also?"

"What Deakin, sir?"

"Hugo Deakin. Lord Deakin."

"No. There is no one here by that name . . . Bates has gone to bed. I'm taking care of you. Now be quiet and I'll fetch you something to drink, and then you must go to sleep again and you'll feel much stronger when you wake."

He was silent and resentful at being treated like a child, and puzzled until she returned. Quietly he drank what she gave him. Then after a little silence, he asked, "Where is my wife?" and Mees Opp, put to the test, lied. She said, "She has gone out in the boat for a little air. The heat has been very hard on her."

For a long time he considered this, then he said, "She must take care not to get lost among the islands."

"She has very good boatmen, sir."

"When will she be back?"

"I don't know, sir."

"What time is it?"

"A little before midnight."

"I want to speak to her. She shouldn't be out alone in a place like Macassar. You can't trust these Malays. She's not able to look after herself."

"This isn't Macassar, sir. She's quite safe here. It's Nivandrum."

"Oh, yes, Nivandrum," and then after a pause, "How long have I been ill?"

"Eight days, sir." She did not wait for him to speak again, but said, "Now I'll go out and you try to sleep."

"I don't want to sleep. I haven't time to sleep. There's too much to be done."

"You won't be able to do any of it unless you go to sleep and get strong again. The more you sleep the stronger you'll be."

Slowly Mees Opp, with the instinct which amounted almost to genius, was beginning to understand him, to reconstruct his personality and his character out of those fragments of speech which emerged weakly from his confusion. What his wife had said was true. His vitality was immense—that he should be able to speak thus even in a weak voice, that there should be any coherence whatever in what he said.

For the first time he looked at her quite directly as if he saw her for the first time. Then he said, "Perhaps you are right, but I wish you could stop those damned drums. I hate them."

"I'm afraid that's not possible, sir," she said patiently. "In a little while you won't hear them. I'll leave you now to sleep. I'll be in the next room. If you want anything, I've put the bell inside you here on the bed. It's tied to your wrist by a string so that you can't lose it. You've only to ring and I'll come in."

Then he closed his eyes and she went out of the room until she knew that he was asleep, for she had no intention of sleeping herself until Lady Groton came in. And she knew that he would sleep, because she had made the draught almost double to make certain that he would not wake again before morning and ask whether she had come in.

So she was still awake when Lady Groton returned a little after three. She had been sitting by the window, as idle as she ever was, thinking about the money which she would be paid for saving the life of Lord Groton and what she would do with it back in the capital at the hospital. Even a moderate amount would pay for new floors and a new roof over the ward where the maternity cases were sheltered. And she thought for a time about the crippled woman, pleased that she had had no word from Mrs. Badoki, who was to send a message if things went badly. Then just before she saw the canoe with Dantry and Lady Groton in it push off in the late moonlight from the island opposite she saw another canoe leave the landing stage—the woman Léah setting off to do her hocus-pocus with a witch doctor somewhere among the islands. Well, she had defeated Léah. Lord Groton had passed the worst and with his vitality he was certain now to recover. Then came the knock and Lady Groton came in, and once again she thought how pretty she was and, a little wickedly, that women as pretty as that shouldn't be hampered. They should have what they wanted, because they were the blessed of the gods.

She rose and closed the door between the two rooms as she always did so that they should not disturb the patient, and Lady Groton only smiled at her without speaking until the door was closed. Then she said, "How is he?"

"All right. He wakened and talked a little."

"Did he ask for me?"

"Yes, I put him off."

For a moment there was a silence while the two women looked at each other, Lady Groton thinking, "Does she know? Of course she does. Dare I to talk as if I assumed that she knew? She knows so much—everything." Aloud she said, "What did you tell him?"

"That you had gone out in the boat for air."

"What did he say?"

"To send you in when you returned." Mees Opp hesitated and then said, "But I gave him a sleeping draught . . . a rather large dose to make sure he would sleep. What you said is true. His vitality is immense."

"That was kind of you." It was a noncommittal remark, which might be interpreted in many ways, but she rather fancied that Mees Opp would understand how it was meant.

[493]

She did, for she said, "I thought that would be the best thing to do under the circumstances."

"You are a wonderful woman."

"No, I try to understand things. I don't know much about the world. It isn't easy sometimes the way people behave . . . so complicated and everything."

Then Lady Groton plunged. She said, "I'm never going back to him."

In a low voice Mees Opp answered, "I guessed that."

"How?"

She smiled. "By the look in your face. When I first came I knew there was something wrong, but I didn't know what it was. Then I began to understand."

"You don't think I'm a horrible woman?"

"I don't know. How could I judge when I know so little? What is he like—Mr. Dantry, I mean?"

"Bad, like me . . . only like me he never meant to be bad. He never really meant to hurt anyone."

"Yes, that happens sometimes," but uncompromisingly Mees Opp continued, "that makes it understandable, but it doesn't make it any easier for the others."

"You're thinking about his wife."

Mees Opp hesitated for a moment. Then she said, "You see, I brought his wife into the world long ago. I've known her always. He should never have taken up with her. That may be his fault or it may not. That woman Léah sent her to his house to wait for him in his bedroom—to catch him." She looked directly at Lady Groton and added, "You mustn't think the girl is a bad girl. She was in love with him. She still is. I suppose she always will be. You see, the trouble is that she's a half-caste. If she had been a pure native, it wouldn't have made so much difference. He shouldn't have married her. I don't know why he did."

Lady Groton looked at the bracelets on her wrist. "He thought it was all finished when he married her . . . he thought he was staying here forever. He thought he would never see me again."

"Then he *was* a very old friend?"

Lady Groton was silent for a moment, still looking at the bracelets as if somehow they fascinated her. Then she said, "Yes, very old. In a way the only friend I've ever had . . . the only friend in that way. I'm not superstitious but it does seem as if it was meant to be, as if it would be wrong if we tried to change it. Can you understand that?"

"Yes."

"It's all so complicated."

[494]

"Things like that always are. Sometimes, out here, the complications are worse."

"I don't know much about it here. I've never been out until this visit." Quickly she looked up from the bracelets and said, "I'm not boring you, am I? When you ought to be sleeping?"

"No, you're not boring me," and as she spoke Lady Groton thought, "No, no one ever bores you. Everyone is human and interesting and in need of sympathy and help. How lucky you are! That's something you can never lose, something that has nothing to do with love or money or anything."

"Don't think too badly of me," she said.

"I'm not judging you," said Mees Opp quite simply. "That's not for me to do. Besides, in order to judge, one needs to know so much."

Lady Groton, with a nod of her head, indicated the closed door and said, "I shouldn't tell him yet, should I . . . that I'm never going back to him?"

"No, I shouldn't tell him yet. It might undo a lot of what we've been trying to do."

"And there's one more thing we oughtn't to tell him . . . about this Mr. Clapton, who has arrived. You see, he found out why my husband was here and has come to get in ahead of him. Even if my husband hears the sound of his motor launch you mustn't tell him. Say it's the revenue cutter belonging to the Ranee."

"I understand."

"Later, when he is stronger, we can tell him. It will be bad enough then."

"I see."

She rose and said, "Now, I'll go and let you sleep." She took the fat hand of Mees Opp that looked so clumsy and was so delicate and said, "It was good of you to stay awake until I came in, and it was good of you to listen to me. I've never talked to anyone like that before." She looked directly at Mees Opp and added, "And it was good of you to lie for me." Then an idea came to her, and turning away a little she unfastened the two wide bracelets from her wrist and held them out to Mees Opp. "Here," she said. "Take these," and as she did it she knew that this was a melodramatic gesture and that it made her feel self-conscious, but she thought too, "That's how I feel now. Tomorrow I might change. And I want her to have them."

"No," said Mees Opp, "I couldn't."

"Please take them. They're not for you. They're for your hospital."

For a moment Mees Opp, her heart beating wildly, said in a low voice, "Well, if it's that, I could take them." Tears came into her pale eyes and in a low voice she said, "Thank you."

Lady Groton, shy and a little ashamed, ran out of the room.

When she had gone Mees Opp stood for a long time with the bracelets in her hand looking at the door, astonished, puzzled that in Lady Groton, of all people, she had discovered a kind of childishness, an innocence. When she turned away she held the bracelets under the light moving them this way and that so that the emeralds and diamonds caught the light and gave back gleams of red and blue fire. Then she seated herself, still holding the bracelets now close to her near-sighted eyes, now far away, now pressing them against her fat, sallow cheeks. They were beautiful, but it was not of their beauty she was thinking; to her they meant new floors and a new roof, an electrical plant and an X-ray machine.

41

Afterward, long afterward, whenever the horror of that day returned against her will to Lady Groton, it seemed to her that there had been something hurried and unreal about it, as if Fate, like a playwright aware of the climax ahead, had hurried everything so that none of the effect would be lost. There was something overintense about everything connected with that day; the heat seemed more terrible, the colors more brilliant; the hours seemed to race ahead.

She wakened late, not as usual about ten o'clock to go back to bed again to sleep until five, but a little before noon with a sensation of heavy weariness and of having lost something out of her life. Then while she was bathing, Mees Opp knocked at the door and said, "Your husband is awake. He seems much better. He asked to see you," and after she had said she would come at once, she thought, "He is really extraordinary—Albert. He will be well enough to go away in a week and then I shall be free."

She did not want to see him again. Not so long ago she would have gone away, perhaps leaving a note, and never have seen him again, but now it was different. She would have to go to him and be kind and patient, and in the end she would have to break things off tactfully and gently, hurting him as little as possible. She *had* to do all this.

So reluctantly she went, thinking of him as he had been on that first day of the illness, moaning, sodden and helpless, but when she opened the door and went in, it was quite different. The purple, apoplectic look, as if with the least show of bad temper he might burst, was gone, and he lay now in the teakwood and mother-of-pearl bed, weak and pale, so weak that as she came in he only turned his eyes toward her instead of his whole head, and all at once she felt sorry for him again, but in a new way, not sorry for him as Albert Simpson, Lord Groton, whose spectacular life had been so barren and empty, but simply as a man, any man, a particle of the human race, ill and suffering and weak, and helpless. There was something shameful in the spectacle—that man, the all-conquering, the braggart, the brute, could be so fragile, so easily destructible.

And when he spoke the sound of his voice shocked her by its weakness. It had a curious reedlike quality. She understood, almost at once, that he expected her to kiss him, casually, lightly on the cheek as she had often done because it seemed to reassure him and put him off from boring her with questions and conversation and because a casual embrace cost her nothing. For a moment she struggled to gain control of herself, thinking, "I can't do it now. I can't. But I must. It means so much to him," and bending down she kissed him on the forehead, and he looked pleased, so wistfully pleased for the great Lord Groton, that she felt a little sick and thought, "A Judas kiss if ever there was one."

Then brightly she said, "Well, everything's all right. You were very ill but now you're going to be well again. Everything is going to be all right."

The weak voice said, "Sit here on the bed near me." And she sat down on the edge of the bed although she would have preferred sitting in the farthest corner of the room. He took her hand and it was cool, almost cold in the heat, and a little clammy.

"It must have been boring for you," he said, "in this heat with nothing to do. What did you do to amuse yourself?"

She answered him quite honestly, "I slept during most of the day and in the evening I dined with Tom Dantry. Thank God he was here. It made all the difference."

He looked away from her scowling, and after a moment he said, "That damned midwife won't say when I'll be strong enough to get out of here and finish my job."

"She told me a fortnight at the earliest, but it depends on you—how well you obey orders and behave yourself."

Suddenly he closed his eyes and a curious shiver ran through the whole heavy body; it was a curious animal, physical thing like the effort of a great bull to shake off a terrier. She understood what its meaning was. He found it insupportable to be chained thus by weakness to his bed when there was so much to be done, so much that had to be accomplished.

"I should think she was a very good doctor."

A little of the old spirit returned to him and he said, scornfully, "A woman and a half-caste!"

"She'll keep her mouth shut and she's making you well. What more can you ask? I think you've been very lucky to have her."

"She's so ugly I have to close my eyes when she comes near me."

How like him that was! That he should see, as he always did, only the exterior of things, that he could appreciate best something that was pretty and trivial and brainless. Perhaps that is why he took to me . . . that and because I was a queen's goddaughter.

Aloud she said, "I don't think she's ugly at all. And besides, she's a very remarkable woman." She wanted to add, angrily, "Worth fifty of you," but he was too weak for her to wound him with wits that were so much sharper than his.

He said, "Would you like to get out of this heat?"

"No, not now . . . not, at least, until you're quite well."

The shadow of a grin came across his face and he said, "No, it wouldn't look well if you went away and then I died. It wouldn't look very well under the circumstances."

"What do you mean by that? You might as well be frank."

But she never heard his answer, for at that moment from near at hand just by the little landing stage there came a series of sputtering explosions, the unmistakable sound of the engine of a launch being started. He heard it at once. She saw from his eyes that he forgot her, he forgot Dantry, he forgot everything save the menace to the great coup he had planned. Looking at her with the old sharp glance of the shrewd businessman, he said, "What is that?"

She knew the look. He had looked at her so many times in that way when she lied to him and discovered nothing. But now it was different and it seemed to her terribly difficult to lie to him with success. But she made a valiant effort.

She said, "It's a launch. It's the revenue cutter."

He raised himself with an effort on one elbow straining a little as if he meant to get out of the bed and go to the window. And below the window he would see Clapton standing by the launch, healthy and sunburned and vigorous as he himself had once been, Hugo Deakin's agent, stealing everything from him just at the moment of accomplishment. If she permitted him to go to the window the sight of Clapton might kill him. She might help him out of bed and across the floor to the window and then he would be dead, and she would be free forever. It all went through her head, even the picture of him dying of bafflement and rage. The sense of guilt weighed on her too. It was not, she knew now, *her* telegram that had brought Clapton here, but it might have been. It was only an accident that she was not guilty. And here was Albert, struggling, and she pushing him back into the bed to save him. Why was she saving him? Nobody wanted him saved. Even that brother she had never seen would want him dead, because then he would have all the money which until now had been doled out to him in bits and pieces.

She was astonished a little to find herself stronger than he, to discover that she could push him back into the bed. She tried to behave quietly, naturally, without any sign of strain or emotion.

She kept saying, "No, Albert, you mustn't. You're too weak. I tell you it's

[498]

nothing but a revenue boat." Then she found herself calling "Mees Opp! Mees Opp!" and the door opened and Mees Opp came in.

But by then he was weak and exhausted and lay back mumbling to himself, his face wet with sweat. The sound of the motor went on sputtering and then halting and she thought wildly, "Will it never go away? I must tell Clapton not to bring it here because the noise disturbs the patient." To Mees Opp she said, "He heard the revenue cutter and thought it was something else. I told him he mustn't try to get out of bed."

Mees Opp bent over him urging him to be quiet, but he would not look at her but only at his wife. Presently he managed to say, "Are you telling the truth?"

"Of course I'm telling the truth. Why should I lie?"

Then he was quiet again, and Mees Opp said, "You mustn't excite yourself like this. If you do, you won't be able to see your wife. Now you must rest again. Your wife will go away and let you sleep."

But he answered stubbornly, like a small child, "No, I want her here by me till I go to sleep."

The motor was going now and suddenly the sound changed and it moved off, with Clapton aboard, on his way among the islands to find the best sites for piers and warehouses and petrol tanks. The sound of the motor had a kind of horror for her.

She said, "It's all right, Albert. I'll stay till you're asleep," and to Mees Opp, she said, "It's all right. He'll be quiet. I'll keep him in order."

Once he opened his eyes and looked at her simply, frankly, in a way that was new to her, and she thought, "It is awful. It's horrible." For she saw suddenly that with the clairvoyance of illness and perhaps of death he saw and understood things which he could not have known otherwise. He *knew* somehow that he was betrayed, that he was alone, and he had chosen to turn to her.

Closing his eyes he reached out with one hand to touch her hand, and she remained there seated on the edge of the bed, uncomfortable, hot, miserable, wanting to escape as much from her own sense of shame as from the sight of Groton who made her conscious of it. It was not that he had become a good man or that he had changed now in illness with death so near at hand, but that the imminence of death had given him a kind of dignity which he had never had before and turned him human as he had never been. And now she saw herself very clearly for the first time as she had been through the years of their life together; she saw herself with all her shallowness and triviality, her passion for luxury and sensation, her faithlessness and neurotic searching. Alone in that room she saw herself and Albert not as Lord and Lady Groton with money and prestige and importance, but simply as a man and a woman, stripped of everything, simply two human creatures who had failed miserably in everything, and that, somehow, brought him nearer to her than he had ever been.

She did not know how long she remained there, but she knew that once when quietly she tried to escape from him and so from herself, he had opened his eyes and looked at her and she had been forced to pretend that she was only going to the window to adjust the shutter so that he might have more air. She returned to the bed and again his hand reached out to touch hers, not to clasp it, but simply to touch it. The contact of his flesh to hers was full of pain as if his touch burned her and she thought, "Even now with all he knows. With everything he suspects, he still thinks me better than I am," for at that moment it seemed to her that it was impossible to sink lower than she had been through all the years they had spent together.

And then after a long time he seemed to sleep and the hand slipped away from hers and quietly, terrified lest she disturb and waken him, she slipped from the side of the bed and went softly out of the room into the room where Mees Opp was.

On the broad face of Mees Opp there was a new look which had not been there before as if she too had suddenly divined that he was to die in spite of anything they could do for him.

Lady Groton said, "I knew it would be bad for him."

"It would have been worse if you had not seen him. He would have fussed without resting all day. You mustn't reproach yourself with that." Without speaking, but by something which passed between them, they conveyed to each other that they both knew he was finished.

Mees Opp said, "I think he will sleep now for a time, perhaps for the rest of the day."

"I will tell that Mr. Clapton not to bring the launch here beneath the window."

"That's difficult," said Mees Opp. "He will be able to hear it even far away among the islands. If he wakens again I will give him something to make him sleep. His heart is very sound and it's better that he be quiet."

So she left Mees Opp and went back to her own room, and even though she took a sleeping draught she slept only fitfully, waking and falling asleep again, frightened and filled with dread of something she could not define. Certainly it was not the death of Albert, for during the time she had sat there by him on the bed she had come to understand that it was better for him to die than to go on living, surrounded by betrayals and disappointments. He should die now when his power was absolute and his wealth immeasurable. That was what he would have wanted if he had had the choice.

Late in the afternoon when the sun was already sinking into the Indian Ocean, she was awakened by the sound of shouting and confusion which came from somewhere belowstairs and almost at once she leaped out of the bed thinking, "Something terrible is happening! Perhaps something terrible is happening to Tom!" and throwing a wrapper about her, she ran into the hallway to the head of the great stairs, and at the same time there came from the great hall below the sound of a pistol shot. From the top of the stairs she saw the whole scene. On the floor lay Groton, dressed in pyjamas and near him a revolver. Rasmussen was there and Mees Opp and Léah and the *ayah* and two of the bearers.

Mees Opp was calling out to Rasmussen, "Help me to get him upstairs again."

She ran down the stairs, and as she reached the bottom, Mees Opp, who was still struggling to raise Groton, turned and said, "It is all right. Nothing has happened."

Together Mees Opp and Rasmussen managed to get the sick man up the stairs. He was shaking now with a chill and he kept muttering incoherent speeches of which only a word was distinguishable now and then . . . words and names . . . like "betrayal" and "Deakin" and "Dantry." He tried to struggle and escape, but he was too weak now and too impotent. There was a kind of sickening horror in the scene of which Lady Groton was acutely aware . . . the horror of the staring terrified eyes of the bearers, of Rasmussen's sullen anger over this new confusion and disturbance, of Groton's helplessness, and the greedy, gloating evil look in the eyes of Léah who followed them all the way to the very side of Groton's bed. It was Mees Opp who discovered her, and turning, she said, "Go away, Léah, there is nothing for you to do here."

Léah looked back at her with hatred and then she said, vindictively, "He is evil. He will never go away," and vanished from the room.

When he was quiet once more in the bed, Mees Opp sent the others away all save Lady Groton. To her she said, "I thought Bates was with him. I was lying down for a little time. I don't know where he got the revolver."

"He always has one with him wherever he goes. What did he mean to do?"

"I don't think he knew what he meant to do. It was delirium, anger, about everything. He'll be all right now. I won't leave him. You can go back to your room. It will be all right."

But Mees Opp did know what he meant to do. She knew that he had got a muddled idea that it was Dantry who had betrayed him to Lord Deakin and in delirium he had set out to kill him.

When Lady Groton had gone, Mees Opp sent one of the bearers for hot water, but in a few moments the boy returned saying that there were no servants in the kitchen, because they had been terrified by the sight and sound of the pistol and had all run away. And Léah too had disappeared. Rasmussen had looked everywhere for her but could not find her. He himself was downstairs in the kitchen preparing the hot water. It would be ready in a few minutes. Rasmussen, the boy said, had sworn at him and driven him from the room.

A little later when Mees Opp sent for Bates, the boy returned saying that he too had disappeared, that no one had seen him for hours, and when she sent Rasmussen himself to find Bates, the hotelkeeper, sullen and glowering, returned to say that he was nowhere on the island.

In her own room Lady Groton realized that it was already long after the usual hour when she crossed to Dantry's house, and she thought, "He will be wondering why I have not come." And then she saw that after all it was impossible for her to join him tonight. With Albert dying she could not go away leaving him alone with Mees Opp. Already, in her happiness, she had behaved shabbily enough; there were, after all, things which she could not do. So she decided to send him a note explaining why she had not come, but even while she was writing it she thought, "No, a note is no good. He will want to see me. I will go myself for a little while and explain what is happening and then come back again. That will do no one any harm." Even to see Tom for a few moments had become to her a pleasure, a necessity, worth all the years of her life that had gone before.

So she tore up the note and while she was dressing there was a knock at the door and Mees Opp came in.

"I'm sorry to disturb you," she said, "but have you seen Bates?"

"No, isn't he here?"

"The bearer tried to find him and then Rasmussen went to look himself. Rasmussen says that he is nowhere on the island and that nobody has seen him for hours."

For a moment Lady Groton was silent and again she was frightened, for now it seemed to her that anything at all might happen in this strange place. Then she said, "It's very odd. I don't think he's been off the island since we came here. Did you look in his room?"

"Yes. I went myself. He wasn't there. There wasn't even any baggage."

42

At twilight Dantry went to the cookhouse to start making the supper for the two of them. He worked for a long time preparing the vegetables and mixing the complicated curry as Silas had taught him to do. In the heat and stillness he worked, waiting for the moment when she would come along the path to join him, and presently when she did not appear he grew alarmed and went twice to the landing stage in the hope of seeing the *wallum* boat poled by the decrepit boatmen on its way from the hotel to the island, and at last when there was no sign of her he went to the terrace and lighted the lantern which was, he knew, visible from the hotel.

He had no desire to cross the channel, to go to the hotel in search of her. He did not want to see Rasmussen or that snob Lansbury, or even Mees Opp, and so he waited, thinking, "Perhaps he has wakened and forbidden her to leave. Perhaps he has been abusing her," and he told himself that if she did not appear in ten minutes he would go to the hotel and bring her back himself, by force if necessary, this time for good and always, never to return. It did not matter if Groton died; it did not matter what scandal followed. For he was changed now; he had been changing ever since that night when he had returned to find her asleep on the Indian bed.

Then while he stood peering across the channel he noticed something metallic which glittered among the cushions in the light from the old lantern, and crossing to the Indian bed he picked up the pistol which Maria had left behind. He knew it at once as Sandy's old-fashioned lugger and at once he divined how it had come there, at least that it must have been brought there by Maria. Perhaps the act was a part of some hocus-pocus which Léah had taught her. And at the same time he was alarmed because the sight of the pistol brought back to him the uneasy feeling of dread which he had forgotten in the happiness of the last four days. And he thought, "There is some dirty work about! Anything might happen to her in this bloody place!" and leaving the pistol on the table he went down the stairs to the edge of the water, and there in the hot stillness he heard the sound of water rushing past the prow of a boat, and in a moment out of the blackness against the glow of light from the Grand Oriental Hotel appeared the silhouettes of her boat and its two ancient boatmen.

She had seen him standing on the little landing stage before her own boat emerged from the darkness, and at sight of his straight form against the glow from the old lantern the feeling of depression left her and she was wildly, hysterically happy, thinking, "He is all right! Nothing has happened to him. If anything had happened to him now I would be as bad as possible . . . really bad. I would destroy myself and everyone else with evil."

He leaped aboard the boat to help her ashore saying, "Where have you been? What has happened? Why are you late?" and she answered, "I'll tell you all that. There is so much to tell."

And as the *wallum* boat drew away into the darkness again she tried to explain to him about Groton, about the arrival of Clapton, about the scene in the great hall. She said, "I can't stay tonight. I must go back at once."

"Why?"

"Because he is dying."

"Did Mees Opp say so?"

"No, but I know he is dying . . ."

[503]

"I don't want you to leave me ever again. It doesn't matter whether he dies or not. It doesn't matter what happens."

The speech brought her a wild sense of happiness, but she knew too that she must go back. She thought, "I mustn't be a fool. I mustn't lose my head now." And she said, "I shouldn't have come at all. I meant to send you a note. But I couldn't help myself. I had to come." And then she saw the pistol lying on the table and thought, "Now I shall have to tell him about her."

In the excitement and delight of the first night she had forgotten the whole incident, and then afterward she had not told him because she did not want to alarm him and because the story would bring the figure of the girl once more between them. She picked up the pistol and he said, "It's mine. I was just cleaning it to take along when we go away."

At that she smiled and said, "It's nice of you not to want to alarm me, but it isn't your pistol. I know who it belongs to and how it came here," and she told him the whole story of Maria's visit, and when she had finished he said, looking at her with wonder, "Weren't you afraid?"

"No, because then it didn't matter whether I lived or not. You had gone away I thought forever." And after a little silence she said, "Clapton says she has gone mad," and a silence fell between them and she thought, "Perhaps it will always be like this. Perhaps she will always be there between us no matter where we go."

Then he put his arm about her and said, "She isn't mad. That isn't true and you mustn't think it. I went off today in the canoe to find out. . . ." Then quickly he released her and said, "What you need is a drink. I'll fetch some champagne."

"I can't stay," she repeated. "I have to go back . . . just tonight. I'm afraid he may waken and ask for me. I talked to him today."

"What did he say?"

"Nothing. He was confused and afraid."

"How afraid?"

For a moment she did not answer him and then she said, "Afraid of weakness, of illness, of defeat, of death. . . ." And as she spoke her eyes filled with hysterical tears.

"You can't be sorry for him."

"I don't know whether it's because I'm sorry for him. It's something deeper and wider than that. It's as if I couldn't help crying because we're all such bloody fools . . . you and me and that ass Lansbury and even Bates and the *ayah* with her fisherman . . . everybody in the world but . . ."

"But who?"

"Mees Opp."

Mockingly he said, "You and your Mees Opp. She's getting to be an obsession. I'm beginning to think it's Mees Opp and not that hag Léah who has the evil eye. What has she been doing to you?"

"I don't know, only she's made me ashamed. I can't explain or understand anything any more."

"Probably it's the heat."

"The heat doesn't get inside of you," and she thought, "I must go back, but I want to stay. I want to stay here forever." She felt weak and helpless now for the first time. She had never loved him so much as now that he had changed.

43

It was true that Léah had disappeared from the island. In the confusion that followed the scene with Lord Groton in the great hall, she slipped away in the twilight in her canoe across the lagoons to that island bordered by mangrove swamps where the bloody image of the River God was hidden. There, alone, she sacrificed to him the last goat that remained. By the time the ceremony was finished it was quite dark, and in the darkness she said a prayer asking the god to bring her courage and strength and success in overcoming the charms of the white men and most of all the charms of Mees Opp who was making the great *burra sahib* well again, for in her heart she believed that the magic of Mees Opp was even stronger than that of the River God.

Then in the darkness she made her way back again through the mud to the canoe, and once away from the dark island she turned toward Sandy's compound on the mainland. Her canoe she kept moving in the shadow of the shore where the light from the fire in Sandy's compound or the light from the moon would not reveal it, black against the water. When she had come within a few feet of the landing stage she stopped the canoe with a single stroke, and after waiting for a moment, she raised her head and began to howl like a jackal. Three times she howled and then waited, watching the compound and the figures seated about the fire gossiping and playing drums. When none of them showed any signs of alarm she howled again three times and again waited, and then in the shadows of the palm trees on the shore she saw the figure of Maria approaching, moving from clump to clump of bougainvillea and bamboo, always on the side away from the little group about the fire. Then slowly she moved her canoe inshore and Maria stepped into it.

The girl was trembling, and Léah said in a voice of authority, in the language of the place, "You must not be frightened. You must not tremble," and the girl answered, "I'm not frightened."

Then before they moved off from the shadow of the shore, Léah took up a parcel wrapped in newspaper from the bottom of the canoe and tearing open the paper she took out a revolver. Carefully she explained to the girl how it worked, and when Maria understood, Léah took cartridges and loaded the revolver and then said, "Leave it here beside me until the time comes," and taking up the paddle she turned the canoe and set out again back toward the islands, moving always in the shadow of the land. In front of her Maria sat very still, quiet now, no longer trembling, as if hypnotized by the narrow black eyes of Rasmussen's wife.

44

On the terrace Lady Groton stayed on and on. She ate none of the curry but took a little fruit and drank champagne, aware that long ago she should have returned to the hotel. With each moment she grew more troubled, and now and then in the midst of their talk she would sit quite silent for a moment filled with dread. The drums no longer sounded romantic but a little sinister. The heat, that still damp heat of the night, pressed down upon her with the feeling of solid weight. And presently she said "I'm frightened. I'm afraid now to go back to the hotel."

"Why? There is nothing to be afraid of."

"I don't know why. Something awful is going to happen."

"It's only the heat and your nerves. You never need be afraid again. You're safe so long as you're with me."

"Oh, it isn't that anything is going to happen to us. We're lucky. We've always been too lucky."

In silence, he put his arm about her and drew her close to him, and in silence they remained like that listening to the drums, and slowly she began to feel less taut, less frightened, as if she drew strength from him. She found herself thinking, "Maybe it is nerves. If only it would rain. If something would only break the terrible heat." And she imagined floods and torrents of water descending, bringing with it coolness and peace.

Presently she said, "I am serious about going back now. What time is it?"

He leaned back a little to see the awful noisy old clock inside the door of his bedroom, and at the same moment there was the sound of two explosions in quick succession. The sound came to them muffled by the heavy air, from the direction of the Grand Oriental Hotel. She felt his body stiffen suddenly, and she said, "It's only Clapton's launch," and after a second he answered, "That wasn't a launch. It was a revolver shot."

Before he finished speaking the sound of two more shots came to them from across the water, and then the sound of excited voices calling and then again silence. For a long time they listened without speaking and then quietly she said, "What is it? For God's sake, what is it?"

He stood up, saying, "Perhaps we'd better go over there," and hysterically she said, "No, you mustn't." And at the same time she thought, "Bates has shot Clapton to cover up his villainy," but immediately she knew that Bates was not like that. He was a coward and there was no violence in his villainy.

Dantry said, "You stay here. I will go over. Something has happened."

"No, if you go, I'll go with you."

Then he said, "There is someone coming across the channel in a canoe," and together they stood peering over the rail of the balcony, and suddenly out of the darkness, above the sound of the drums, a voice came toward them from the canoe, *"Sahib! Sahib!"* The high-pitched voice of an islander shrill now with fear like the voice of a frightened animal.

In the language of the islands Tom called out, "I'm here. What is it?" And the voice came back, "The *burra sahib* has been shot."

She understood the words *"burra sahib,"* and in a whisper she said, "Albert. Why Albert? It couldn't be Albert."

Back across the water went Dantry's voice. "Tell them I am coming."

Turning to her, he said, "Will you stay here?"

"No, that is out of the question."

"Then come along."

Together they hurried down the stairs to the canoe, never saying a word. All the way across the channel while Dantry paddled frantically they were silent, because there was nothing to say, because whatever there was to say had no need of being spoken. She thought, "I was right. I knew it! Poor Albert! Why should he have shot himself? Why should he have done it when he was going to die anyway?" And she was aware of a kind of horror at the sound of the shots, two isolated reports and then two more, as if he had had to finish what he had begun messily. Yet she could not quite believe that Albert had tried to kill himself. He was not the sort. He was the kind that went on fighting even after everything was lost.

At the landing stage he helped her out of the canoe. There in the shadows stood one of Groton's boatmen. As they passed him he said, in his own tongue, "She is shot too."

"Who?" asked Dantry.

"Maria. . . ."

Out of the brief exchange of words, she understood only the word "Maria." Dantry did not stop but started running along the path. Following him she kept crying out, "What did he say? For God's sake, what did he say?" But Dantry did not wait. By the time she reached the great arched doorway he was halfway up the stairs, his sandals gone, running in his bare feet. That was something she remembered long afterward—the horror of those bare, hurrying feet just ahead of her on the stairs.

By the time she had reached the top of the stairs he had disappeared, but she went at once to Groton's room. As she reached it the door opened, and the ruddy bulk of Clapton's form blocked the doorway. He said, "Don't come in. He is dead. There is nothing you can do."

"But I want to come in. I must come in."

She did not know what had happened, but she knew that she must enter the room, that she must look at Albert dead, that she must go through the whole horror whatever it was, for which she was responsible, for which in the end she must atone. She had to go through it to the very end, for her own sake and Tom's to atone and save what they had found. "Please," she said, "I must. I have to . . . I must. Don't you understand? I'm not afraid. I have to." And as Clapton gave way to her she said, "What is it? What has happened?"

"That woman . . . Maria, shot him and then herself."

Wildly she thought, "She must have believed it was my room. She must have done it by mistake. It is me she must have hated. It must have been me she meant to shoot."

She was in the room then, and by the yellow light of the lamp she saw the figure of Albert lying in the teakwood and mother-of-pearl bed exactly as she had left him, as if he were still asleep. His hand lay outstretched as it had been when he reached out to touch her for comfort; only on the thin cotton sheet there was a small spot of red. Tom was standing by the bed, and just behind him was Rasmussen looking white and shaken, and Lansbury looking effete and ridiculous in Cossack pyjamas of black satin. And one of the coolies was in the room and the *ayah*, the white of her big eyes showing in terror. Behind her Clapton whispered, "He was asleep. He never knew what happened."

"But why? Why?" And then she heard Tom saying, "Where is Maria?" And Clapton, who suddenly seemed officious and horrible to her, said, "In the other room. That half-caste doctor woman is with her. She wanted to speak to you. That's why I sent to the islands."

Tom, it seemed to her, had changed into a Tom she had not seen before, ever. The color had gone out of the sun-tanned face so that he looked green and ill in the yellow light from the paraffin lamp, but the jaw had become hard at the angle and the lips drawn and full of determination. Even in the midst of all the horror and confusion she was conscious of how much she loved him, that she had never loved him so much as in this very moment.

He looked at her quickly and said, "You'd better go to your own room." She started to speak, meaning to refuse, and then she thought, "No, that will only worry him," so she pretended to go, thinking all the time, "I can't funk it now. I've got to go through it to the very end." His face softened a little and he said, "I'll come to you in a moment. I've got to clear up this bloody mess," and then he hurried past her into the room where Mees Opp sat by the side of the wounded Maria.

When he was gone she turned to Clapton and said, "Please go away and take that coolie and the *ayah* with you. I don't see why they're here." Clapton started to protest, but she said, not weak and frightened any more but angry now, because she loathed him for his officiousness and vulgarity, "No, no. Don't you understand? It's my husband. I want to be alone here. I'm quite all right. If you have any sense or feeling, get out of here."

In her voice there was a kind of fury which awed Clapton, overcoming even his feeling that all women and especially this one, were fools and incompetent. He said to the *ayah* and the coolie, "Clear out of here," and then went himself, closing the door behind him.

When he had gone she went slowly to the side of the bed, a little frightened, but aware that she must do what she was doing. Gently she sat on the edge where she had sat that very morning while he fell asleep, and then slowly her hand moved toward his until she touched it. Then softly as if he could still hear her, she said, "Why couldn't we have been decent toward each other? Why couldn't we have understood each other? Why couldn't we have known that we were both weak and silly and vain and human? Why was it that we were never even friends?"

She saw everything now, their folly, their madness, their vanity, their weakness; but now it was too late.

45

In Mees Opp's room Dantry was kneeling beside the bed where Maria lay dying, with her great eyes turned toward him. By the window, turned a little away, as if she were looking out across the islands, stood Mees Opp. She had done her best to save the life of the girl, and he did not mind her standing there now in the room with them. He did not mind even her hearing what Maria was saying to him, painfully, with little gasps, because the moment he saw Mees Opp he knew at once that it was all right. In the strain, the intensity of the moment, he saw with a kind of clairvoyance what it was Alix had seen in her.

Maria was saying, slowly, painfully: "It was because I wanted you to be happy." The eyelids trembled for an instant, and then with a great effort she managed to say, "Léah said you would not be happy unless you were both free . . . now you are free . . . you are both free . . . and no one is to blame . . . but me."

Then suddenly she was dead, and he was holding her hand saying, "You mustn't die, Maria, you mustn't. It's going to be all right. . . ." Then he turned to Mees Opp and cried, "You must do something. You must save her," and Mees Opp coming toward him, took the wrist of Maria in her great fat hand and said, "There isn't anything that can be done. There isn't anything that can save her."

Then she crossed the hands of Maria on her breast after the fashion of the Christian people of the country and said to him, "You'd better go in to her. There isn't anything you can do here."

Rising from beside the bed, he asked, "Did you hear what she said?"

"Yes," said Mees Opp.

Fury colored his voice. "It was that bitch, Léah. It was her doing."

Mees Opp only repeated, "Go to her. That's the good you can do now. I'll stay here."

He said, "Where is the revolver?"

"There on the table."

Crossing the room, he picked it up and looked at it slowly, carefully. Then he said, "It isn't Sandy's gun. It's Rasmussen's. It was Léah who gave it to her. We've got to find Léah. She's the guilty one."

"I'll find Léah. You go in to her now."

And when he had gone, Mees Opp thought, "So Léah *did* help the River God to keep the harbor closed. It was Léah who made her shoot him when I stopped her poisoning him. I should have guessed what she was doing. I should have known because I know these people. It's my fault too. The others couldn't have guessed, but I should have known." And after a long time she thought, "It's the fault of so many people and so many things. It began so long ago. . . ."

In Groton's room he found Alix still sitting on the edge of the horrible teakwood bed, touching Groton's hand, looking down at him with a curious look of wonder in her face, fascinated, as if she were a little mad. She did not even look at him as he crossed the room toward her. Then he raised her gently from the edge of the bed and said, "You mustn't do that."

"It's all right," she said. "I'm quite calm. . . ."

Then gently he drew the cheap cotton sheet over the dead face of Groton, and she thought, with a sudden hysterical desire to giggle, "It's true. It's just like the cinema. They *do* cover the faces of people when they die."

Then he put his arms about her and they stood thus in silence for a long time, and presently he said, "You mustn't take it too hard. It was that woman Léah who did it." And he told her as quietly, as quickly as he could what had happened in the other room. When he had finished, she said quietly, "No, it wasn't like that. That wasn't the reason. I know what it was. It came to me while I was sitting here alone with him. It happened because we were the three most selfish people in the world—you and I and Albert. None of us ever thought of anything save what we wanted. And now we've had to pay for it. Everything came out of that, and it isn't finished yet."

In a quiet voice he said, "It was the worst thing that could have happened . . . the very worst. I suppose that we'll get through it . . . somehow."

"That is part of it."

And she began to cry suddenly, hysterically almost in silence, her body shaking while he tried to comfort her, and even in the midst of the hysteria which was like a physical illness, she experienced faint intimations of happiness that it was Tom who was comforting her, that now in the crisis and the tragedy, he was strong again. He had changed from the moment the sound of the pistol shots had come to them muffled by the hot damp air across the water.

She thought, "I'm not alone now. I'll never be alone again, no matter what happens." But near her, near them both, in the yellow half-light, lay Albert and that poor girl, Maria, dead now. And they would always be there, quite near to her and Tom, as long as they lived.

Then the door of Mees Opp's room opened softly and Mees Opp came in. She said, "There's no use in staying here. Go to your own room. I'll take care of everything. I'll give you something to take to make you sleep." But Lady Groton thought, "No. I can't do that. It would be cheating. I cannot sleep. I mustn't cheat. I must see it through to the end."

Dantry knew too that there was no sleep for him, so when he had taken her to her own room, through a corridor filled with wide-eyed islanders, he left her, saying, "I'll be back presently. Lie down and try to sleep." She wanted to say, "Don't leave. I can't be left alone . . . now." But she only said, "If you need me, come for me . . . whatever it is, no matter what."

"I shan't need you. There's Mees Opp."

"You see, I was right about Mees Opp."

46

But when they tried to find Léah she had disappeared, and when he asked Rasmussen where she was, Rasmussen answered sullenly that he did not know.

"She had been going out every night somewhere among the islands."

"I know where she has been going, and you do too."

Rasmussen was silent. "She drove Maria to do it. Maria told me." It was odd how calm he felt now, how suddenly capable and detached like a Grand Inquisitor.

[511]

Sullenly Rasmussen, who once had been his friend, looked away from him and said, "It wasn't all her fault."

"It's enough her fault to be a case for the police."

"She never wanted him here or you either," said Rasmussen. "She was right. You didn't belong here."

And when he asked for Bates no one could find him either, and then a coolie who listened to the questioning came forward still shaken with terror and said, "White man coolie gone away."

"Gone away where?" asked Dantry.

"By train . . . today . . . noontime."

So that was it. Rats deserting the ship. For a moment he felt a wild desire to get into his canoe and set out among the islands to find Léah and bring her back, but almost at once he knew that finding her would be an impossibility. She knew coves and inlets and lagoons which he had never discovered. By tomorrow she would be in the high mountains, thinking that the death of Groton had saved Nivandrum. She would be in some jungle village where they would never find her until everything was finished and it was too late to do anything about it. And in his heart he too knew that it wasn't altogether Léah who was to blame. What Rasmussen had said was true. It wasn't any good running Léah to earth. Even she hadn't got what she wanted, because Clapton was here now and the harbor would be opened and they would perhaps pull down his own house and build petrol tanks where it had once stood. It did not matter now, any of that. He and Alix would have to leave Nivandrum and never see it again.

And suddenly feeling baffled and collapsed, he left the great vaulted hall filled with peering islanders, and the sullen Rasmussen and Lansbury in his ridiculous black satin pyjamas hysterically excited and offering asinine advice . . . the great vaulted hall where he had seen the lovely island for the first time through the arched doorway and thought, "I have come home. I have found peace."

As he reached the foot of the lovely stairway, he saw Sandy coming through the doorway, a Sandy, collapsed like himself, no longer plump and humorous, but dazed and hurt, and he thought, "He is coming to fetch Maria, whom he loved, who is dead now. And it is my fault that she is dead. That I can never escape or forget so long as I live. No, I can't speak to him now . . . not now . . . perhaps some day. I'm not yet man enough for that."

Sandy did not see him, because the whole room and all the silent awestricken faces in it were blurred and indistinct. Without speaking to them he went up the stairs to find Mees Opp. She would help him. She would know what to do.

[512]

47

In her room Dantry found Lady Groton still awake. She was sitting by the light at her dressing table with a packet of papers in front of her. She was very white and holding in her hand a letter.

When he came in he said, "What are you doing?"

"I couldn't lie in the darkness. I lighted the lamp. Look," and she handed him a note. "Bates has gone away."

"I know."

Then he read the letter. It was short, and said:

Lady Groton,

When Your Ladyship receives this I will have gone away. I am leaving with you some papers which may be of interest. I witnessed the will. His Lordship did not like Mr. Lansbury so he said nothing to him about it. I did not send your telegram because I had already sent one three days before. You were right in what you thought. But what I did was not criminal. I cannot go to jail for it. I am going to retire. If you should want to reach me, send a letter care of the Postmaster, Manchester. I could explain to you why I did a great many things, but perhaps you might not understand. The world is changing and men like His Lordship are finished. The world has had enough of them. By the time he is well enough to persecute me, I will be disappeared. Please believe in my good wishes for yourself.

Herbert Ernest Bates.

When he had finished reading, he looked at her and said, "What does he mean by the telegram?"

Then quietly, like a child at confessional, she told him the whole horrible story of the hysterical betrayal, of her shame, of the wild effort to undo what she thought she had done, of her disgust and loathing of herself. The confession brought her relief, for now he knew everything about her, the very worst, that she could be and had been as horrible as it was possible for a wife to be.

"It was only a mistake that I was not to blame. I had meant to betray him. I had meant to ruin him. I hated him . . . or at least I hated him until yesterday."

"What changed you then?"

"I don't know. . . . It was you partly . . . and Mees Opp too, I think."

"You were right about Mees Opp. She has the good eye just as that bitch Léah has the evil eye."

She turned again to the dressing table and said, "But that's not all. He knew everything. He must have known. But he never said anything all those years. . . . He never did anything until the night before he was ill. We had a quarrel then and I hurt him, deliberately. He must have gone back to his room and written those names."

She handed him a sheet of note paper on which was written:

Packy (Boxer)
Sir Henry Leatham
Pierre de Couloisy
Deauville 1931 (?)
Monte Carlo (Tom Burchard)

He looked away from the list down at her and she said, "He was right about some of them. He may have guessed, or Bates may have hinted. Bates knew too much. It's all true. I was trying to find what I never found until now." The tears came into her eyes and she said, "Now you know. If you never want to see me again, it doesn't matter. I'll understand. There isn't anything more that I can tell you, except that I've been mean and trivial and selfish and vain and a cheat."

He looked at her for a long time and then said, "We're pretty much of a cut, my dear . . . and anyway, whether we like it or not, we're chained together now for the rest of our lives by what has happened. Wherever we go, whatever happens to us, the story will follow us, and it won't get any better because it's confused and mixed up, and it won't improve with retelling. It'll grow worse and worse."

Then there was a knock at the door and when Dantry called out, "Who is it?" Mees Opp answered, and Lady Groton whispered, "Tell her to come in."

When she saw Lady Groton sitting by the light, she said, "You should be in the bed." Then firmly she said, "You mustn't have silly ideas. You're doing no one any good by sitting up, reproaching yourself. I've brought you this. Take it and rest, and then tomorrow we shall see."

Dantry said, "She's right. You must take it," and Lady Groton obeyed him, too weary, too weak to resist any longer.

Then Mees Opp said, "And now I'll leave you both. I can manage everything. You had better stay with her until she is asleep. And if you need anything come to me."

She went out and Lady Groton lay on the bed while Dantry sat beside her, stroking her forehead until presently she closed her eyes. The murmur and confusion had died away belowstairs and there was only the distant sound of a drum or two among the islands. Just before she went to sleep she opened her eyes and said, taking his hand and pressing, "We've got to climb out of it somehow, Tom . . ."

In the morning when Mees Opp came in she found them there together, Lady Groton on the bed, Dantry asleep sitting up in the chair by her side.

48

When she wakened it was dark, and the only light came through the window from a fire somewhere outside, near at hand. Confused, she looked about her and in the shadows discovered Tom sitting beside her, and then hazily she remembered all the horror of the night before, where she was, and why Tom was there in her room in the Grand Oriental Hotel.

She heard him saying, "That's better now. You've slept for hours . . . the whole of a day."

"Have you been here?"

"Nearly all the time. I slept too."

"Where is the fire?"

"It's a funeral pyre. It's Groton's."

Then, feeling strangely embarrassed, she was silent, and he said, "Mees Opp took charge of it. She's managed everything."

"It was good of her, but I've had enough of that."

"Of what?"

"Of having people do things for me. It's always been like that. Someone has always done the unpleasant things."

"I know what you mean."

"We've got to get clear of that . . . the first thing of all."

"We're going away tomorrow."

"Where are we to go?"

"To the capital. You see, there has to be a kind of inquest. It isn't as if Groton were just a beachcomber who came to a violent end."

She wanted to say, "I won't go, they can't make me. I can't stand any more," but she knew that it was no good saying that. The thing had to be faced to the very end. She would have to go through it all, even if it went on forever, until she died. In a way it was only beginning. Coldly now, her nerves rested, she considered what lay ahead of them . . . the horrible inquest and the newspapers which, pray God, they would never see, and all the stories that would go the rounds of London, New York and Paris, Deauville and Cannes and Monte Carlo. Bitterly she thought, "Well, it's made the summer for a lot of people. What a lot they'll have to talk about!" And as Tom had said, the stories would grow more and more complicated and evil and decadent. Then quite clearly she saw that never again could they go back into that world, that never again would she enter a hotel or a restaurant or step aboard a ship, even here in the East, without knowing that all about her people were saying, "That is Lady Groton. You remember the awful story? And that's the man with her, who was her lover at the time. It was his native wife who did the shooting." Maybe it was better that both of them die too, because it wasn't only the story that would always follow them, but the memory of that horrible night with Albert dead on the teakwood bed and the girl Maria dying in the next room.

Outside in the stifling heat the flames of the pyre faded a little and she thought, "What shall I do with his ashes? I can send them to his brother— that brother he never allowed me to see."

And then she was aware of a roaring sound, strange and terrifying. It came suddenly without warning, and at the same time the light from the distant flames went out and the room was in darkness. Beside her Tom pressed her hand and she heard him saying, "It's the rain. The monsoon has broken."

It was a wonderful sound which eased her nerves and seemed suddenly to envelop them both, shutting out all else. They sat thus hand in hand for a long time, and presently Tom said, "I've been thinking what we'll do."

"Yes."

"I talked to Mees Opp. We must hide away."

"Forever. For always," she said.

"We can go to her."

"She has enough troubles without us."

"She wanted it. . . . D'you know what she said? She said that there were illnesses of the spirit as well as of the body. She said people sometimes died when the spirit was ill. She said it often happened out here."

"I know," she said. The freshness of the rain had come into the room now, changing everything. The heat no longer seemed to bear down like a heavy weight and through the windows drifted a fine mist. Then there was a knock at the door and Mees Opp came in quietly. She said, "I've brought you some port and some broth. It will be a little cooler now that the rains have broken."

She went away again, and presently against the horizon over on the mainland near Sandy's compound a new fire appeared, leaping up suddenly, undefeated even by the downpour of the monsoon rain. The light from the flames was at once reflected and diffused by the falling rain so that the glow seemed to fill all the sky and force its light even in the rooms of the Grand Oriental Hotel. Dantry turned his head slowly and sat watching it, thinking, "It will always be there, for the rest of my life, haunting me . . . the light of those two fires."

49

They took three days to make the journey by lagoon and across country to the capital, going in easy stages because of the heat and the rains, sleeping the night in the huts of the island people. It was a dreary journey. Even the healthy cheerfulness of Mees Opp who accompanied them, made it no better, but only a little worse, for the cheerfulness of one so active, who occupied herself only with the troubles of others, only made their weariness and despair the more powerful. There were moments when the optimism of the half-caste doctor seemed almost obscene, and moments in the darkness when Lady Groton and Dantry, each lying awake and alone with the sound of the pouring monsoon rain on the thatched roof, wanted no longer to live, when they would have died but for the fact that God had given them everything, including bodies that were healthy and strong in spite of all their dissipation and recklessness. To her it seemed a kind of punishment that she should be forced to live when she preferred fever and death. They had each other now perhaps forever, but each was as ashamed now of the other as of himself. That was the worst of all, and the best too.

It was Mees Opp who proposed that they should stay with her at the hospital.

"It won't be luxurious or even comfortable," she said, "and I suppose the Magistrate will want you to stay in his house. You might be happier there."

But they both rejected the idea of staying with any European now, to be pitied and discreetly questioned, to be patronized and made the butts of morbid curiosity. Anything was better than that . . . even hard beds and rains and insects and fever.

The news of Mees Opp's return went before them, and when they arrived at last at the hospital compound they found the place decorated with flowers and paper garlands and banners, all dripping in the rains, and a waiting crowd of men and women and small children which sang for no apparent reason, since Mees Opp was a half-caste of Dutch origin, "God Save the King" to the accompaniment of an awful brass band. The crowd hung garlands on Mees Opp until her heavy figure was hidden beneath jasmine and marigold and temple flowers. They cheered and danced, and Dantry and Lady Groton behind her, jostled and ignored, watched in silence. And presently Mees Opp and the swarthy Mrs. Badoki took them into Mees Opp's little house which was to be theirs until the whole ugly business was finished and they went away.

The Magistrate made the inquest as easy as possible, but Lord Groton had been a great and powerful man in the West, and his death by violence, even for the sake of his wife and her lover, could not be passed over lightly. And so the torture had to be gone through again, all the hideous questions about Lady Groton's rendezvous each night with Dantry, the questions about Maria, about Lord Groton's illness and the sinister Léah; and with each question, in spite of anything the Magistrate could do to soften the answers, the case became more and more clear against them, not of guilt or at least of direct guilt in the actual death of Groton and Maria, but of their own weakness and selfishness, their own ruthlessness and self-indulgence. And in spite of anything the Magistrate could do, each question, each answer made it clearer that it was they who had killed Groton and Maria.

The awful business was over at last, and when it was finished the Magistrate shook hands with them and again offered them the hospitality of his own house until they were ready to leave. But again, thanking him, they refused and together left the court and set out for the hospital compound.

As they came down the steps the rain ceased for a little time, and the sun, coming out, turned the drops of water on the drenched trees to quicksilver. Along the narrow road from the Magistrate's court to the hospital they walked slowly in silence, half-suffocated by the terrible heat. It was Lady Groton who spoke first. She said, "And now . . . what are we to do? Where are we to go?" They could not go now to Bombay or Singapore or Madras or Colombo, to be pounced upon by journalists, to be stared at by every passenger on the ship, by every man and woman in every hotel and bar. They could board no train, no ship.

Almost shyly Dantry said, "We could stay here."

"That's what I want to do."

"Perhaps that's the best of all." And after a moment he added, "I don't mean for a day or two."

"No, longer then, for weeks. . . ."

They would stay here hidden away until they were rested and the story had grown dim. Neither of them believed that it would ever be altogether forgotten, any more than they believed that they would themselves be able to forget what had happened in that hideous *chambre de luxe* of the Grand Oriental Hotel. But the memory of it might grow dim, as things did with time.

They were silent for a time, walking side by side, close to each other in the hot sun, and presently ahead of them far down the long avenue of Java fig trees the bedraggled arch of welcome erected to celebrate the return of Mees Opp came into sight. At the same time they both became aware that they were no longer alone. Behind them at a little distance a crowd followed, a crowd made up of islanders, naked urchins, and old men and women and among them a half-dozen half-castes. It was the crowd which had waited outside the office of the Magistrate during the hearing, squatting on its haunches under the banyan trees in the rain, chewing betel nut and gossiping and turning over and over the bits of news passed out to it from time to time by the scarlet-clad *chuprassi*. At each house, from out of each pathway, new individuals came out to swell its numbers. It seemed to be a quiet and orderly crowd: the only sound which came from it was an occasional laugh raised by a gibe or quip in a dialect which Dantry knew too slightly to be able to understand.

For three or four minutes the two of them walked in silence, each pretending to the other that he was unaware of the disorderly troop of natives which followed them. Then from behind them there arose a solitary howl of derision and then another, and unconsciously, against their wills they walked a little more rapidly. But the rabble behind them walked faster too, keeping always just a little way off. Still neither of them looked at the other, and Dantry thought, "Not even here . . . we can't even stay here."

Then he felt something strike his shoulder a glancing blow and a half-rotten mango fell between them. Then another and another and an over-ripe papaya struck him full in the back, the rotten pulp spreading over his shirt, and between his teeth he said fiercely, "Run! Go ahead! I'll follow you."

But she would not leave him, and there was nothing to do now but to turn and face the mob. This he did, threatening them in the tongue of the Nivandrum islanders. But he spoke with an awkward accent and the dialect sounded strange here in the capital, and although the crowd halted its advance as he turned, his threats were only answered by jeers and shouts of laughter. Among the tormentors he recognized suddenly two of Sandy's boys, and then among the dark faces, one stood out clearly, apart from all the others. He knew the close-set black eyes and the long nose. It was Léah.

Then a mango struck Lady Groton's hat, and his nerves gave way. Hysterically, he turned and shouted at her, "Go on. For God's sake, go on and stop being a heroic ass!"

She looked at him for the fraction of a second with an expression of hurt astonishment in her blue eyes. Another rotten mango struck her and then she turned and ran. And as she ran she saw waddling toward her on tired, sore feet through the bedraggled flowers and garlands of the arch of welcome, the heavy, ugly figure of Mees Opp who had been born with nothing, coming out to rescue them.

VI

Good Time Bessie

ONCE long ago he was a matinée idol, of the good old-fashioned kind. Everyone knew him when he walked through Peacock Alley at the old Waldorf, and palpitating young women used to stand outside the stage door waiting to see him come out and climb into a hansom and drive off without ever looking to right or left. He must have been a dapper fellow because even as an old man with very little money, living in one room of a dusty old-fashioned hotel on the upper West Side, he managed somehow to give the appearance of a rather sporting old gentleman who had an excellent valet. He wasn't one to give in to circumstances, and he loved life. The terrible changes he had seen in the theater and in the world and in his own circumstances never succeeded in discouraging him or breaking his spirit.

I knew him through his daughter, and I used to go sometimes with her to call on him. He was inclined to live in the past and tell stories of what to him was the Golden Age of New York. Whenever he talked of it, it certainly sounded so, and so it may have been. He loved the island of Manhattan with a profound passion and had no desire to leave it, even in summer. In the Golden Age, he said, there wasn't any "season" in the theater. It went on the whole year round, winter and summer, and so he never got into the habit of leaving town save occasionally on an outing to Staten Island or Jersey City or when his company made a tour; and then he was miserable. He used to tell some tall stories, and he told me this one. I am leaving it in his words because he told it so much better than I could possibly do it. I retire to the role of commentator and give place to him.

His room was not very large and it had a tiny narrow view of the North River, framed on both sides by apartment houses. It was a neat room, a room as dapper as the old gentleman himself. There was a bed in one corner, a table, an easy chair and two straight chairs, a small library made up almost entirely of collections of plays, and myriads of photographs, most of them rather yellow and spotted—of Ada Rehan and Rose Coghlan, the Drews,

[520]

Lester Wallack and dozens of others. He had lived through three generations of the theater and known in two of them at least everybody of the least importance.

But this is the story the old gentleman told me, while he rocked and smoked a big cigar out of the box I brought him. I lay on the bed listening and upsetting him a little, I think, because I disturbed the neatness of his room. But the stiff chairs were impossible for any length of time.

2

"Bessie," he said, "was a big woman made on the scale they no longer make 'em . . . the kind of woman who warmed a man's heart and made a light come into his eyes. I used to see it happen again and again. I remember her as she looked when she used to come into Jack's early in the morning after the night spots like Rector's and Churchill's had begun to turn out their lights. The door would open and in would come Bessie with two or three men—sometimes there were a half-dozen—and when she came into the room something came into it with her which was not there before. Everyone looked up and at first sight of her there was always a little hush and then two or three people—hicks or people who didn't know Broadway would say, 'That must be Bessie Devine.' They knew her from her picture in the papers or from the little cards you got with cigarettes . . . pictures sometimes in tights and sometimes in a short spangled skirt. Her corsets must have been reinforced with steel because God never meant her to have a wasp waist. I ought to know if anyone did. She was built like Juno rather than Venus with big breasts and hips that were on the same scale as her vitality and her big warm nature . . . She had honey-colored hair and blue eyes and the complexion of a peach. Her voice was loud and deep and when she laughed you could hear her all over the restaurant. Whenever she had had a little too much Irish whisky—she hated champagne and called it a "sissy drink"—it would turn warm and a little husky.

"Nothing ever seemed to dim that vitality and health of hers. She could drink and do without sleep and raise hell for days at a time and still look as blooming and fresh as a strawberry, fresh-picked with the dew still on it. She was too big to be a good dancer, and she never took the trouble to learn how to sing properly. Part of her charm for audiences lay in her amateurish quality; she never quite learned how to wait for a laugh or to put over her points. She always just missed them with a lazy indifference which in itself made you laugh. I think toward the end, it grew into a kind of technique or method which was all her own. If she hadn't broken her neck, she might have lived to be a fine performer, but she didn't live long enough to take any of it seriously. There were too many things in life that were more fun than worrying about being professional—things like eating and drinking and loving and giving people a good time. I think she liked the stage simply because it was fun. She liked cracking jokes with the stage hands and the girls in the chorus. What always got across the footlights was her colossal vitality. The tired people in the audience fed off it. When she came on, a kind of wave of pleasure and fun went right through the whole house.

"Probably you wouldn't know what the theater was like at the time she flourished but it wasn't anything like it is today. It was fun then . . . I'm talking about the end of the nineties when you were nothing but a kid. And everybody came to see it and people liked the theater because it was the theater. It hadn't been corrupted by a lot of art ideas, and critics didn't come to a new play just to find out whether it fitted into their own ideas of art or the ideas they were trying to work out in plays they were writing themselves. If a play was good entertainment they liked it. And in those days actors were actors, boy! They didn't try to make an impression by doing nothing at all, or by going through a bag of tricks that they'd been told was art. They each had their own way and everything was free and easy and every actor gave everything he had to give, and that was what the public wanted. They liked an actor to tear up the carpet and break things.

"No, something is wrong with Americans nowadays. They've all got kind of pallid and anemic, and the theater along with them. But back in the nineties the theater was the theater—the way it was in the time of Molière and Shakespeare. People didn't go to it just to say, 'Oh, isn't she real,' and 'Isn't that set wonderful!' Stage designers were just scene painters and the play was all the better for it. There weren't a lot of interior decorators cluttering up the stage with a lot of stuff that would get them a big hand on the opening night and then ruin a play by cluttering it all up with antique furniture and plush drapes. And actors were content to be actors. They didn't try to mix with society people any more than society people tried to mix with them. *They* knew where the fun was. It was in the theater and Rector's and Delmonico's and not in a Fifth Avenue drawing-room. I guess the movies have spoiled things too by taking away from the theater its best audience. I mean all those people who used to sit in the balconies and nigger heaven. They didn't want any grim realism. They wanted illusion and grandeur and splendor and real comedy like the nasty kind that Molière gave 'em.

"Well, anyway, there's no use going on about all that. I only bring it up to give you some idea of the kind of background Bessie had and the kind of person she was. There aren't any like her any more. As I said, she couldn't act, not according to our standards, but she was a hell of a lot better actress than most of these mincing respectable school marms that pass as actresses

[522]

nowadays. No, men were men, and women were women in those days, and love affairs were love affairs.

"The first time I ever saw Bessie she was playing in *The Minx*, a kind of second role . . . you know, the friend of the heroine . . . and she was a great foil for little Herminie Ross who played the title role. Herminie was small with a little face like a Persian pussycat and a great little comedienne, and Bessie was big and blond with a big voice and a hearty laugh, and together they made the show, which wasn't so much of a show at that. And the moment I laid eyes on Bessie I took a quick look at the program to find out what her name was and said to myself, 'That's the girl for me!'

"Let me see, that's about thirty-five or forty years ago. That would make me about thirty-two at the time . . . just the right age, not too young to be a sap and not too old so that I couldn't take it, right all the way to the limit. Boy! I used to stay up all night and then go home and make love till three in the afternoon and be at the theater fresh as a daisy at a quarter to eight. I was in the company at Wallack's that season, but just then I was playing only three nights a week so the rest of the time I had off except for rehearsals.

"Well, by the time the curtain came down on the last act of *The Minx* I was worked into a lather about this Bessie Devine. About the middle of the second act I forgot all about the play and all about the part Bessie was supposed to be portraying. She was just a woman to me—a woman called Bessie Devine I'd never seen before, who was my kind of woman. So when the curtain calls were over I went around backstage to call on Herminie Ross. She wasn't my type at all, with her little pussycat ways, and she knew it too, so there wasn't any trouble. We were good friends the way a man and a woman can be when they know they like each other and don't want anything from each other. I found her in her dressing room, sort of smothered in flowers with a lot of Johnnies waiting around. That was more her school . . . Johnnies with top coats and mustaches and hansom cabs at the door. I told her she was great in that part, which she was, and after a minute she got the dress, boys out of her dressing room and when they were gone, she looked at me and said, 'I know what you're after. It's not me. It's Bessie you want to meet.' You see she knew my type.

"I said, yes, it was, and she said, 'I knew if you saw her, you'd fall. She's not very ladylike but then you don't like 'em that way.'

"She put on some sort of a flossy wrap and said to her maid, 'Look after those diamonds, Cleora, till I come back,' and we went out the door through all the Johnnies and across to the other side of the stage. They gave me dirty looks. They always hated good-looking actors, I guess because they knew that the actors got for nothing what cost them diamonds and flowers and hansom cabs.

"Herminie didn't knock on the door; she just pushed it open. There was a squeal and I saw Bessie snatch up a dressing gown and hold it before her. No costume could have become her more. She clutched it all in a lump so that beneath the edge of it I caught sight of her big fine legs and above it a glimpse of her big breasts. Her long blond hair was undone and fell over her white shoulders.

"I expected a scene to follow the squeal. I'd been through the same sort of surprise often enough before and usually there were screams of indignation and bad language, even from ladies who had no temerity whatever at showing themselves under almost any other circumstances. But Bessie seemed to take it all naturally as a joke.

"She laughed and said, 'You almost caught me. Better luck next time.'

"Herminie started to introduce me but Bessie said, 'Oh, you don't need to go into that. I've seen him plenty of times over at Wallack's.' Still clutching the dressing gown to her with one hand she held out the other. 'Sure, I know Mr. Davenport. I go over to Wallack's every time I have a moment off to learn how to act.'

"And then I caught sight of an odd little woman sitting in the background. She was small and rather withered in appearance and dressed in clothes which gave the impression of being too big for her. They weren't actually, but everything she wore seemed to be oversized as if she had withered away since she got them. She wore an enormous fur around her neck and an enormous hat with plumes which seemed to extinguish her like a candle snuffer. The hat and furs must have cost a lot once but they were shabby now. The plumes drooped wearily and the furs had a plucked look.

"Graciously, as if she were fully dressed and wearing a tiara instead of being stark naked save for a dressing gown stained with make-up pressed against her stomach, she turned and said, 'Meet my sister, Mrs. Rafferty.'

"Mrs. Rafferty gave me a faded smile and Bessie said, 'Don't go away, Mr. Davenport. Just give me a minute to slip something on and you can come in.'

"'Sure,' I said. 'I'll wait. Get dressed and we'll get something to eat.'

"'Fine,' said Bessie and closed the door.

"Outside I thanked Herminie and asked, 'Who's Mrs. Rafferty? Ought I to ask her too?'

"'No,' said Herminie. 'That's only her sister. She's got six children and her husband drinks. Bessie has to look after 'em all. Whenever Mrs. Rafferty appears it means there's been trouble at home. Probably Rafferty is in jail.'

"And with that Herminie crossed the stage and went back to her pussycat nest with the flowers and the diamonds guarded by Cleora and the Johnnies waiting outside. It struck me as funny that there weren't any flowers in Bessie's dressing room, and certainly there wasn't a single diamond. It was just a bare ugly dressing room, empty save for her own clothes.

"And then out of the darkness in the wings came the figure of 'Bink'

[524]

Mallory, not dressed up the way he always was in the evening but still in a checked suit with a top coat and a brown derby. His big red face looked depressed and when he grinned it was a melancholy grin which didn't do justice to all the gold teeth he had.

"He said, 'Hello,' and I said, 'Hello. What's the matter? Why aren't you dressed up?'

"'I just got in from Long Branch. They gave me a spring cleaning down at the track today and I need considerable cheerin' up. So I came along to see Bessie and get a laugh. I ain't in the way, am I?'"

"'No,' I said. 'Not in *my* way. Not exactly. I just met her for the first time. I asked her out for supper. I'm not in your way, am I?'"

"'No. I just want some fun and a couple of good laughs. We can all go out together. I'll clear out early. I ain't had any sleep for two nights.'

"And just then we were joined by somebody else coming out of the shadows and it was Harry Peel, who'd just finished his act at the Victoria Roof. He must have been awful funny that night at Hammerstein's because there wasn't any comedy left in him. He had a face a mile long.

"'Hello, boys,' he said, 'waiting for Bessie? Hope I'm not in the way?'

"'No. Come along and eat.'

"'I've just had a row with the management,' he said, 'and walked out, and I needed that dough. God knows when I'll get another good booking. I want to go and get drunk.'

"So the three of us waited there till Bessie got her clothes on, exchanging stories and talking Broadway gossip. It struck me as funny that there weren't any Johnnies outside the door waiting for Bessie . . . but only an actor, a race-track man and a comic juggler. And then Bessie came out, looking big and beautiful and healthy, dressed all in black with a black feather boa which trailed on the floor and a big black hat covered with ostrich plumes. Something came out the door with her . . . health and vigor and good nature and love, I think. Love for everybody and everything. She wanted everybody to have a good time.

"So the four of us went to Rector's for a time and then to Jack's and there Harry Peel left us. He was drunk and happy again. Bessie had done that to him with her stories. She had a way of seeing funny things that happened during the day on the street, in restaurants, among the stage hands, and afterward she would recount them, not always in the most delicate language but in an irresistibly funny fashion. In spite of being no actress at all she was a good mimic. She could re-create for you any character which had caught her attention during the day. Harry Peel had forgotten about his quarrel and his lost job. Tomorrow he'd get up with fresh spirits and a new point of view, ready to begin all over again.

"About five o'clock 'Bink' Mallory with his checked suit and brown derby bade us good night and I was left to see Bessie home. That was what I was waiting for all the time but now when the time came, I didn't know exactly how to cope with Bessie. Maybe I should say I didn't exactly know how to approach what was on my mind. You'd have said that it was the easiest thing in the world to say to a woman like Bessie, 'I'm crazy about you. Take me home with you,' but it wasn't. God knows I wasn't any novice at such things and I knew at least twenty ways of leading up to the subject, but none of them seemed to fit Bessie. Suddenly, left alone with her, all my slick Casanova tricks just curled up and died.

"I've had about forty years to think it over and I've come to the conclusion that Bessie had a peculiar quality which most girls I knew never had. She was on the level, more on the level than any woman I ever knew, and somehow when you'd tried to pull a fast one with Bessie you were ashamed of yourself because you knew she wouldn't do that kind of thing to you. Nobody ever pretended that Bessie was pure as the driven snow, but whenever she was generous with her favors there was a reason for it and the reason wasn't money.

"Anyway, we got into a hansom. I drove her home just at dawn to the old Hoffman House where she was living then, and all the way there I never made a pass at her or even a suggestive remark. We just talked like any two nice people that like each other—about the milk wagons, and the show and about acting. And when we left each other I asked if I could see her again soon and she said, 'Sure, come on around any night.'"

3

"When I came home that night, Lester heard me open the door and got up as usual to make me a cup of tea. Lester was my valet. He was a little Cockney I found in London when I was over there with Ada Rehan. He wanted to come to the States so I brought him home with me. We were both kids then. I must have been about twenty-four or five and Lester was about twenty-one. He'd been with me for eight years when I first met Bessie and he had a kind of worship for me, like a faithful dog. He hadn't any life of his own. He was small and ugly and he didn't seem to know anyone or how to make any friends. He just kept to my flat, and the only fun he had was when people came in and we had a party and he could wait on them and look at the beautiful women and the sporting men. He'd trained himself to wake the moment he heard my key turn in the lock and then he'd get up and make me tea and see that I got safely to bed.

"I was never able to discover what went on inside his head. Sometimes I used to think nothing went on in there, but I guess there must have been something because there never was a better servant. I used to tell him a good many things . . . the kind of things I didn't tell to anyone else, just for the pleasure it gave me to see his eyes light up and a funny grin that would curl up one side of his ugly little face. And that way he had a kind of life of his own, which wasn't real, of course, but came to him through me. Years afterward I found out that I was pretty close to being right about it. In some funny way he got to imagining that he was *me*, and that all the escapades I went through were really happening to him too. He'd spent a good part of his life being hungry and beaten and he knew he was little and ugly and so he was afraid of ever trying anything on his own. He worked it all out somehow. I suppose when I was out all night he was with me in a funny way, seeing all the rowdy men and the beautiful women I saw. Of course he never did go out and he never did go with me. He managed it in a kind of dream life. It was just the same whether he was awake or asleep.

"Anyway, there he was when I came home and he said, as he poured my tea, 'Miss Ransom came in tonight, sir.' She was a girl from the Casino chorus that I'd been carrying on with for some time.

"'Did she wait?' I asked him.

"'No, she didn't,' he said. 'I didn't let her in.'

"'Why?' I asked him.

"'Because I found her picture torn up in your wastepaper basket, sir. I was afraid she might come in and break things up.'

"'That's right, Lester,' I said. 'That's just what she would have done. If she comes back again always keep the door on the chain. She's the kind that gets cold mad and smashes things up. It's all over with Miss Ransom, Lester.'

"'I'm glad of that, sir.'

"'Why, Lester?' I asked him.

"'If you'll excuse me, sir, I always thought you couldn't count on her.'

"That was exactly it. She was a nice girl but you couldn't count on her and she had tantrums; sometimes right in a restaurant she'd throw all the dishes on the floor and begin to scream. I didn't care much for that. I didn't mind breaking it off. The funny thing was that Lester knew all about it. He'd sort of been going through the affair with me. He'd had a half-dozen pictures of Polly Ransom, which he'd cut out of newspapers and theatrical magazines, pinned to the wall of his room for months, just as if he was the one who was carrying on with her. When I looked into his room the next day they were all gone.

"The next night I went to *The Minx* again, only instead of going out front I came behind stage and spent my time between Herminie's dressing room and Bessie's. When one was on the stage I went to sit in the dressing room of the other, and so I came to learn a lot about Bessie while she was before the footlights and Herminie was waiting to go on. Usually Herminie couldn't bear any other pretty woman who happened to be in the same company with her, but Bessie she didn't seem to mind. She even liked her, and while I sat talking with her I began to understand why. Bessie wasn't in any sense a rival. On the stage she served as a foil to Herminie and made Herminie seem even more *petite*, and certainly more young than she really was, and off the stage she didn't offer any competition, at least any competition that Herminie need worry about. I began to learn why there weren't any Johnnies waiting for Bessie and why there weren't flowers and diamonds in her dressing room.

"It seemed that she couldn't stomach Johnnies. She was born on Ninth Avenue and she didn't like flossy manners and what she called 'clubmen.' In the first place their dandified manners made her nervous and in the second place they bored her. And gentlemen, she said, were 'dirty' when they made love. Afterward when we were living together she explained what it was she meant. It took her a long time because she wasn't very good at words, but I finally discovered that what she objected to was their condescension. Most of them felt, she said, that they were so damned superior to you that they were doing you a favor and soiling themselves in the process. And she wouldn't have any of that. So whenever some Johnny turned up, she told him right out that it wasn't any use trying to hang around because she never went out with clubmen. What she liked, Herminie said, was fellow actors and sports and often enough chaps who were down on their luck.

"'She just goes around looking for fellows who are broke. She can spot 'em a mile off,' Herminie used to say. 'So she doesn't come out very well where diamonds and flowers are concerned. God knows she could use a few jewels and a little cash now and then. She never has any. She's always giving it away. That girl just hasn't got any sense about money. She ought to cut loose from that family of hers . . . the Raffertys and all her brothers and sisters and uncles and aunts and God knows what. As if they weren't enough she's always paying the rent for chorus girls and doctors' bills for stage hands. What's going to become of her? A girl has to look out for herself in this business. If Bessie had any sense she could have a cold hundred thousand laid away right now. And she hasn't got a dime.'

"Well, all that didn't exactly put me off Bessie. Anyway, you knew that if she liked you, she *liked* you. She wasn't just pretending to get out of you what she could. What Herminie said explained a lot of other things about Bessie . . . why it was so hard to get down to brass tacks on that first evening and why every now and then, right in the midst of all her laughing and good nature, her face would suddenly grow sad when she thought nobody was watching her, and sometimes you'd hear her sigh, very quietly, as if she didn't want anybody to hear her. You see, all the time, down underneath all that good-time manner, she knew what it was all about.

[528]

She knew the human race was pretty sad and tragic, only she refused to admit it and she wasn't going to let anybody else suspect what she knew. She was just born that way . . . *knowing*, and I always had a feeling that she took the responsibility for the whole mess on her own big handsome shoulders and did her best to straighten it out. She was always taking over the troubles of other people, and didn't want you to know about it. It would have made her feel sort of ashamed.

"Well, to make a long story short, Bessie and I took up together. It must have been love because God knows on her side she couldn't have expected anything else from an actor making a couple of hundred dollars a week. We had a little flat of two rooms where we used to meet. Lester stayed on in the other flat to take care of it and I didn't see so much of him. Sometimes I wouldn't come home for two or three days, and that upset him terribly. He worried over not being able to get up in the morning when I came in to make my tea, and he fussed because he couldn't look me over from head to foot every time I went out to see that I was turned out the way a gentleman should be. And his own dreary little life got drearier and drearier because after Bessie became my sweetheart, I didn't have any more of those parties he used to like so much, when he could pour drinks and listen to the talk of all the sports and the beautiful women.

"Once or twice he said to me, very respectfully, 'Sir, you ought to bring Miss Devine around here some time to show her what a nice flat you have and how well it's kept.' There was a little reproach in his voice as if I'd insulted him somehow by not bringing her to see what a good, devoted servant he was. I kept promising to bring her around and have a party for her but I kept putting it off and then it was too late and Bessie was where she couldn't ever go to parties again.

"It was the happiest time in my life. God knows I've known plenty of women but never one that could touch Bessie. Life was full of excitement and fun twenty-four hours of the day. We were together for about six months and then my father died out in Kansas City and I had to go out there to my mother. It was in August, I remember, and hotter than Hades. I left Lester in the flat and said good-by to Bessie, telling her I'd be back in ten days or so. Well, there was trouble about the will and my mother was sick and all broken up and I couldn't leave her, and so ten days got to be two weeks and then three and then four. Bessie wasn't much at writing letters but I used to hear from her about once a week, little short letters full of bad spelling with news of New York and a lot of stories and jokes she'd picked up during the week. They always made me laugh and feel better. I couldn't read all of them to my mother because some of the stories weren't exactly the kind you could tell to nice old ladies, but I used to read her parts of them and they'd make her laugh and feel much better. It was as if Bessie

[529]

had the power of putting some of her big hearty self into an envelope to send out to me in Kansas City. I've always thought it was as much Bessie's letters as the doctors themselves that helped my mother to get well that time.

"Anyway, she began to get strong again and I bought my ticket for a Friday to go back to Bessie and work and then on a Wednesday I got a telegram from Herminie Ross. I'll never forget that telegram. For me it was just as if the world had suddenly come to an end. It was like getting up one morning to find that the whole universe had gone cock-eyed and the sun had failed to come up. Bessie was dead. She'd been killed in an accident during a political outing in Hoboken.

"I took the next train back and when I got to my flat Lester wasn't there. It was the first time in all our life together he hadn't come to the door when I rang the bell. I went to the janitor and he gave me a note. He said it was from Lester and that he had written it himself for Lester because Lester couldn't read or write. When I opened it I discovered the second blow at the foundations of my life. Lester was gone.

"The janitor had written for him something like this:

Dear sir;
I regret to say that I have had to leave. I cannot tell you the reason. I was very satisfied with the place and you have always been more than kind to me, but I have to go. Something has happened. I could not face you again on account of shame. Forgive me, sir, if I ask God to bless and keep you.
Your devoted servant,
Lester Bitts.

"Then for a day or two I forgot all about Lester. Bessie was the only one I could think of . . . Bessie whom I would never see again.

"Herminie told me the story. It seemed that Bessie had been asked to be the guest of honor at a Democratic political picnic and rally over in Hoboken and as she always said yes, she accepted, and was crowned Queen of the Rally on a throne. She must have looked wonderful because that was just the sort of big human background in which she belonged. You could just see her there in the midst of all those families drinking beer and enjoying themselves . . . Bessie seated on a throne with a crown on her head and a stein of beer in one hand . . . big and handsome and good natured.

"The accident happened late in the afternoon. It seemed that three breweries had sent beer trucks with their finest big horses drawing them . . . six big Percherons on each truck. They took part in a kind of pageant. It was good advertisement too for the breweries. About five o'clock Bessie got the notion that as Queen of the occasion she wanted to drive one of the trucks, and as everybody was feeling gay, they let her do it. Still wearing her crown she climbed up to the seat and took the reins. There was a driver beside her to show her how to drive six big brewery horses at once, but he'd had a little too much beer and he and Bessie began to laugh and the horses got out of hand and started to gallop. When the driver snatched the reins from her and tried to straighten them out, they got tangled. The horses went faster and faster with Bessie and the driver laughing and clinging to the high seat, until they crashed into a corner of the grandstand and the whole truck went over with Bessie and the driver underneath. When they finally righted the truck and pulled her out, she was dead.

"We gave her a wonderful funeral. Everybody on Broadway came and hordes of people, mostly shabby men and women down on their luck whom nobody had ever seen. They were, I guess, all people whom Bessie had helped. And all the Rafferty family were there and the uncles and aunts and cousins from Ninth Avenue. There were masses and masses of flowers from blankets of roses down to scrubby little bunches of nasturtiums. I hope there's an afterlife and that Bessie was able to see what was going on. She would have loved her own funeral."

4

"I wasn't the only one who missed her. There were all those down and outers who came to the funeral, and people in places like Rector's and Jack's would suddenly miss something, not quite knowing what it was, and then as the evening wore on they would discover that what they missed was Bessie. They didn't see her sweep in with her plumes and feather boas and they didn't hear her loud laugh. The table in Jack's and at Rector's where actors and sporting men once gathered like flies on honey, was empty now. Something was gone.

"As for Lester I thought that some day he'd just walk in the door and go about his work again without saying anything. A week passed and then another and then another and finally I got in a little Filipino to take his place, planning to fire him when Lester returned; but Lester never came back. I got the police to looking for him—Mike Regan at the Forty-sixth Street station was a friend of mine and he saw that they searched thoroughly —but they never found hide nor hair of him. It was easy enough for him to disappear because he hadn't any friends or connections except me and so there wasn't anybody you could question about him. When I showed his note to the police they said, 'What was he ashamed of? What'd he steal? Didn't you miss nothing?' And I said, 'No, I didn't miss anything.' All my diamond studs and my two fancy watches—everything of any value I found locked in my strong box just the way they always were. Lester had left the key with the janitor. As a matter of fact, there was one thing missing but I never spoke of it to the police partly because it seemed so unimportant and partly because I had a feeling—you know, one of those feelings you can't account for which are always right—that I'd better leave the whole thing lie. The only thing missing was a picture of Bessie, cabinet size, in an evening dress with hat, plumes and boa.

"The police gave up the problem of Lester and I began to settle down. I wasn't very old—only in my middle thirties—but somehow after Bessie, I never had any more fun larruping around. Right in the middle of a love affair I'd begin to be bored and start comparing the woman to Bessie and then that would be the end of it. So one day I married Minnie Sands. She was just a kid then, playing ingenues in our company. I never regretted it. It was one of those good old-fashioned stage marriages that don't happen any more, with kids born in dressing rooms and carried along on tour to sleep in trunk lids and bureau drawers. I've been lucky all my life. Bessie was one kind of luck and Minnie another and both of 'em were okay.

"And in the meanwhile Herminie Ross married one of her Johnnies. She's still alive and you read about her now and then in the society columns, a respected and fashionable old lady. She gives a lot of her money to charity and works on Actors' Relief Boards. After Bessie died and Herminie got married I didn't see much of her until one day about ten years ago I was asked to speak at one of those high-brow drama meetings, and there sitting next to me at the speakers' table was Herminie. She hadn't changed very much and gradually we got to talking about the old days, and when lunch was over, she said to me, 'Why don't you come home with me for a cup of tea? We can talk there without having everybody listen in on us.' I knew she was dying to let down her hair and talk, but she didn't want to in front of all the other society women at the lunch. And that was just what she did. She had done well for herself, as well as poor Bessie had done poorly, but in her heart Herminie was still a trouper and sometimes, she said, she nearly died for wanting to talk about the old days.

"I stayed until eight o'clock and then it was she told me why Lester had disappeared. All the time she and Bessie were playing in *The Minx* they used to tell each other all their adventures, usually before the show, because afterward there never was any time, what with all Herminie's admirers trouping in and out. Bessie used to tell her everything and one night Bessie came in and said to her, 'Herminie, every night I come in now for a week or more there's been a little man standing under the street lamp outside the stage door. I think he wants to speak to me from the way he looks at me. I don't know what he wants but I guess if it was a touch he'd have spoken of it before now. I feel kind of sorry for him, hanging around like that. He looks so scared and unhappy.'

"So Herminie said, 'Why don't you speak to him?' and Bessie said, 'All right, I will.'

[532]

"Well, Herminie didn't hear any more about it for about a week and then one night Bessie came in early to the theater and came straight to Herminie's dressing room and said she had a funny story to tell her.

"She said, 'I did speak to the little man and I took him home with me.' And Herminie said, 'What do you mean took him home with you?'

"'Just that,' said Bessie. 'I took him home with me. He's been with me for a week, day and night.'

"'What about Jack?' asked Herminie, meaning me, and Bessie said, 'It's all right. What he don't know won't hurt him, and anyway some day he'll understand. Wait until you hear the story.'

"It seemed that when she did speak to the little man, he was so frightened he couldn't answer her at first and then slowly she got out of him that it *was* her he'd been waiting to see night after night under the lamppost. He was afraid he'd annoyed her and he said that all he ever asked was just the chance to look at her as she came in and out of the theater, if it didn't upset her. He said she didn't need to bother with a poor little thing like him with so many other men wanting to make love to her and marry her. He didn't know it, of course, but he'd said just the right thing, about the only thing he could have said to make Bessie notice him, only I guess he was so scared at the moment that he didn't even want to say the right thing. Anyway, he was just Bessie's dish—somebody scared and abused and humble. So she said, 'Come along and have a bite to eat.' But he thanked her and said he couldn't go to any restaurant. 'It's all right,' he said, 'if you'll just let me look at you every night and say good evening sometimes.' He kept addressing her very respectfully as 'Madam' which made Bessie laugh. So she said, 'All right. You're coming home with me and I'll cook you up something. You look as if you hadn't had a square meal for months.'

"When they got home Bessie made it into a real party. She opened champagne for him and Irish whisky for herself and they sat down to have a big time. All the time the little man was scared to death and tongue-tied. She couldn't get anything out of him for a long time but 'yes' and 'no' until presently the champagne began to work and then he talked about himself, and Bessie drew him out.

"She found out that he'd been an orphan since he was three years old and that he'd worked hard ever since he was a kid and nobody had ever loved him. 'I guess I was too ugly,' he said, 'and too measly for any woman ever to look at me.' Anyway, no woman ever did from the time he was a kid. 'But inside,' he said, 'I'm just like any other man. I fall in love but nothing ever comes of it. I wouldn't dare ask any woman to speak to me.' And then Bessie got out of him that he'd been beaten and kicked and abused so much as a child that all he ever wanted to do was shrink away from people

[533]

and hide, for fear of a blow or a nasty crack. So he didn't know anybody at all.

"Well, by this time the whisky Bessie was drinking had begun to work on her too and she began to cry over his story and said, 'I'll tell you what you're going to do. You're going to stay here with me. I'll fix things up for you.'

"And so, still trembling and frightened, the little man stayed on. For more than a week except when she was at the theater, Bessie cosseted and cared for him . . . this poor little man who had never been loved by any creature and had never been a woman's lover or known what love was. And Bessie confided in Herminie her belief that when she had finished with him he'd be a different man. He wouldn't be scared or timid ever again and anyway he wouldn't die without ever having known the love of a woman. And what a woman! One who couldn't be bought for any amount of money or diamonds.

"Herminie said that he came with Bessie to the theater every night and was there waiting when the curtain went down, but he never came inside. He waited for her under the lamppost at the end of the stage door alley. He'd stay there from a quarter to eight when he left Bessie until midnight when she came out again. He hadn't anything else to do. And sometimes he'd see Herminie coming out with three or four admirers wearing all her orchids and diamonds. And then Bessie would come out alone and take him home with her.

"It was Herminie who discovered who he was. One night Bessie's sister Mrs. Rafferty came into her dressing room with an extra load of troubles and so Bessie was late, and when Herminie came out the little man was standing by the lamppost. At sight of her he turned away quickly into the shadows but this time he didn't turn quickly enough. She saw that it was Lester.

"But Bessie never found out because she never again came into Herminie's dressing room for a gossip. The next day she went to Hoboken to be Queen of the Rally and Herminie never saw her again alive."

5

"When I left Herminie's swell house on Fifth Avenue that night, I didn't go home but went straight to Jack's and had dinner in a corner, all alone. Somehow or other the occasion demanded it. There didn't seem to be any other place in New York that was fitting and proper and in a way the melancholy state of that grand old restaurant was right too. Prohibition had come in and Jack's was on its last legs. There weren't any actors or sporting men. There wasn't anyone there save a few dreary people eating here and there alone or in twos and threes; but there were the ghosts of Diamond Jim Brady and Herminie Ross and Edna MacCauley and Good Time Bessie. There was, I think, even the ghost of myself.

"I ate alone, served by a tired, somewhat untidy waiter, who moved about as if he were serving ghosts. And I thought about what Herminie, sitting in her expensive, decorated drawing-room had told me. Bessie, long ago had been right, when she said, 'Some day he'll understand.' I did understand. If I had discovered about Lester twenty-five years before, I would have been crazy with anger and jealousy at both of them, never seeing that what Bessie had done was perhaps the kindest thing she had ever done in a life that was given over to doing kind things for other people. There was in the story something so fantastically grand and human, that what I cared and thought was of no importance. Like in the old story of the Juggler of Notre Dame, I think God understood. Bessie gave the only thing she had to give, and believe me it was no small gift. Sitting there over my oysters I was sure now that Lester had been there at the funeral, lost somewhere in the great crowd, hiding from me . . . the only other person besides Bessie that he had loved.

"Only one thing tormented me and that was a terrible curiosity to know what had become of Lester in the twenty-five years since he left the note written for him by the janitor. Perhaps, I thought, it changed his whole life. Perhaps he's married now with children and grandchildren, maybe living right here in New York somewhere near me. Or maybe he forgot his fear of women and became a lady killer. Or maybe . . . but everything I tried to figure out about him was wrong, I found out in the end.

"My wife died and my children got married and I wasn't any longer a leading man but a character actor and jobs got scarcer and scarcer. The pictures never seemed to have any use for me and the new people who came to Broadway didn't remember me even if they'd ever heard of me. And so to make ends meet, I gave up my flat and came up here to live. It isn't a very good hotel but it's clean and neat and the rooms are big with high ceilings, and I can't complain about life. I've had a lot of fun and that's the thing that's important. I can sit here and look at the river and have a lot of fun just thinking about it all.

"Anyway, I'd been here only a day or two when I heard a quarrel going on downstairs in the lobby back of the screen that hides the entrance to the service elevator and I heard somebody speak Bessie Devine's name, which I hadn't heard for years and then somebody, somebody young, said, 'Bessie Devine, my eye! There wasn't any such person!' and the young voice laughed and the old voice said, 'You don't know what you're talking about . . . you and your silly moving picture magazines.'

"Waiting for the elevator, I managed to peek through a crack in the screen and there standing with two or three suits, freshly pressed and on hangers, was Lester. There couldn't be any mistake. Nobody ever had such an ugly face as Lester's. It was so ugly that age made little difference to it. And he had the poorest little rickety body in the world, because as a child he'd never had enough to eat.

"I didn't speak to him then but I sent for Jimmy, the bellboy he'd been quarreling with. Jimmy is a nice kid who grew up to be the porter. And I asked him about Lester, because it *was* Lester all right. There wasn't any mistake. And Jimmy said, 'Oh, he's nuts! He's a good hotel valet and harmless but completely nuts.' And when I asked him why, he said, 'Oh, all he does is talk about the good old days and a love affair he had with some dame called Bessie Devine. He says that everybody knew her and she was a big star, but none of the boys around here ever heard of her, and anyway, can you imagine any big star havin' a love affair with an ugly little runt like that.' And then I told him not to tease Lester any more because there once was a big handsome actress called Bessie Devine and that it was true that she'd had a love affair with Lester; but when I got all through, you could see he didn't believe me any more than he'd believed Lester.

"So I sent for Lester and when he saw me he didn't believe it at first and then he turned white and began to shake all over, and then he cried. But I told him it was all right because it had all happened so long ago that it couldn't possibly make any difference except to bring a couple of old men like ourselves both closer together than we had ever been, and that we must be friends because that's what Bessie would have liked more than anything in the world. And so we came to know each other all over again, in a different way. We talked a lot about Bessie but we never talked openly about what had happened between him and her, and presently I began to understand what the effect of the affair on him had been all these years. It wasn't at all what I thought. Because it was the only thing which had ever happened to him all his life and because it was so incredible and tremendous, it seemed to have unsettled his mind. And as he grew older he couldn't think about anything else . . . only just this wonderful thing that had happened to him. And then whenever he got a little acquainted with anybody he'd tell them the story. At first he didn't use her name but when nobody believed him and said, 'Well, if it really happened to you, what was her name?' and he'd tell it, but that only made it worse because then nobody would believe that Bessie Devine whom everybody knew at Rector's and Jack's, had ever slept with this ugly little valet. And as the years passed he began to find people who had never even heard of Bessie Devine and, like Jimmy the bell-hop, said there wasn't any such person. So it only got worse and worse, until that day he and I found each other again as old men, and after that he didn't care. You see at last, after more than thirty years, he'd found someone who believed his story."

6

"So that's the end of the story," the old gentleman said. "Lester insists on looking after me just the way he did thirty-five years ago. It makes him kind of happy, so I let him do it."

Just then there was a knock on the door and the old actor said, "Come in." The door opened and in came Lester carrying a worn gray suit on a coat hanger. It was freshly pressed and I understood why the old gentleman always looked so well turned out instead of looking shabby and untidy. I understood too why the room was so neat and spotless. The valet was unmistakably Lester. I never saw an uglier, more misshapen little man.

"Lester," said the old gentleman, "this is a friend of mine. I've just been telling him about Bessie. He's too young to remember her."

Lester gave a slight glance of distaste at the sight of me, sprawled in ungentlemanly fashion on the untidy bed and then said, "Yes, sir. I'm pleased to know you." A light came into the poor little Cockney face. "Bessie, sir. That was a great woman. I think she was the greatest woman I ever knew."

VII

That Which Never Returns

THE captain paused for a moment on the edge of the deck, his face turned upward in the dim tropic darkness. He was young, much younger than the lean, middle-aged man who stood at the rail of the little schooner, and he appeared anxious and troubled. Bendham, the older man, seemed only bored; so listless and so indifferent that the boredom was like an illness.

"I oughtn't to go ashore," said the boyish captain.

"Go ashore," said the older man wearily.

"The river is rising, sir. What will you do if she breaks her moorings?"

"She won't. We're safe behind the point. I've moored in this spot before— a hundred times."

"I don't like to leave you, sir." The "sir" he added out of deference to Bendham's age and his position as owner of the schooner, and grudgingly too out of respect for the older man's superior experience as a navigator in this part of the world.

Bendham's boredom vanished in a sudden gust of rudeness. "My God, man, I knew every eddy in this river before you were born."

The captain, snubbed, descended the short ladder and sprang into the dory. Bendham remained at the rail watching the little boat making its perilous way across the rising water toward the distant settlement.

"My God, won't they ever leave me alone?" and he felt the thought so intensely that he spoke it aloud, savagely.

He was alone now save for his wife who lay asleep below deck and the Malay who had remained on board to serve him. On his mat, the Malay sat aft on the little schooner, and Bendham was aware that the yellow man was watching him, just as one becomes aware of being watched by a cat of whose presence one is altogether ignorant. Even the Malays seemed different, he thought. Once he had liked and understood them. Now he was aware that he distrusted them and that they disliked him. He could not understand a change like that.

He turned to the Malay. "Go to sleep," he said in the man's own dialect. "I shan't need you. Go below deck."

The Malay silently rolled up his mat and disappeared down the companionway with the naked tread of a cat and Bendham felt a quick sense of relief. He was alone on the deck.

He was hungry for solitude. "I am," he thought, "like a sick animal"; yet there appeared to be nothing the matter with him. It was no tropical fever, for he knew all the varieties of fever from long experience. He had no appetite but then, even as a boy, he had never had an appetite in weather like this. Yes, he was like a sick animal which wanted to hide away and die. It was the worst of all sicknesses—an illness of the nerves.

It was hot, horribly hot, with the menace of fresh, torrential downpours in the air. The atmosphere, he thought, must nearly have reached the point of saturation. It was difficult to breathe. In the dim light of the moon he looked about him at the raging river filled with grass, uprooted saplings, wrecked bamboo huts and coconut palms. The river would rise, he calculated, for perhaps another forty-eight hours, and no more than that. Never in all the years of his experience had it risen higher.

On both sides of him lay the long black lines of the shore. He knew what was there—a solid wall of dripping jungle, broken only by the squalid settlement with its score of twinkling lights. Now and again the moon came from behind the ragged storm clouds and turned the churning river to molten silver.

The insects became intolerable, whole clouds of them of a million sizes and shapes, buzzing and whirring, attracted through the moist night by the schooner's lights. He went inside a kind of tent made of netting which had been erected by the Malay so that he could remain on deck, because he found it impossible to sleep or even to breathe below deck. It was near the bow among the crates of plant specimens he had been collecting during the past six weeks.

Inside the little tent there were two deck chairs and a rattan table with several glasses, a fresh bottle of whisky, a bottle of soda water, a shaded oil light with the wick turned low, and a bowl of rapidly melting ice from the American refrigerating machine below deck. "Oh," he thought, "I travel in luxury now—different from the first time I saw this river." And then bitterly, he thought, "So what!"

He lifted the netting quickly to prevent the insects from entering and slipped inside. He poured himself a drink and put no ice in it. Ice made you hotter rather than cooler. Then he lay back in the deck chair drumming the edge with his long, lean, brown fingers. He was a long, thin man with a handsome narrow head covered with graying, curly black hair. His skin was yellow tan, a color acquired permanently before he was thirty-five from fevers and long exposure to the sun. He was lean and tough with unquestionable powers of resistance; but he was neat, too, nervous and too well controlled, one of those men who by instinct and long habit never betray an emotion, and so turn knotted and tense in their very souls.

The night was still and yet not still. There was no sound produced by man, but a million sounds made by nature itself—the monotonous buzzing of insects, the gurgling sounds of the river, the bump of an occasional log against the side of the schooner. Once there was the wild cry of a panther somewhere in the jungle and almost immediately the solitary scream of a monkey. He was aware of a wholly primitive world all about him, filled with creeping, crawling, flying, climbing and swimming things—a primitive world in which eating and sleeping, reproducing and escaping death were the beginning and the end—a world, he thought, with a queer sense of relief, which was with all its savagery, simple. He had known it once intimately. He had lived that kind of life. Why, he asked himself, was it impossible to recapture it? Twelve years was not a long time.

For twelve years had passed since he went back to England, a rich man, and during those twelve years he had grown richer and richer, and life oddly enough had grown more and more unsatisfactory. He could not say why wealth had not made it simple. His whole existence had on the contrary grown steadily more intolerable and now, when he could endure it no longer, he had come back again to that world where he had made his fortune before he was thirty-six. That primitive world was unchanged. He was here in the midst of it. He had come halfway round the world to satisfy the horrible nostalgia, yet he could not find his way back. It stood apart, a long distance off, mocking him. Somewhere along the way he had gotten tangled in stocks and shares and the responsibilities and conventions of another world.

He felt suddenly that he was stifling and that the only thing which could save him would be to find himself alone in a cave of ice where there was no other life but his own. If he could be alone again, alone in the world with nothing save his own health and spirit, as he had been at twenty-two, he might recover the thing which had gone away forever, that something—he could not say what—which had given him courage and direction. And then immediately he felt cold and chilled by the kind of chill which was altogether new in his long experience with fevers. He took another drink, raw whisky this time, and became agonizingly aware again of the roar of the insects. It seemed to fill all the world, growing louder and louder, intolerable and suffocating. He extinguished the lamp and waited for a time, only to discover that it was not the lamp which attracted the insects. The air itself was filled with them. The sound was unescapable. He decided to drink himself into unconsciousness. "Otherwise," he thought, "I will go mad."

2

And then he saw the light. He did not know how long he had been sitting there when he heard the sharp, sudden clamor of mongrels in the settlement on the shore. The lights one by one had gone out until there were now but two or three and one of them was moving. It was no will-o'-the-wisp, for it moved evenly on the low ground by the river below the settlement, in a straight line. Someone was walking there, carrying a light. There was nothing unusual in that. He could not say why it fascinated him. "Perhaps," he thought, "I'm a little drunk." He looked at his watch. It was two o'clock in the morning.

In his imagination he saw the settlement, a cluster of houses swarming with natives and in the midst the squalid house of the Portuguese governor. Through the roar of insects he heard the dogs barking again. He thought, "Perhaps it's Mason and the crew coming back. Why can't they leave me in peace?" Alone! But he wasn't alone! Below deck lay Jenny sleeping quietly through the intolerable night. His wife. She was always there, young, pretty, calm, a perfect wife. Yes, damn her, a perfect wife, thinking only of him. He could hear again her voice as she stepped off the pier at Singapore, "I thought I'd surprise you, darling, so I came by the Canadian Pacific." And before he could answer she had kissed him in that way of hers, so strange and passionate in a woman so soft, gentle and well-bred, a way which filled him with distaste, because it made him feel that she was always trying to gain possession of him, or at least of that part of him which he meant to surrender to no one. And yet his body was weak: nearly always he yielded, and afterward was sick in his spirit, because, with passion spent, he knew she had won again.

He closed his eyes. Why had he not put her at once on the P and O boat and shipped her home? Why had he not escaped then and there her awful devotion, that dreadful singleness in her determination to be a perfect wife? There she was below deck, sleeping calmly through the intolerable heat and damp as if she were in her own bed in her father's house beside the quiet river in Devon. She never complained. She was never in the wrong. You could never put your finger on what she did, saying, "It is this," or "It is that which makes me hate her." Even these dreadful nights had no effect upon her. She did not fall ill. She did not mind the insects. No, she belonged to a different, intolerable breed, and she was spoiling his solitude by bringing with her a part of that life which he wanted so desperately to escape. So long as it clung to him he would never find his way back. But then once, long ago, he too had slept unaware of heat and discomfort. Perhaps it was only because she was young.

He thought, "I must not let her become an obsession. I must not blame her for everything." But he kept having thoughts which frightened him again with the suspicion that he was going mad.

When he opened his eyes again he saw that the light was no longer moving along the shore. The dogs were no longer barking and the light was on the water, and he knew now it was not Mason and the crew returning, for the light did not move with the steady roll of the dory; it bobbed and flickered and slithered from side to side. It was, he knew, a native craft, light as paper, and he wondered what mysterious and urgent errand could have engaged so fragile a craft on such a night. But the sense of his own misery overpowered his curiosity. He did not rise from his chair to follow the movements of the light which came toward him like a will-o'-the-wisp across the surface of the swollen river. He simply closed his eyes, still vaguely aware of the buzzing of insects which was like distant thunder. His thoughts slipped backward over the past leading him to wonder, "If I had done this or that, would it have been different? Would I have grown less tired and sick of everything? I am rich. I am successful. I have a beautiful wife. I need only children to have everything and I am not sure that I want to bring children into this lousy world."

And after a long time, in the midst of his brooding, he was startled suddenly by the sound of something bumping gently against the side of the schooner. He thought at once, "It is a log," but a log would have struck the schooner and slipped past on its way to the sea, and this sound continued bumping gently and irregularly. Then he remembered the bobbing craft and the will-o'-the-wisp, and a sudden wild excitement took possession of him. It was as if twenty years had suddenly slipped from him and he was a young man again on the deck of a dhow, waiting on the edge of the jungle, pistol in hand, with every nerve throbbing.

The long, thin brown hands clasped the edge of the deck chair and his body stiffened with the effort of listening. His heart beat more rapidly and he was aware suddenly that he was alive again as he had once been. The whisky filled him with a pleasant fuzziness, and he knew that in the profound depths of his soul danger, even death, was a matter of indifference. The great thing was that he felt alive again, for the first time, he thought, in years and years, since the night he had said good-by to Albertine de Jongh and the old life on the edge of the jungle clearing.

The light bumping sound continued and through it he heard another sound, that of footsteps on the ladder. They climbed upward and presently he heard someone walking on the deck, coming toward him. The moon had disappeared again under a black cloud and it was quite impossible to distinguish anything through the swarms of insects gathered on the netting.

The steps came directly to the little canopy of netting, which was lifted suddenly with the quick, experienced gesture of one who had lived long in the tropics, and he was aware in the faint light from the dimmed lamp of a figure dressed all in white linen. It wore jodhpurs made of linen and a linen jacket, a topi with a veil to protect the face from the swarming insects. But the figure, despite the clothes, was not that of a man. It was female, round, voluptuous, even fat. Under the jacket he discerned the heavy modeling of the large overflowing breasts.

A hand threw the veil up over the helmet with a gesture unmistakably feminine and hauntingly familiar. It was impossible to discern the features but a voice said, "Hello, Jim," and the world ceased any longer to have reality. He felt violently ill.

The sound of the voice, like the will-o'-the-wisp, and the footsteps sent him backward years and years. Someone who seemed not to be himself, said, "Tina, for God's sake."

And almost at once he was certain that he was mad or delirious. This fat, coarse woman could not be Tina. Yet Tina's voice answered him, "I was staying with the governor. I heard you were here." It was a warm, husky voice with the faint accent which was neither Dutch nor French nor Russian. There was no other voice like it in all the world, and no other accent. It did not astonish him that he recognized her thus: he would have known that voice and accent anywhere. She spoke casually, as if they had seen each other for the last time only yesterday instead of twelve years ago.

And in a second he relived a whole decade of his existence that was past forever—nights on the river, nights in the bar of the Raffles Hotel in Singapore, the Hotel des Indes in Batavia, nights in Sumatra, in Macassar, in Samarang, and nights on that ancient schooner *Artemis*, long since bleaching her bones among the muck and mangroves of an island not a hundred miles from where he sat.

He heard her saying, "Will you offer me a drink?" and recovered himself. He turned up the light and looked at her for a long time in silence. He saw then how shockingly fat she had grown. The voluptuous curves had all swelled into pure corpulence. The face was puffy and badly painted. The sensuous mouth had gone shapeless. She smiled at him cynically and displayed two gold teeth he had never seen. Only the eyes were unchanged, fine, brilliant and exciting. For a second he felt again the faint warmth of a flame which once had nearly devoured him. But the warmth was not for this woman but this woman's eyes and husky voice and for something which was a memory—the memory of Albertine de Jongh, part Dutch and Russian and French, but one-eighth Malay. It was the Malay which in the end had claimed her body. "Staying with the governor." He knew what that meant and he knew the governor, a fat, greasy, Portuguese with a green skin.

She did not seem to resent his examination. She looked at him smiling,

"Yes, I have changed," and she lighted a cigarette with all the indifference of a Malay. "But so have you. Life is like that."

He asked a banal question, "Did you bring a boatman?"

"No, I came alone." She nodded her head toward the settlement. "He was drunk, so I came secretly. He is very jealous."

"You're a fool to come alone on this river."

She looked at him in an odd way. "We've been through much worse than that together." She treated the rising river with scorn.

And again he saw not this fat woman but the Albertine de Jongh of years before with a fine, beautiful body, tanned by the sun—his woman but his companion too, as good as any man on an adventure. He knew that body but not this one. For no reason at all he thought of his wife, young, blond and cool below deck, so protected, and soft and luxurious. That was what his spoiled body wanted now—not Albertine, this fat monument to lechery.

The visitor sat down and the deck chair creaked beneath her weight. She seemed to find nothing unusual in her strange midnight visit. It was as if they had parted only yesterday.

3

It was not easy to recapture the past. It was not easy to grow used to each other once again and sit talking like old friends, because they had been so much more than friends. It was not easy for Bendham to sit there opposite this fat Malay woman with the fine eyes and warm voice thinking all the while of Albertine de Jongh as he saw her for the first time in the bar of the Hotel des Indes. But for the eyes and the voice, he would have believed this was another woman and been indifferent, but he kept seeing the eyes and hearing the voice, and they kept bringing back not only unwelcome visions of Albertine de Jongh on the deck of the *Artemis* or swimming naked on a white coral beach, but of wild dark rivers and native villages and brilliant sunlight and a light sky filled with stars. It was not easy and they felt their way toward each other in little banal questions and speeches. But it was easier for her. She appeared to accept what had happened as inevitable, and in him there still lurked fierce rebellion and despair.

She said, "You. You have done well for yourself. I've followed your career from time to time, when I came across English papers. You must be very rich."

"I am very rich. And you?"

She took a drink of whisky before answering him. "Me—I still have a little of what you gave me."

"I'll see that you have more."

She laughed, "No. I don't need more." And he thought that she looked at him with scorn but he could not be sure. "I have all I need. I'm going to quit him when the next boat comes in." She nodded toward the settlement. "He doesn't know it. He won't know until I've gone. Then I'm going to Penang."

Dimly he saw that although the Malay in her had claimed her body, it had not claimed her mind. Inside the fat, painted body, behind the fine eyes the mind was a European mind and it knew where to strike to hurt him most. She was telling him that she was satisfied with her life and was, in a way, happy, that at least she had peace, and she was telling him that all his money meant nothing to her. She had found something which you could not buy.

"And then what?"

"I shall take a house and grow old and die."

"Peace," she was saying, "Peace. I have Peace." She did not even resent his having paid her off and left her twelve years before when he left the East to become a power, a rich man in London, to settle and marry and become a personage. Power! Wealth! Personage! The words were bitter in his thoughts. He kept seeing the rubber plantation at Anao and the veranda and Albertine de Jongh and felt again the pang and the misgiving he knew on the day he rode through the opening in the jungle saying good-by forever to the old life. He remembered how he had turned to look back for the last time with a sudden sickness at leaving. He saw her again standing there on the veranda, perfectly still, not moving, not speaking, not calling after him but silent and rigid, resentful at his going, but silent. In that moment too the Malay had taken possession of her. He wondered, "What if I had turned back then instead of going on."

"You stopped writing to me," he said. "I was afraid you were dead."

"I read that you had married." She shrugged her fat shoulders like a French woman. "After that . . . besides it was all finished."

"No," he said. "Things like that are never finished."

He heard the haunting husky voice again, beautiful against the drone of the insects. "When I heard you were on board this schooner I had to see you once more—for the last time. We shan't meet again. I wanted to see you." She hesitated for a moment and he had the impression that she meant to say more and checked herself. By the light of the oil lamp he saw a look in her dark eyes that sent a wave of warmth through him. They were so near to each other for an instant and then immediately so remote.

She laughed, "So I got Portago drunk. He won't wake until noon to-morrow. And I came." She lighted another cigarette. "Maybe I shouldn't have come." Looking away from him she said, "I didn't come to annoy you. I don't want any money. I shan't ever bother you again—ever."

He did not answer her and she said, "You look ill and tired. Fever?"

[545]

"No. No fever. Not, at least, fever of the body."

"You ought never to have come back to the tropics. You can't stand it."

He burst out fiercely, "Why not? I'm as good as I ever was."

"No, Jim. Neither of us are, but that isn't what I meant." After a silence she said, looking at him sharply, "Why did you come back?"

He asked himself what she was driving at. "I came back to look out for my properties," and as if he had forgotten, "to collect plants. They're all there in those boxes on the deck. They're for a museum."

"Collect plants," she repeated in a voice gentle but tinged with acid. "That's a good name for what I'm doing too," and she nodded again toward the settlement. "Collect plants. We all have to do something until it's time to die."

4

Presently she smiled and said, "I passed Patna three months ago, so near that I saw the *Artemis*. She was half-buried in the mud. The mangroves are growing over her. There's not much left of her but a skeleton."

A skeleton. He did not answer her. He thought, "A skeleton."

She continued, "I spent Christmas at the Hotel des Indes. It's just the same. Old Vermaeren is the same, balder and fatter, a little."

No, he thought, it was impossible. Everything had changed. "Balder and fatter." And he decided to abandon his plan of revisiting Batavia.

But she continued, maddeningly, to dredge the past, dragging up memories which he had meant to die. "I see by the papers that you made a fine match—a woman young, pretty, distinguished—as it should have been. You were meant for that. I was never good enough for you."

"My God. Good enough for me!"

"No, not in that way. I went with you as far as I could go. I'd only have spoiled things. A Eurasian is beyond the borders and I was too well known in this part of the world. Everybody knew I was your woman. I keep imagining you at great dinners. People in hotels cluster and whisper when you pass—'there goes Bendham, the great rubber magnate.' You're a great man, Jim. I always knew you'd be. But I couldn't go with you. I went as far as I could."

He was aware that she was bringing back their old intimacy in spite of anything he could do, and he kept fighting against it. She was, in a strange way, insinuating her gross, painted self between him and the pretty gentle woman below deck. No matter how he struggled she was taking possession of him. He wanted to ask her if he seemed changed, but he dared not risk it. Time and change creep on so slowly that one is unaware of them. You could only see it if you had avoided mirrors for ten years.

"I heard that she is with you," she said, and looked at him sharply.

"Yes, she is below deck. She minds nothing—not even this heat."

"A good wife. She never annoys you. Wonderfully faithful and devoted."

How did she know that? How could she know that Jenny was like a parasite liana? Devoted, faithful, unscrupulous, pure and sensual—that was it. She was the worst thing a woman can be—puritan and sensual.

Suddenly his nerves gave way and he burst out violently, "What are you trying to do to me?"

She answered him calmly, "Nothing. I'm interested, curious. That's rational—even if I am a Eurasian, I'm a woman. I'm glad you found a good wife to care for you."

"Oh, she cares for me. She never allows me out of her sight." And at once he was ashamed of the outburst and the bitterness. He began suddenly to hate this gross, tawdry reminder of his past. She would not change now. It was too late. She would change no more than old Vermaeren at the Hotel des Indes, or himself. She could no more change than the skeleton of the *Artemis* could turn itself once more into a living ship. You could not go back. He wanted her to go.

"I don't ask to meet her," she was saying. "But I should like to see her," she laughed, "from a safe distance. Are you bringing her ashore?"

"Not here." He had meant to stay here. He had meant to take her ashore, but now he could not stay. He could not escape soon enough. If only Mason and the crew would return he could leave at once. If only this awful woman would go and leave him in peace instead of sitting there, gross and dreadful, a mockery of himself and all his life and ambitions. His nerves cried out, but he betrayed himself only by the tenseness of the lean fingers. If only she would stop looking at him in that prying way, seeing inside him all the disgust and despair and yearning which he was determined to conceal. It was the damned native in her which gave her that power. As she grew older the Malay blood claimed her.

With a great effort he gathered control of himself, "Don't stay, Tina. Go back to the settlement."

She smiled, "Across this river?" And he knew she was mocking him again. He did not answer her. He wished the river would swallow her up. "I don't mind going. I'm not afraid," she added, speaking slowly. "I'm not afraid of anything. I'm satisfied. I've seen you again."

And as she rose he heard another voice, clear, fresh and cool, calling, "Jim, Jim, where are you?" and was aware that the worst thing of all had happened. Jenny had wakened and was coming to look after him, as if he were a child and she the nurse.

Tina looked at him sharply and he did not address her. He answered the other woman, his wife, "I'm here. It's all right. You can go back to bed."

But it was too late. Tina was determined to see the other woman. She had lifted the netting and Jenny was moving toward her. The wife wore a night dress of pale crepe de Chine, embroidered and lacy with red Morocco slippers and a lacy little jacket. She looked pretty and young—so much younger than himself or Tina. The two women, it seemed to him, could not have been more different. For an instant it seemed to him that as they stood facing each other, they were symbols of his two lives and he knew that in the end he belonged to the gross adventurous one, fearless and defiant like a man, to whom all life, even to the end as a fat old woman in Penang, was an adventure. He had always belonged to her since that first night so long ago in the bar of the Hotel des Indes.

With a great effort he said, "This is my wife," and to Jenny he said, "This is Miss de Jongh, an old friend. She heard I was here and came out to see me."

The two women bowed and the wife, if she suspected anything, behaved perfectly. She always behaved perfectly, damn her. She was always civilized and well-bred. He thought now that her perfection would drive him mad. Suddenly it was the other woman, gross and horrible, whom he wanted to stay on the schooner. He heard his wife inviting Tina to stay the night.

"No," said Tina, "your husband thinks I should leave."

The wife protested but Tina said, "No, I must return. There are good reasons." And again she nodded toward the shore and the Portuguese governor. He said nothing but stood dumbly, watching a comedy which he felt was vile and disgusting.

The insects buzzed and the damp heat was like a blanket. Bendham thought, "I hate them both. I can bear it no longer."

Then he saw Tina lifting her flabby bulk, with extraordinary expertness, over the rail to the ladder. He moved to the rail and found that his wife, the soft, white pretty wife he hated, was there before him. Tina slipped from the ladder to the frail, bobbing craft with a wonderful dexterity. He could see her white figure dimly in the light from the ship's lantern.

"You must come again," his wife was saying.

"I think not," said Tina. The little craft bobbed off on the churning river. A solitary monkey screamed on the distant shore, and again the thought occurred to Bendham that these two women were symbols of his two lives. The one was gone now, moving across the river toward the settlement, slipping always farther and farther from him, never to return. The other, beside him, was there forever, until he died. He could never escape. And for the last time he heard Albertine de Jongh's golden voice. She called out, "Good night," and disappeared.

He felt a sudden mad impulse to push his wife into the swollen river. It was so easy. His head buzzed and he heard her saying, "Jim. What are you doing? For God's sake what's the matter?" and the sound of her voice restored his sense of reason. He was holding her by both arms with the grip of a vise. He released her suddenly and put his hands over his eyes.

"Jim, my poor Jim. Come to bed. What you need is sleep. You haven't slept for days."

She began to stroke his head gently but he stepped away from her, aware that he hated her with an unbearable intensity. The touch of her white, pretty hands filled him with loathing.

"Go away," he said dully. "Go away."

She tried to persuade him but he shook her off with such savagery that she withdrew to a little distance and stood looking at him.

"Do you hear me?" he cried bitterly. "Go below for God's sake and your own. Get out of my sight. I want to be alone."

Silently she disappeared down the companionway and as he turned he saw that the bobbing light had reached the shore. The dogs began to bark again distantly. The light disappeared and he was alone. There were only the insects, millions of them, buzzing and roaring all about him. He could not breathe.

5

In the morning when Mason and the crew returned they found Mrs. Bendham on the deck with the Malay. She was hysterical and fainted when they told her that Bendham had not come ashore at the settlement. There was no trace of him on the schooner. The body was never found.

The European newspapers printed biographies of James Bendham and long eulogies of his career, relating how he had gone to the East as a boy to build up the great rubber plantations which now supplied half the world with rubber. It was, they pointed out, a romantic career ranging from a boy's adventurous poverty to the fabulous wealth and success of a great capitalist. He had vanished from his schooner-yacht a few weeks before he was destined to receive a peerage.

But none of the eulogies concerned themselves with the soul of Bendham.

In the settlement among the natives a strange rumor came into existence. They said that Madame de Jongh, the governor's woman who had disappeared, was a witch and that she had gone out in the middle of the night to destroy the great Tuan Bendham on his own ship. Among themselves they said that he had done her a great wrong twelve years earlier and that she had avenged herself.

And in the bar of the Hotel des Indes, Albertine de Jongh, who was on her way to Penang to grow old and die, sat on a high stool and conversed in her golden voice about old times with old Vermaeren, the proprietor, who had grown even fatter and balder than when she had last seen him.

"He was not made for that life," she said. "He was not meant to grow old. He belonged to me always. He could not bear to lose that which never returns."

VIII

Better Than Life

BECAUSE they rarely had boarders who had to be in an office at eight-thirty or nine o'clock, Mrs. Lefferty and Maggie did not rise until nearly eight. It was Maggie who got up first to be downstairs and start the fire in the kitchen because she was the cook. A little later Mrs. Lefferty rose, put on a black dress (she had worn nothing but black ever since Mr. Lefferty died twelve years before and very little else before that event), joined Maggie and had a cup of strong coffee at the kitchen table. Then by eight-thirty or a quarter to nine the boarders began to appear in the dining room —old Mr. Van Diver, Miss Flint, Mr. Boldini and Mr. Salmon who were always with them, and occasionally a transient or two. Mrs. Lefferty sat at the head of the table, poured the coffee, dished out the oatmeal and the eggs and led the conversation. Luckily, she always wakened in high spirits, for Miss Flint nearly always had a headache in the mornings, Mr. Boldini suffered from chronic biliousness and Mr. Salmon in the early morning always seemed to be in a kind of haze, confused and poetic and a little sullen. Only Mr. Van Diver was bright and gay because he was so old that he slept very little and so his day had already begun hours before the others were out of their beds. As a rule he wakened and was washed and dressed and reading a motion picture magazine a little after daybreak, so that by the time breakfast was ready he was already in full possession of all his faculties save his memory.

After breakfast Mrs. Lefferty cleared the table, put the dishes on the dumb-waiter and whisked them down to Maggie. Then if it was her turn, she put on her hat and coat and went out to do the marketing, and if it happened to be Maggie's turn, she at once set about cleaning the house and doing up the rooms. While she did Mr. Boldini's room, he took his poodle for an airing. A little while later Mr. Salmon went out, he said, to visit editors and publishers, and with relief she threw open his windows (which he always kept closed at night) and made up his bed. She sometimes argued with him about the windows, telling him that it was lack of air which gave him such a pallor, but nothing could persuade Mr. Salmon. As a young man he had had a pallor and as he passed middle age and threatened to become stout and ruddy in a Jewish way, he fought to keep his youthful pallor because it was an impressive part of the picture he had made of himself long ago.

Old Mr. Van Diver never left the house until nightfall, so while she did up his room, he took a motion picture magazine and went downstairs to sit in the parlor among poor Miss Minnie's Victorian furniture. Miss Flint always did her own room. If there were transients Mrs. Lefferty did their rooms last with very little interest because they rarely stayed long enough for her to feel that they had become a part of her life. Either they had come to her boardinghouse because they wanted to hide or because they were a little broke, and as soon as the reasons were removed they disappeared.

The four star boarders—Miss Flint, Mr. Van Diver, Mr. Boldini and Mr. Salmon—had been there for so long that their lives and hers seemed to have become entangled and grown together beyond separation. Mrs. Lefferty and Maggie were both affectionate, easy-going and creatures of habit, all of which was a handicap in keepers of boardinghouses. The transients nearly always seemed to them violent creatures blown in by the wind from the strange hard outside world, to be blown out again after a week or two, always mysterious and remote and cantankerous, never fitting the leisurely old-fashioned tempo of the establishment. None of that inner circle of boarders, the permanents, at Mrs. Lefferty's ever seemed to be in a hurry like the people one met outside the house, rushing for the bus or the subway or the elevated, dashing about in taxis and motors. In the middle of Manhattan Island, Mrs. Lefferty's boardinghouse was an island where time seemed to have stood still. Mrs. Lefferty would never have taken transients save that the income from them gave her and Maggie a tiny margin that permitted them to keep the place going for Miss Flint, Mr. Boldini and the rest.

A little before noon Mrs. Lefferty went down to the kitchen and helped Maggie finish the preparations for lunch. Then she went upstairs again and sounded the bronze Chinese gong in the lower hall, just as she had done when poor Miss Minnie was still alive, every day in her life since she was twenty-three years old. At lunch everyone was, as a rule, cheerful, and after lunch they all had coffee in the parlor. That was where Miss Minnie had always had it and Mrs. Lefferty continued the custom because it was elegant and also because it made old Mr. Van Diver feel at home, as if nothing had changed. She felt sorry for him because his mind was failing and at times he didn't seem to realize that he was old and poverty-stricken and living in a boardinghouse, and Miss Flint knew that having coffee in the parlor was the proper thing to do because they had always had coffee in the parlor in all the fine houses where once, long ago, she had gone to sew.

[551]

When coffee was finished Mrs. Lefferty went downstairs to help Maggie with the dishes and then dressed and went out to the pictures. Now and then, rarely, Maggie went with her but usually Maggie preferred to take a nap or soak the feet she had been standing on for eighteen hours a day for thirty-one years. About six Mrs. Lefferty came in again, climbed the stairs and wakened Maggie who was a great sleeper and but for alarm clocks and Mrs. Lefferty would have slept, as Mrs. Lefferty said, "until the trump of doom." Together they got ready the evening meal and after supper Mrs. Lefferty left Miss Flint to serve the coffee in the parlor while she descended to the kitchen to have her own coffee off a shelf while she helped Maggie with the dishes. This she did in order to gain time so that she might get upstairs to the rummy game a little earlier. When the dishes were finished she put out the cat and Maggie turned out the lights and they went upstairs to find Miss Flint, Mr. Boldini and Mr. Salmon already gathered impatiently about the card table with old Mr. Van Diver dozing or reading a movie magazine in poor Miss Minnie's plush armchair by the fire.

There were no stakes in the rummy game because none of them could afford to play for money, but they kept a running score of the games, month after month, year after year, and played with passion. Mrs. Lefferty, who was full of tricks and played every night, had eighteen hundred and thirty-four games; Miss Flint, who was less successful because there were times when she seemed foggy and unable to give her full attention, had fourteen hundred and three. Mr. Boldini, who was handicapped by having to be absent when he had a professional engagement, had twelve hundred and forty-five, and Mr. Salmon, who was frequently called away by his muse, had eleven hundred and sixty-three. Because Mr. Boldini and Mr. Salmon were unable to play every night, they were each allowed the value of one and a half games for every game they won. As Mr. Salmon grew older his muse called him less and less frequently and he had been able to catch up a little on the general score.

About midnight Mrs. Lefferty brought up a cold snack from the kitchen and then they all went to bed.

Every day with Mrs. Lefferty was exactly the same except Sundays when sometimes she went to Mass, and on the first and the fifteenth of each month when she and Maggie took an evening off to go over their hopelessly muddled accounts in an effort to discover whether they were making or losing money, something which they never did discover until the insurance came due or the taxes had to be paid. Always after these evenings spent over the accounts, the meals became noticeably slimmer and the cuts of meat a little poorer. This would last for three or four days and then the generous, carefree spirits of Mrs. Lefferty and Maggie would defeat their sense of impending doom, and the food would become excellent again and plentiful until the next day of reckoning.

The truth was that Mrs. Lefferty was an incurable romantic, and that the reckless temperament of her partner, Maggie, did not help. If she had not begun life as a kitchen maid too early to have learned in school much more than the merest elements of reading, writing and arithmetic, she might have been a writer instead of keeping a boardinghouse in the sixties too near the elevated. She would have had a great popular success, for in all her romances, in all the stories she was always making up about her boarders and the people she met while marketing, the ending was always perfectly happy or so sad that it wrung the heart and so was almost more satisfactory than if it had been happy.

Mrs. Lefferty's imaginings had very little to do with what was known as "life"; there was, even in the blackest moments of her "stories," no evil or bitterness but at worst only the rather mechanical plottings of the "villain"; there was never any misery, nor any irony nor any real malice. Mrs. Lefferty never even made people into villains unless it was necessary to the story; and even then in her heart she knew all the time that they were not really villains but only made up that way like actors on the stage. She knew from her reading of the picture magazines that all the vamps and villains were in private life good, kindly, respectable people who either had large families or adopted large ones, and spent their evenings at home knitting or reading books of philosophy. Being just able to read, her awe of the printed word was so great that she believed whatever she saw in print.

That was the way she felt about people in real life—they were never really bad. When they seemed to be bad they were only playing parts; and watching them playing parts gave Mrs. Lefferty a deep satisfaction, even when she herself suffered from their evil actions. Thus twice she and Maggie had lost all their small savings because she became fascinated by gentlemen who came to see her and discuss investments. Thus life was always interesting to Mrs. Lefferty, whether she was cleaning the rooms or shopping on Third Avenue or helping Maggie in the kitchen, and there were moments when she grew a little confused in the head, not knowing where what went on about her in the boardinghouse ended and where what went on while she was in the picture house across the street began.

Aside from the fact that optimism was a part of her romantic nature, Mrs. Lefferty remained incurable because somehow, in some mysterious fashion her romantic imaginings were always coming true. She knew in her heart that the two gentlemen who had swindled her had not gone out of her life forever but would one day return bringing all her money and a lot of profit besides. She was certain that some day luck would turn for Miss

Flint and that once again Mr. Boldini would be "the sensation of three continents," that Mr. Salmon would be a famous writer, and that Maggie's daughter Sarah Jane would settle down and "get a break" and cease to be a burden and a worry. Mr. Van Diver was much too old to have any ending but the inevitable one and Mrs. Lefferty, taking care of him, was planning as happy an ending as possible.

Only in the case of her son Tommy did she ever have any doubts and those only came to her at times in the middle of the night when she lay awake unable to sleep, and kept seeing Tom as a little boy playing in the back garden of poor Miss Minnie's house on Murray Hill with Maggie's Sarah Jane. Watching them long ago when poor Mr. Lefferty and Maggie's husband Mr. Ryan were still alive, she had imagined all sorts of wonderful stories about them both. But Sarah Jane hadn't turned out so well and it was more than five years since she had heard anything at all from Tommy.

To ease her heartache she told herself that it was really not Tom's fault that he had neglected and forgotten her but because poor Miss Minnie had paid for his music lessons and sent him to college. Mrs. Lefferty still had old world ideas and she was not at all certain of the virtues of democracy. It did no good, she felt, to educate people above their stations in life. It only made them feel restless and insecure. Being ambitious, Mrs. Lefferty knew wisely, did not make you happier. Even if you gained your ambitions, it didn't make you any happier because you only wanted more. The important thing in life, Mrs. Lefferty believed, was not to make a great deal of money nor to win a great deal of glory but to have a good time and help others to have a good time. After all, that was the only important thing when you got to be old and the only thing you could take into the grave with you. If people had always to be wanting things in order to be happy, then there was a curse on them.

That was the trouble with Tommy. He would have made an excellent butler like his father, with his good looks and his gentlemanly air, but education had put ideas into his head and unsettled him. It was really his father's fault. Because he was an Ulsterman, he had been ambitious and wanted a better life for his son; if he had been south of Ireland like herself and Maggie he would have known better. It was Mr. Lefferty who let poor Miss Minnie educate Tom and teach him to play the piano.

And it was American ideas and those dancing lessons that poor Miss Minnie had given Sarah Jane which had sent her off into the chorus with ideas about becoming a famous actress, instead of being content with being a good typist and coming home regularly with her money. Sarah Jane was always coming and going, returning to live with her mother and Mrs. Lefferty when she was out of a job and dead broke. Choruses, Mrs. Lefferty observed, seemed to work in a spasmodic fashion for two or three months at a time with long gaps in between, and Sarah Jane never seemed to get one of those "breaks" Mrs. Lefferty was always reading about in the picture magazines. Just the same she knew that Maggie was lucky to have her come home at all, instead of never seeing her the way she never saw Tommy, not knowing what had become of him or whether he was alive or dead. She had his picture and his baby shoes and sometimes in the night when she could not sleep she got them out and looked at them and the baby shoes always made her see him crawling about the floors of the servants' sitting room in poor Miss Minnie's "big house" or climbing the dark back stairs which always infuriated his father who might at any moment descend the stairs with a tray full of things. Those were happy days! Because Mrs. Lefferty was a romantic she forgot whatever was unpleasant and so she remembered nothing at all about the endless stairs of poor Miss Minnie's "big house" and the carrying of coal and hot water and the tantrums of "the old gentleman," Miss Minnie's father, and the fact that the house had been overlarge and understaffed. Sometimes a horrible suspicion came to her that Tommy had disappeared because he was ashamed that his mother had been a housemaid and now kept a boardinghouse. Once long ago in the Grand Central Station she had seen him talking to another boy about his own age, a nice boy dressed like a gentleman, but Tommy seemed not to see her. She was never sure whether he had seen her or not and she had never had the courage to ask him and now, perhaps, it was too late and she would never know.

It was only at night that she thought much about Tommy because in the daytime she was too busy, what with Maggie and herself seeing to the whole house and the buying to do, which meant listening to the troubles of all the friends she had made at the grocer's and the butcher's and the chain stores. She had a great many friends for she had no shyness. If she liked a person's looks she had a friendly "good morning" and something about the spinach or the chops or the weather. Sometimes people were standoffish and sometimes they were not, but very few held out for long against her faint Cork brogue and her grin which seemed to say, "Well, the world is a fine place, and it's a fine morning for sure and Myers hasn't any right to charge that much a pound for rumpsteak." And so she knew almost everybody—the young housewives who needed advice about cuts and such things, the tired, shabby, respectable, middle-aged women with husbands out of work trying to keep up their respectability and dignity with only twenty-five cents to spend, and even the one or two cooks from the "big houses." There weren't many "big houses" because the neighborhood was run-down and shabby-re-spectable, not a grand neighborhood like Murray Hill in the days of poor Miss Minnie and "the old gentleman," where there were only big houses and fine carriages and coachmen.

[555]

2

Miss Minnie had been dead for ten years but she still lived so far as Mrs. Lefferty and Maggie were concerned. They had both gone to the funeral in Long Island, wrapped in yards of hired crepe, and seen her with their own eyes laid away in the earth of the old cemetery alongside "the old gentleman" and her mother, among the other Randolphs, the last Randolph who would ever be buried there because Miss Minerva Randolph was the last of them. There weren't many people there—just the clergyman and old Mr. Van Diver and two or three elderly respectable friends of Miss Minerva. By the time she died she hadn't many friends left because she was not only the last of her family, but almost the last of a generation and of a whole society which had lived quietly and well and had very nearly disappeared. And when Maggie and Mrs. Lefferty came back to the empty house they wept and keened not only because poor Miss Minnie was gone but because without her, the world itself seemed to have come to an end.

Poor Miss Minnie had been their mistress, their charge, the figure about which their whole world revolved since they had come from Ireland long ago. They had seen her grow from a thin, delicate, middle-aged spinster into an old lady, waiting upon her, worrying about her health, fetching her cushions and delicacies, never once seeing that they too had changed, from young apple-cheeked girls into women past middle age. They had both come home to Miss Minnie's house from their weddings, in the old days when it was a grand house on Murray Hill, Mrs. Lefferty married to Miss Minnie's butler and Maggie to Mr. Ryan, the coachman. In her house Maggie's Sarah Jane and Mrs. Lefferty's Tommy had been born. In her house Mr. Lefferty had died of pneumonia contracted when he rose on one winter night and went downstairs in his nightshirt to help Miss Minnie calm "the old gentleman" who was in one of his tantrums. To Miss Minnie's house Mr. Ryan had been brought home to die after his horses shied at "one of those new horseless carriages" and threw him out on his head in Central Park. To Mrs. Lefferty and Maggie, sitting in their crepe in the servants' sitting room of the house near the elevated where Miss Minnie had come when "the old gentleman" died, the world had come to an end. Not only had they lost poor Miss Minnie but there would no longer be a house with fine walnut furniture and the remnants of beautiful china, and a beautiful linen closet, but Mrs. Lefferty and Maggie would have to find new places and perhaps be separated and Sarah Jane and Tom could no longer live at home.

And then the day after the funeral Miss Minnie's lawyer, old Mr. Prendergast, came to the house and called Mrs. Lefferty and Maggie into the long tunnel of a drawing room and told them that Miss Minerva had left the house to the two of them with everything in it and all the money she had left from the great fortune founded by her grandfather which, if everything went well, would be about enough to pay the taxes and insurance. Mr. Prendergast advised them to sell the house and its contents and invest the money, but neither Mrs. Lefferty nor Maggie could bring herself to do such a thing. Sell all that furniture they had always lived with? It would be like being evicted. Anyway neither of them wanted to retire. They could not imagine what retirement would be like. What could they do with themselves?

Mr. Prendergast painted a bright picture of the joys of living on one's income, but neither Mrs. Lefferty nor Maggie was moved. They would not have been moved if the prospective incomes had been ten times greater than the figures which Mr. Prendergast made on a bit of paper showed they would be.

Ten years afterward Mrs. Lefferty and Maggie still spoke of Miss Minerva as if she were still alive, calling her "poor Miss Minnie" or simply "she," discussing what she would have liked and what she would have thought and said and done. There was wisdom in their calling her "poor Miss Minnie." They had always felt sorry for her, from the beginning when they had come into the house fresh from Ireland, for the emptiness of her life and the tyranny of "the old gentleman." She may have had money and been beyond the need of working with her hands, but in their hearts Mrs. Lefferty and Maggie knew this was nothing, because she had never known what it was like to have the love of a fine upstanding man like Mr. Lefferty or a big good-natured fellow like Mr. Ryan, and she had never had any children and never any fun.

Miss Minnie, they were vaguely aware, had been a relic of a New York that was gone forever, a New York which had already begun to wither and fade when they stepped off the boat long ago at Castle Garden. Miss Minnie had lived gently and discreetly and well while the world into which she was born withered all about her, until at last "the old gentleman" died and she had no longer to take care of him and put up with his tyrannies and pretend to him that they were still as rich as ever. When Mr. Ryan was killed Miss Minnie gave up the horses and when Mr. Lefferty died she did not take on another butler, and put off "the old gentleman's" rages over the indignity of having no manservant in the house by explaining that she could not find a man as satisfactory as Lefferty; and all the time she knew that they were living no longer off income but off capital. But being a timid soul she was unwilling and afraid to let her father know they were no longer rich and no longer of very much importance. In the big house on Murray Hill, Maggie, belowstairs, and Mrs. Lefferty, above, went on doing all the work, and when "the old gentleman" died, Miss Minnie quickly sold the big house on Murray Hill and bought the nondescript brownstone front in the sixties near the elevated, where she lived until she died.

It was an ordinary four-story brownstone house like a score of others in the same street, with a high stoop and a tunnel-like parlor. At that time it still stood within the limits of gentility. One house farther east would have been too near the tenements and one farther west would have been too expensive for the money Miss Minnie had left out of the ruin. As it was, she managed to get along; nothing would have induced her to suffer the indignities of an apartment house or a hotel. She couldn't, she said, feel comfortable and genteel living in the same building with a hundred other people whom she had never even met.

She was a little, dry, withered old lady. As often as she could afford it, she had friends to tea or to dinner, always the same friends because there were not more than a half dozen who remained out of the world in which she had spent her youth and middle age. They were old ladies and gentlemen as gentle and dry and withered as herself, timid and a little frightened of automobiles and subways and skyscrapers. One by one they died until there remained only old Miss Tilton who long ago had sat next to her at Miss Waterbury's School for Young Ladies in Washington Square and old Mr. Van Diver who had been courting her for forty years. After she came down in the world to the brownstone house, she never bought any more new clothes but wore out the dozens of old dresses that filled the closets, strange, fussy garments of heavy, durable purple or black satin and grosgrain. She gradually became deaf, not so deaf that conversation was difficult, but only so deaf that she could not hear the sordid noise of the elevated trains passing a couple of hundred feet from her door.

She never said anything about it, but Maggie's Sarah Jane and Mrs. Lefferty's Tommy went on living in the new house. It would not have been genteel to say anything, even if she had not in her heart felt that they were like her own grandchildren, denied to her by her long devotion to her father and to virtues which no one any longer regarded. An extraordinary love existed between Miss Minnie and Maggie and Mrs. Lefferty. None of them ever spoke of it. Miss Minnie knew that it would not have been genteel, and Maggie and Mrs. Lefferty would never have dreamed of giving any sign that they were aware of it. But they all knew that it existed. It existed because the three of them, so different in character and circumstances—Miss Minnie with her desiccated correctness, Maggie with her terrible temper and Mrs. Lefferty with her good-natured romanticism—were simple and good.

When Maggie and Mrs. Lefferty were left the house, there seemed only one thing to do in order to keep it going and that was to open a boardinghouse. It was all there, ready and waiting, furniture and all, in a good location save that it was a little too near the elevated. And they knew, because they had known poor Miss Minnie for so long, that the plan would have pleased her. They talked it all out in terms of what poor Miss Minnie would have thought and said and done. It was Maggie's opinion that poor Miss Minnie had left them the house, hoping that they would go on living there.

So Mrs. Lefferty, because of her appearance and because she had been a housemaid all her life, was obviously the choice as nominal proprietress. She was plump and pleasant with humorous eyes and a kindly manner, so kindly that she sometimes failed in one aspect of her duties; she would have been swindled again and again but for Maggie's peasant shrewdness. Mrs. Lefferty's romantic imagination made her want to believe the stories her boarders told her partly because their tales of pending inheritance and vast checks gone astray and huge projects with success just around the corner, were always so much more exciting than the simple truth that they were broke and that there was no prospect of ever paying her.

Sometimes as in the case of Miss Flint, the seamstress, and the Great Boldini, weeks passed without any payment being made, but Mrs. Lefferty and Maggie knew that when they had money they would pay, and besides they were almost members of the family; at least they were members of the club. Old Mr. Van Diver had only thirty dollars a month when he first came to them and when stocks began to go bad, this was cut to twenty dollars. He paid Maggie and Mrs. Lefferty everything he received, simply turning over to them the endorsed checks. He did not smoke, and like poor Miss Minnie, he had enough clothes left from his prosperous days to last him until he died. The sum he paid them scarcely covered the cost of his food, but they could not turn him out. For forty years he had been devoted to poor Miss Minnie. For thirty years he had called three times a week and come to supper every Sunday evening. For thirty years he and poor Miss Minnie had waited for "the old gentleman" to die or give his permission for them to marry, and when at last he died it was too late and the habit of courtship had become fixed and agreeable. Not only were they too old, they were too poor to marry. And so one day about three years after Miss Minnie died, old Mr. Van Diver came to the door and asked Mrs. Lefferty to take him as a lodger. Trembling and shy, he told her that if she did not take him he would have to go to a charitable institution. He told her exactly how much money he had. So while he sat in the familiar parlor, Mrs. Lefferty went belowstairs to consult Maggie. Her own mind was made up, but she was afraid of Maggie who sometimes lost her Irish temper and told Mrs. Lefferty that before long they would be paying boarders to stay with them.

Belowstairs, Maggie was busy with the supper. She was a squat little woman, very fat and built rather like a hippopotamus. For thirty-seven of her fifty years she had lived between the basement and the top floor. For thirty years she had been constantly on her feet and so she waddled a little as she walked. She wore her gray hair yanked back from her plain face and twisted into a tight screw on the top of her head. Worn in that fashion it took simply a jerk and a twist to do it in the morning and it never came down, and the danger of hairs in the soup was practically nonexistent. Her face and her nature alike would have been hard save for her sense of the comic and the twinkle in her blue eyes which betrayed her. Without it she might have been a murderess, not one who employed slow poison, but one who used a meat cleaver. Mrs. Lefferty knew that in the old days, when Mr. Ryan the coachman, came home drunk, Maggie gave him a beating, big as he was, which kept him in order for weeks afterward. She was a black Catholic and a Fenian. She would, as she bluntly said, have gone to the grave a virgin like poor Miss Minnie, before she would have married an Orangeman like Mr. Lefferty. Sometimes Mrs. Lefferty, corrupted by the Ulsterman husband, long since dead, missed Mass and confession, but Maggie had missed neither the one nor the other since the day she was confirmed.

So when Mrs. Lefferty proposed Mr. Van Diver as a boarder at thirty dollars a month Maggie, oddly enough, did not fly into a temper. She only said, "We'll have to do it, I guess. Poor Miss Minnie, God rest her soul, would like to know that he's well taken care of." Both of them referred to their late mistress as "Poor Miss Minnie, God rest her soul" so that for a long time after the Great Boldini, who never learned English very well, came to the boardinghouse, he had an idea that *"Godresthersoul"* was Miss Minnie's last name.

So they took in Mr. Van Diver and his few belongings—some books, a few worn suits of clothes, a gold-headed stick and a photograph of Miss Minnie taken during her twenties in which she wore a dress with a bustle in a gentle storm of artificial snow. From the beginning the old gentleman was happy. He never went out save after nightfall because his clothes were shabby and he lived in gentle terror of a world which moved too rapidly and too noisily for him. He was very clean and gentle and retiring and as Mrs. Lefferty said, "He gave class to the house."

Mrs. Lefferty gave him all her motion picture magazines to read, and because he was so old that he did not remember what he read, they were always new to him and he read them over and over again until at last they fell apart and were used by Maggie to start the kitchen fire in the morning. In all his life he had never been inside a moving picture theater, but, at eighty, virtually his only reading was stories about the stars and their lives. It opened a whole new world to him in which everyone seemed to rise from poverty to riches with amazing rapidity, a world in which existed none of the baser motives and weakness of life, where everyone was happy and pure and rejoiced only in doing good for others. He had not seen many beautiful women in his life and no naked ones whatever and the pages of Mrs. Lefferty's magazines seemed filled with little else; he regarded the pictures with a certain gentle wistfulness, and regret that he had been a young man in the days when bathing beauties wore costumes with ankle-length skirts, high collars and long sleeves. He and Mrs. Lefferty talked a great deal together about the picture stars and presently he began to use the phrases he read in the magazines as freely as Mrs. Lefferty herself. It gave them pleasure that Myrna Loy "had got a break" at last and for days the two of them were troubled after reading an article entitled, "Is Baby Le Roy Through?"

The magazines stood in a huge pile in the corner of his room, mounting higher and higher each month until at last the worn ones were carted off by Maggie, a whole compendium of extravagant romance, beauty and excitement, out of a world which to Mr. Van Diver in his childishness was as wonderful as the Arabian Nights.

At last Mrs. Lefferty took him for the first time to see a picture with Miss Ileana Dangerfield, whom he thought the most beautiful of all, in "Love or Die." But he found that the pictures hurt his eyes and gave him a headache and that Miss Dangerfield, seen from all angles and portraying all emotions, was rather like a great many of the girls he passed on the street during his excursions after nightfall, and not nearly so beautiful as in the carefully posed photograph at the edge of her swimming pool just outside the *galleria* of her lovely house in Hot Water Canyon. So he never went again and gradually he forgot the shock of reality and slipped back again into the lovely hazy world of the magazines.

As he grew older and his mind a little more confused there were moments when, living in poor Miss Minnie's house, surrounded by the furniture and the pictures and the carpets he had known for forty years, he forgot that she had been dead for a long time, and now and then when he found himself alone with Mrs. Lefferty in the parlor, he would look up and ask gently just as he had done in the old days, if Miss Minnie would be down soon, and Mrs. Lefferty would always reply in a friendly way, "You know where poor Miss Minnie is, Mr. Van Diver," as if she were not in her grave but had just gone round the corner on an errand.

Mr. Van Diver, like poor Miss Minnie, belonged to a world that had vanished and Mrs. Lefferty and Maggie belonged to one that was rapidly vanishing. There weren't any more Irish servants like themselves, belonging for their lifetimes to one family—witty, sloppy, slap-dash, good-humored and devoted. Even boardinghouses like theirs with sober respectable pasts, where the lodgers all sat down at one table like a large family and knew each other's failures, disappointments, vanities and weaknesses and which piece of chicken each one preferred, were rapidly going the way of poor Miss Minnie

[561]

and Mr. Van Diver. Nowadays, Mrs. Lefferty knew, people who had no homes lived in vast mechanical structures divided into cubicles, with the sexes segregated as often as not, where the food appeared mysteriously out of the walls into which the laundry in turn disappeared to come back mysteriously fresh and clean in a few days. Maggie and Mrs. Lefferty and their boardinghouse were swiftly becoming as odd and incongruous in the New York of the thirties as the horseless carriage which frightened Mr. Ryan's horse and killed him, had been in the New York of the nineties.

And so slowly they had come to be a shelter and a refuge for those who in the march of time had lagged behind and found in turkey-red carpets and high ceilings, pullman drawing rooms and old-fashioned chandeliers, a refuge and a solace which they could not find in hotels and furnished flats.

That was why Miss Flint had come to them and why after nine years was still with them. All her life she had been a "sewing woman" who went out by the day to make the dresses of whole families in the days when the rows of brownstone houses lay monotonous and respectable in a gigantic gridiron across the whole of Manhattan north of Thirty-fourth Street. But slowly everything had changed for Miss Flint. People no longer had in "the sewing woman" spring and fall to stay day after day and sometimes overnight, gossiping, wielding her scissors, her mouth full of pins. Something had happened which Miss Flint, a little puzzled and hurt, could never quite understand. People didn't seem to have big families any longer and if there were children, their parents seemed to buy their clothes, as Miss Flint said scornfully, "ready-made." She still had one or two clients, ladies like herself who were no longer young and could not abide buying things off the racks. Twice a year she visited them to "go over" their dresses, but most of the time she stayed in her room at Mrs. Lefferty's working in melancholy solitude on the crocheted bags she sold occasionally at the Women's Exchange.

It was not only that she was left miserably poor by the decline of her fortunes; it was much more than that, for in the old days she had led a kind of exciting vicarious existence in which she knew everything about family life and almost everything about matrimony, going to houses where there were big families, knowing their griefs and pleasures, their joys and their disappointments, hearing fresh bits of gossip, and bringing gossip with her from house to house along with her scissors and pins. Then she had been a person of importance. There were even families who had looked forward to her coming. Now no one looked forward to seeing her. Nobody knew that she existed, or cared whether she lived or died. Mrs. Lefferty and Mrs. Ryan were kind to her and Mrs. Lefferty sometimes took her to the pictures, but after all, as Miss Flint, who was a snob, knew, they were only a pair of Irish servants who had set up a boardinghouse and were not genteel like the people she had worked for in the old days. She had never taken her meals with the servants. Either she had eaten alone in the sewing room or at the table with the family.

Miss Flint dyed her hair now in order to make herself look more "youthful," not discreetly, but a strange, flaming red, which resembled the color of no hair on land or sea. She did it herself in the bathroom and because she was unfamiliar with the art of hairdressing and too nearsighted to read the directions correctly, she may have been guilty of some error in the use of the dye. In any case the unnaturalness of the shade did not seem to trouble her; rather she flaunted it as if she thought it becoming to her tired, raddled face. There were times when the sight of poor respectable Miss Flint coming down the steps of the boardinghouse on her way to the Women's Exchange with a crocheted bag, was almost too much to be borne by Maggie who said, "Sure and she gets herself up like a madame."

She did her own room and mended the sheets and pillow cases and napkins as a contribution toward the board and lodging with which she had never been able to catch up during the nine years she had lived with them. She spent no money except on whisky which she used "medicinally," and always wakened in the morning with a bad headache. Lately she had returned home from the Women's Exchange again and again with the story that she had been "followed"; twice the man dared to come almost to the door itself. When she recounted these stories Mrs. Lefferty and Maggie listened sympathetically, pretending that they believed them, but after she had gone upstairs Maggie said one night, "Sure and she's lucky to have only one man following her. It's a wonder there ain't a whole crowd the way she gets herself up."

And there was Mr. Boldini whom Mrs. Lefferty and Maggie sometimes called with a kind of pride, "The Great Boldini." He was not much better pay than Miss Flint or Mr. Van Diver but they were attached to him because long ago he had been their first boarder. In those prosperous days he had been in and out a good deal, now staying for a week, now away on tour for four or five weeks at a time. Occasionally when he was what he called "at liberty," he was with them for as long as three months at a time, but as the years passed, the engagements grew steadily fewer and fewer until at last he seemed to be "at liberty" most of the time and became a "permanent."

He was a tall man of about sixty who looked rather like a bloodhound, with large hypnotic Mussolini eyes, a sallow skin, and hair which he wore very long and, like Miss Flint, dyed to give himself a youthful appearance. His clothes, like those of Mr. Van Diver, showed signs of once, a long time ago, having cost a great deal of money. It was the Great Boldini who, as the Original Boarder, occupied what had once been poor Miss Minnie's sitting room at the front of the house overlooking the picture theater so much frequented by Mrs. Lefferty; but the room no longer bore, save in shape, the slightest resemblance to the room where Miss Minnie spent the last years of her life. The closets which once contained her starched and whale-boned clothing were now filled with costumes—Spanish, Turkish, Indian and Chinese together with a great many which were created in a moment of fantasy by some creator as Roman. Once bright and gay, they were faded now and their gold and silver braid and embroidery was tarnished beyond repair; but the Great Boldini clung to them, keeping them wrapped carefully in newspapers and sprinkled with camphor.

The shelves on which Miss Minnie's hats once stood were burdened with turbans, berets, Roman helmets and headdresses with plumes, carefully put away against the day when Mr. Boldini would stage his great "comeback" and be able to pay all he owed Mrs. Lefferty and Maggie. Luckily the house was old-fashioned and the closets were enormous for Mr. Boldini had stowed away in them not only his own costumes but those of a whole troupe as well. In the past when great magicians were still held in esteem, he had believed in giving his act novelty by changing the costumes of his troupe each season; and being of an economical nature, he had always kept them as his own property.

The walls were covered with photographs of himself in all his various costumes, some framed, some merely fastened to the wall with thumbtacks. In some of them he was surrounded by his troupe of "Fourteen Performers, Fourteen Magicians, Jugglers and Acrobats." And in one corner, where they were a great nuisance to Mrs. Lefferty because they gathered dust, stood a huge pile of books filled with clippings. Once or twice Mrs. Lefferty had suggested storing them in the attic but the Great Boldini objected and she had not the heart to pursue the idea because she knew that he liked to have them at hand where he might read them over and over. They were the only reading Mr. Boldini ever did. There might be wars, floods, catastrophes, but the Great Boldini lived on in happy ignorance of them, lost in the raptures of reading the notices he had got long ago in London and New York, Berlin and Budapest, Bombay and Singapore and Shanghai. Whenever he was embarrassingly far behind with his rent he got out the books and read aloud to Mrs. Lefferty the clippings about his invitation performances before the Kaiser and the Emperor of Austria, and Mrs. Lefferty was impressed, never noticing that royalty had fallen to an estate very nearly as low as that of the Great Boldini. Nowadays his agent, hounded by Mr. Boldini, occasionally produced a three-day engagement in some picture house in the "sticks" but the bulk of his income came from pulling rabbits out of top hats at children's parties. The very families which once had engaged Miss Flint to make up their children's clothes for the year now spent their money in engaging Mr. Boldini to perform tricks.

In one corner of the room there was a large and shabby basket with a cushion in it. Here slept Fanto, Mr. Boldini's poodle. He was no longer a young dog for he had already had a career as part of his master's act in the days when vaudeville was still prosperous; but despite his rheumatism, he was as clever as he had ever been and none of his tricks had been forgotten. Sometimes he performed with Mr. Boldini at children's parties where he always experienced a greater success than his master. For Fanto Mr. Boldini charged extra. His agents announced him as "The Great Boldini. With Fanto, the World's Most Extraordinary Dog, Fifty Dollars. Without Fanto, Thirty-five Dollars." The billing was incorrect, for of the two Fanto was certainly the star and always had much the greater success. They loved each other, but like a husband and wife in "a double," professional jealousy sometimes disturbed the happiness of their relationship. On the occasions when the children, delighted by Fanto, shouted for more and more tricks from him, Mr. Boldini was always a little hurt and outdid himself to regain prestige, and Fanto, aware of his own success, barked and turned somersaults and heartlessly thrust his master into the background. When Mr. Boldini had engagements without Fanto, the poodle would sulk jealously at home, melancholy and heartbroken, or would lavish his affections on Mrs. Lefferty and scarcely notice Mr. Boldini on his return. At such times he would follow Mrs. Lefferty about the house, from room to room, while she did her work, and from her he learned all sorts of new tricks. He would fetch her scrubbing brush and dust cloth and he even learned to help her make the beds, holding the sheets gently in his dull old teeth on one side of the bed while Mrs. Lefferty drew them smooth and tight on the opposite side. He did all this joyfully with wild barkings and waggings of the tail which sometimes made Mrs. Lefferty helpless with laughter so that she had to sit down for a moment in the midst of her work.

In the beginning Mrs. Lefferty had been dubious about allowing dogs in the house. Poor Miss Minnie had always preferred cats, so until Fanto came neither Mrs. Lefferty nor Maggie knew anything about dogs. They took poor Miss Minnie's opinion that they were untidy beasts. But once Fanto was allowed inside the door he made forever secure not only his own place but that of his master as well, for although there were times, at the bimonthly reckonings, when Mrs. Lefferty and Maggie would have been willing to see Mr. Boldini leave, they could never bring themselves to see Fanto go. Once as a joke Mrs. Lefferty, working on the third floor, put Fanto into the dumb-waiter and sent him down to the kitchen where Maggie, opening it in the expectation of finding a wastepaper basket or some soiled linen, was nearly knocked down by the joyful Fanto, barking and wagging his tail. After that whenever Fanto had finished helping Mrs. Lefferty with her work, he jumped into the dumb-waiter and rode down to the kitchen where Maggie wickedly fed him all sorts of delicious tidbits outside the dull diet of vegetables, rice and dog biscuit which Mr. Boldini prescribed for his rheumatism.

Sometimes when Mr. Boldini had engagements at picture houses in places like Troy or New Haven or Atlantic City, he would be gone for a whole week and then Fanto's basket was moved up to Mrs. Lefferty's room on the fourth floor because, Fanto, left alone, would droop and grow melancholy and actually become ill. Occasionally, about three times a year, one end of poor Miss Minnie's parlor was cleared of its clutter of Victorian furniture and the Great Boldini and Fanto, with the finest of professional manners, would go through a whole performance of magic and tricks before an audience made up of old Mr. Van Diver, Miss Flint, Mr. Salmon, Mrs. Lefferty and Maggie, who always finished the evening, her eyes popping with excitement and real terror, by saying, "Sure, and it's all black magic!" And as the months and years passed it became more and more evident to Mrs. Lefferty and Maggie that no matter how far behind the Great Boldini became with his board and lodging, they would have to keep him on.

Mr. René Salmon, né Joseph Solomon, was, financially speaking, the rod and staff of the establishment. Luckily, for he was a poet, he received three hundred dollars a month quite regularly from his father who owned the extremely prosperous Boston Store in Great Falls, Indiana. Mr. Solomon, senior, a delightful old gentleman over eighty years old, had for more than thirty years found it worth three hundred dollars a month to be able to open a magazine now and then and read poems filled with sentiments, either very high-flown or completely incomprehensible, bearing the signature of René Salmon. He always kept the magazines in a pile in the corner of his office and showed them to citizens of Great Falls and the girls in the shop saying, "Who'd have thought that my Joe would ever get to be a famous poet?" He even thought it worth a few hundred dollars more from time to time to bring out Joe's poems in limited editions in bindings which he thought a little loud but accepted in his humbleness as beyond his understanding. And when Joe came back to Great Falls, which he did about once every six or seven years, he read his poetry before palpitating assemblies of middle-aged women who would have died rather than admit that they understood none of it, and before somewhat puzzled congresses of businessmen who understood only the dirtier parts. With them he had a great success during his "breast and buttock" period and fell into unpopularity with his poems written during what he called the "Freudian Influence."

Mr. Salmon, like the others at Mrs. Lefferty's, was a relic, although of a vintage somewhat later than that of Miss Flint and old Mr. Van Diver. He had begun his career a little before the turn of the century when Mouquin's was Mouquin's and poets were creatures full of light who dressed in such

[566]

a way that there could be no doubt of their calling. At that time he had come fresh from the West, a dark, slender, good-looking boy with large gazelle eyes, who attracted notice as much by his physical beauty as by his talents. He wrote poems about the High Road and Golden Girls and the Joy of Living, for at that time, long before the war, New York was a joyous place, comfortable and secure and gentle, where a joy might still be found in living, not the hysterical, frantic excitement of life which left Mr. Salmon, as a poet past middle age, bewildered, frustrated and stranded, but a gentle, rich kind of joy. Not only did he frequent Mouquin's and sit elbow to elbow with the great literary men of his time; he was invited to read his poems in the salons of female poets and patrons of the artistic where he had, although he failed to understand it at the time, a greater success from his beauty than from his verse. The "free" languid ladies would watch him as he read, hearing nothing of the dubious music of his verse, but absorbed completely in the music of his gazelle eyes, his thick, dark, curling hair and the pure line of his throat above the black flowing tie. Life was easy then; there were always plenty of women, good wine and tobacco and talk, and on the three hundred dollars a month which came from the Boston Store in Great Falls, he lived like a king. He knew John Drew and Richard Watson Gilder and Richard Harding Davis and once he was invited to dinner by Robert Underwood Johnson.

Then the war came, and that lovely world of Golden Girls and the Joy of Living was shattered beyond all repair, and when the bewildered Mr. Salmon wakened among the fragments, he was over forty and no longer a somewhat corrupt and opportunist gazelle-eyed boy but a middle-aged man with a paunch and bags beneath the gazelle eyes, and Greenwich Village had taken the place of Mouquin's. Richard Harding Davis was dead and all the figures of the Happy Period, both men and women, had become old and tired. Luckily he still had enough resilience and adaptability to cope with the situation, and before long he was sitting in a room in Eighth Street surrounded by another group of admiring ladies, no longer languid New York females with salons, but plainly dressed and rather plain ladies no longer in their first youth who had come from high schools and kitchens of comfortable homes in the Middle West and New England to be "free" in the Village. Despite his paunch and the bags under his eyes, René Salmon was not yet out of the running, for he had two great advantages—his three hundred a month which was about one hundred times as much money as anyone else in the Village possessed, and he had a wonderful technique, learned from the ladies of the good old Golden Girl period. And so for a time he became a kind of king in a flat painted black and orange with red curtains, where there were always plenty of cigarettes and gin and whisky. At this period Mr. Salmon also brought his poetry up to date. He began to write verse full of breasts and buttocks and freedom, touched, as he expressed it, "with a harsh animal beauty," and under the strain his liver began to give way.

And then after a little time that world crashed too, not in a violent explosion of war like the world of the High Road and the Joy of Living, but slowly, crumbling bit by bit like a jerry-built house constructed upon a fraudulent foundation. It was the tourists and the uptown drunks and prohibition which ruined the Village. It became intolerable to Mr. Salmon and it had proved too great a strain on his health and left him with dyspepsia and a tendency to bilious attacks as well as forty or fifty extra pounds of weight, which made him seem less and less like a poet and more and more like Mr. Solomon who ran the Boston Store in Great Falls.

It was too late for him to change again and impossible for him, who had known the ease and splendor of the Happy Period, ever to adapt himself to the raucous bitter realities of a New York dominated by speakeasies and night clubs. So he went into retreat, temporarily, he thought, at Mrs. Lefferty's, and while he was there had himself psychoanalyzed.

From that time on the "Freudian Influence" made itself apparent, and instead of writing poems about breasts and buttocks, he wrote, virtually the same poems over again, about mountains and hillocks, Maypoles and serpents, wells and horses and balloons, all of which confused the businessmen back in Great Falls who had never felt lasciviously about any of these things and did not understand the poet's excitement over them.

Back in Great Falls, old Mr. Solomon began to grow a little alarmed by two things—the suspicion that his son Joe was going a little potty, and the fact that for the past few years Joe's "pomes" appeared less and less frequently in the magazines; and presently, about five years after Mr. Salmon came to Mrs. Lefferty's to live, old Mr. Solomon wrote timidly suggesting that since the poetic vein of his son seemed to be running out and Mr. Solomon himself was growing old, it might be a good idea if Joe came home and took over the Boston Store. To which Joe responded with a great sheaf of poems of the Village and the "Freudian period" which he said he meant to bring out in a privately printed edition. They only succeeded in shocking and puzzling the old gentleman. René, né Joe, wrote that all editors were nincompoops and prudes and that naturally they would not publish poems about breasts and buttocks and did not understand the deeper significance of the poems written during the "Freudian period."

He had neither the desire nor the intention to go home and take over the Boston Store and he was very happy at Mrs. Lefferty's, for by the time his psychoanalysis, which took nearly two years, was finished, he found himself very much at home there. In that obsolete establishment where time stood still, with Maggie and Mrs. Lefferty, old Mr. Van Diver, Miss Flint,

Mr. Boldini and the eternal presence of poor Miss Minnie, he found again something of the peace and security of the old days at the turn of the century. It was the old play done over again by a new cast. The characters were the same, only the values had changed. Mrs. Lefferty and Maggie with their awe of anyone who could read and write without difficulty, would listen, eyes and mouth wide open, while he read his poetry, understanding not a word of it and accepting the blame for themselves, because they were not properly educated. They and the bedizened Miss Flint, with her conviction of her fatal effect upon all men, took the place of the palpitating ladies with literary salons. Miss Flint understood no more of the poetry than Mrs. Lefferty and Maggie but out of the confusion of Maypoles and mountains, serpents and cisterns, her distracted mind gained a muddled, half-voluptuous excitement filled with the intimations of carnal pleasures she had never known; and afterward, aided by the "medicinal" whisky, she experienced the most strange and exciting dreams. Now and then, about twice a month, she spent twenty-five cents out of what they paid her at the Women's Exchange for one of her bags, on a gardenia which she left on the mat outside Mr. Salmon's door. The first one, unluckily, was discovered by Mrs. Lefferty instead of Mr. Salmon, and, puzzled by the discovery of a gardenia apparently fallen miraculously from heaven, Mrs. Lefferty picked it up and put it in a vase in the parlor. At supper she discussed the miraculous flower before the blushing Miss Flint who said nothing whatever of its origin. Mr. Salmon only smirked and implied that it was a sign from the gods, indicating his genius. Afterward in private, a bridling Miss Flint explained to Mrs. Lefferty, and from then on Mrs. Lefferty always left the gardenias respectfully on Mr. Salmon's doormat.

So Mr. Salmon, nearing sixty, still had a life that was carefree and filled with adulation, a life which perhaps he could have found nowhere else in New York of the nineteen-thirties. Only the values had changed; and nature itself had been unkind, changing the appearance of Mr. Salmon bit by bit, maliciously, without his becoming aware of it. He still wore his hair long and "touched it up" but he was a little bald in front and despite the flowing black tie and the large black felt hat which both screamed "Poet!" at every passer-by, he no longer looked like a gazelle-eyed boy poet but a prosperous businessman who needed a haircut. For a year or more he had written almost no verse but was engaged upon his memoirs.

3

Into the quiet of this small lost world, Maggie's daughter came and went, sometimes appearing quietly, sometimes returning noisily in a burst of drama, for she was one of those personalities which appear to project excitement, to create disaster, calamity and farce.

Sarah Jane had a "career," spotty, checkered and full of ups and downs, a career which somehow, no matter what the opportunities, never seemed to arrive anywhere. Luckily for the career she resembled the squat flat-footed Maggie scarcely at all. She had Maggie's quick temper, and her sense of the ridiculous, but physically nature had been kind to her, permitting her to resemble her father, the big, florid, wild, handsome Mr. Ryan, the coachman, to whose charm even poor Miss Minnie had succumbed despite his drinking and his habit of overturning the victoria by running it into trees. She was tall, and even the most severe dieting, upon which she embarked spasmodically, could not make her beauty anything but one of curves. She would have served admirably as a model for Mr. Salmon's poems of the "Village Period" which so excited the Great Falls businessmen; those features of the human anatomy to which Mr. Salmon referred so freely were not only remarkably developed in Sarah Jane but she displayed no desire to hide them. On the contrary, covered by one layer of flimsy cloth, she displayed them with an engaging frankness and generosity to the entire world. Her naturally red hair she had changed long ago to a color which even old Mr. Van Diver, from his reading of the motion picture magazines, knew was "platinum."

At home she was known as Sarah Jane, a name suggested long ago by poor Miss Minnie, but when she crossed Sixth Avenue into the world of theaters and night clubs, she was known simply as "Sal" and sometimes as "Big Sal." Because she was at once bold and beautiful, hot-tempered, honest, provocative and virtuous, she was always in trouble and rarely able to hold a job. The great Mr. Ziegfeld had attempted her glorification and when he gave it up Mr. Carrol used her as a siren, captured nude, so that her only costume was a fish net with a mesh so large that anything less heroically built than Sarah Jane could have slipped away without an effort. But he too had to give up helping Sarah Jane on her way to fame, for like Mr. Ziegfeld he found that having Sarah Jane in the theater was exactly like keeping a package of nitroglycerin lying about. After that she got a job in a Shubert revue, but that was no good either. Once she threw another girl down two flights of stairs and on one occasion an admirer, enraged because Sarah Jane would not give in, eased his feelings by smashing all the mirrors in the dressing room she shared with eight other show girls.

That was really Sarah Jane's trouble; she would never give in, either in her quarrels with other show girls or to the advances of admirers and so all the "breaks" that came her way eventually shriveled up and died. At times she used language which would have startled a longshoreman and there was nothing she did not know, but technically she remained "a good girl." Only the more experienced and hard-boiled denizens of Broadway believed this and they believed it only because they "*knew,*" for Sarah Jane's appearance was scarcely that of a well-behaved young woman. Along Broadway some of the more flippant called her "Virgie" when they were well out of her reach, and flashy lady-killers had been known to make large wagers on the score of her assailability, but all of them had lost their money and some of them had lost teeth or gained black eyes as well. There were even times when old Maggie, bewildered by Sarah Jane's clothes and behavior, did not believe she was "a good girl," and then between the two of them would break out a row which shook the whole boardinghouse. But it *was* true, because Maggie had put the fear of God into Sarah Jane as a child and because being Irish, and Roman Catholic, she had a wholesome terror of hell, and finally because after she found out about the wagers of which she was the subject, she made up her mind to "show them."

She would not have minded being married so long as it did not interfere with her "career" but she had never been asked by a man whom she did not hold in contempt. On one or two occasions she could have married rather feeble young men who would have given her Rolls-Royces and diamonds, but the honesty which came to her from Maggie always spoiled everything; she couldn't have a man about for whom she felt contempt. She wanted someone like Mr. Ryan, the coachman. Now and then her maternal instinct was touched and she felt sorry for the rich little "pip-squeaks" who sent her orchids, but in the end she couldn't do it. Once long ago when she and Tommy were twenty, she had thought about marrying him and fulfilling the dream of Maggie and Mrs. Lefferty; but Tommy never asked her, and anyway they knew each other too well and both of them were ambitious and they were always fighting.

Her "career," as Maggie sometimes observed during their rows, seemed to move backward. She had begun with Mr. Ziegfeld and for six years she had been slipping down and down. Each job was a little less good than the one before until presently she found it very difficult to get work at all save in fly-by-night restaurants which opened and went into bankruptcy with extraordinary rapidity. Every now and then a manager who had forgotten her reputation or did not know her would "discover" her, a statuesque beauty who seemed all the more remarkable for being surrounded by middle-aged and broken-down chorus girls, but always within a day or two he was informed by a friend that he had only rediscovered "Sal" and that he might just as well bring a package of dynamite to rehearsals.

Her presence at the boardinghouse during those periods when, like Mr. Boldini, she was "at liberty," always brought troubles and disturbances of the somnolent peace which otherwise enveloped the place. She had a way of upsetting the "relics," of filling their heads with new ideas, of making them think, even old Mr. Van Diver, that they were young again and skittish. She never brought home any money because she never had any and sometimes Maggie and Mrs. Lefferty loaned her a few dollars out of the slender store which kept them out of ruin.

One evening about eleven o'clock while the rummy game was in progress in poor Miss Minnie's parlor and Mr. Boldini, with a look of triumph, was in the act of laying down four aces and three kings, Sarah Jane had one of her dramatic homecomings. It was preceded by the sound of rushing footsteps on the steps of the brownstone stoop and of someone trying frantically to open the door. Then came Sarah Jane's voice crying, "Let me in! Let me in!" and the sound of a violent smack followed by a flow of sulphurous language. Fanto, barking wildly, sprang from his chair and ran to the door.

Mrs. Lefferty followed him and when she opened the door she discovered Sarah Jane and a small, dark, ugly little man seated on the floor with his back in the corner, shielding his face with raised hands. Sarah Jane held a revolver in one hand and was kicking him, saying, "You rat! I'll teach you to pull a gun on me."

At the sight of Mrs. Lefferty she rushed into the house and closed the door. Mrs. Lefferty double-bolted it and Sarah Jane threw the revolver down on poor Miss Minnie's table of teakwood inlaid with mother-of-pearl and said, "The rat! The white slaver! He had the nerve to pull a gat on me," and without another word ran up the stairs to Maggie's room.

Mrs. Lefferty went to the parlor window and watched Sarah Jane's unfortunate admirer limp down the stairs, climb into a taxicab and drive away.

Then she turned and said, as if nothing had happened, "It's Miss Flint's deal." In her determination to beat Mr. Boldini, even with his meld of four aces and three kings, she forgot all about Sarah Jane and no one at the table even mentioned her or asked the cause of her latest stormy return. This was partly because they were used to her homecomings and partly because all of them found something a little shameful and upsetting about their violence, something out of another day, almost of another civilization which until Sarah Jane came into the house they had managed to keep at a distance. It was something which disturbed them all and at times even frightened them. They went on with the game in the well-bred silence of complete gentility, as if all of them—even old Mr. Van Diver in his childishness—had an unspoken agreement to treat Sarah Jane and her escapades either as nonexistent or as something which the demands of gentility made it necessary to ignore. Miss 1935 crashing a party given in 1890 was something difficult to carry off.

But this was an attitude possible to carry out only as long as Sarah Jane herself remained in the background; once she came into the room—handsome, reckless, glowing with the excitement of her violent homecoming—

it was impossible to pretend that she did not exist or had never happened at all. On this occasion while they went on with the game, Sarah Jane remained closeted abovestairs with Maggie. She remained, so to speak, in the background or at least out of sight, but to their ears she was violently present, for fragments of the quarrel going on on the fourth floor kept penetrating the parlor . . . shouts from Maggie of "Sure, and I ought to shut you up with the sisters for a time. Your poor father must be rollin' in his grave," and, "You're a bad girl! Don't tell me you aren't!" With Sarah Jane shouting back, "I'll do as I please and you can't stop me. No man has ever laid hands on me without bein' slapped for it."

Once it had been difficult to pretend that Maggie and Sarah Jane weren't having a row, but long ago the rummy players had become so used to it that it no longer disturbed their game. Indeed they all knew all the taunts and accusations, the reproaches and answers and threats which were hurled back and forth, all meaningless and without result and giving both participants a great deal of fun. But presently there was silence and a few minutes later Sarah Jane herself appeared in quest of company and beer and at sight of her, Mrs. Lefferty did not wait for Mr. Salmon to deal, but quietly took up the cards, the pencil and the score and put them away in poor Miss Minnie's *secrétaire*. She knew that the game was finished for that night.

When she came into the room something happened to everyone in it except Mrs. Lefferty who had known her for too long and spanked her out of too many tantrums to be impressed by her now. Mr. Boldini became very Italian and full of old-world courtesy, quips and elegant speeches. Mr. Salmon smirked, deftly ruffled his hair and disarranged his flowing tie to give himself a more Bohemian appearance, and experienced a sudden return of youth which made him remember the ladies of his earlier days, none of whom was ever as young or as handsome as Sarah Jane. As for Miss Flint, instead of glowing and relaxing, she grew as rigid as the wife of Lot after she had satisfied her curiosity about the friends she had left behind in Sodom. Old Mr. Van Diver, who never joined in the games because he could never remember the cards that had been played, put down his moving picture magazine, smoothed his hair and began to chuckle. All the while Mrs. Lefferty had been hoping that for once Sarah Jane would not appear to provoke a quarrel between Mr. Boldini and Mr. Salmon and throw Miss Flint into a fit of sulks, but she had known too that the hope was vain. Sarah Jane only stayed out of sight, when, broke and discouraged, she came home quietly by the areaway and the kitchen door.

Now she sat down in the midst of them, crossed her legs, lighted a cigarette and said, "Can you *imagine*? He was gonna make me into a torch singer. He took me to his studio to give me a lesson and after about five minutes, I said, 'Yeah, well, I never heard that called a singing lesson before.' The dirty little white slaver! And when I beat it, he followed me right to the door in a taxicab. Can you *imagine*? With a gat too . . . as if I didn't know enough to manage a guy with a gat! Torch singing!"

Breathlessly she went on with the whole story, about how Mr. Myers had "discovered her" and was going to open a night club and give her all sorts of "breaks." She threw away one cigarette and lighted another. "Breaks!" she said, "I know all about breaks! They always mean the same thing. All men are beasts!"

"You never said a truer word," said Miss Flint. Then, unbending a little she told about *her* experiences, beginning with her earliest disillusionment and finishing with the story of being followed home—all the way—from the Women's Exchange by a "young Italian-looking man about thirty" only yesterday. Then in order to show that she didn't include Mr. Salmon, who was a poet, among "all men," she bridled a little and asked him for a cigarette and sat back in her chair, smoking, with her lips pursed, the cigarette held between her thumb and first finger with the little finger sticking well out, tossing her head a little so that the long, oriental earrings made a jangling noise against her scrawny neck.

"I remember," she said, "once when I was sewing for Mrs. Willoughby . . . you know the Willoughbys who used to have that big house at the corner of Madison Avenue and Seventieth Street, very fashionable they were in those days. . . . Well, while I was there, making up the spring clothes for the children, a young man attacked Dorothy, that was the oldest daughter . . . she's Mrs. Jackson Durant now . . . right in the front parlor . . . her own front parlor."

Mrs. Lefferty, watching her, knew that Miss Flint had reached the second stage. First the presence of Sarah Jane made her bristle and then it made her feel fast and Bohemian. "The minute Sarah Jane comes home," Mrs. Lefferty thought, "everybody goes cockeyed." And in disgust, scarcely able to stand the spectacle of Mr. Salmon's smirks and Miss Flint's bridlings and Mr. Boldini's fatuous compliments, she went off downstairs for beer and sandwiches.

The party lasted until one o'clock and before going up to her room, Sarah Jane announced to Mrs. Lefferty's dismay that she thought that now she was home she might as well stay for a while and have a rest.

Left alone, putting the room in order, Mrs. Lefferty considered the growing problem of Sarah Jane and the equally growing problem of making ends meet. Sarah Jane was a good girl at heart and Mrs. Lefferty loved her and it made Maggie happy to have her home. But aside from the extra burden upon an already tottering budget, Mrs. Lefferty disliked the effect on the boarders. Even her good-natured soul was annoyed and a little revolted at the display of sex which Sarah Jane's presence aroused in Mr. Salmon, Mr.

[574]

Boldini, Miss Flint and even poor tottering old Mr. Van Diver. Sure it was shameful and disgusting. Why, even Fanto became a different dog. And she was upset too at the thought of what poor Miss Minnie would think of the goings on in her house, with her front stoop defiled by the presence of a man like Mr. Myers. With poor Miss Minnie sex had been kept in its place. Never once in forty years had Mr. Van Diver so much as kissed her. And unlike Sarah Jane poor Miss Minnie had kept her figure so well covered beneath cotton underwear, whalebone and padding that even Mrs. Lefferty had never had any idea what it was like.

And as she carried the remnants of the supper to the kitchen and put out the lights, there were tears in her eyes, tears of jealousy of Maggie at having Sarah Jane back in the house, sleeping in the room next to her where she could see her and talk to her and wait on her. Five years was such a long time. There were moments now when she thought that perhaps Tommy was dead and maybe buried some place outside consecrated ground with no one to care for his grave. Tommy, who loved her, wouldn't have stayed away so long without a sign, if he were still alive.

She felt so bad that she took a little drink of Irish whisky, "medicinally" like Miss Flint, and that warmed her and by the time she had taken off her woolens and was in bed she was her old optimistic self again and knew that somewhere, out in the great world of which she knew nothing, Tommy was all right and would one day come back to her.

Sarah Jane would get her "break" and Tommy would come home in a big comfortable automobile with a cut glass light in the top, rich and successful, to take her away to live in a fine palace. Once started on a story like this, she lay for a long time sleepless, building it up, putting in details, making it more and more like a moving picture, seeing it all happen on the screen of the picture house across the street. It was a beautiful story. Tommy had gone away to South America and discovered a big mine full of gold and hadn't told her anything about it because he wanted to surprise her by driving up in front of the house in a big car. He would buy her a big house and she and Maggie would move into it and take all poor Miss Minnie's lovely furniture with them and then Sarah Jane would be "discovered" and become a great movie star and she and Tommy would get married. She was just at the end of the story, with Sarah Jane and Tommy at the altar when through the half-waking dream came the sound of the doorbell ringing violently, and she thought, "There he is now! He's come home at three o'clock in the morning to make the surprise better."

While she put on a wrapper and twisted her thin hair into a screw on the top of her head, she knew that when she opened the door Tommy would be there. It couldn't be anybody else ringing the bell at this hour of the night. The bell kept up its wild clamor, ringing the way it rang when Sarah

Jane was on the stoop pursued by an admirer. As she went down the stairs, there was something in the desperate sound of the bell which frightened her. Suddenly she felt old and afraid and, with a feeling of sickness, she knew all at once that the whole dream had been made up and foolish and that probably Tommy was dead and she would never see him again.

But when she opened the door, cautiously on the chain, and called out, "Who's there? What is it?" Tommy's voice answered her, a voice she would have known anywhere in the world, a voice which she knew better than her own. It said, "It's Tommy. Let me in!" And suddenly Mrs. Lefferty was sure that when she opened the door she would find a beautiful automobile with a cut glass light in the top, waiting at the curb.

But when she opened the door, she caught only a glimpse of a taxi-cab driving away. It was Tommy all right, but a Tommy so changed that for a moment she doubted the truth. And there was a man with him, a big man who was cockeyed and wore his hat pulled far down over one eye.

They came in and Mrs. Lefferty threw her arms about Tommy, crying out, "Tommy! Tommy!" over and over again and then she stood back a little and looked at him, frightened a little because he was so pale and thin and looked so sallow and shabby. He was still a good-looking boy with big dark blue eyes (like Mr. Lefferty's) and a big generous mouth, but his body seemed to have shrunk and shriveled inside his clothes.

And then somehow they were in poor Miss Minnie's parlor, with Tommy looking around at the furniture he had known all his life, and the big man said, "I guess it's a long time since you seen Tommy."

"Five years!" said Mrs. Lefferty, tearfully. "More than five years."

The big man was about forty with a red face and big shoulders. He stood now with his hat in his hand, a cigarette hanging from his lips.

Tommy was still shy and embarrassed. He didn't say anything but she knew from the way he looked at her that he was glad to be back. He asked, "Have you got anything to eat, Ma?"

"Sure, and what would you both like to drink?"

Tommy wanted beer and Mr. Grasselli, which was the name of the big man with the cockeye, wanted whisky.

"You set right down here, both of you, and I'll go and fetch it. You're going to stay a while, ain't you, Tommy?"

"Yeah, Ma, I'm going to stay a while."

She kept staring at him, still not sure whether she was dreaming or not. He hadn't come back with a big automobile but it didn't matter now. The only thing that mattered was that here he was back in poor Miss Minnie's parlor as if he had never gone away.

"My friend, Mr. Grasselli, wants a room for a time. Have you got one, Ma?"

"Yes. On the second floor at the back."

"Mebbe I could have the little room next to him."

"Sure, Tommy, anything you want."

"He doesn't like to be alone."

She thought it was funny that a big man like Mr. Grasselli didn't like to be alone. You'd have thought he wasn't afraid of anything.

"Well, I'll get some cheese and cold ham and some drinks."

"Sure," said Mr. Grasselli, "that would be fine."

She went downstairs thinking that she did not like Mr. Grasselli's face and wishing he wasn't there so she could talk to Tommy and hear about why he had never written to her. He was alive! He wasn't dead! She and Maggie would feed him up. In a little while he'd look like he used to as a little boy.

4

When she had gone, Mr. Grasselli put out the light and went over and pulled aside the lace curtains to look out of the window. Opposite there was the darkened façade of Mrs. Lefferty's favorite moving picture theater. The street was empty. It lay shabby, obscure, characterless, lined by rows of old-fashioned, shabby, respectable brownstone façades. Then Mr. Grasselli turned back and surveyed the room with a grin.

"Sure," he said, "this is all right. It's great. Where did they find all this stuff?"

"It belonged to an old lady called Miss Randolph. She left it all to my mother." And for a second it occurred even to Tommy that it was odd to see his "friend" Mr. Grasselli standing there in poor Miss Minnie's parlor among all her things.

"Well," said Mr. Grasselli, "it ought to be worth a lot of money some day to a museum. They oughta pay a big price for it."

From the direction of the dining room there came a sudden violent rumbling sound and Mr. Grasselli started and jumped behind poor Miss Minnie's old-fashioned piano.

"Put on the lights," he said, with his hand in his pocket.

Tommy put on the lights. "It's all right," he said. "It's only the dumb-waiter." And a moment later Mrs. Lefferty appeared with a tray burdened with cold ham and chicken and sandwiches, beer and whisky and glasses and a large pot of coffee.

In silence Tommy and Mr. Grasselli ate everything on the tray. They ate, Mrs. Lefferty thought, as if they had not eaten for days, and when it was all gone she went downstairs for more, a little troubled by the thought of what Maggie would say when she found that all of tomorrow's lunch had been eaten up. At last they had enough and Mr. Grasselli said he thought it would be a good idea if they all went to bed, "Because," he said, "this is a kind of rest cure I'm taking. I'm gonna stay in bed a good part of the time. I'm not goin' out much."

Secretly Mrs. Lefferty regretted the news because it would mean a new interruption of the non-stop rummy tournament.

"Mr. Grasselli," said Tommy, "didn't bring any baggage. I'm going out in the morning to buy him some things and get my own stuff."

5

When she had made up the beds and everything was ready and she had shown Mr. Grasselli to his room, she lingered for a moment in Tommy's room, watching him with a beaming face, thinking how much more refined he was than his friend, Mr. Grasselli, and how nice he talked. She wanted to stay and talk to Tommy, to find out where he had been and what had happened to him and why he'd never written to her, but when she saw how gray and tired he seemed, she had not the heart to keep him awake any longer.

Anxiously she asked again, "You're goin' to say a while, ain't you?"

"Yes, Ma."

"And you'll never run off like that again?"

He looked away from her at the floor and at last said, "No, Ma."

"Why didn't you ever write and tell me where you was?"

"Because I didn't want to come home till I was successful. I wouldn't have come home now only . . ." He did not finish the sentence, save by a weary gesture.

"I know, Tommy."

She bent down and kissed him and he put his arm about her waist and leaned his head against her plump body. It was a tiny gesture but it made Mrs. Lefferty feel warm and triumphant.

"Never mind," she said, "everything's goin' to be fine. You're goin' to be a big success. What line have you been tryin'?"

"Writing songs . . . lately. I've tried a lot of things . . . too many things, I guess."

She knew now, with his head resting against her side, that she was glad he hadn't come home in a big automobile with a cut glass light in the roof. Now she could feed him up and see that he got plenty of sleep so that he'd get good and strong to start all over again. All her life she had been taking care of people—first poor Miss Minnie and "the old gentleman" and after that all the boarders and the people she met when she went to market. She knew now that she didn't want Tommy to take care of her. She had never wanted it. She wouldn't have felt right. She wouldn't have known how to act in a big car and a big house. No, this was a lot better story than the one she had imagined.

As she said good night, she added, "Sarah Jane is home again."

Without interest, he said, "Is she?"

"She's out of a job."

"Too bad," said Tommy, "but it isn't exactly news."

"She's had a bad time lately. She never gets a break. She had to sell that beautiful silver fox."

"I guess some of her bad luck is her own fault."

"She's a good girl."

"Yeah," said Tommy, "that's her trouble. She's made an issue of it. Even I can't . . ." He didn't finish the sentence so Mrs. Lefferty never knew what it was he meant to say.

She asked him, "What were you going to say?" But he only answered, "I don't know. I've forgotten."

Then she left him, wondering that he showed so little interest in Sarah Jane who was like a sister to him.

It was nearly four o'clock when Mrs. Lefferty finally fell asleep but she was up again at eight, helping Maggie and seeing that everyone got enough to eat at breakfast and that old Mr. Van Diver didn't forget to take the medicine for his heart. She had just finished clearing away the table and was on her way to do the rooms when Maggie appeared carrying a letter from old Mr. Prendergast, poor Miss Minnie's lawyer. Maggie always let her read all the letters because she wasn't very good at reading herself, and it was the day when the check from Mr. Prendergast was due so she wasn't alarmed until she tore open the letter and found there wasn't any check in it. Instead there was a note from old Mr. Prendergast saying that there weren't any dividends from the stock poor Miss Minnie had left them and he did not know when there would be any. And he said there wasn't much use in trying to sell the stocks now as they weren't worth anything.

The truth was that old Mr. Prendergast was himself a "relic" belonging to a simpler age. He had failed them not because he was careless or dishonest but because he was not shrewd and mean enough to cope with the stock market and its "riggers." He wrote a long explanation of how it had all come about but Mrs. Lefferty and Maggie did not understand a word of it. Besides if there wasn't any more money, it wasn't any use in worrying about why there wasn't.

Maggie and Mrs. Lefferty had the same thought, "What was to become of old Mr. Van Diver and poor Miss Flint and Mr. Boldini?"

For a moment Mrs. Lefferty could think of nothing to say. At last she said, "Something will turn up. It'll be all right. It always is." But her voice was a little weak this time, because it was the first time she had ever had any doubts. She and Maggie weren't as young as they once were and they needed money now on account of Tommy and Sarah Jane. But a story like theirs, which had begun so pretty with poor Miss Minnie leaving them everything, couldn't have a bad ending. That kind of story never did. It had to come out right.

6

It was after two o'clock in the afternoon when Sarah Jane wakened at last, rose lazily, dressed and went down to the kitchen. It was too late to have lunch with the boarders but, that, she thought, was all the better for her figure. Now she wouldn't be tempted. She'd just have a cup of coffee with Maggie in the kitchen.

She found her mother dealing with the remains of lunch just sent down on the dumb-waiter by Mrs. Lefferty.

"You'll have to get up for your meals if you're goin' to get anything around this house," said Maggie.

"I don't want any meals. All I want is a cup of coffee."

But as she drank the coffee the fragrance of hamburger steak was wafted to her nostrils and she traced the scent to the pan on the stove where Maggie was keeping warm what was left. "I guess I'll just have a bit of steak," she said.

"Sure," said Maggie, "I don't believe in this dietin'. It ain't natural for any big strong woman to diet herself. How about some potatoes with the steak?"

"If there's any gravy I'll have just a bit," said Sarah Jane.

When her mother returned with the plate it bore not only the hamburger and potatoes and gravy but also a large helping of beans. About this Sarah Jane made no comment whatever, and while she ate she caught sight of a large slice of lemon meringue pie, the last left on the plate, and thinking that another mouthful or two did not much matter now, she had that too. And then as she picked up the *Daily Mirror* she had another cup of coffee.

While she was eating, Maggie said, "Tommy's come home."

"Has he?"

"Yes. Sure, you take it as if he'd only gone away yesterday."

"It doesn't seem so long."

She wasn't listening very closely to what her mother said because she had gotten interested in a story in the *Mirror* about Monk Maguire, the Beer Baron, who was being sought by Federal officials on an income tax charge. She had known Monk, off and on, mostly in the days when he was the head of a bootlegging ring, when he owned a couple of speakeasies and the Villa Paradise night club. She had worked there once for a couple of weeks untii she had that fight with Renée LeClaire, the fan dancer, about who had the best *exposé*.

"Five years," said Maggie, seating herself before a large lunch she had constructed out of the remnants from abovestairs. "Five years it is . . . it was the year that Mr. Ziegfeld gave you your first job. He ain't so well, Bridget says."

Sarah Jane, still lost in reading about Monk Maguire, said, "What's the matter with him?"

"I don't know. I guess he's just run-down. I told Bridget to give him a lot of that swamp root tonic."

To this Sarah Jane made no response whatever.

"He brought a friend back with him. He's gonna stay as a boarder."

"Yeah?" said Sarah Jane.

"His name is Mr. Grasselli."

"Never heard of him."

Then slowly Maggie began to show signs of becoming irritated by Sarah Jane's lack of interest. Her face grew a little redder and a wicked light appeared in her blue eyes.

"I should think you'd be interested . . . with Tommy brought up alongside of you like a twin."

"WELL, can you beat it!" exclaimed Sarah Jane. "That's what I call fast work."

"What?" asked Maggie.

"About me and Mr. Myers and the vestibule. *Imagine,* already. And it ain't three o'clock yet."

"I hope it ain't one of them scandals again."

"Listen," said Sarah Jane, reading from the *Mirror.* "It says, 'Early this morning Abe Myers was trying to explain away a black eye and a missing front tooth. Said he fell downstairs. Wiseacres say . . . (here Sarah Jane stumbled for a moment) *Cherchez la femme* . . . a femme known around Broadway hot spots as Sal. Well, Abe's in good company. A lot of other fellows have lost bets on Sal, along with their front teeth.'" Sarah Jane threw down the paper. "The bastard!" she said. "If I'd known he was bettin' I'd have given him more than he got."

"Bettin' on what?" said Maggie.

"That he could make me. Why, the little rat!"

"Well," said Maggie, growing still redder. "If it ain't a scandal I don't know what you'd call it."

"It's only a coupla lines," said Sarah Jane. "Why, the last time . . ."

"Your poor father ain't allowed to rest in his grave and poor Miss Minnie . . ."

"*Poor* Miss Minnie is right. She never had any fun . . ."

And then Maggie exploded. Reaching across the table she gave Sarah Jane a slap that was heard by the boarders having coffee upstairs in the parlor. "I'll teach you to be disrespectful about the dead. I'll teach you to speak like that of poor Miss Minnie . . ."

Tears of pain came into Sarah Jane's eyes, but she took the slap. Maggie was the only person in the world who could slap her and not be knocked down.

7

Abovestairs in the parlor an air of dullness and futility hung over the boarders. It affected even old Mr. Van Diver, although there were moments when he did not know quite why he felt dull. Lunch, approached in the expectancy of having not only Sarah Jane to brighten the table but Tommy and his "friend" as well, had ended in full disappointment, since none of them had appeared and the boarders had only themselves to look at and to listen to. For the news of Tommy's return had gotten quickly about, as well as that of the arrival of a new "transient." Once the arrival of a "transient" had been frowned upon as an invasion upon the circle and something which disturbed the atmosphere, but now it had been so long since there had been a "transient" in their midst that they were willing to welcome almost anyone. Only Mrs. Lefferty was in high spirits but she found herself quite unable to raise the spirits of the others. She was aware that Miss Flint and Mr. Boldini and Mr. Salmon felt a kind of actual resentment toward her as if the food she had put on the table were spoiled. They drifted away quickly after their coffee as if they had been asked to an entertainment which had not come up to expectations.

On the second floor, Tommy and his friend still slept. Three times Mrs. Lefferty went to their doors, but each time she discovered only the unmistakable sounds of slumber. Mr. Grasselli, she discovered, had even locked his door, which she thought odd and even faintly insulting. Nobody in the house ever locked his door. What on earth was there in the house to lock one's door against?

It was nearly five o'clock when at last Tommy did wake and have a bath and dress himself. When she heard him moving about, she went in to tell him that when he was ready, she would be in the kitchen with something for him to eat. He said that he didn't want much and that he was going out right away to buy a razor and a toothbrush for Mr. Grasselli and bring his own clothes.

"I forgot to tell you," he said, "that Mr. Grasselli would like to have his meals in his own room."

"Why can't he come down to the table like everyone else?"

For a moment Tommy hesitated and then said, "You see he's having a kind of nervous breakdown and he can't see people without getting upset."

"It'll make a lot of extra work."

"He'll pay extra for it."

Mrs. Lefferty was silent for a moment, considering. Now that old Mr. Prendergast didn't have any more money for them, every penny could be used. Somehow or other she and Maggie would manage the meals. It would mean maybe fifty cents a day sheer profit, except for her legs. She remembered that Mr. Salmon had been like that when he first came, that time when he was going to see a fancy doctor about himself. He had been very uppity about the other boarders, but in the end he had turned out to be really the best of them all.

"All right," she said, "I guess I can manage."

"And he doesn't want to see anybody," said Tommy. "Will it bother you if he stays in his room while you make it up?"

"Yes, it'll bother me. I can't bear to have somebody sitting around in the room I'm working in. I always make all the others get out."

"I guess he'd pay extra for that too," said Tommy.

"He must have a lot of money to throw around . . . paying extra just to sit in his own room to watch his bed being made up. Maybe we can work that out too, but I should think he'd be better off in a hospital."

"No," said Tommy, "he can't stand hospitals. They make him worse."

"All right, being he's a friend of yours."

As she was leaving the room Tommy asked, "Has Sarah Jane gone out?"

"Yes. She's gone to fetch her clothes."

"When will she be back?"

"I don't know. She's just gone."

Tommy went on arranging his tie. "Okay," he said, without looking at her.

But Mrs. Lefferty was suspicious. She said, "What's the matter with you and Sarah Jane?"

"Nothing."

"Why don't you want to see her?"

"I didn't say I didn't want to see her. I just asked if she'd gone out."

But that didn't fool Mrs. Lefferty. She went downstairs to the kitchen but she wasn't deceived. She knew there was some kind of mystery.

8

At the kitchen table something happened to Tommy. Perhaps it was the sight of the familiar kitchen itself, unchanged after so many years, with the same old-fashioned chairs, with Maggie's worn raincoat and battered hat with a feather hanging against the wall, with the same plates and tea cups which he had noticed for the first time when he was spanked for breaking one of them as a little boy of four in the kitchen of poor Miss Minnie's big house on Murray Hill . . . Perhaps it was that in all the suffering he had known during the five missing years, he had become more human and honest and much nearer to reality and truth, sloughing off all the pride and falsity and vanity which had corrupted him . . . Perhaps it was nothing more than the presence of the two fried eggs which lay on the plate before him, swimming in browned butter, fried as only his mother and Maggie knew how to fry them, eggs such as he had neither seen nor tasted since he left home, either in cheap eating places or cafeterias or in great hotels and expensive restaurants . . . Perhaps it was simply the sight and the smell of those two humble eggs rousing a long train of memories, of his father long since dead, of his mother as a young woman taking care of him, protecting him as she was still trying to do with all the warmth and simplicity of her nature. Whatever the reason Tommy underwent a sudden change. He became another person, a person who seemed, after those five hard years, almost a stranger, even to himself.

Mrs. Lefferty, with a leap of the heart, saw it almost at once. She knew it not only by the look in his eye, but by the tone of his voice, by the way he looked at her simply and directly as he had done long ago before he went away to college. He had come back to her, not only the Tommy who had gone away five years ago, but the Tommy he had been before poor Miss Minnie sent him away to be educated—the Tommy, her boy, who had been born in poor Miss Minnie's house and grown up there along with herself and Sarah Jane and Mr. Ryan and poor Mr. Lefferty, before he had got his head filled with ideas that he was better than all of them.

And presently, quite easily, he was telling her what had happened to him since he went away, how he had planned to be rich and successful and some day have enough money to buy a place in the country for her and Maggie. He told her about the fine job he had got in the mills belonging to the father of one of the boys he had known in college, and how quickly all that dream had vanished at the first sign of bad business, how his friend and his father had quickly rid themselves of him and forgotten him at the first threat to their own security; how one by one, he had tried other college friends, how some had put him off with smooth words and others had simply told him to get out, and how he had wandered from job to job, trying to gain a foothold anywhere, even on the lowest rung of the ladder of success, and finally how he had been content to do anything at all simply to get a place to sleep and enough food to keep him alive, and how sometimes he went without anything to eat at all for days at a time, and how at last Mr. Grasselli had befriended him and given him a job as a kind of secretary and manager of his personal affairs.

[584]

It was a long story and Mrs. Lefferty cried while she listened, mostly at the thought of Tommy going hungry when there was always so much good food at home. Mrs. Lefferty believed every word he spoke, for it was a believable story despite the fact that it was not quite true. The facts themselves were true enough but bare facts add up so rarely to make the total sum of truth. It was not that Tommy distorted the truth; it was that he left out part of it.

He did not tell her that he had disappeared because he was ashamed of her and Maggie and the noisy Sarah Jane, because he had never had a home like other boys, uncluttered by eccentric boarders, to which he might bring his friends. He did not tell her that while he was in college he had pretended to be an orphan and the nephew of poor Miss Minnie, and how afterward when he set out to make his own way, he had thought his mother and Maggie and Sarah Jane too great a handicap for any young man to carry who planned to get on in the world. He did not tell her of his wild ambition to become rich overnight. And he did not tell her all the low things he had done from time to time simply in order to be able to go on living. And he did not tell her what Mr. Grasselli's business was.

Lately, he said, he had gone back to playing the piano and that he was more thankful now than he had ever been to poor Miss Minnie for the lessons she had paid for long ago. He told her that he was writing songs but that he hadn't had much success as yet because it was so hard to get a "break." And he asked her if they could have poor Miss Minnie's piano tuned so that he could work at home.

When he had finished, Mrs. Lefferty held her peace and did not tell him, as she had meant to do, of her own troubles and the letter from old Mr. Prendergast and the menace of taxes and insurance which hung over her and Maggie's head. Poor Tommy! she thought. He had enough to bear.

When he had finished his coffee, he put on his hat and went out to buy a toothbrush and razor for Mr. Grasselli and to fetch his own things. But again he told her only part of the truth, for he was going out to do a great deal more than that. When he returned he brought with him two suitcases which seemed singularly heavy. It astounded Mrs. Lefferty when she made up his room the next day that they seemed to have contained nothing more than one suit of clothes, some underwear, three shirts and Mr. Grasselli's razor and toothbrush.

9

For nearly a year Sarah Jane had known that Tommy was alive; for most of that time she knew where he was and for a part of the time she suspected, at least, what he was doing. But Tommy had made her promise not to tell.

It was a promise Sarah Jane would have broken if she had seen fit to do so; she kept it because she had no more desire than Tommy to tell Mrs. Lefferty and because, oddly enough, Tommy was the only person in the world, save Maggie, who could ever exert even the faintest control over Sarah Jane.

There was a whole world known well, even intimately, to Sarah Jane which she left outside the door once she returned to the boardinghouse. She never brought it any nearer than the vestibule, as she had done with Mr. Myers, although the aroma of it still clung to her sometimes and excited faintly all of Mrs. Lefferty's boarders with its intimation of things going on in the world which they had never dreamed of. It was a world made up of confidence men and chiselers, pimps and drug addicts, dubious, second-rate gangsters and gunmen's molls and middle-aged broken-down chorus girls, a whole world filled with the Hogarthian gusto which Sarah Jane's wild nature had need of from time to time.

During the years in which she kept slipping downward from the eminence upon which Mr. Ziegfeld had placed her in the beginning, she gradually found a greater and greater need of that gusto. By circumstance she slipped into it and by nature she did not dislike it for it bucked her up at moments when the prospect of a "career" seemed beyond the possibility of realization. There was a kind of what-the-hell atmosphere which she liked; and being Sarah Jane, she was able to take care of herself and never quite succumb to its blandishments, no matter how broke she got to be. When worst came to worst, she always found a refuge in the boardinghouse. It was a world which existed in the forties and fifties between Sixth and Ninth Avenues and in it Sarah Jane was known as something apart, a special character, a curiosity who was always welcomed on account of her health and gusto and good looks. Her mere appearance in that tired, sick and cynical world served to raise the spirits of its inhabitants, just as her presence in the boardinghouse raised the spirits of Mr. Salmon and Mr. Boldini. "Sal" was something special and by her honesty and violence and physical strength, she drew respect from a world which respected nothing else.

In the fifties, not far from Eighth Avenue, there was a kind of all-night lunch with a false front much frequented by those who belonged to that lost shabby world. To the uninitiated it displayed a shabby, sordid façade with the legend THE EXCELSIOR CAFE AND LUNCH ROOM stenciled in chipped and fading paint on the dusty windows. Beneath the legend one saw displayed piles of fly-specked fruit and immortal vegetables made of wax whose brilliance was dimmed by a coating of Eighth Avenue dust. If you didn't know the place, the best you could expect was a bad snack cooked and served by a Greek known as Pete. You could eat and go away again without suspecting anything. But of course you would never have chosen to eat there because it was the last place within a radius of five blocks where anyone would have chosen to eat. It did not, however, depend on the trade attracted by Pete's frightful concoctions to keep it going.

Those who knew the place entered, exchanged a word or two with Pete and then walked directly through a door which was marked "Lavatory." To a stranger this would have appeared a fabulous place capable of swallowing up whole armies of people who entered and never came out. The secret was simple. There was a lavatory behind the door but there was also a long hallway which led into a back room. This, unofficially, was known as the Excelsior Club.

The ceiling of the room was low and the room completely airless save when someone opened the door leading into a dreary back areaway in order to save those inside from suffocation by cigarette smoke. The floor was covered with sawdust, and beer was the fashionable drink. Here congregated a large part of that world which Sarah Jane found from time to time exciting. The police knew about it and from time to time paid the place a visit in the casual hope of picking up a couple of characters they were looking for; but they never had much luck and they never knew quite why because they did not know about the electric button hidden just beneath the grill where Pete cooked his hamburgers.

At sight of policemen or detectives Pete would become completely absorbed in his cooking and unnoticed press the button which rang an electric bell hidden behind the piano in the back room. If somebody happened to be playing the piano at that moment, he would stop abruptly, strike a sour chord and then continue as if nothing had happened. If he was not playing, anyone could hear the bell and by the time the officers of the law had negotiated the long passage marked "Lavatory" the wanted ones would have slipped out into the areaway through a cellar and out into the freedom of Eighth Avenue. The only time the police ever caught anyone was the night that Albany May was insulted by Pete and out of revenge cut the wires with her nail scissors. It settled a double grudge for Albany May because the police caught Young Dansy alias Hyman Breuer who had walked out on Albany May, and sent him up the river for seven years.

Sarah Jane came and went, to and from the Excelsior Club, miraculously escaping any trouble more serious than an occasional scandal like that of Mr. Myers and the vestibule.

And then one night when she came in, there was a new man playing the piano. She did not notice him at first. In any case it was almost impossible to see him at the far end of the room through the fog of cigarette smoke. It was only when he began playing Irish tunes like "Kathleen Mavourneen" and "Mother Machree" that she noticed something different about the music, some quality which together with the music itself made her cry without quite knowing why. It made her think first of the good old days in poor

Miss Minnie's house on Murray Hill with herself and Maggie and Mr. and Mrs. Lefferty all sitting about listening to the miraculous Tommy playing tunes which brought tears to all their eyes, poor Tommy who was probably dead by now and buried somewhere in a pauper's grave. She hadn't thought of Tommy for quite a while and now, crying into her beer and thinking of him, she was ashamed of herself to be sitting there in the Excelsior Club surrounded by bums. And then slowly, as she listened, it seemed to her that it must be Tommy himself or Tommy's ghost who was playing the piano because she had never heard anyone play "When Irish Eyes Are Smiling" like that with little trills all through it.

Rising halfway out of her seat, she peered through the cigarette smoke at the back of the pianist's head. It was . . . no, it couldn't be . . . exactly like the back of Tommy's head. She knew the way the curly black hair grew close and vigorous. But it couldn't be Tommy . . . Tommy would never be playing the piano in a joint like the Excelsior Club . . . not the Tommy who had had a college education and wanted to be a swell. She was about to cross the room and make certain when "Irish Eyes" was suddenly interrupted by an especially sour chord. Three members of the Excelsior Club, two men and a girl called Quick Time Bessie, rose·hastily and disappeared through the door into the areaway, and then two "dicks" came in. They walked around the room and when they passed her table, they said, "Hello, Sal," with a kind of good-humored affection and then went out. The piano player began a new selection called, "Just a Little Bit of Dublin."

While she waited for the "dicks" to make their round of the tables all sorts of things happened to Sarah Jane's emotional nature. She was crying, not simply moved now by the music, but by all the memories which the sight of the back of the piano player's head had roused without warning. She cried over the big house on Murray Hill and poor Miss Minnie herself, and over her own muddled career and lost opportunities and because she was getting old (she was twenty-four) and because of Tommy, not the Tommy who had pretended not to know her in a swell speakeasy five years before, but the Tommy she had played with as a child, the Tommy she had always protected, the Tommy she was once in love with. That Tommy, she knew now, out of her hard experience, was the nicest man she had ever met. And she cried because the man playing the piano couldn't be Tommy, because Tommy was dead by now.

But when the detectives, empty-handed, had gone away, she pushed the table violently away from her, rose and went all the way across the room to make certain. Before she reached the piano she knew that the player *was* Tommy, a Tommy who looked tired and thin and played the piano dully, without enthusiasm, a cigarette hanging from his lips . . . a Tommy who she knew at once was crushed. The old gay funny look wasn't there. He looked much older and his whole body seemed to droop.

She took a chair and placed it beside him and sat down and even then he seemed completely unaware of her presence. He went on playing absent-mindedly, as if his spirit had left his body there functioning mechanically and gone away.

"Poor Tommy," she thought, and from the depths of her rich nature there arose a knowledge of all that had happened to him during the missing years. She saw everything. She thought, "I'll take him home and look after him. Maybe I'll marry him. He needs somebody." And suddenly she felt in love all over again, not as she had been at seventeen when he came home from college, so changed and grand, but in another way, knowing that of the two she was the strong one who could cope with the world and protect him. It was the same direct brusque richness of nature which made her say at once the wrong thing.

She said, "Hello, smart guy!"

He turned and looked at her, not seeing her at first, as if he had to wait for his spirit to rejoin his mechanically functioning body. Then he said, as if he'd never gone away at all, "What are you doing here?"

He went right on playing because that was his job and because he could do it without effort or concentration.

"Where have you been?" asked Sarah Jane.

Tommy raised one hand from the piano to chuck his smoked-out ciga-rette. Then he went right on again. "Chicago, St. Louis, San Francisco, Panama . . . a lot of places."

"Never sending a word to your poor old mother."

"Leave my poor old mother out of it."

"She's been nearly crazy sometimes."

"Yeah? You don't need to tell me about that." He looked away from her and went into another tune.

"Will you come home with me tonight and surprise her?"

"No," said Tommy.

"Why not?"

"I can't go yet."

"Why not?"

"Not till I get on my feet again. I've got a lot to atone for. I've got to pay."

"Don't turn mick on me," said Sarah Jane.

"Well, I'm not going, and if you tell her anything, you'll regret it."

She knew all about that. That was Tommy's stiff-necked pride, that Orangeman stubbornness he had come by from Mr. Lefferty.

"I've got plans," he said. "You keep out of it. I don't suppose you can, but anyway I'm warning you."

[589]

"I'm gonna tell her," said Sarah Jane.

"If you tell her, I'll go away again and never come back. You'll spoil everything just when I'm beginning to get on my feet again."

"Well, you ain't on your feet yet. This job ain't so hot."

"This job isn't everything. I've got other plans . . . maybe in a week, maybe in a month . . . you'll see." His thin shoulders stiffened a little defiantly. "I don't want her to know I'm playing the piano in a clip joint."

"This isn't any clip joint."

"I guess you know it better than I do. What does Maggie think about your being in a place like this?"

"She doesn't know it. Can I help you out . . . a little cash or something?"

"You don't look so prosperous yourself. Are you working?"

"No," said Sarah Jane.

"What's the matter? A looker like you ought to be able to get a job any time."

"That's the trouble," said Sarah Jane.

"How?"

"They're never satisfied with me being only an actress."

"I get you."

"I was just thinking about the old days. All that mick music made me think about it."

"Yeah," said Tommy, "so was I. That's how I came to be playing it."

"Tommy."

"Yeah?"

"I'm sort of fed up."

"You don't know the meaning of the word."

She wanted to say something to reach him but she did not know what to say or how to say it. He turned away from her. She saw the cords at the back of his neck stand out and his jaw suddenly grow hard and then she knew there wasn't anything to be done, not right now anyway.

"Where'll I find you?" she asked. "Here?"

"Yeah . . . off and on."

10

But the next night when she returned to the Excelsior Club he was gone and she did not see him again for weeks although she went from place to place with only that in mind. And then one night she saw him again in a big Broadway restaurant, well-dressed and looking almost prosperous although he was still pale and thin and his shoulders drooped. From across the room she watched him without his being aware of her presence, disapproving of the company in which he found himself, noticing that he did not

[590]

feel at home in the small circle of chiselers and cheap racketeers which surrounded him; and presently, unable to resist the impulse any longer, she crossed the room and spoke to him.

When he had left the table she said to him abruptly, "You'll end up in the cooler."

"What about yourself?" he asked. "Your company isn't so hot."

"I can take care of myself," said Sarah Jane.

"Meaning that I can't?"

"Yeah, that's it."

"How would it be if you minded your own business?"

"Okay."

She went away and again for a long time she did not see him, and when she did see him again he was still in bad company and again she spoke her mind and again they quarreled. But she worried about him and in spite of everything she could not get him out of her mind. She knew him well enough to know how hard it was to reach him. It wasn't weakness that got him into bad company; Tommy was hard enough. It was, she knew, ambition and impatience. He wanted to get on so desperately. All his life he had been looking for a short cut and Sarah Jane knew by now there wasn't any such thing, at least there wasn't any short cut that didn't get you into trouble.

She didn't mind his ambition. She herself knew about that. She was only afraid that he might be tempted to do something that would get him into a scrape. But she did not know how to penetrate the hard shell of his pride and resentment and rediscover him, the real Tommy who she knew was there all the time. For the first time in her life she regretted the fiery temper that was forever defeating her; the other defeats, the quarrels with managers, the fights with other girls, the brawls with men who had bet on her powers of resistance . . . none of these did she regret because there was always the compensating fun and excitement which accompanied them. Now she wished earnestly that she could control herself just long enough to talk Tommy into reason. She wanted to talk to him gently, to get *through*, to make him understand how she felt, but each time she saw him she spoiled everything right at the start by opening the conversation with a smart crack.

She had a feeling—indeed she knew it each time she saw him—that he was lonely and wanted to be friendly, perhaps more than anything else on earth, and she knew all the time that beneath the complications of pride and impatience and bitterness, he was as fond of her as he had ever been. There were even times when for a moment everything seemed between them as it had been long ago at home when poor Miss Minnie was still alive. Now and then he would look at her suddenly, just for a second, with the old look of teasing good-humor in his blue eyes, in a way which made her feel subdued and a little faint and not at all like the overpowering character she was supposed to be. And then she would think, "If only I could get him away somewhere, maybe in the country, till he could pull himself together. I could do it if he'd let me." But almost immediately she found herself compelled to laugh at the picture of them both in the country, bored, not knowing one tree or flower from another, wondering what to do with themselves. They belonged, she knew, forever to the asphalt. Besides he would not let her help him, and after a long time she divined the reason; it was because he was *both* proud and ashamed, and in his stubbornness he would not admit these things, least of all to himself.

So week after week, month after month, they saw each other infrequently and nearly every time the encounters ended in smart cracks and insults. And then suddenly Tommy inexplicably came home, bringing with him the mysterious Mr. Grasselli, and the moment Sarah Jane heard of it, she grew suspicious. She knew her way about. She didn't like the smell of Mr. Grasselli and she determined to find out who he was and why he had chosen to become a pensioner of Maggie and Mrs. Lefferty.

II

But finding out who Mr. Grasselli was, was no easy matter.

None of the boarders ever saw him, not even Miss Flint who, driven by the curiosity of a gossipy nature and by a kind of obscure romantic conviction that perhaps Mr. Grasselli was the man who had been waiting for her all these years, found excuses to go up and down the stairs several times a day and even managed to linger on Mr. Grasselli's landing for an hour or two at a time in the pretense of mending the curtains. No one saw him but Tommy and Mrs. Lefferty—not even Maggie.

He had his meals in his room and paid Mrs. Lefferty not the fifty cents a day she had counted upon but two dollars a day extra for the privilege. He insisted on paying two dollars a day more for the privilege of remaining in his room while she cleaned it and made up the bed. And he voluntarily added ten dollars a week to the regular sum she asked of him for board and lodging. In short, for Maggie and Mrs. Lefferty, Mr. Grasselli turned out to be a small gold mine, and in a way the most satisfactory boarder they had ever had, better even than Mr. Salmon. Not only did he pay his room and board regularly like Mr. Salmon but he paid a lot more. But Maggie and Mrs. Lefferty both knew that even if they filled every room in the house with gold mines like Mr. Grasselli, they still would not have enough money for the interest and taxes and insurance when the day of reckoning came. Maggie did not worry much about it because she had always left these things to Mrs. Lefferty and Mrs. Lefferty, feeling that in any case there was noth-

[592]

ing to do, waited for something to turn up, convinced in her romantic optimism that the story which had begun long ago when she and Maggie went as green Irish girls to poor Miss Minnie's big house, could not have a tragic ending. Stories never turned out like that. Nobody would even sit through a picture that had that kind of an ending.

Tommy brought in newspapers for Mr. Grasselli, a good many of which Mrs. Lefferty had never seen before—*Variety,* the *Daily Mirror,* the *Daily News,* the *American,* the *Racing Form* and the *Hollywood Reporter.* Tommy said he read them not so much for the international and political news as to keep in touch with his friends. Now and then, about once a week, Tommy went out and returned with a visitor for Mr. Grasselli, a short rather plump Jewish gentleman with thick glasses, dressed very quietly and respectably, and always carrying a leather dispatch case with a gold lock on it. He would remain in Mr. Grasselli's room for a couple of hours and then go away again. Tommy told Mrs. Lefferty that his name was "Mr. Hirsh" but "you'd be surprised if you knew who he really was." That was the nearest Tommy ever came to giving away a hint of Mr. Grasselli's true identity.

Slowly the thing became an obsession with Sarah Jane. When she was not in bed eating chocolates and reading the *Daily Mirror* and the picture magazines and putting on weight, she spent all her time in trying to discover who Mr. Grasselli was. From Tommy she could gain not the slightest hint. They did not see each other very often even though they lived now in the same house, for Tommy, at the moment, was just a little afraid of Sarah Jane and Sarah Jane shrewdly divined that the time for breaking down Tommy would never arrive so long as Mr. Grasselli was there in the house troubling Tommy's conscience. For she knew almost at once that there was something shady about Mr. Grasselli and that Tommy was worried. In a way Mr. Grasselli, mysterious, always hidden in his room behind locked doors, became a kind of mortal enemy of Sarah Jane, an obstacle blocking her path, baffling her, defeating her, and that was not a good position for Mr. Grasselli or anyone else to be in.

Now and then she encountered Tommy working over his songs at poor Miss Minnie's piano which had been tuned and put thoroughly in order. She did not hesitate to attack him on the subject of Mr. Grasselli. One day she said, "If you want to get yourself into trouble, it's okay by me (which wasn't true) but you haven't any right to drag your mother and Ma into it."

"Who's dragging them into anything?" asked Tommy.

"Don't try to kid me."

"I'm not trying to kid anybody. It's a damned shame that a man can't come here and have a rest without every boarder in the house getting sick with curiosity. You behave like old Flint hanging around the stairway pretending to mend the curtains."

"What's he hidin' from?"

"He's not hiding from anything. Go on away and let me work."

"You might give me an idea of one of your songs, unless you're afraid Mr. Boldini or me or somebody else is gonna steal them from you."

"Sure," said Tommy, "I didn't know you were interested."

So Sarah Jane sat down and lighted a cigarette and listened while he played. At first she lay back in poor Miss Minnie's armchair, relaxed and not very sanguine in her expectations. Then slowly, as Tommy played, she sat up a little in the chair, and by the time he had finished, she was sitting on the edge.

"Jeez . . ." she said, "that's good! Where'd you learn to do that?"

"Haven't you ever heard about genius?" asked Tommy.

"What d'you mean . . . genius?"

"How it's born and not made."

"Why don't you get it published?"

Tommy wheeled round on the old-fashioned piano stool and said, "Did you ever try to get a song published?"

"No," said Sarah Jane, "I never wrote any."

"Well, just try to get a hearing some time."

"What's it called?" asked Sarah Jane.

"I kind of like 'The Up and Down' as a title."

"Who's gonna write the words?"

"I wrote them myself."

"Jeez," said Sarah Jane. "Let's see it."

He handed her the manuscript and she looked over it. When she handed it back to him she said, "Well, what d'you know about that? It looks like the real thing . . . all written out and everything. I didn't know you were so smart. Where'd you learn to write out music?"

"Well, that's one of the things I learned wandering about."

The shoe was suddenly on the other foot and both of them were aware of it. Sarah Jane was not treating him now as if he were a naughty, half-witted child who had to be taken care of. She was impressed and in her simplicity she collapsed at once. The fact that she was impressed changed her, and Tommy saw that too, right away. He swelled a little with pride. He lost the defensive air of indifference and defeat. His eyes became brighter and the color came into his pale face. It was as if the old Tommy had suddenly returned. Sarah Jane noticed it at once and thought, "Maybe that's done it. Maybe if I keep on telling him he's God himself, I can get through to him." The emotion wasn't false, either. The song, she thought, was swell.

"Got any others?"

"Yes," said Tommy, "if you can spare a minute from bed to listen to them."

He played three others, singing the words in the husky tenor voice which she loved. When he had finished, she said, "You're wonderful. Maybe you'd let me take a crack at singing one of 'em?"

"Since when do you sing?"

"I've always sung."

"Yeah, I remember," said Tommy, "you and poor Miss Minnie's cats."

Miraculously Sarah Jane kept her temper. "Well, I *do* sing," she said. "I've sung in public even . . . twice . . . not very good places but I got away with it."

"Okay," said Tommy without enthusiasm, "if you want to try."

"Sure I do."

So they chose a comedy song, "What Am I Gonna Do Now?" There was a great deal of difficulty over the key but at last they found it and Sarah Jane sang from the manuscript leaning against poor Miss Minnie's piano, and when she finished Tommy looked up at her.

"Not bad," he said, patronizingly, "not bad at all."

"Thanks," said Sarah Jane. "Jeez . . . we ought to make a team. We'd be good."

"Yeah," said Tommy, "but not so good at starving to death."

"We could get a break some place."

"Where?"

"Well, I don't know. We could get somebody to take us on. Of course I can sing it better than I did. I'd never seen it before. I've got ideas about how to build it up."

"When did you take lessons?" asked Tommy.

"I never took any lessons. You don't need any lessons to sing a song like that."

"Thanks," said Tommy.

"I didn't mean it that way. You know what I meant. If a girl's got any talent, she ought to work a song like that out her own way. She ought to trust her instin't."

"I suppose you would take a *few* suggestions."

"Sure," said Sarah Jane, "from the composer. Give me a chance to work it up."

"Okay. Maybe that'll keep you from annoying Mr. Grasselli."

"Sure," said Sarah Jane.

She had never lost her temper once. Although a score of smart cracks came into her head, she had managed to suppress every one of them. When she went up to her room again, she couldn't quite believe what had happened, but she was glad, because for a minute or two she had recovered the old Tommy, quick, humorous, lovable. "Jeez . . ." she thought, "mebbe love makes you keep your temper. Mebbe I'm in love. Mebbe that's the way it feels." And then suddenly a great revelation came to her. Maybe that was what had been her trouble all along. Maybe that was why she never seemed able to get along with men. Maybe you had to keep telling them all the time that they were God himself.

After that she went down now and then to work with Tommy in the afternoons. It was fun. It was like the old days. Tommy's disposition improved and she didn't feel restless any more, wanting to go out as soon as midnight came round to see lights and people and drop in at places like the Excelsior Club. She began to see that maybe it wasn't all Tommy's fault. Now that they were working together and she kept telling him he was wonderful, it was just like the old days.

12

But she didn't leave Mr. Grasselli in peace. She knew perfectly well that he wasn't having any nervous breakdown and that he was in the house for no good reason. Most likely, she thought, he was hiding away, whoever he was. And because she had no intention of getting into trouble like a fool, without knowing why, she began a campaign to find out about Mr. Grasselli, Tommy or no Tommy.

At first she began on Mrs. Lefferty, questioning her, but she didn't find out anything because Mrs. Lefferty really didn't know anything, except that one day when she had gone into the deep closet where he kept his clothes and picked up one of his suitcases to move it out of her way, it fell open and revealed three revolvers and a big complicated piece of machinery which must have been a gun. She couldn't say because she'd never seen anything like it before. When it happened, she said Mr. Grasselli got very mad and followed her into the closet and asked her what she was poking around in there for. Then she lost her temper and told him she wasn't poking around but only doing her work and if he didn't like it he could leave, as she had enough trouble carrying up his meals and having him sitting around watching her while she worked, and besides she wasn't used to having boarders who kept guns in their closets. After that he quieted down and said it was all right so long as she didn't mention it to anyone else.

That was exactly what Sarah Jane had expected. After the story, she tried to get Mrs. Lefferty to let her go into the room and pretend to be helping with the work, but Mrs. Lefferty wouldn't agree to that. In the first place, she'd promised Mr. Grasselli and in the second place except when she had lost her temper as she did over the gun incident, she had no desire to lose the best boarder they had.

"He means a lot of money," she told Sarah Jane, "and believe me we need it just now. I don't know what we'd do without him."

And Sarah Jane soon discovered that it wasn't any good waiting around the hall for a glimpse of him. After spending two whole afternoons on the landing just above with a box of chocolates and a picture magazine, she gave that up as too boring.

And then she had an inspiration. Now and then Mr. Grasselli did have to go to the bathroom. These visits she discovered were made either late at night or early in the morning when there was no one about. Even if you got up early or waited up late it didn't do any good. She tried it a couple of times but all she saw was a glimpse of a man in a red dressing gown with a hat pulled far down over one side of his face. The door to the bathroom was only three feet from his own door and in the half-light from the single bulb at the far end of the hall you couldn't see anything at all. So at last she came to the conclusion that there wasn't anything to do but go right into the bathroom and hide and catch him as he came in.

At the end of the bathroom there was a sort of shallow curtained alcove where Mrs. Lefferty kept towels and soap and here one night, after pretending to everyone including Tommy that she had gone to bed, Sarah Jane concealed herself and waited. When Mr. Grasselli came into the room she planned to emerge from the alcove and pretend innocently that she had only come for a towel or a cake of soap.

A little after midnight she hid herself but Mr. Grasselli never went to sleep until two or three in the morning and so was in no hurry about his bath and she had a long boring wait in which she developed a terrible case of fidgets with nothing to do and nothing to read and nothing to amuse herself but her own thoughts. She must have been there for more than an hour when she heard his door opening and his step in the hallway. Peeking out from between the curtains she saw the door of the bathroom open a few inches and one eye peer round the corner to make certain the coast was clear. When the eye discovered the room was empty the door opened and the rest of Mr. Grasselli came into the room, and she knew at once who Mr. Grasselli was.

Pushing the curtains back she came out and as she emerged Mr. Grasselli's hand went swiftly into the pocket of his dressing gown. And then when he saw that it was only Big Sal, he took it out again.

Sarah Jane said, "So *you're* Mr. Grasselli!"

"Yeah, and you've got a nerve spying on me."

"I wasn't spying. I came after a piece of soap."

He knew that wasn't true and he didn't pretend to believe it.

"I oughta gone away," he said, "when I discovered you was livin' here."

"I'm not gonna bite you." Then she didn't pretend any more. "I only wanted to know what Tommy had got himself mixed up with."

"Well, now you see."

"I knew he was mixed up with something that was gonna get us all into trouble."

"Well, don't worry. I'll beat it now. Anyway nobody would have got into any trouble. They only want me on account of income tax."

"Yeah, I read that in the papers. It was kinda dumb of me not to guess you and Mr. Grasselli was the same. Nice of you to get us all in trouble. I suppose we'll all get pinched now."

"No. None of you'll get pinched. I'm gonna give myself up when the time comes. Only the case ain't ready yet. We're just preparing it. When it's ready I'll beat it an nobody'll ever know I was staying here. They can't ship me up the river. They haven't got anything on me. Only we got to make everything tight before we take a chance."

"Give me a cigarette," said Sarah Jane. "I've been sittin' behind that curtain for an hour without anything to smoke. I thought you were never gonna take a bath."

He gave her a cigarette and held a match for her. He knew it wasn't any use trying to threaten Sal or bully her because there really wasn't anything she was afraid of. But if you could get on the right side of her everything would be okay. So he began feeling his way.

"I suppose you'll go right out and tell everybody up and down Broadway."

"I wasn't gonna tell anybody at all. It's none of my business if the government is after your money. Go on, turn on the water. I'm not gonna stay."

Mr. Grasselli, alias Monk Maguire, turned on the water meekly and Sarah Jane asked, "What ever made you think of comin' here anyway?"

"It was Tommy suggested it."

"How was Tommy mixed up with you?"

"He wasn't mixed up with me. I liked the way he played a hot piano and I told him I'd help to get his music published, and then I asked him if he knew about a good hideaway. It had to be a place in New York where I could see my lawyer. I didn't even want any of the boys to know where I was. They're all kind of nervy just now and one of 'em might squeal to get himself off. And he said he knew a boardinghouse that would be the last place in the world anybody would think of looking for Monk Maguire. He was right, all right. Nobody would ever think of looking for me here. Only he didn't tell me before I came that you was here in the same house."

"He didn't know it then," said Sarah Jane. "Did he tell you after?"

"No, I heard your voice. I'd know that voice any place. Well, what are you gonna do about it?"

"I'm not gonna do anything. If you're gonna give yourself up without any trouble, you might as well stay on till the time comes. Ma and Mrs. Lefferty need the money pretty bad . . . worse I guess than any of us know."

"I've never seen your mother yet, but I like Tommy's mother. She's on the level. She keeps makin' me think of my own old woman, lookin' after me as if I was her own."

"You must get awful sick of that one room."

"I am beginning to feel a little nuts from being shut up so much." He leaned over the tub and felt the bath water.

"Why don't you come down for meals? That would be a change."

"I'm not so hot about being seen just now."

Sarah Jane laughed. "None of them would ever know. You oughta see the rest of 'em. Why, they ain't even alive. At least they don't live in New York. They're a lot of fossils." And she proceeded to give him a brief description of old Mr. Van Diver and Miss Flint, Mr. Boldini and Mr. Salmon. "You're safe as a church with them around. Sure, they'd make you laugh . . ."

"Well, mebbe I'll think about it. It's kinda like beginning a sentence already, being shut up all the time in that room. I'm gettin' awful sick of the wall paper. About midnight it begins to crawl."

Sarah Jane opened the door and went out. "Have a good bath," she said, over her shoulder. "And don't worry about me. Silent as the grave."

"Oke," said Mr. Grasselli, beginning to take off his dressing gown.

"And don't forget about Tommy," said Sarah Jane. "He needs a break pretty bad. If he don't get one he's gonna go to pieces."

"I won't forget him," Mr. Grasselli called from behind the closed door.

And then the worst happened. As she passed Tommy's door, it opened and Tommy's head was thrust out. His hair was tousled and his face red with anger, and at sight of him Sarah Jane was not so much frightened as smitten with a sudden terrible feeling of love for him, because he looked exactly like Tommy as a little boy.

"Now you've done it," he said, "spoiled everything with your spying."

"I haven't spoiled anything. I've just kind of cleared up the situation."

"Yeah?" He began to swear at her.

"Calm down! Calm down! He's not gonna beat it. He's staying right here and he's even coming down to meals. Leave him to me. I know him better than you do."

"He was going to give me a break," said Tommy. "He could have helped both of us."

"He mighta talked about it before," said Sarah Jane. "Now he's gonna do it, believe me, he's gonna."

"Better not try any monkey business with Monk."

"Listen, Tommy, I know guys like Monk Maguire. I know what kind of a rat he is. Help you when everything's goin' fine and he can use you and forget all about you the rest of the time. I know that kind of a rat . . . you oughta seen him when I came out from behind the curtain . . . scared stiff! Just leave it to me. Go on back to bed. I've been waitin' for years for a break like this."

13

It was a lot better than she had hoped. After she was in bed she lay awake for a long time thinking how dumb she was not to have guessed that Mr. Grasselli was Monk Maguire. She knew all about Monk. She'd even worked for him a couple of times in his Glass Slipper Night Club. She knew everything about him, even back in the days of prohibition when he was a bootlegger and speakeasy king. She knew about his night clubs and the money he put up to back shows and about his interest in the "drug" business. And most important of all, she knew that at heart he was a coward. She knew that all the lot were like that. They were brave enough when they worked in gangs, full of bullying courage when everything was going well, but once a guy like Monk Maguire found himself on the way out, he collapsed. She knew that it wasn't only Monk Maguire that was scared now but most of his friends and rivals. The government had them scared. They all went around quaking on the inside. She knew Monk was quaking as soon as she stepped out from behind the curtain. He didn't deserve any pity or any soft treatment; playing on the level didn't get you anywhere with a mug like him. The sooner she got Tommy out of that jam the better, because he was too innocent to cope with anything like Monk Maguire.

And she knew now who the respectable "Mr. Hirsh" with his dispatch case was. He was Mr. Berolzheimer, the smart lawyer that Monk always hired to get himself out of a jam.

Sarah Jane, lying awake until early morning, laid her plans.

14

The next evening Mr. Grasselli came out of his retirement and appeared at dinner all dressed up in a dinner coat and a black tie, his sandy hair all oiled and shiny. His appearance was the greatest moment in the history of Mrs. Lefferty's boardinghouse. For two weeks, the boarders had been aware of Mr. Grasselli's presence in the same house; for two weeks they had speculated upon his identity, his past, his appearance, his present condition, and now suddenly on an hour's warning he had appeared to become one of them. Maggie made up a couple of special dishes for the occasion. Mrs. Lefferty put on her best dress and Miss Flint, making a supreme effort, hastily ran up a concoction made of the bottom of one dress and the top of another. She it was who appeared the most deeply affected by his presence. She giggled and bridled, shaking her oriental earrings, and whenever she talked, she was completely incoherent.

For two weeks, ever since the arrival of Mr. Grasselli, the idea of him had obsessed her. There was something so exciting about the presence of a strange man mysteriously hidden in the same house with her that after the first two or three days she came and went to the Women's Exchange in the greatest peace. Thinking about Mr. Grasselli she entirely forgot about being molested. In the solitude of her own room she invented the wildest fancies about Mr. Grasselli—how after all these years he had come to her—the man for whom she had been waiting all her life; how one day there would be a knock at her door and on opening it she would find Mr. Grasselli standing there to say he was *the man*. And slowly she had come to believe these things just as she had once believed that she could not walk a block without being followed at once. So when Mr. Grasselli came down the stairs and entered poor Miss Minnie's parlor she had thought, "Here *he* comes."

He was not exactly what she had thought *he* would be. He was not handsome and she had not exactly expected him to be a little wall-eyed, but he had other qualities. Perhaps it was the hardness of his jaw and the cruel twist of the lips, the coldness in the shallow blue eyes, in which she found compensation. He was, she thought, exactly like the heroes Miss Ethel M. Dell always wrote of . . . masterful, cruel, with one eye a different color from the other (only Mr. Grasselli was wall-eyed instead). In any case *he* was a success, perhaps because his appearance was completely a surprise.

Mr. Boldini and Mr. Salmon bristled a little at the appearance of another male boarder, and Mr. Salmon became aware at once that Mr. Grasselli did not speak like a gentleman. At his corner of the table old Mr. Van Diver chortled and chuckled to himself, pleased and faintly aware through the haze of immense age that there was excitement about and that everyone was happy.

Oddly enough the only one at the table who felt uncomfortable was the newcomer. Mr. Grasselli had been through a great deal and he had seen a great deal more and he was altogether far from being an innocent, but never before had he encountered that atmosphere of gentility which reigned at Mrs. Lefferty's. Never before had he seen such courtly old-fashioned manners as those of old Mr. Van Diver and Mr. Boldini, Mr. Salmon and Miss Flint and Mrs. Lefferty herself. Belonging to a New York which none of them knew, a raucous, noisy, scrambling place where he reigned for a time as king, the elegant leisurely New York he encountered in poor Miss Minnie's house was something which made him feel clumsy and brutal and now and then brought him close to a peculiar kind of terror worse than anything he had ever felt, even in a tight spot covered by a sawed-off shot gun.

And afterward in the "drawing room" (which was a word Mr. Grasselli had never even heard) while Mrs. Lefferty sat pouring out coffee as poor Miss Minnie had done evening after evening for nearly sixty years, his fear and awkwardness increased. He became, also for the first time in his life, conscious of his own language, and aware that very often he expressed himself in words and expressions which the other boarders seemed to find quite as new as he found the name of the room in which they were sitting. And Miss Flint fascinated and terrified him, because he had never seen anyone like her before, sitting all bedizened and coquettish, bolt upright on the edge of one of the chairs that were so funny-looking. He told himself, in words which had never even been thought, let alone been spoken, before in poor Miss Minnie's drawing room, what was the matter with Miss Flint. She could be cured, he thought, only now it was probably too late and it would be very difficult to find anyone to undertake the task.

But on the whole the dinner went off extremely well save for one incident which occurred just as they were finishing something which Mrs. Lefferty called "the sweet." Mr. Grasselli sat between Mrs. Lefferty and Sarah Jane opposite the screen which hid the dumb-waiter, and suddenly without warning from behind the screen came the sound of breaking china and a muttered imprecation. At the same time one blue eye became visible at the joint of the screen and Mr. Grasselli's hand flew into the pocket of his dinner jacket.

"It's all right," said Sarah Jane. "It's only Ma trying to get a look at you. She's knocked something off the table."

15

After dinner Mrs. Lefferty and the boarders were aching to return to the non-stop rummy game but none of them were impolite enough to propose it until Sarah Jane, feeling that the atmosphere was becoming more and more arid and strained, asked Mr. Grasselli if he played rummy. He didn't, he said, but he played all kinds of cards and liked playing. He said that he guessed he could learn.

"They don't play for money," said Sarah Jane.

"Okay," said Mr. Grasselli.

"If you're all gonna play cards, I guess I'll take Tommy to the movies."

So Mrs. Lefferty fetched "the old gentleman's" gaming table and they all sat down to play. The game relieved the atmosphere enormously and after a little while Mr. Grasselli, with the worn playing cards in his fat ugly hands, began to feel more at home. He picked up the game very quickly and after the second hand no longer needed the solicitous help and advice of Miss Flint. And when the second game went to him, Mrs. Lefferty took out the copy book in which she kept the running score and wrote "Mr. Grasselli" and under it the figure one.

"Now," she said to Mr. Grasselli, "you're one of us."

During the third game Sarah Jane and Tommy returned from the movies across the street and sat down to watch. Until that point Mrs. Lefferty had been showing her usual skill and was far ahead, but from the moment Sarah Jane and Tommy returned, she seemed unable to keep her mind on the game. She kept getting caught with cards she should have played and discarding cards which were of the greatest advantage to Mr. Boldini who sat next to her.

It was, she knew, the first time that Sarah Jane and Tommy had gone out together in more than five years, and the sight of them, coming in out of the rain, both looking happy, filled her heart with warmth. She couldn't keep her mind on the game for thinking about them and watching them slyly, out of the corner of her eye. She couldn't help thinking how wonderful it would be if they took a fancy to each other and got married and settled down, so that she and Maggie didn't have to be worrying about them all the time. Tommy, she saw, was already looking plumper and healthier for the quiet well-fed life he had been living. "If only that would happen," she kept thinking, and then suddenly her heart would feel cold when she remembered the interest and the taxes and the insurance. "Maybe," she thought, "we won't have any home at all this time next year." But the story, she knew, couldn't turn out wrong. Something had to turn up.

Mr. Boldini won the game, principally by the aid of Mrs. Lefferty's mistakes, and while Mrs. Lefferty put away the cards and the score, he excused himself and took Fanto for his nightly airing.

"That's a funny-looking dog," Mr. Grasselli observed, "I've never seen one like that except on the stage."

"Fanto's been on the stage," said Miss Flint eagerly, "and he knows the most wonderful tricks. You'd never believe what he can do, Mr. Grasselli." And then she asked Mr. Salmon for a cigarette to show that she was playing no favorites, and leaned back in her chair puffing at it in the most genteel and spinsterish fashion.

"Sure," said Mrs. Lefferty, "and Mr. Boldini is a magician . . . a wonderful magician. Sometimes he does tricks that makes the hair stand up on your head."

"They ought to give a performance for Mr. Grasselli. About twice a year Mr. Boldini gives a performance just for us."

"I kinda remember that name from somewhere. Did he used to play the Palace—in the old days?"

"Sure," said Sarah Jane, "he used to travel with a whole company . . . the Great Boldini and Troupe."

[603]

"D'you mean he's the *Great* Boldini?"

"Sure," said Mrs. Lefferty with pride, "you ought to see his clippings. He's done tricks for the Kaiser and the Emperor of Austria."

And then Mr. Boldini returned with Fanto who made his entrance walking on his hind legs, and Mrs. Lefferty suggested the performance.

"Of course," said Mr. Boldini. "What about the end of the week? We've got some new tricks we've been practicing. We'd like to try them out. How about it, Fanto?" And the poodle went into an outburst of happy barking.

"And Mr. Salmon could read his poems," said Miss Flint.

"Oh . . . no . . . not really . . . I couldn't," said Mr. Salmon.

"He's a wonderful poet," said Miss Flint.

"But I haven't written any for a long time. I've been so busy on my memoirs," said Mr. Salmon.

"Sure and the old ones are good enough for us," said Mrs. Lefferty.

"If you'll read your poems, Mr. Salmon, Tommy and I will play and sing for you all," said Sarah Jane.

This was not entirely an innocent remark. In the first place she thought Mr. Salmon's poems were the funniest things she'd ever heard, funnier than anything she had ever found in the theater, funnier even than Mr. Boldini when he was giving a performance. And in the second place it would give her and Tommy a good chance to show Monk what they could do. By Friday they'd have four or five songs all worked up and ready.

"That would be wonderful," said Miss Flint, "just like a vaudeville program."

"Will you, Mr. Salmon?" asked Mrs. Lefferty.

"If you insist," said Mr. Salmon.

"All right then," said Mrs. Lefferty, "Friday night."

Then they all went to bed. The evening had been a success and Mr. Grasselli fitted into the society of poor Miss Minnie's drawing room far more gracefully than Mrs. Lefferty had thought possible. She helped old Mr. Van Diver upstairs to his room and brought him the latest moving picture classic to read when he wakened in the morning and then went off to bed thinking about Sarah Jane and Tommy and how after all things seemed to be working themselves out, all save the money.

16

After that Mr. Grasselli came down every evening to dinner, and every evening there was a rummy game and every evening he won more often than anyone else. After the second night they let him do all the dealing because he seemed to know how to do it better than any of them and the game went so much faster, and so he became a kind of croupier in the gambling hell of poor Miss Minnie's drawing room. Sometimes Tommy stayed in and played the piano and once he went out again with Sarah Jane to the pictures. Then on Thursday, the day before Mr. Boldini's performance, two things happened.

In the morning Sarah Jane came upon Mrs. Lefferty sitting on a chair in Mr. Boldini's room with a letter in her hand, weeping. When she questioned her, Mrs. Lefferty simply handed her the letter. It was brief. It said that the interest was overdue and that something would have to be done about it. The bank, said the letter, had been lenient and put up with delays in the past but under present conditions, it could no longer continue such a policy.

"So that's it!" said Sarah Jane. She knew now that all along she had been aware that there was something wrong but she hadn't imagined that it was as bad as this.

"It isn't only that," sobbed Mrs. Lefferty, "there's the insurance and the taxes."

Sarah Jane sat down opposite her and took a pencil and some paper from Mr. Boldini's desk. "Now tell me the whole story." So Mrs. Lefferty told her all about everything, about their struggle to make ends meet and about how little Mr. Van Diver paid and how much Miss Flint and Mr. Boldini owed them and how for a long time until Mr. Grasselli turned up there hadn't been any transients at all.

"You'd better sell everything and clear out. How much would you have left?"

Mrs. Lefferty didn't know. She only knew the assessed value of the house. So Sarah Jane took that and did some figuring. She wasn't very good at arithmetic but after a long struggle she managed to discover that when everything was washed up they'd have practically nothing at all.

"That wouldn't do any good," she said.

"Besides I couldn't do that anyway . . . no matter what happens," said Mrs. Lefferty.

"Why not?"

"We couldn't sell poor Miss Minnie's things . . . not after she left them for us to keep."

"Poor Miss Minnie won't know anything about it."

"Don't talk like that," said Mrs. Lefferty sharply. "Poor Miss Minnie knows everything we do. It's blasphemous." She blew her nose and added, "Anyway we couldn't. What would become of Mr. Van Diver and Miss Flint and Mr. Boldini? Somebody's got to keep a home for them. Mr. Van Diver couldn't go to Ward's Island . . . a man like him to die in the poorhouse after he was poor Miss Minnie's friend for forty years."

"How much do you have to have right now?" asked Sarah Jane.

"I don't know exactly," said Mrs. Lefferty.

After another struggle Sarah Jane got it out of her and wrote it all down. The interest and taxes and insurance and some bills that hadn't been paid. Again she did some figuring and at last she said, "Leave it to me. I guess the bank can wait a day or two more."

"I'm sure something will turn up," said Mrs. Lefferty.

That made Sarah Jane a little impatient. "The only thing I can see," she said, "is the process servers." And then almost at once she was sorry for speaking sharply and went over and kissed Mrs. Lefferty and told her everything would be all right. She was a little ashamed of herself because she knew suddenly that she hadn't made it any easier for Mrs. Lefferty and Maggie by living off them and borrowing money from them. It struck her for the first time that Maggie and Mrs. Lefferty weren't so young any more. They couldn't go on working, looking after people, forever. She didn't know exactly what she was going to do but she meant to do something. The idea did not come to her until late that same evening when she was watching the rummy game.

Somehow the spirit had been going out of the game, slowly, bit by bit, night by night. In four nights Miss Flint hadn't won a game nor had Mr. Salmon. Mr. Boldini had won a single game and Mrs. Lefferty had won two. All the others had gone to Mr. Grasselli. And now the game wasn't fun any longer, because Mr. Grasselli had all the luck. Mr. Boldini's face had grown long and solemn and Mr. Salmon never stopped complaining about his bad luck, and even Miss Flint, despite her admiration for Mr. Grasselli, found no pleasure in the spectacle of his perpetual success. And then Sarah Jane, watching, discovered the reason. Mr. Grasselli was stacking the cards. Once she was suspicious, twice she was very nearly sure and on the third occasion there was no doubt. After that she saw him do it again and again.

For a second she very nearly lost her temper and made a big scene. Two weeks ago she would have done it, but now that things were going so well with Tommy, her temper wasn't quite so bad, and after a second of heroic control, she kept silent. Mr. Grasselli won the game and after that everybody went to bed. While Mrs. Lefferty was putting away the cards, Sarah Jane said to Mr. Grasselli, in a low voice, "Wait a minute, Monk, I want to tell you something."

"Okay," he answered, "but lay off that name."

"All right, Mr. Grasselli." Then she said to Tommy and Mrs. Lefferty, "I'll be up in a minute. I want to talk to Mr. Grasselli about something confidential. I'll put out the lights."

[606]

Tommy looked at her curiously, and Sarah Jane's heart gave a sudden leap. This time it wasn't a look of anger because she might be stirring up trouble for Mr. Grasselli. It was a look of jealousy. There was no mistake about it.

But Tommy and his mother went upstairs and when they were well out of hearing, she said to Mr. Grasselli, "Well, of all the cheap, lousy bastards!"

"What's the matter now?"

"Palming the cards in a game with a lot of old women."

"Who was palming any cards?"

"Listen, I wasn't born yesterday. I saw you do it not once but twenty times."

"So what?"

"It would be bad enough if you were taking their money . . . but you're taking their fun from 'em . . . about the only fun they have."

"I never thought of that. My God, I've got to have a little fun myself. I guess it's a kind of habit . . . hard to break. . . . When I get cards in my hand . . . I guess I'm goin' nuts here anyway, bein' shut up all the time."

"You oughta be ashamed of yourself."

"I am ashamed of myself. I won't do it again, only I've got to have a little fun now and then." He was ashamed. He couldn't look at her, even with his one good eye. She had never hoped for that—a Monk Maguire who was ashamed.

"Sure. Well, I can tell you how to have some fun. I can tell you how you can square yourself."

Mr. Grasselli finally looked at her. "What?" he asked.

"Sit down."

Mr. Grasselli sat down.

"The old girls are broke," said Sarah Jane. "They're gonna lose the house if something isn't done."

"What, for instance?"

"Some money."

"How much?"

"I'll tell you in a minute. Wait till I tell you the story first."

She told him the story, all of it, from the very beginning, all about poor Miss Minnie and Tommy and herself, and the boarders who had found a little corner of peace in a city which frightened them.

"You see," said Sarah Jane, "it isn't only Ma and Tommy's mother. It's all the rest of them. They'll all have to go to flophouses or Ward's Island. See?"

"Yeah, I see," said Mr. Grasselli, "I like Mrs. Lefferty. She makes me

[607]

think of my old woman. She's been dead for ten years, God rest her soul." For a moment something glistened in Mr. Grasselli's good eye. "How much?"

"They got to have it right away. About two thousand."

"Oh," said Mr. Grasselli. "Two grand! I thought you was talking about real money. Sure, they can have it . . . tomorrow, as soon as Tommy can get it from my lawyer. What are they gonna do after that?"

The words of Mrs. Lefferty came to Sarah Jane's lips, "Something'll turn up." She didn't doubt it now. This first step was so easy that the rest seemed nothing. Anyway it was still six months or a year away before they had to worry. Maybe her mother and Mrs. Lefferty *were* right. Maybe a story like theirs couldn't have a bad ending.

Mr. Grasselli went upstairs and when Sarah Jane had turned out the lights she followed him. Just as she expected, Tommy's head appeared in the doorway of his room.

"What were you doing downstairs?" he asked.

"Business," said Sarah Jane.

"Don't pull that stuff on me."

"I'm not pulling anything on you."

"Well, take it from me. Don't get mixed up with that guy. I'll beat you up first. If Maggie isn't strong enough, I am."

"Good," said Sarah Jane, "you might gang up on me. When do we begin?"

"I should think you'd try to keep straight in the same house with your own mother."

That made Sarah Jane lose her temper for the first time in two weeks, perhaps because it came too near to the subject about which so many bets had been made.

"Listen, you! No man has ever touched me. See? And if you think I'm gonna begin with a rat like that, you're nuts."

Tommy looked at her for half a minute without speaking. "Do you mean that?" he asked. "Is that true?"

"You've got a hell of a nerve thinkin' it isn't."

"What did you expect me to think? The way you act and talk, the people you go around with."

"I thought you had a little idea of what I was like. My God, you're dumb! Go to bed and sleep it off."

And in disgust she walked off and left him. It was only after she had gone that he remembered he still had not found out what her business with Mr. Grasselli had been.

She told him in the morning when Mr. Grasselli sent him with a note to "Mr. Hirsh" instructing him to pay over two thousand dollars. Mr. Grasselli hadn't any money or securities in the bank. They were all in the keeping of "Mr. Hirsh" where the government couldn't find out about them.

[608]

17

On Friday at lunch Mr. Boldini made a disappointing announcement. His performance, he said, would not be ready for that evening. It would have to be postponed for another week. He had some new tricks. He and Fanto had been rehearsing steadily but Fanto, he explained, was not quite ready for his part and might break down. This, as a professional and experienced performer, the Great Boldini was not willing to risk. The new tricks, he said, would be stupendous, something that had never before been attempted on the stage. The other boarders, he implied, were being greatly honored by being allowed to see the first performance.

A murmur of disappointment went around the table and Sarah Jane glanced quickly at Mr. Grasselli, half-expecting him to say that he was sorry but that he wouldn't be here to witness the performance because he would have to leave before then. But he said nothing at all. He seemed to take the announcement philosophically.

Sarah Jane was aware that at any time Mr. Grasselli might decide to give himself up and once he was out of the house she knew he would be of no further use to her. Out of long experience she knew exactly how those things happened. Once he escaped, he would be too busy to see her or Tommy. He would forget all about them because their usefulness was finished. He would put them off again and again until at last their patience was gone and their hopes wearied. And so would come to an end one more sterile opportunity. She was aware too that even now when he came down to meals and played cards every evening he was beginning to be fed up. For that she didn't blame him. It wasn't a very exciting life after you had been used to crowds and bright lights and gambling for big stakes. She knew all about that. It was only the presence of Tommy which kept her quiet and subdued. Without Tommy she would long ago have found her way out of the house at midnight to go to the Excelsior Club or some other place like it.

Once her temper over Tommy's suspicions had died down, she came to see that he wasn't to blame for what he had believed, any more than Maggie, driven at times beyond endurance, was to blame because she didn't believe that her daughter was "a good girl." But she was aware that the announcement had brought about another change in Tommy's attitude toward her. It seemed to bring her one more step nearer to the Tommy she knew was the real one. It was as if he had opened a door, letting her come a little nearer to him. Those moments when he would suddenly withdraw just when she was feeling very near to him, failed to occur during the next two or three days. He seemed to relax and he no longer bristled when she came upon him suddenly while he was working, but accepted her presence, easily, almost, thought Sarah Jane, too easily.

There were times too when it seemed to her that they would never get anywhere, because they were too used to each other and because Tommy accepted her as a pal and a sister rather than someone who was no relation to him. This she found very subtle and difficult to combat, much more difficult than the problem of her own temper. The trouble was, she knew, that she had begun all wrong at the moment when he had come back into her life. She might have been strange and aloof and different, a mysterious Sarah Jane, who roused his interest, but instead of that she had gone right up to him and greeted him with a smart crack, just as if they had parted only the day before instead of having been four years without seeing each other.

Thinking about it, there were moments when, in her own room, she acted out for herself how she *should* have behaved; this she did by raising her head, lowering her eyelids, moving with the old show-girl walk she knew so well. She would study her big, handsome face in the mirror trying one expression after another in order to appear seductive and mysterious. But before very long she always broke down and laughed because she looked so funny. In her heart, she knew it was impossible for her to be mysterious and aloof and seductive. If it had been possible she would have been a big movie star long before now. She would have given in, either in marriage or otherwise, to one of those ten or fifteen men who could have given her a boost upward on the ladder of success and fame. No, there was nothing doing. It wasn't her type. She wasn't any good as a glamour girl.

Nowadays, she knew, you had to have something special to get on. Good looks weren't enough. Thinking about it, she felt sure that she really had something special, some kind of message or interpretation which she might project to the millions who went to theaters and picture houses, but what it was, she seemed unable to discover. What she needed, she thought, was someone to take her in hand and exploit her the way Mr. Von Sternberg had built up Miss Dietrich. Only it was too late to expect that now; she had been about Broadway for too long. Too many people knew her too well. Nobody would believe that "Big Sal" could be anything more than "good company." She was, she felt, after all her experience in musicals, revues and night clubs, a little shopworn. After all Mr. Ziegfeld had tried and Mr. Carrol and Mr. Shubert and all of them had given it up.

And so after a time, her rehearsals of seduction and mystery in front of the mirror degenerated into a travesty of all the tricks she had observed in the movie queens, done for her own amusement during the hours when she had nothing to do. She got out the make-up box which hadn't been used for so long that most of the materials had begun to dry up, and made up her face to give it a faraway look and plastered her eyelashes with mascara and drew over her own ripe generous lips a cupid's bow which had nothing to do with nature. The result made her laugh so loudly that Maggie came into her room one evening to find out what was the matter and thought one of them had gone crazy when Sarah Jane turned toward the door and she saw the mask which Sarah Jane had created on top of her own face. "Sure," said Maggie, "you'd better go out and get yourself something to do or they'll be shuttin' you up."

And finally she shaved off her eyebrows and with a pencil created new ones, arched far above the ones she had inherited from Mr. Ryan, the coachman. The false eyebrows with the veiled mascara look gave her a surprised, rather half-witted expression, as if she had just been startled out of a deep slumber. "Languor," she thought, "is no name for it." And made up as she was, she went downstairs to poor Miss Minnie's drawing room where Tommy was working at the piano.

He did not hear her enter but when she was quite close to him, he turned, looked suddenly frightened, and said, "What's the matter with you? Have you gone nuts?"

She didn't answer him but walked across the room, languorously seated herself on poor Miss Minnie's "love seat" and lighted a cigarette. Then it was that Tommy burst into roars of laughter. When he finished, he suddenly said, "I've got it."

"What?" said Sarah Jane, sprawling back into a comfortable Sarah Jane position.

"An idea!"

"What is it?" she asked.

"Wait till I get it worked out. Go on away and leave me in peace." And almost at once he took up a piece of paper and began working as if she weren't in the room.

"That, I suppose," said Sarah Jane, "is genius."

But there was something else which troubled her about Tommy. He had never told her anything of what had happened to him during the five years he had been away, nothing beyond the mere statement that he had been in "Chicago, St. Louis, Panama and a lot of other places." And slowly she began to be suspicious. There were times when in the midst of a mood of gayety he would suddenly grow quiet and still and a shadow would come across his face and he would look old and tired again and a little gray, and she would want to say, "What's the matter? Tell me about it." But she did not dare for fear of driving him still further from her. Whatever it was that changed him thus, suddenly, was, she knew, something which took him far from her, something that seemed to undo all the good she had accomplished, all the progress she had made. He would become remote again and almost hostile as he had been on that first evening in the Excelsior

Club. His mother didn't seem to notice anything. She was too happy at having him home again where she could look after him.

Now and then late at night Sarah Jane sometimes felt tired, for the first time in her life. It was not physical weariness, but a tiredness that affected her head, what with Tommy to worry about, and wondering what was to become of Mrs. Lefferty and Maggie, and how long it would be before they all got a "break" and how long before Mr. Grasselli would leave them to give himself up. She supposed it was because she had never had to use her head much up to now. All her life she had been free as the wind and now suddenly, she found herself having to think and to look after everyone around her. She was even beginning to feel the way her mother and Mrs. Lefferty felt about old Mr. Van Diver and the other boarders. Somebody had to look out for them, because they weren't able to look out for themselves. They were all like babies, even Mr. Salmon with his funny poetry and his "memoirs" which no one was ever going to read.

18

Mr. Grasselli had been right. Mrs. Lefferty's boardinghouse was the last place in New York that they even thought of looking for him. Nearly every day the name of Monk Maguire appeared in the papers. Again and again there were pictures of him, pictures, it is true, which bore no resemblance whatever to him. When he saw them he was thankful that he had always made war on photographers and pulled his hat over his eyes and his coat about his ears every time one had appeared on the horizon. Nearly all the pictures were photographs of a hat or an elbow or a back, which might have belonged to any man on the street. And he was lucky too, he knew, in the fact that practically nobody at Mrs. Lefferty's except Tommy and Sarah Jane ever read the tabloid papers. The scandals, the orgies, the murders, the breach of promise suits, the florid gossip which illumined their pages like fireworks, had no interest for the others. To Mr. Van Diver it would have been like reading about life in China, and for Miss Flint and Mr. Boldini and Mr. Salmon it was much the same. It was all a world of which they knew nothing, and in which they had no interest. So Mr. Grasselli kept his fingers crossed.

"Mr. Hirsh," he thought, hadn't been very quick about fixing up his case. He kept saying that what would help them most was an "adjournment." If they could get a delay, the feeling against Monk Maguire wouldn't be so strong. The public would get bored with the idea and the jury wouldn't be hostile, especially as he was going to prove that the income which the government wanted to tax all came out of bootlegging and the public didn't think that much of a crime. When he complained to "Mr. Hirsh" about how bored he was, the lawyer suggested that he leave town to which Mr. Grasselli replied, "I can't do that. I've got too many interests I've got to keep my eye on. The way things are now, everything would go to pieces if they knew I wasn't right here in town keeping an eye on them."

"Sure," said "Mr. Hirsh," "then you'd better stay right here. You couldn't find a better place."

"Yeah, that's right. But what if somebody took to following you?"

"How could they follow me? I got that fixed too. When I'm coming here, I never go out the front door of the apartment. I've got a way of coming out half a block away. I take a taxi. How could anybody follow me?"

"How's it all gonna come out?" Mr. Grasselli always asked anxiously.

"Okay. You leave it to me and don't rush things. I'll get you off."

"Mebbe I'd better beat it."

"No. You don't need to beat it."

So "Mr. Hirsh" would go away and Mr. Grasselli would sink back in bed (where he spent the whole morning) and begin all over again to read about himself and look at the pictures of overcoats and hats and elbows.

The truth was that Sarah Jane had spoiled a lot of his fun when she caught him cheating. For Mr. Grasselli, playing cards without stakes or cheating was no fun at all. But since he had stopped palming the cards, the spirit came back into the game for the other boarders. Miss Flint won a game and Mr. Boldini and Mr. Salmon two or three apiece. But after a couple of nights, Mr. Grasselli began stacking the cards again. He couldn't do it when Sarah Jane stayed at home and watched, but he did it every time she was not there.

19

At last the night of the performance arrived. Mrs. Lefferty arranged to have supper a little early so that she and Maggie could both be up in the drawing room by nine o'clock. Everybody was excited, even Mr. Grasselli, to whom the performance offered at least a change from the inevitable routine of rummy. Miss Flint seemed to be almost beside herself and at dinner talked incessantly, mostly to Mr. Grasselli, about the families she had known and worked for in the old days. After supper while Mrs. Lefferty was downstairs helping Maggie, she acted as hostess in Mrs. Lefferty's place, pouring out the coffee with the air of a duchess. When Mrs. Lefferty came up at last from the kitchen, she brought with her a bottle of old brandy, one of the last bottles that remained from the remnants of "the old gentleman's" cellar left them by poor Miss Minnie. When Mr. Grasselli tasted it, his eyes closed a little and he smacked his lips. "What is that?"

[613]

he asked, and Mrs. Lefferty showed him the bottle so covered with dust and mold that the label was no longer legible.

"Jeez!" said Mr. Grasselli, "that's great stuff. There ain't any like that around any more. That's worth a lot of money. How much of it have you got?"

"I don't know," said Mrs. Lefferty, swelling a little with pride. "Maybe twenty-five. Maybe a few more. We don't use it much."

"Twenty-five bottles of that liquid gold!" said Mr. Grasselli. "D'you want to sell it?"

"I don't know," said Mrs. Lefferty. "I'd have to talk to Maggie about it. I don't know what poor Miss Minnie would think of selling it."

"Whenever you want to sell it, let me know. I'll make an offer right now of fifteen dollars apiece for every bottle you'll sell me."

"I wouldn't want to cheat you," said Mrs. Lefferty. "Did you say fifteen dollars?"

"You ain't cheatin' me and I said fifteen dollars!"

Then Maggie appeared, not from the kitchen but from upstairs where she had gone to change, in a purple dress, wearing poor Miss Minnie's gold watch that pinned on with a gold fleur-de-lis. All day her hair had been done up in kid curlers and now it had blossomed forth in an elaborate coiffure with rolls on the side and the back instead of the usual tight screw which adorned the top of her head.

While Sarah Jane and Mrs. Lefferty arranged the room, Tommy, with a cigarette hanging from one corner of his mouth, played the piano in order to build up the mood. All the chairs and the "love seat" were removed from the end of the tunnel-like room where the piano stood, leaving it empty for a stage with two entrances, one into the dining room and one into the back hall. Then Mrs. Lefferty drew the curtains which in winter divided the room in half to keep in the heat and keep out draughts, and the illusion of a small theater was complete.

At the opposite end the audience seated itself, Mr. Van Diver chuckling with an excitement which he understood only vaguely, Mr. Boldini a little nervous and Mr. Salmon with his tie and hair carefully ruffled, already getting into the mood. In the center of the audience in a large chair Mr. Grasselli had been given the seat of honor and next to him in a smaller chair drawn very close to his, sat Miss Flint like the Queen Consort. For the occasion she had tied a bit of black velvet about her throat and wore a butterfly of rhinestones given her long ago by one of her employers, pinned in her flaming hair. She clutched her handkerchief in her hand, and kept saying, "Oh, I've never been so excited." She kept smoking incessantly. The smoke of her cigarette drifted upward and mingled with that from the expensive cigar made especially for Mr. Grasselli in Havana.

Presently Mr. Salmon retired and everything was ready and Sarah Jane stood up and announced that the program was about to begin. Mr. Salmon, she said, would open the program by reading two or three of his poems. After that would appear the Great Boldini and Fanto, the wonder dog, and it would close with an act by Tommy Lefferty and Sarah Jane Ryan, "Ryan and Lefferty," she said, "in a few songs."

Then Tommy left the piano and came to sit in the audience and Sarah Jane went to summon Mr. Salmon, who had retired upstairs in order to make an entrance and suddenly, as if they were in a real theater, the audience lowered their voices and conversed in whispers. "Oh, I'm so excited," said Miss Flint.

20

Mr. Salmon chose two poems out of his "Village" period. One was called, "In Praise of Venus" and the other, "The Tea Shop Under the El."

Long ago as a handsome gazelle-eyed boy with an open throat reading before the literary ladies of the days before the war, he had acquired a special and impressive technique, in which there remained traces of the Oscar Wilde influence. First of all he had to have a table against which to lean at moments when, apparently overcome by his own poetry, he grew weak and vaporous. He never stood on both feet but on one or the other, the legs slightly bent at the knees, so that while he read he moved with a faint swaying motion like that of an elephant in the zoo. His eyes were rolled upward and out, above his audience. At times, when overcome by some rapturous passage, the pupils would disappear entirely. And he had a special voice, with a deep organ quality which he never used on other occasions when his voice was rather lean and high-pitched.

Now, as Tommy pulled back the curtains, he took his place languorously beside poor Miss Minnie's table of teakwood inlaid with mother-of-pearl. For a moment he seemed to go into a trance waiting for the audience to grow calm and Miss Flint to overcome the excitement which had taken possession of her at the idea of sitting beside Mr. Grasselli and hearing Mr. Salmon read his poems all at the same time. Then clearing his throat he began:

> Oh, Venus, born of hot and languorous seas,
> Creature of breasts and buttocks and dimpled thighs

At the second line Mr. Grasselli began to feel nervous. Something about Mr. Salmon's poem, recited in the genteel surroundings of poor Miss Minnie's drawing room, seemed to him indecent. And the words . . . they were words which Mr. Grasselli had never used, words indeed which he had never heard spoken before. He knew all the female charms well enough but by other more vulgar words which would have offended him much less than the words Mr. Salmon used because he was accustomed to them. By the middle of the poem he began stealing glances to right and to left to see how the ladies were taking it. The faces of Maggie and Mrs. Lefferty were perfectly blank and filled with that look of awe which they both felt at any demonstration of literacy. On the angular, sagging face of Miss Flint there was a look of rapture as if Mr. Salmon's ode had been written to herself instead of Venus Anadyomene. It made Mr. Grasselli suddenly suspect the authenticity of that atmosphere of gentility which made him feel so ill at ease. By the tenth line Mr. Grasselli alias Monk Maguire was blushing and when it was finished he looked quickly over his shoulder at Sarah Jane, reproachfully, as if she herself had sat in the nude for this effort of Mr. Salmon.

There was a faint patter of applause to which the shocked Mr. Grasselli contributed nothing as a way of showing his disapproval. Then Mr. Salmon, after a bow, cleared his throat again and announced, "The next verse was written a great many years ago when I lived in Eighth Street. Some of you never knew Greenwich Village when it was the American Parnassus. Some of you are not old enough to have known it. I hope my few lines will give you an impression of what it was like during those Golden Days. The poem is called, 'The Tea Shop Under the El.' It is written in free verse."

He began:

Beneath the El obscured by the grim shadow of a prison,
Nymphs and fauns disported by the light of ancient candles on tables of ebony
    and lacquer red
Venus, enshrined, gave blessing to the revels
Unseen, reclining on her bed of clouds. . . .

As he read, recognition slowly dawned on Mr. Grasselli. The second poem like the first was filled with references to the more unmentionable parts of female anatomy, still designated by those refined words which Mr. Grasselli found so offensive; but this time Mr. Grasselli was less shocked than transported to the realm of wonder because before Mr. Salmon was half through the reading, Mr. Grasselli recognized the background of the poem. He knew that little tearoom beneath the El. It was the Tinker Bell Tea Shoppe and he figured out that he knew it at about the same time Mr. Salmon had written the poem, and his wonder was born of the fact that to Mr. Salmon it had looked so completely different from the way it had appeared to himself. He knew it very well because he had begun his career in a small room just above it where he established a flourishing business in

[616]

cocaine and heroin, and try as he would, he could never remember having seen any of the nymphs and fauns Mr. Salmon wrote about going in or out of the tearoom doors. The only nymphs he had ever seen frequenting the joint were rather scrawny middle-aged spinsters wearing batik blouses and a great deal of art jewelry; and as for the fauns, well, what Mr. Grasselli thought of them was better left unsaid.

At the close of the poem Sarah Jane seemed suddenly to be overcome by an attack made up of equal parts of coughing and sneezing and ran from the room. Maggie looked after her severely and then after a moment's pause Mr. Salmon said, "The next poem belongs to an earlier period. Indeed, this recital might almost be called retrospective, as I have gone backwards, you might say, to my origins. This little bit of verse was written long ago at a time when life was beautiful and easy and New York was a place full of kindliness and gentility and talent. Golden days they were, when I first came to that New York out of the Middle West. The verse is called 'The Open Road.'"

Again he cleared his throat and began:

> Oh, to be out on the open road,
> When the sun is up and the dew is wet.

It was, in fact, the poem which had been Mr. Salmon's greatest early success and long ago in the New York of the Golden Days it had been printed on postcards and souvenir calendars, the glorification of nature written by a poet who never left the city if he could help it and had never walked a step when it was possible to be transported. Mr. Grasselli liked this one better than the others and listened attentively, but the sense he got from it was scarcely the sense which the poet intended. The picture Mr. Grasselli had in his mind's eye was of a troupe of Bronx débutantes dressed in knickerbockers, silk stockings and high heels, hiking up the Hudson to Bear Mountain.

This time he joined in the applause. The sentiment of "The Open Road" struck him especially strongly after being shut up for a month at Mrs. Lefferty's with the possibility ahead of him of several years at Atlanta, if "Mr. Hirsh" happened to be wrong in his judgment. "That's great," he said.

Mrs. Lefferty leaned forward and said, "Isn't he wonderful?" and Miss Flint echoed, "Wonderful! Wonderful!" and Mr. Salmon came toward them and sat down, beaming. After all nothing had changed in nearly forty years since he first read "The Open Road" as a boy of twenty in Mrs. Van Rensselaer's drawing room on Sixteenth Street.

Then Mr. Boldini excused himself to go and fetch Fanto, and Tommy set about preparing the stage for the magician's act. He pushed the screen a little nearer the front, shoved poor Miss Minnie's table to one side and again seated himself at the piano and began to play. Sarah Jane, who seemed to have recovered her coughing fit, returned, and took her place in the audience, but traces of the attack still remained for every time she looked at Mr. Salmon it began all over again.

The appearance of Mr. Boldini was heralded by the wild barking of Fanto as he and his master descended the stairs from Mr. Boldini's room where the poodle had been shut up to keep his nerves quiet. Fanto knew he was going to perform and now he could not restrain his delight. It took Mr. Boldini nearly five minutes before he could quiet him enough to begin. Then he gave the signal and Tommy stopped playing and Fanto and the Great Boldini made their entrance.

The entrance came as something of a surprise to everyone for even Maggie and Mrs. Lefferty, as often as they had seen him go through his repertoire of old-fashioned tricks, had never seen him in costume before. He had chosen to appear as a Roman and was dressed in a suit of mail made of papier-mâché and painted bronze. Here and there the papier-mâché had given way beneath some ancient strain and cracked, leaving the bronze paint chipped and missing in spots. On his head he wore a helmet of pseudo-Roman design with a plume of black horsehair which fell to his shoulders and became confused with his own long, black, dyed hair. Beneath the coat of mail he wore a sort of kilt which left his bony knees exposed, and fastened about his throat and hanging down the back he wore a long cloak of faded purple pierced by a great many moth holes. One thing about the costume he had either failed to notice or been blind to: the armor had been made, in the classic Roman fashion, upon the model of a heroic warrior with all the muscles of massive trunk molded in high relief. Looking at it, one expected it to be accompanied by limbs of herculean proportions; instead, there emerged from the openings in the armor only Mr. Boldini's own skinny withered legs covered with black, coarse hair. The effect was that of a spider with a large body rearing into the air.

The sight, after the strain of Mr. Salmon's embarrassing words, was too much for Mr. Grasselli. He grew red in the face and choked and then snorted and went into a coughing fit like Sarah Jane. While he coughed and stuffed a handkerchief into his mouth, the Great Boldini waited with an expression of resignation on his face. Beside him Fanto wriggled and wagged his tail in impatience to show off before an audience. When Mr. Grasselli had recovered himself, Mr. Boldini in his spectral tragedian's voice enriched by a heavy Trieste accent said, "Ladies and Gentlemen: This evening I am going to exhibit to you a few tricks which I hope will hold your attention. One or two of them have defied the efforts of whole committees to understand. I regret that I have not my troupe with me and that the stage is too small to employ all the apparatus which would be necessary to give you such an entertainment as I should feel worthy of the Great Boldini. However, we shall do our best. And now I take pleasure in introducing to you Fanto, the World's Wonder Dog."

At the sound of his name Fanto stood on his hind legs and made a bow. He did not bark because he was too well trained and he understood now that with Mr. Boldini all in costume, he was giving a real performance as he had done long ago on a stage in the days when, as a young dog, he had traveled over half the world with a whole troupe of fellow actors; he did not bark, but inwardly he was shaking with excitement and despite anything he could do a little whimpering sound came out of him from time to time. Once the bow was made, he scurried about fetching colored handkerchiefs and wands and other bits of apparatus of which Mr. Boldini had need. This he did with the expertness of an old actor, keeping one eye on the audience, quite aware that he was already having a success behind the back of his master. He heard the faint discreet murmur of Miss Flint saying, "Oh, the darling! Isn't he cute?" and gave a faint wag of his short tail in answer to the flattery. He heard the faint, suppressed chuckles of Mr. Grasselli, and he was aware of the silent steady love and admiration of Mrs. Lefferty and Maggie, sitting there very quiet, a little terrified as they always were by Mr. Boldini's tricks. He *knew* . . . he and Maggie and Mrs. Lefferty had jokes together that Mr. Boldini, standing there dressed up in Roman costume, trying to attract *all* the attention, knew nothing about. Mr. Boldini didn't know about the way he helped Mrs. Lefferty make the beds or about the dumb-waiter trick. In spite of his fourteen years, in spite of his rheumatism, Fanto felt young again and gay and important.

The Great Boldini went on with his tricks. There wasn't anything extraordinary about them. They were tricks which might impress Maggie and Mrs. Lefferty but Mr. Grasselli and Tommy and Sarah Jane had seen them all a hundred times, better done often enough, because now Mr. Boldini was getting old and his hands were not so sure any more and worst of all, in spite of everything, he was bored by his own tricks. He didn't sweep cages full of birds out of the air or saw young women in two before your very eyes. He contented himself with the tricks he passed off at the children's parties, simple ones in which he produced odd objects out of the plumed Roman helmet and from beneath the flowing moth-eaten cloak, and slowly as he worked, he became aware that a terrible thing was happening, the same terrible thing which happened nearly always nowadays when he and Fanto appeared together at children's parties. Fanto, his "stooge," was stealing the show. His audience was more interested in Fanto than in the Great Boldini; and worst of all, as Mr. Boldini noticed from the corner of his eye, Fanto knew it and was showing off. He was insufferable, wagging his tail and whimpering and looking to the audience for approbation. Pangs of jealousy attacked the Great Boldini, and the more Miss Flint murmured and the more Mr. Grasselli chuckled, the deeper did the pangs gnaw into Mr. Boldini's heart. He knew that he was not holding his audience and he suspected, rightly, that behind his back Fanto was behaving like an elderly female star, grimacing and sitting up and turning somersaults in order to kill the performance of his master. And slowly the jealousy transformed itself into fury. He knew what he would do. He would punish Fanto. The new and wonderful tricks he had been rehearsing depended more upon Fanto than upon himself, and Fanto, whimpering and impatient, was longing for the moment when he might show off. Desperately Mr. Boldini kept trying to annex to himself the success Fanto was having behind his back. Inwardly furious, he would turn suddenly and pat Fanto's head and murmur with bitter enthusiasm, loud enough for his audience to hear, "Good old fellow!" and "Clever dog!" He would give the poodle a patronizing glance over his shoulder and then chuckle, with bitter artificiality, as much as to say, "Haven't I trained him well? Isn't he a clever dog?" And all the time he was longing to pinch the incorrigible Fanto's ear or give him a good smack to put him in his place.

Behind the frozen smile he turned on the poodle, he came to a decision. He thought, "Very well, young man, I'll fix you! We won't do the new tricks at all!" And so instead of withdrawing for a moment to put Fanto into a travesty of his own Roman costume for the new tricks, he went suddenly into the goldfish trick, the breath-taker with which he always finished his act.

Fanto knew the goldfish trick! He knew it was the end of the act. Vaguely he suspected that he had been betrayed. For a moment, in astonishment, he stopped wriggling with joy and then suddenly sat up on his haunches, very grave, all his joy gone, a chastened and well-behaved dog. It was as if he said, "I'll be good, if you'll only let me do the new tricks." Mr. Boldini made a professional tour of the audience holding out the purple cape to show that he concealed nothing beneath it and while he passed before Maggie and Mrs. Lefferty and Mr. Grasselli and Miss Flint (who was a little upset by the proximity of Mr. Boldini in so scanty a costume) Fanto remained on his haunches, still as a statue. He did not move a muscle while Mr. Boldini returned to the stage, faced his audience and impressively paused for a moment before producing a bowl of live goldfish out of the air itself. Then Fanto acted. With a swift jerk of his teeth he snatched the Great Boldini's moth-eaten Roman cloak and from beneath it fell the bowl of goldfish, water and all, on poor Miss Minnie's Axminster carpet. The score was even!

For a moment there was a dreadful silence while the startled goldfish attempted to get their bearings and swim away over poor Miss Minnie's faded carpet; then came the explosion. The sight of the goldfish was one too much for Mr. Grasselli. He began to laugh softly at first and then louder and louder, and at the first chuckle Tommy and Sarah Jane were with him. Only Miss Flint and Maggie and Mrs. Lefferty gave forth sounds of disappointment and sympathy. They had been waiting for this last great coup, sitting forward on the edge of their chairs. They had really been working with Mr. Boldini all the time, straining every nerve and muscle to make certain that this wonderful trick would come off properly before Mr. Grasselli; and now everything was ruined. Maggie leaned over to Sarah Jane and in a fierce whisper said, "Shut your face before I give you a good slap." And Mrs. Lefferty dashed for a cloth to rescue the struggling goldfish and save poor Miss Minnie's carpet. There on the front of the stage beside a Great Boldini who was shattered, stood Fanto on his hind legs barking joyously and taking his bow.

Nothing could check the laughter. Mr. Grasselli shook in a terrifying way, clapping his hands together at the same time to create an applause which was worse than if he had kept silent because each clap was patronizing. Sarah Jane began to grow red in the face and choke again. Tommy howled. Maggie and Miss Flint glared at the offenders but nothing could stop the awful mirth. It was all the more terrible because they were laughing not merely at Fanto and Mr. Boldini's mishap; it was more profound and devastating than that. It was the New York of 1935 laughing at the New York of poor Miss Minnie, of Miss Flint and Mr. Salmon and Mr. Boldini, laughing at poor Miss Minnie's furniture and Miss Flint's clothes and stories of the families for whom she had once worked, at Mr. Salmon's poems and old Mr. Van Diver's long and placid devotion to poor Miss Minnie, at poor Mr. Boldini's old-fashioned tricks and the mere idea that a magician could ever have interested large and childlike audiences. If Mr. Boldini's tricks had been the most impressive in the world Mr. Grasselli and Sarah Jane and Tommy would still have laughed in the same uncontrollable way because the laughter was an accumulation, heroic in proportion, that came from days and weeks of suppression. And the worst was that everyone in the room, even Maggie, understood this dimly.

Mr. Boldini dashed suddenly from the stage but Fanto lingered for a moment longer to savor to the full his triumph and success.

"That's great," said Mr. Grasselli, gasping for breath, "that's one of the best acts I ever seen."

"It wasn't meant to be like that. It's a wonderful trick," said Miss Flint with a frozen dignity. "Fanto is a naughty dog. I can't imagine what got into him."

When the wreckage had been cleared and the panting goldfish rescued, they waited for Mr. Boldini before beginning "A Few Songs by Ryan and

Lefferty." They waited for five minutes and then ten and then fifteen and then Mr. Grasselli had some more brandy and at last Mrs. Lefferty rose and said, "Maybe I'd better see what is the matter," and left to go up to Mr. Boldini's room.

Upstairs she knocked once and then twice but there was no response and, alarmed, thinking that Mr. Boldini in his humiliation might have done something terrible, she pushed open the door. There was no light in the room but by the light from the hall she saw that Mr. Boldini, still in his papier-mâché armor, was lying on the bed. In his basket in the corner Fanto lay curled up, looking up at her, the very picture of dejection. His ears drooped and his large brown eyes regarded Mrs. Lefferty mournfully. She knew that Mr. Boldini had not struck him, but she knew that Fanto and his master had had a quarrel and she could tell from Fanto's dejected expression that accusations had been hurled at him. It was difficult to say which figure was the more tragic—Mr. Boldini in his Roman armor or poor Fanto shrinking with shame in his basket. Mr. Boldini did not even turn his head when she entered and for a moment she thought he might be dead, but when she touched his shoulder he turned his mournful bloodhound face toward her and she saw that there were tears in his eyes.

"Sure," she said, patting his shoulder, "it was nothing at all. It was a great success. Mr. Grasselli said he never seen such a funny act."

At this Mr. Boldini gave a great sigh and a groan and turned his face to the wall.

"They're waiting for you . . . Tommy and Sarah Jane . . . to begin their act."

At this Mr. Boldini gave a great snort of anger. Mr. Grasselli and Tommy and Sarah Jane had laughed. He could still hear the awful sound of their laughing.

"No," he said, "I couldn't go down. I couldn't face them."

"Sure, and you'll spoil all the fun."

"No. Never again . . . never again." Tears began to come out of the large eyes.

"You're taking it too hard. Maybe some brandy would make you feel better."

Mr. Boldini made no response. Mrs. Lefferty said, "Sure, I'll bring you some brandy and they can begin the act and then you can come down."

She fetched a fresh bottle of brandy and a glass and left them on the table by his side and then returned to the drawing room.

"I guess we'd better go on with the program," she said. "He's all broken up. Maybe he'll come down later."

So Tommy went to the piano and Sarah Jane retired to the dining room to make ready.

It wasn't easy. Both of them were aware of that. Now that the uproarious mirth over Mr. Boldini was finished, there was a reaction, a lassitude, a faint weariness on the part of the audience, of which Tommy and Sarah Jane and even Mr. Grasselli were aware. A part of their public—Miss Flint and Mr. Salmon and Maggie—were definitely hostile, because they all knew somehow that it wasn't only Mr. Boldini but themselves as well who had roused the outburst of mirth. It was as if they sat there like a first night audience, saying, "Come on. Show us, if you're so good!" The laughter had divided the audience into two camps—the party of 1935 and the party of 1890.

Mr. Grasselli had another brandy and then Sarah Jane signaled that she was ready and Tommy began to play. Turning to the audience he said, "This one is called 'Tit for Tat.'"

Nobody had ever heard one of Tommy's songs through to the end and nobody had ever heard Sarah Jane sing one of them. The most that any of the audience had ever been permitted was a snatch or two of song drifting upstairs from behind the closed doors of the drawing room where the two "artists" worked in the late afternoons. Some of the snatches had sounded good and some of them had sounded merely detached and a little confused. Now for the first time they presented the whole, and astonishingly, it was good. Even the 1890 faction admitted it grudgingly.

Sarah Jane had put on a black evening dress, cut very simply and very low, and she wore about her throat, tied carelessly, an immense scarf of plain white silk. The costume made her appear slimmer than she really was yet it concealed none of the generous exciting curves of her heroic figure and it threw the attention at once to her face, a part of her which, despite its beauty, was usually a little overlooked by the public in its interest in other features of Sarah Jane. For the first time Mr. Grasselli thought, "The girl's got a face. She ain't just all body. She ain't just simply a show girl." As she leaned against the end of poor Miss Minnie's old square piano, waiting to sing, Mr. Grasselli sat a little further forward in his chair. Sarah Jane noticed this. It was what she had been waiting for. Now she had to produce the goods and dazzle him. Clearing her throat and gritting her teeth she prepared to give him the works.

And when she began to sing, Mr. Grasselli discovered that Sarah Jane not only had a face, she also had a voice. It wasn't exactly a voice for grand opera, although the volume would have filled any vast auditorium, but it was a voice that did something to you. Mr. Grasselli, at least, was aware that it did something to him. It was low and deep and rich and somebody—it must have been Tommy—had taught her how to use it. She did not shake her shoulders and get hot or do any hi-de-ho. She just stood perfectly still, and allowed her voice and singing to convey how she felt about the music, and her voice made the spine of Mr. Grasselli tingle agreeably. And it was good music too. It was the first time that Mr. Grasselli had ever really listened to Tommy's music, the first time he had really seen that there was something in it. "Tit for Tat" was a swell song. The rhythm of it not only penetrated the critical consciousness of Mr. Grasselli, who might have been expected to understand such things, but Maggie felt it, grudgingly for she was still out of temper with Sarah Jane, and Mrs. Lefferty and even old Mr. Van Diver who at the second chorus began to hum softly off the key to himself. As for Miss Flint, she appeared to be enchanted by the song and began to sway a little in sympathy, to tap the tip of her slipper on the floor and set her oriental earrings to jangling.

When Sarah Jane reached the end, there was a burst of applause and she noticed that Mr. Grasselli was applauding loudly and was quite red in the face, although it was impossible to tell whether this had been caused by enthusiasm or by brandy.

Then they sang another called "Here We Are in Love," and put a great deal of feeling into it and Mr. Grasselli sat still further forward in his chair and about the middle of the song it occurred to him that he didn't know Sarah Jane at all. She wasn't just "Big Sal" that he'd known about Broadway for five or six years, a big good-looking show girl who was always getting into some kind of scrape. She wasn't dumb; she couldn't be dumb and sing like that. You had to have brains and feeling to sing like that. Sarah Jane had never been the type that appealed to him. He had never liked those big, handsome women; he preferred little cuddly blond ones; but now suddenly Sarah Jane began to appeal to him. He could feel the appeal stealing over him slowly, creeping outward from his head and his imagination to the very ends of his big ungainly body. Sarah Jane had changed. He was sure of that, but he did not know why she had changed. He did not understand that for the first time in her life, Sarah Jane was in love, richly, deeply, violently in love and when she fell in love she did it in a big violent way as she did everything else. She wasn't only doing her best for herself; she was working to put over Tommy's songs as well. In her heart, although she wanted a "break" she didn't really care about herself. She was straining every nerve for Tommy's sake.

Then after the second song she retired to the dining room and there was another wait of five minutes, and then suddenly she appeared between the dining room curtains, a Sarah Jane none of them but Tommy and Maggie had ever seen before because she was made up as a siren, the way she had been the day she came downstairs and frightened Tommy into an idea. Her face was dead white and her eyebrows appeared to have risen in astonishment or terror of something she had seen and then remained there high on her forehead without coming down again. The lashes, veiling her half-closed eyes, seemed to be at least an inch long and very thick, and the mouth,

[624]

created by nature full and voluptuous, had been blocked out and recreated into a mouth which promised a perverse voluptuousness beyond even the imagination of Mr. Grasselli. It was a Sarah Jane which made Maggie think that one of them had gone a little crazy and that nobody who looked like that could possibly be "a good girl." The sight of her made the room very still until she again leaned against the end of the old square piano, and Tommy said, "This one is called, 'I'm Nada McSweeney, the Glamour Girl.'" And then the silence was broken by a laugh, a loud belly laugh from Mr. Grasselli who had seen the point.

The song itself was funny. Tommy had hit it and in the lyric he told the story of Mary McSweeney who had been "discovered" and put into pictures, and how they blocked out her mouth and stuck on eyelashes and changed eyebrows and taught her to speak in a bass voice, and altered her figure and changed her name to Nada, until her own mother didn't know her and wouldn't let her in the house. And as she sang Sarah Jane changed the pitch of her voice, ever so little now and then, lifted an eyebrow, or read a line with a faint accent. The gestures, the intonations were nothing at all, the merest outlines, but so skillfully were they done that in turn she created Garbo and Marlene Dietrich and Katharine Hepburn and Myrna Loy and a half-dozen others so that everyone in the room except Mrs. Lefferty was pleased; even old Mr. Van Diver who only knew them from his movie magazines, got exactly what she was doing and began to laugh. Mr. Grasselli laughed hardest of all, slapping his thick knees with his big red hands.

She sang:

I'm Garbo, I'm Dietrich, I'm Hepburn, I'm Loy.

She had won her audience, even the hostile audience of the nineties. When she had finished there was a lot of applause and Mr. Grasselli kept saying, "That's great. . . . Say, I'd never have thought it. Say, that's great!" Only Mrs. Lefferty seemed not quite enthusiastic. She applauded a little feebly as if something in Sarah Jane's behavior troubled her.

Led by Mr. Grasselli they called for more but there wasn't any more, because, as Sarah Jane said, "That's all we've got ready. Tommy's got a lot more songs but I haven't got them worked up."

"Sing them over again," said Mr. Grasselli; so Sarah Jane sang them all over again, but this time differently, imitating a different star with each verse, and Mr. Grasselli laughed so hard that Mrs. Lefferty became alarmed for fear he might injure himself. But behind his laughter he was *seeing* Sarah Jane very clearly. He had begun to discover what it was Sarah Jane had . . . that special something which he had never been able to define or clarify— Sarah Jane, Mr. Grasselli saw in a moment of revelation, was a great comedienne . . . a better comedienne than she was a singer; and she was a pretty good singer too. The trouble was that nobody had ever before been able to see beyond her beauty and her famous figure. They'd never let her do anything but show the body that nature, lavish and benevolent, had given her, never suspecting that Sarah Jane had other assets, more lasting, which might carry her to fame and keep her going long after her body had grown too fat and fan dancers were as old-fashioned and funny as Mr. Boldini's tricks.

When she had gone through the songs twice, Sarah Jane had to stop for breath and everybody had a drink and talked about how they couldn't believe Tommy's songs were so good and Sarah Jane could sing like that, and every now and then Mr. Grasselli would smite his thigh and say, "Yeah, that was great! Say, I never guessed you had it in you." And they all felt so well that Mrs. Lefferty decided to go upstairs and fetch Mr. Boldini. Sarah Jane said that if he'd come down, she'd sing the songs all over again.

So again Mrs. Lefferty opened the door of Mr. Boldini's room when he failed to answer her knock, and again she found him lying in his armor with his face to the wall, only this time when she shook his shoulder he didn't respond at all. Terrified, she turned him over and discovered that he was still breathing. He wasn't dead at all. The air was filled with the fragrance of "the old gentleman's" brandy, and when Mrs. Lefferty looked at the bottle she saw that he had drunk up the whole fifteen dollars' worth. Fanto wasn't in his basket at all. He was lying curled up at the foot of the bed, but his eyes were still mournful and filled with shame.

So Mrs. Lefferty with a good deal of effort got the armor off and put Mr. Boldini beneath the sheets and opened the window and as she left, she thought, "No, I couldn't turn him out. What would become of him?"

Downstairs she said, "Mr. Boldini can't come down. He's not feeling so well."

The statement dampened the gayety and Miss Flint said, "It isn't serious, is it?"

"No," said Mrs. Lefferty. "He'll be all right in the morning. What about a game of rummy?"

So they played one game of rummy which Mr. Grasselli lost because Sarah Jane, still made up as a glamour girl, was there to keep an eye on him. It went to Mr. Salmon who had won only two or three games since Mr. Grasselli had entered the contest. Then Mrs. Lefferty produced supper and a miraculous bottle of "the old gentleman's" champagne but it wasn't any good because Mrs. Lefferty, who didn't know about champagne, had left it in the cellar for too long. It had been there for nearly thirty years and it wasn't champagne any longer. So everyone had beer instead and enjoyed it just as much and at last about two in the morning they went upstairs and Mrs. Lefferty turned out the lights.

At the bottom of the stairs Mrs. Lefferty called to Sarah Jane and Sarah

Jane waited for her. She had been aware that something was troubling Mrs. Lefferty, that Mrs. Lefferty was the only one of her public whom she had not succeeded in winning, and she suspected that now she was to find out the reason. Mrs. Lefferty looked a little saddened and said, "That wasn't very kind of you."

"What wasn't kind?" asked Sarah Jane.

"What you did to Katharine Hepburn."

"What did I do?"

"You made fun of her. She isn't like that. She's *real*. She's just a nice, wholesome, honest girl. She's one of my favorites."

"All right," said Sarah Jane, "the next time I'll make her real."

She allowed Mrs. Lefferty to go up the stairs ahead of her. The old lady felt better now, and she fell to thinking what a nice evening it had been save for Mr. Boldini's mishap. In the end everything was turning out for the best what with Tommy and Sarah Jane getting on together again and staying home evenings to work on the songs. Maybe it was all going to come out all right after all. There was only one cloud over her happiness and that was the two thousand dollars that came from Mr. Grasselli. Sarah Jane said not to worry about that, but she couldn't take it as easily as Sarah Jane took it. She wasn't "modern" like Sarah Jane. A debt was a debt and she could not think how she was ever going to save enough to pay him back nor how she was going to manage things when the next payments came due. It hadn't really helped at all. It had only made things worse.

21

After Mrs. Lefferty had disappeared around the curve of the stairway Sarah Jane knocked on Tommy's door and he thrust out his head. He looked suddenly white and tired and collapsed again and Sarah Jane, to cheer him up, said, "Well, we got over big with Monk."

But Tommy was carrying the weight of five years of disappointment and disillusionment. He looked at her and said, "So what?" and that made Sarah Jane angry.

"What's the matter with you? Haven't you got any guts?"

"I don't believe the moon is made of green cheese."

"Trying to help you is like trying to lift the Empire State with one hand."

Then Tommy lost his temper. "Nobody asked you to help me," he said, and closed the door, leaving her standing alone in the hall, all her excitement and pleasure gone. The old Tommy had vanished right there before her eyes, and she knew that he wouldn't come back again for days, not until that mood of defeat and despair left him. She thought, "I've got to make him talk and tell me everything. He won't be any good until he gets that load off his mind, whatever it is. He's done something he's awful ashamed of."

In his own room, Mr. Grasselli got into a bathrobe and as he opened the door to go for his bath he discovered Miss Flint waiting in the hallway outside. He said, "Oh, hello!" with exaggerated casualness for he was not at all sure what she wanted or what she might do. At sight of him Miss Flint giggled and said, "I've got a surprise for you."

"What d'you mean, a surprise?"

She shook her finger at him. "I know who you really are."

Mr. Grasselli didn't like this. He looked at her for a moment and then said, "Well, who am I?" and Miss Flint opened her beaded bag (one of those she had never been able to sell at the Women's Exchange) and pulled out a clipping from a newspaper.

"Look," she said, "I found it in the kitchen."

It was a picture of the missing Monk Maguire but how she had ever divined that Monk Maguire and Mr. Grasselli were one and the same man, Mr. Grasselli was unable to discover. It was one of the usual pictures, perhaps a little more generous than most, for it showed about a quarter of his face with his bad eye.

"I knew by the eyes," she said in a voice filled with romantic overtones. Then she put her finger to her lips and the long earrings jangled. "But I won't tell," she said. "Nobody could drag it from me. I can keep a secret." And she left him suddenly and went on upstairs, still bridling and giggling, to the tiny room which had once been poor Miss Minnie's linen closet. In bewilderment, Mr. Grasselli stood there until she was partway up the stairway, long enough to see her lean over the rail, shake her earrings at him once more, put her finger to her lips and say, "Mum's the word."

Then she vanished, shaking with romantic excitement. She was feeling young again and almost up to date. She knew a gangster. Better than that, she knew him almost intimately. It never occurred to her that she had not yet caught up with the times and that before long gangsters would be as old-fashioned as poor Miss Minnie's furniture.

Inside the bathroom Mr. Grasselli swore loudly and eloquently while he waited for the water to fill the tub. Now, he knew, he would have to clear out, for his instinct, if not his experience, told him that Miss Flint, despite all her breathless promises, could never keep a secret like that. She could never resist throwing dark hints to the others in the house, to the people at the Women's Exchange. Luckily she never saw anyone else. Apparently she knew no one else. Mr. Grasselli was in a fury because it had happened just at the moment when he was becoming reconciled to life at Mrs. Lefferty's, and now he would have to find a new hiding place where he could still keep an eye on his business and make his presence felt by his subordinates. And try as he would, he could think of no place so secure as Mrs. Lefferty's—until Miss Flint had made her discovery.

When he had finished his bath, he got into bed, turned on the radio and took up the papers to read about himself and look again at the photographs of hats and elbows and backs. And while he read and looked, he listened to the radio, turning from one station to another, in order to get one torch singer after another, for "the old gentleman's" brandy had worn off a bit now and the discovery of Miss Flint had helped to sober him, and he wanted to see whether Sarah Jane was as good as he thought she was or whether it had only been the brandy. He listened to one torch singer after another until he had heard four and then he decided that he was right. Sarah Jane was better than any of them and Tommy's music was a lot better than most of the stuff that was coming out of the air from over half the United States into his room at Mrs. Lefferty's. And suddenly Mr. Grasselli's great idea came to him.

Once the inspiration had lost its novelty he was surprised that he hadn't thought of it before. It made him decide to stay on at Mrs. Lefferty's despite even the peril of Miss Flint. It was a lucky idea, for the next morning when "Mr. Hirsh" appeared he brought the news that the trial had been adjourned for six weeks since the defendant couldn't be located and that meant that Mr. Grasselli would have to remain in hiding until "Mr. Hirsh" felt the case was watertight and the time ripe for acquittal. With the great idea under way, Mr. Grasselli wouldn't have to be bored any longer.

22

He was a man of great energy and, like all people of vitality, he had to be doing things, creating new projects and realizing new plans. In a way that had been the secret of his great success. He had enough energy to do ten times the work of his competitors, and if one thing didn't succeed at once he always had ready a half-dozen other projects. He was never forced, like his competitors, to wait around and think up something new or to follow where others had blazed the way. Mr. Grasselli, in the realm of corruption, had always been a pioneer and an innovator; in that lay the source of much of his pride. Backed by the merest suggestion of education and diverted in the proper direction, his energy and ingenuity might have carried him to great heights in another world. That they had always been turned in the wrong direction was not precisely his fault; he was not to blame, for example, because he had been brought up in miserable poverty in slums where it was impossible for any boy to take the right path; nor was it his fault that his father had spent half his life in prison and his mother had been a drunkard. Mr. Grasselli, it might have been said, had done the best he

[629]

could with his talents considering his background, his education and the examples which surrounded him. He had accomplished a number of things, not much more corrupt than the things which got by as honest undertakings in the world of "big business." He had established a watertight drug ring and made a fortune out of bootlegging and established three of the best speakeasies in existence, one which had attracted racketeers, another which had had the most fashionable clientele in town and a third, which had done the biggest business of all, designed just for dull people, who wanted to feel at the same time safe and reckless. And he had organized and given his "protection" to the laundry business and the undertaking trade in the suburbs surrounding New York, a bit of pioneering which brought him in a large income. He was always full of plans and looking for new fields to conquer and his boredom at Mrs. Lefferty's had come about largely from the fact that the atmosphere of the place and the necessity of his keeping in hiding made it impossible to carry out any of these projects. It was, he had discovered long ago, no use to send lieutenants to arrange things; they lacked his presence and above all else the prestige of his name, which was worth a great deal of money, and they never planned things in a big way; they were likely in their small-mindedness to become absorbed in details and lose the forest for the trees. "Mr. Hirsh" was the only man with talents, which in the matter of seeing things in a large way, he felt approached his own, and "Mr. Hirsh" could scarcely be expected to take over his business. He had a large clientele of his own and he was kept pretty busy simply with keeping Mr. Grasselli himself out of jail.

23

The next day neither Mr. Boldini nor Mr. Grasselli left their rooms. When Mrs. Lefferty brought coffee for Mr. Boldini, he only groaned in response to her cheery "good morning." She left him alone and took Fanto for a walk and when she returned and went up at the usual hour to do Mr. Grasselli's room, he told her not to come back until three o'clock and that he wanted no lunch.

This was a disappointment to Sarah Jane for she had meant to take him aside and press the question of Tommy's songs. He had, she knew, plenty of connections and plenty of influence along Broadway. He could get them sung and even published. Now that she had got in the small end of the wedge, she had no intention of giving up, and she was afraid that a good deal of Mr. Grasselli's enthusiasm had been alcoholic and that once it was passed he would cool off a little, and need further prodding. It was not the first time that a gentleman after four or five drinks had told Sarah Jane she was a great artist.

[630]

And then in the afternoon just as she and Tommy had begun to work in the drawing room, Mrs. Lefferty appeared with the news that Mr. Grasselli would like to talk business with her in his bedroom.

At the announcement, Tommy stopped playing the piano and said, "Why his bedroom?"

"Well, I guess he ain't feelin' so well," said Mrs. Lefferty.

"He's got a nerve," said Tommy.

"Leave it to me," said Sarah Jane. "I can take care of myself."

"Make him come down here."

Sarah Jane faced him across the piano. "Listen!" she said, "I've been passing up breaks for years and this one I'm not gonna pass up. Take it or leave it."

"All right," said Tommy, "leave me out of the whole thing."

"Nuts!" said Sarah Jane and left the room.

She found Mr. Grasselli in his red dressing gown propped up in bed surrounded by bicarbonate of soda, the *Daily Mirror*, *Variety*, and a lot of legal papers which "Mr. Hirsh" had just left. As Sarah Jane entered, he turned off the radio and said, "Shut the door."

"No," said Sarah Jane.

"Why not?"

"On account of . . ."

"On account of what?"

"On account of the old girls wouldn't like it."

She sat down and Mr. Grasselli said, "Well, I'm gonna become a permanent, I guess, unless Nutsy Flint chases me out."

"Why? What's she done?"

"Well, in the first place, she goes around heaving and panting, and in the second place she's found out who I am."

"How?"

"By the pictures in the paper."

"How could she tell by them?"

"I don't know. I guess it must have been my cockeye."

"Never mind, I'll fix her."

"How?"

"I'll tell her that if she breathes a word they'll take her for a ride."

"Okay. I've got an idea."

"Yeah?"

"Yeah." He paused to light one of his expensive Havana cigars. "Boardinghouses is kinda out of date."

"I'll say they are."

"My givin' money to the old girls ain't gonna save the place. It's got to be put on a payin' basis."

"Yeah," said Sarah Jane. "How?"

"Well. What about a night club?"

"Are you crazy? Can you imagine Ma and Mrs. Lefferty runnin' a night club?"

"They wouldn't run it."

"Who would?"

"I would. I gotta stay shut up here at least another six weeks, and I gotta have something to amuse me."

"It'll take you six weeks to get it goin'."

"Not me. I've got a couple of guys that'll make all the changes it needs in ten days. Anyway, that's not so tough. I don't plan to make a lot of changes."

"What are you gonna do?"

Mr. Grasselli regarded his cigar thoughtfully and then looked at Sarah Jane for a moment without speaking. She did not like the look; she had seen it before too many times. It meant that Mr. Grasselli was interested in her, and that his interest was not, as she had hoped, confined entirely to her art.

"Well," he said, "I plan to keep it pretty much as it is. I'd kinda like to get the atmosphere we had last night . . . you know, kind of old-fashioned and cozy, a sort of homelike night club."

"Yeah," said Sarah Jane, "if you can make a homelike night club I'll go right to Macy's tomorrow."

"I plan to keep a lot of the furniture and the curtains and things like that so as not to lose the atmosphere." Mr. Grasselli began to feel the enthusiasm of an artist and make gestures like a window-draper. "And then I've thought of a good name, too." He looked at Sarah Jane with pride.

"What?"

"The Golden Nineties! It ain't exactly original. It was Mr. Salmon's poems that give me the idea. I think the time's just ripe for something like that to go in a big way."

"The place ain't big enough."

"Yeah, that's just it. I plan to keep it small and exclusive, see? And expensive. And have specialties to eat . . . make it an eating place where you get good food, not just one of these dumps where you pay a lot of dough for bad liquor and garbage. I wanta make it small and classy, see? With just a coupla acts to amuse the clients."

"What, for instance?"

"Well, you and Tommy doin' four or five songs." He looked at her again in that interested way which she didn't like. "What d'you think of the idea?"

"It sounds kinda nuts to me."

"Who are the tenants next door?"

"There's a box factory on one side and a couple of budding architects on the other."

"Well, I guess they won't complain, then. They won't be in nights. Yeah, I'd like to put you and Tommy on and Mr. Boldini and his act."

"Mr. Boldini?"

"Sure. Just the way he was. I never seen anything funnier. We could make the dog the star of the act and let Mr. Boldini play straight, see? Make them speeches just the way he does with that long face of his and then have the dog spoil his tricks every time."

"You mean, make the Great Boldini into a stooge?"

"That's it."

"You're crazy. You'd never get him to do that."

"Not even if there was money in it?"

"I doubt it."

"Your mother and Mrs. Lefferty would have to give me the basement and the first two floors. I can make a fortune for 'em quick. I don't want no profits. This is just to amuse me, see?"

"Yeah," said Sarah Jane. She saw clearly enough but she was trying to keep from showing her excitement. For the first time she was getting a break and she was getting one for Tommy, if only it didn't turn out the way it always did, the way those glances of Mr. Grasselli's made her suspect it might.

"We'd just have specialties . . . for dinner and for after the theayter. . . . Your old woman could superintend the kitchen . . . you know, Irish stew and corned beef and cabbage, the way she makes 'em. I never tasted 'em as good anywhere."

"I don't know if the two old girls would do it."

"Why not? I'll get 'em out of the red in the first month."

"Well, on account of they wouldn't think it was respectful to Miss Minnie."

"I get you. Well, tell 'em it would be a lot less respectful if all Miss Minnie's stuff went at auction. What d'you think about it? A great little idea, ain't it?"

"Sure."

"We can have a lot of fun together . . . especially you and me."

"Don't kid yourself about that," said Sarah Jane.

"Now don't get mad. I ain't got any bets with anybody."

"When d'you want to begin?"

"Tomorrow morning. I already talked about it to 'Mr. Hirsh.' He thinks it's a great idea. He can get men in here to work in twenty-four hours. It's up to you, see?"

"How?"

"You gotta bring the old girls around. I've got to have some fun or I gotta find a new boardinghouse. And you might ask Tommy to write a coupla 'nineties' numbers. I can kind of see you all dressed up, singing a coupla old sob songs."

"Okay," said Sarah Jane, "but don't get any ideas about me mixed up in it."

[633]

"Why not? I could do a lot for a girl like you."

"Well, I mean it. I'm not kidding and I'm not mad either. Only it just won't work so don't let your mind dwell on it." She rose to go and he said, "Okay, only tell me all about it some time. You've got a psychology that interests me."

"Mebbe I will in a pinch," said Sarah Jane.

"And don't forget Miss Flint."

"Don't worry. I'll scare the bejeezis out of her."

24

She couldn't take the thing up at once with Maggie and Mrs. Lefferty because Maggie was asleep, resting her feet and Mrs. Lefferty was across the street seeing the new Hepburn picture. And she knew that Mr. Boldini wasn't in any mood to discuss becoming a "stooge" for his own dog; so she went downstairs and told Tommy all about it.

He listened while she told him everything and when she had finished, he said, "Well, what's the answer?"

"What d'you mean? What's the answer?"

"Well, what's he gettin' out of it?"

"Nothing . . . I guess, but amusement."

Tommy looked at her sharply, masterfully, as if he were already married to her and beat her every time she looked at another man. It was a look that Sarah Jane loved. It made her feel all warm inside and every time he looked at her that way, she knew that his spirit was coming back and that he was a little nearer to being the old Tommy who as a little boy had always bullied her, and that was what Sarah Jane wanted more than anything else in the world. She wanted to be bullied by the man she was in love with.

"Why did he want to talk to you alone in his bedroom?"

"He's known me for a long time and I guess he thinks you're temperamental."

She wanted, out of vanity, to tell him that Mr. Grasselli had been making passes at her, but her instinct told her that this bit of information she could use to more advantage a little later on. Right now it might spoil everything. So she held her tongue and said, "Listen, everything between me and him is on the level. He's scared of me."

"It had better be," said Tommy.

"What about working up a coupla 'nineties' songs like he suggested? You know . . . something comic, like 'In the Baggage Coach Ahead,' or 'Down by the Wayside She Fell,' only kind of modern with a good tune you could dance to."

"I can't turn out songs like sausages."

"Well, I guess it won't hurt your genius this once. It don't matter if they're lousy as long as they're funny. We've got three or four *good* songs already. If you listen to me, they'll be playing 'Tit for Tat' and 'Here We Are in Love' over every hick station all over the country before we're open a week."

"Okay."

"You get to work on the songs, I'll do the rest of it."

"Okay."

When she left Tommy she went down to the kitchen and went through the whole pile of *Daily Mirrors* that Maggie kept in the corner to start the fires with each morning. Near the bottom she found what she wanted. Then she poured herself a cup of tea from the kettle of black liquid Maggie kept stewing all day on the back of the stove and sat down at the kitchen table. In about five minutes, as she expected, Miss Flint appeared for her afternoon cup of tea, and from the way she entered, tossing her head a little, Sarah Jane knew that she was thinking about Mr. Grasselli.

"Oh, hello!" said Miss Flint, very flip and modern.

"Hello," said Sarah Jane, "I thought I'd join you in a cup of tea."

"That's nice," said Miss Flint, pouring herself a cup of Maggie's witch's broth.

"I just had an idea," said Sarah Jane. "I wanted to talk to you about it."

"Yes?" said Miss Flint, blowing on her tea.

"I want a coupla dresses . . . old-fashioned ones . . . you know, the kind they used to wear in the nineties. It's for a number I'm building up. You'd know how to make them, wouldn't you? I mean dresses with a lot of ruffles and flounces and lace and stuff, you know?"

"I guess I haven't forgotten how," said Miss Flint.

"Have you got any ideas?"

"Well, maybe I could remember some of the ones I made when I used to go out. I made some wonderful dresses for Mrs. Pierrepont Wycherly, when she was young—you know the one that lives now at the corner of Park Avenue and Sixty-first Street, the one that founded the home for stray cats."

"Yeah," said Sarah Jane. "Can you draw?"

"Yes . . . a little bit."

While she talked, Sarah Jane kept turning the pages of her newspaper, looking up now and then to watch Miss Flint, noticing how she had undergone two changes recently, one when Mr. Grasselli first came downstairs and she had ceased to be "followed," and now a new one when she discovered who Mr. Grasselli really was.

"Well," she said, "make me a picture of a coupla dresses. Only I want 'em funny. You know, everything a little bit exaggerated."

"I don't know whether I could do *that*," said Miss Flint.

"Oh, yes you could, if you tried. I'll help you. I'm good at that kind of thing." Sarah Jane turned a page of her *Daily Mirror* casually and took another sip of black tea. "Isn't it awful," she said, "what goes on in New York?"

"Why?" said Miss Flint. "What's going on?"

"Why, it's in the papers every day. Just listen to this," and Sarah Jane began to read:

Workers on a North River dredge early yesterday morning made a gruesome discovery when the shovel of the dredge dumped on to the deck a barrel containing the body of a man who had been tortured, strangled and his body placed in a barrel which was filled with liquid cement. Late this afternoon the body was identified as that of Buzzy Leibowitz alias Buzz the Whizz alias Little Hermy, a member of the notorious Valparaiso gang.

The impact of the barrel striking the deck cracked open the cement which encased the body, exposing it, naked and mutilated, but in a remarkable state of preservation owing to the cement which shut out all air.

Sarah Jane looked up from her paper. "Isn't that terrible?" she asked.

"Horrible," said Miss Flint in a weak voice.

"But listen to this!" said Sarah Jane.

An autopsy showed that the victim had been tortured before being killed. The head and feet were tied together and the body covered with small wounds. About the neck there still remained the wire with which the victim had been garroted.

"What is garroted?" asked Miss Flint in a whisper.

"I don't know exactly," said Sarah Jane, "but I think it means slow strangulation. Listen!"

It is believed by the police that the victim was murdered for squealing.

"Squealing," said Sarah Jane, "means betraying somebody." With one eye she regarded Miss Flint and saw that she had gone quite white. The rouge stood out on her cheeks in hard spots and her lips were trembling a little. She had forgotten all about her tea.

"Aren't you going to finish your tea?" she asked.

"I don't feel like it," said Miss Flint in a whisper.

"Listen," said Sarah Jane. And this time, although she regarded the newspaper again, she allowed her fancy to insert a line of her own creation:

It is believed [she read] that Little Hermy talked too much and let slip a clue by which the police were able to arrest two other members of the gang. The body was identified by certain scars and dental work. The gold teeth for which Little Hermy was famous, had been wrenched from his jaws, probably while he was still alive.

[636]

Miss Flint's hand went quickly to her jaw, and little beads of perspiration came out on her forehead.

"Look," said Sarah Jane. "Here's the picture of the barrel." She handed the paper across the table but Miss Flint recoiled from it.

"No . . . no . . . I couldn't look at it," she said, and then rising unsteadily, she added, "I think I'll go upstairs and lie down. I don't feel very well."

"Don't forget about the dresses," Sarah Jane called after her. "I'll be wanting them in about ten days."

When she had gone Sarah Jane put the tea cups in the sink and thrust the paper into the stove. She thought, "Well, I guess that fixed her," and went upstairs to waken Maggie and see if Mrs. Lefferty had come in yet from the Hepburn picture.

25

When she told the plan to her mother, Maggie looked at her with a fishy eye untainted by Sarah Jane's enthusiasm, and said, "No good will come of it, and how can I go into the night club business at my age?"

Mrs. Lefferty received the news with a more open mind, warmed, as always, by the romantic character of her imagination. While she listened, wonderful stories began to create themselves in her brain, dazzling stories of fame and fortune and success. She saw herself branching out into a chain of night clubs, making a fortune once a month, providing for her boarders a life full of splendor and luxury. She saw Sarah Jane becoming an opera star and Tommy becoming a famous composer. And at the end just before the picture faded, Tommy would drive up in a large motor with a cut glass light in the roof.

Seated about the kitchen table they talked until Maggie, glancing at the clock, said, "Sure, and while we go on gassin', it's gettin' later and later and there won't be any supper for the boarders we *have* got."

But Sarah Jane kept worrying her, even after Maggie had begun making the dinner, and at last she got them both to admit that they wouldn't mind taking a try at a night club except for what poor Miss Minnie would think. Somehow they couldn't see people drinking and cavorting in poor Miss Minnie's parlor.

But Sarah Jane had her answer ready. "I guess poor Miss Minnie would feel a lot worse if she saw her furniture being sold off at auction to anybody who came along."

Maggie turned indignantly from the kettle filled with boiling potatoes, "Sure, and who's sellin' poor Miss Minnie's furniture to anybody who comes along?"

"What's gonna happen?" asked Sarah Jane, "the next time you have to pay interest and taxes and things? What Mr. Grasselli said is true. Boardinghouses are out of date. There's no money in them any more. You already owe him two thousand dollars. You can't go on borrowing from him forever."

"That's right," said Mrs. Lefferty. "I don't know what we're gonna do, Maggie. Poor Miss Minnie wouldn't want her furniture sold up and us thrown out on the street."

But Maggie had one more argument. "And what d'you think Father McGuffy would say if he heard I was runnin' a shindig like that? Sure, I'd never be able to go to confession again."

"Father McGuffy would tell you to do it," said Sarah Jane.

"And what do you know about Father McGuffy . . . you who haven't set your foot in a church since God knows when?"

"I'll tell Father McGuffy for you."

"And I can tell him myself, thanks."

"And will you do it, if Father McGuffy says it's all right? Will you do it if I begin going again to Mass and confession?"

Maggie dropped her spoon in astonishment. "Sure," she said, "if you'd begin goin' to Mass again I'd be willing to walk along the Third Avenue El naked as the day I was born. It's an awful thing for a mother to know that she'll get to Paradise some day and that if she waited till the trump of doom she'd never see her child there."

"All right. I'll go to Mass again."

"We'll see," said Maggie, but Sarah Jane knew she had won and she knew that she had Mrs. Lefferty on her side. There was a look in Mrs. Lefferty's blue eyes, the look that came into them whenever somebody offered her tickets in a raffle, or sold her worthless stock that was going to make her a millionaire. Sarah Jane knew that look. Mrs. Lefferty was making up stories. She knew that she had won, but she decided she'd take the trouble anyway to pay a visit to Father McGuffy and explain it to him, just in case her mother remained stubborn. It was hard to choose between the stubbornness of Maggie and the stubbornness of her daughter, but Sarah Jane knew that she had youth on the side of her own stubbornness. Sometimes when Maggie was tired and her feet hurt, she gave in.

She left them and went upstairs to Tommy, whom she found working on the new songs. He already had a melody for one of them, a melody that was haunted by intimations of Mr. Salmon's Golden Nineties but was at the same time catchy and a good dance tune. It wasn't, she knew, any use going to work on Mr. Boldini until he felt better. When she and Tommy had gone over the new songs a couple of times, she left him and went upstairs to report to Mr. Grasselli. She was proud of her progress. Everything was practically set. She only had to call on Father McGuffy and wait till Mr. Boldini had recovered and they could go ahead.

Mr. Grasselli thought they could go ahead anyway. He wrote out a telegram. "Take that out and send it to 'Mr. Hirsh,'" he said. "That'll get things started."

"It looks good, don't it?" said Sarah Jane.

"You're a great little kid." He gave her a pinch and was rewarded by a good slap.

"Lay off that," she said. "This is on the level or I'm out of it."

"Okay," said Mr. Grasselli. "Did you fix Miss Flint?"

"I fixed her all right," said Sarah Jane.

That night when Miss Flint came down to dinner she looked pale despite all the rouge she had put on, and once or twice she dropped her fork with a loud clatter. It was clear that he fascinated her more than ever but for some reason she appeared to have forgotten her coquetry. During the rummy game she became confused and played the wrong cards, and at eleven she complained of a "sick headache" and went upstairs to bed.

26

Before Maggie and Mrs. Lefferty had time to consider what had happened, three men appeared at the kitchen door and said they had come to make over the drying shed in the back yard. When Maggie asked indignantly who had sent them and what they were doing to the drying shed, they said that a "Mr. Hirsh" had sent them and that they were to look it over to see whether it could be made into an addition to the kitchen. She told them sharply that she didn't need any more kitchen than she had already and she would have sent them away but for the sudden appearance of Sarah Jane who conducted them through the kitchen and showed them where they were to go to work. About an hour later a contractor arrived and Sarah Jane and Tommy took him through the first and second floors showing him what he was to do.

There weren't many changes. Poor Miss Minnie's Axminster carpet was to be taken up and a floor of hardwood put down in its place, and the opening between the dining room and the tunnel-like drawing room had to be widened. In the kitchen two more stoves and an extra sink had to be installed. "Mr. Hirsh" got in touch with the right men to buy small tables, chairs, linen and silver but there wasn't much to buy because Mr. Grasselli always had a lot of table linen and silver stored away, the residue of one of his other night clubs. The first time since Minnie had come to the house, perhaps for the first time in all its existence, it was thrown into a hubbub of activity. The moment the workmen disappeared Mr. Grasselli would descend and inspect what they had done and have a lot of new ideas. A remarkable change came over him. Now that he had a project under way, his spirits rose. He no longer sulked in his room, and no longer became ill at times with boredom. He even ceased to stack the cards in the rummy game whether Sarah Jane was absent or not.

As for Maggie, she took up an embattled position in the kitchen and, surrounded by workmen and dust and débris, refused to be moved. If the workmen got in her way, she berated them until presently they came to live in half-humorous terror of her. And on the third day after Mr. Grasselli's gigantic operations had begun, she put on her hat with the plumes and went to see Father McGuffy. But Sarah Jane had been there first and told him the whole story, truthfully, except for slipping over the true identity of Mr. Grasselli; so Father McGuffy told Maggie that he saw no harm in her running an ordinary restaurant (which was how Sarah Jane had described the project) especially as she was a good woman and came regularly to confession and with Mrs. Lefferty (the backslider) was doing a good Christian work in taking care of old Mr. Van Diver and Miss Flint and Mr. Boldini. So long as she didn't turn them out into the world, there was nothing wicked in the project.

But Maggie had no intention of turning them out, or Mrs. Lefferty either. It required a good deal of ingenuity to keep them there and give them three meals a day while all the renovations were going on, what with workmen about and the house being torn down over their heads, but Maggie and Mrs. Lefferty managed it. They simply had the meals in the servants' sitting room instead of the dining room and Sarah Jane gave up her own room to share Maggie's. They played rummy in the evening either in Mr. Grasselli's room or in the torn up drawing room. When Mr. Grasselli proposed that all of them, except himself, take their meals in a restaurant to make things easier, Maggie and Mrs. Lefferty rejected the idea with vigor. Nobody would feel at home in a restaurant, and what about poor Mr. Van Diver? He was already confused out of his wits by the hammering and the pounding and the fact that he could not remember from one hour to another why there was such confusion and disorder in the house. What would he think of eating in a restaurant? Now and then, whimpering, he would come to Mrs. Lefferty to ask whether they were pulling down the house over his head and when he would have to leave.

Only old Mr. Van Diver and Miss Flint seemed to be disturbed, for even Mr. Boldini, once he had been brought round, grew excited, and Mr. Salmon seemed to take on a new youth, because he became aware presently that he was being brought up to date in spite of himself and that perhaps out of all the confusion, his genius might be reborn and he might go into a "fourth period" of creation. But Miss Flint seemed odd and depressed. Except at rare moments, she no longer tossed her head until the earrings jangled, and when she went out to the Women's Exchange now she always wore a veil, a relic of the nineties so thick that Sarah Jane wondered how she could see where she was going. Once more she took to being "followed," only now it was not by young men who were attracted by her charms but what she referred to as "rough individuals" who were bent on a more dark and sinister purpose. She scarcely spoke at all when Mr. Grasselli was about, and whenever he was not looking at her she stared at him fascinated with a look of mingled terror and admiration in her eyes.

27

The "bringing-round" of Mr. Boldini was accomplished by Sarah Jane. She did it craftily, waiting for two days until Mr. Boldini appeared a little less yellow and depressed. When the effects of the awful night had passed and the first workman had appeared in the house, she allowed Mrs. Lefferty to tell him that Mr. Grasselli was planning to turn the place into a night club. This news he received with dubious enthusiasm, for he was still feeling embittered about everything even faintly connected with the show business. Sarah Jane allowed him a day of reflection and recovery during which Mr. Boldini's bitterness about the fiasco of his performance became transformed, as Sarah Jane had hoped, back into the old bitterness at being unable any longer to find a job save at children's parties. And on the fourth day, Sarah Jane knocked and bustled into his room full of enthusiasm and excitement.

"I've got news for you, Mr. Boldini," she said.

Raising his large yellow eyes, he regarded her dismally, as if the mere sight of anyone so young and so enthusiastic depressed him.

"What?" he asked with indifference.

"I've got a job for you?"

"What kind of a job?"

"A job as a magician . . . a regular job, seven nights a week."

"Where?"

"Right here in the house," said Sarah Jane. "You won't even have to go out."

He began to display a faint interest and instead of looking out of the window regarded Sarah Jane for the first time. Even Fanto looked up and wagged his tail as if he too were beginning, after his disgrace and triumph, to take an interest in life.

"Yes," said Sarah Jane, "Mr. Grasselli thought you were wonderful."

"Mr. Grasselli," said Mr. Boldini in a hollow voice, "laughed. He laughed the hardest of all."

That made Sarah Jane see that it was going to be difficult to persuade Mr. Boldini.

"That was it . . . he appreciated it. That's the way he showed he liked it."

"What does he want me to do?"

"He wants you to put on the act just as it was, with a few small changes."

She saw from the way he looked at her that he was beginning to be suspicious. "What changes?" he asked, in the same hollow voice.

"Well, you see, it's like this." Then suddenly she found that she had begun without knowing where she was going. She coughed and said, "It's difficult to explain . . . but you see, he liked the finish. He wants to make it all like that."

"You mean the part where everybody laughed?" He glanced suddenly at Fanto's basket and Fanto cowered with shame.

"Well, not exactly, only he wants to make it into a laugh act. See? He thinks it would be one of the greatest acts ever."

For a moment Mr. Boldini stared at her as if he could not believe his ears; then all the dewlaps and ridges and furrows in his bloodhound face contracted until he became the picture of outraged Roman dignity.

"Do you know what you're asking, young woman? Asking me, the Great Boldini, to make a prostitute of myself!"

"No, not *that*, Mr. Boldini! You get me wrong."

"Me, the Great Boldini, who has been president of the International Society of Magicians!" He began to thump himself on the chest so hard that Sarah Jane became alarmed. "Me!" he continued, "who has given command performances before the Emperors of Germany and Austria!"

Shouting the last words he turned his back to her and stood staring into the street. Sarah Jane waited for a moment and then said, "Listen, Mr. Boldini, it isn't like that. Look at me, for example. Well, I was known as the most beautiful show girl on Broadway. Mr. Ziegfeld, God rest his soul, glorified me. Mr. Carrol put me on as Lady Godiva. I've been a fan dancer and a balloon dancer, but d'you know what I'm going to do? I'm going to be a comic. Why? Because show girls and fan dancers have gone out of fashion. The public is sick of 'em. They want to laugh, see? It's just like boarding-houses and magicians. They've gone out of date too. And the Kaiser and the Emperor of Austria. Where are they now?"

Mr. Boldini, it seemed, did not know the whereabouts of the Kaiser and the Emperor of Austria. He turned suddenly and gave her a single swift look of fury. But Sarah Jane meant to drive home her point, "Name me a single magician that's making a good living. Just name me one!" She paused but Mr. Boldini, it seemed, couldn't think of any, so the question became purely rhetorical. "No, the public is sick of magicians . . . anyway of magicians playing straight. Houdini ruined them. The public knows all about magic." Again he turned and glared at her, but she continued, "No, Mr. Boldini, times have changed, and we artists have to change with it. See? An artist isn't any good unless he keeps up to date." Then in a more quiet mood she said, "All Mr. Grasselli wants you to do is to do your magician's act up to date and teach Fanto to be a clown."

Mr. Boldini gave Fanto another savage look and again Fanto cowered with shame. "That's easy enough. That's all he is—a clown! There isn't a drop of artist's blood in him."

"Clowns can be artists, Mr. Boldini, just the same as you and me."

"Well," said Mr. Boldini, turning from the window. "What does he want me to do?"

But Sarah Jane didn't tell him at once. "There'll be a lot of money in it."

"How much?" asked Mr. Boldini.

"Well, maybe as much as seventy-five dollars a week."

"I get thirty-five dollars a performance already without Fanto—and fifty with him."

"Yes, but you only work about once every two or three weeks."

"During the school holidays I work sometimes as much as four times a week."

"All right. Maybe Mr. Grasselli would pay you a hundred a week." Mr. Grasselli had said he'd pay up to a hundred and twenty-five if Mr. Boldini was as good as he was the night Fanto ruined his act, but Sarah Jane didn't tell him this. She wanted to keep the extra twenty-five as a margin with which to bargain against Mr. Boldini's dignity, the Society of Magicians and the two emperors.

Suddenly, without warning, Mr. Boldini became indignant again, so indignant that he slipped back into his richest Trieste accent. "You ask me to become a feeder, a stooge for my dog . . . that ungrateful clown of a dog."

"No," said Sarah Jane, "it's not like that at all. He just wants Fanto to learn some new tricks."

While they talked, Fanto in his basket was swept back and forth like a pendulum between the poles of emotion. When Sarah Jane spoke he pricked up his ears and wagged his tail and when Mr. Boldini referred to him, he was covered with shame and dejection.

"I'll tell you something," said Sarah Jane confidentially. "If you leave it to me I think I could get him up to a hundred and twenty-five a week and if we're successful, Mr. Grasselli might put us into a revue he's got an interest in."

This time Mr. Boldini didn't answer but turned away again to the window, not indignantly now, but thoughtfully, lost perhaps in considering that if he took the job he might be able to pay Mrs. Lefferty what he owed her, that he might become famous again, that he might have money enough to live again in the Astor Hotel.

"All right," he said, "I'll think it over."

"I'll tell Mr. Grasselli." She knew Mr. Boldini meant to do it. She had

[643]

known a lot of Italians and she knew he was talking like this just to save his face and pretend that he was giving in as a favor to her and Mr. Grasselli. "Mr. Grasselli," said Sarah Jane, "will show you what he means. Maybe he'll help you work out the act."

"Who is Mr. Grasselli that he should tell me?" asked Mr. Boldini.

"Don't worry. He knows all about show business. He's backed a lot of shows."

As she left the room she noticed that there was a new expression in Mr. Boldini's melancholy face, an expression she had never seen there before. For the first time he looked as if he expected something a little better than the worst.

28

That afternoon Mr. Grasselli himself honored Mr. Boldini by a call in his room and there, after Mr. Boldini had gone through another fine performance of indignation and wounded dignity and breast beating, they got down to brass tacks and discussed the act. It was not difficult, Mr. Grasselli said. Mr. Boldini would only have to keep the speeches and gestures he already made, losing none of their solemnity and impressiveness, and Fanto would have to learn a few new tricks, or rather change a little the tricks he already knew, turning them into impudence and comedy. The trouble, Mr. Grasselli knew from the beginning, would be in forcing Mr. Boldini to play "straight," to suppress his jealousy of Fanto and abandon all attempts to horn in on Fanto's success.

They went to work at once and for days they rehearsed the act above the din of hammering and pounding from belowstairs. They worked in poor Miss Minnie's bedroom, now occupied by Mr. Grasselli, because it was the biggest, with Mr. Grasselli lying in bed smoking a cigar and Mr. Boldini and Fanto performing at the far end.

From the very beginning the dog was easy. He soon gathered what was wanted of him and asked nothing better than to play the role of clown. But Mr. Boldini was a problem. It was, Mr. Grasselli discovered, like trying to make Sarah Bernhardt stand by and hold the handkerchief for a troupe of acrobats. All during the performance he kept regarding his audience with one eye, telling Mr. Grasselli by the smug expression in his bloodhound countenance that he knew how good the dog was, and wasn't he cute, and of course he couldn't have learned all those tricks save for Mr. Boldini himself. And at first as Fanto spoiled one trick after another for him, he would turn, instead of giving an exhibition of that divine indignation which had driven Mr. Grasselli to hysterical laughter, and pat the dog's head to show that there was

[644]

no ill feeling, and to take for himself a little of the glory of Fanto's cleverness. Then Mr. Grasselli would sit up in bed indignantly and say, "No, not like that, Mr. Boldini! You've got to be mad at the dog! Get me? You've got to be funny!"

That was a fatal suggestion, for nothing could be more terrible than the result of telling Mr. Boldini to be funny. He wasn't a comedian. He wasn't even an actor, but he was convinced that he was both; and his idea of being funny was to take the audience into his confidence and let them know how funny he was being. With a patience he had never known before Mr. Grasselli labored with Mr. Boldini until he came to the verge of giving up the whole thing as a bad job, and then by accident he found out how he could get the effect he wanted.

"Listen," he said, with exaggerated patience, "get this in your mind, Mr. Boldini. I know it's the hardest thing in the world to get a ham to play a ham. See? You're a broken-down ham magician and every time you do a trick your dog spoils it and that makes you mad. Get me?"

But while he was talking an expression came over Mr. Boldini's face that very nearly frightened Mr. Grasselli.

"So I'm a ham, am I?" he cried. "A broken-down ham magician . . . me! The Great Boldini! You tell me that?"

Mr. Grasselli held up his hand. "Now, listen, Mr. Boldini, I didn't say you were a ham. I was just telling you you must think of yourself as a ham. That's what acting is, ain't it? That's what great art is. Now listen, be sensible and go ahead with the act."

Fuming, Mr. Boldini went ahead with the act and miraculously in his fury and wounded vanity, he gave exactly the effect that Mr. Grasselli wanted. Crushing out his cigar, Mr. Grasselli lay back in bed and laughed, very nearly as hard as he had laughed on that first night. "That's it!" he said. "That's exactly it!"

Mr. Boldini beamed, and Fanto, the clown, aware that he had at last got the laugh he wanted, barked and wagged his tail frantically.

"You're a great artist, Mr. Boldini," said Mr. Grasselli, "when you do it like that. Let's do it again and see if we can hold it."

But when he did it again, in a good humor now, Mr. Boldini fell back into his old tricks, smirking sidewise at the audience, giving Fanto patronizing glances and trying to keep the stage all for himself. It was terrible. But Mr. Grasselli had discovered his secret. You had to make Mr. Boldini mad to get the effect you wanted. Only you had to use the secret discreetly. If you kept making Mr. Boldini mad at rehearsals his rage would have the edge off it by the time he came to give a performance. So craftily Mr. Grasselli said, "That's great! You've got it. That's great!" and bided his time.

[645]

29

In the meanwhile Tommy and Sarah Jane were making progress with their songs and Miss Flint was making progress with Sarah Jane's dresses.

Tommy had written two "nineties" songs and Sarah Jane was learning them. One was called "The Poorhouse with You" and the other "She Was the Bartender's Sister." Now they had five good songs. Sarah Jane worked at them giving them everything she had, taking a tip now and then from Mr. Grasselli when she thought it was a good one and rejecting others when she thought they were bad, for she was aware of a sudden new confidence, different from anything she had ever known before, not like the confidence she had felt as a fan dancer or as Lady Godiva when she simply displayed with generosity what a lascivious nature had bestowed upon her. That was just luck and she hadn't anything to do with it. This confidence was different. It was Tommy who told her that it was what you called "creative confidence." She knew how a song ought to be sung. She knew when she was right and when she was wrong. And best of all, Tommy trusted and praised her. Now and then he would stop playing and look at her with something close to awe in his blue eyes and say, "You've got it, baby! I don't know where it came from, but you've got it!" That always made her feel faint with happiness.

But Tommy didn't seem properly excited about their début. As the time drew nearer, as the alterations were finished, one by one, and the tables and chairs and linen and silver began to arrive, he seemed to grow more and more depressed and nervous. When Sarah Jane questioned him directly he said it wasn't anything, but he always looked away from her and she was sure again that there was something troubling him which she knew nothing about, something which had happened while he had been away from her for five years.

Miss Flint had a good deal of trouble over the dresses. She remembered the design she had made for Mrs. Pierrepont Wycherly but just how the intricacies of their ruffles and stays, lace and passementerie were put together she had forgotten. It took a great many fittings, which were hard on Sarah Jane's temper, and Miss Flint, heavily veiled, had to make a good many trips to shops, because Sarah Jane was a good deal bigger than Mrs. Pierrepont Wycherly and Miss Flint found that she was always underbuying. During the fittings Sarah Jane accidentally revealed that she shared Miss Flint's awful secret and after that the sewing woman never talked except on one subject —Mr. Grasselli alias Monk Maguire. She no longer referred to him by name but only as "he" or by sinister nods of the head in the direction of his room belowstairs. She asked questions until Sarah Jane thought she was going crazy. Most of the answers she did not herself know and some of them she made up, as when Miss Flint asked, "How many men d'you think *he's* taken for a ride?" and Sarah Jane replied, "Oh, I suppose about thirty or forty . . . roughly, that is . . . about thirty or forty." And with a mixture of terror and admiration in her voice, Miss Flint answered, "I suppose he's what you'd call a modern Robin Hood."

"Not exactly," said Sarah Jane, "not exactly a Robin Hood."

But the dresses went ahead well. There wasn't any need of having Miss Flint exaggerate their lines and cut and ornament. What Miss Flint regarded as making them "straight" was funnier than anything Sarah Jane could think up in the way of exaggeration. What annoyed Sarah Jane was having to buy a corset and pull in her generous Venus de Milo waist to suit the styles of the nineties. After she bought it, she always put it on when practicing "The Poorhouse with You," and "She Was the Bartender's Sister" so that she would feel used to it because it was the first time she had ever worn such a thing. In that kind of corset, she discovered, you had to breathe in a special way.

But Miss Flint herself seemed to grow thinner and more wrinkled and silent and about four days before the opening she developed a tic which made one eye and her mouth twitch without ceasing. Mr. Salmon noticed this, and out of his knowledge of psychoanalysis, decided that there was something troubling Miss Flint's "subconscious."

30

And then suddenly the alterations were all finished and the chairs and tables installed and Maggie's two assistants arrived and in the afternoon there was a final rehearsal of cooks and waiters, captained by Victor Leontopopulos, a headwaiter who had served Mr. Grasselli at the openings and closings of countless night clubs and speakeasies. And at three o'clock, behind closed and curtained doors in poor Miss Minnie's drawing room, the performers held a rehearsal under the eye of Mr. Grasselli, the impresario. The act of "Ryan and Lefferty in a Few Songs" went perfectly, but Mr. Boldini was terrible. Sarah Jane and Tommy, watching, were aware of this and it troubled Sarah Jane that Mr. Grasselli either did not notice how terrible it was or he did not seem to mind. When she drew him aside after the rehearsal and said, "Old Boldini is going to be terrible," he only grinned at her and replied, "Never mind. He's going to be great. You wait and see."

"You're nuts if you think that," said Sarah Jane.

Then the worst happened about eight o'clock in the evening when Tommy didn't come down to dinner. He sent word by his mother that he didn't feel very well and wanted to lie down for a while in the dark. When Mrs. Lefferty told her the news, Sarah Jane was aware that all along she had known this was going to happen. Her instinct had told her, if she had only listened to it, that Tommy was still a broken reed that under pressure might collapse completely.

When she had eaten a quick but substantial dinner (for Sarah Jane was so healthy that she could not work on an empty stomach and nothing upset her appetite) she hurried up to Tommy's room and knocked.

In response to his "Come in" she entered and found him lying in the dark on his bed. By the light from the hall, she found her way to the foot of the bed and stood there looking down at him. He didn't even stir and made no effort to speak until she said, "Well?"

Then he said, "It's no use. I can't do it. You've got to find another piano player."

Suddenly she was angry and scornful. Fury blazed up inside her, but in the next second, remembering what she had learned, she counted ten before speaking and then said, "You must be crazy. I can't get a piano player at this hour. And anyway he couldn't do those songs the way we do them. Not even Paderewski could do it."

"I can't," said Tommy. "That's all there is to it."

"What's the matter with you?"

"I don't know . . . nerves, I guess . . . jitters. What you call neurasthenia. I'm scared."

Quietly she came round the end of the bed and sat on the edge of it by his side. "Listen," she said. "You can't do that. You can't let us all down . . . not now, when everything is ready."

"I can't," said Tommy in a low voice. "I guess I'm going nuts. I've been trying to think of the music and I can't even remember it. I guess I'm going nuts. If I went on to play I wouldn't know what I was playing."

Then she was aware by the dim light from the hall that there were tears on his cheek. He said almost in a whisper, "I don't want to act like this. I can't help it. It isn't my fault, Sally."

Her heart suddenly leaped. He had called her Sally long ago when they played together in the back garden at poor Miss Minnie's house on Murray Hill; but he had never called her that since he came home. She knew suddenly that she didn't care about "The Golden Nineties" or her career or anything. She only cared about Tommy. But she knew too that she had, somehow, to make him go through with their performance for his own sake more than for any other reason. She had to make him do it in order to save him.

"Don't you see?" he said, "I'm nuts or something."

She had to think quickly and skillfully; she knew that she could not risk making a mistake. After a little silence in which she abandoned thought and allowed her instinct to tell her what to do, she asked, "Is it on account of something that happened while you were away?"

He didn't answer her, and after another silence she said, "Was it something you did?" and in a whisper, he said, "Yes."

Then suddenly she reached over and took his hand. It was the first time they had touched each other since he came back, and the feel of his hand brought a lump in her throat, a lump caused as much by happiness as by pity. In the dark she felt his hand take hers and press it tightly, almost hysterically, as if he depended on her. Then she said, "Tell me. What is it?" But he didn't speak.

"Tell me," she said. "It'll do you good. You know, don't you, that I'm all for you . . . that I'd do anything for you? You know that, don't you, Tommy?"

"Yes."

"Well, tell me then . . . what was it . . . ?"

After a long silence, he said, "I was in jail."

That didn't surprise her, because it was what she expected. "What for?" she asked.

"Bootlegging . . . in Detroit."

She laughed. She couldn't, in her relief, help herself. "That doesn't matter," she said. "Bootlegging wasn't any crime. Everybody did it . . . everybody was guilty . . . people who drank were just as guilty. Nobody cares about that."

"I beat it," he said. "I got out of jail by a trick and beat it."

"Well," said Sarah Jane, "that was very smart of you. So what? All that's finished. Nobody's gonna bother you about that. All that's squashed."

"It wasn't only that," said Tommy.

"What else? Go on! It'll do you good to talk."

"It was a lot of other things I did."

"What?"

"It's no use talking about. A lot of things . . . little things I'm ashamed of. I don't know how or why I did them except that sometimes it was on account of getting a meal or a place to sleep. D'you know what it's like, Sally, to be hungry and cold and sleepy and have nothing to eat and no place to go? Maybe I was kind of weak. But then it seemed to me anything was better than that."

She pressed his hand again softly. "Go on," she said, "tell me. I get it all."

"It's no good telling you some of the things. I'm ashamed to. I'm ashamed because I was ashamed of you and Ma and Maggie. I thought I was too good for you all until I found out I wasn't good enough."

"I know," said Sarah Jane, "I knew all that."

"How did you know?"

"I'm not so dumb."

"I guess that's what's the matter with me. I'm sick inside."

[649]

"It don't matter, now," said Sarah Jane. "It's all finished. You weren't the same as Ma and me and your mother. You're kind of a genius too, I guess . . . sensitive like. You were kind of different and you got to know a different kind of people. That's all washed up now. We're both down to brass tacks again. That's why I know everything is gonna be swell for both of us. I'll bring you a drink and you'll be all right."

"No," said Tommy, with a sudden return of hysteria. "I can't! I can't sit up there in front of all those people. I can't remember anything. It's all kind of come back at once in a heap. I can't explain exactly—only all I want to do is to hide—like this in the dark."

So now, she knew, there was only one thing left to do, and again she knew she mustn't do the wrong thing. It had to be just right. She didn't know anything about neurosis and she didn't know anything about psychoanalysis but she did know a lot about people, and about men. So for a second time she abandoned thought and trusted her instinct.

"Tommy," she said.

Out of the darkness his voice answered her, tired and frightened. "Yes?"

"Tommy, would you marry me?"

There was a silence and then he asked, "Do you really mean that? You're not kidding me?"

"I never meant anything so much in my life. I've always been in love with you, I guess. Anyway since I was about sixteen years old. Now, there it is! How do you feel about it?"

He pulled her hand up to his lips and kissed it. "There," he said. "That's how I feel. I guess I always felt the same way about you, only I was a fool. I didn't know it till just lately . . . I wanted to ask you only I didn't dare."

"Why?" asked Sally. "I tried to make you see it."

"I couldn't, because I was so ashamed of myself, and I didn't have anything to offer . . . nothing at all but failure. I didn't even have any guts. And you could marry all kinds of guys with money and Rolls-Royces and diamonds."

"Oh!" said Sarah Jane. "Those squirts! You needn't have worried about them."

In the darkness he pulled himself up and sat cross-legged on the bed. "Gee!" he said, "Gee! I'm still sort of afraid of you, Sally."

She leaned across toward him. "And now I can look after you," she said, "and keep you out of trouble. You oughtn't ever to get mixed up with people like Monk. You don't know how to manage 'em. See, from now on, you can just work at your music and not worry about anything at all."

Then suddenly he put his arms about her. He didn't speak at all but only kept saying, "Sally! My God, Sally!"

Then they both knew that it had been waiting for them all along, all the time, for years, and now when it came to them it was better than anything

[650]

they had dreamed of because they *knew* each other. They had known each other always. There wasn't any strangeness. There wasn't anything they had to find out about each other.

31

At about eleven-fifteen the first clients began to arrive and about a quarter to twelve poor Miss Minnie's drawing room and dining room were filled to capacity. Victor Leontopopulos had even set up two small tables in the hall and one against the back of the piano itself. In the dining room near the dumb-waiter and the screen from behind which Maggie had given Mr. Grasselli a fright, there was a special table reserved for Mrs. Lefferty and the boarders, and here early in the evening Miss Flint and Mr. Salmon had installed themselves. Mr. Boldini and Sarah Jane and Tommy could not appear of course until after their performances; Mrs. Lefferty was still bustling about now upstairs and now down and now in the kitchen where an embattled Maggie, her face red and her eyes shining with the light of crisis, was directing the putting together of more last minute corned beef hash and Irish stew. Mr. Van Diver was kept in his room until Mrs. Lefferty was ready to sit down because she knew that if he came down alone and found the rooms where he had courted poor Miss Minnie filled with a noisy pushing crowd of strangers, he might do anything. He might even think that Ward's Island was a better place to live.

Mr. Salmon, in a dinner jacket but still wearing his flowing tie, sat by the side of Miss Flint at the center of the table. For the great occasion she had made herself a new dress out of three old ones and some of the pieces left over from Sarah Jane's costumes. Around her sagging throat she wore the bit of black velvet and in her flaming hair the butterfly of rhinestones, and from somewhere she had produced a *lorgnon* which Mr. Salmon had never seen before, and which she now held before her nearsighted eyes from time to time to regard the patrons. These in turn stared back at her, not quite sure whether she was simply a bit of atmosphere like the curtains and the pictures or whether she was one of the performers. Mr. Salmon, watching her, from time to time out of the corner of his eye, noticed that her "subconscious" was still troubled by something. Her mouth and eyes still twitched, worse than ever.

A moment or two after they were seated Victor Leontopopulos came over to the table and asked them what they would have to eat, handing them a menu filled with a list of Maggie's specialties which made them feel all at the same time at home and very strange, because it was the first time in all the years they had been here that they had seen Maggie's dinners set down in cold print. When they said they would wait for the others, Mr. Leontopopulos invited them to have a bottle of champagne, tactfully adding that he had received instructions that they were to have everything and that it would all be "on the house." So they had a bottle of champagne and presently Mrs. Lefferty with old Mr. Van Diver in tow appeared through the passage from behind the screen and joined them and Mr. Leontopopulos bounced up to the table with another bottle of champagne.

Mrs. Lefferty wore a fine purple dress with poor Miss Minnie's seed pearls and looked very handsome, handsomer than Mr. Salmon had ever seen her look, and old Mr. Van Diver wore a white tie and an odd old-fashioned tail coat which had turned a little green along the seams and been restored to something of its original color by Mrs. Lefferty with the aid of a bottle of India ink.

Mr. Grasselli, opener and closer of night clubs and speakeasies, had done his work well. The room was full of important people, not diplomats and statesmen and great bankers, but people who were important in the world of Broadway and Hollywood and the show business, and that was the world that mattered so far as Maggie and Tommy and Mr. Boldini were concerned. If Sarah Jane had chosen an audience before which to show what she and Tommy could do, this would have been it. They had come in response to whispers sent along Mr. Grasselli's grapevine of communications. The news had reached them that this new place was going to be good, that there was a new singer who was a wow, and a magician act completely new that was something unique, and that the food was something to write home about.

And so they were all there, agents and actors, motion picture people, columnists and newspapermen, racketeers and chiselers, and people generally who were in the "know." Taken as an audience, as a picture as a whole they alarmed Mr. Salmon and Mrs. Lefferty; made no impression whatever on Mr. Van Diver, and only added to the terror of poor Miss Flint, whose eyes and mouth took to twitching harder than ever at sight of them. And Mrs. Lefferty, with a sinking of the heart, suddenly understood what had happened; this, all this crowd about her, was the New York of 1935. It had stormed and taken possession of poor Miss Minnie's house. The sight of them made her unhappy and she knew that she would not be happy again until they were gone, all of them, forever, no matter how much money they poured into her pockets, and poor Miss Minnie's house was once more the home of Maggie and herself and the boarders. Suddenly it wasn't fun and exciting like making up a story. She didn't like any of their faces any more than Miss Flint liked them. They weren't poor Miss Minnie's kind or her own. They were cheap.

Mr. Leontopopulos brought another bottle of champagne. They were all enjoying it and Mrs. Lefferty said it was kind of him to think of them. It was the first time in her life that Miss Flint had ever tasted champagne and she thought it was lovely. Mr. Salmon filled her glass twice and then three times and then four. And then suddenly without warning from behind the screen which hid the dumb-waiter just beside them appeared a face which was at once terrifying and familiar. It was Miss Flint who saw it first and she gave a faint scream, which attracted the notice of the others. What she saw was like something out of a nightmare, out of one of those dreams which she had been having, night after night, of late. It was Mr. Grasselli, but a Mr. Grasselli none of them had ever seen before. His hair and new-grown mustache were dyed black, not a natural kind of black, but the black of shoe-blacking put on in the bathroom by himself, and he wore a pair of dark glasses which made it impossible to tell that he was wall-eyed. But worst of all was his skin which looked terrible for some reason. The reason was, after all, simple enough. It was the same skin—the pale, faintly freckled skin that goes with reddish hair; it was the black hair and mustache which gave it a leprous appearance. The whole face resembled more than anything else, the face of a walking corpse.

Miss Flint stifled her scream and Mr. Salmon pressed upon her another glass of champagne, and then the spectral face of Mr. Grasselli disappeared again behind the screen.

32

It disappeared at the arrival in the hallway of Mr. Boldini in his Roman costume accompanied by a panting and whimpering Fanto, a number of wands and rings and colored handkerchiefs and a bowl of live goldfish. Fanto was scarcely more excited than Mr. Boldini but the magician managed to conceal his excitement beneath an expression of such smugness that at sight of him Mr. Grasselli thought, "I'll have to make him mad as hell or he's gonna be terrible."

Then Tommy appeared, looking, Mr. Grasselli thought, like a stranger. In his dinner jacket he looked very smart and he held himself very straight and there was color in his face and a challenging twinkle in his blue eyes. Mr. Grasselli looked at him hard; this couldn't be the Tommy who a couple of hours before had been too sick with stage fright to join the others at dinner. Then he drew Tommy aside. "Listen," he said, "I forgot all about a master of ceremonies. You've got to be it. You've got to introduce old Boldini."

Tommy, staring at him, said, "I've never made a speech in my life."

"Well, this time you've got to do it, see? And get away with it."

"I'll get away with it," said Tommy, still staring.

"And lay it on thick," said Mr. Grasselli. "*Too* thick. Get me?"

"Yeah," said Tommy.

"What are you staring at?" asked Mr. Grasselli.

"That make-up you've got on."

"Is it okay?" asked Mr. Grasselli.

"Your own mother wouldn't know you. It's all right, if it don't scare away all the trade."

"Oke. Then get on with it."

Tommy gave a signal to the tiny orchestra that sat pressed against the piano and there was a roll of drums and he stepped forward into the tiny space left just before the widened doorway from the drawing room into the dining room. Mrs. Lefferty, from her end of the table, was just able to see him and she, like Mr. Grasselli, was startled by the change in him. This was the old confident, bright, dapper Tommy who Maggie always said reminded her of Jimmy Walker.

With the greatest of professional airs, he waited for the murmur to die away. Then he said, "Ladies and Gentlemen: I thank you in behalf of the management, the performers, the staff and myself for coming here tonight. As you see (here he looked all round the room) we are crowded to the doors. In spite of every effort we have had to turn away a large crowd. We are doing our best. I hope you will like the place and that you find the food as good as we hope."

From the back of the room a voice said, "Great!" and from another corner a second voice said "Swell!" Listening behind the screen, Maggie heard these compliments and beamed.

Then Tommy went on, "I hope you will like our performers of whom," he said modestly, "I am one. In any case the management hopes to give you something new. The first number on the program will be the Great Boldini and his dog Fanto (from behind the screen came the sound of a joyous bark, quickly stifled). There he is now," said Tommy.

Then continuing, "The Great Boldini scarcely needs an introduction. A good many of you have seen him before in the days when he was touring the four quarters of the earth, before he went into retirement. In those days he was a headliner and gave command performances before the Kaiser and the Emperor of Austria. After a retirement of years he has been induced to appear again after much persuasion on the part of the management. I think I also ought to say that his costume has been in retirement with him. The Great Boldini—King of International Magicians!"

Then he made a little bow, received a round of applause, and retired.

Mr. Boldini did not come out at once but that was because Mr. Grasselli was preparing him for his appearance. In the half-darkness behind the screen Mr. Grasselli said, "Now listen, you old ham! Remember you're a lousy broken-down magician and this is your chance to come back. Get on there and do your stuff. And for God's sake, try not to ham it!"

A look of fury crossed the bloodhound face. The mouth opened to speak but no words came out because before he could speak Mr. Grasselli with the aid of his foot sent him through the doorway on to the tiny stage, preceded by a barking, joyous Fanto.

33

The entrance of Mr. Boldini savored less of pomp and dignity than of rage. The very suddenness with which he appeared to have been projected upon the scene was in itself comic, and the costume with its exaggerated muscles molded in papier-mâché, which had moved Mr. Grasselli to such uproarious mirth, had a similar effect upon the audience. And Tommy's speech too had done its part, for he had scarcely prepared the audience for the appearance of an elderly magician with a bloodhound countenance who resembled a somewhat hairy spider in Roman costume.

There was a wave of laughter and when Mr. Boldini glared at the audience in rage, they took it as a part of his role and began to laugh all over again. In a fury he began the act, feeling against Fanto the same genuine resentment he had felt on the night when Fanto ruined everything, so that each time Fanto mischievously ruined his best planned trick, he was really angry, and each time the audience laughed at his anger, their laughter served only to increase it.

Fanto was perfect, for he liked an audience, a big audience, and he was aware somehow that now he was the star of the act; there wasn't any longer any doubt about it. Mr. Boldini was his stooge. He made all the men laugh and he charmed the women and the minute Mr. Boldini turned his back for a moment, to make one of his pompous speeches, Fanto turned a somersault or stood on his head to attract attention to himself. The goldfish trick was a triumph, and when Fanto upset the bowl on the floor, there was a tempest of laughter and applause.

Then the act was suddenly over and Mr. Boldini and Fanto were called back again and again. It was only then that Mr. Boldini grasped the fact that he had been a success, and he was never aware that all the time, while he was playing the act in a blind rage, the audience had believed that the rage was acting, that he was a superb "dead-pan" comic. He had been so angry that never once had it occurred to him to wink at the audience or to give Fanto a patronizing pat on the head. And now, as the lovely sound of applause came rolling back to him, everything was changed; he forgot his anger and convinced himself that he had meant it that way. He had not been really angry; he was only acting. He even forgave Mr. Grasselli.

As for Fanto, he was beside himself, and after Mr. Boldini had taken his last bow and was turning to go up the stairs, Fanto turned, ran past him and had a final bow in which his master played no part. It was, after all, his right as the star.

34

At the boarders' table everyone drank another glass of champagne to the health of Mr. Boldini and Fanto, and a moment later Mr. Grasselli appeared to take a chair exactly opposite Miss Flint with his back to the audience so that the most anyone could see was the back of a man who appeared to have very black hair.

"What'd I tell you?" he said. "I know an act when I see one. Here's to Boldini and Fanto." He raised his glass, and everyone, including Miss Flint, drank a second health. But Miss Flint's hand had begun to tremble a little.

Then for a little time the customers tried to dance by all crowding on the tiny square of floor and then one by one they all gave it up and then there was another roll of drums and Tommy appeared again and made another graceful speech about "Ryan and Lefferty in a Few Songs," and when he had finished Mrs. Lefferty beamed and said, "I never heard a better speech. That's what education does. If it hadn't been for poor Miss Minnie . . . sending him to college and all . . ."

And then Maggie, having finished in the kitchen, appeared with her hair done in rolls and wearing the gold fleur-de-lis watch and pin that poor Miss Minnie had left her, and once again those in the audience who saw her could not make her out any more than they had been able to make out Miss Flint and Mr. Salmon and old Mr. Van Diver and Mrs. Lefferty and even Mr. Grasselli in his strange make-up, and put the whole table down once and for all as "atmosphere," a table of "extras" hired like the furniture and the curtains.

35

In the corner by the door, Mr. Malkowsky, the great foreign movie director and his assistant, took a sudden interest when Sarah Jane appeared in the same simple black dress and white scarf which she had used before. Mr. Malkowsky discovered things in her that most of the audience who knew her at once as "Sal" accepted without examining critically. Mr. Malkowsky, to whom "Sal" was a stranger, saw her in a different way and noticed that when she came into the room the drums didn't have to roll in order to get silence. He noticed that when she walked there was in her walk a kind of beauty which a lot of actresses spent their lives working to acquire. He noticed the shrewdness with which she had costumed herself, wearing a simple dress which revealed the beauty of her body but threw the attention to her face; and when she began to sing, he noticed that her voice, which was not a great voice, had in it a quality that sent a thrill down your spine. He noticed all these things.

[656]

His assistant noticed none of them; like the rest of the audience he only knew that she was "good." But his whole career, the whole of his success, had been built not out of his own reactions and opinions, but of observing those of Mr. Malkowsky and then saying it first. He knew the signs of Mr. Malkowsky's enthusiasm . . . the faint quivering of the acquiline nose, the moistening of the lips above the black Assyrian beard as if he were about to sit down to a good meal, the light that came into his eye. So after watching all these things, when Sarah Jane had finished her first song, the assistant said it first. He said, "She's great, isn't she?"

"Yes," said Mr. Malkowsky, keeping his eye on Sarah Jane and not paying much attention to the assistant. That, his assistant knew, was one of the surest of signs. This enthusiasm was deeper than he had imagined.

Then Sarah Jane sang "Here We Are in Love," the second of her numbers, and at the end they would not let her go away but kept calling to her and Tommy to come back. There were cries of "Sal! We want Sal!" They all knew her. They were friendly toward her as a Broadway character and now when they were surprised by what she could do, they were pleased.

So she came back and sang "Here We Are in Love" all over again and then when they would not let her go she retired for a moment, and returned with her special make-up to sing, "I'm Nada McSweeney, the Glamour Girl."

This came as a surprise to Mr. Malkowsky who had not thought of her as a comedienne, but it pleased him too, although now and then something in the imitations struck very close to Mr. Malkowsky himself. But he took it good-humoredly and when she finished, "I'm Garbo, I'm Dietrich, I'm Hepburn, I'm Loy," he pounded his fat hands together hysterically, and his assistant pounded his in imitation.

Then Tommy announced that they would return shortly with a couple of more songs, and the public tried again to dance and again gave it up.

At their table in the corner by the screen Mrs. Lefferty and Maggie and the boarders, all save Miss Flint, were delirious with excitement. It was all better than they had hoped, better even than anything Mrs. Lefferty had made up in her story. She turned to Mr. Grasselli and said, "Is it always like this?"

And Mr. Grasselli said, "No, I never seen anything like it before." Then he leaned over and whispered to Mrs. Lefferty, "Maybe you'd better do something about Miss Flint. She looks to me as if she was gonna be sick."

Mrs. Lefferty looked at her and had the same idea. Miss Flint was staring sullenly through eyes that were a little glazed, directly at Mr. Grasselli. She had been staring at him like that for a long time, her face frozen except for the twitch of the eyes and at the corners of the mouth. It was rather a terrifying look in which defiance, terror and challenge were mingled, and it made Mr. Grasselli feel very uncomfortable.

"Maybe you'd better take her up and put her to bed," he whispered to Mrs. Lefferty.

"Maybe I had," said Mrs. Lefferty. Then she got up and bent over Miss Flint and suggested that they both go upstairs and have some bicarbonate of soda, and Miss Flint, strangely enough, agreed with docility. But once in the room that had been poor Miss Minnie's linen closet, she refused to go to bed.

"No," she kept saying, "I'll be feeling better in a little while. Just leave me alone." She lay down on the bed fully corseted and dressed. "No," she said, "I won't go to bed. I'll be all right."

So at last Mrs. Lefferty closed the door and left her, and as soon as Mrs. Lefferty had gone, Miss Flint rose and put on her raincoat over her evening dress and put on her hat and her thick veil right on top of the rhinestone butterfly. Then she opened the door a little way and peered out and when she saw there was no one about, she went into the hall. At each turn of the stairway she executed the same reconnoitering tactics until she reached the first floor where, in an unsteady dash, she went through the door and down the front steps, to the astonishment of the doorman who had noticed no one who even faintly resembled her entering the house.

36

The "nineties" songs had the same success as the earlier ones, and in his corner Mr. Malkowsky's enthusiasm grew. At the end he turned to his assistant and said, "Vell, wot do you tink of her?"

"What do *you* think?" asked the assistant.

"She's vunderful. She's just vot ve've been looking for."

"That's just what I was thinking," said the assistant. "She's remarkable. She's got immense possibilities. Maybe I'd better arrange for a test to see how she photographs."

"Ve don't need any tests," said Mr. Malkowsky. "An artiste is an artiste, Bergman. It ain't got anything to do vit celluloid and sound apparatus. I vant to hear her speak. I vant to talk to her. I vant to hear her woice. Anyvay I'm gonna give her a chanct."

"Should I go and bring her over here?"

"Sure. Vot you tink?"

"Mebbe the coast'll want a test."

"Listen, Bergman, I don't do vot the coast says. The coast does vot I say. Vot kind of a contrict d'you tink I got?"

"All right. I'll go and get her."

So Mr. Bergman, the assistant, went over to the boarders' table where Tommy and Sarah Jane had gone to join the others. The table was surrounded now by old friends of "Sal," by people who pretended they were old friends, by people who wanted to know her, by people who had given her an extra push when she was on the way down, but Sarah Jane wasn't deceived by any of it, because she'd been in the game too long. What she did know was that this was success. When they came running like that it meant the real stuff, more than compliments and applause and everything. They all knew she was a success and they were all pushing and crowding like a subway crowd to get aboard the boat.

Mr. Bergman, the assistant, made his way through the throng and bent over her. "Excuse me," he said, "I'm assistant director with Colossal Pictures. I've got Mr. Malkowsky, the great foreign director, with me, and he wants to know if you'll have a glass of champagne with him."

"Sure," said Sarah Jane, rising.

The moment she saw Mr. Malkowsky, she thought, "He's a 'phony.'" She could tell it by the black Assyrian beard, by the unctuous voice, by the way he rose and kissed her hand. But almost at once she thought, "So what? Even if he is a phony, mebbe I can use him. I'll feed him up. What's the difference, if he 'discovers' me?"

So she fed him up, playing up to the shiny beard and the hand kissing and the unctuous voice, and when she left the table, Mr. Malkowsky said, "Vell, I expect you then to have lunch mit me tomorrow at one at the Valdorf."

"I'll be there," said Sarah Jane.

When she had gone, Mr. Malkowsky said, "She's vonderful! I tink I make a discovery."

"She's marvelous," said Mr. Bergman, the assistant. "Colossal! You've got a wonderful eye for talent."

Mr. Malkowsky beamed. "Vell," he said, "I tink I go back and send a telegram to de coast. Ve can still catch the night rate. Funny, she vass just the type I vass looking for."

37

When she got back to the table Mr. Grasselli had disappeared, because success had attracted to the table too many people that knew him. People came and went. Agents suggested meetings and one revue producer talked about a show he had in the fall, if Sarah Jane was "interested." She said she didn't know. She could tell him later. She had a good many plans to consider.

Finally about four in the morning there wasn't anyone left in the room but Sarah Jane and Tommy and a couple of tired waiters. They had expected that Mr. Grasselli would return, but he never did, so Sarah Jane said, "Let's go up and see him."

In the upper hallway, Tommy suddenly put his arms about her and said, "Well, we pulled it off, didn't we?"

"I'll say we did."

"And none of 'em knew why we were so good."

Sarah Jane laughed and kissed him and he said, "There was even a song publisher playing around . . . old Herman from Beck and Herman."

"There'll be a lot more," said Sarah Jane.

"When d'you want to get married?"

"Any time . . . tonight or tomorrow."

"Can't tonight." He looked at her. "We're as good as married now."

"No," said Sarah Jane, "it would upset the old girls. Ma would begin worrying about purgatory."

"They had a good time, didn't they?"

"Sure, but I don't think they really liked it."

"Guess you're right at that. It's not their dish."

"I kinda think they were still worrying about whether poor Miss Minnie was snooping about."

"I'll bet she liked it," said Tommy, "especially about you and me. I think she kind of always wanted that."

"Sure she did." She gave him a great hug and said, "Let's go and talk to Monk. I've gotta go to lunch tomorrow with Mr. Malkowsky, the great foreign director, and I gotta look fresh and young."

The old hostile, jealous look that pleased her came into Tommy's blue eyes, "What kind of a guy is he?"

"Don't worry. He ain't that kind. I sized him up."

She went to Mr. Grasselli's door and knocked and when there was no answer Tommy pushed it open. Still there wasn't any sign of Mr. Grasselli and when they turned on the lights the room was empty.

"That's funny," said Tommy.

"Maybe he's in the bathroom."

But he wasn't in the bathroom. They went all over the house but they couldn't find any trace of Mr. Grasselli. Then it occurred to Tommy to ask the doorman. The doorman would know. He'd worked at Mr. Grasselli's joints for years. Tommy found him back of the screen changing out of his uniform. He was a squat, powerfully built fellow sometimes used as an assistant bouncer.

Tommy described Mr. Grasselli's appearance, his black hair and mustache.

"Sure," said the doorman, "I seen him goin' out. A coupla cops had him.

I kinda noticed him because he was so funny lookin' . . . like a walkin' corpse. He looked kinda familiar to me, only funny."

If the cops had him there wasn't any use pretending any longer that Mr. Grasselli wasn't Monk Maguire, so Tommy said, "You know who he was, don't you?"

"No, who?"

"It was Monk."

"Jeez!" said the doorman, "I knew he was familiar."

38

Sarah Jane, it was decided, should go to bed in order to be young and fresh for Mr. Malkowsky, so Tommy went off alone around the corner to the police station. He found the sergeant and a couple of sleepy policemen and when he asked for Monk Maguire, the sergeant said, "And what d'you wanta see *him* for?"

"Because I work for him."

"How?" asked the sergeant.

"I play the piano in his joint."

"Oh," said the sergeant. "Well, that's different. He ain't here."

"Where is he?"

"They took him to headquarters, but there ain't no use in going way down there. You couldn't see him. Better wait till the morning."

"Okay," said Tommy. "Thanks."

As he turned to leave, the sergeant said, "Wait a minute. Mebbe you could tell us about the old dame we've got shut up here."

"Mebbe," said Tommy. "What does she look like?"

The sergeant described her—dyed red hair, lots of paint, a heavy veil and a kind of diamond butterfly in her hair.

"Sure," said Tommy, "I know who she is. She lives at my mother's boardinghouse. How did she get here?"

"Well, I'll tell you," said the sergeant.

It seemed that about two-thirty in the morning Miss Flint, in a state of hysteria, came into the police station and asked to be locked up. When they said they couldn't lock her up for doing nothing and asked why she wanted to be locked up, she said it was because she was scared. When they asked by what, she said she was always being followed and that they were trying to take her for a ride. At first, because of poor respectable Miss Flint's appearance, they believed her story, only they couldn't think of any joint in the neighborhood that had a madame who resembled Miss Flint. And then it dawned on them that maybe Miss Flint had had a little too much to drink, and they began to question her and soon discovered that she was trying to hide something. At last after a half-hour of questions during which she nearly drove them crazy trying to follow her, they discovered that she knew where Monk Maguire was and that she was scared out of her wits by her knowledge. So finally they broke her down. She said nobody in the boardinghouse but herself had guessed the secret but if they wanted to get him, they could go right over there now and pick him up, only they had to remember that he had dyed his hair and mustache, and was wearing dark glasses.

Then the sergeant thanked her and told her she might as well go home, but she begged instead that they shut her up. She wouldn't feel safe outside of jail. She wouldn't be able to close an eye. She'd heard, she said, that Monk's gang meant to strangle her and put her body in a barrel and fill it up with cement. So in the end they yielded and locked her up in a cell and almost at once she had gone to sleep.

"Mebbe I'd better have a look at her," said Tommy.

"Sure," said the sergeant. "Murphy, take the gentleman in to see the lady."

They went along a corridor and at last came to the cell where Miss Flint was locked out of harm's way. She was asleep, very sound asleep. The police had taken off her hat and coat and veil and put a blanket over her. The butterfly of rhinestones still glittered jauntily in the flaming hair.

When Tommy returned, the sergeant said, "Better let her stay here to-night and sleep it off. We'll bring her home in the morning."

"Thanks," said Tommy. "Good night."

Tommy understood. The champagne *and* Mr. Grasselli's strange make-up had been too much for her. He didn't blame her. It would, he thought, have been too much for almost anybody.

39

Tommy didn't wake until noon and by then Mrs. Lefferty and Maggie had already discovered the disappearance of Mr. Grasselli and Miss Flint. An elopement, they decided, was scarcely likely, so Mrs. Lefferty went round to the police station, and there for the first time she learned the true identity of Mr. Grasselli. It came as a shock, such a shock that she had to sit down and have some brandy and be fanned. They knew her at the station house, so they didn't have any suspicions that she had been consciously providing the notorious Monk Maguire with a place of refuge.

Then when she had recovered from the first shock, she found out all about Miss Flint. Miss Flint, the day sergeant said, was still sleeping peacefully, but by now, he thought, she ought to be able to go home. So accompanied by Mrs. Lefferty, they went to the cell and roused Miss Flint. She waked slowly and at the sight of Mrs. Lefferty burst into tears and flung herself into Mrs. Lefferty's plump arms.

"Never mind, dearie," said Mrs. Lefferty patting her back, "we're going home now. They've told me the whole story. It's going to be all right."

"Oh," cried Miss Flint, "we can't go home alone."

"Why not?" said Mrs. Lefferty.

"They'll surely get us now."

"Who'll get us?"

"Mr. Grasselli's mob," sobbed Miss Flint.

Here the sergeant, grinning, intervened, "Sure, don't you worry, Mrs. Lefferty," he said. "I'll send Officer Leibowitz around with you. That'll keep her quiet."

"Oh, I'm so ashamed of myself," sobbed Miss Flint. "I don't know what came over me . . . to get you into all this trouble."

"There ain't any trouble," said Mrs. Lefferty, continuing to pat Miss Flint's skinny back. "Sure, dearie, stop your worryin'."

Officer Leibowitz came forward to escort the two ladies home. He was a respectable Jewish policeman, with a large family, and after he had taken a good look at Miss Flint, painted and dyed and still bedecked in a ball gown, with the diamond butterfly in her Titian hair, he went up to the sergeant and began whispering to him.

"Sure," said the sergeant, "take 'em home in a taxi. I guess the city can pay for it."

"Oh," cried Miss Flint, "I'm so ashamed. I'm so mortified. I don't know how it happened. I don't know how I got mixed up in it all."

"Come on, ladies," said Officer Leibowitz.

Outside he summoned a taxicab and for the first time in their lives, Miss Flint and Mrs. Lefferty had a ride in an automobile.

40

But at home there was a fresh calamity, one which to Maggie and Mrs. Lefferty was far worse than the scandal of Mr. Grasselli's identity and the night spent by Miss Flint in a cell at the police station, for in this new calamity there was a tragedy which touched them both and destroyed forever the few remnants of dubious joy that remained over the success of the opening of the Golden Nineties.

After Mrs. Lefferty and Maggie had put Miss Flint to bed and given her calming medicines, they met Mr. Boldini on the stairs. He had been looking for them. His bloodhound countenance was the apotheosis of melancholy and the tears streamed from his eyes.

"A terrible thing has happened," he said. Then he began to sob and it took Maggie and Mrs. Lefferty quite a little while to calm him. Then he said, still sobbing, "Fanto is dead!"

"Dead!" said Mrs. Lefferty. "But what was the matter with him? He was in wonderful spirits last night."

She leaned against the stair rail trying to realize what it was that Mr. Boldini was telling her. Fanto couldn't be dead, not the Fanto who had been so joyous only last night.

"When I woke up this morning," said Mr. Boldini, "he was still in his basket, curled up the way he always was, but when I called him he didn't get up. He didn't even open his eyes and wag his tail. I went over to him and . . . he was dead!" And Mr. Boldini began to sob again. "He's been with me for fourteen years . . . ever since he was a puppy . . . my best friend!"

And then the three of them, without speaking, went softly along the hall to Mr. Boldini's room and opened the door.

There in his basket, curled up as he had always been, lay Fanto. He looked happy. He looked, Maggie said, as if he had died wagging his tail.

"Sure, he had a good time," said Maggie. "And he had fun last night."

"Yes," said Mr. Boldini, "he never had such a success before."

"It must have been the excitement," said Mrs. Lefferty.

"Sure," said Maggie, "with his rheumatism. It was too much for his heart." She leaned down and touched Fanto's head. It was her way of saying good-by to him. She and Mrs. Lefferty were thinking the same thing. Fanto wouldn't be there any more to help Mrs. Lefferty make the beds. He wouldn't be there to spring out of the dumb-waiter to surprise Maggie. He wouldn't ever again give them a performance, wagging his tail, and turning somersaults and standing on his head.

41

After Tommy had risen and had some breakfast and heard about Miss Flint being home and Fanto being dead, he went to police headquarters to see Mr. Grasselli. He found him in a cell having a late lunch which he had sent out for, and he seemed to be taking the whole affair philosophically. Without the dark glasses now you saw not only the pale freckled skin but the pale blue eyes, one of them aslant. He looked, with the dyed hair and mustache, more than ever like something out of the Chamber of Horrors.

"It didn't make any difference," he said. "I was gonna give myself up anyway on Monday. It was all fixed. 'Mr. Hirsh' had it all arranged. He says everything is gonna come out all right. A coupla days don't make any difference. Say, but that was a swell opening, wasn't it?"

"Yes," said Tommy.

"I guess you and Sarah Jane oughta be pretty well fixed. You two got a break anyway. You oughta be getting contracts right along now."

"It looks kinda good," said Tommy.

"If I can do anything, let me know."

"Sure," said Tommy.

"Are the old ladies pleased?"

"No, I think they're kinda mad this morning."

"Why?"

"On account of everything that happened. They think poor Miss Minnie wouldn't have liked it."

"I get you . . . not respectable."

"That's it."

"Well, what d'you expect of show business? I guess even old Boldini will get a break out of this if he don't lose his head and ham it."

"No," said Tommy, "that's finished."

"How finished?"

"Fanto is dead."

"Dead . . . that dog?"

"Sure . . . the excitement was too much for him."

Something like a tear appeared in Mr. Grasselli's eye. "Say, that was a wonderful dog," he said. "That was the swellest dog I ever seen. He was almost 'uman."

"Yeah," said Tommy, "he was. The old girls can't get over that."

There was a little silence and then Mr. Grasselli looked up from his lunch and said, "There's one thing I'd kinda like to ask you."

"What?"

"What happened to you last night between eight o'clock and eleven? I never seen such a change in anybody."

Tommy grinned. "Well," he said, "it was like this." And he told Mr. Grasselli about what had happened between him and Sarah Jane.

When he had finished, Mr. Grasselli, with a little spaghetti still hanging from the corner of his mouth, grinned back at him. "So that was it," he said. "I get it."

"What?"

"About Sal being so upstage."

"Yeah," said Tommy, "that was it." He rose and picked up his hat and called the turnkey. "Well, I guess I'd better go," he said.

"If there's anything I can do," said Mr. Grasselli, "let me know. You don't need to worry about the club. Leontopopulos can manage that."

"Okay. Thanks. It'll be all right if the old girls don't kick up a row. Of course, old Boldini's act is finished."

"Yeah, that's finished. Here, I almost forgot," said Mr. Grasselli, reaching in his pocket. "Take this for Fanto's funeral. Tell 'em to bury him in the dog cemetery. It's a nice place. One of my girls has got a coupla Pomeranians buried out there." He counted out some bills and then said, "And take this extra to put up a monument. A dog like that oughta have a monument . . . more than a lotta 'umans oughta have. I guess three hundred dollars oughta cover it. If it ain't enough, lemme know."

"Thanks," said Tommy.

"And tell Sal that she musta scared old Flint too hard."

42

Lunch scarcely happened at all that day. Both Sarah Jane and Tommy were absent, Miss Flint was indisposed, and Mr. Boldini didn't feel like eating anything, so in the end Maggie and Mrs. Lefferty sat down with old Mr. Van Diver and Mr. Salmon in the servants' dining room to a meal in which none of them save old Mr. Van Diver found any pleasure. Mr. Salmon was suffering from a headache, Mrs. Lefferty was a little dazed, and Maggie had fallen into a Gaelic state of brooding. But old Mr. Van Diver didn't notice anything. He ate and chuckled and talked in his squeaky voice as if nothing unusual had happened. Although Mrs. Lefferty had told him everything—about Fanto and Mr. Grasselli and Miss Flint—he had forgotten it all in the next half-hour.

It was Maggie's brooding that worried Mrs. Lefferty. She hadn't brooded like this in years, and when she brooded, Mrs. Lefferty always knew that an explosion was certain to follow and Maggie, brooding, was a terrifying spectacle. She grew silent and stared into space. The corners of her mouth went down and a wild look came into her blue eyes. At such times she appeared to function mechanically, as if her spirit had left her body. She could ask and answer questions. She could cook and even rise from the table to serve the food, but you had the impression that it wasn't Maggie who was doing it, but an automaton. Maggie wasn't there at all. She had gone away somewhere into solitude. And the brooding had the power of projecting itself so that it settled down like a thick fog over all the world about her.

When lunch was finished, she went about her work, still brooding. Only once did she give a hint of what was troubling her and that was when she suddenly said abruptly to Mrs. Lefferty, "I told you poor Miss Minnie wouldn't have liked it." Every time she went near the dumb-waiter out of which poor Fanto would never spring again, the look in her eyes became more baleful.

Even when Sarah Jane returned home filled with the news of her interview with the great foreign director, Mr. Malkowsky, it didn't cheer her.

She showed no joy at the news that Sarah Jane already practically had a contract for Hollywood and that she had already had two offers to sing in night clubs. Even when Tommy came in with the news that very likely three of his songs were going to be published and would be sung over the radio, she did not show any signs of pleasure. For a second, when Tommy produced Mr. Grasselli's three hundred dollars for Fanto's funeral and monument, the grim lines of her face relaxed a little, but she only muttered, "It's tainted money. We oughtn't to touch it."

And when at last Tommy and Sarah Jane told her and Mrs. Lefferty that they were going to be married at City Hall, she merely said grimly, "Well, it's about time you made up your minds. And you're not gonna be married in City Hall. No daughter of mine is gonna be married outside the Church. You're gonna be married by Father McGuffy, a proper marriage that is a marriage."

Sarah Jane said to Mrs. Lefferty, "What's the matter with Ma?"

"I don't know," she said. "I guess it's all the trouble. She hasn't been like this for years."

Mrs. Lefferty did not brood. She was merely frightened. She was frightened by all that had happened and what still lay ahead of them and she was frightened by Maggie's brooding. But most of all she was frightened because the story she had made up seemed to have gotten out of hand. It was all coming out just as she had planned it, the way her stories always did, sooner or later, only it seemed to be happening with too great a violence and distortion. Tommy and Sarah Jane had got their "breaks." They were even going to be married and they were going to have money. And Mr. Grasselli, "the villain" (who was really a nice generous man at heart), was in jail. And the night club was a success and they wouldn't have to worry over where the interest and taxes and insurance were coming from. All that was fine, only Tommy's and Sarah Jane's luck was too good, and the club was too much of a success, and everything, except poor Fanto, was going too well. Somehow the story, it seemed, had run away with her and she didn't know how to stop it. It made her nervous. And like Maggie, she didn't like the cheap, unhealthy people that success had brought into their lives . . . people like Mr. Grasselli, and Victor Leontopopulos and Mr. Malkowsky, the big foreign director, and all those people who had crowded about the table to congratulate Sarah Jane. Now she wanted to stop the story where it was. It had gone far enough.

43

It was Maggie who stopped it!
About seven in the evening she went up to Mr. Boldini's room with Mrs.

Lefferty to help choose out of a catalogue which Mr. Boldini had got, a casket in which to lay Fanto away. The three of them studied all the designs and the prices and finally agreed on a gray basket coffin trimmed with silver. It was more than Maggie could bear, going over that catalogue, with poor Fanto lying there dead right beside them. The look in her eye became a little fiercer, and suddenly she left the room without a word and went directly to the kitchen.

At a table in the far end, her two assistants, a pair of men whom Victor Leontopopulos had engaged, were busy preparing corned beef hash. The sight of them was too much for Maggie.

She advanced toward them and said, "Get out of here, both of you, as fast as your legs can carry you."

They were both timid fellows and they looked at her in astonishment. One of them said, "What's the matter?"

"Never mind what's the matter," said Maggie. "Get out. See?"

The more timid of the two rose and went to the sink to wash his hands. The bolder said, "You can't fire us like that. What have we done?"

But Maggie had already taken up a strategic position by the stove. She took up a kettle filled with boiling water and advanced on the objector.

"Don't argue with me. Get out of here before I scald you both."

That made him give in. The boiling water was bad enough but the embattled look in Maggie's eye was worse. Both assistants reached for their hats and coats and keeping close along the wall, well out of Maggie's range, they slunk out of the door into the areaway.

When they had gone, Maggie locked the door and then went to the stove where the Irish stew was boiling in three large kettles. One by one she emptied these into the large garbage cans that Mr. Grasselli had had installed. When she had done that she took the corned beef hash and likewise did away with it. Then she poured herself a cup of "tea" from the kettle of black liquid on the back of the stove and rang the bell that she used to summon Mrs. Lefferty from abovestairs.

When Mrs. Lefferty appeared she said, "Tell the boarders not to come down tonight."

"Why?" said Mrs. Lefferty.

"Because it ain't gonna be safe. I'll fix up some cocoa and bread and butter and jam and you can take it up to 'em. There ain't gonna be anything else to eat come out of this kitchen tonight."

"What about upstairs?" said Mrs. Lefferty.

"They might as well call it off. There ain't gonna be any night club. Anyway there ain't gonna be anything to eat."

"Oh," said Mrs. Lefferty. She knew now that the storm had broken. While she stood watching Maggie timidly, Maggie assembled on the table beside her several teacups, a half-dozen plates and a soup tureen.

"What's the tureen for?" asked Mrs. Lefferty.

"It's for that Greek when he comes down to make trouble. I never liked Greeks anyway. And you'd better go right upstairs and keep outa the way, Bridget. . . . I'll send the cocoa and stuff up on the dumb-waiter when it's ready."

So Mrs. Lefferty went away. It was not desertion, because she knew Maggie could take care of herself, and Maggie, in her present mood drinking black tea, was a spectacle that always terrified the gentler Mrs. Lefferty. In the back of her brain, as she climbed the stairs, there was the memory of another scene very like this in the kitchen of the big house on Murray Hill when "the old gentleman" in one of his most cantankerous moods had come downstairs himself to discharge Maggie after poor Miss Minnie, in hysterics, had refused, for the first time in her life, to obey him. "The old gentleman" had never had a chance against Maggie, and Mrs. Lefferty guessed that if Maggie could put to rout "the old gentleman," a Greek like Mr. Leontopopulos would be no trouble at all. So Mrs. Lefferty retreated to her room at the top of the house, closed the door, and waited for the sounds of strife.

In a little while, as Maggie expected, there was the sound of footsteps on the stairs, the unmistakable hated sound of the feet of Mr. Leontopopulos who had dared to put on airs and try to order her about in her own kitchen. Stimulated by the black tea, she listened until his unsuspecting feet reached the bottom step and then, just as he opened the door, she flung a plate with all her might. But Mr. Leontopopulos saw it coming and ducked. It struck the door and smashed into a thousand pieces.

When the crash died away, the head waiter opened the door an inch or two but before he could speak, another plate struck it so hard that it was flung shut in his face. The third time he made no attempt to communicate with Maggie face to face, but spoke from behind the shelter of the door.

"What do you mean," asked Mr. Leontopopulos, very grand in his safety behind the door, "by discharging your helpers?"

"You'd better not come in here unless you want your head broke," said Maggie.

"Where's the supper?" asked Mr. Leontopopulos.

"In the garbage can," said Maggie.

Mr. Leontopopulos considered this disaster for a moment. Then he said, "Either you get the supper or get out and let someone else get it."

"Nobody is coming into this kitchen tonight," said Maggie. "There ain't gonna be any supper."

"What's the matter?" in a conciliatory tone.

"Never mind what's the matter. It's none of your business what's the matter."

Another silence and then Mr. Leontopopulos decided to take a firmer tone.

"I'm the manager of this place," he said, "and you're under my orders. Mr. Grasselli has left me in charge."

"That jailbird!" said Maggie scornfully. "He's in the cooler where he belongs."

"Well," said Mr. Leontopopulos, "I'll get the police. A contract is a contract."

"Sure," said Maggie, "a contract is a contract, only there ain't any in this affair. This is my house and my kitchen and nobody's coming into it."

So Mr. Leontopopulos retired temporarily. A little later he returned and again tried arguing through the door, but with no greater success, and at last he appealed to Tommy and Sarah Jane, but this did no good whatever because in her brooding, Maggie conceived the idea that after all they were to blame because it was on account of them that Mr. Grasselli and all those other people got into the house.

"Sure," said Maggie, "if it hadn't been for you that Grasselli would never have come here at all."

The siege continued, without result, until about eleven-thirty when not Maggie but Mr. Leontopopulos gave in. He was forced to tell the arriving patrons that there wasn't any food but sandwiches which he sent out for at a neighboring restaurant; and at last about midnight, he decided to surrender entirely and announce that "owing to a disagreement in the management" the place was closed.

So among all Mr. Grasselli's speakeasy and night club ventures, the Golden Nineties held a record. It had opened one night and closed the next, and never had a club had a greater prospect of success.

44

When Tommy, a little shamefacedly, told Mr. Grasselli the story in a cell at the Tombs, Mr. Grasselli only laughed. He laughed hard and long at the story of Maggie in the kitchen drinking black tea and throwing plates every time Mr. Leontopopulos put his head in the door. He laughed almost as hard as he had laughed at Mr. Boldini's first performance.

"That's the first time anybody ever fixed Victor Leontopopulos. He's the toughest egg in the whole racket." Then when his mirth had died down a little, he said, "Well, I wasn't countin' on makin' anything out of it. It's up to the old girls. But what are they gonna do now?"

"Well, I guess if Sally and I get along, we'll be able to help 'em out."

"Mebbe it was a nut idea anyway . . . the whole thing," said Mr. Grasselli, after a moment's reflection. "The nineties is buried and I suppose we oughta let 'em stay buried. As I said to Boldini, you can't expect a ham to play a ham."

And then suddenly Tommy saw a light. He understood it all. The whole venture had grown out of that first performance when he and Sarah Jane and Mr. Grasselli had laughed at the nineties. The whole idea had been based on making money out of making fun of Maggie and Mrs. Lefferty, Mr. Boldini and Mr. Salmon, Miss Flint and old Mr. Van Diver. He knew now why the brooding Maggie had exploded.

45

Three weeks later Sarah Jane and Tommy were properly married by Father McGuffy. Nobody came to the wedding except Maggie and Mrs. Lefferty and the boarders. It was Miss Flint's first venture outside the house since she had "squealed," but her terror had died away a little beneath the assurances offered by everyone about her and by the message Tommy brought her from Mr. Grasselli that it didn't matter because he had meant to give himself up anyway, and that he didn't harbor any feelings of vengeance. She even consented to go to the wedding without being heavily veiled.

The rest of the story came out just as Mrs. Lefferty imagined except for Mr. Grasselli. What happened to him was a surprise, and Mrs. Lefferty, who knew that he wasn't really a villain but good at heart, thought they treated him badly. She didn't know exactly what she meant by "they" but anyway "they" wouldn't let him out on bail and after a short trial, "they" found him guilty of evading income tax and "they" gave him seven years in Atlanta. The truth, which Mrs. Lefferty never quite grasped, was that "mobsters" like Mr. Grasselli were already a little out of date. Juries and judges weren't afraid of them any longer. Like Mr. Salmon, Miss Flint and Mr. Van Diver, they had begun to belong to an epoch.

On the day Mr. Grasselli went off to Atlanta, just as he was boarding the train, a messenger boy came running along the platform shouting "Mr. Maguire! Mr. Maguire!" He had two packages for Mr. Grasselli. One was a large box of cigars with Sarah Jane's card in it and the other was a tiny bouquet of flowers. When he opened the flowers, Mr. Maguire found inside a card on which was written in precise, even finicky handwriting, "Bon voyage, from Malvina Flint."

Sarah Jane got her contract from Mr. Malkowsky and made a lot of money in the meanwhile singing in a couple of night clubs, and Tommy got his songs published and, largely through Sarah Jane's connivings, got a contract for the coast. Two or three days before they left, the final chapter of Mrs. Lefferty's "story" happened exactly as she had pictured it. There was a ring at the door and Tommy was standing there all dressed in fine clothes and he said, "You and Maggie put on your hats and come on for a ride." And then she saw waiting at the foot of the stoop a fine, shiny new automobile.

It wasn't quite as big as she had pictured and the light in the top wasn't cut glass; it was only frosted. But Mrs. Lefferty thought maybe that was better. It kept the story in hand.

It was the first ride Maggie had ever had in an automobile and the first Mrs. Lefferty had had, if you didn't count the ride home from the station house with Miss Flint and Officer Leibowitz. Tommy took them up Riverside Drive to see the Washington Bridge and then up the Grand Concourse and by that time it was getting dark. On the way home Tommy said, "As soon as Sally and I get our bearings in Hollywood we're gonna send for you both. It's a wonderful place. I've been there."

"When?" asked Mrs. Lefferty.

"When I was away," said Tommy.

She and Maggie didn't talk much more but seemed to fall into a silence from which it was impossible to rouse them and when at last they drove up again in front of poor Miss Minnie's house, Mrs. Lefferty said, "It's a wonderful automobile, and it's kind of you and Sarah Jane to think about taking us to Hollywood, but we couldn't go."

"No," said Maggie, "it ain't possible."

"Why?" asked Tommy.

"What would become of Miss Flint and old Mr. Van Diver and Mr. Boldini?"

"You can send us a little money from time to time, if you want," said Maggie. "It'll cost you less than keepin' us in Hollywood."

46

That night after supper Miss Flint poured the coffee while Mrs. Lefferty helped Maggie with the dishes, and as soon as dinner was over, Mrs. Lefferty got out "the old gentleman's" gaming table and the perpetual rummy score and said, "You begin dealing, Miss Flint."

The room was almost the way it had always been, save that beneath poor Miss Minnie's Axminster carpet there was now a floor of hardwood and the opening between the dining room and the drawing room was wider than it used to be. Mr. Boldini won the first game and Mrs. Lefferty the second. In his corner Mr. Van Diver looked at the picture magazines and chortled to himself, and about eleven o'clock Mrs. Lefferty went downstairs to fetch beer and sandwiches. Nothing was changed except that poor Fanto wasn't there. There was a new poodle, a puppy called "Flic" which Sarah Jane and Tommy had bought to comfort Mr. Boldini. And now they had a radio because Mr.

Grasselli said he wouldn't need the one he had in his room and they might as well keep it.

While they ate and drank, Mrs. Lefferty turned to what was known as "Sarah Jane's station" and in a little while Sarah Jane was singing "Here We Are in Love" right there beside them—"just as if she was in the room."

"Isn't it wonderful?" said Mrs. Lefferty.

"Yes," said Maggie, "if only poor Miss Minnie could be here."

IX

Aunt Flora

FROM her bedroom window Margaret could see the two boys seated on a big wood packing case near the stable door. They sat side by side, Dejection and Boredom, kicking their heels against the box and listening to the hollow sounds they made. As she watched them she thought, "That's exactly how I feel. Poor kids!" Sitting listlessly in the damp midsummer heat, she watched them for a long time, all thought suspended, like one hypnotized by the steady monotonous rhythmical thumping sound made by the heels of her small sons, and presently the thought came to her vaguely that they ought not to be making that dreadful noise with Uncle Hughie's body in the house waiting for Mr. Prescott to come and read the service and bury it. But she had not the energy to rise and walk the whole length of the garden to bid them stop the racket. After all, what were they to do, poor kids, with their holiday postponed for three days in this awful heat because Uncle Hughie whom they had never seen or heard of had died?

Then from the far end of the house she heard a voice, irritated and disagreeable, saying, "No, and when I say no I mean no." Margaret knew the voice and the accent. It was unmistakable. It issued from the fat throat of Mrs. Svenson, the cook, and the sound of it made Margaret feel faintly ill. It was silly, of course, to let quarreling and ill nature among other people upset you. She knew that she should have gone down and told Mrs. Svenson that she must not shout in that fashion so that she could be heard all over the house. She knew that if she had any character that is what she would have done, but she could not do it. She told herself that it was much too hot to trouble and she even made excuses to herself for Mrs. Svenson, telling herself that a fat woman like Mrs. Svenson must suffer terribly working over a hot stove on a day like this. But she knew that the reasons for her failure were far more simple and direct. She was merely weak. A woman who was a good housekeeper would have descended it for no other reason than to preserve her prestige. That was what the women she knew always did, but

[674]

the other women were always losing their servants and Mrs. Svenson had been with her for ten years.

It was silly to be afraid of emotional scenes. Her dread of them, she reflected, probably came of being brought up in a large family which loved drama and allowed its emotions to run wild. In stories and in books, families like that could be entertaining but in life they were quite another matter. Perhaps it was better to be brought up as Tom had been in a family where everything was ordered and calm, where servants were put in their places and no one ever raised his voice in anger. Perhaps there was something to be said for the cold self-containedness of the Landons.

Presently she rose and with a sigh drew the black broadcloth skirt over her head. She did it without haste and when she had hooked it, she sat down once more before the window. She tried to find excuses for herself, knowing all the time why she dawdled with her dressing. It was not really on account of the heat, but because she could not bear to face the boredom of going downstairs and talking to Aunt Kate and Cousin Henry until the rector arrived and the funeral service began. "Why," she thought, "do people have to wear black because somebody died—especially somebody like Uncle Hughie?"

Black was hot and ugly and stuffy, especially on a day like this when one ought to be in a bathing suit diving off a pier into cool salt water. That was where they all would be if Uncle Hughie had not died.

Through her thoughts she became drearily aware of a new sound, new, metallic and dreadful. Looking toward the stables whence she knew that it must come, she saw that the boys had abandoned kicking the packing case for a new amusement. They had found an empty gasoline tin and were beating it with sticks. "Now," she thought, "I shall have to go down. Tom will never notice the noise but Aunt Kate will say that they are disrespectful and horribly brought up."

She did not see why she should care what Aunt Kate or any of Tom's relatives thought, but the fact remained that she did care, perhaps because she was expected to care and perhaps because she disliked giving Aunt Kate the pleasure of an opportunity for criticism. As she fastened her blouse she reflected that she herself really was a ridiculous person. She was always planning revolts and setting up ideals of independence and common sense, but in the end she always degenerated into the kind of conventional hypocritical person which the Landons expected her to be. Regarding herself in the mirror she thought, "How red and hot I look. But some day I'll show them. I'll revolt."

She did not really care what the boys did—they could even burn down the house—so long as they were healthy and full of vitality.

Turning toward the window again, she saw that Tom was showing

Aunt Kate and Cousin Henry the garden. He seemed utterly unaware of the awful din his sons were making, but Aunt Kate lost no time in speaking of it. Margaret saw her saying something to Tom and then heard him calling to the boys. They stopped beating the gasoline drum and disappeared into the stable. Margaret viewed their disappearance with alarm. It was better to have them in sight beating the tin than out of sight, occupied with heaven knew what mischief.

From the window she regarded Aunt Kate coldly. She was a thin woman with transparent hands, dressed now in the blackest of mourning which she always appeared to wear with satisfaction and even triumph as if she said, "Well, one more gone and I'm still here as vigorous as ever." Margaret reflected that Aunt Kate and Cousin Henry had never missed a funeral which they had even the faintest excuse for attending. Certainly neither of them would have missed Uncle Hughie's burial. But you could not much blame her. If you had not seen your brother in forty years, you would probably come any distance, even if it was only to see what he looked like as he lay in his coffin.

Then suddenly Margaret laughed aloud, remembering Aunt Kate's remark when she left the coffin just before they closed it. "He still has the Landon ears." As if that were the finest thing she could think of him, as if she had expected him to lose them because for forty-four years he had been the black sheep of the family. Perhaps Aunt Kate thought that considering the way he had behaved, Uncle Hughie no longer had any right to the ears.

Fascinated, she watched Tom taking Aunt Kate and Cousin Henry from flower to flower, and shrub to shrub. She wondered what he was saying because he knew nothing whatever about gardens. He did not know a rose from a petunia. He must have been desperate with boredom to have suggested a tour of the garden. She could see Aunt Kate speaking from time to time and guessed what she was saying—that the verbenas did not seem to be flourishing (which alas was true) and that the zinnias hadn't much color and the delphiniums seeemed to have suffered from the heat.

But the sight of Tom, so big and good-natured and patient, made her forget Aunt Kate and filled her with a tumult of affection, so that all at once she was ashamed of herself and afraid. She was ashamed that she was irritated by the heat and because she hated Aunt Kate and because she was angry that Uncle Hughie's death had upset all the plans of Tom and herself and the boys. And she was afraid lest God, impatient with the pettiness of one to whom He had given everything in the world, might punish her by taking something from her.

Then she saw that the other relatives, Cousin Herbert and Aunt Carrie and Cousin Mabel, had come out of the house and were wandering about the garden. She knew they were saying, "Why doesn't Margaret come down? It never took any woman as long as that to dress." Which, again, was true.

The boys did not reappear from the stable and she knew that they would not come out so long as the menace of relatives hovered upon the horizon. They were terribly quiet, so quiet that she tried not to think of all the things which they might be doing.

She heard a motor arriving and thought, "It must be Banks bringing Aunt Flora. Now I shall have to go down." But when she looked out she saw that it was only Tom's sister Ethel arriving. The motor like everything else belonging to Ethel looked smart, hard and expensive. It glittered with chromium plate. No tiny scratch marred the beauty of its mulberry enamel. From the shelter of the chintz curtains she watched Ethel descend and swoop into the house. "Smart, hard, expensive and empty," thought Margaret. "She's empty because she's always been rich and doesn't know the value of anything."

She wondered why Ethel had troubled to come to the funeral. It was extraordinary how close were the ties of Tom's family. Ethel had never seen Uncle Hughie alive and she would never see him dead now that the coffin was closed. But she was being respectable and doing her duty.

The sound of Ethel's motor brought back to her all the horror of the problem of Aunt Flora whom none of them had ever seen although she had been Uncle Hughie's wife for thirty years; Aunt Flora who had kept a boardinghouse in Capetown. She could not picture the meeting of Aunt Flora with the others, neither with the solid ones like Aunt Kate nor the fashionable ones like Ethel. She knew what would happen. She could feel the chill of ice which would mark Aunt Flora's reception. They would treat her as if she had no right to be there, as if she should have known better than to force herself into the circle of the Landons simply because their black sheep had married her. Only Tom would be polite—Tom on whom all the family troubles had been dumped ever since he was a man.

Not even Tom had ever seen Aunt Flora. He had letters from her often enough, and sometimes amused he brought the letters home to show to Margaret. From them they had formed their opinion of Aunt Flora. Of all Uncle Hughie's brothers and sisters and nieces and nephews, it was only to Tom that Aunt Flora wrote because Uncle Hughie had made Tom his heir and because when Tom's grandfather and Uncle Hughie's father lay dying the old man sent for Tom and asked him to look after the affairs of his black sheep son. The family always wished its disagreeable tasks upon Tom.

2

The story of Uncle Hughie's disgrace and exile began before Tom was born. It was known vaguely to the rest of the family but only Tom knew it all for Tom had heard it all, because he had heard Uncle Hughie's side as well. Twice Uncle Hughie had reappeared in New York—a little gray man, with a head too big for his body, dressed flashily in the style of a touring actor. He never saw any of his relatives but Tom.

"I know them," he used to say. "They don't want to see me. They've always been ashamed of me—Kate and all the others. Anyway, what would be the good of seeing them? It's been years and years since Pa sent me away and we're strangers now. I won't annoy them." And after a pause he had added wistfully, "But I'd like to come and see you when I'm in town if it doesn't trouble you."

The visits, separated by eleven years, were brief enough. Without any warning he appeared to lunch with Tom and asked what members of the family had died since he last heard from them. With the politeness of a day long gone by he would sit on the edge of his chair holding his gray derby on his knees with his gray cotton gloves laid politely inside, and talk half the morning and all through lunch. Sometimes he took to reciting scenes from dramas in which he had played small parts—that of a butler or merely of a "walk-on." But he always knew the roles of the principal actors and recited speeches in a high falsetto voice in the most melodramatic fashion. He was a bore. That was the only thing Tom had against him. For otherwise he was harmless enough and not at all what you would expect a black sheep to be. But after all, two visits in forty years was not much to put up with.

When he had tired of reciting, he would talk about Tom being his heir and executor as if he had a great fortune which would benefit Tom and Tom's children, but Tom knew that the income left Uncle Hughie by his father had dwindled and dwindled until at length it had disappeared. Tom knew because for eight years he had been supporting Uncle Hughie out of his own pocket. He had even sent him extra sums over what the income was supposed to be, when Uncle Hughie had been ill or had gotten into trouble of some sort.

Tom knew there was nothing very wrong with Uncle Hughie. It was simply that for forty years he had been regarded as the family black sheep until in the end he had come to think of himself as a ne'er-do-well and a disgrace. It was impossible to convince the rest of the family that he was really a harmless fellow, a little eccentric and not solid and conventional like the rest of the Landons. And sometimes Tom wondered at the harshness of a generation which had sent Hughie off to South Africa as a boy of twenty because he had been "fast" and liked women and gambling. From Uncle Hughie himself he knew the story of that scene which had taken place forty years ago when a woman came one Sunday morning as Hughie's father was setting out for church to demand that his son make her an honest woman.

"A blackmailer!" said Uncle Hughie, telling the story. "Ruined her! She was a girl about town when I was in kilts."

But the old man never forgave Hughie for the shame which had been brought one Sunday morning to his respectable Washington Square door-step, and that was the end of Hughie. He was simply dumped on the world and paid a hundred and fifty dollars a month so long as he kept out of sight of the rest of the Landons.

There were moments on those two visits when Uncle Hughie was not a bore, and that was when he talked about the life he had led. Some of the stories, like the one of the shipwreck on the coral reef in the South Seas and his marriage to a native belle, were so steep that Tom did not believe them, but they fascinated him none the less. Uncle Hughie had been a sheepherder and a barman, an actor and at one time, when he was overtaken by one of his periodical seizures of remorse he had been a revivalist preacher in a small way, lecturing at a mission in the slums of Melbourne on the evils of loose living. Tom, respectable and dutiful, sitting in his office high above the North River, had listened, fascinated, with a slow envy in his heart.

And then, on both occasions, Uncle Hughie, after lunch was finished, had said, "Well, my boy, I'll drop in tomorrow," and the first time he had not dropped in again until eleven years had passed. The second time he did not reappear until his body arrived in a coffin from Montreal.

Through both visits and through all Uncle Hughie's letters there had run the saga of Flora. There were times when, judging from the letters, Flora and Uncle Hughie appeared to be living together in peace and amity. At such times, Uncle Hughie merely wrote, "Your Aunt Flora is with me again." He always called her "your Aunt Flora" as if gently he sought to gain a position for her in the gallery of Landon women and a respect which clearly she did not deserve. But try as he would, Tom could never see Aunt Flora among the others, either those who were well-off and respectable, or those who were rich and fashionable. Alas, Aunt Flora's letters would have betrayed her even if Uncle Hughie, in off moments, had not written of her as "that damned virago your Aunt Flora," "that she-devil," and "that vulgar woman who has been a millstone around my neck."

For Aunt Flora's letters were masterpieces of illiteracy and vituperation and she only wrote at the times when Uncle Hughie had escaped from her and she wanted money. Her life for thirty years, it seemed, had been spent in losing and recapturing Uncle Hughie. Tom, receiving her letters, was convinced at last that she must be a despicable woman to have pursued the old man for half a lifetime simply for the sake of that pitiful pension of a hundred and fifty dollars a month. She had pursued him from South Africa to Melbourne and from Melbourne to San Francisco, and then for the last four years both Uncle Hughie and Aunt Flora had kept silent. Tom did not even know where they were until he had received the telegram from Montreal saying "Your Uncle Hughie is dead. Please wire funds." So he knew then that Aunt Flora was in possession at the end.

[679]

3

And now she was on her way to the funeral. She would arrive now any moment, driven up from the station by Banks, the chauffeur.

While Tom went around the garden, trying to explain about the flowers and shrubs to Aunt Kate and Cousin Henry one part of his distracted mind was occupied with the problem of Aunt Flora. Phrases from those old abusive letters kept running through his head, "That old reprobate, your uncle"—"That drunken scoundrel"—"That good for nothing waster"—"The day I met him was the most evil day of my life." He saw again the illiterate handwriting and the misspelled words of abuse. She would be awful. Try as he would, he could not see her among all the others. Aunt Kate and Cousin Henry and Ethel. She would probably cry and scream and throw herself on the coffin.

He was no snob, but he hated scenes and emotion, and he liked life to be kept in well-ordered layers. In life some elements mixed and others did not. No good could come of mixing Aunt Flora with all the others.

And then he saw Margaret coming toward them across the lawn and at sight of her he experienced a feeling of relief. Margaret he could count upon. Margaret would understand and take Aunt Flora under her wing and keep her in order and protect her from the hostile looks and awful silence of Uncle Hughie's brothers and sisters and nephews and nieces.

Margaret said, "We'd better go in. Mr. Prescott is here."

Aunt Kate's expression changed mechanically from one of rapture over the flowers to one appropriate to funerals and the arrival of the rector, and together they started toward the house. Cleverly Margaret managed to fall behind a little, drawing Tom with her and when they were at a safe distance, she said, "We'll have to wait for Aunt Flora."

"Of course."

"I don't see what's happened to her."

"The train is probably late."

"You're sure Banks understood about meeting her?"

"Of course. She wrote that she'd be wearing a crepe veil."

Margaret began to worry. "There might be another woman with a crepe veil."

Tom laughed, "Well, Banks could eliminate. There couldn't be ten or a dozen."

"No, I suppose not."

Then before they had reached the house Margaret had found another cause to worry. "Don't you think you'd better see what the boys are doing?"

"They're all right. What could they possibly do? Do you want me to fetch them?"

"No. There isn't any reason why they should have to go to the funeral."

The hour of the funeral was set for eleven and already it was half past and there was still no sign of Aunt Flora. Margaret went to the window where she had a view of the avenue and part of the road leading to the village, but she saw no sign of Banks or Uncle Hughie's widow. Aunt Kate was talking to Ethel, who was very smart in black. Margaret saw them pretending to be cordial as if Aunt Kate did not think Ethel extravagant, frivolous and a little vulgar and as if Ethel did not consider Aunt Kate a dowdy bore. They were being *too* polite and *too* animated. Margaret knew that they never met save at funerals or weddings in the family. Uncle Henry and Cousin Herbert and Aunt Carrie, fat and perspiring, stood talking to Mr. Prescott, the rector. All about were relatives disliking and mistrusting each other, separated by a thousand elements, by wealth, by taste, by character, by morality. Here they were all brought together by the corpse of Uncle Hughie whom some of them had not seen for more than forty years and some had not seen at all. Margaret, still watching the window, experienced a sudden feeling of suffocation. Who were these strangers who had been imposed upon her by the simple act of her marriage to Tom? Why were they here in her house? She would not have chosen them for friends, not one of them. She did not think that even Tom would have chosen them. Yet here they were, all collected about the coffin of the little man whom they had exiled and ignored. They respected death, perhaps because they were all afraid of death.

Then all at once it seemed to her that the little man in the closed coffin had had a better life than any of them, for at least he had been free.

She heard a motor and saw her own well-worn car approaching up the long drive. "Now for it," she thought. She would have to be kind to Aunt Flora no matter how horrible she was—she and Tom—for nobody else would be kind to her. The Landons had no patience with people who were poor and common and in hard luck.

As she walked out of the room into the hall to welcome Uncle Hughie's widow she had in her mind a very clear picture of her. It was created out of what Tom had told her at night when they lay in the darkness side by side, and out of the letters which Tom had shown her now and then with a twinkle of amusement in his blue eyes, never dreaming that one day Aunt Flora would turn up thus in their lives. As she closed the screen door a new horror came to her. What was to become of Aunt Flora now that Uncle Hughie was dead? Someone would have to look out for her. Someone would have to support her. In her heart she knew it would be Tom, because no one else in the family would do anything about it.

The motor drove up to the steps. The picture in Margaret's mind was of a big coarse woman, overdressed and swathed in ostentatious crepe, purchased with Tom's money, a woman with a dreadful voice and an offensive, tactless, overcordial manner. But the door opened and out of the motor stepped a woman who was not at all what she had expected.

She was small and as she threw the crepe veil back over her hat, Margaret saw that her hair was gray and that she must be about sixty. She wore gold-rimmed spectacles and behind them her eyes were swollen with weeping. It was rather a kind, amiable face and it wore a look of humbleness and apology as if she were saying, "I'm sorry you've had all this trouble." In spite of the heat she wore a long coat which came to her ankles. It was not black but of some checked material. Beneath it Margaret caught a glimpse of a navy-blue dress and suddenly she knew that Aunt Flora had put on the awful coat because the dress underneath was shabby. She wore black cotton gloves and carried a black leather handbag which was worn gray at the edges.

"I'm Mrs. Landon," said Margaret with an unnatural brightness, "Tom's wife. I meant to come to meet you but at the last minute there were too many things that had to be done. I hope you didn't have trouble finding the chauffeur." It was a lie she had prepared because she could not face the horror of the trip alone with Aunt Flora all the way from the station, and now when she came to utter it, she was ashamed. For some reason she was more ashamed than she had ever been in all her life.

"No," said Aunt Flora, "he found me right away. I'm afraid I'm late and have made you a lot of trouble. But it wasn't my fault. The train was held up." It was not the voice of a shrew which Margaret heard.

In the hall, she found herself faced with a new problem. Should she ask Aunt Flora if she wanted to take off the awful checked coat and expose the shabbiness of the blue dress underneath? Then she knew that she must ask her as if she had noticed nothing at all strange about the costume, and she shuddered at the thought of Aunt Flora entering the living room to face all the Landons in that awful checked coat.

"Would you like to take off your coat?" she asked.

"No, I don't think so. I've had a bad cold," she answered with quiet dignity that bewildered Margaret, thinking of the abusive letters.

4

In the living room they were all waiting with an air of impatience and when Margaret came in with Aunt Flora she saw a shudder pass through Aunt Kate and a look of astonishment on the face of the fashionable Ethel. She knew that they had found Aunt Flora even worse than they had feared.

But Aunt Flora seemed unaware of their astonishment or their displeasure. She held out the hand covered with the black cotton glove, simply, murmuring a "Pleased to meet you," and, "It's a pleasure, I'm sure."

They did not make it any easier for her. They did not say that they were pleased to meet Hughie's wife after so many years. There was no grace in the Landons. Margaret saw them suddenly with a blinding light. They were smug with the inevitable smugness of people who had always been rich, dull with that dullness in which the prosperous are inevitably embalmed. They were bores, all of them, in the way that only the rich can be boring.

Then she heard Aunt Kate saying, "I suppose we might as well get on with the service."

Margaret slipped her arm through Aunt Flora's and led her into the long room where Uncle Hughie lay in his closed coffin. She knew that taking Aunt Flora's arm was an ostentatious gesture, but she was aware that Aunt Flora was becoming an issue, a cause, a crusade. She meant to protect Aunt Flora from the others. The awful letters did not matter now, nor her life-long hounding of Uncle Hughie. She led the old lady to a chair and sat beside her, and Mr. Prescott, the rector, stood up. There was a hush broken only by the little sighs and stirrings which were the sign of the family boredom at having to go through this last service for the one of them who had never kept their rules.

Then Tom came and sat on the other side of Aunt Flora and turning a little, smiled at the old lady, and Margaret felt suddenly that she could not survive·the love she felt for him. She felt tears coming to her eyes, not for Uncle Hughie but for the honesty and simplicity which were in Tom's blue eyes.

"'I am the Resurrection and the Life,'" said Mr. Prescott, "'and whosoever believeth in me shall not perish but have eternal life.'"

The black veil covered Aunt Flora's spectacles once more, but through it Margaret saw that tears were running down the old lady's face.

"'For a thousand years in thy sight are but as yesterday, seeing that the past is as a watch in the night . . .'"

Suddenly Margaret too began to cry. She had not expected to cry at the funeral. She had pictured herself as going through it briskly and cheerfully. She did not know why she was crying unless it was on account of Aunt Flora's old checked coat. There was something about it . . .

"'So teach us to number our days that we may apply our hearts to wisdom.'"

5

The little white church stood beside a lake and in the hot sunlight the old tombstones shone white against the willows and lilacs. Here the Landons had all been buried for generations and here Uncle Hughie had come at last after all his wanderings to take his place beside the mother who had died when he was born, near the father who had sent him away long ago to die without ever seeing his son again.

The heat hovered over the white road distorting the outline of the white phlox in bloom by the edge of the lake and the outline of Ethel's smart motor upon which the white dust lay as a sacrilege. Margaret stood close by the old lady in the checked coat, holding tight to the thin hand in the black cotton glove. When they lowered the coffin into the grave she felt the thin hand contract suddenly and heard Aunt Flora murmur, "My poor little man! My poor little man!"

Then suddenly it was over and they were making their way back once more to the motors. Aunt Kate was blowing her nose loudly and Ethel was brushing angrily at the white dust on her immaculate black skirt.

6

But for Margaret it was not over. There was still the dreadful lunch to be gone through with Aunt Flora, nervous and timid at her side and all the others making conversation, stupid and forced; Aunt Kate trying to find out just how rich Ethel was and Cousin Henry trying to discover what Tom had paid for the land he had just bought behind the stables.

All the way back from the churchyard they rode in silence—Tom and Margaret and Aunt Flora. Margaret stared out of the window with a feeling of dullness, as if the whole occasion had worked itself up to a climax which had failed to arrive.

When they reached the house she said to Aunt Flora, "Would you like to go up to my room before lunch?" and the old lady followed her upstairs. At the top she asked Margaret suddenly about the trains.

"There is one at two-fifteen," said Margaret, "but you won't be able to make it. And another at three-twenty. I hope you're not going to rush away just when we've come to know each other."

"No . . . no," said Aunt Flora, "I don't aim to be impolite, but I think I'd better get back as soon as possible. I'm afraid I've made so much trouble already."

"No. You must rest after lunch. You must be very tired."

Aunt Flora did not oppose her. She stood, hesitant in the doorway and Margaret knew suddenly that again it was a question of the checked coat. She did not want to take it off until Margaret had left the room.

"I'll go down and see about the others," said Margaret. "Just come down when you're ready."

A look of gratitude came into the old lady's blue eyes. The hand in the black cotton glove reached out and touched Margaret. "You've been very kind to me," she said quietly. And then Margaret put one arm about her and kissed her gently and went quickly out of the room, filled with an odd shame at the sight of the shabby old lady standing in the middle of her luxurious bedroom.

7

She had kissed Aunt Flora! As she descended the stairs it seemed that she must have lost her mind. Aunt Kate would say that she had simply been unbalanced and hysterical and it occurred to her that Aunt Kate would have been right. The whole day seemed unreal and strange. The burden of the whole thing was on her shoulders. But she had kissed Aunt Flora—the woman who wrote those horrible, abusive, threatening letters in illiterate handwriting. "Perhaps," she thought wildly, "really wicked women are like that—gentle and quiet and timid and disarming." She wondered when Aunt Flora would show her evil side and whether she would go away without ever betraying herself. Margaret remembered having read that female poisoners always had a dovelike air.

She told the others to go into lunch and then went to see the boys who were finishing their meal under the awning on the terrace. She found them in the midst of eating their ice cream and beneath the table they were having a kicking contest, each trying to kick the shins of the other.

"Stop it at once," said Margaret.

"Tommy began it," said John.

"I did not," said Tommy.

"I don't care who started it. I want you both to stop."

"I'm glad there's a funeral," said Tommy. "I've had two helpings of ice cream."

"You mustn't talk like that," said Margaret.

"Well, it's true," said John, "after it spoiled our going away."

"You're going away tonight."

"Yes, but we missed three days."

"You're not to talk like that. Have you been good boys?"

"Yes," said John.

"Yes," said Tommy, but the tone of his voice did not seem too certain. It was Tommy who could never carry off a lie. John was good at it. He was more a Landon and a little like Aunt Kate.

"When you've finished I want you both to go upstairs and take a shower and get into bed until everybody's gone."

"Then we don't have to say good-by?"

"No, I'll tell them you're asleep."

"That's swell," said Tommy.

"You can each take a book to bed with you."

[685]

Then she left them, ashamed that she was always weak with them when Miss Baines wasn't there. No matter how naughty they were she always wanted to laugh at the moment she should have been giving a fine show of firmness.

In the dining room the seventeen relatives sat at the table. Lunch had already begun but the place which Margaret had kept by her side for Aunt Flora was still empty.

"Hughie's wife hasn't come down yet," said Aunt Kate, as if Margaret were blind.

"I suppose she's not feeling too well," said Margaret.

There was a long silence and then Aunt Kate sighed heavily, "Poor Hughie, what he must have gone through," and then quietly they began to talk again, always about Landon affairs and Landon connections. Aunt Kate kept sobbing and blowing her nose although Margaret could not imagine why, since in forty years she had never even troubled to write to Uncle Hughie.

She waited for a long time before going to discover why Aunt Flora had not come down. Perhaps, she thought, the old lady wanted to be alone. The cold fish was finished and the chicken was begun but still Aunt Flora did not appear, and presently Margaret began to think, "Perhaps she has fainted or something awful has happened." What if she died here in the house to upset all their plans once more, and keep the children from the beach, when she had promised them that they should go by the night train?

When she could bear it no longer, she rose and said, "I'm going up to see if anything has happened to her."

To her horror she saw Aunt Kate rising with that look of bright anticipation which came into her eyes at the prospect of disaster. She heard Aunt Kate saying, "I'll go with you."

"No, no. Go on with your lunch."

"Maybe you'll need me," said Aunt Kate with determination.

Then Margaret lost all control of her nerves. She knew only one thing—that Aunt Kate must not go up to her bedroom to torment Aunt Flora and pry into her life and ask her questions about Hughie and perhaps see that shabby blue dress. She knew too that only violence could stop Aunt Kate. She heard herself saying, "Will you please listen to me? This is my house. I don't want you."

She saw the look of triumphant malice on Aunt Kate's face and then ran from the room to escape the dreadful silence. She had put herself in the wrong and delivered herself into the hands of Aunt Kate forever. But somehow, she did not care. Wildly, as she hurried up the stairs, she wished that she had stayed to say more than she said—to say all the things which she had cherished in silence for Tom's sake for so many years. Wildly, she opened the door of her bedroom without knocking.

There on a stiff chair in the middle of the room sat Aunt Flora, still in the checked coat, her small body limp with fatigue, the cotton gloved hands resting in her lap. She had been crying.

Margaret put her arm about her, "Why didn't you lie on the bed or on the chaise longue?"

"I didn't want to rumple the bed," said Aunt Flora, "and the sofa looked so pretty with all the pillows, I didn't think that it was meant to lie on."

"But you haven't had any lunch."

Aunt Flora looked away from her and was silent.

"Do come down and eat something."

There was a little silence and the old lady said, "No, I don't think they'd like me sitting at the table with them."

"That's nonsense. They've been waiting for you. Of course they want you."

"Not if they knew the truth."

"They know the truth."

Aunt Flora drew away from her a little. "No," she said, "they don't know that I'm not Aunt Flora. They don't know that I was never married to Hughie."

For a moment Margaret could think of nothing to say. She thought wildly, "The old lady is tired. She is out of her mind." Finally she said, "It's all right. I'm sure you're mistaken, Aunt Flora. You're upset."

"No. It's true. I don't know what happened to Hughie's wife. She must have died. We haven't heard from her for nearly ten years. I'm just an impostor." She began to cry again. "I've deceived you all. I couldn't help it. I had to come to Hughie's funeral. It was the only way I could come. That's why I signed the telegram with her name."

She was trembling and Margaret helped her to the chaise longue where she forced her to lie down.

"And you've been so good to me," she said. "I'll never forgive myself for the way I've imposed on you. I haven't any right here at all."

Margaret felt an odd sense of relief, because in spite of this strange old lady's confession of deception, she had not deceived her at all. She had known all along that she could not have been the Aunt Flora who wrote those awful letters.

"I'll fetch you some port," she said, "and then we'll have some lunch here all alone where you won't need to see the others."

When she returned the old lady was crying again. She gave her the port and then remembering Aunt Kate, locked the door and took a chair and sat down beside her.

"When you feel better," she said, "talk to me about it. Tell me everything. You'd like to talk about it, wouldn't you?"

"Yes," she murmured, "yes. My poor little man! My poor little man!"

[687]

8

It was a simple story. The old lady told it, leaning back among all the lace and satin of Margaret's chaise longue, looking away from Margaret all the while as if she were living it all over again while she talked.

It began nearly ten years before Uncle Hughie died. "It was in Seattle we met each other," she said. "He was acting a small bit and I was the wardrobe woman. He had an attack of bronchitis and I sort of looked after him. We used to have a bite after the theater together at a lunch wagon or some place like that. I guess his wife wasn't much good. You could see he was the kind of man who'd never had anybody to look after him. I was a widow. My husband died thirty years ago. He was an actor too. So Hughie and I grew fond of each other and the next season we got a job together again. And after that he said it would be easier if I called myself Mrs. Landon. We couldn't get married because he didn't know if Flora was alive or dead—and anyway at our age I guess it didn't matter much." She fell silent for a moment, regarding her hands. "You see there really wasn't ever anything like that between us. We were both old. We were both just kind of lonely and tired, I guess. He was awful tired, Hughie. I guess he was tired of wandering all his life—and lonely. Both of us were old and lonely." She sighed and said again, "My poor little man."

So for eight years they had lived thus. Sometimes they had work and when they did not they lived in one room in a cheap boardinghouse. She taught him to save and make tiny economies. They traveled all one summer with companies that played in tents and at county fairs. Sometimes she played mother parts and then they had more money. "Hughie was used to counting on the money your husband sent him, but I thought it would be better if he was independent. That's why you didn't hear from him. I've had kind of a hard life but I've always been independent and that's a great thing, I guess. Hughie got like that too, toward the end."

They were always happy together. They were even happy the last year when everything went wrong. "I guess Hughie liked having somebody to look after him." But that last year Hughie had a lump in his throat and for a long time he wouldn't go to the doctor about it because doctors cost money and when it began to hurt him he went to the doctor and the doctor said it was a cancer. But it was too late to do anything about it. He hadn't been able to get a job on account of the way he looked, so there wasn't anything for them to do but live on their savings. But boardinghouse proprietors didn't want them because they looked old and poor and because they thought if the other boarders saw Hughie they'd leave. They were in Montreal then and they went from boardinghouse to boardinghouse trying to find some one who would take them in. They must have tried twenty or thirty and at last they found one kept by a woman who had been in the show business like themselves. She had been an acrobat in a circus. She took them in.

"We stayed there until Hughie died," she said. "It was all right. She was a kind woman and the doctor let us have lots of morphine so Hughie didn't suffer much. I think it was all right. I think he was happy." Again she began to cry and again she murmured, "My poor little man!"

When she had finished Margaret could think of nothing to say, and anyway she felt that whatever she could have said would have been stupid and dull. She patted the old lady's hand and she stopped crying and took out a cotton handkerchief and dried her swollen eyes. When she had put her handkerchief back into the pocket of the checked coat she drew out an envelope.

"Here's what was left after the undertaker was paid," she said. "I brought it back to your husband. There's seventy-eight dollars and eighty-five cents."

She laid the envelope in Margaret's lap and Margaret thought, "She could have bought a new dress and coat with that."

She picked up the envelope and pressed it into the old lady's hands, "No, keep that, please. Please keep it."

"No, I couldn't, thank you. I have a little money. It wouldn't be honest. I've always been independent like. I feel better that way. Don't think I don't appreciate it."

"My husband can take it out of Uncle Hughie's estate. He's Uncle Hughie's heir."

"There isn't any estate—anyway nothing but debts. Hughie only learned about money when it was too late. I guess he never knew what it was worth —always having it sent to him all his life."

Margaret thought, "I mustn't argue with her. Later on we can help her some way or another. I won't talk to her about money now."

It seemed to her that all the Landons, all that pompous respectable family were forever in the debt of this woman who was not Aunt Flora at all. She rose to pour another glass of port and as she turned again toward the chaise longue she saw through the open window that smoke was rising from the end of the stable. It rose in a thick white cloud and near the eaves there were little ribbons of flame. For a moment it seemed to her that what she saw was not real at all but only a part of the long nightmare which had begun on rising this morning. With the glass still in her hand, she stood staring as if fascinated. Then in a calm voice she said, "The stables are on fire. I must go and tell them. Stay here and sleep a little if you can. I'll be back at once."

She hurried to the door forgetting that she had locked it against Aunt Kate. Her hands were clumsy and it took her a precious moment to open it. Then she ran down the stairs and called to the parlormaid who was in the hall and burst into the dining room where the men sat smoking. It was all mad and insane.

Then she remembered the horses and followed Tom out of the house into the garden. The horses had to be saved and the children's pony. Everyone was running from the house—all the Landon relatives and the servants, crossing the garden toward the fire. Tom and the groom pulled down the hose and turned on the water, and she herself led out the pony. Then all at once the garden was filled with the village fire apparatus and men running back and forth with lines of hose.

9

In half an hour the fire was out and then Margaret remembered Aunt Flora, who was not Aunt Flora. She had not come out. She was not among the others. She must still be in the bedroom.

But when she arrived all damp and disheveled in her bedroom, the old lady was not there. She looked into the dressing room and ran along the corridor calling "Aunt Flora! Aunt Flora!" because she knew no other name for her. But she was nowhere to be found. Neither upstairs nor down nor in the garden. She called Tom and together they searched, and then the fantastic idea occurred to her that the old lady might have tried to walk to the station and she sent Banks to look for her. But he too returned with no clue. He had not met her and there was no train at that hour by which she could have left.

At dark they had still found no trace of her. Tom telephoned to the police and they abandoned the plan of leaving that night in the hope of finding some clue regarding her strange disappearance. In the end the police said she must have walked to the road and asked for a ride in a passing motor. Tom said that they would find her somewhere but when the police asked her name they had no name to give them, save Aunt Flora, because that was the only name they knew.

Late that night Tommy, who could never hide his own guilt, confessed. While all the family were at the funeral he and John decided to play Indian and John took the feedbin as a blockhouse. It was Tommy who attacked the stronghold and rendered desperate at last by the resistance of the besieged, he had built a fire to smoke his brother out, the way Indians did in books. It was a plan which succeeded and when the game was over, they had hidden their guilt by pushing the remnants of the fire under the bin. "We had to do something," said Tommy, "when we were kept home for three days."

They never heard of Aunt Flora again nor found any trace of her. But that night when Margaret went to bed exhausted, she found beneath her pillow an envelope containing seventy-eight dollars and eighty-five cents and on it was written, "Thank you for being so kind to me."